Camp Pock-a-Wocknee and the DYN-O-MITE Summer of '77

by Eric Glickman

Camp Pock-a-Wocknee and the DYN-O-MITE Summer of '77

Black Panel Press
Toronto, ON
Canada

www.blackpanelpress.com

First Edition
Printed in Canada

ISBN: 978-1-990521-07-2

For Nick, JJ and Duke

All my love to Missy, Paris, Jolie and Trey for their
support and faith in me while I created this book.

And a big thanks to my mom and dad for
sending me to camp when I was a kid.

PROLOGUE

If it wasn't for Camp Pock-a-Wocknee, I wouldn't exist.

———

My parents met as teenagers in the summer of 1956
at Camp Pock-a-Wocknee.

Five summers later, when they were counselors, I was
accidentally conceived by the lake on the last night of camp.
(I think of it like something out of a Bruce Springsteen song,
if Bruce wrote about upper-middle-class suburban Jews.)

I started going to Pock-a-Wocknee when I was 10 years old
and from that summer on I lived my life '10 months for 2' —
suffering through the interminable school year just so
I could get to those 8 magical weeks away at camp.

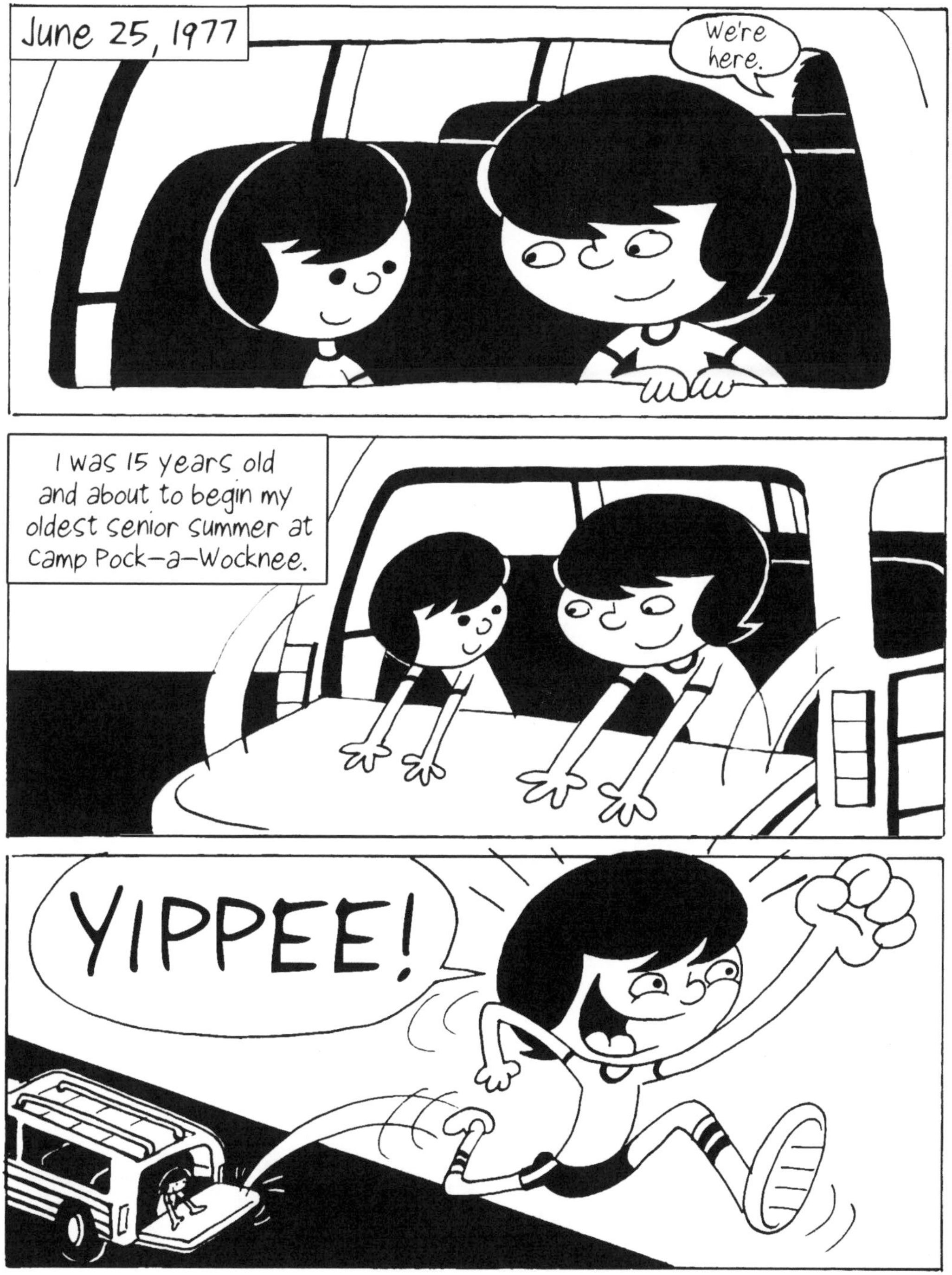

June 25, 1977
We're here.
I was 15 years old and about to begin my oldest senior summer at Camp Pock-a-Wocknee.
YIPPEE!

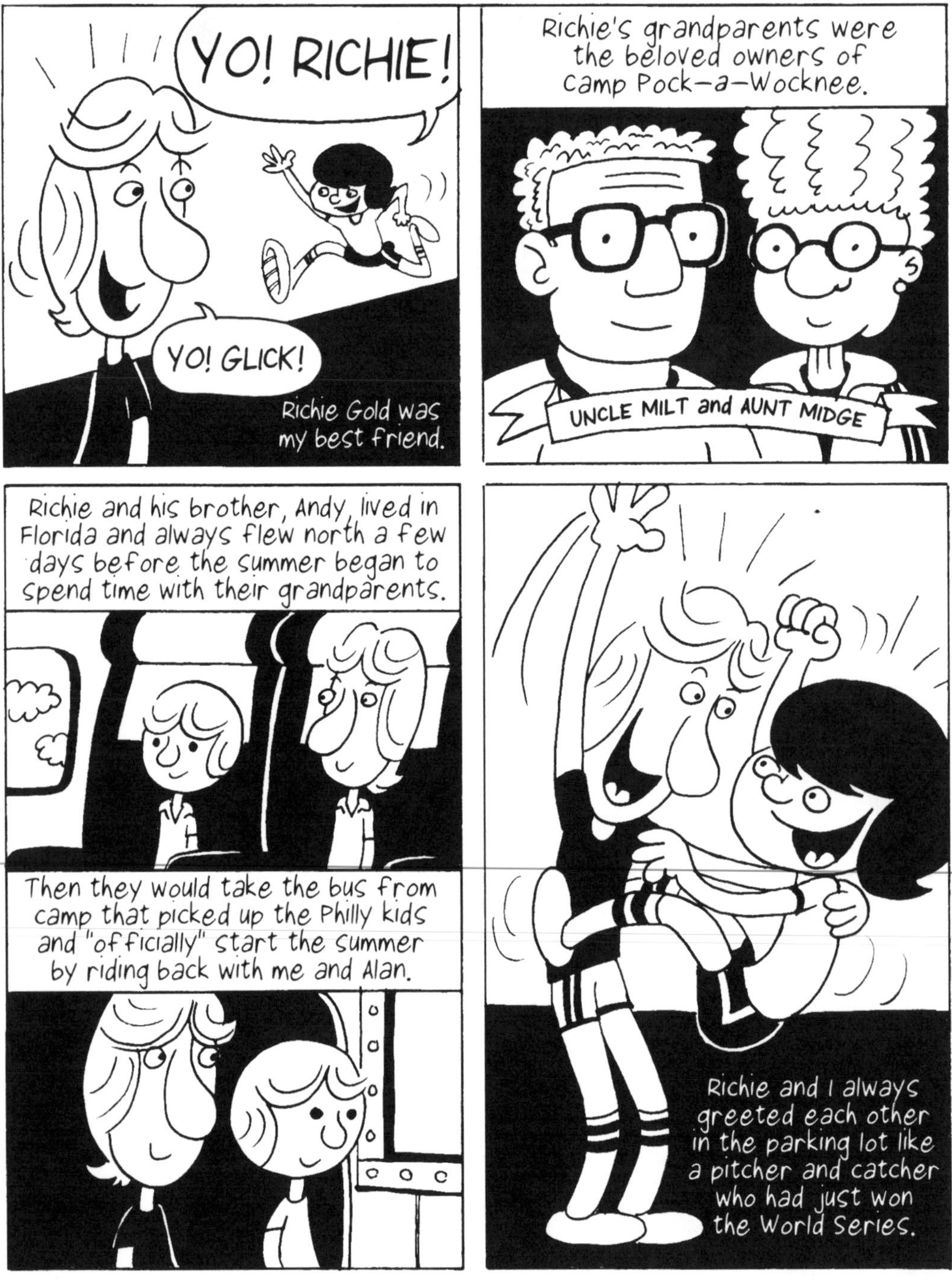
YO! RICHIE!
YO! GLICK!
Richie Gold was my best friend.
Richie's grandparents were the beloved owners of Camp Pock-a-Wocknee.
UNCLE MILT and AUNT MIDGE
Richie and his brother, Andy, lived in Florida and always flew north a few days before the summer began to spend time with their grandparents.
Then they would take the bus from camp that picked up the Philly kids and "officially" start the summer by riding back with me and Alan.
Richie and I always greeted each other in the parking lot like a pitcher and catcher who had just won the World Series.

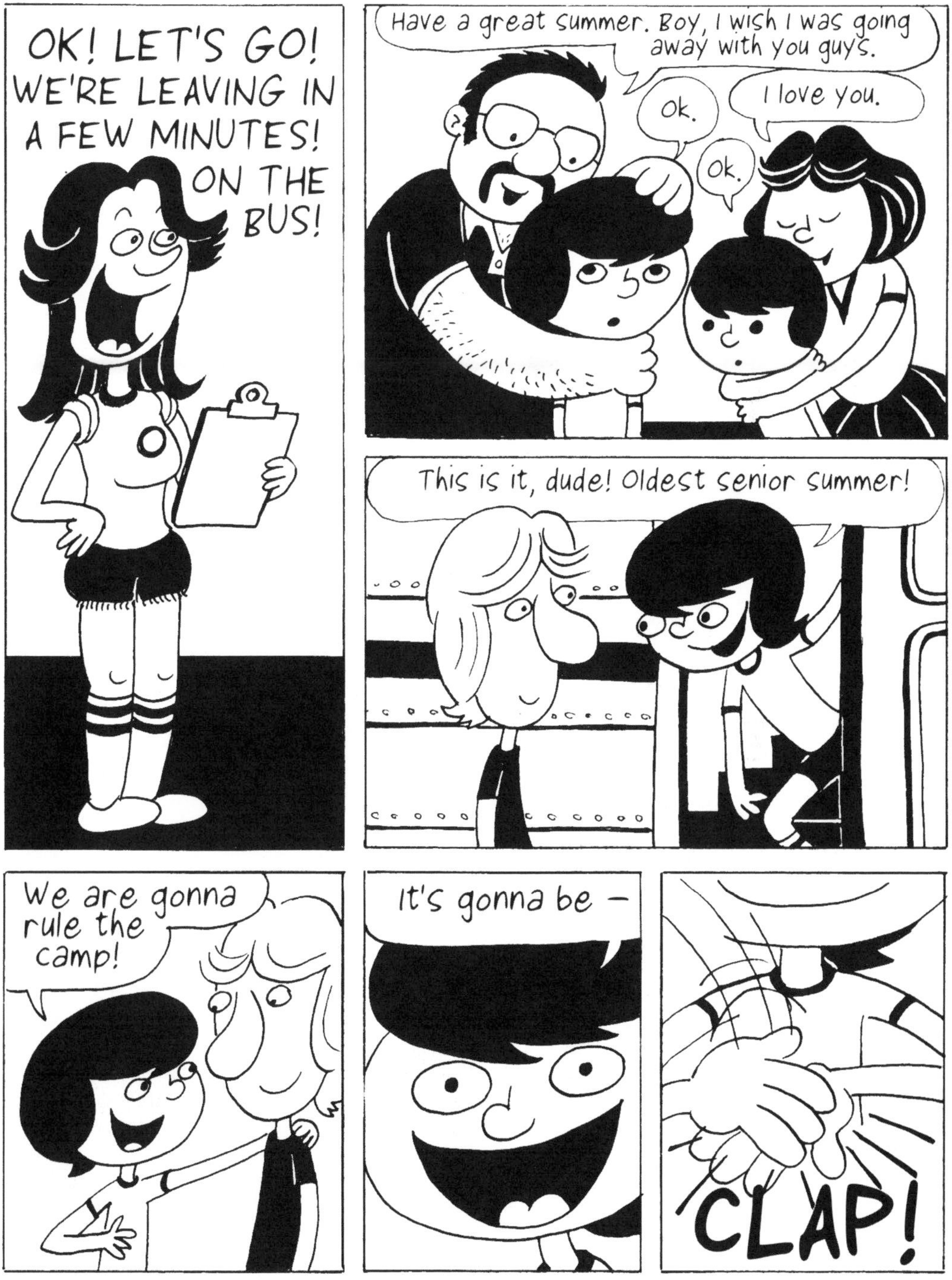
OK! LET'S GO! WE'RE LEAVING IN A FEW MINUTES! ON THE BUS!
Have a great summer. Boy, I wish I was going away with you guys.
Ok.
I love you.
Ok.
This is it, dude! Oldest senior summer!
We are gonna rule the camp!
It's gonna be –
CLAP!

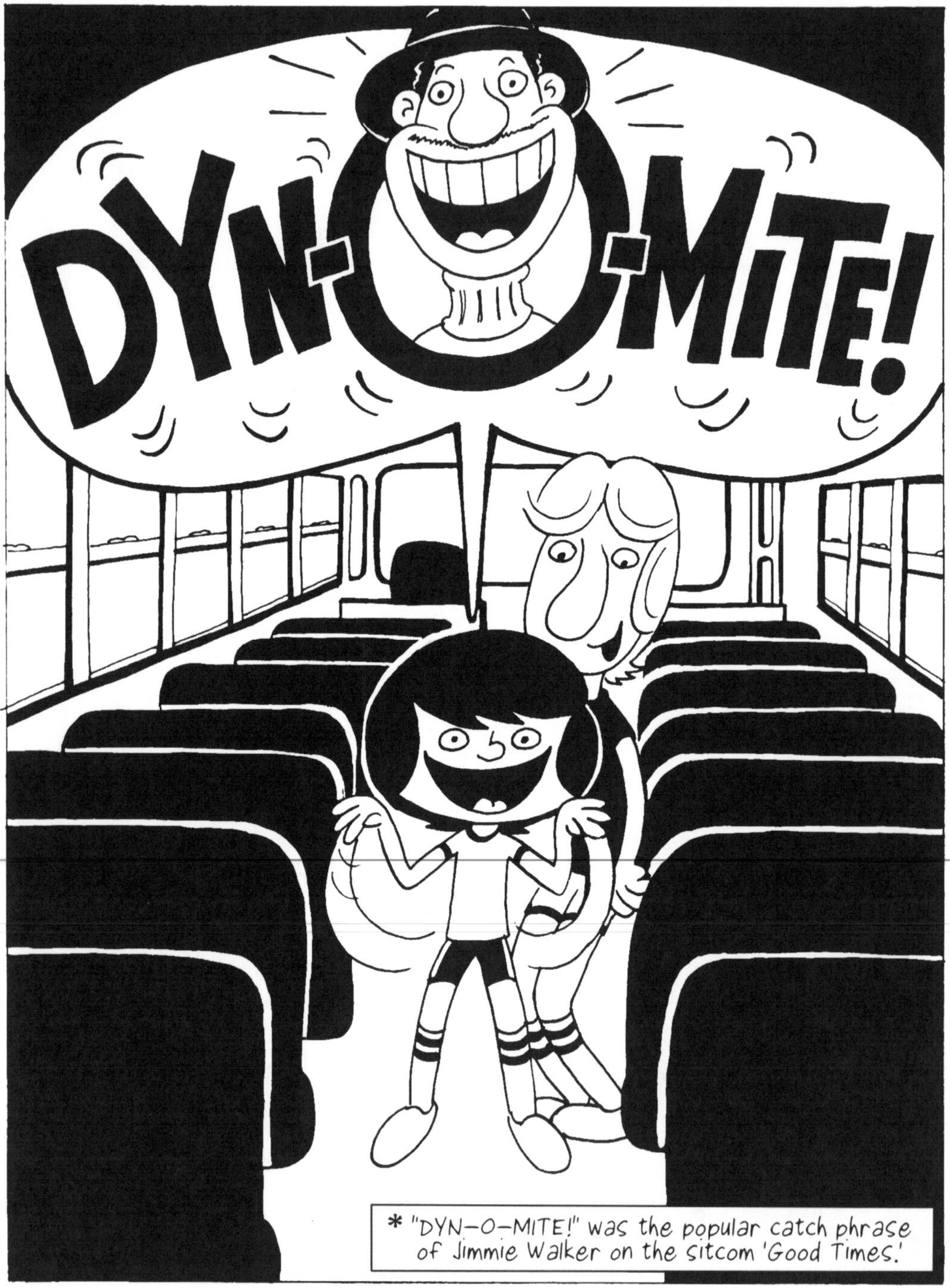
DYN-O-MITE!
* "DYN—O—MITE!" was the popular catch phrase of Jimmie Walker on the sitcom 'Good Times.'

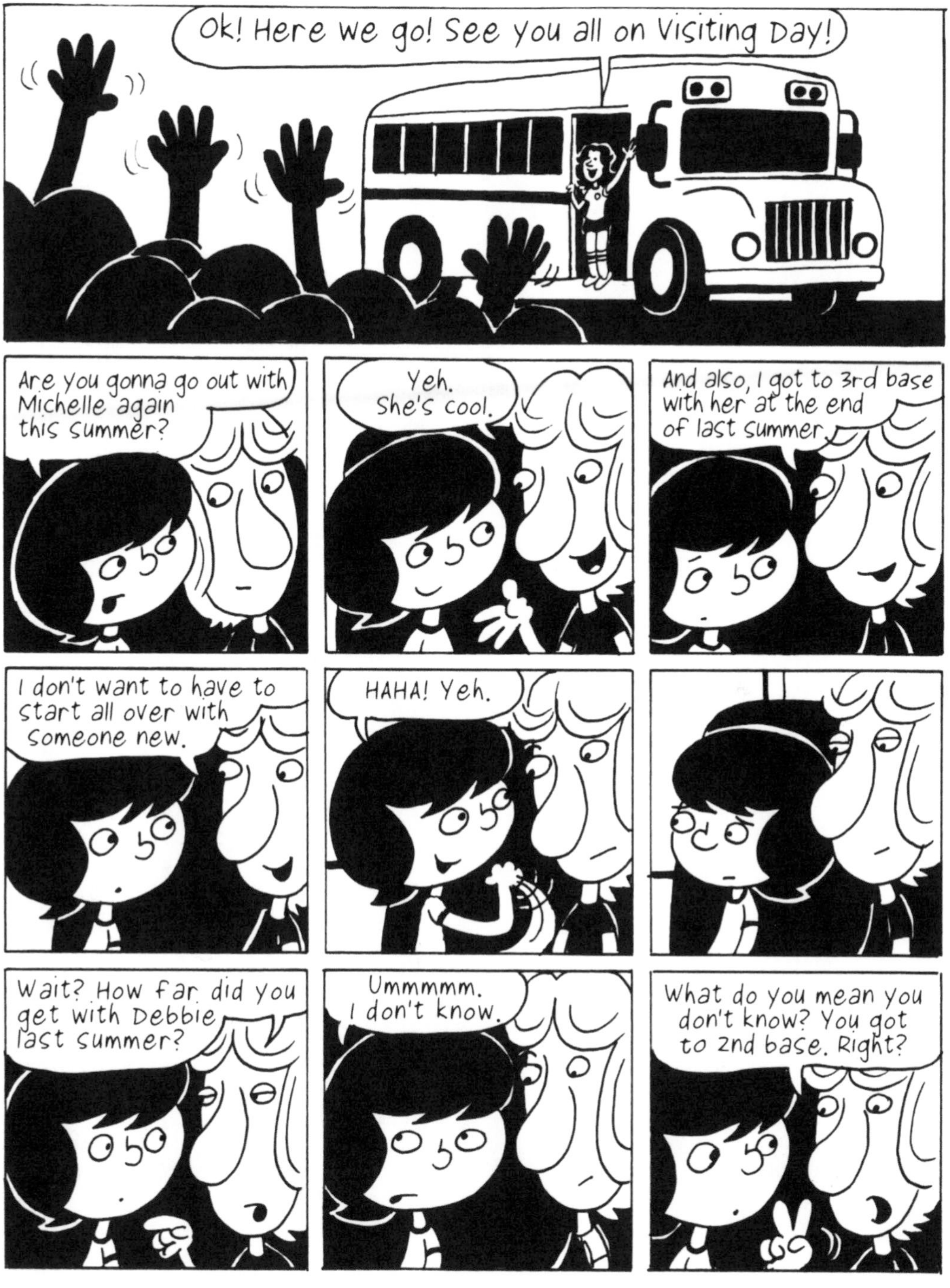
Ok! Here we go! See you all on Visiting Day!
Are you gonna go out with Michelle again this summer?
Yeh. She's cool.
And also, I got to 3rd base with her at the end of last summer.
I don't want to have to start all over with someone new.
HAHA! Yeh.
Wait? How far did you get with Debbie last summer?
Ummmmm. I don't know.
What do you mean you don't know? You got to 2nd base. Right?

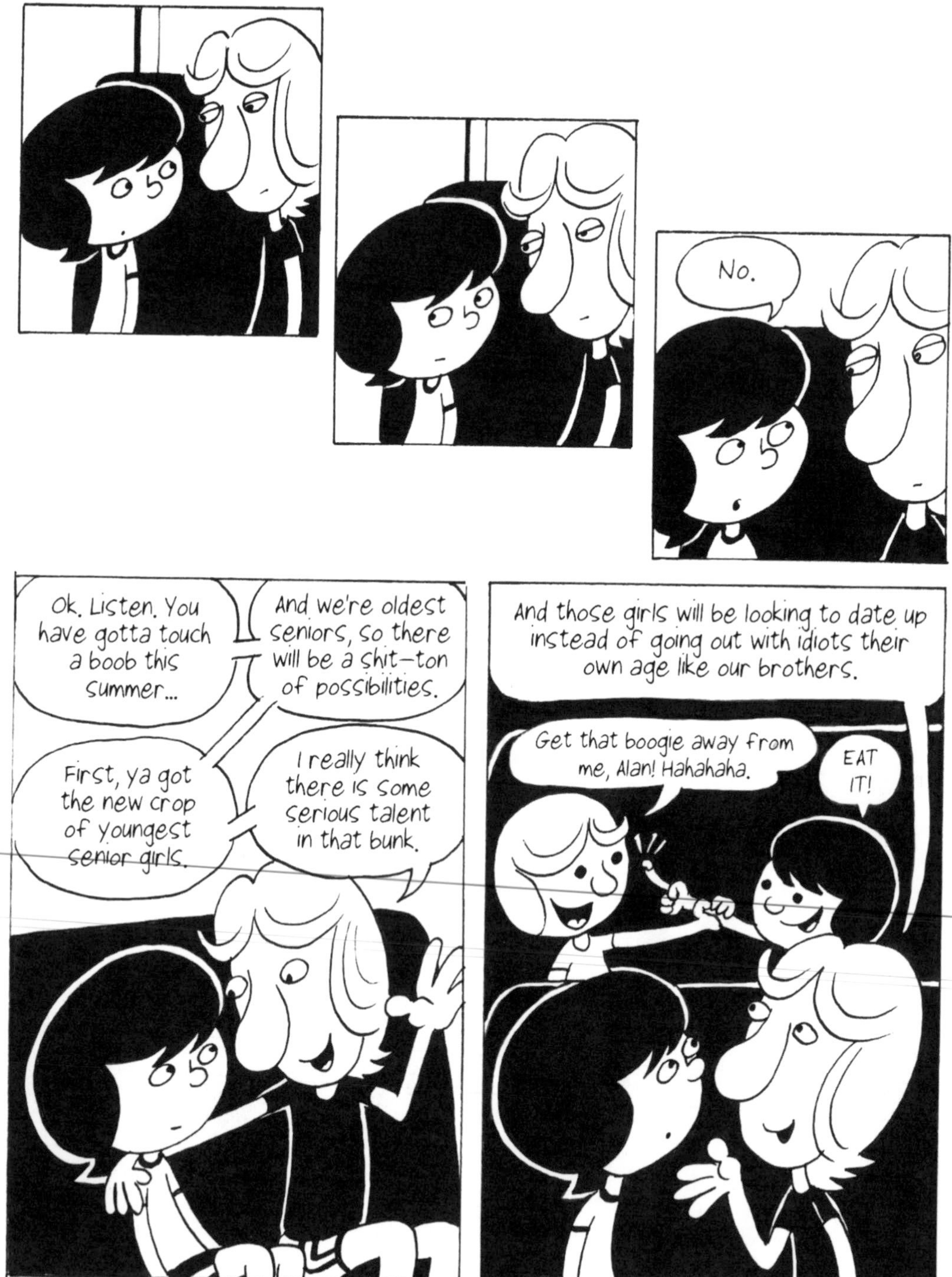
No.
Ok. Listen. You have gotta touch a boob this summer...
And we're oldest seniors, so there will be a shit-ton of possibilities.
First, ya got the new crop of youngest senior girls.
I really think there is some serious talent in that bunk.
And those girls will be looking to date up instead of going out with idiots their own age like our brothers.
Get that boogie away from me, Alan! Hahahaha.
EAT IT!

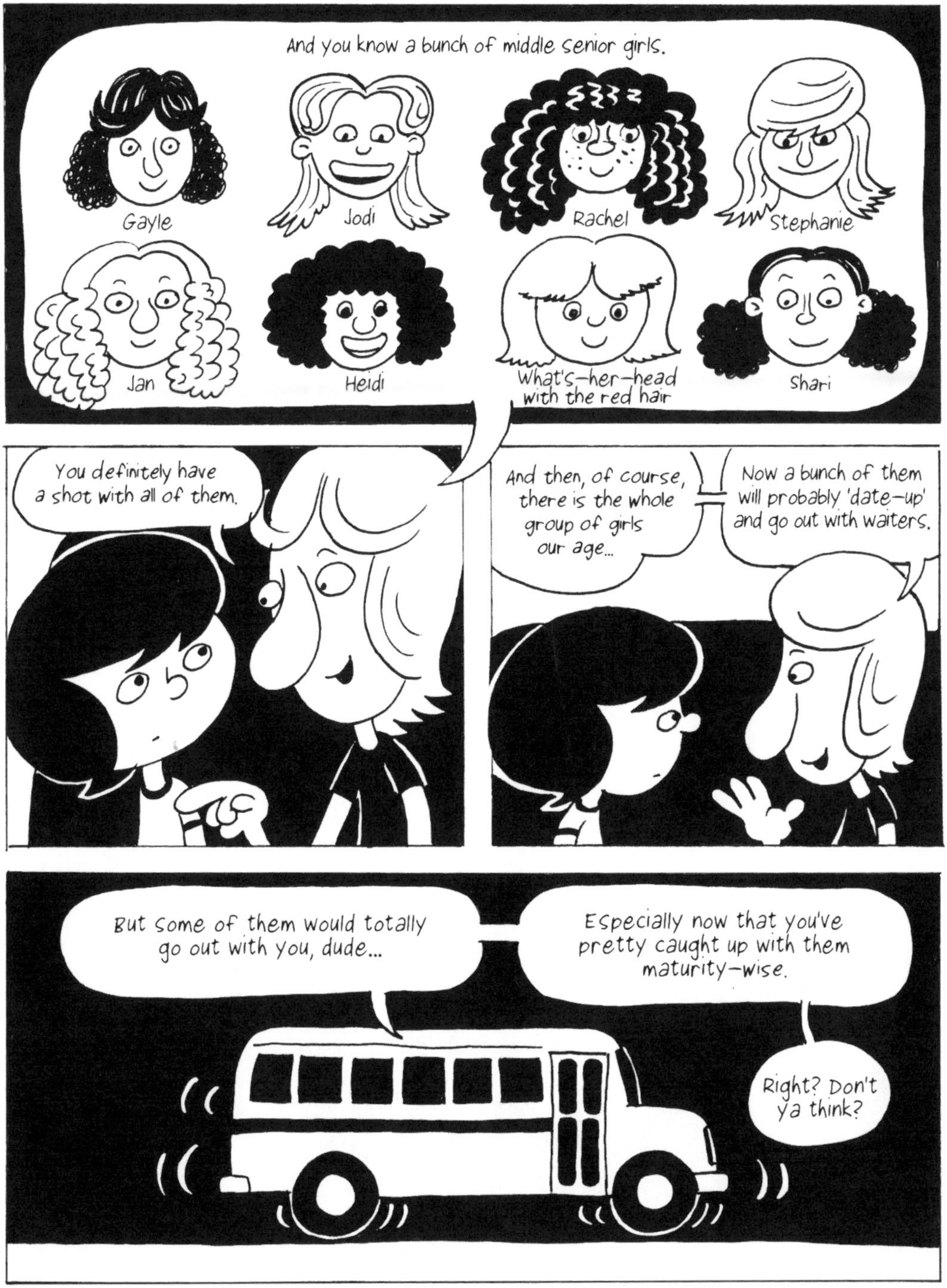

And you know a bunch of middle senior girls.
Gayle
Jodi
Rachel
Stephanie
Jan
Heidi
What's-her-head with the red hair
Shari
You definitely have a shot with all of them.
And then, of course, there is the whole group of girls our age...
Now a bunch of them will probably 'date-up' and go out with waiters.
But some of them would totally go out with you, dude...
Especially now that you've pretty caught up with them maturity-wise.
Right? Don't ya think?

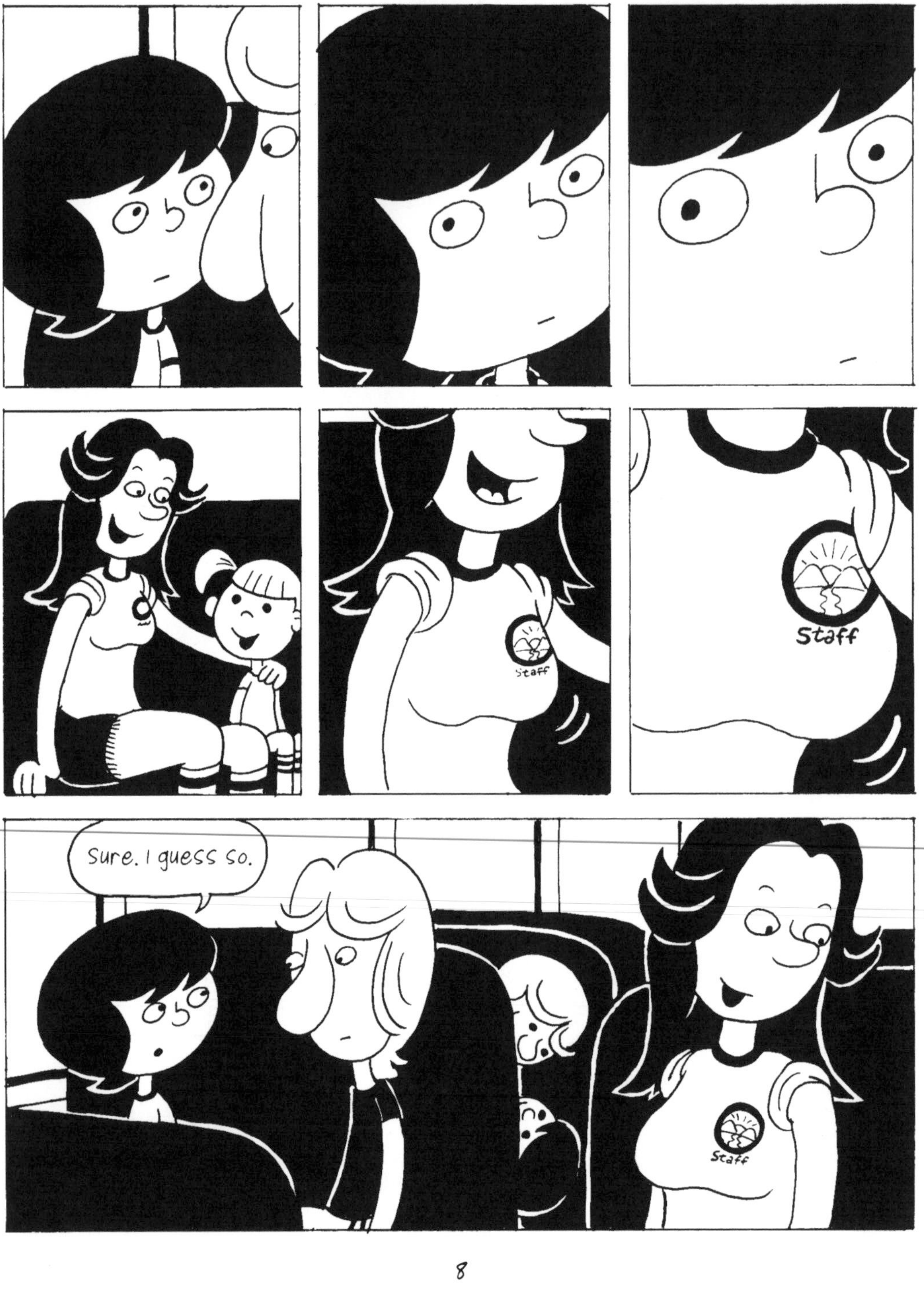
Staff
Staff
Sure. I guess so.
Staff

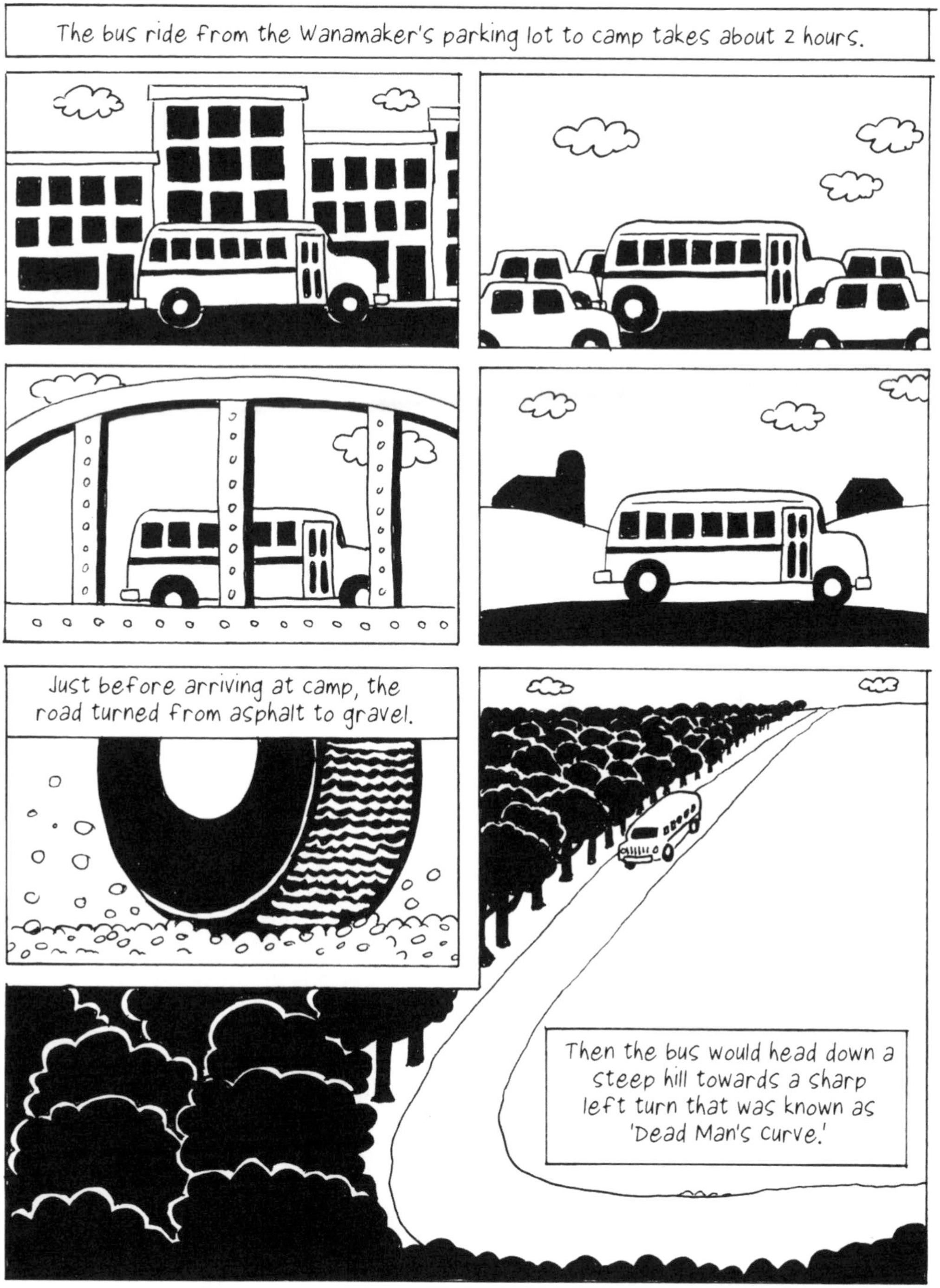
The bus ride from the Wanamaker's parking lot to camp takes about 2 hours.
Just before arriving at camp, the road turned from asphalt to gravel.
Then the bus would head down a steep hill towards a sharp left turn that was known as 'Dead Man's Curve.'

But it wasn't known as "Dead Man's Curve" because of the treacherous terrain, the vertical hill, or the sharp right turn.

Do you think he'll be there?

I mean, yeh. He's always there.

Oh shit.

He's there.

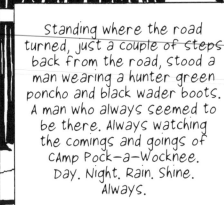

Standing where the road turned, just a couple of steps back from the road, stood a man wearing a hunter green poncho and black wader boots. A man who always seemed to be there. Always watching the comings and goings of Camp Pock-a-Wocknee. Day. Night. Rain. Shine. Always.

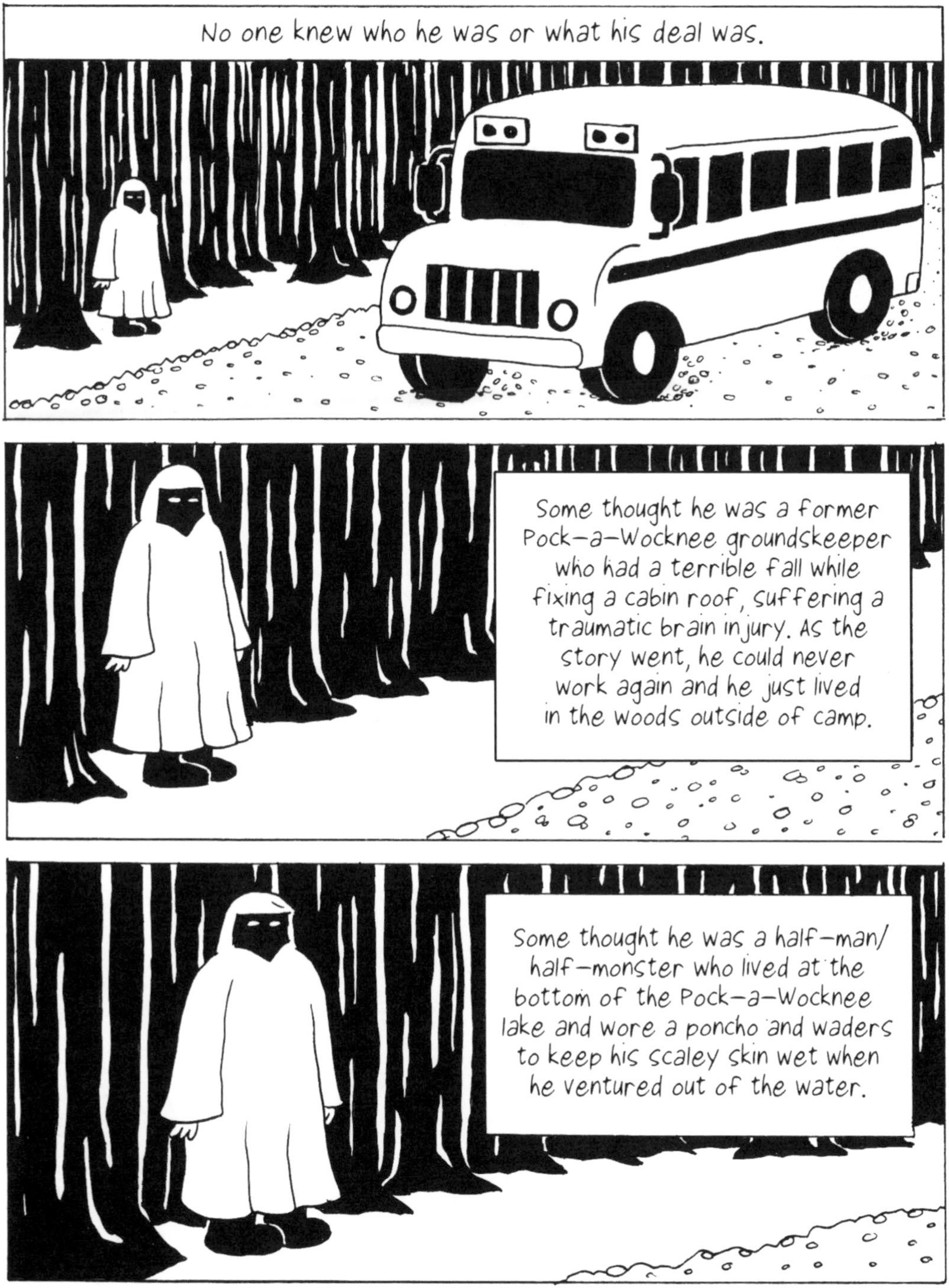
No one knew who he was or what his deal was.
Some thought he was a former Pock-a-Wocknee groundskeeper who had a terrible fall while fixing a cabin roof, suffering a traumatic brain injury. As the story went, he could never work again and he just lived in the woods outside of camp.
Some thought he was a half-man/half-monster who lived at the bottom of the Pock-a-Wocknee lake and wore a poncho and waders to keep his scaley skin wet when he ventured out of the water.

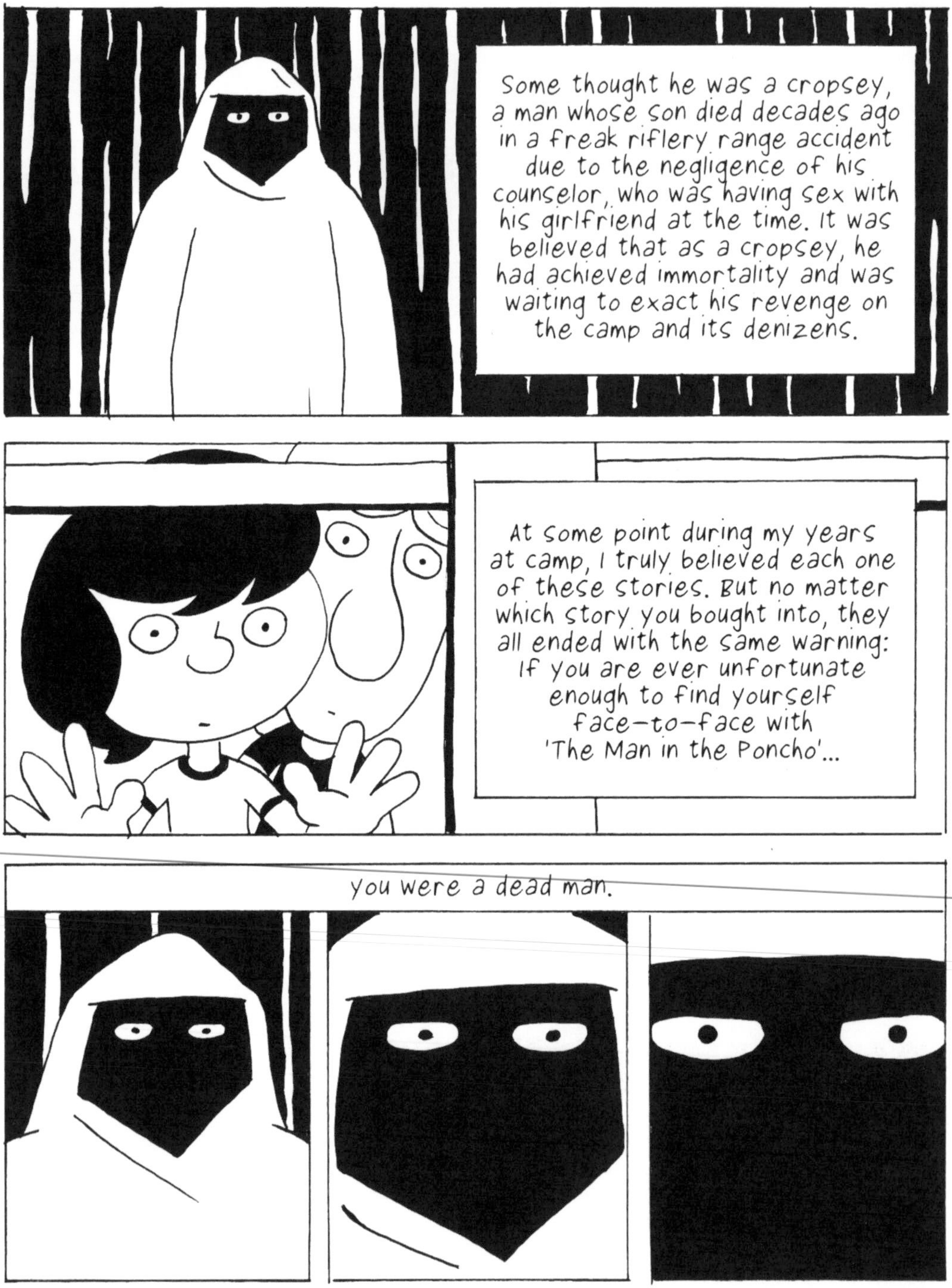
Some thought he was a cropsey, a man whose son died decades ago in a freak riflery range accident due to the negligence of his counselor, who was having sex with his girlfriend at the time. It was believed that as a cropsey, he had achieved immortality and was waiting to exact his revenge on the camp and its denizens.
At some point during my years at camp, I truly believed each one of these stories. But no matter which story you bought into, they all ended with the same warning: If you are ever unfortunate enough to find yourself face-to-face with 'The Man in the Poncho'...
you were a dead man.

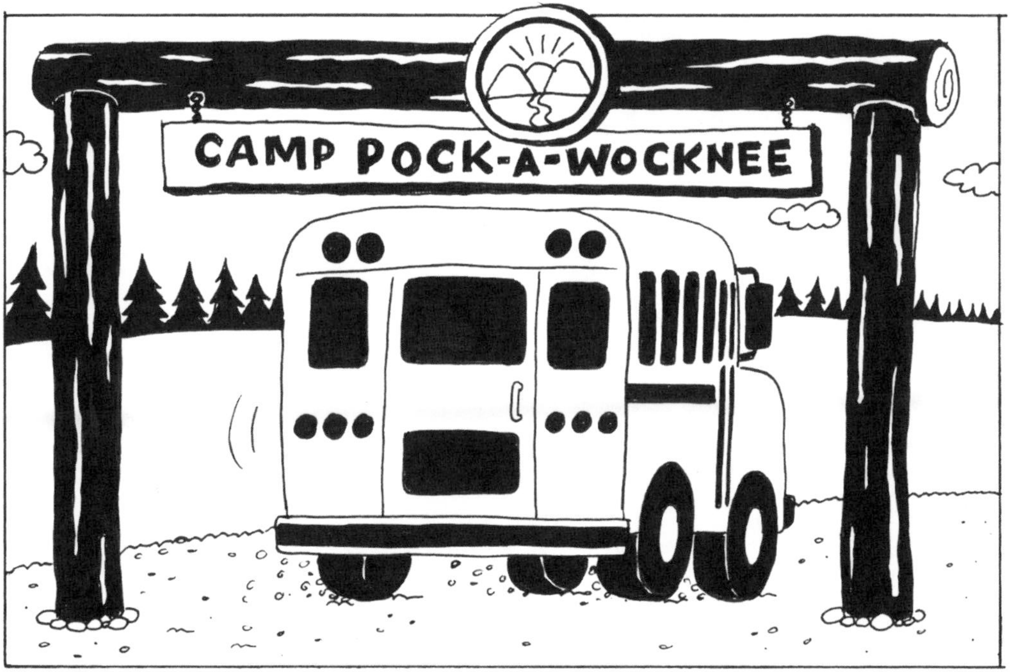
CAMP POCK-A-WOCKNEE

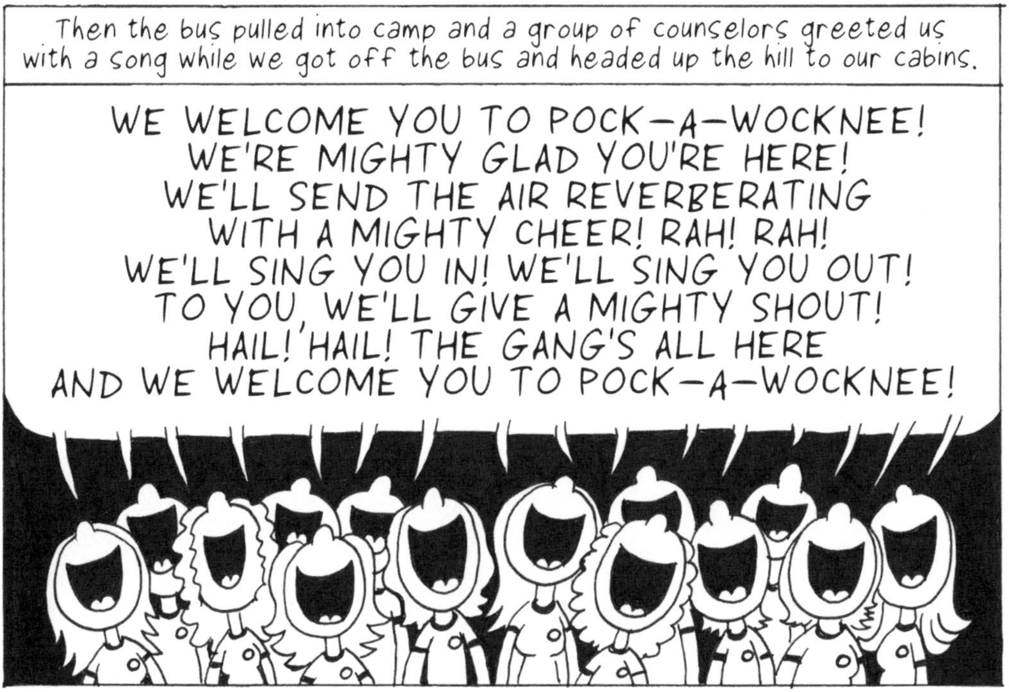
Then the bus pulled into camp and a group of counselors greeted us with a song while we got off the bus and headed up the hill to our cabins.
WE WELCOME YOU TO POCK-A-WOCKNEE! WE'RE MIGHTY GLAD YOU'RE HERE! WE'LL SEND THE AIR REVERBERATING WITH A MIGHTY CHEER! RAH! RAH! WE'LL SING YOU IN! WE'LL SING YOU OUT! TO YOU, WE'LL GIVE A MIGHTY SHOUT! HAIL! HAIL! THE GANG'S ALL HERE AND WE WELCOME YOU TO POCK-A-WOCKNEE!

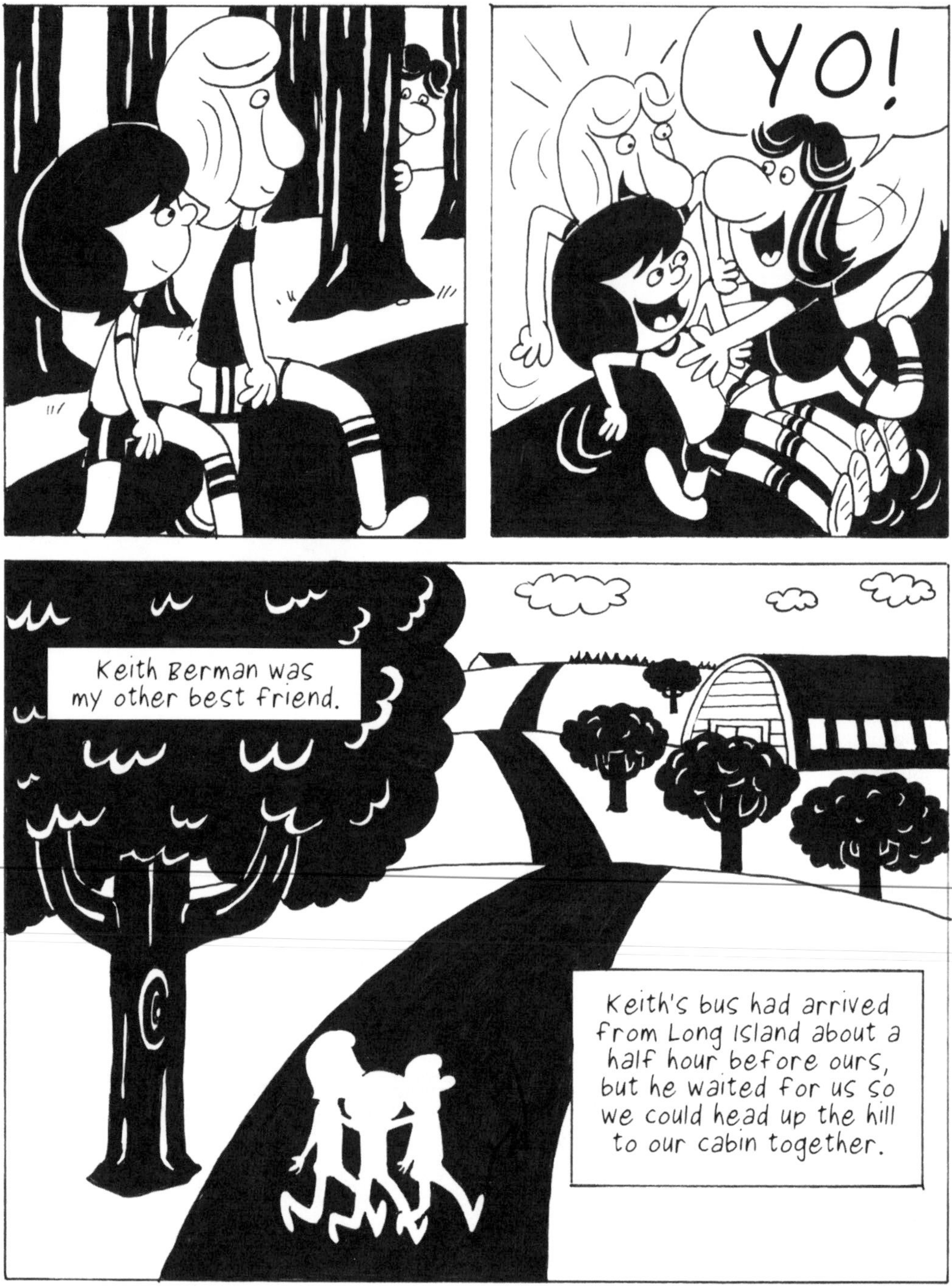
YO!
Keith Berman was my other best friend.
Keith's bus had arrived from Long Island about a half hour before ours, but he waited for us so we could head up the hill to our cabin together.

We walked past the Lower Hill and the cabins we lived in as Juniors.

We made our way to the Upper Hill where the oldest Senior Boys' cabin stood closest to the road.

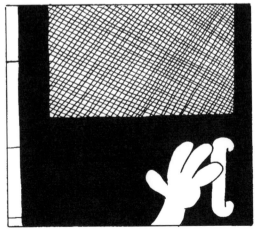

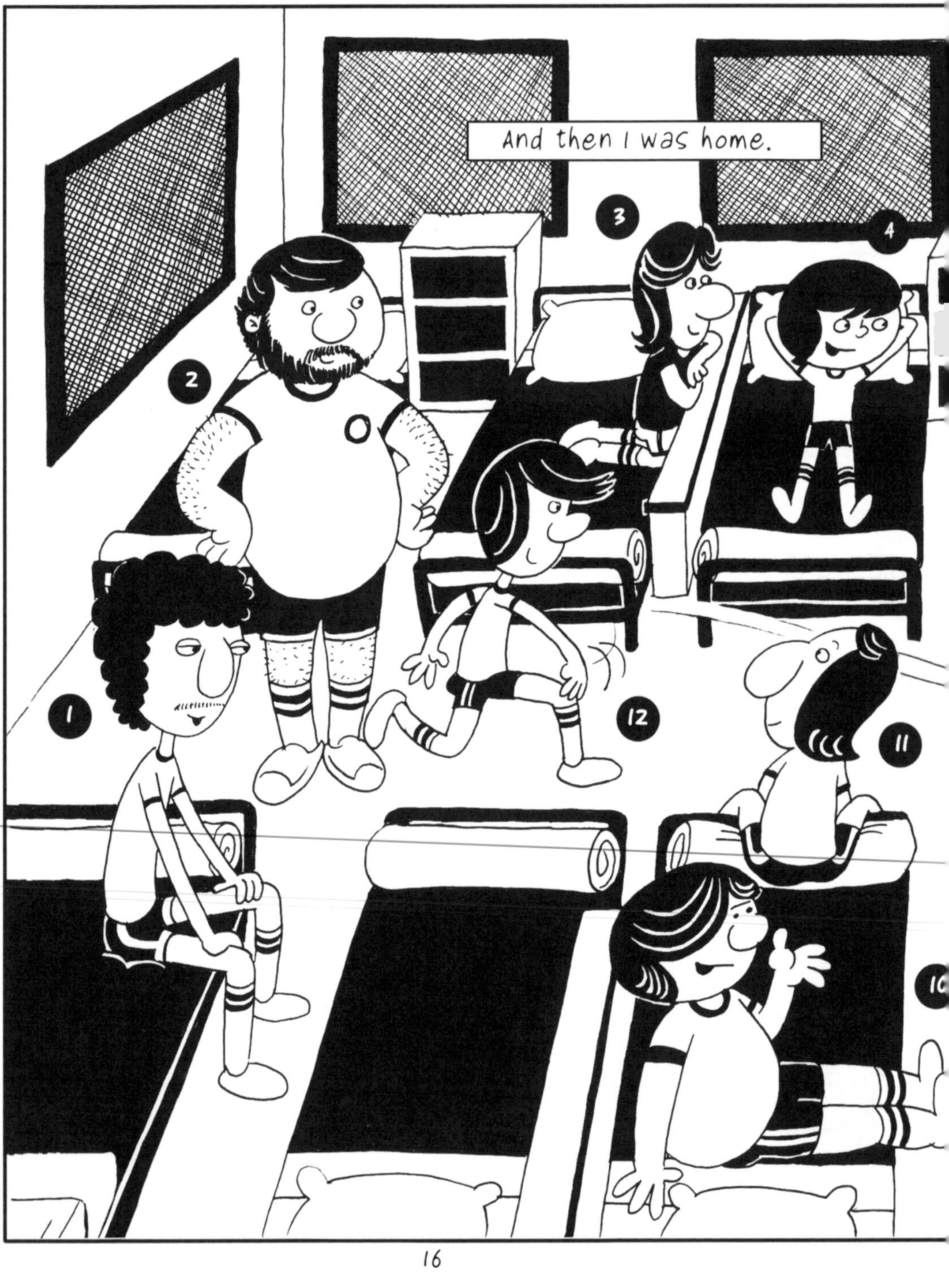
And then I was home.

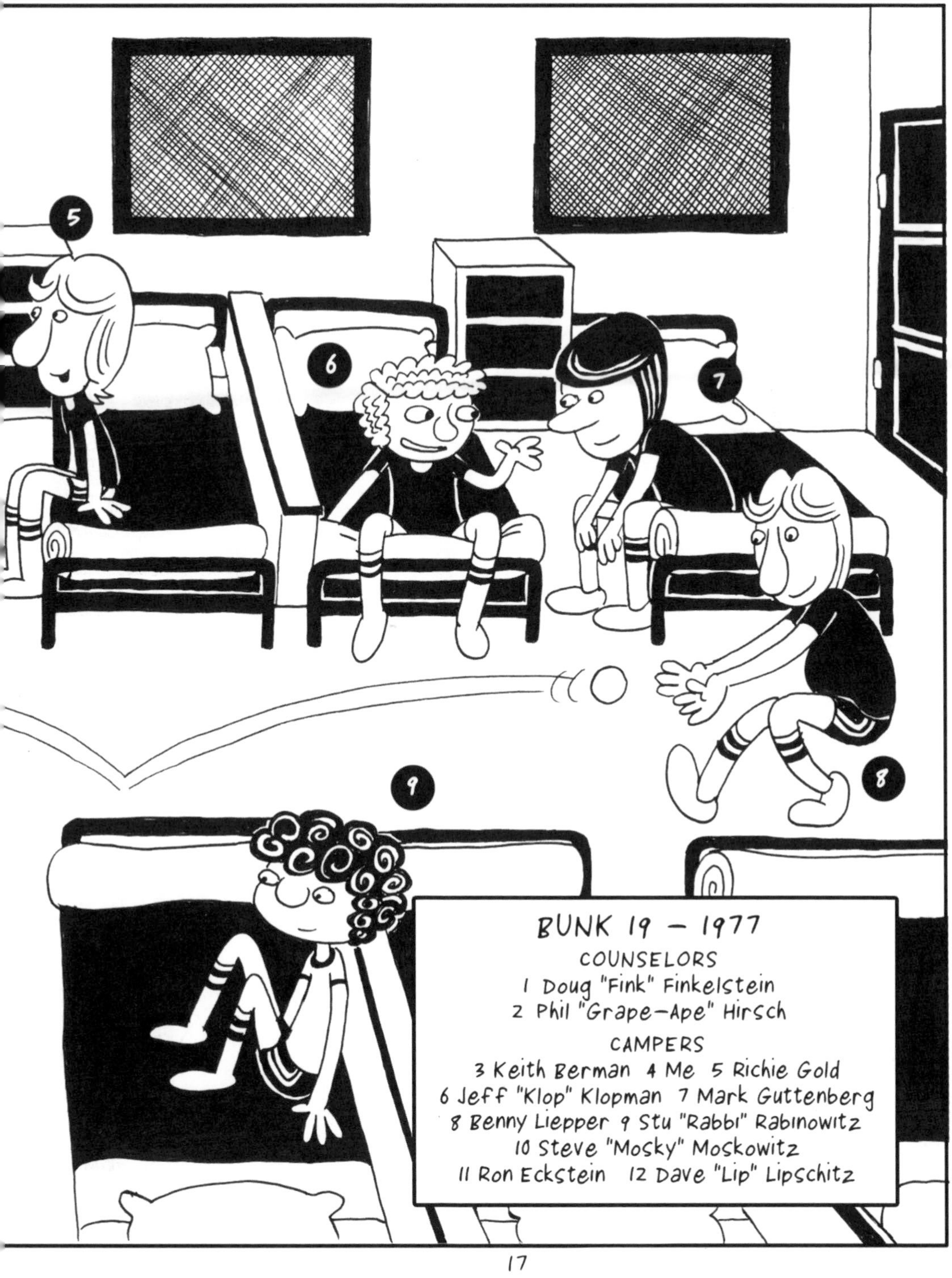
5
6
7
9
8
BUNK 19 — 1977
COUNSELORS
1 Doug "Fink" Finkelstein
2 Phil "Grape-Ape" Hirsch
CAMPERS
3 Keith Berman 4 Me 5 Richie Gold
6 Jeff "Klop" Klopman 7 Mark Guttenberg
8 Benny Liepper 9 Stu "Rabbi" Rabinowitz
10 Steve "Mosky" Moskowitz
11 Ron Eckstein 12 Dave "Lip" Lipschitz

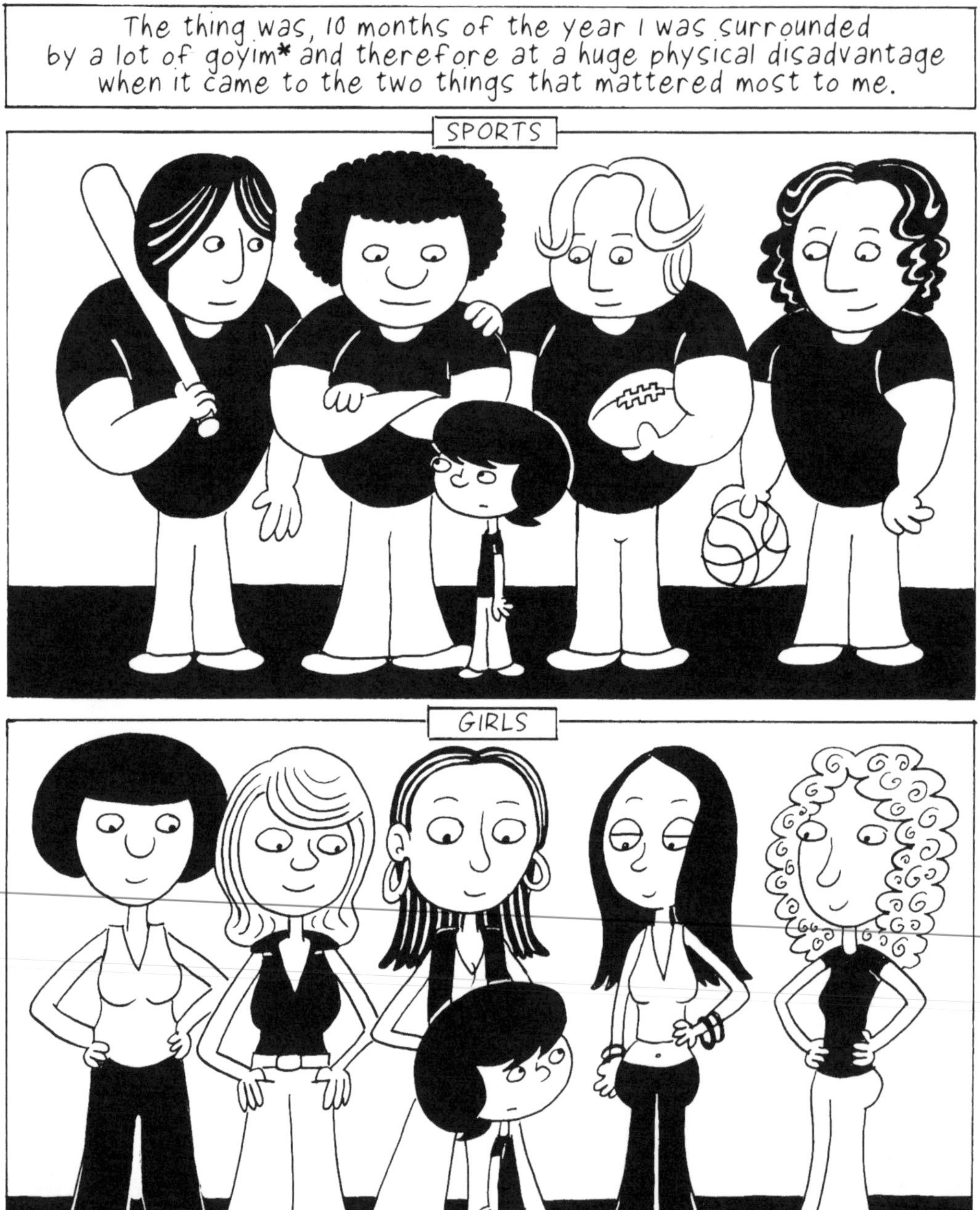
The thing was, 10 months of the year I was surrounded by a lot of goyim* and therefore at a huge physical disadvantage when it came to the two things that mattered most to me.
SPORTS
GIRLS
*Yiddish for 'Non-Jew'

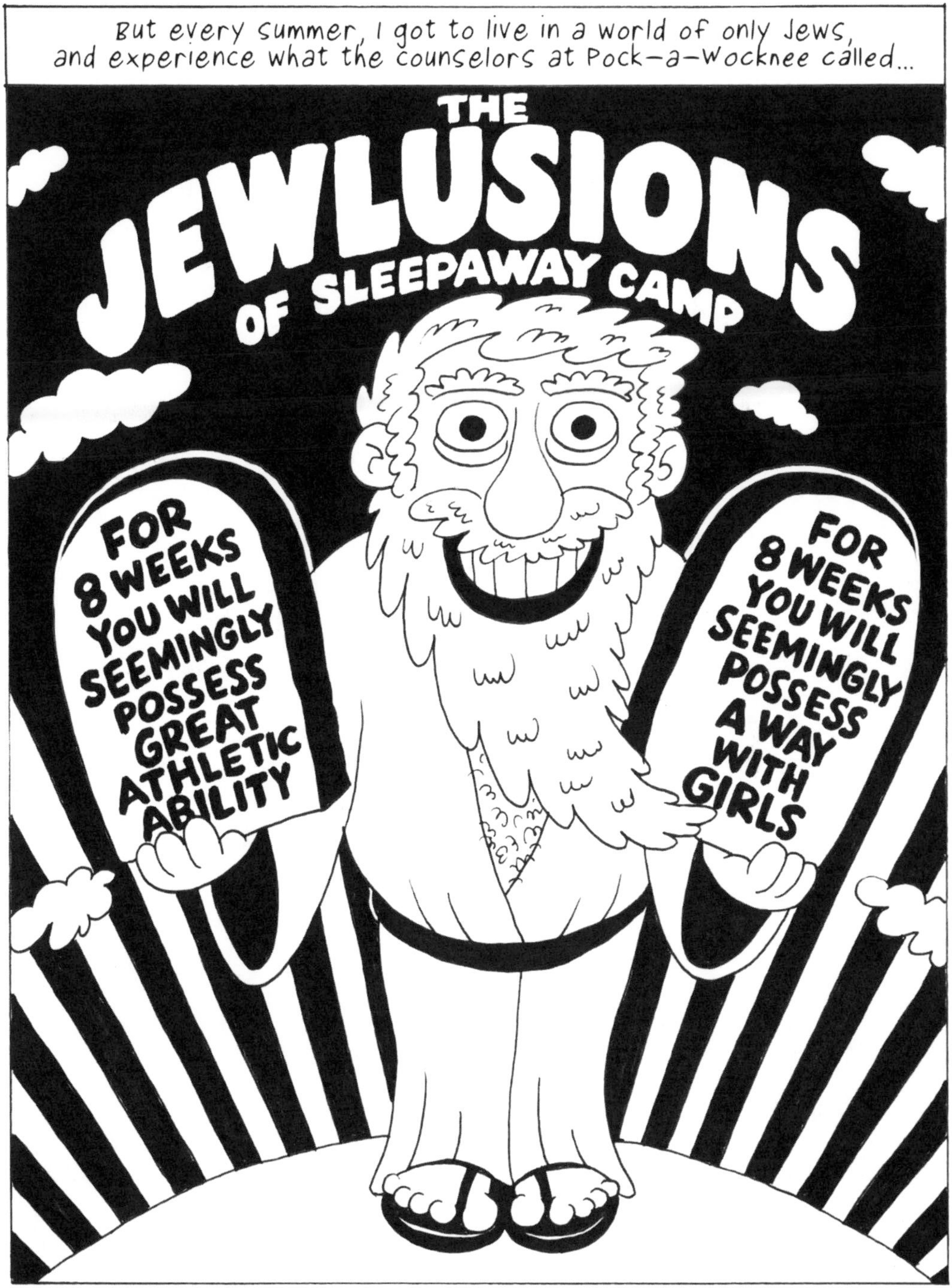
But every summer, I got to live in a world of only Jews, and experience what the counselors at Pock-a-Wocknee called...
THE JEWLUSIONS OF SLEEPAWAY CAMP
FOR 8 WEEKS YOU WILL SEEMINGLY POSSESS GREAT ATHLETIC ABILITY
FOR 8 WEEKS YOU WILL SEEMINGLY POSSESS A WAY WITH GIRLS

The first meal of the summer was always CHEESE BOATS — toasted hoagie roll halves with melted American cheese and tomato sauce.

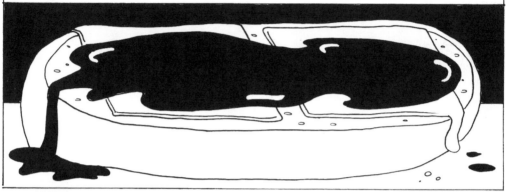

Hey! yo! Chef Ralph! How ya doin'? Ready for another summer?

uf coorz i em redee.

yoo liddell fish-fukker

i havf bin dooing dis sinz yoo werr een yerr daddeez ballz

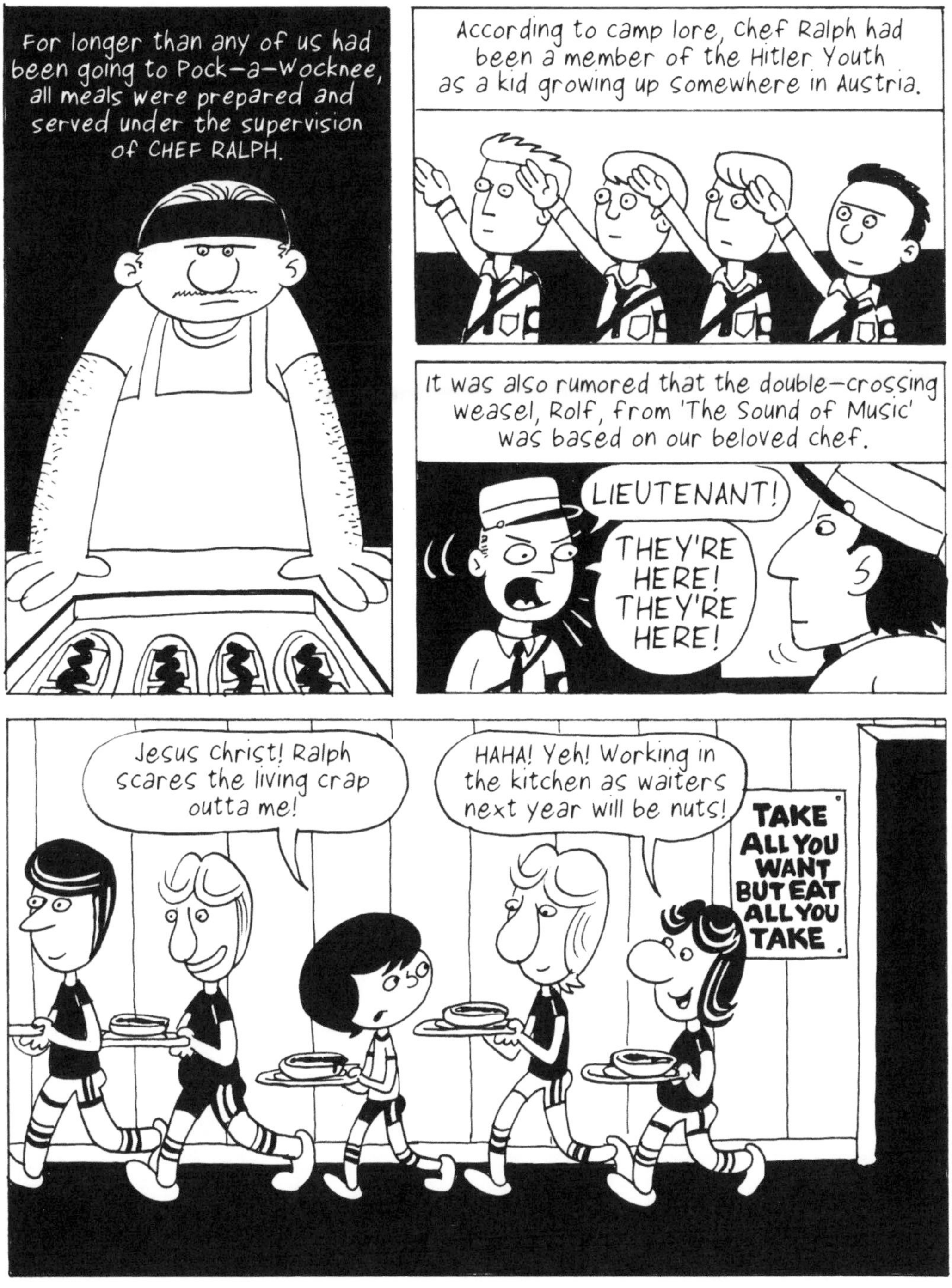
For longer than any of us had been going to Pock-a-Wocknee, all meals were prepared and served under the supervision of CHEF RALPH.
According to camp lore, Chef Ralph had been a member of the Hitler Youth as a kid growing up somewhere in Austria.
It was also rumored that the double-crossing weasel, Rolf, from 'The Sound of Music' was based on our beloved chef.
LIEUTENANT!
THEY'RE HERE! THEY'RE HERE!
Jesus Christ! Ralph scares the living crap outta me!
HAHA! Yeh! Working in the kitchen as waiters next year will be nuts!
TAKE ALL YOU WANT BUT EAT ALL YOU TAKE

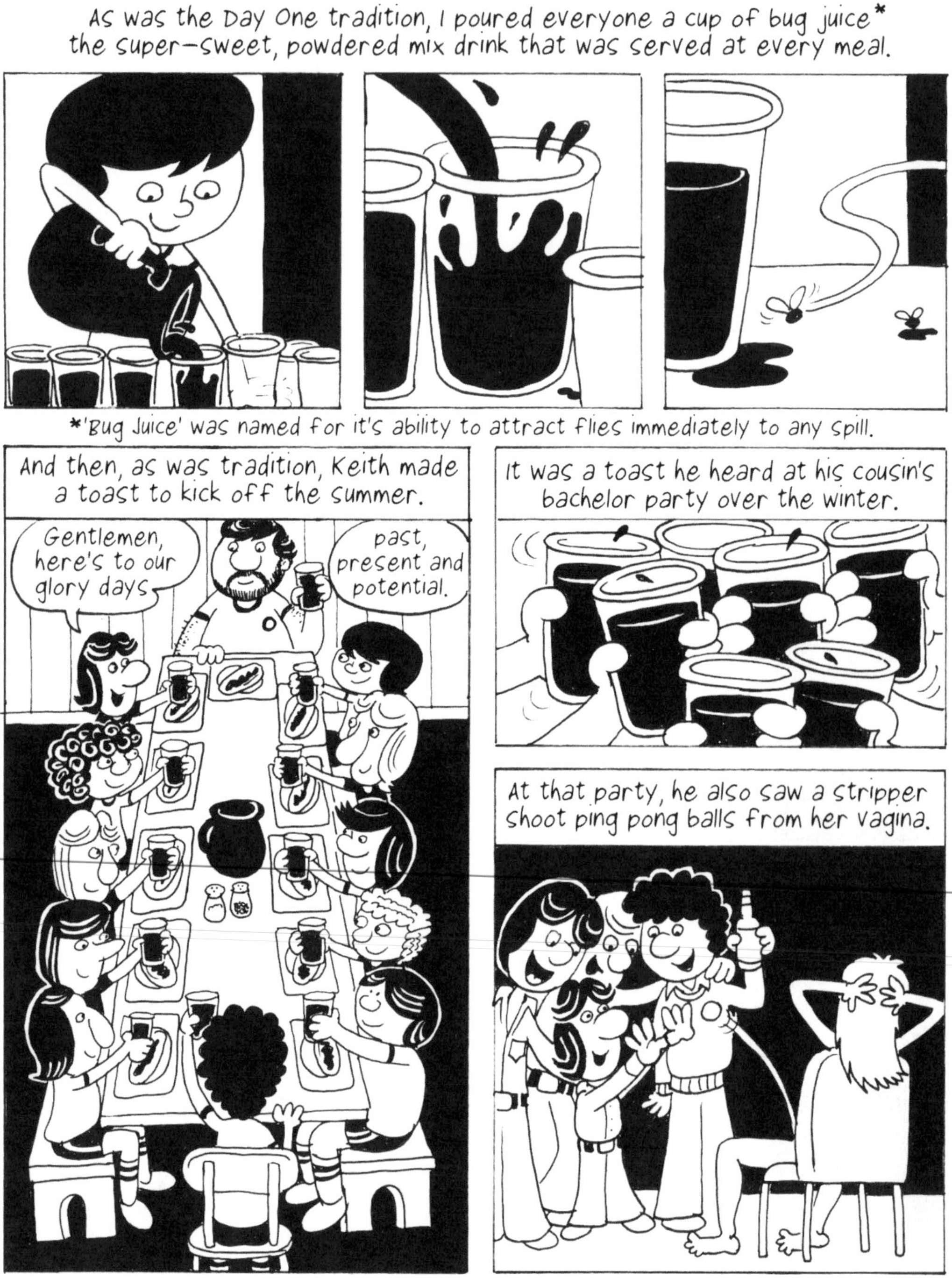

As was the Day One tradition, I poured everyone a cup of bug juice*
the super-sweet, powdered mix drink that was served at every meal.
*'Bug Juice' was named for it's ability to attract flies immediately to any spill.
And then, as was tradition, Keith made a toast to kick off the summer.
Gentlemen, here's to our glory days
past, present and potential.
It was a toast he heard at his cousin's bachelor party over the winter.
At that party, he also saw a stripper shoot ping pong balls from her vagina.

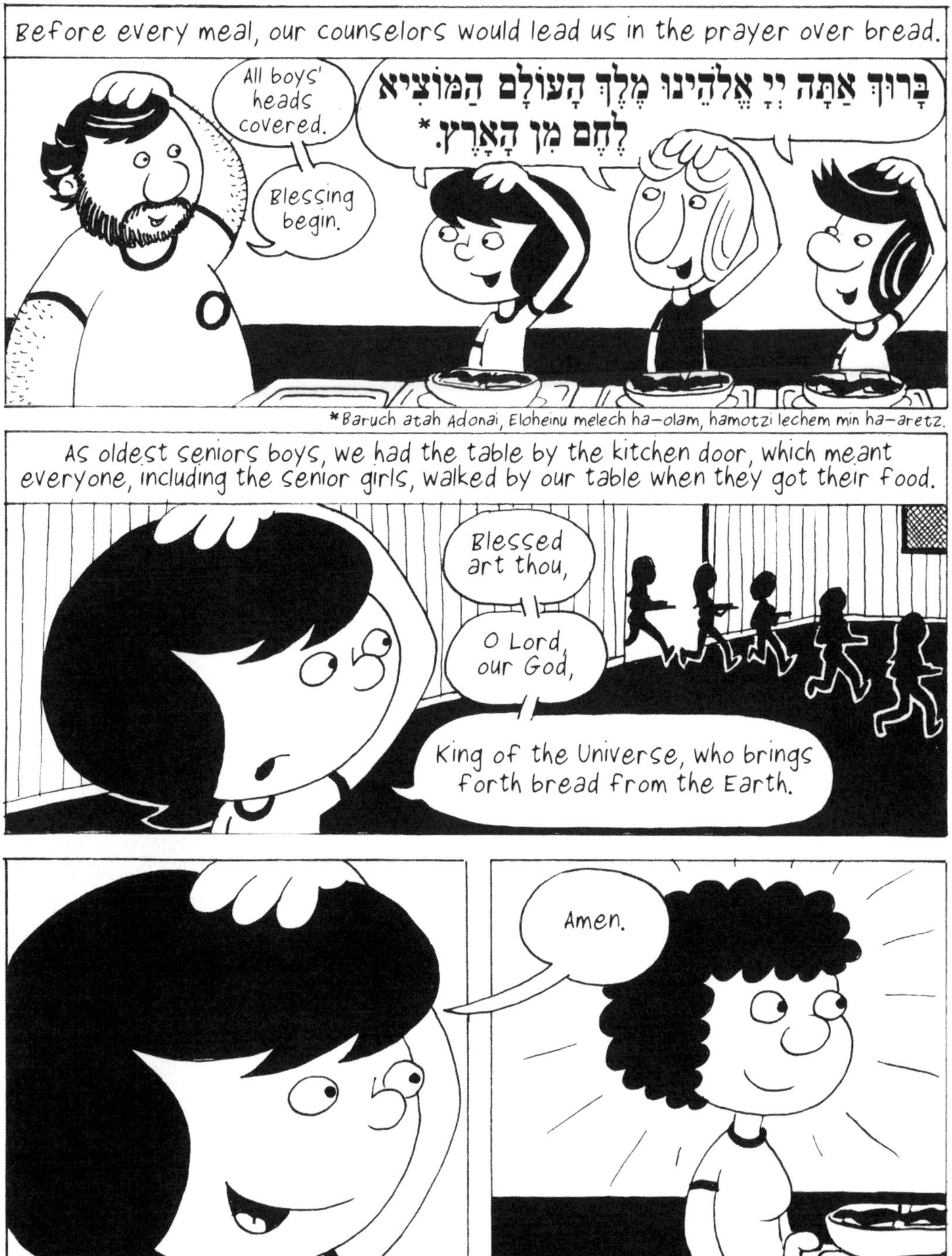
Before every meal, our counselors would lead us in the prayer over bread.
All boys' heads covered.
Blessing begin.
בָּרוּךְ אַתָּה יְיָ אֱלֹהֵינוּ מֶלֶךְ הָעוֹלָם הַמּוֹצִיא לֶחֶם מִן הָאָרֶץ.*
*Baruch atah Adonai, Eloheinu melech ha-olam, hamotzi lechem min ha-aretz.
As oldest seniors boys, we had the table by the kitchen door, which meant everyone, including the senior girls, walked by our table when they got their food.
Blessed art thou,
O Lord, our God,
King of the Universe, who brings forth bread from the Earth.
Amen.

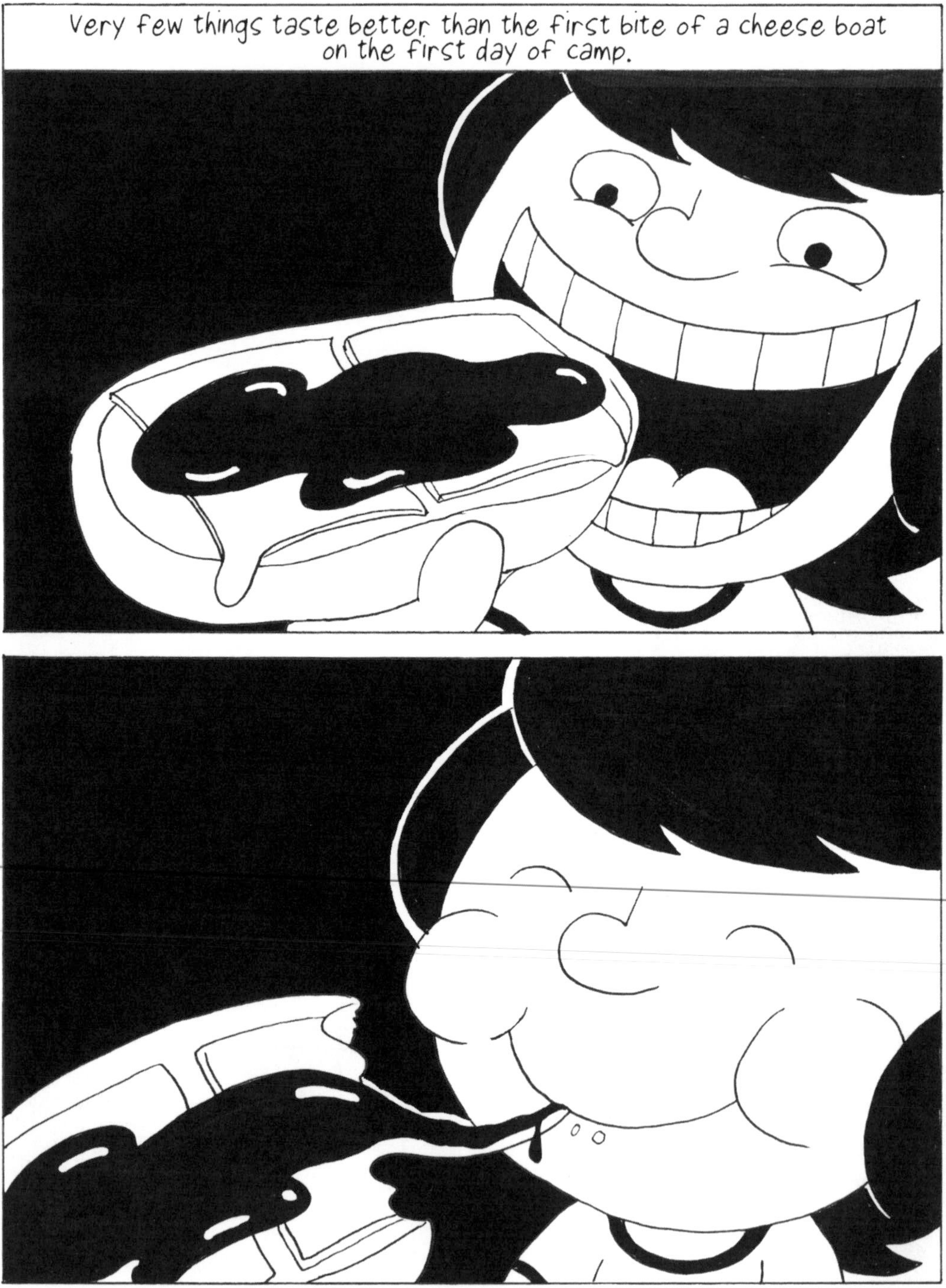
Very few things taste better than the first bite of a cheese boat on the first day of camp.

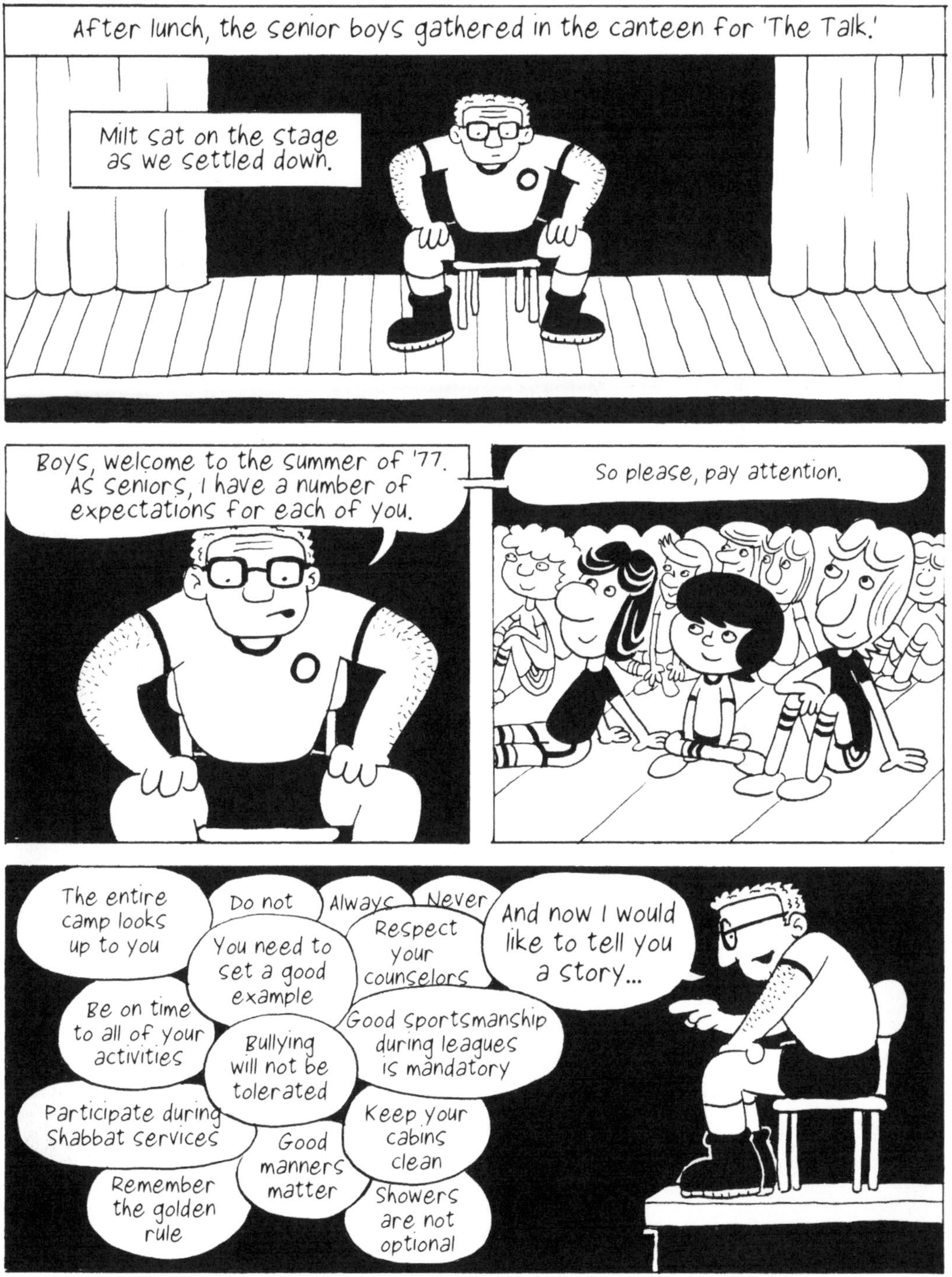

After lunch, the senior boys gathered in the canteen for 'The Talk.'
Milt sat on the stage as we settled down.
Boys, welcome to the summer of '77. As seniors, I have a number of expectations for each of you.
So please, pay attention.
The entire camp looks up to you
Do not
Always
Never
Respect your counselors
You need to set a good example
Be on time to all of your activities
Bullying will not be tolerated
Good sportsmanship during leagues is mandatory
Participate during Shabbat services
Good manners matter
Keep your cabins clean
Remember the golden rule
Showers are not optional
And now I would like to tell you a story...

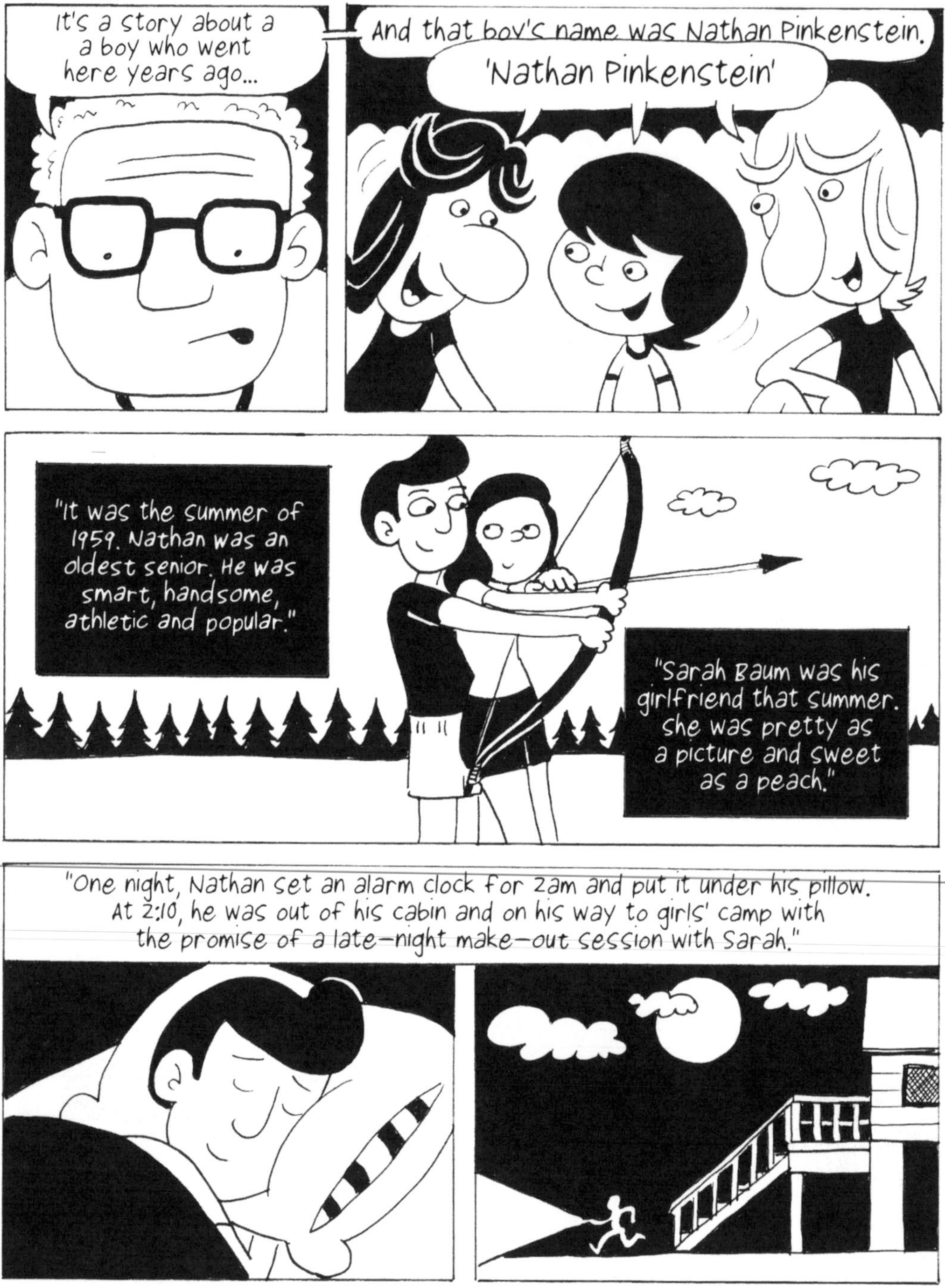
It's a story about a a boy who went here years ago...
And that boy's name was Nathan Pinkenstein.
'Nathan Pinkenstein'
"It was the summer of 1959. Nathan was an oldest senior. He was smart, handsome, athletic and popular."
"Sarah Baum was his girlfriend that summer. she was pretty as a picture and sweet as a peach."
"One night, Nathan set an alarm clock for 2am and put it under his pillow. At 2:10, he was out of his cabin and on his way to girls' camp with the promise of a late-night make-out session with Sarah."

Sarah.

"Now Nathan didn't know that I'm always awake at 2am, typing the morning flyer."

"So when I saw someone running from boys' camp to girls' camp, I followed."

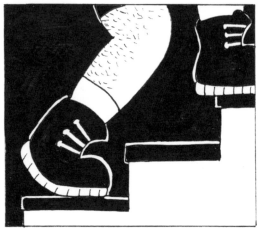

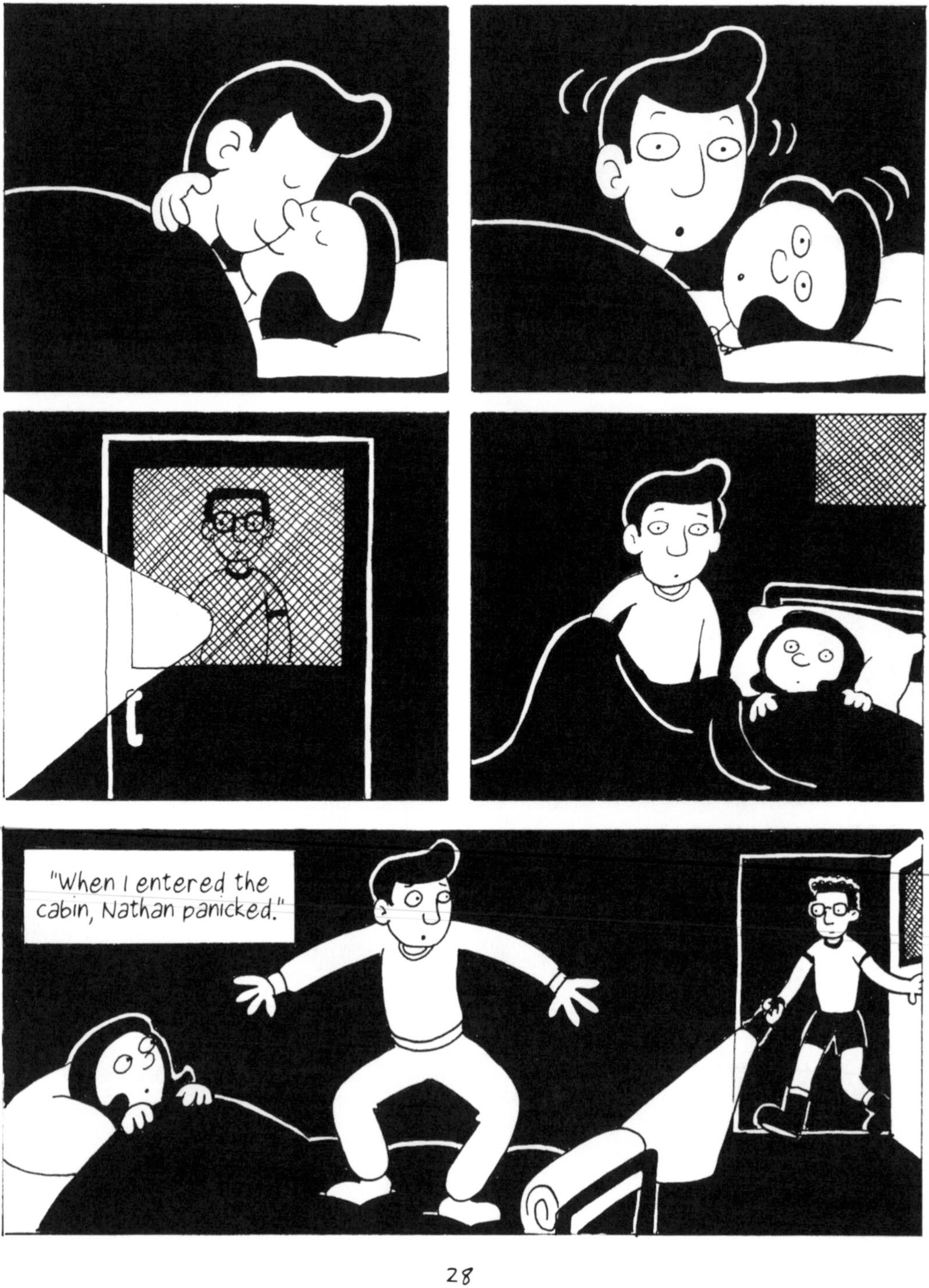
"When I entered the cabin, Nathan panicked."

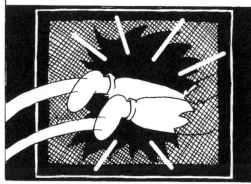

"And looking to escape, he dove through the screen window above Sarah's bed."

"I found Nathan laying on the ground in a heap, holding the side of his head."

"Then I saw a bloody ear hanging by a nail on the side of the cabin."

Nathan Pinkenstein had ripped his ear clean off of his head.

We all sat there in stunned silence, staring up at Milt on the stage.

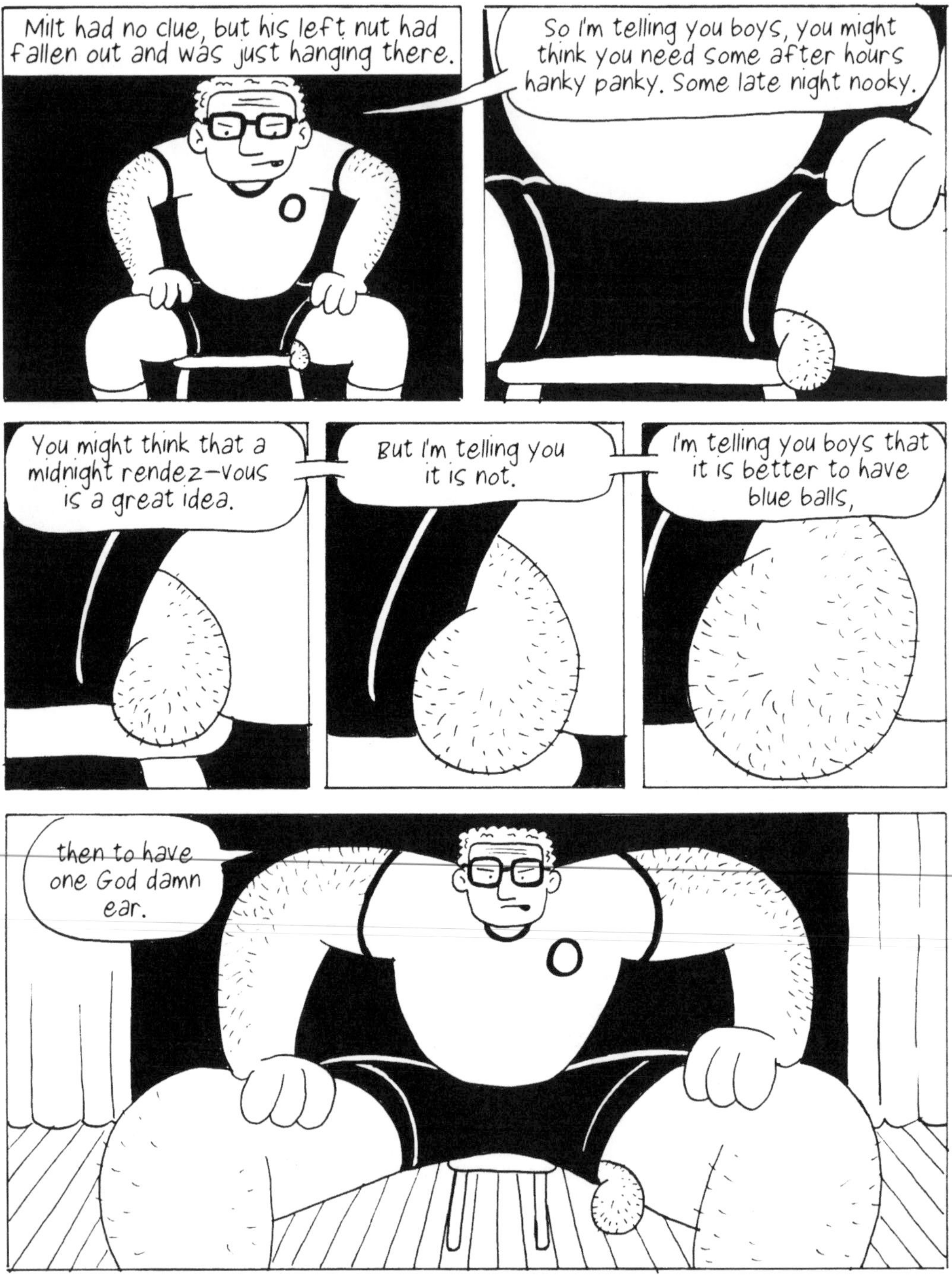
Milt had no clue, but his left nut had fallen out and was just hanging there.
So I'm telling you boys, you might think you need some after hours hanky panky. Some late night nooky.
You might think that a midnight rendez-vous is a great idea.
But I'm telling you it is not.
I'm telling you boys that it is better to have blue balls,
then to have one God damn ear.

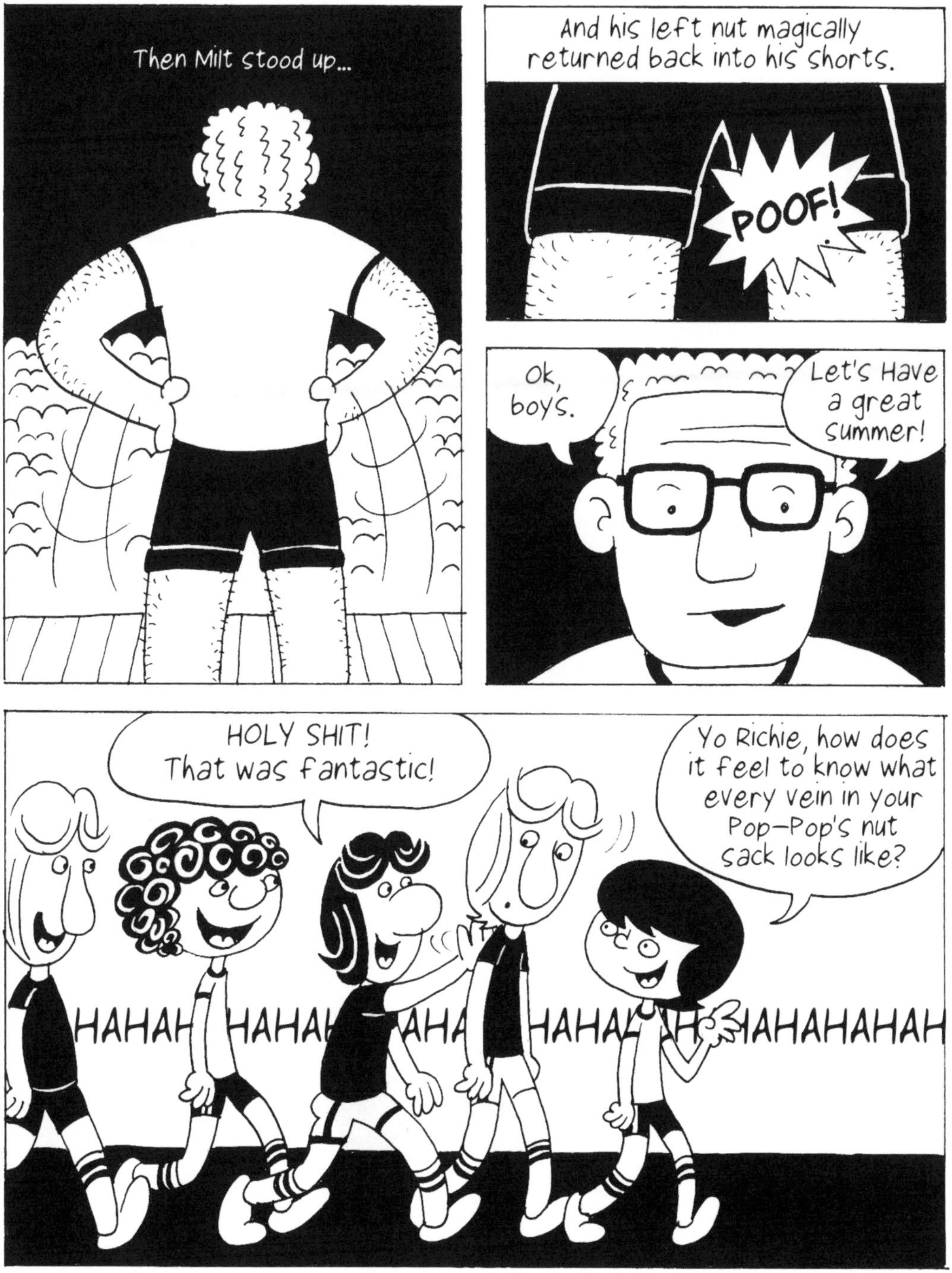
Then Milt stood up...
And his left nut magically returned back into his shorts.
POOF!
Ok, boys.
Let's Have a great summer!
HOLY SHIT! That was fantastic!
Yo Richie, how does it feel to know what every vein in your Pop-Pop's nut sack looks like?
HAHAHAHAHAHAHAHAHAHAHAHAHAHAHAHAHAH

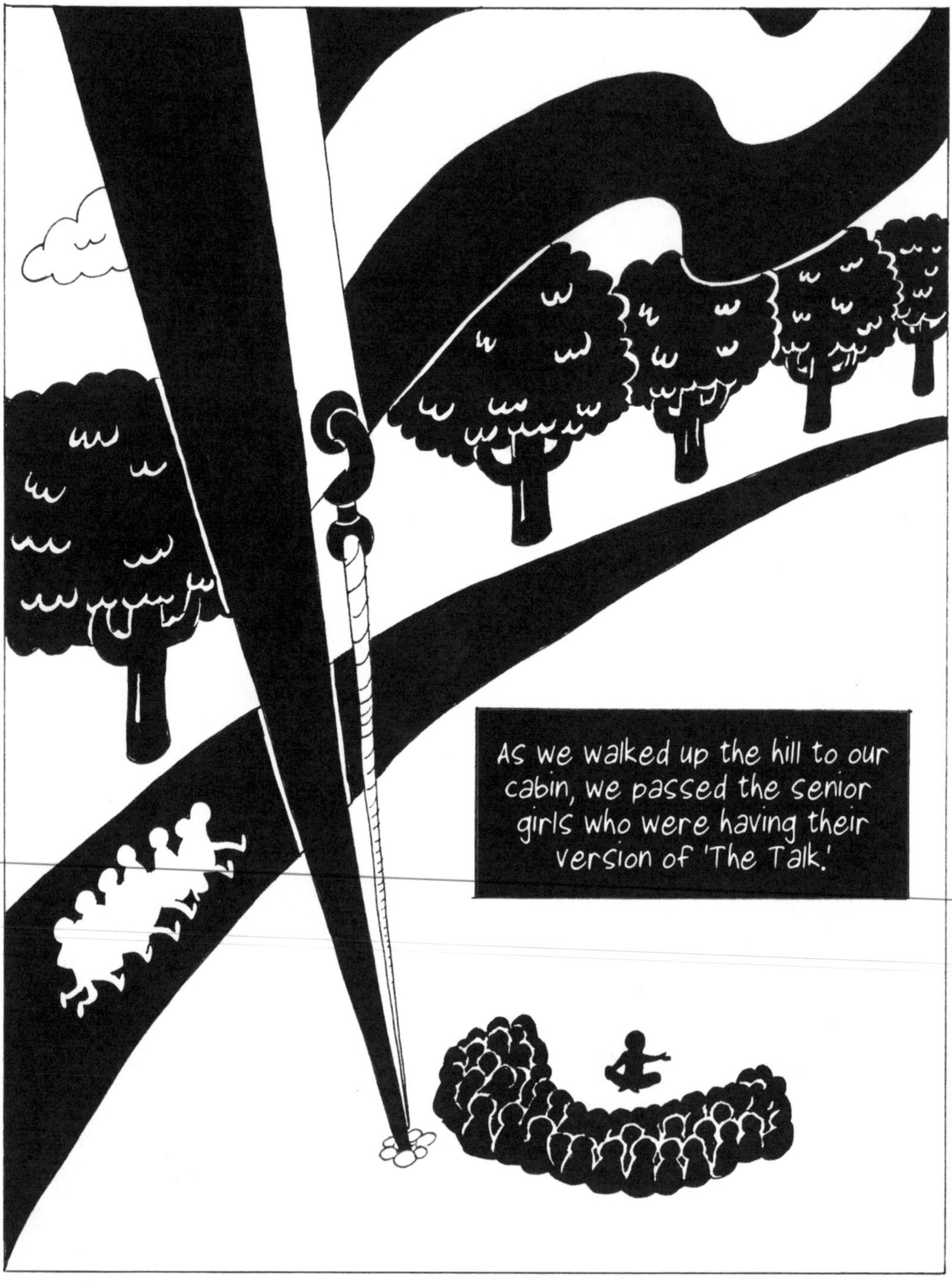
As we walked up the hill to our cabin, we passed the senior girls who were having their version of 'The Talk.'

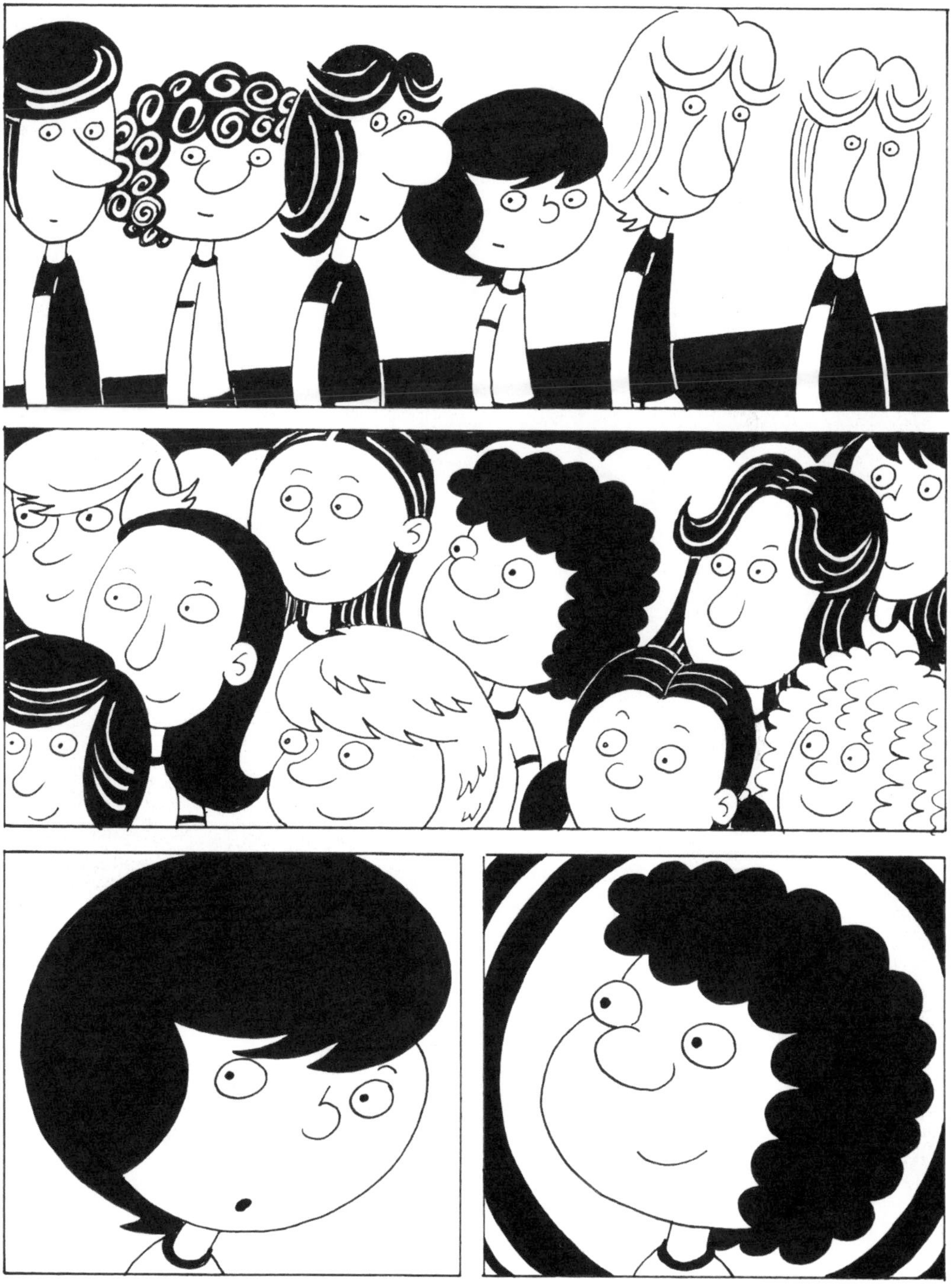

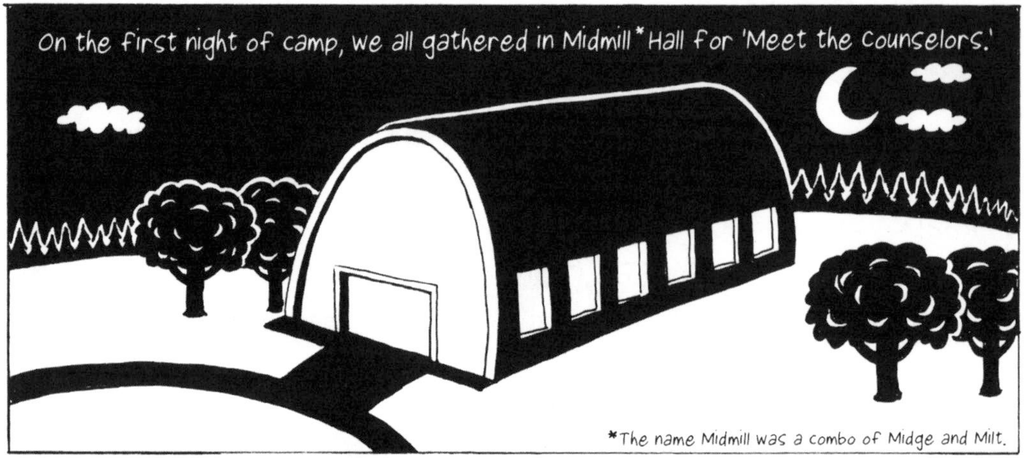
On the first night of camp, we all gathered in Midmill*Hall for 'Meet the Counselors.'
*The name Midmill was a combo of Midge and Milt.

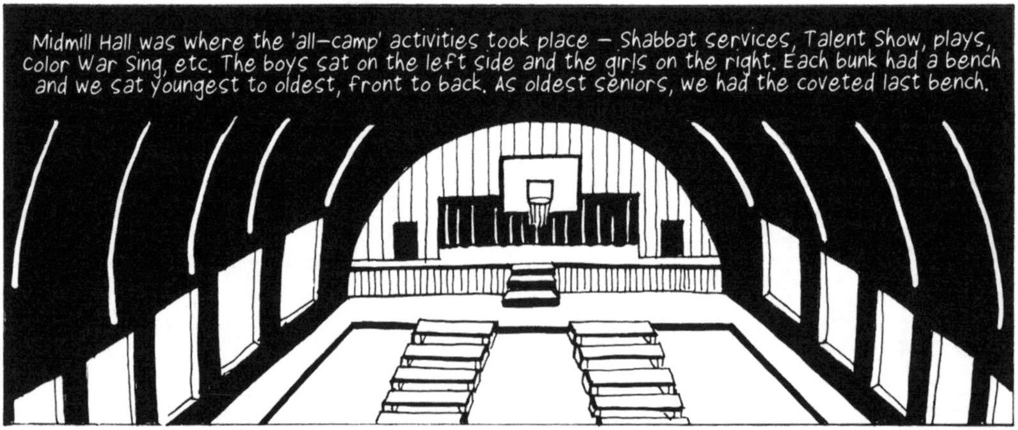
Midmill Hall was where the 'all-camp' activities took place – Shabbat services, Talent Show, plays, Color War Sing, etc. The boys sat on the left side and the girls on the right. Each bunk had a bench and we sat youngest to oldest, front to back. As oldest seniors, we had the coveted last bench.

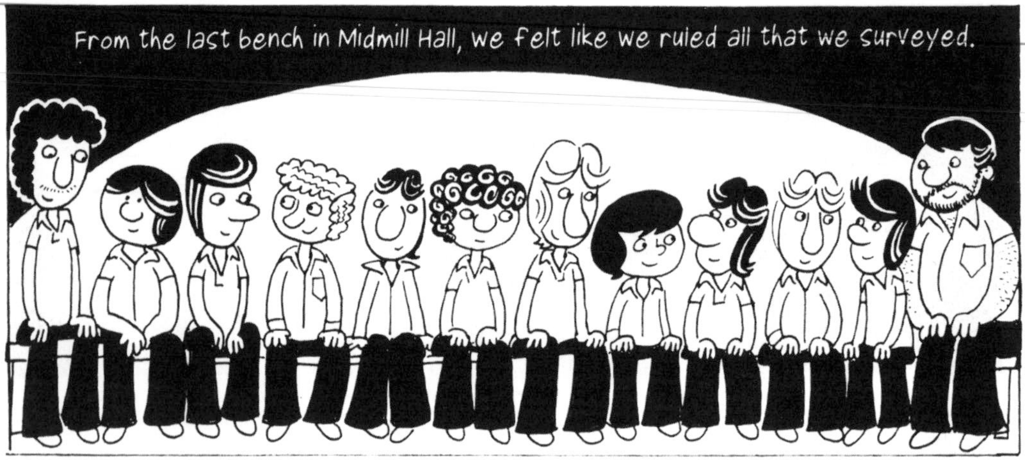
From the last bench in Midmill Hall, we felt like we ruled all that we surveyed.

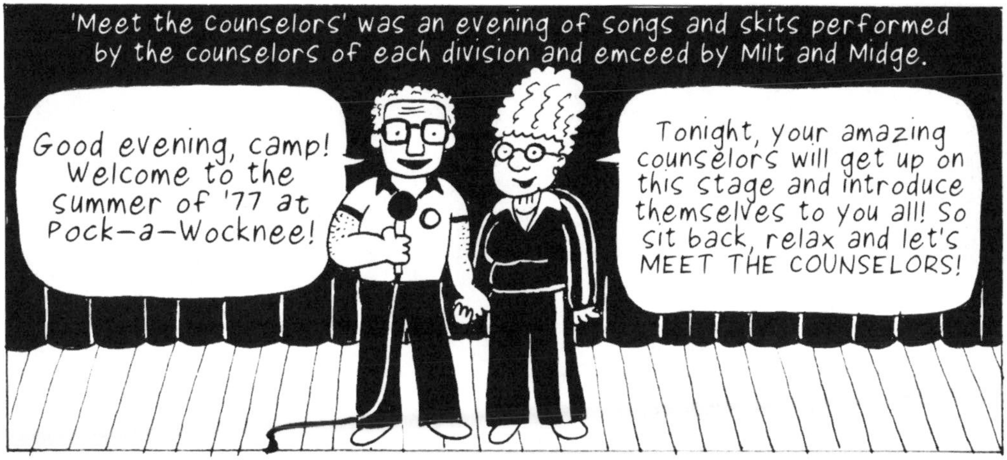
'Meet the Counselors' was an evening of songs and skits performed by the counselors of each division and emceed by Milt and Midge.
Good evening, camp! Welcome to the summer of '77 at Pock-a-Wocknee!
Tonight, your amazing counselors will get up on this stage and introduce themselves to you all! So sit back, relax and let's MEET THE COUNSELORS!

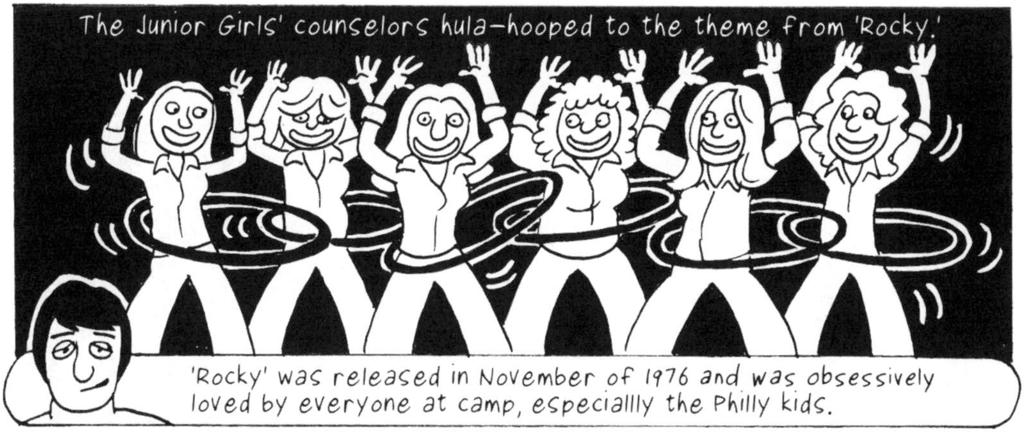
The Junior Girls' counselors hula-hooped to the theme from 'Rocky.'
'Rocky' was released in November of 1976 and was obsessively loved by everyone at camp, especiallly the Philly kids.

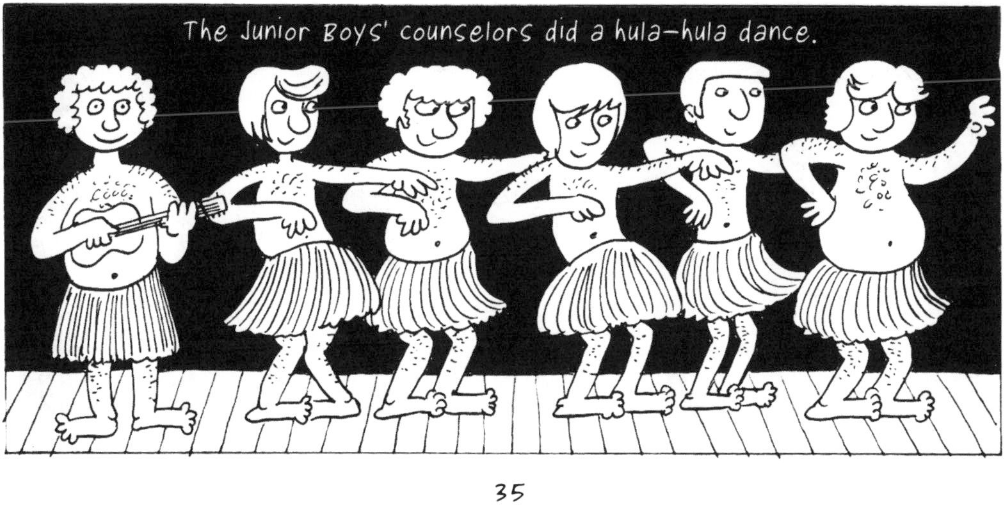
The Junior Boys' counselors did a hula-hula dance.

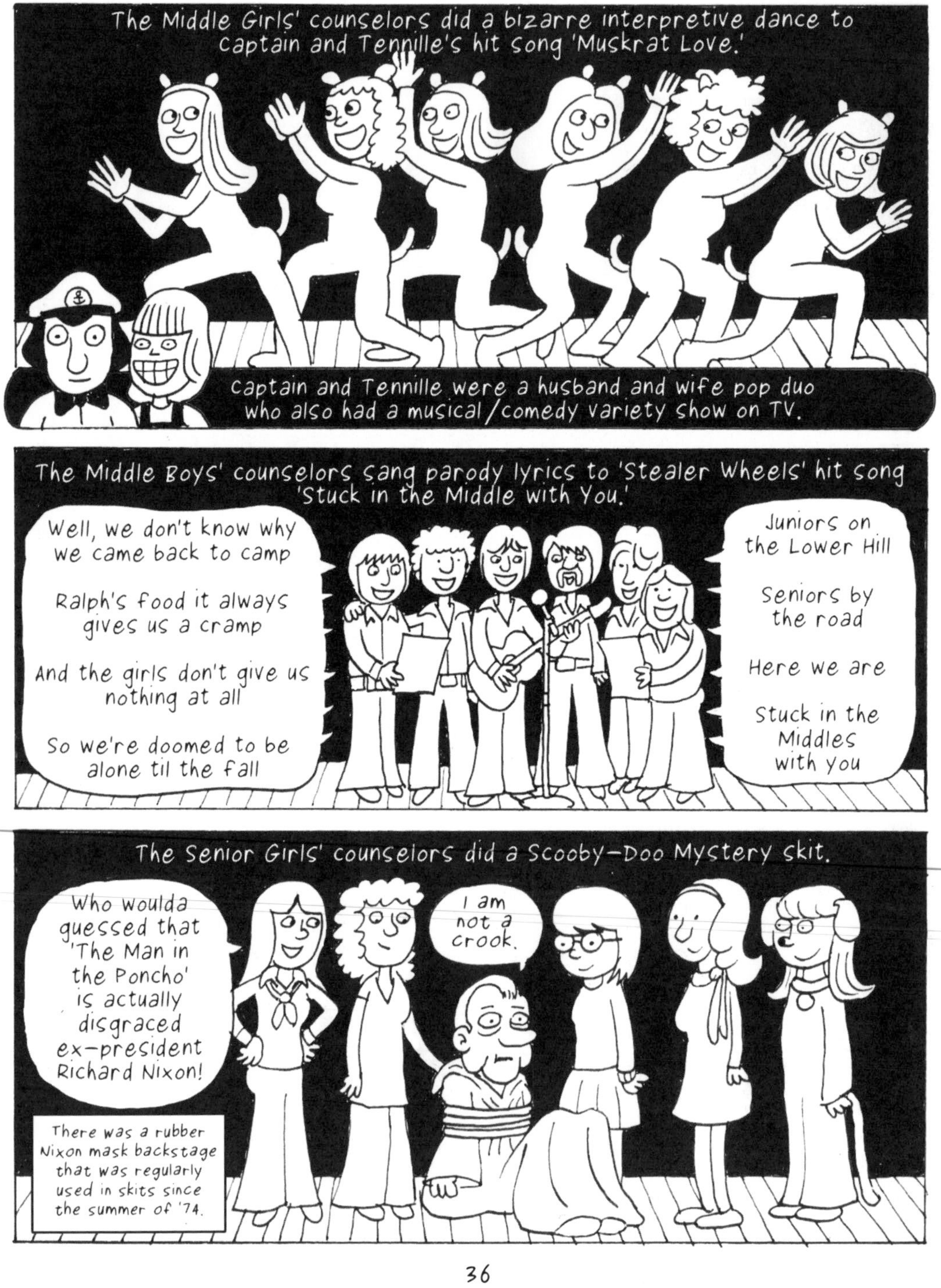
The Middle Girls' counselors did a bizarre interpretive dance to captain and Tennille's hit song 'Muskrat Love.'
captain and Tennille were a husband and wife pop duo who also had a musical/comedy variety show on TV.
The Middle Boys' counselors sang parody lyrics to 'Stealer Wheels' hit song 'Stuck in the Middle with You.'
Well, we don't know why we came back to camp
Ralph's food it always gives us a cramp
And the girls don't give us nothing at all
So we're doomed to be alone til the fall
Juniors on the Lower Hill
Seniors by the road
Here we are
Stuck in the Middles with you
The Senior Girls' counselors did a Scooby-Doo Mystery skit.
Who woulda guessed that 'The Man in the Poncho' is actually disgraced ex-president Richard Nixon!
I am not a crook.
There was a rubber Nixon mask backstage that was regularly used in skits since the summer of '74.

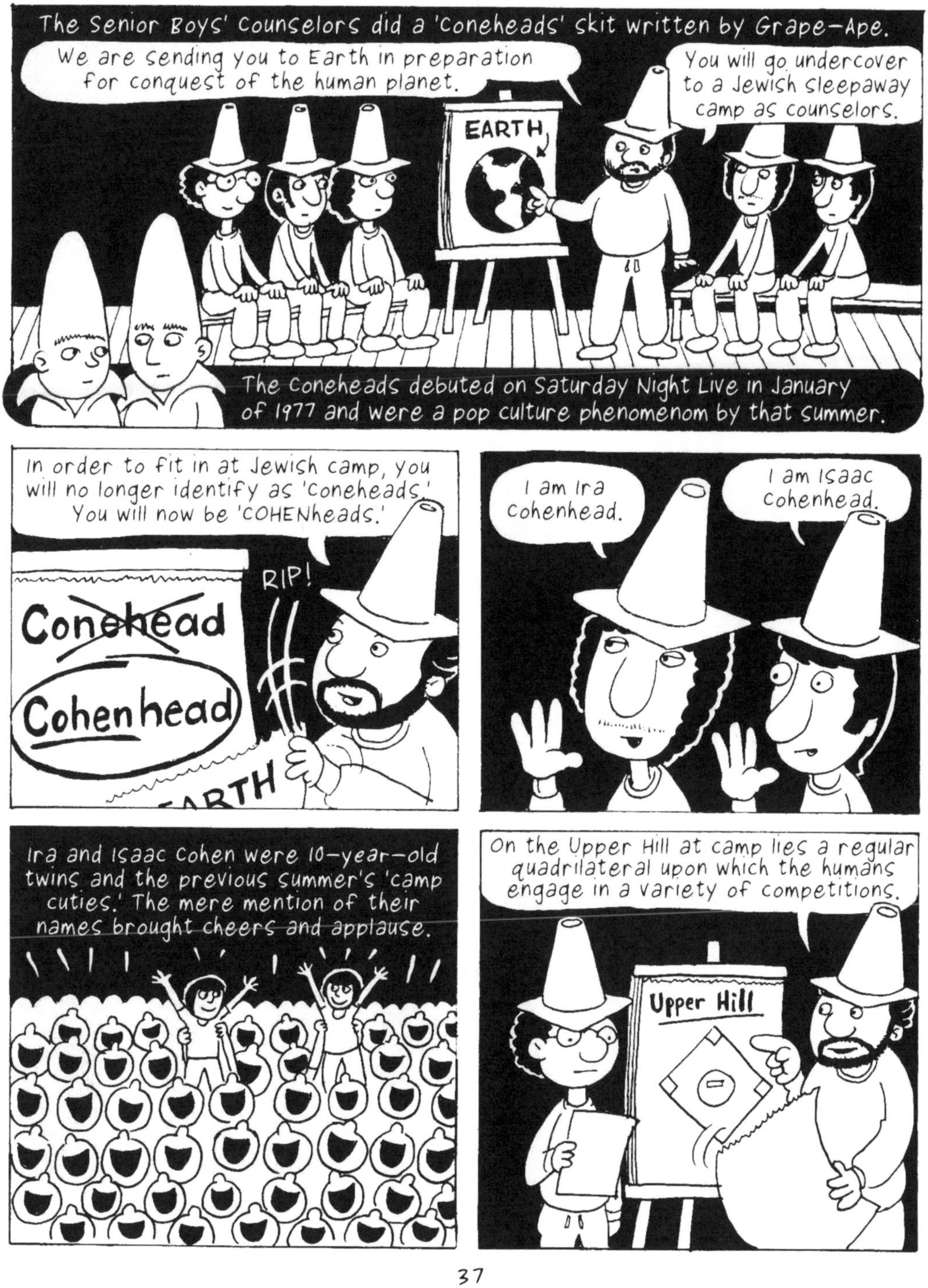
The Senior Boys' Counselors did a 'Coneheads' skit written by Grape-Ape.
We are sending you to Earth in preparation for conquest of the human planet.
You will go undercover to a Jewish sleepaway camp as counselors.
EARTH
The Coneheads debuted on Saturday Night Live in January of 1977 and were a pop culture phenomenom by that summer.
In order to fit in at Jewish camp, you will no longer identify as 'Coneheads.' You will now be 'COHENheads.'
Conehead
Cohenhead
RIP!
EARTH
I am Ira Cohenhead.
I am Isaac Cohenhead.
Ira and Isaac Cohen were 10-year-old twins and the previous summer's 'camp cuties.' The mere mention of their names brought cheers and applause.
On the Upper Hill at camp lies a regular quadrilateral upon which the humans engage in a variety of competitions.
Upper Hill

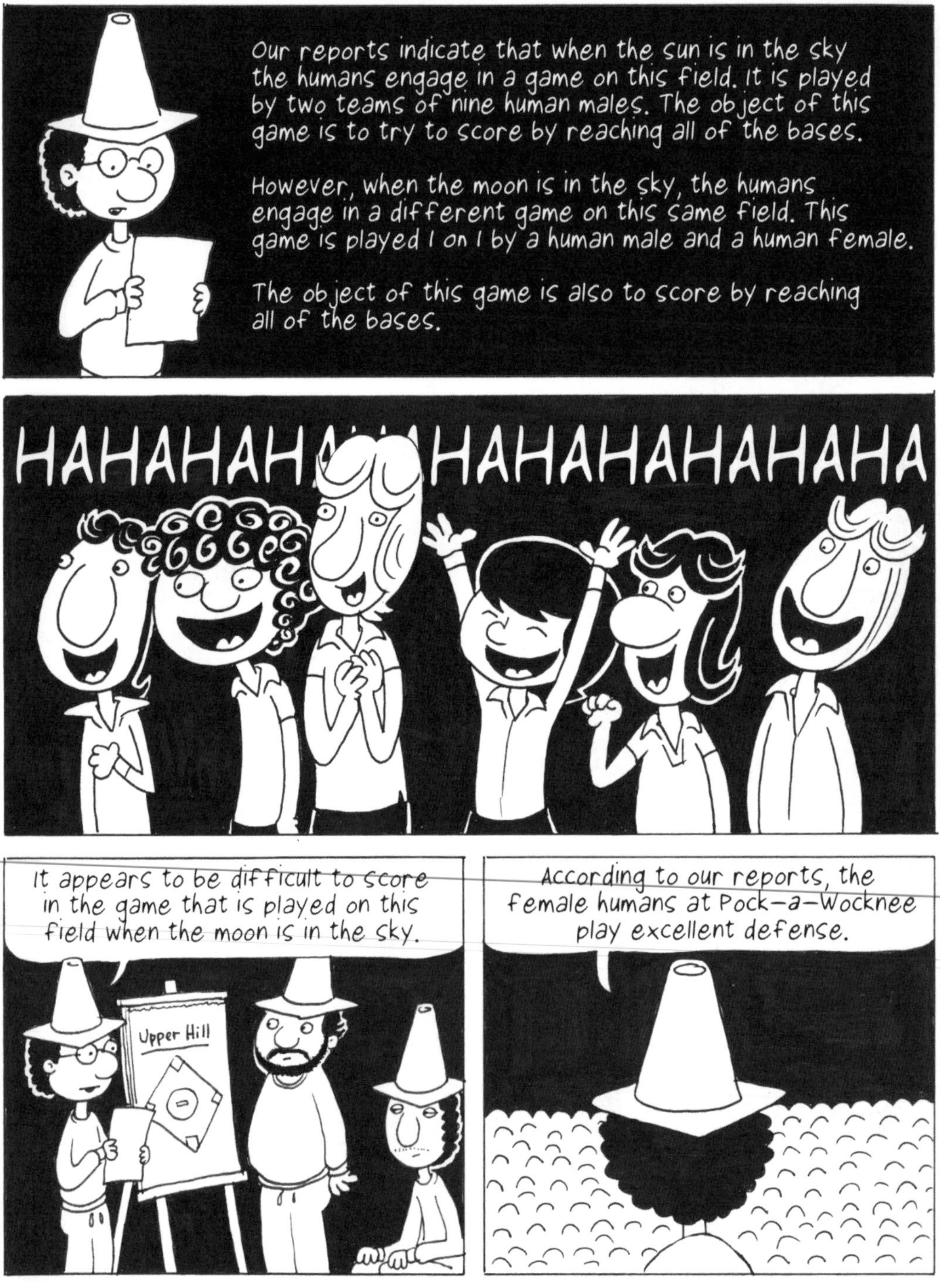
Our reports indicate that when the sun is in the sky the humans engage in a game on this field. It is played by two teams of nine human males. The object of this game is to try to score by reaching all of the bases.
However, when the moon is in the sky, the humans engage in a different game on this same field. This game is played 1 on 1 by a human male and a human female.
The object of this game is also to score by reaching all of the bases.
HAHAHAH HAHAHAHAHAHAHA
It appears to be difficult to score in the game that is played on this field when the moon is in the sky.
Upper Hill
According to our reports, the female humans at Pock-a-Wocknee play excellent defense.

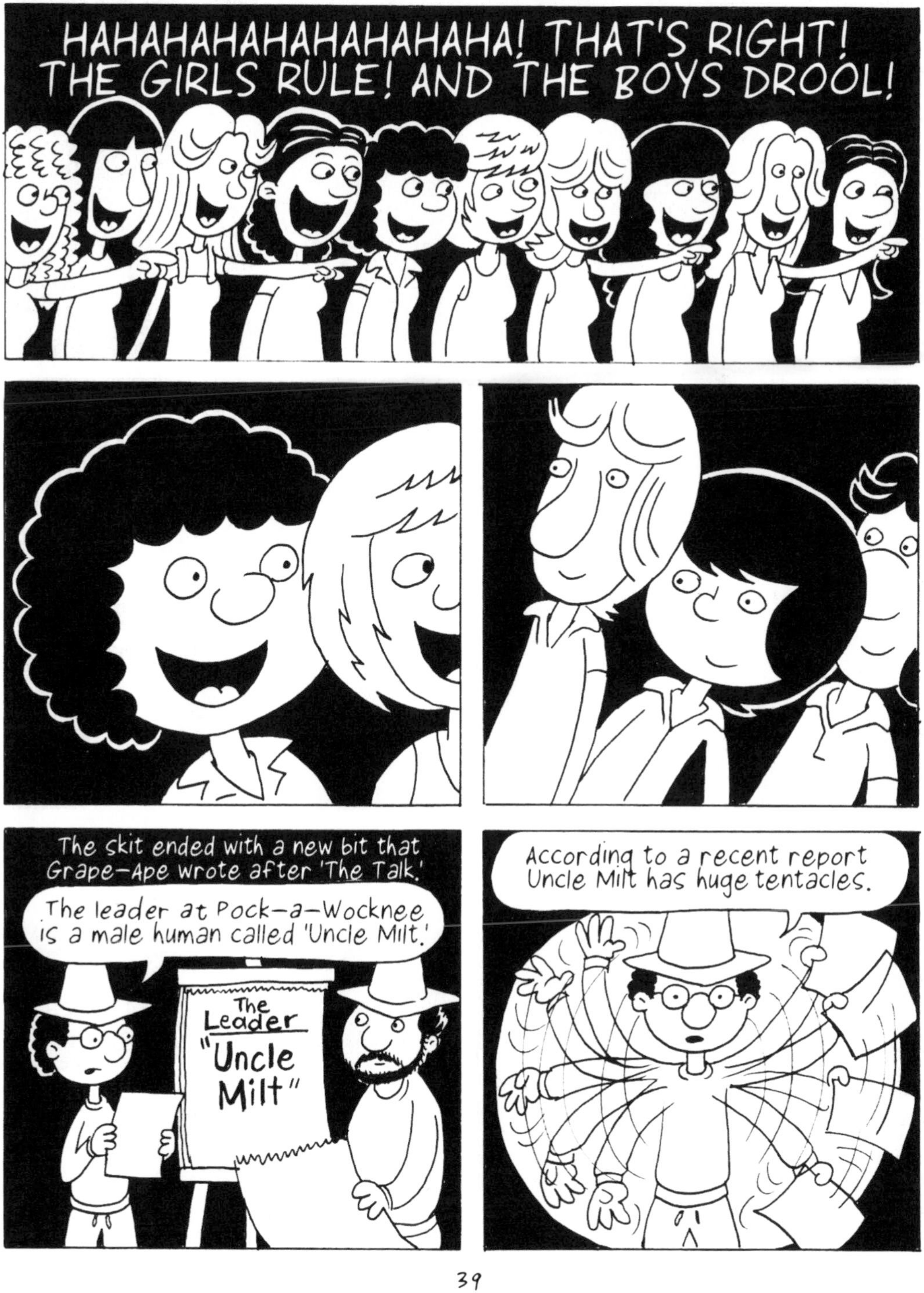
HAHAHAHAHAHAHAHAHAHA! THAT'S RIGHT! THE GIRLS RULE! AND THE BOYS DROOL!
The skit ended with a new bit that Grape-Ape wrote after 'The Talk.'
The leader at Pock-a-Wocknee is a male human called 'Uncle Milt.'
The Leader "Uncle Milt"
According to a recent report Uncle Milt has huge tentacles.

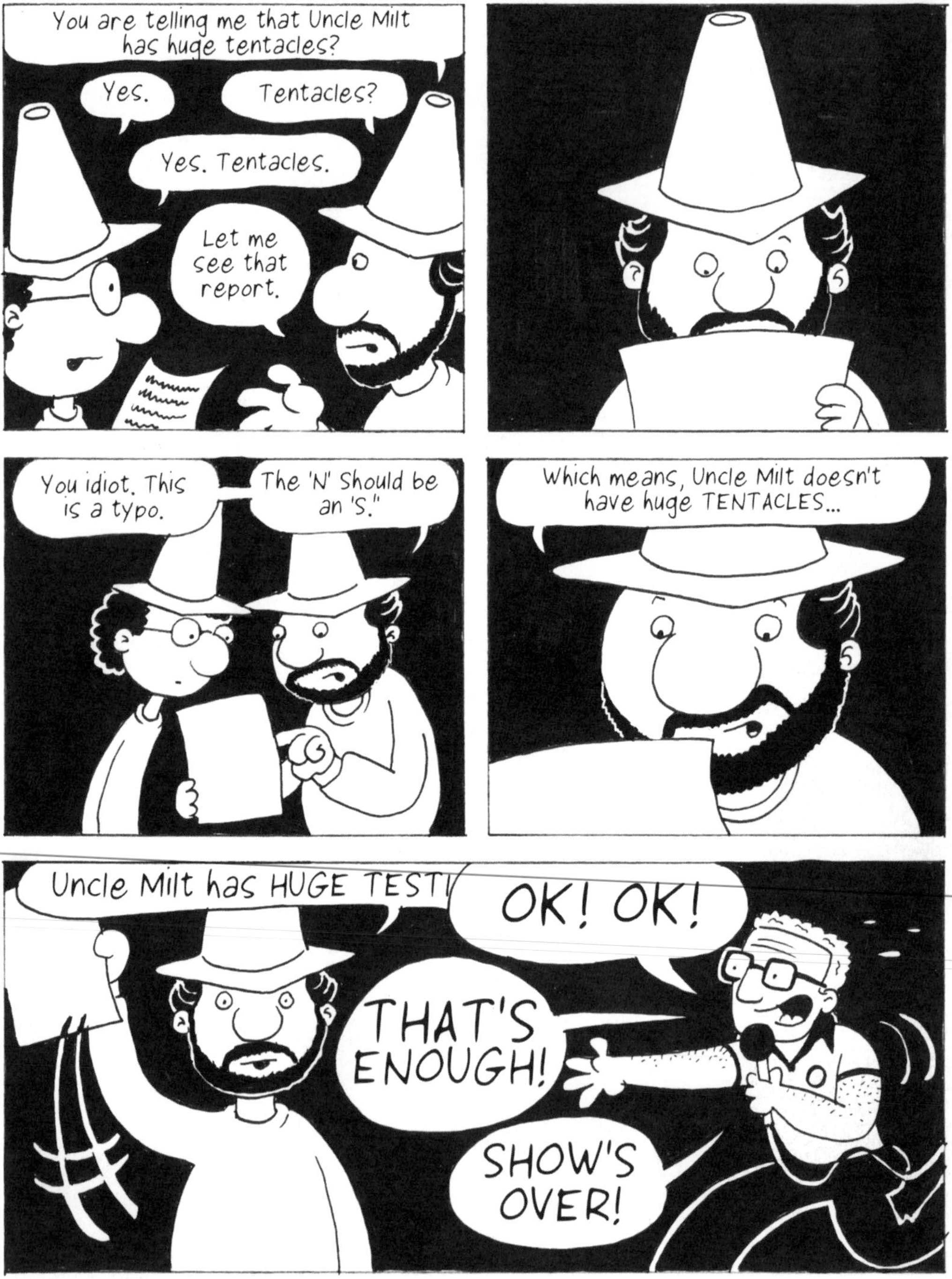
You are telling me that Uncle Milt has huge tentacles?
Yes.
Tentacles?
Yes. Tentacles.
Let me see that report.
You idiot. This is a typo.
The 'N' should be an 'S.'
Which means, Uncle Milt doesn't have huge TENTACLES...
Uncle Milt has HUGE TESTI
OK! OK!
THAT'S ENOUGH!
SHOW'S OVER!

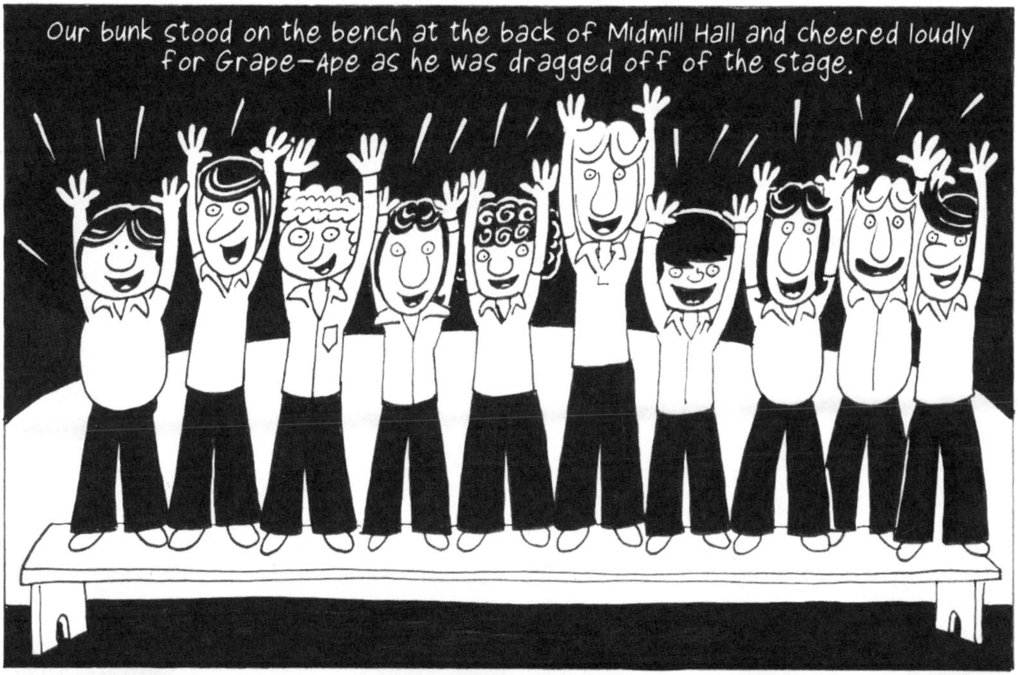
Our bunk stood on the bench at the back of Midmill Hall and cheered loudly for Grape-Ape as he was dragged off of the stage.

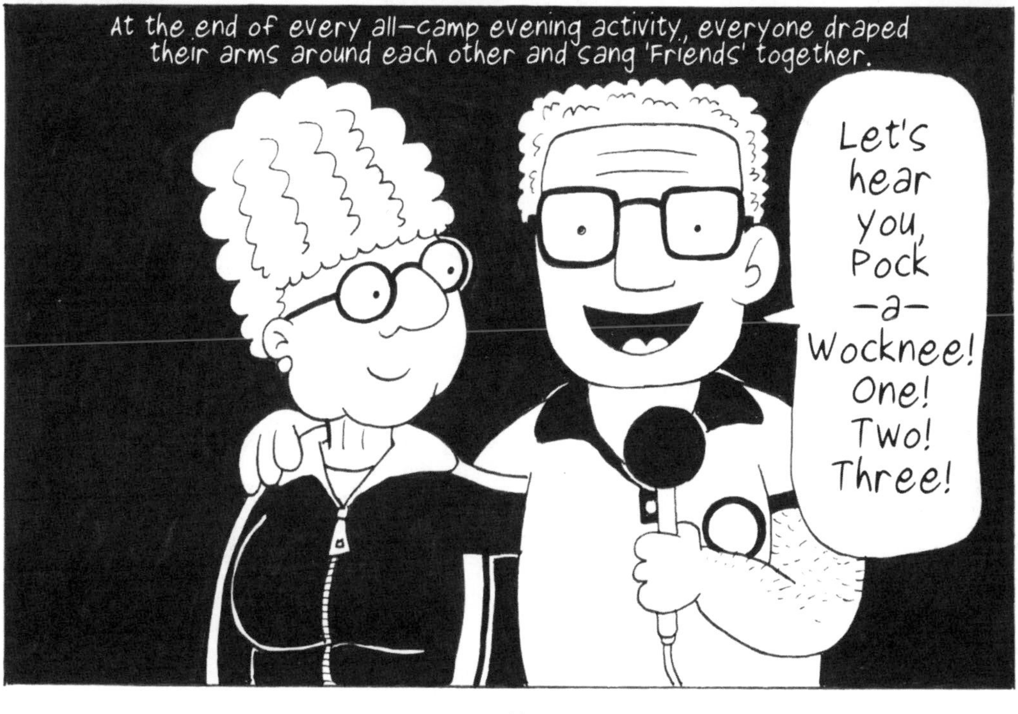
At the end of every all-camp evening activity, everyone draped their arms around each other and sang 'Friends' together.
Let's hear you, Pock-a-Wocknee! One! Two! Three!

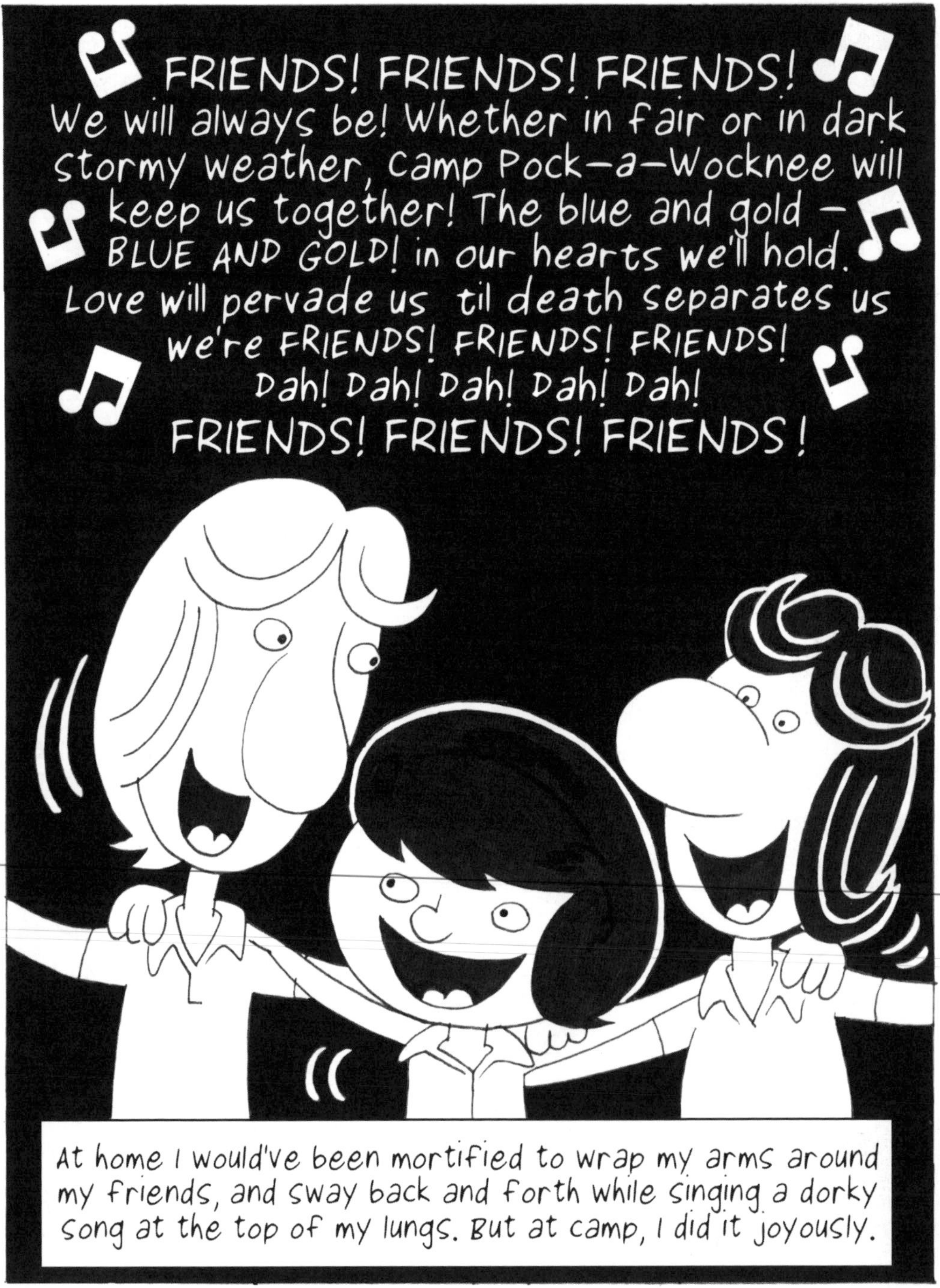
FRIENDS! FRIENDS! FRIENDS!
We will always be! Whether in fair or in dark stormy weather, Camp Pock-a-Wocknee will keep us together! The blue and gold - BLUE AND GOLD! in our hearts we'll hold. Love will pervade us til death separates us we're FRIENDS! FRIENDS! FRIENDS!
Dah! Dah! Dah! Dah! Dah!
FRIENDS! FRIENDS! FRIENDS!
At home I would've been mortified to wrap my arms around my friends, and sway back and forth while singing a dorky song at the top of my lungs. But at camp, I did it joyously.

During the school year, I could barely open my eyes before 2nd period.

But for 8 weeks, I was wide awake from the moment I heard the scratchy sound of a needle on a record before it even found the groove.

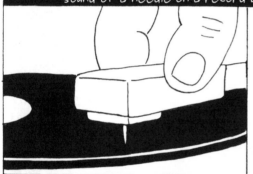

That sound came every morning at 7am when Midge played a 45 of 'Reveille' and blared it over the camp sound system.

BUP—BUP
BUD—DAH
DUP—BUP
BUP
BUD—DAH
DUP—BUP
BUP—BUD—DUH
DUP—BU—BU—DUP

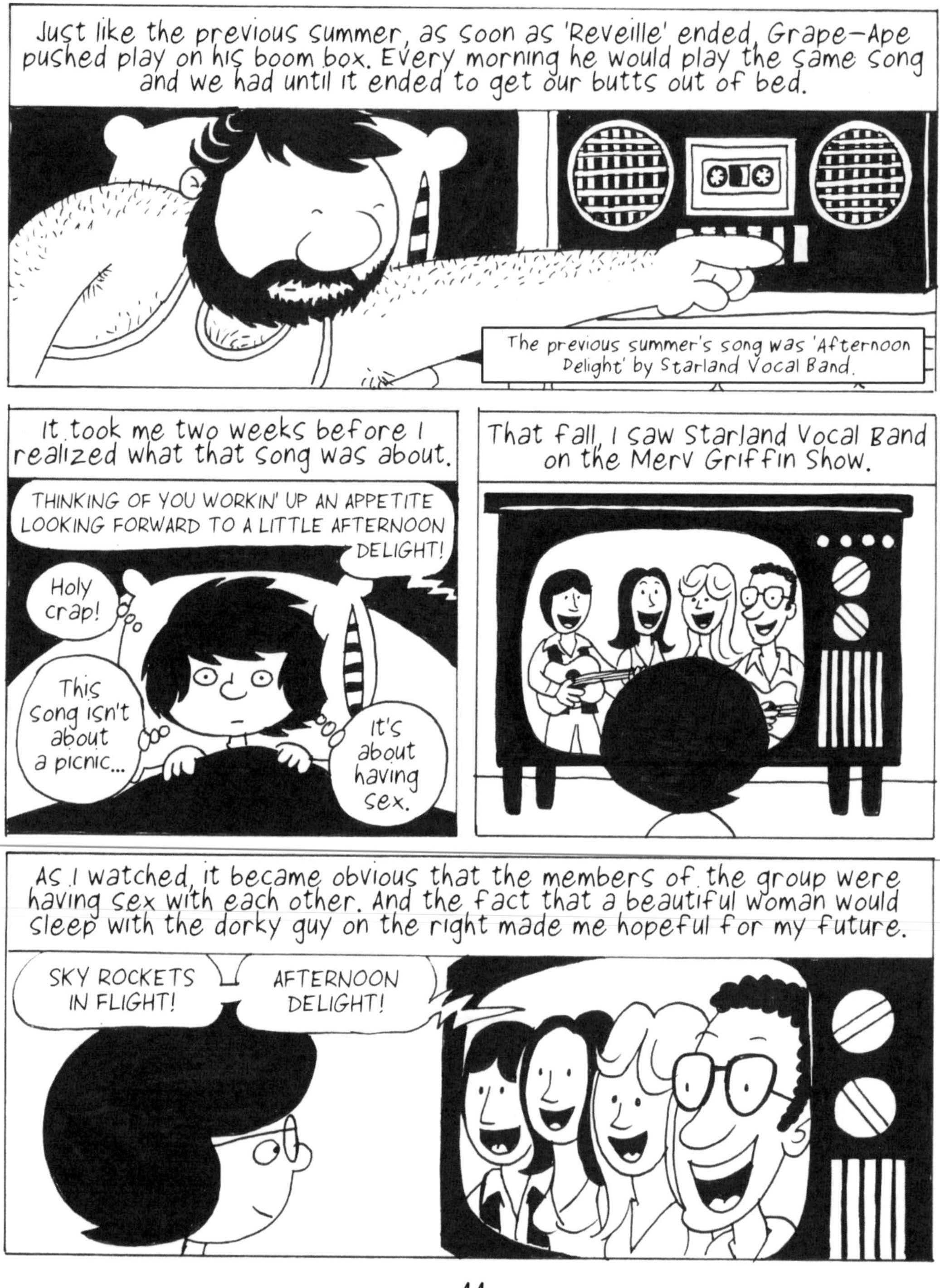
Just like the previous summer, as soon as 'Reveille' ended, Grape-Ape pushed play on his boom box. Every morning he would play the same song and we had until it ended to get our butts out of bed.
The previous summer's song was 'Afternoon Delight' by Starland Vocal Band.
It took me two weeks before I realized what that song was about.
THINKING OF YOU WORKIN' UP AN APPETITE LOOKING FORWARD TO A LITTLE AFTERNOON DELIGHT!
Holy crap!
This song isn't about a picnic...
It's about having sex.
That fall, I saw Starland Vocal Band on the Merv Griffin Show.
As I watched, it became obvious that the members of the group were having sex with each other. And the fact that a beautiful woman would sleep with the dorky guy on the right made me hopeful for my future.
SKY ROCKETS IN FLIGHT!
AFTERNOON DELIGHT!

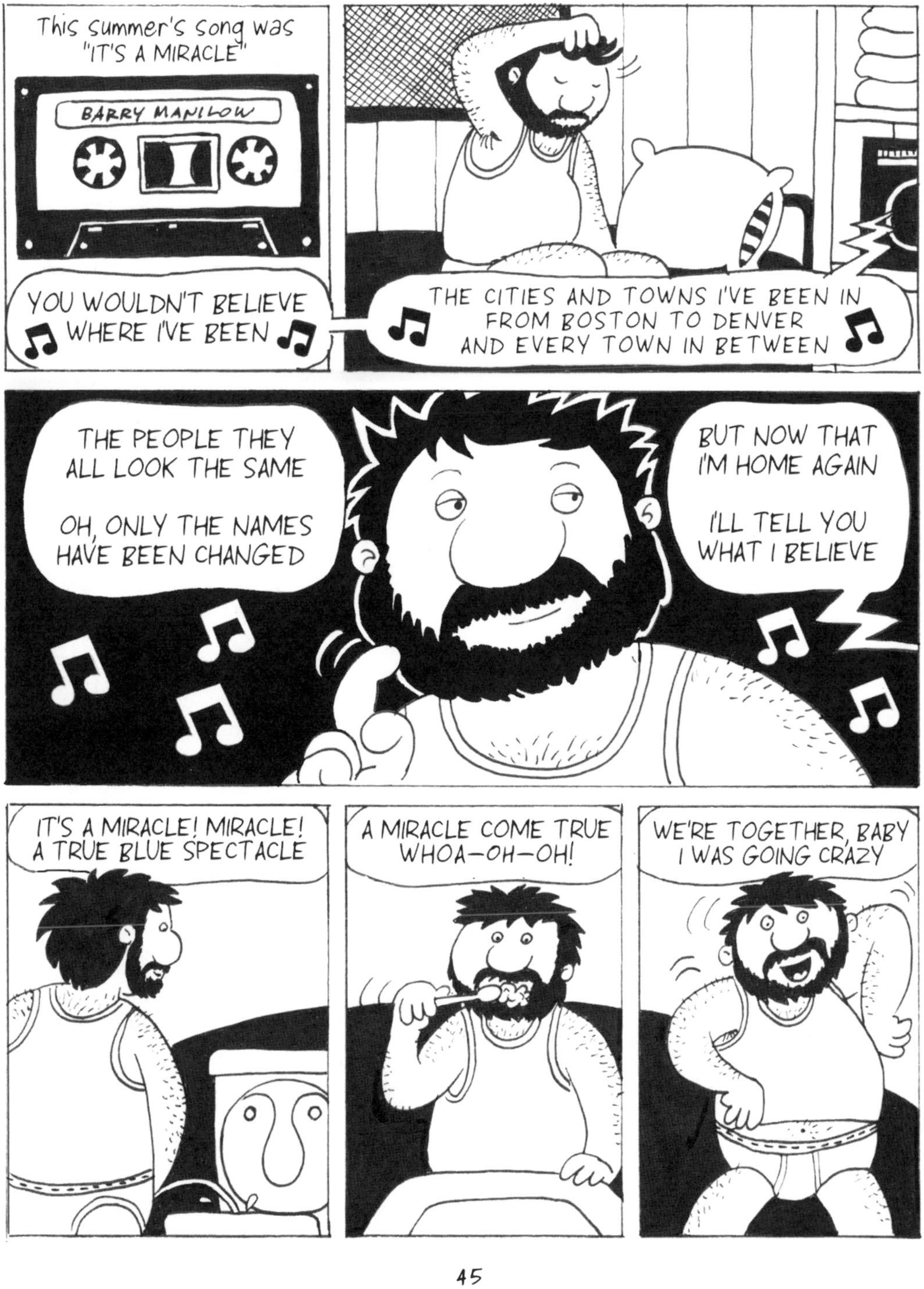
This summer's song was "IT'S A MIRACLE"
BARRY MANILOW
YOU WOULDN'T BELIEVE WHERE I'VE BEEN
THE CITIES AND TOWNS I'VE BEEN IN FROM BOSTON TO DENVER AND EVERY TOWN IN BETWEEN
THE PEOPLE THEY ALL LOOK THE SAME
OH, ONLY THE NAMES HAVE BEEN CHANGED
BUT NOW THAT I'M HOME AGAIN
I'LL TELL YOU WHAT I BELIEVE
IT'S A MIRACLE! MIRACLE! A TRUE BLUE SPECTACLE
A MIRACLE COME TRUE WHOA-OH-OH!
WE'RE TOGETHER, BABY I WAS GOING CRAZY

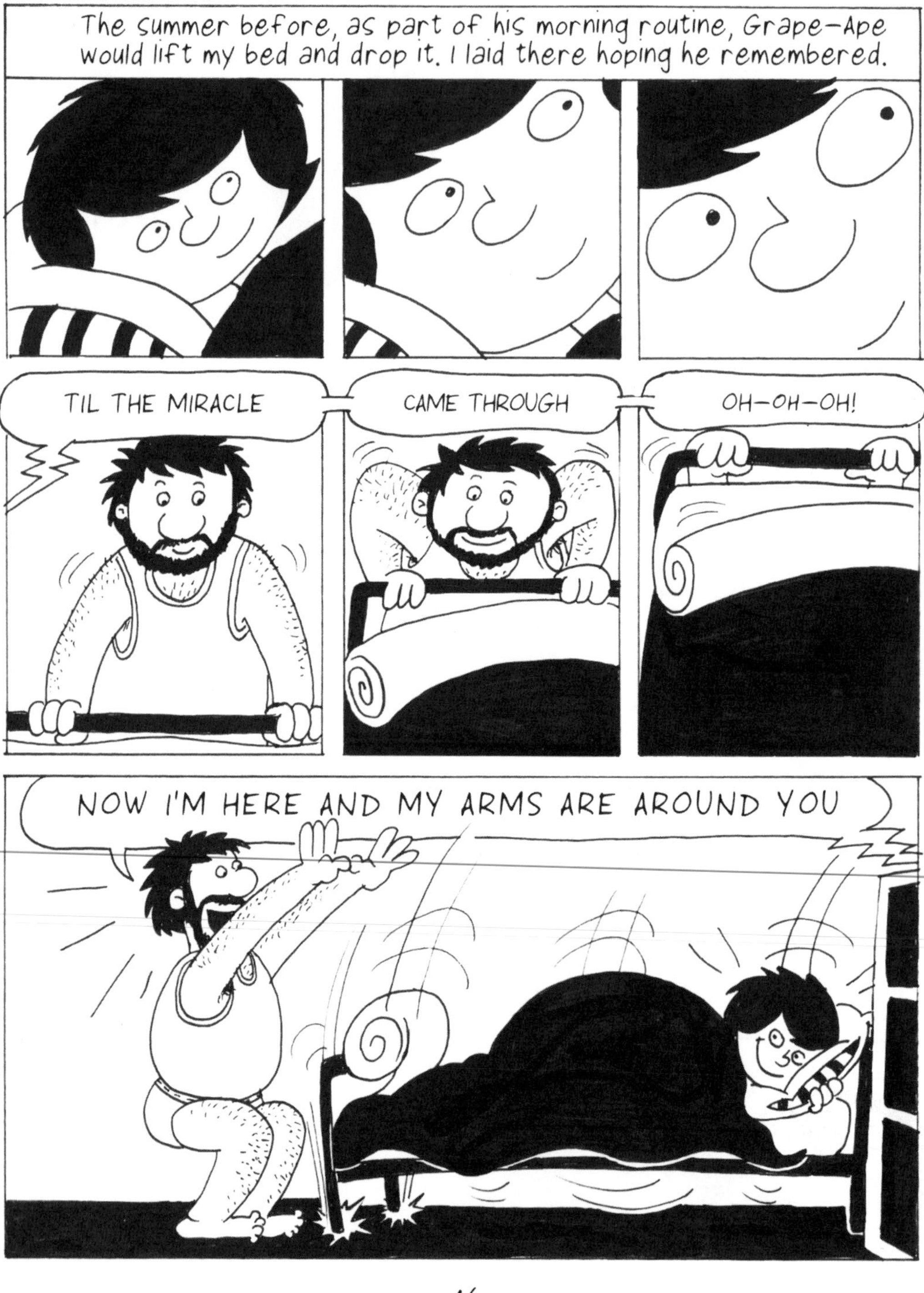
The summer before, as part of his morning routine, Grape-Ape would lift my bed and drop it. I laid there hoping he remembered.
TIL THE MIRACLE
CAME THROUGH
OH-OH-OH!
NOW I'M HERE AND MY ARMS ARE AROUND YOU

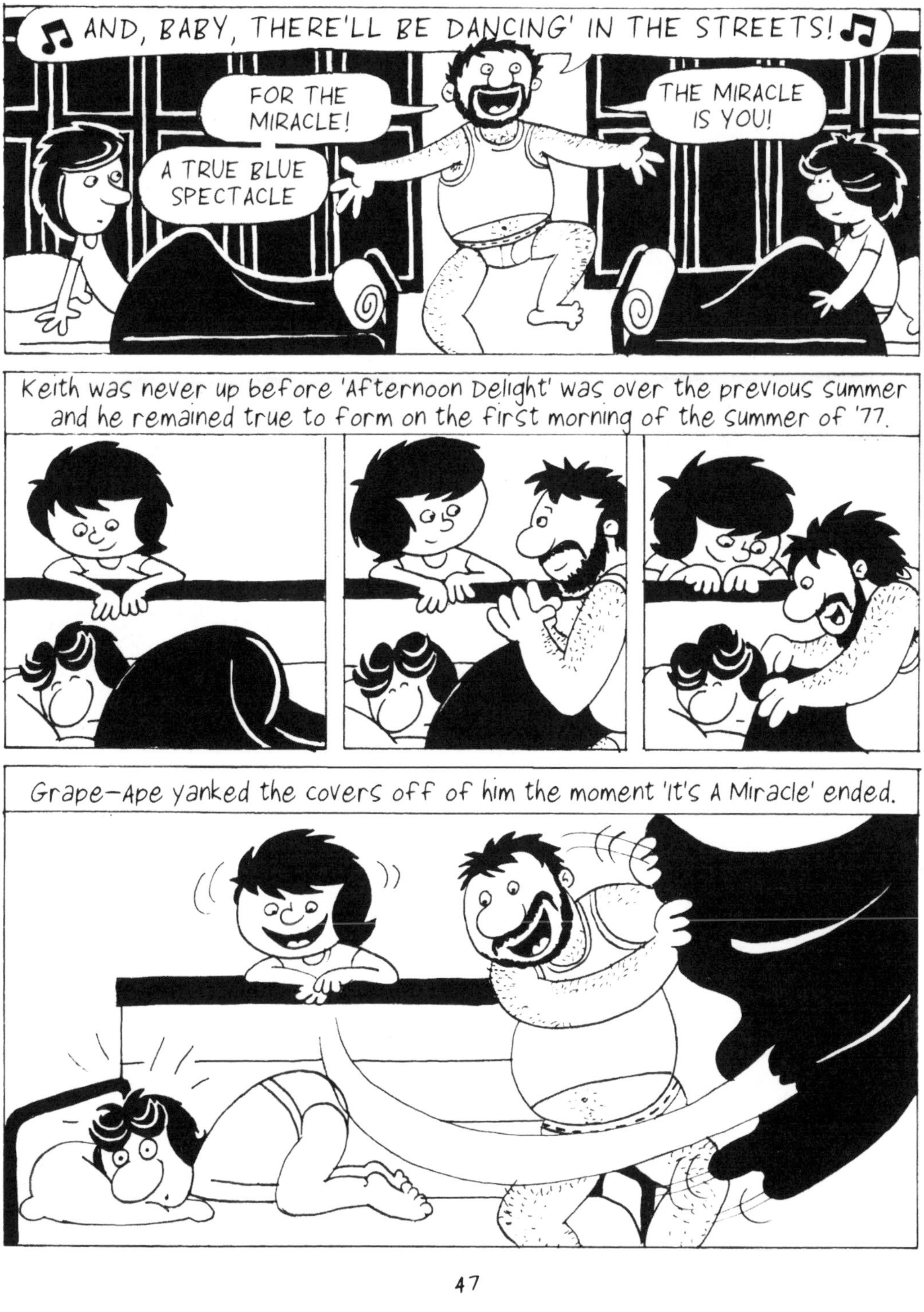
FOR THE MIRACLE!
A TRUE BLUE SPECTACLE
THE MIRACLE IS YOU!
♫ AND, BABY, THERE'LL BE DANCING' IN THE STREETS! ♫
Keith was never up before 'Afternoon Delight' was over the previous summer and he remained true to form on the first morning of the summer of '77.
Grape-Ape yanked the covers off of him the moment 'It's A Miracle' ended.

We all pissed in the left stall without flushing.

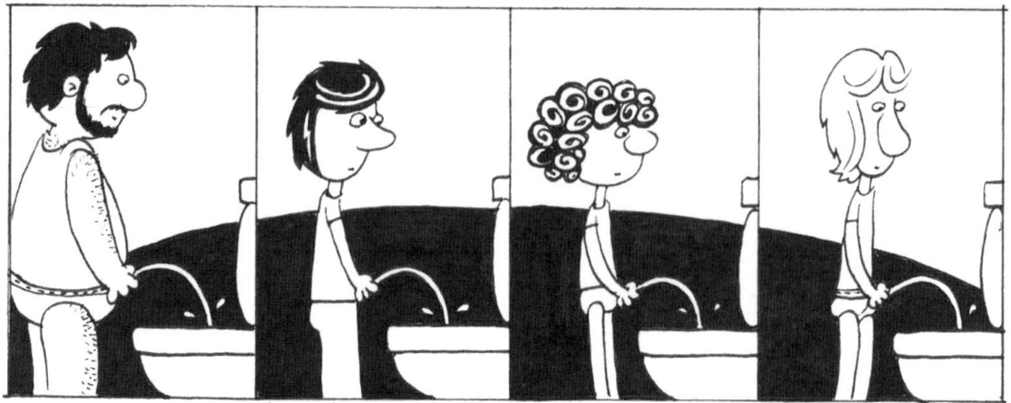

It was the continuation of last summer's seemingly futile attempt

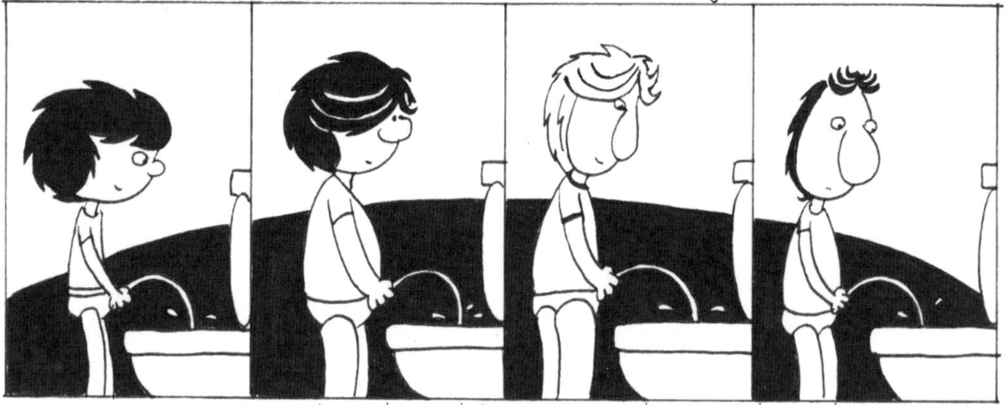

to overflow the toilet with our collective morning urine.

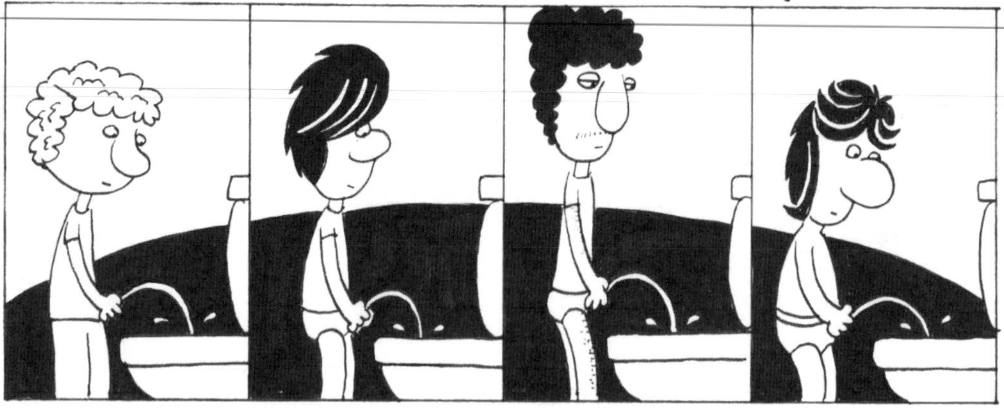

On the first morning of our oldest senior summer, we once again failed.

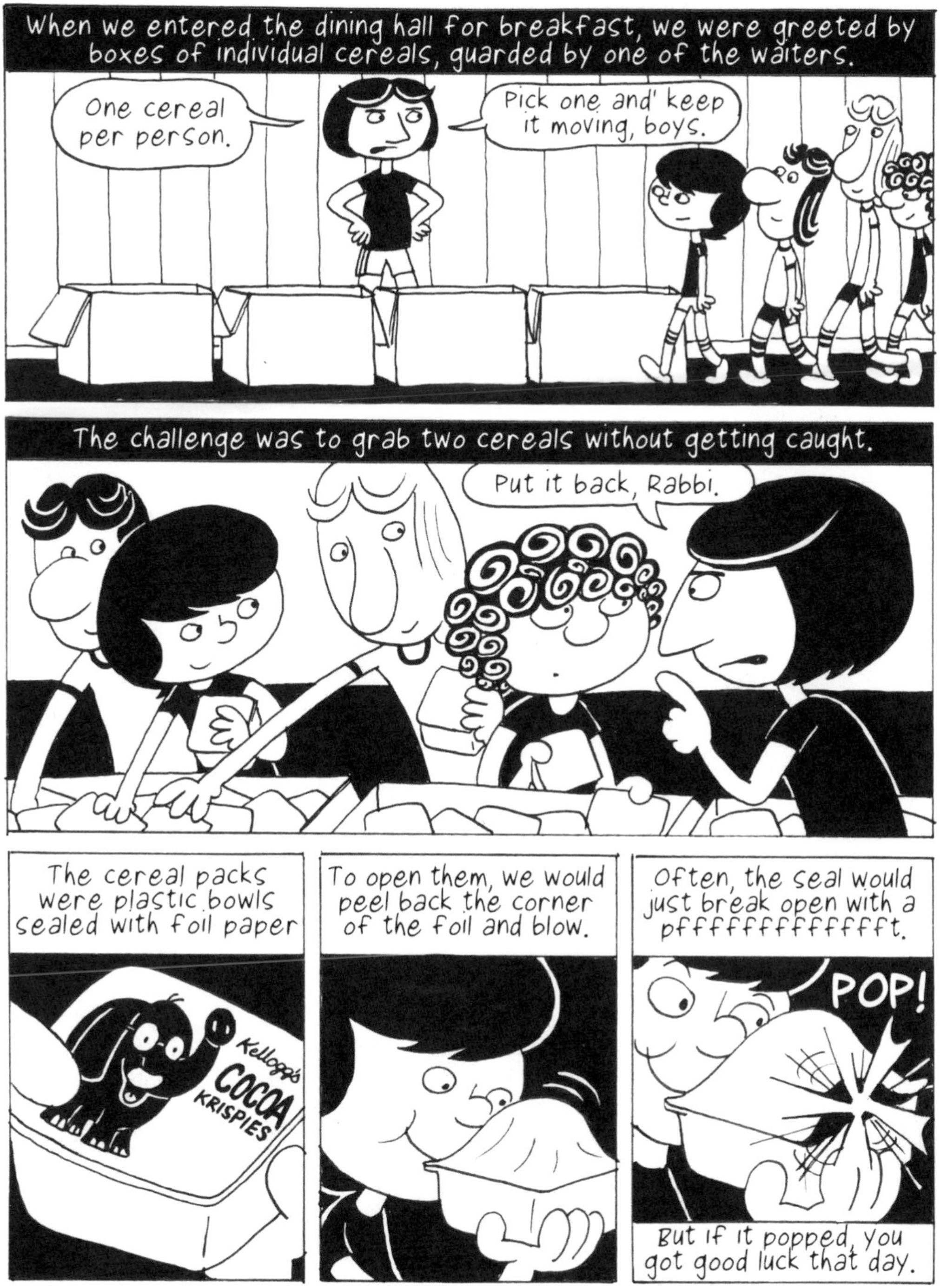
When we entered the dining hall for breakfast, we were greeted by boxes of individual cereals, guarded by one of the waiters.
One cereal per person.
Pick one and' keep it moving, boys.
The challenge was to grab two cereals without getting caught.
Put it back, Rabbi.
The cereal packs were plastic bowls sealed with foil paper
Kellogg's COCOA KRISPIES
To open them, we would peel back the corner of the foil and blow.
Often, the seal would just break open with a pfffffffffffft.
POP!
But if it popped, you got good luck that day.

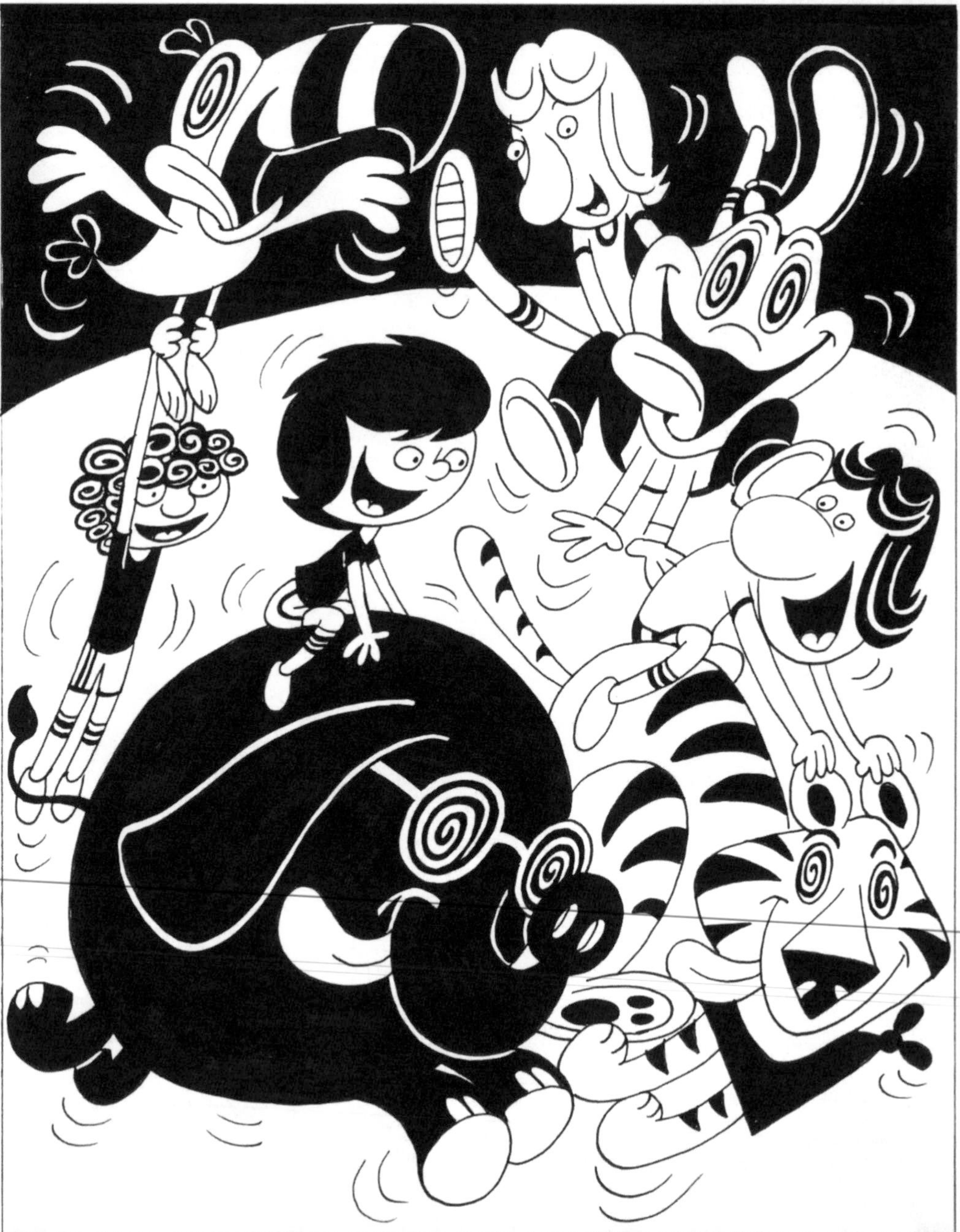

Then we rode those sugar beasts for all they were worth.

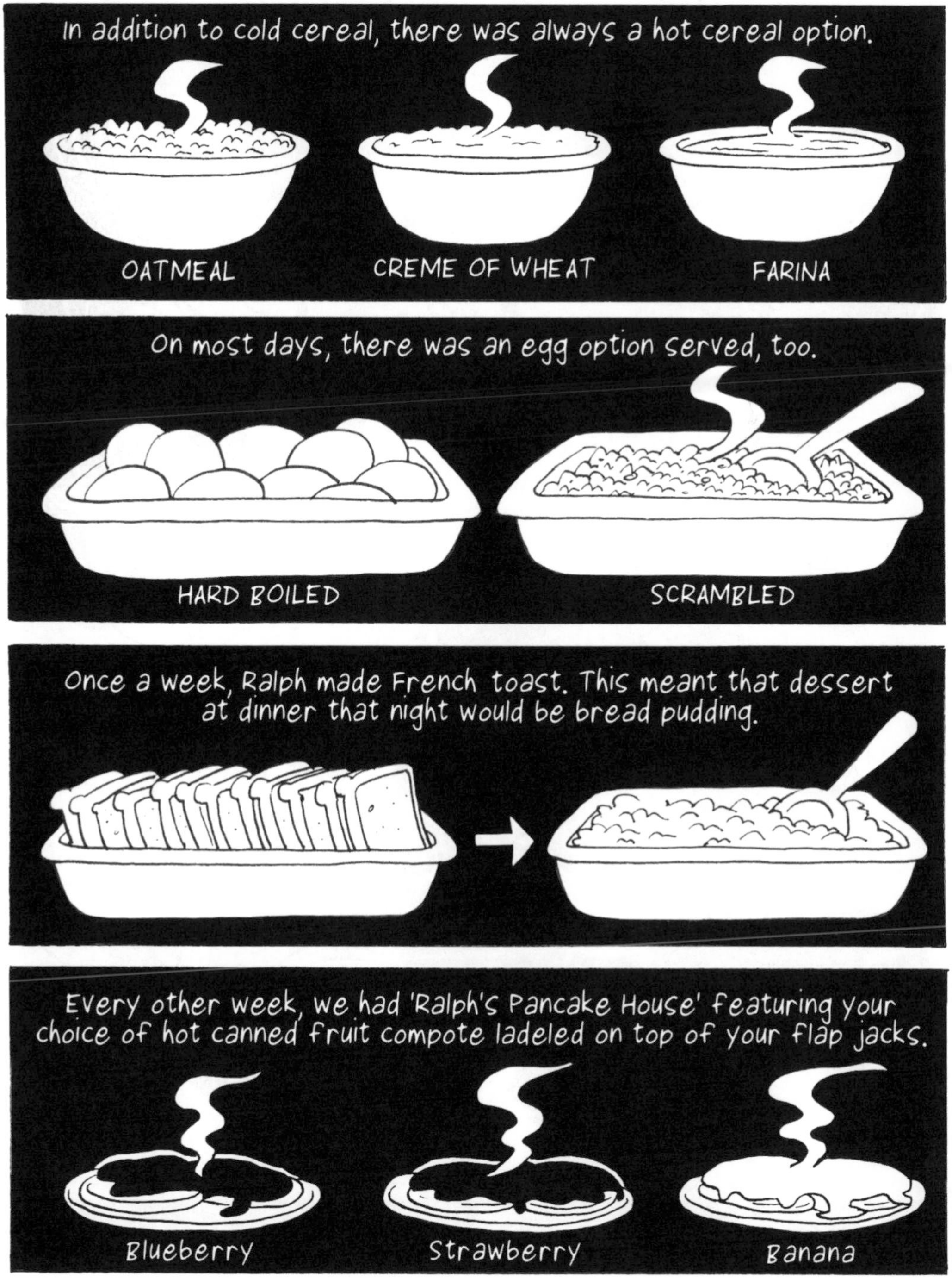
In addition to cold cereal, there was always a hot cereal option.
OATMEAL
CREME OF WHEAT
FARINA
On most days, there was an egg option served, too.
HARD BOILED
SCRAMBLED
Once a week, Ralph made French toast. This meant that dessert at dinner that night would be bread pudding.
Every other week, we had 'Ralph's Pancake House' featuring your choice of hot canned fruit compote ladeled on top of your flap jacks.
Blueberry
Strawberry
Banana

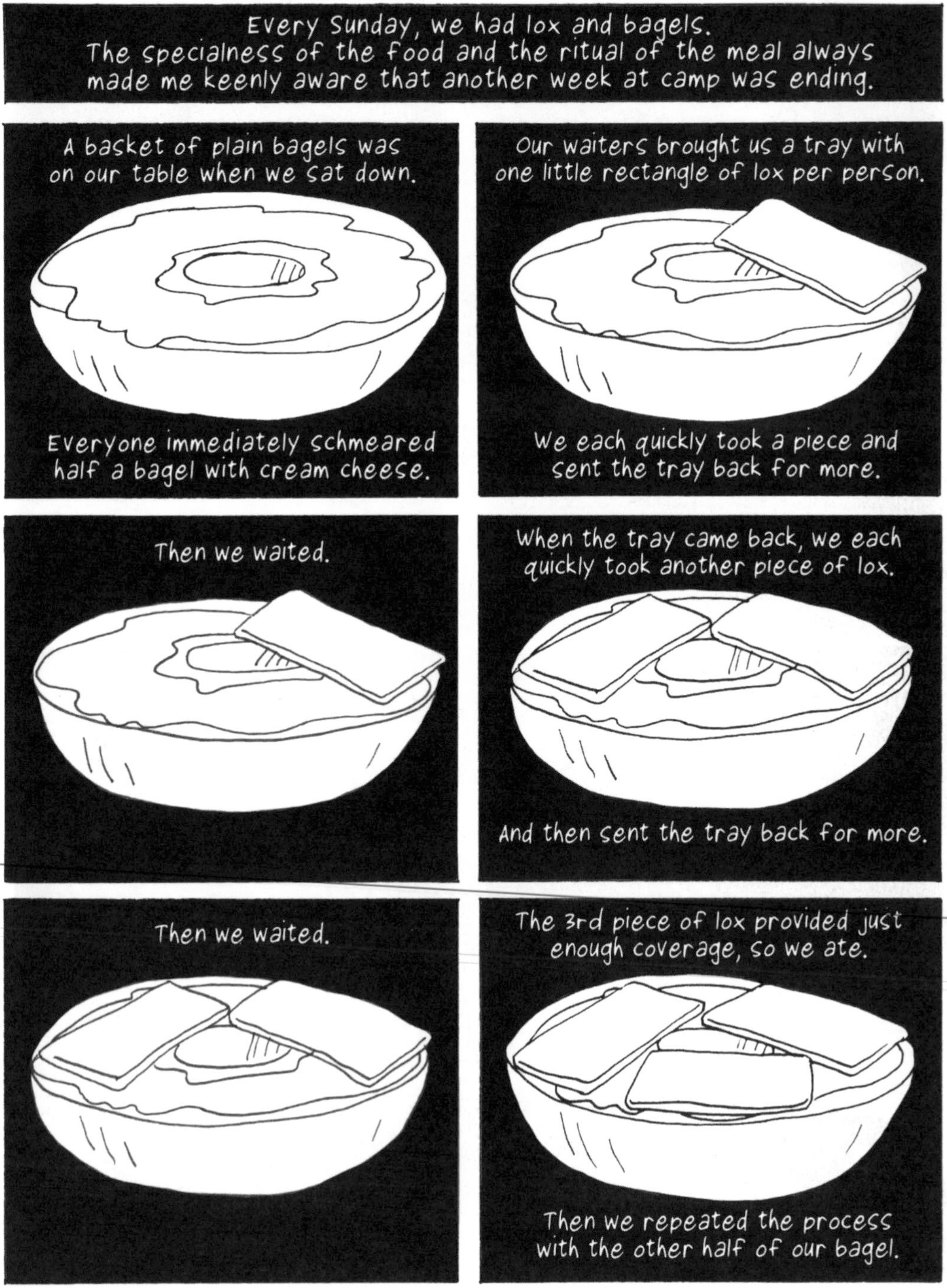

Every Sunday, we had lox and bagels.
The specialness of the food and the ritual of the meal always
made me keenly aware that another week at camp was ending.

A basket of plain bagels was
on our table when we sat down.

Everyone immediately schmeared
half a bagel with cream cheese.

Our waiters brought us a tray with
one little rectangle of lox per person.

We each quickly took a piece and
sent the tray back for more.

Then we waited.

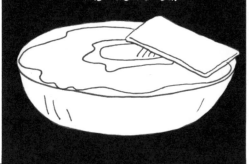

When the tray came back, we each
quickly took another piece of lox.

And then sent the tray back for more.

Then we waited.

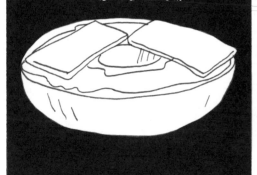

The 3rd piece of lox provided just
enough coverage, so we ate.

Then we repeated the process
with the other half of our bagel.

After breakfast, we had clean-up and inspection.

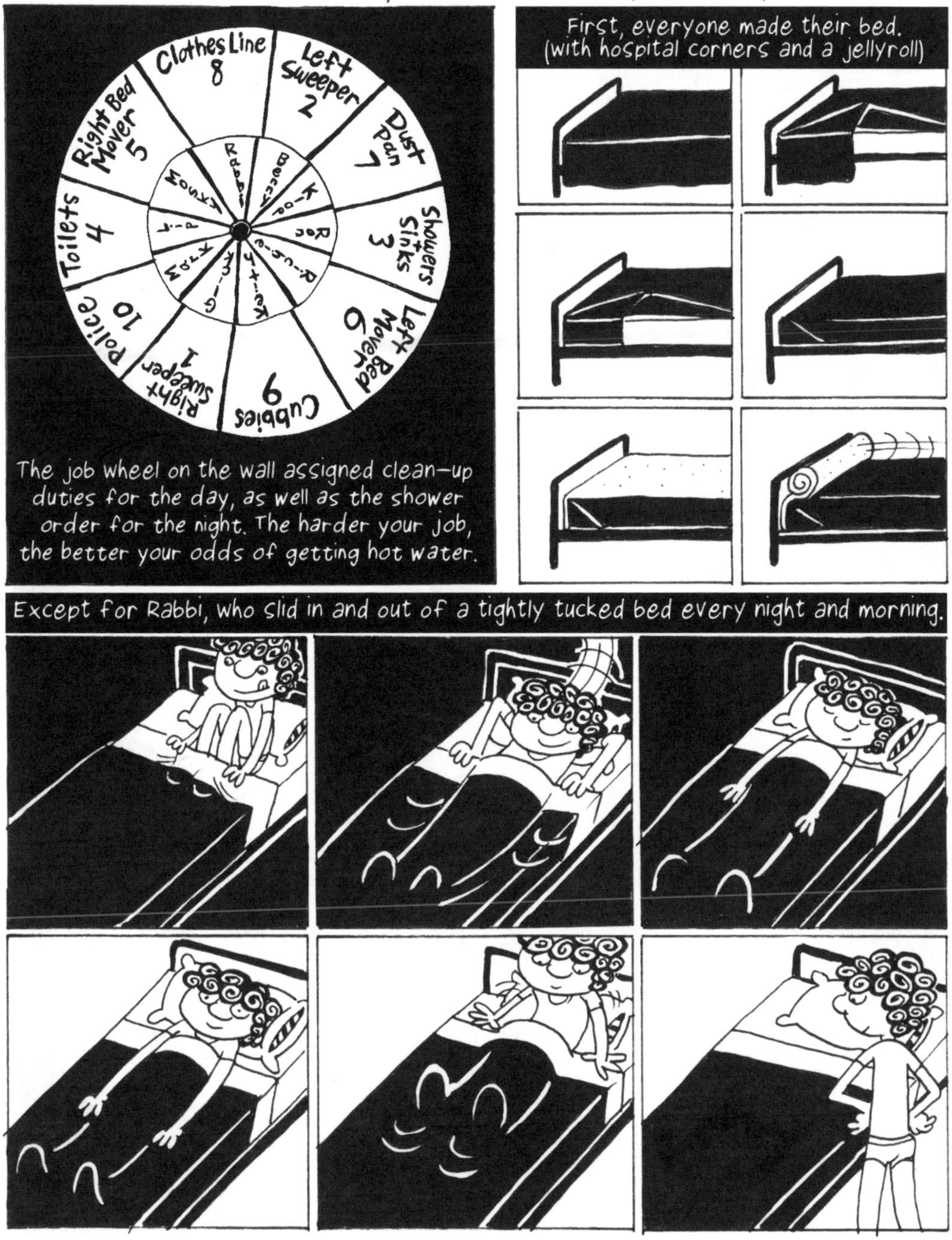
Clothes Line 8
Left Sweeper 2
Dust Pan 7
Showers Sinks 3
Left Bed Mover 6
Cubbies 9
Right Sweeper 1
Police 10
Toilets 4
Right Bed Mover 5
Rabbi
The job wheel on the wall assigned clean-up duties for the day, as well as the shower order for the night. The harder your job, the better your odds of getting hot water.
First, everyone made their bed. (with hospital corners and a jellyroll)
Except for Rabbi, who slid in and out of a tightly tucked bed every night and morning.

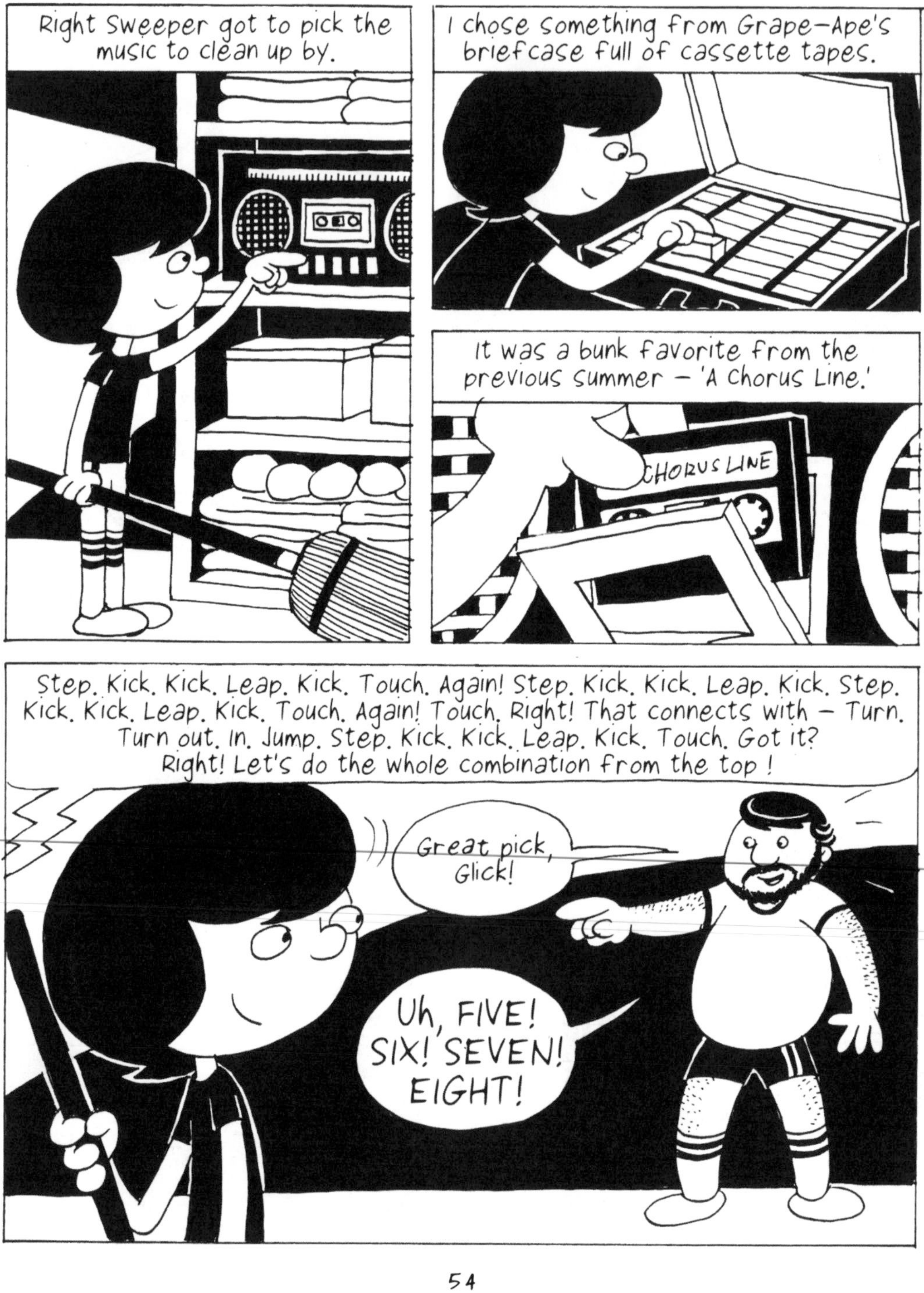
Right Sweeper got to pick the music to clean up by.
I chose something from Grape-Ape's briefcase full of cassette tapes.
It was a bunk favorite from the previous summer – 'A Chorus Line.'
CHORUS LINE
Step. Kick. Kick. Leap. Kick. Touch. Again! Step. Kick. Kick. Leap. Kick. Step. Kick. Kick. Leap. Kick. Touch. Again! Touch. Right! That connects with – Turn. Turn out. In. Jump. Step. Kick. Kick. Leap. Kick. Touch. Got it? Right! Let's do the whole combination from the top!
Great pick, Glick!
Uh, FIVE! SIX! SEVEN! EIGHT!

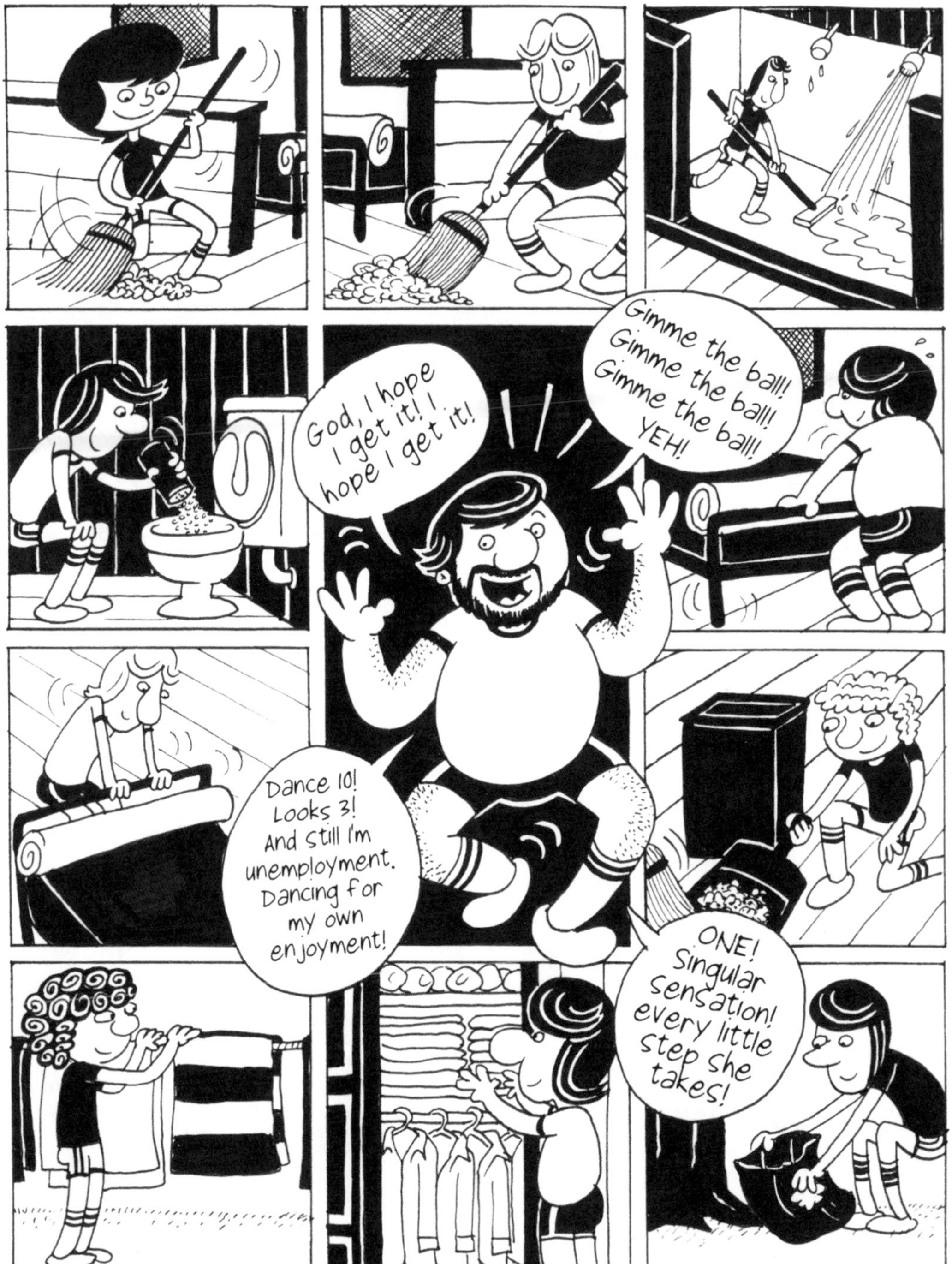
God, I hope I get it! I hope I get it!
Gimme the ball! Gimme the ball! Gimme the ball! YEH!
Dance 10! Looks 3! And still I'm unemployment. Dancing for my own enjoyment!
ONE! Singular sensation! every little step she takes!

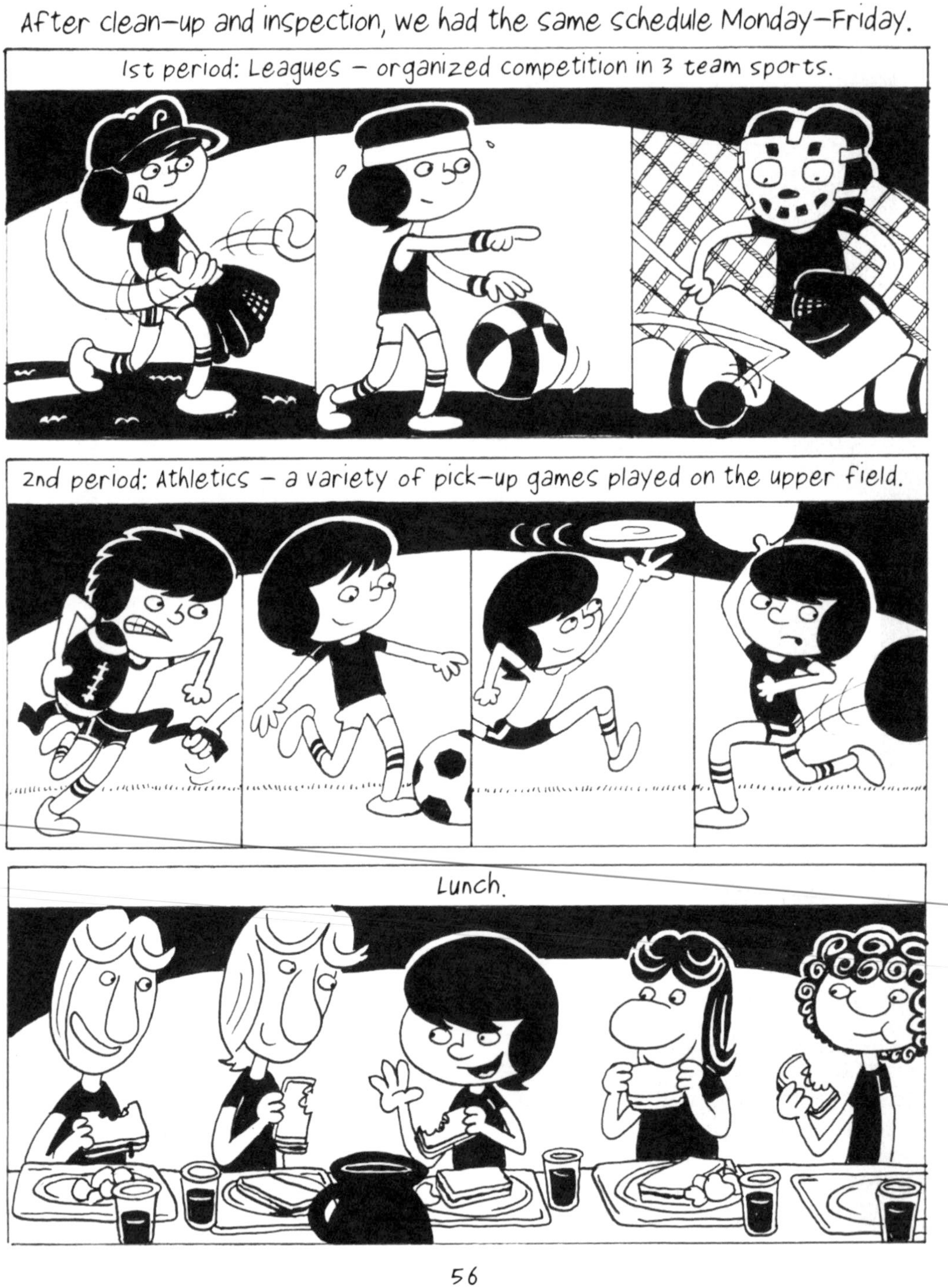
After clean-up and inspection, we had the same schedule Monday-Friday.
1st period: Leagues - organized competition in 3 team sports.
2nd period: Athletics - a variety of pick-up games played on the upper field.
Lunch.

Rest Hour

After lunch, all campers returned to their cabins to relax before afternoon activities began.

It was a chance to just hang out, listen to music, write letters home, take a nap, or read a magazine.

Rest Hour was also a great opportunity to earn or win Cokes.

Sodas were 25 cents from the vending machine in the canteen, and 'a Coke' was the defacto monetary unit at Pock—a—Wocknee.

We played rafter ball, cards, and quoits for 'a Coke.' We did dares for 'a Coke.' And we gave back massages for 'a Coke.'

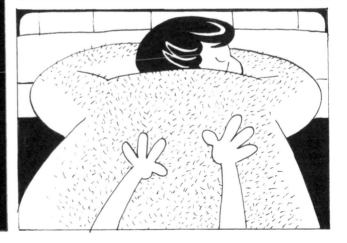

RAFTER BALL: A baseball game was simulated by tossing a tennis ball up and trying to bounce it on top of the rafter.

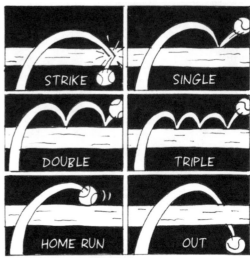

STRIKE

SINGLE

DOUBLE

TRIPLE

HOME RUN

OUT

QUOITS: Two one-pound rubber rings (quoits) per player are alternately tossed towards an angled board with a short post in the middle. Only quoits that land on the board can score. The quoit closest to the pin gets 1 point. If a player has two quoits closer than his opponent, he gets 2 points. A quoit that encircles the pin is 'a ringer' and is worth 5 points. If a player 'tops' his opponent's ringer with a ringer, the first ringer is worth nothing and the subsequent ringer is worth 10 points. A quoit that lands leaning against the pin is 'a leaner' and worth 3 points. Any quoit that remains upside-down is 'dead' and worth no points. Games are to 21.

One. Two. Three. Spit!

58

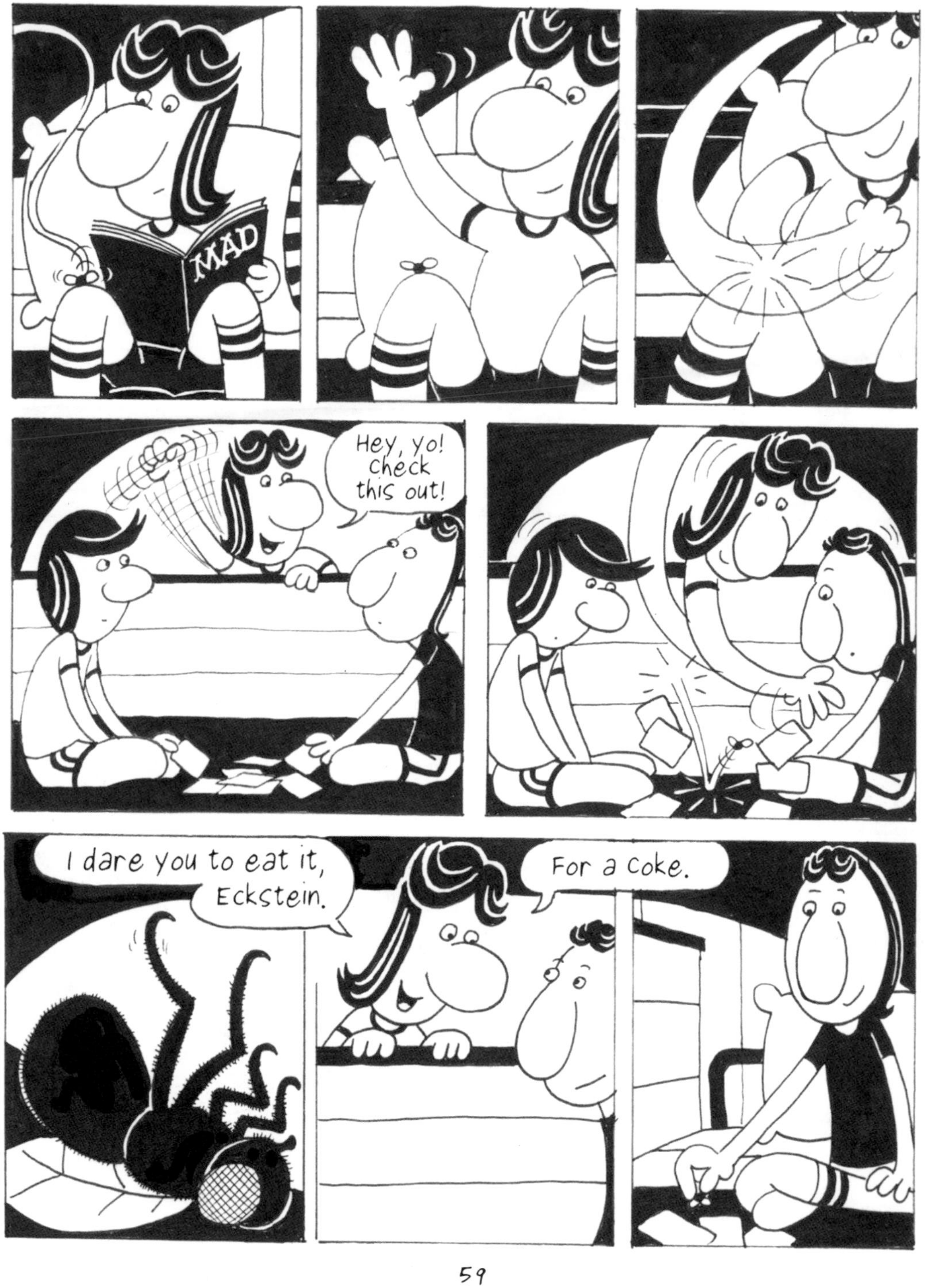
Hey, yo! check this out!
I dare you to eat it, Eckstein.
For a coke.

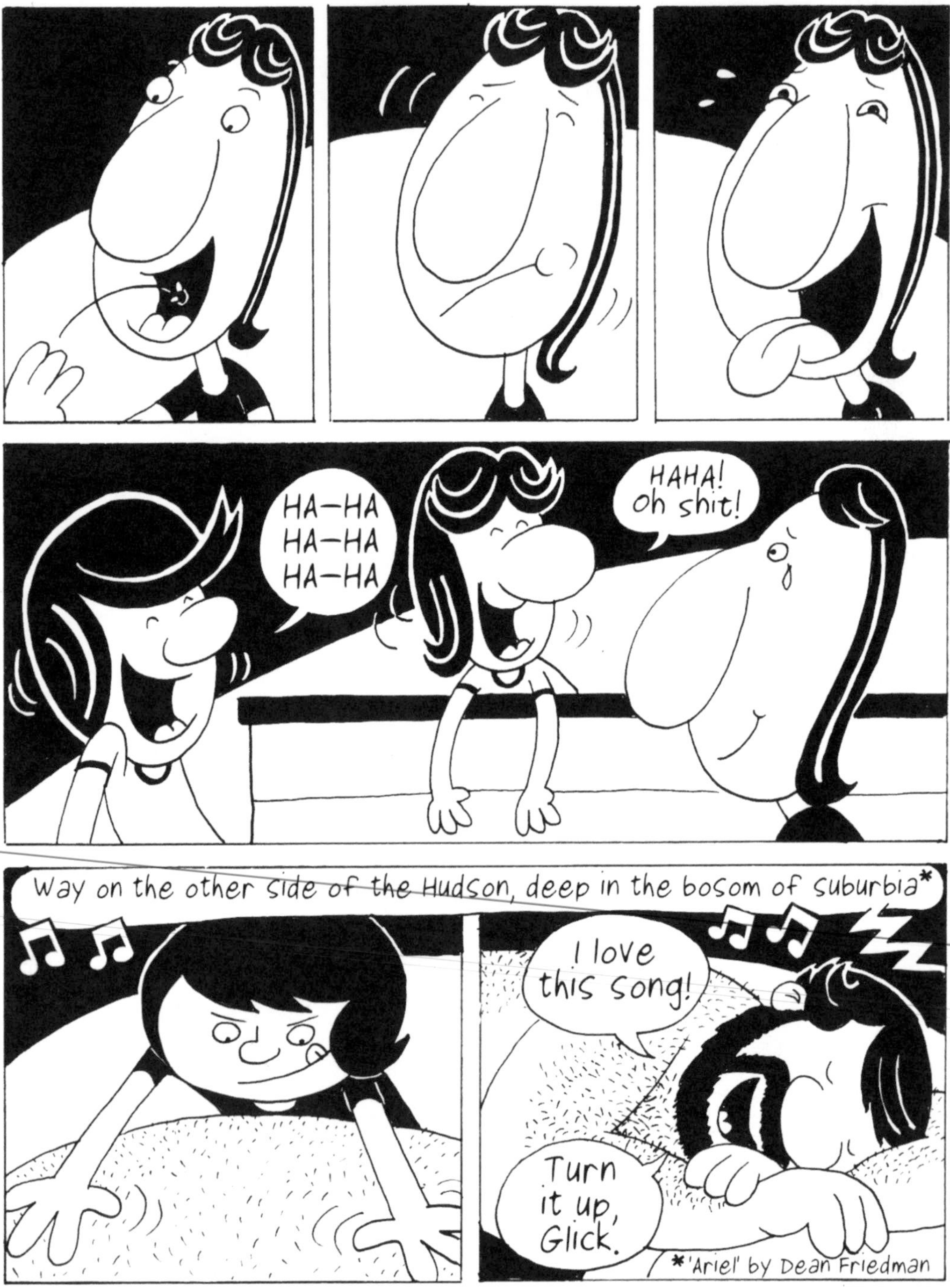
HA-HA
HA-HA
HA-HA
HAHA!
Oh shit!
Way on the other side of the Hudson, deep in the bosom of suburbia*
I love this song!
Turn it up, Glick.
*'Ariel' by Dean Friedman

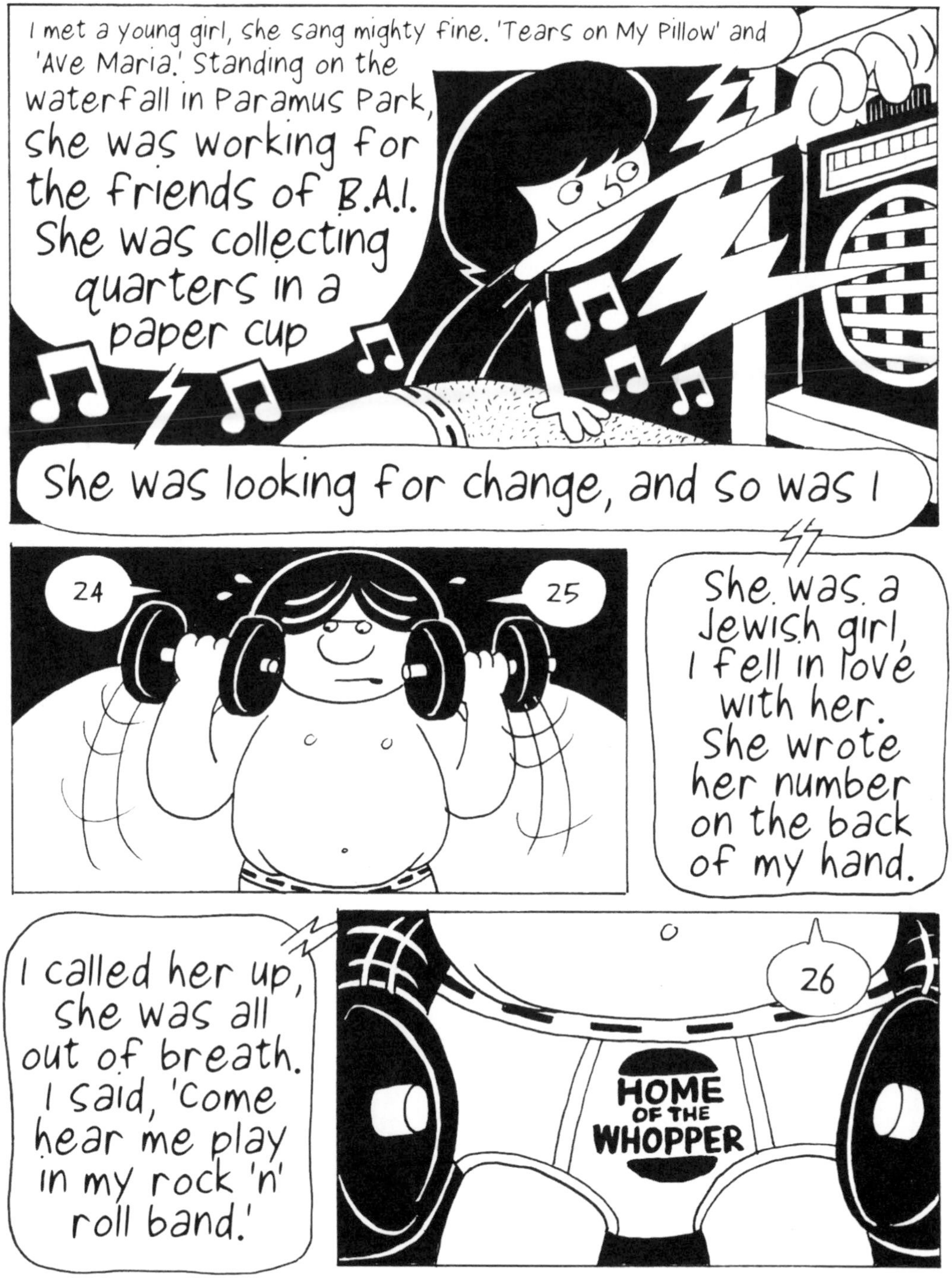

I met a young girl, she sang mighty fine. 'Tears on My Pillow' and 'Ave Maria.' Standing on the waterfall in Paramus Park, she was working for the friends of B.A.I. She was collecting quarters in a paper cup
She was looking for change, and so was I
24
25
She was a Jewish girl, I fell in love with her. She wrote her number on the back of my hand.
I called her up, she was all out of breath. I said, 'Come hear me play in my rock 'n' roll band.'
26
HOME OF THE WHOPPER

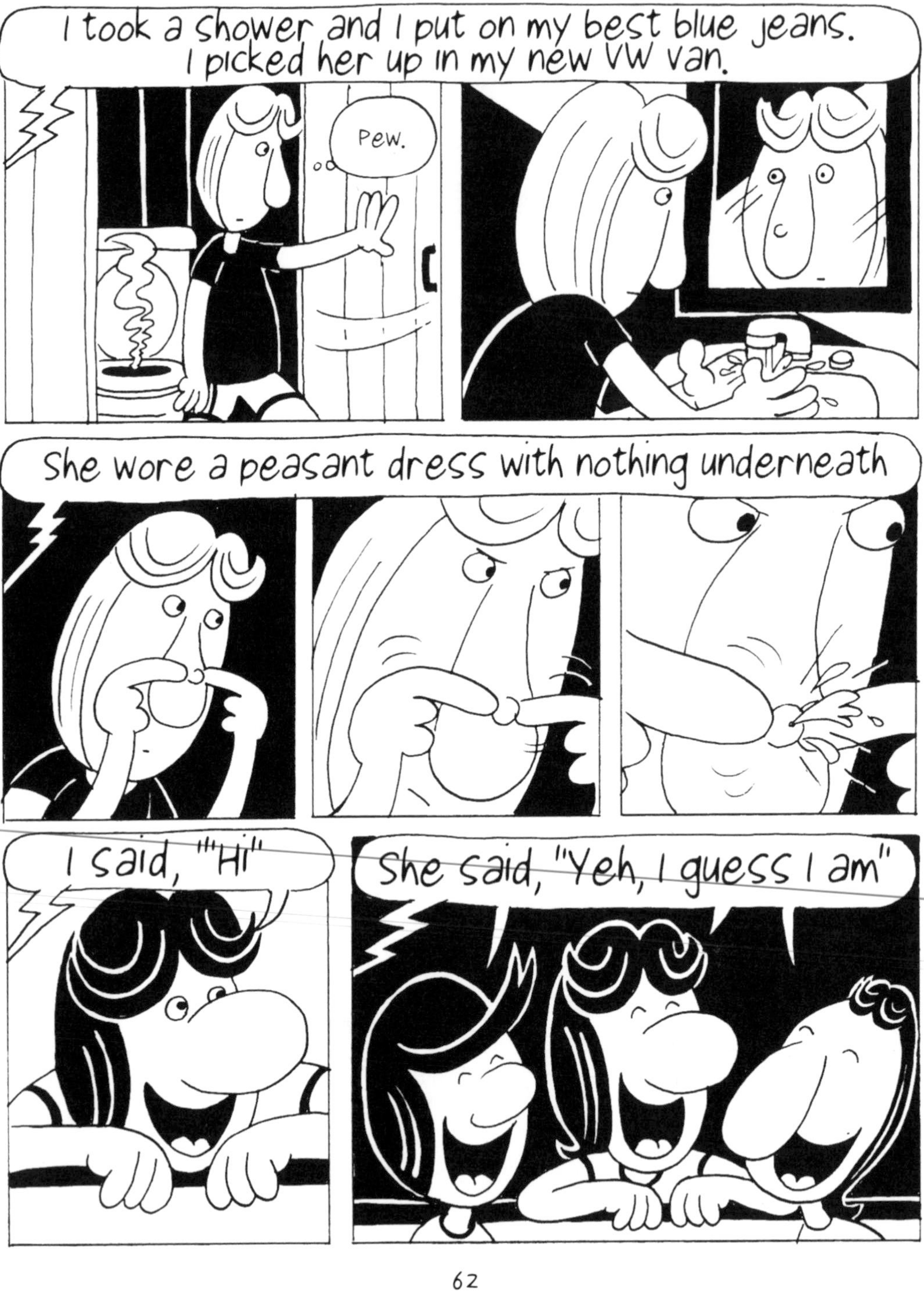
I took a shower and I put on my best blue jeans.
I picked her up in my new VW van.
Pew.
She wore a peasant dress with nothing underneath
I said, "Hi"
She said, "Yeh, I guess I am"

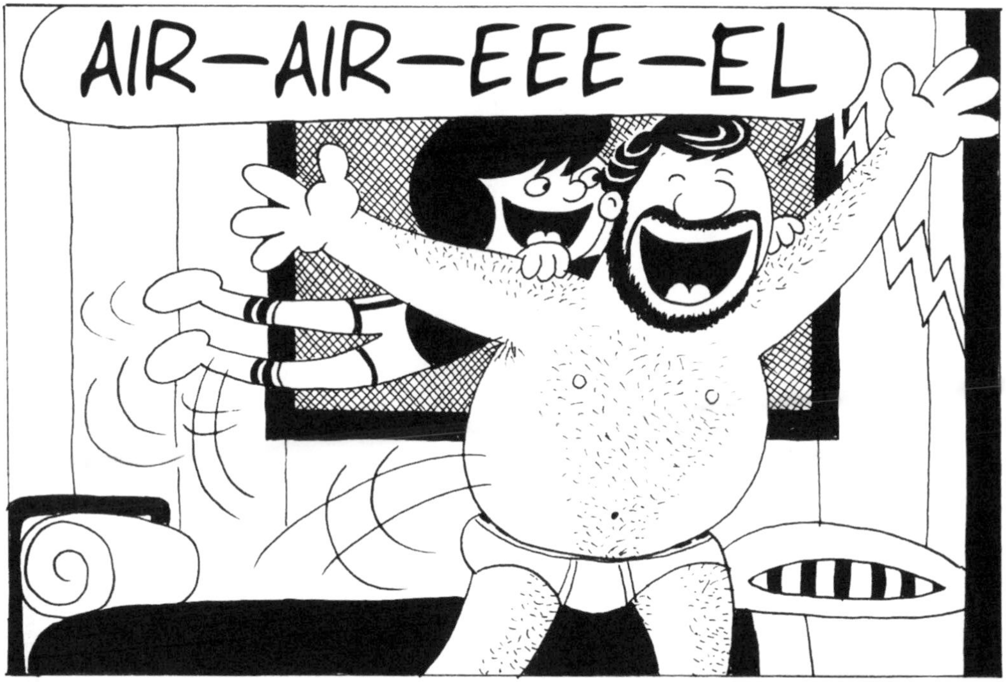
AIR—AIR—EEE—EL

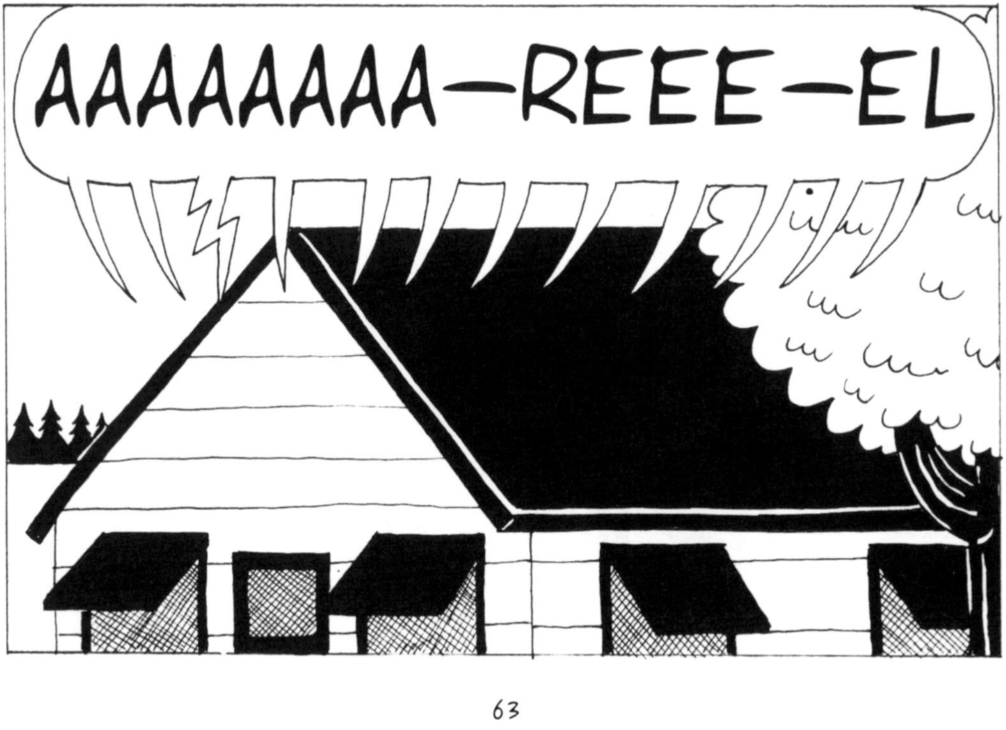
AAAAAAAA—REEE—EL

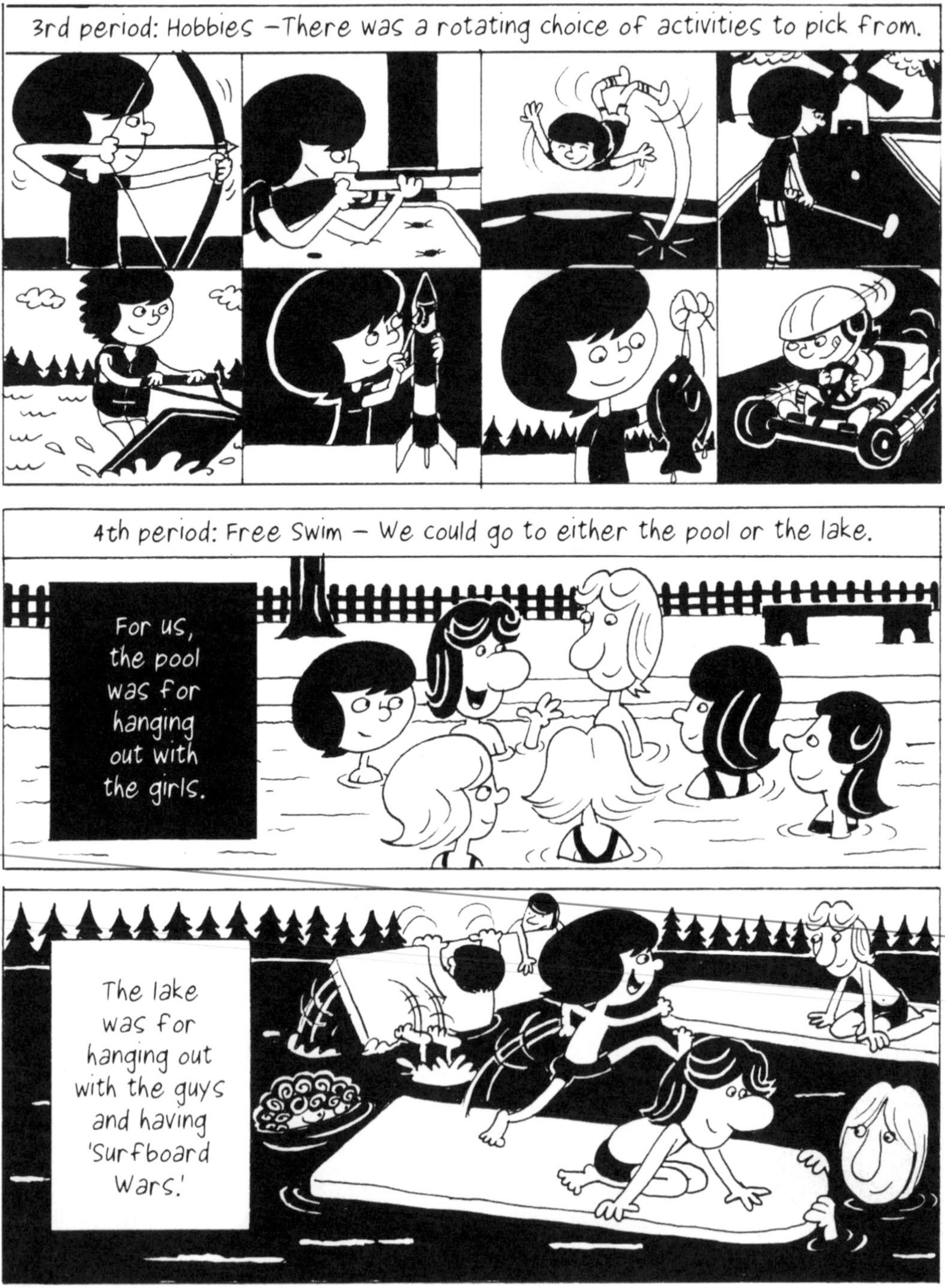

3rd period: Hobbies –There was a rotating choice of activities to pick from.
4th period: Free Swim – We could go to either the pool or the lake.
For us, the pool was for hanging out with the girls.
The lake was for hanging out with the guys and having 'Surfboard Wars.'

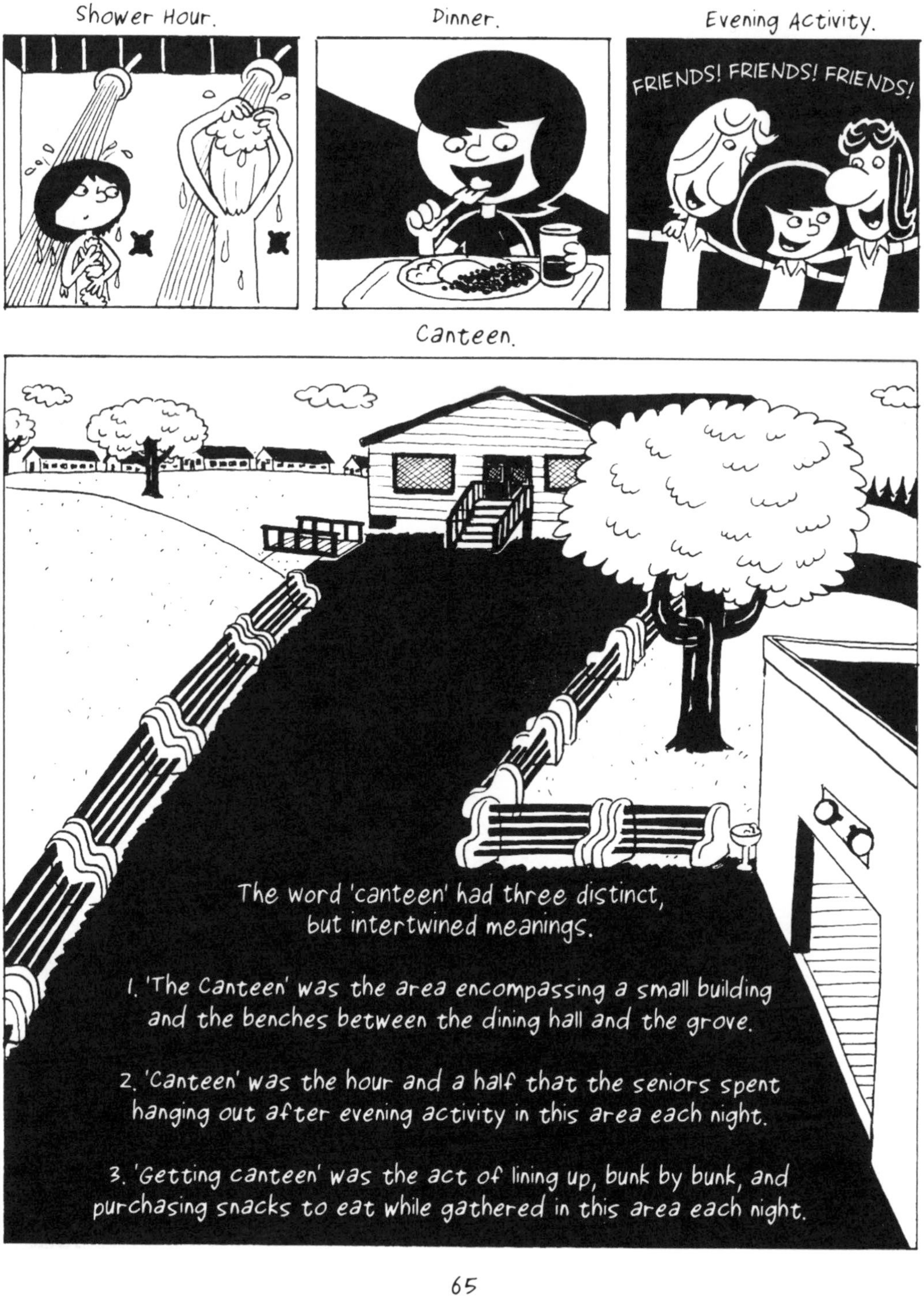
Shower Hour.
Dinner.
Evening Activity.
FRIENDS! FRIENDS! FRIENDS!
Canteen.
The word 'canteen' had three distinct, but intertwined meanings.
1. 'The Canteen' was the area encompassing a small building and the benches between the dining hall and the grove.
2. 'Canteen' was the hour and a half that the seniors spent hanging out after evening activity in this area each night.
3. 'Getting canteen' was the act of lining up, bunk by bunk, and purchasing snacks to eat while gathered in this area each night.

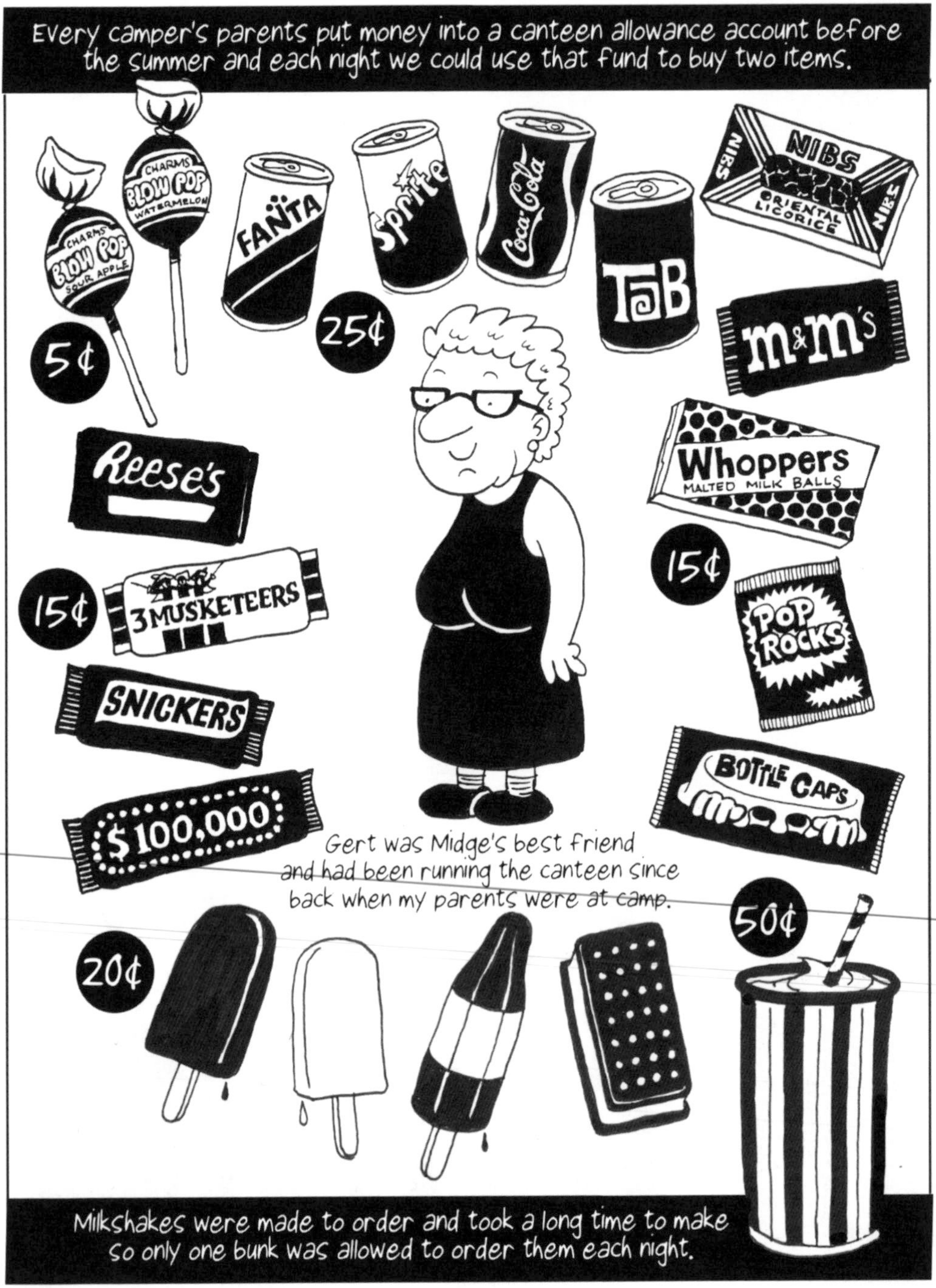
Every camper's parents put money into a canteen allowance account before the summer and each night we could use that fund to buy two items.
CHARMS BLOW POP SOUR APPLE
CHARMS BLOW POP WATERMELON
5¢
FANTA
Sprite
Coca-Cola
TaB
25¢
NIBS ORIENTAL LICORICE
m&m's
Reese's
Whoppers MALTED MILK BALLS
15¢
3 MUSKETEERS
15¢
POP ROCKS
SNICKERS
BOTTLE CAPS
$100,000
Gert was Midge's best friend and had been running the canteen since back when my parents were at camp.
50¢
20¢
Milkshakes were made to order and took a long time to make so only one bunk was allowed to order them each night.

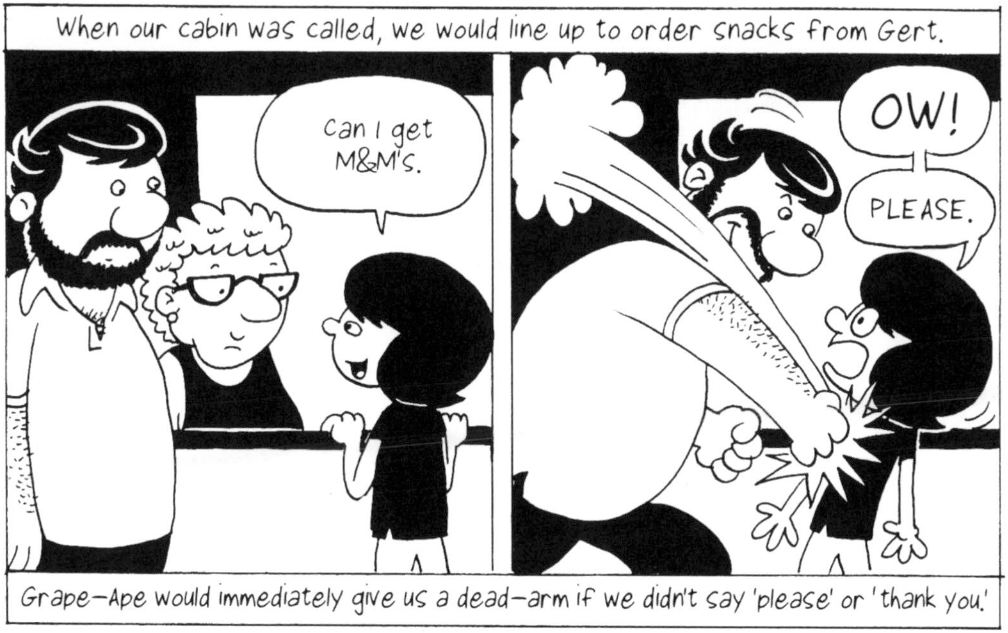
When our cabin was called, we would line up to order snacks from Gert.
Can I get M&M's.
OW!
PLEASE.
Grape—Ape would immediately give us a dead—arm if we didn't say 'please' or 'thank you.'

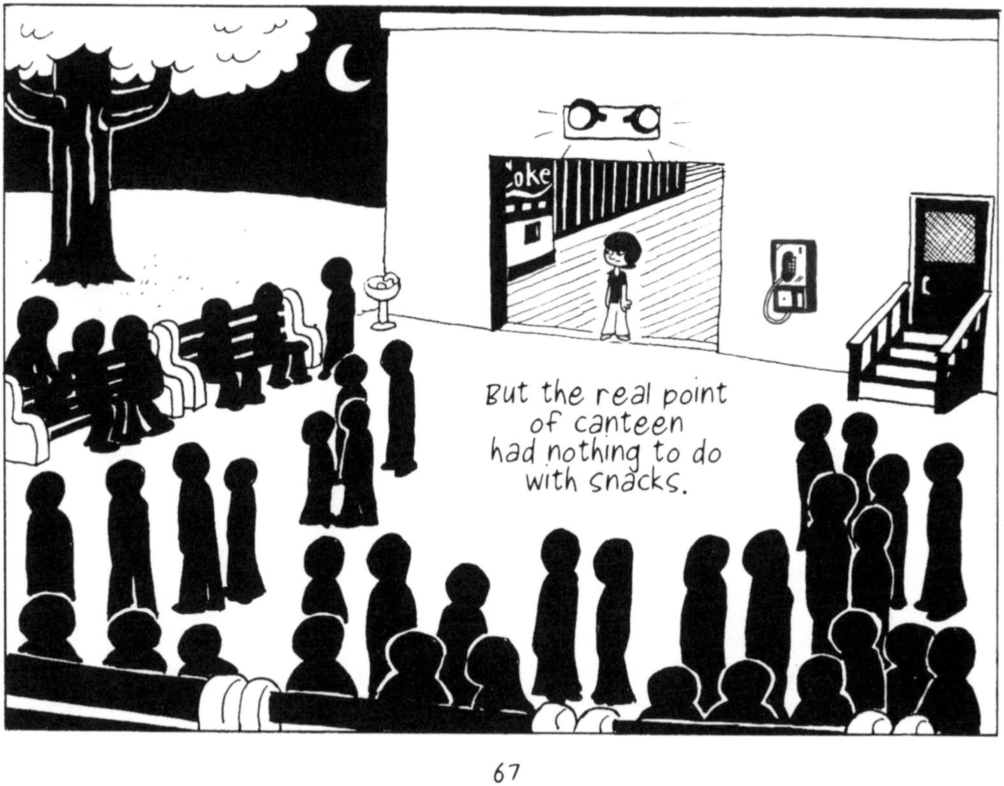
Coke
But the real point of canteen had nothing to do with snacks.

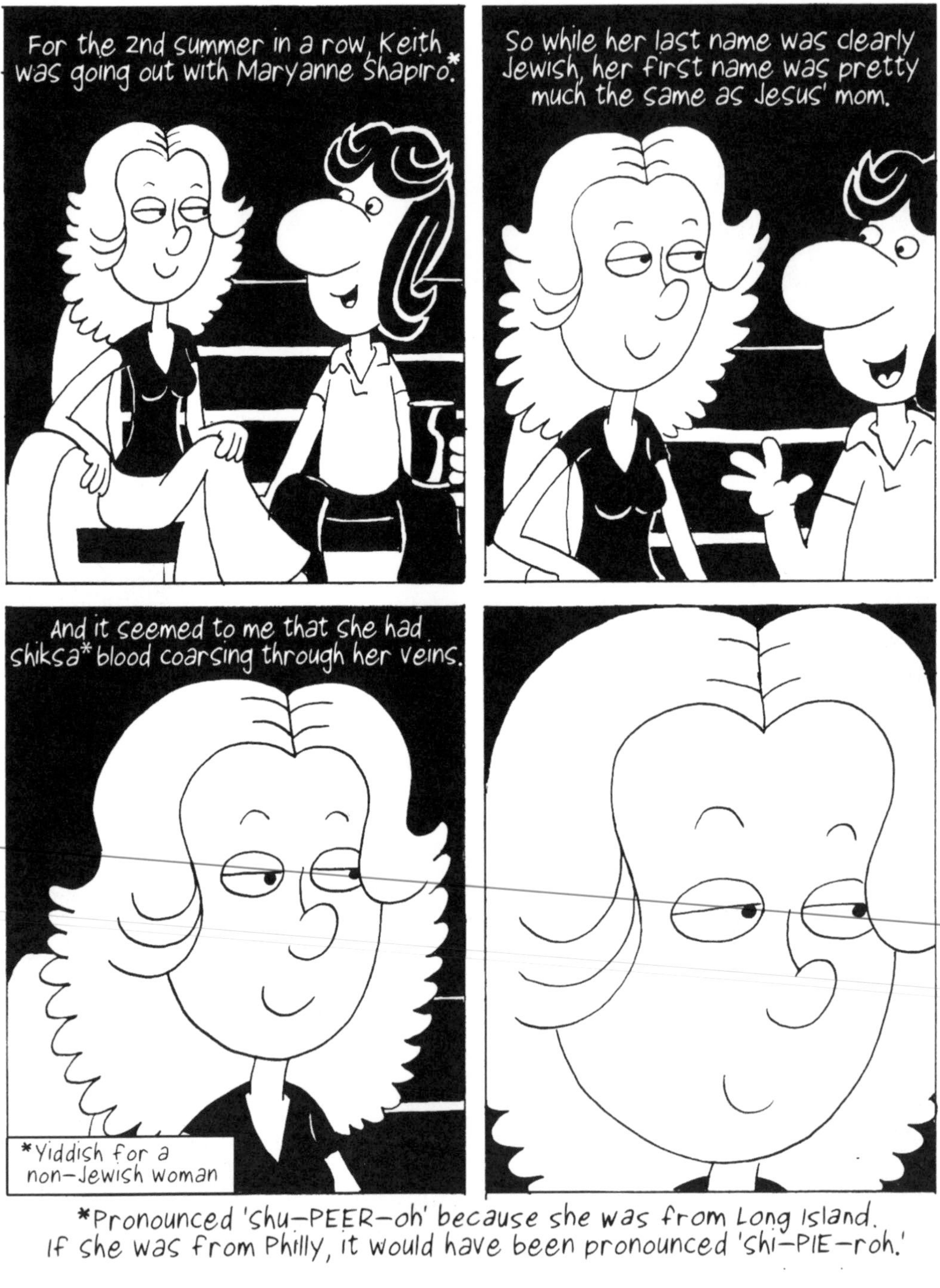
For the 2nd summer in a row, Keith was going out with Maryanne Shapiro.*
So while her last name was clearly Jewish, her first name was pretty much the same as Jesus' mom.
And it seemed to me that she had shiksa* blood coarsing through her veins.
*Yiddish for a non-Jewish woman

*Pronounced 'Shu-PEER-oh' because she was from Long Island. If she was from Philly, it would have been pronounced 'Shi-PIE-roh.'

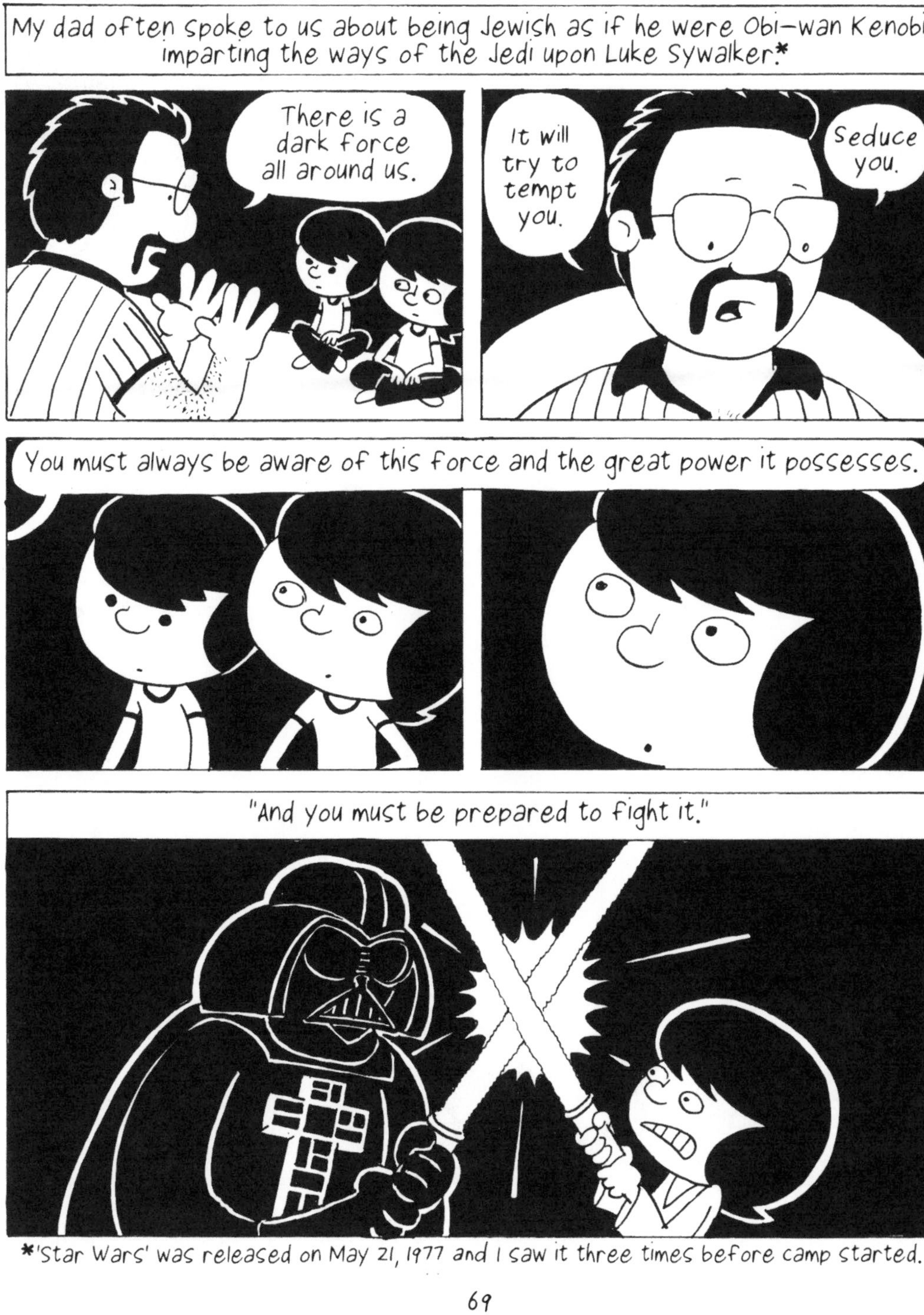
My dad often spoke to us about being Jewish as if he were Obi–wan Kenobi imparting the ways of the Jedi upon Luke Sywalker.*
There is a dark force all around us.
It will try to tempt you.
Seduce you.
You must always be aware of this force and the great power it possesses.
"And you must be prepared to fight it."

*'Star Wars' was released on May 21, 1977 and I saw it three times before camp started.

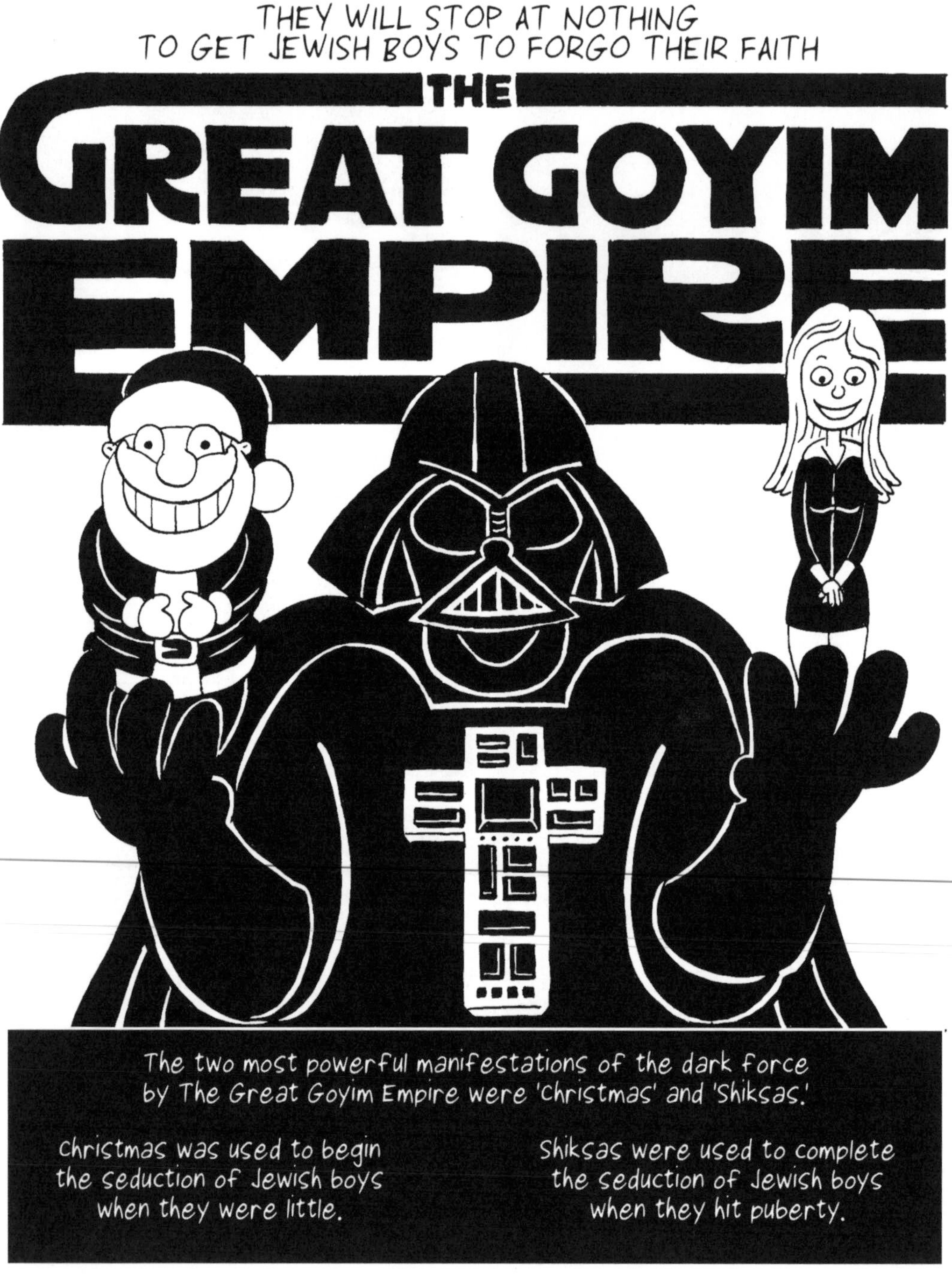
THEY WILL STOP AT NOTHING
TO GET JEWISH BOYS TO FORGO THEIR FAITH
THE
GREAT GOYIM
EMPIRE
The two most powerful manifestations of the dark force
by The Great Goyim Empire were 'Christmas' and 'Shiksas.'
Christmas was used to begin
the seduction of Jewish boys
when they were little.
Shiksas were used to complete
the seduction of Jewish boys
when they hit puberty.

To combat these incredibly effectual forces, American Jewish parents did two things:

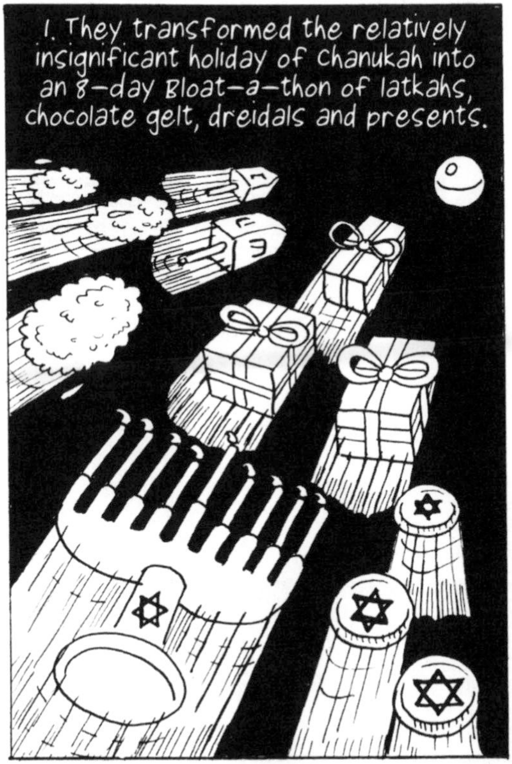
1. They transformed the relatively insignificant holiday of Chanukah into an 8-day Bloat-a-thon of latkahs, chocolate gelt, dreidals and presents.

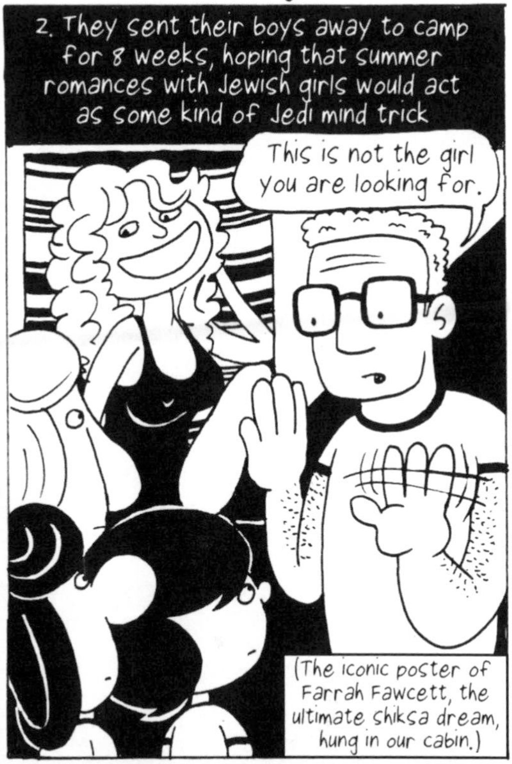
2. They sent their boys away to camp for 8 weeks, hoping that summer romances with Jewish girls would act as some kind of Jedi mind trick
This is not the girl you are looking for.
(The iconic poster of Farrah Fawcett, the ultimate shiksa dream, hung in our cabin.)

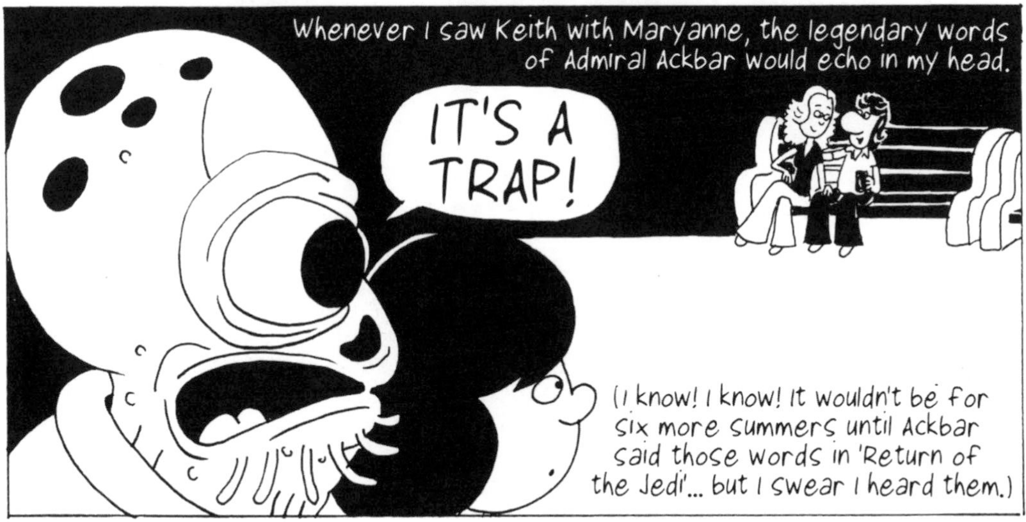
Whenever I saw Keith with Maryanne, the legendary words of Admiral Ackbar would echo in my head.
IT'S A TRAP!
(I know! I know! It wouldn't be for six more summers until Ackbar said those words in 'Return of the Jedi'... but I swear I heard them.)

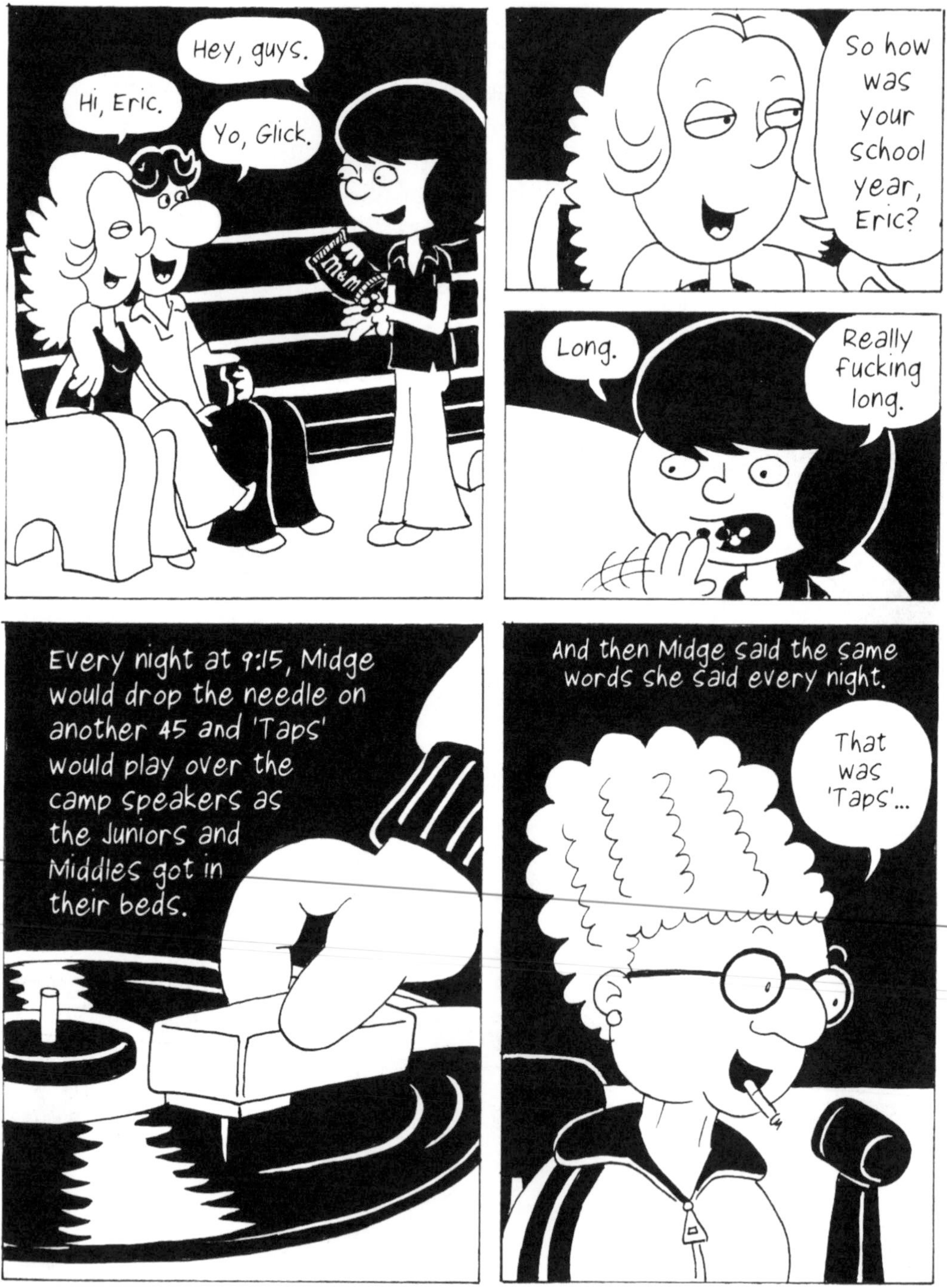
Hey, guys.
Hi, Eric.
Yo, Glick.
So how was your school year, Eric?
Long.
Really fucking long.
Every night at 9:15, Midge would drop the needle on another 45 and 'Taps' would play over the camp speakers as the Juniors and Middles got in their beds.
And then Midge said the same words she said every night.
That was 'Taps'...

Good night Boys' camp. Good night Girls' camp.

And remember...

Pock—a—Wocknee loves you!

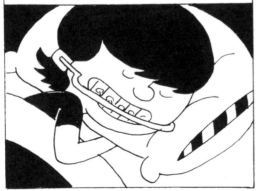

When I was younger, I would happily fall asleep moments after 'Taps'.

Now, I stood there with my stomach in a knot, trying to figure out how to approach that curly—haired girl.

The next night, at the senior campfire, I got a chance.

pffff!
pffff!
pfff!

Mine is perfect. Ya want it?

sure.

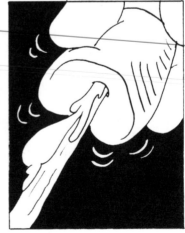

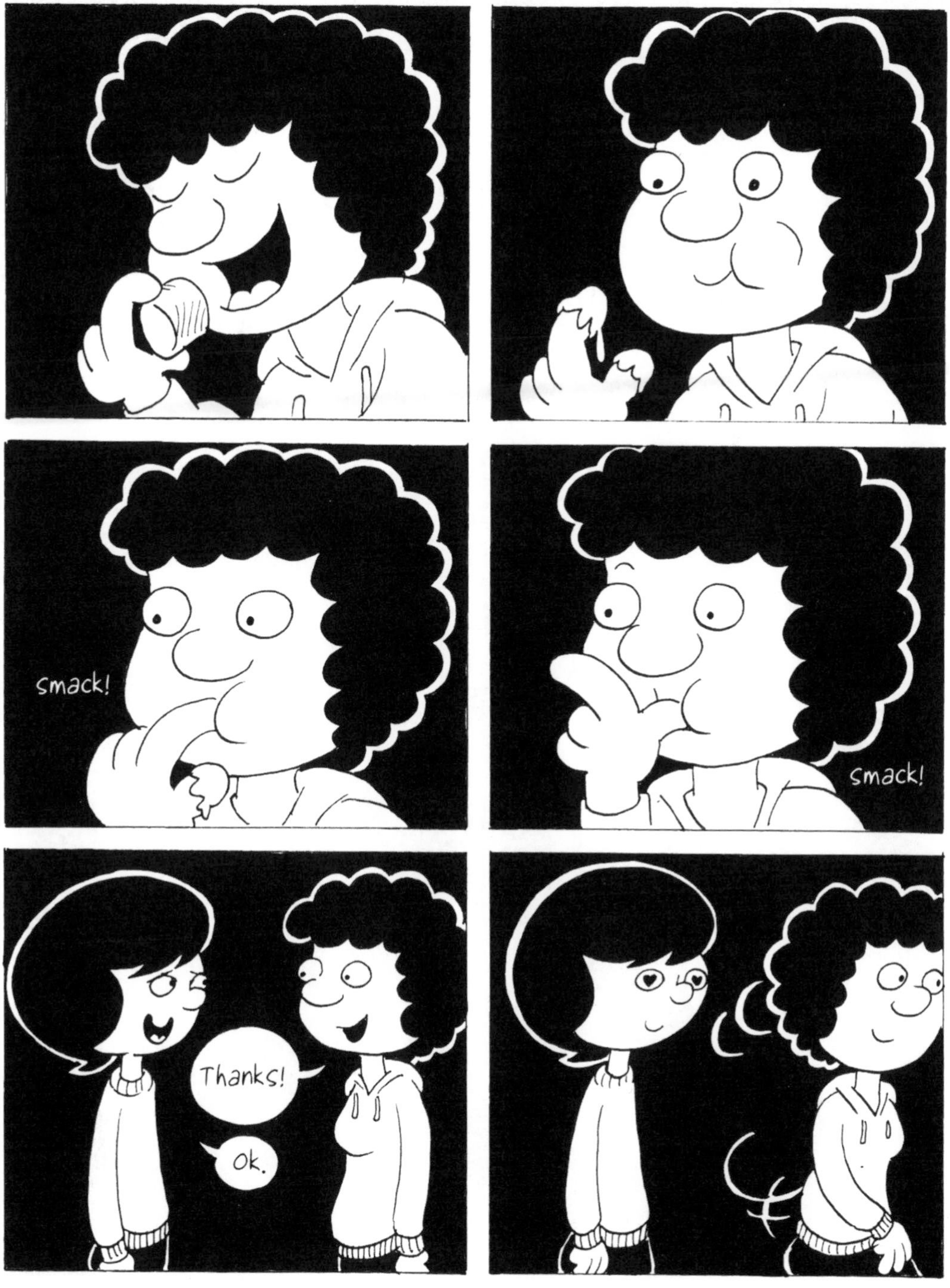
smack!
smack!
Thanks!
Ok.

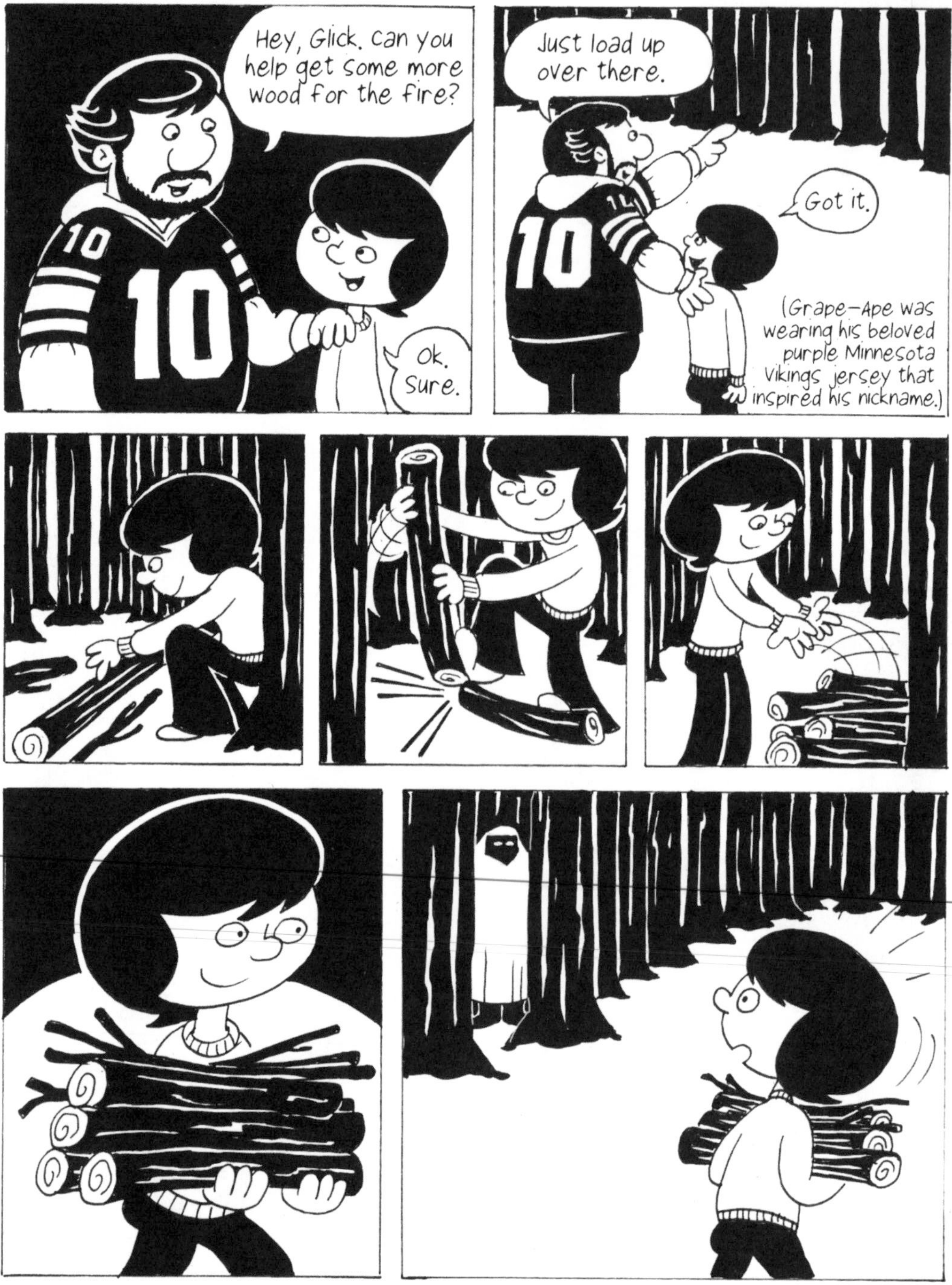
Hey, Glick. Can you help get some more wood for the fire?
Ok. Sure.
Just load up over there.
Got it.
(Grape-Ape was wearing his beloved purple Minnesota Vikings jersey that inspired his nickname.)

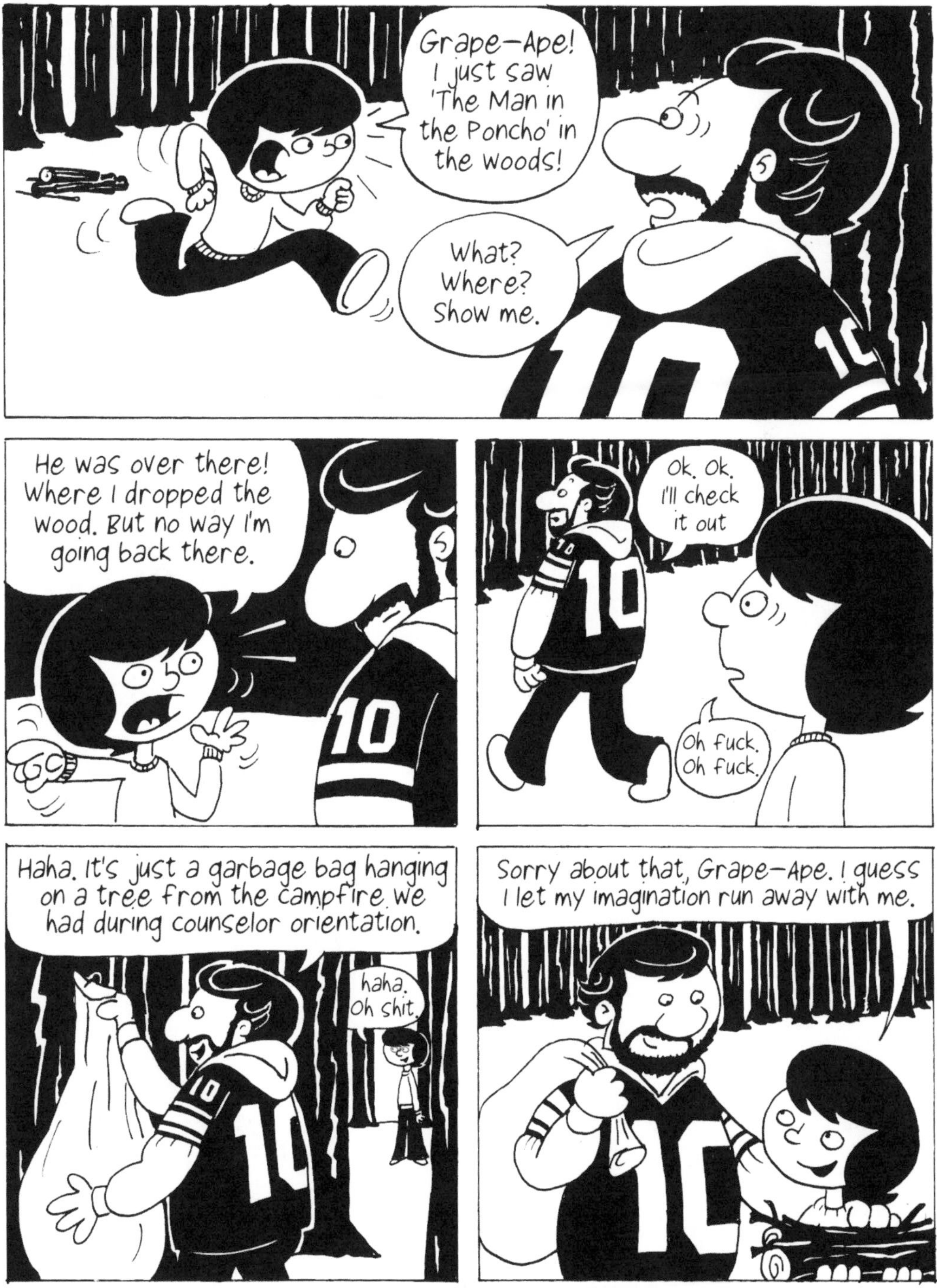
Grape-Ape! I just saw 'The Man in the Poncho' in the woods!
What? Where? Show me.
He was over there! Where I dropped the wood. But no way I'm going back there.
Ok. Ok. I'll check it out
Oh fuck. Oh fuck.
Haha. It's just a garbage bag hanging on a tree from the campfire we had during counselor orientation.
haha. Oh shit.
Sorry about that, Grape-Ape. I guess I let my imagination run away with me.

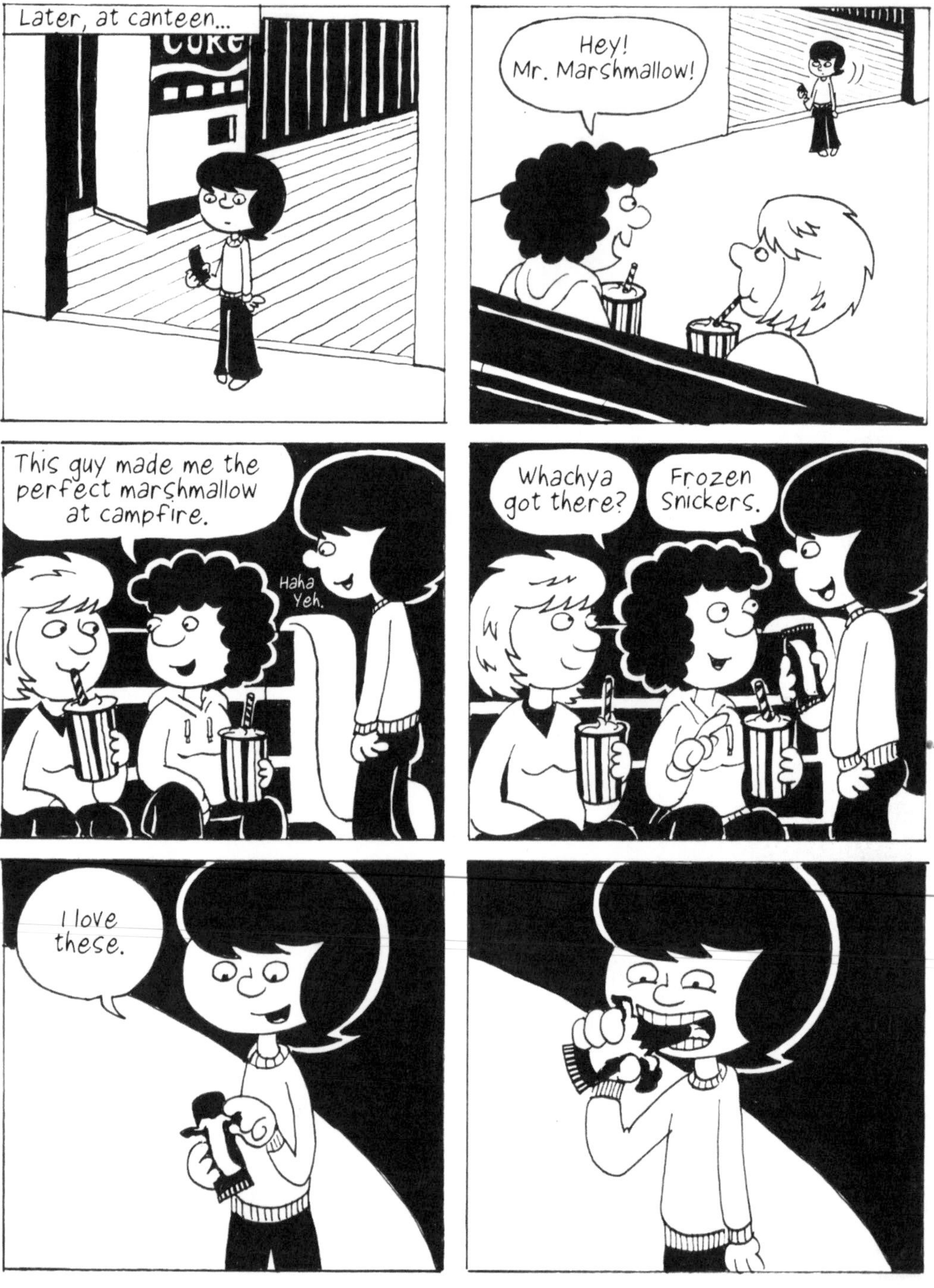
Later, at canteen...
COKE
Hey! Mr. Marshmallow!
This guy made me the perfect marshmallow at campfire.
Haha Yeh.
Whachya got there?
Frozen Snickers.
I love these.

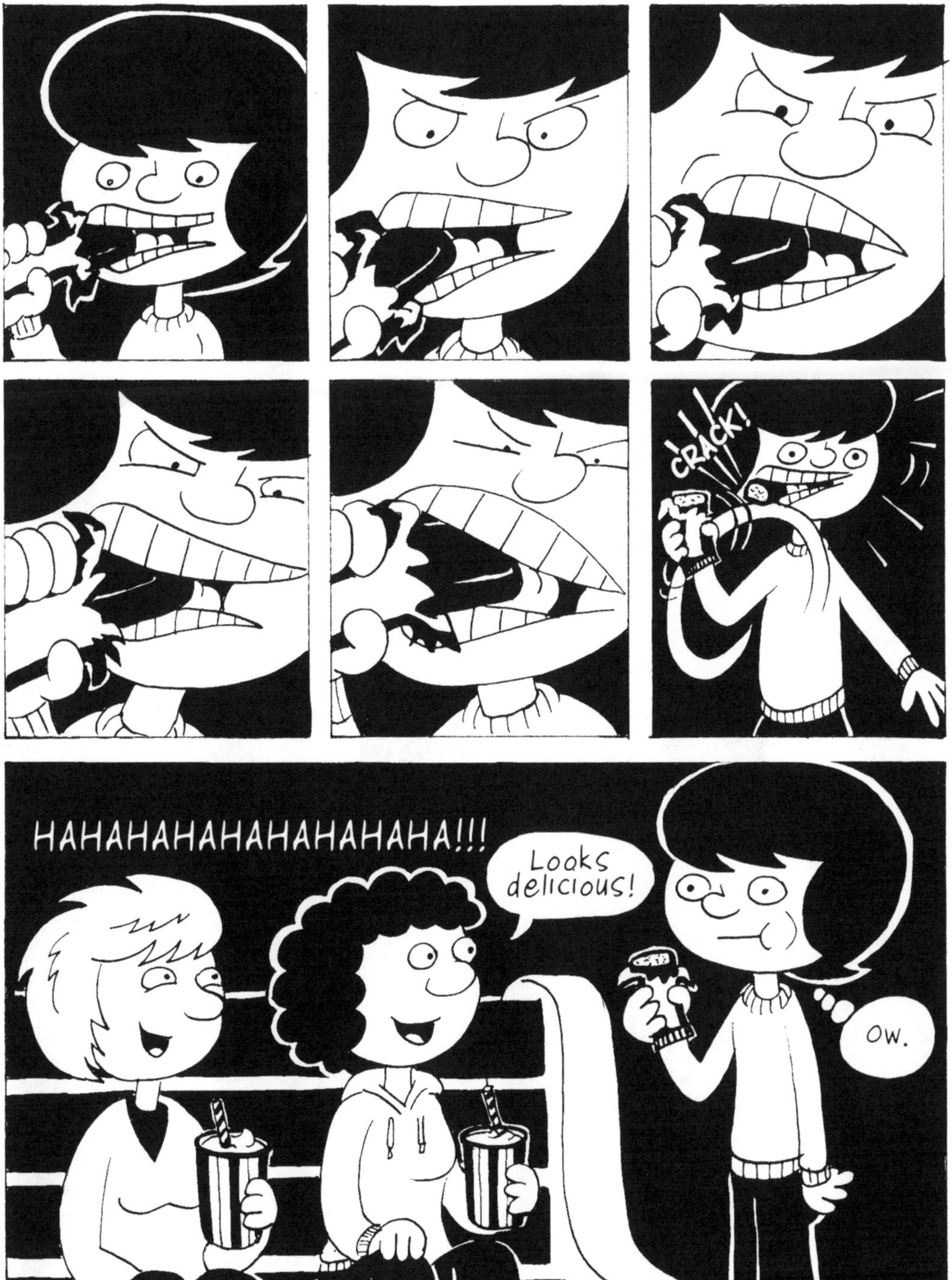
CRACK!
HAHAHAHAHAHAHAHAHA!!!
Looks delicious!
OW.

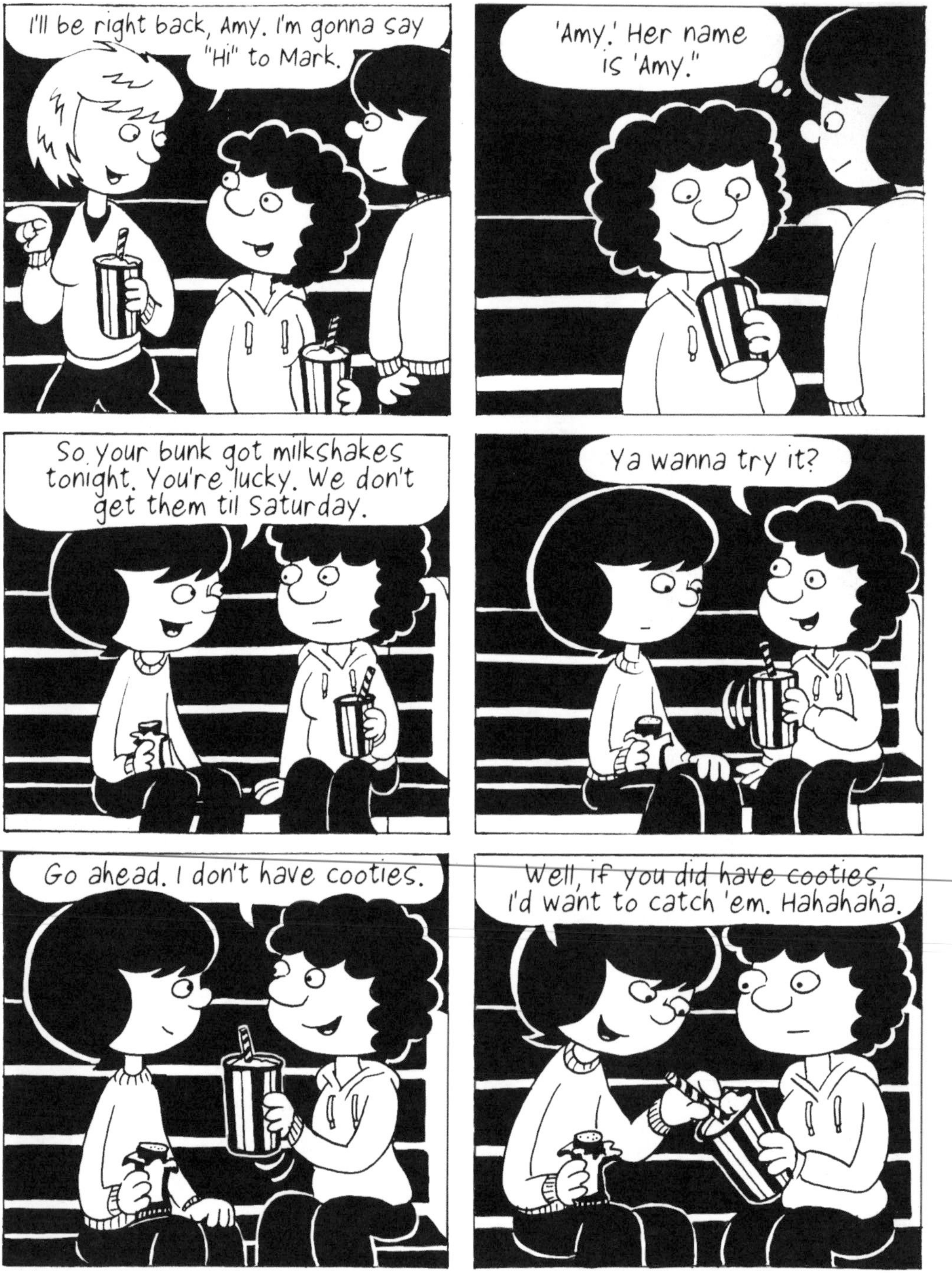
I'll be right back, Amy. I'm gonna say "Hi" to Mark.
'Amy.' Her name is 'Amy.'
So your bunk got milkshakes tonight. You're lucky. We don't get them til Saturday.
Ya wanna try it?
Go ahead. I don't have cooties.
Well, if you did have cooties, I'd want to catch 'em. Hahahaha.

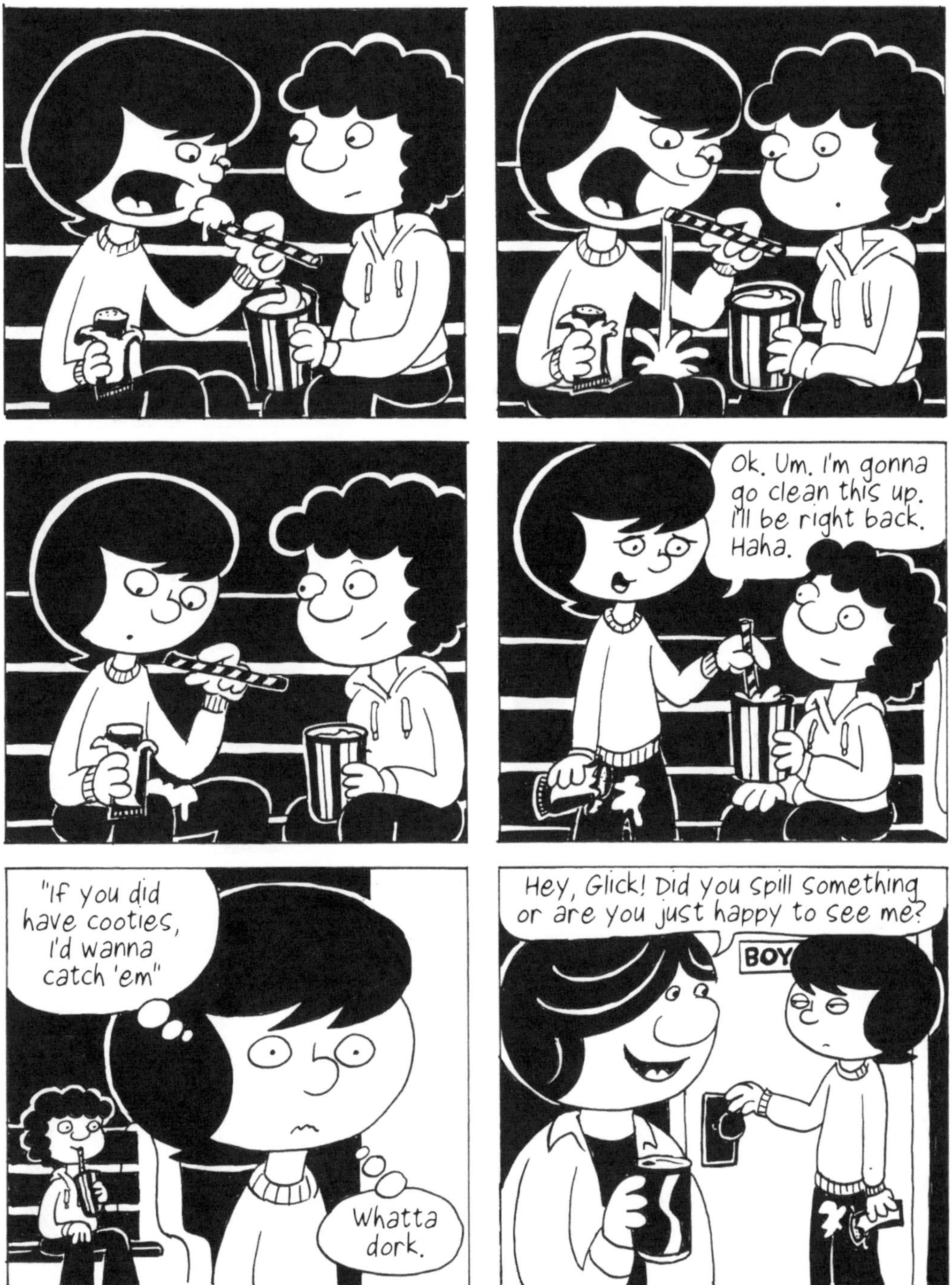
Ok. Um. I'm gonna go clean this up. I'll be right back. Haha.
"If you did have cooties, I'd wanna catch 'em"
Whatta dork.
Hey, Glick! Did you spill something or are you just happy to see me?
BOY

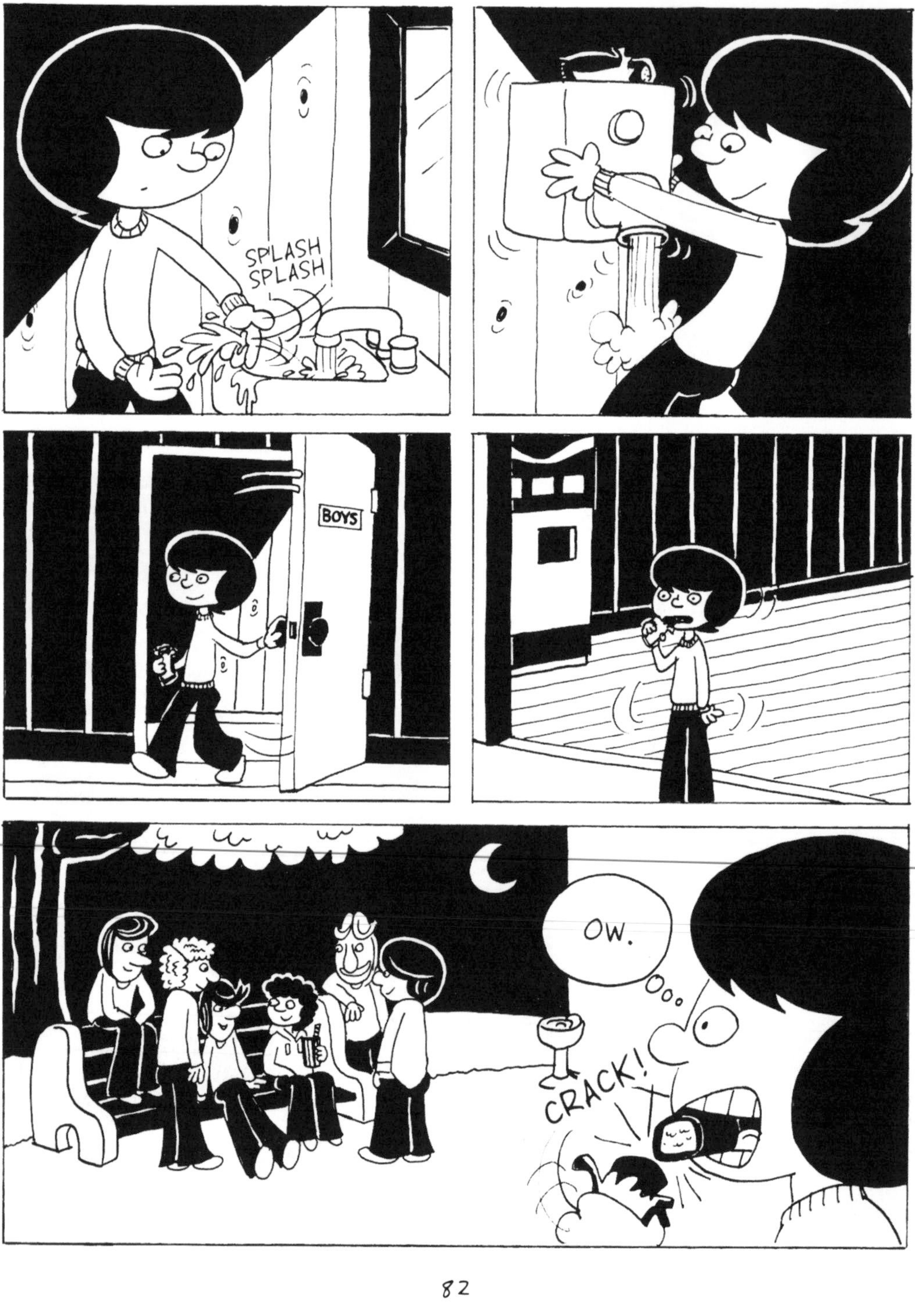
SPLASH
SPLASH
BOYS
OW.
CRACK!

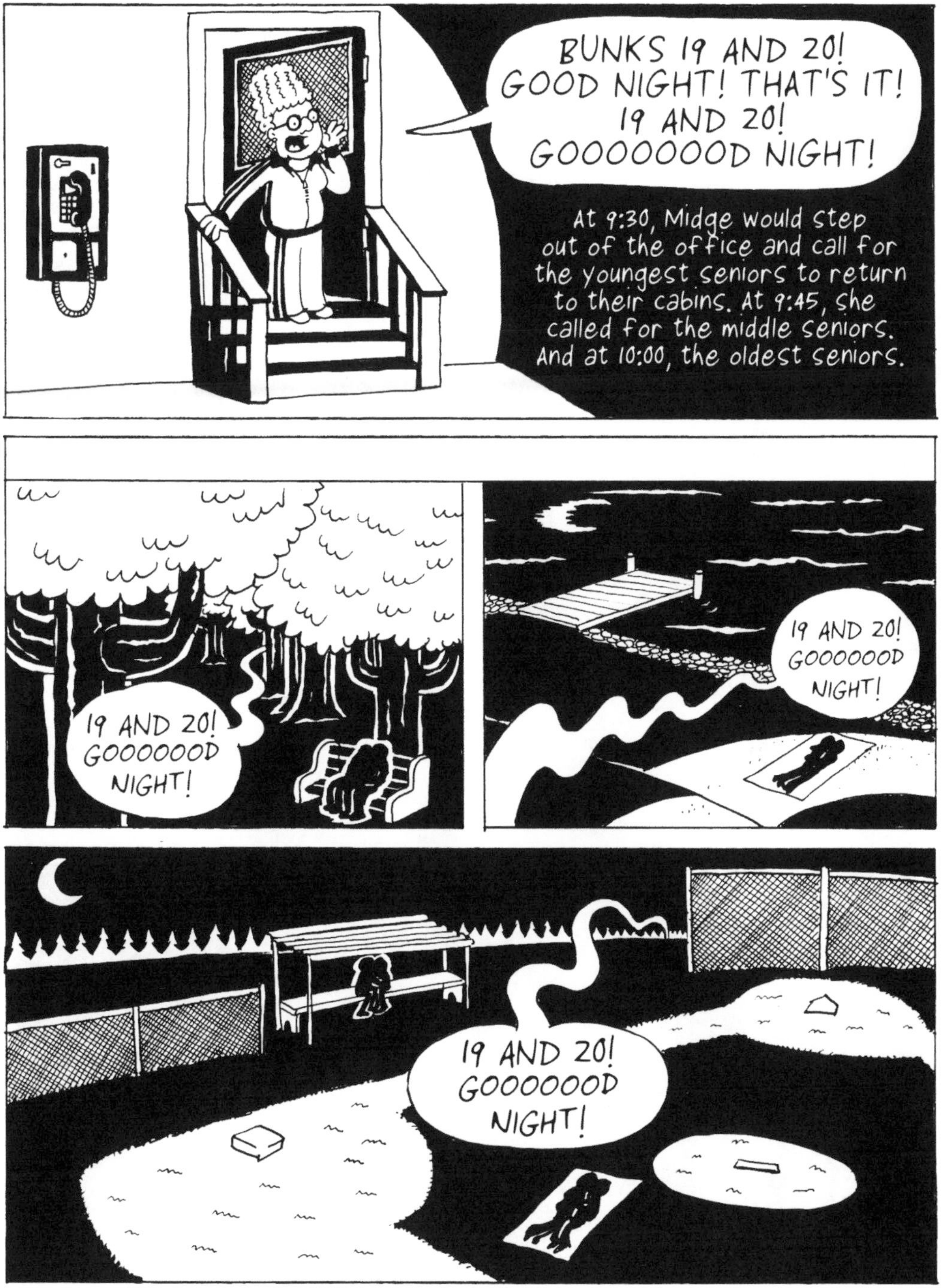
BUNKS 19 AND 20! GOOD NIGHT! THAT'S IT! 19 AND 20! GOOOOOOOD NIGHT!
At 9:30, Midge would step out of the office and call for the youngest seniors to return to their cabins. At 9:45, she called for the middle seniors. And at 10:00, the oldest seniors.
19 AND 20! GOOOOOOD NIGHT!
19 AND 20! GOOOOOOD NIGHT!
19 AND 20! GOOOOOOD NIGHT!

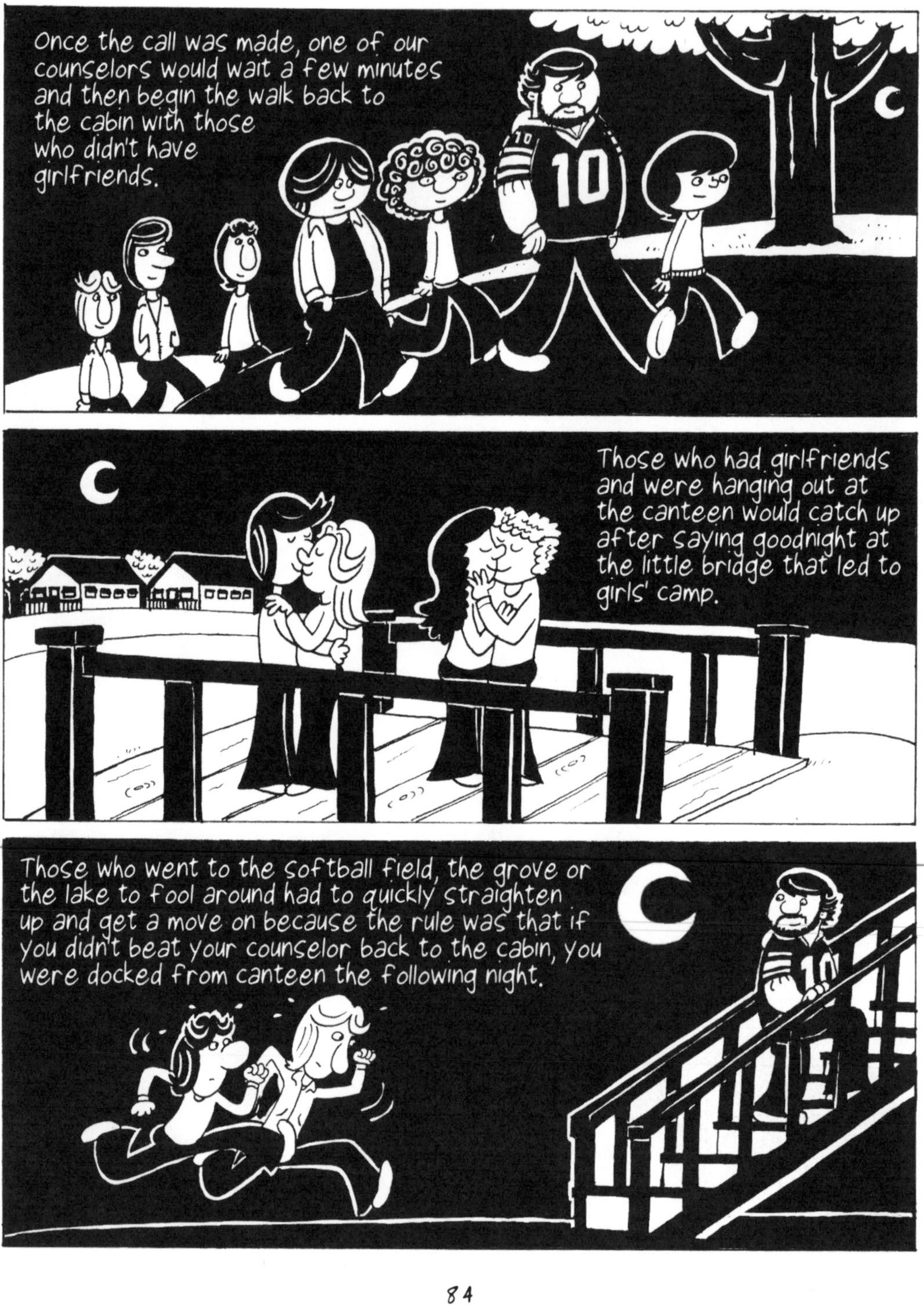
Once the call was made, one of our counselors would wait a few minutes and then begin the walk back to the cabin with those who didn't have girlfriends.
10
Those who had girlfriends and were hanging out at the canteen would catch up after saying goodnight at the little bridge that led to girls' camp.
Those who went to the softball field, the grove or the lake to fool around had to quickly straighten up and get a move on because the rule was that if you didn't beat your counselor back to the cabin, you were docked from canteen the following night.

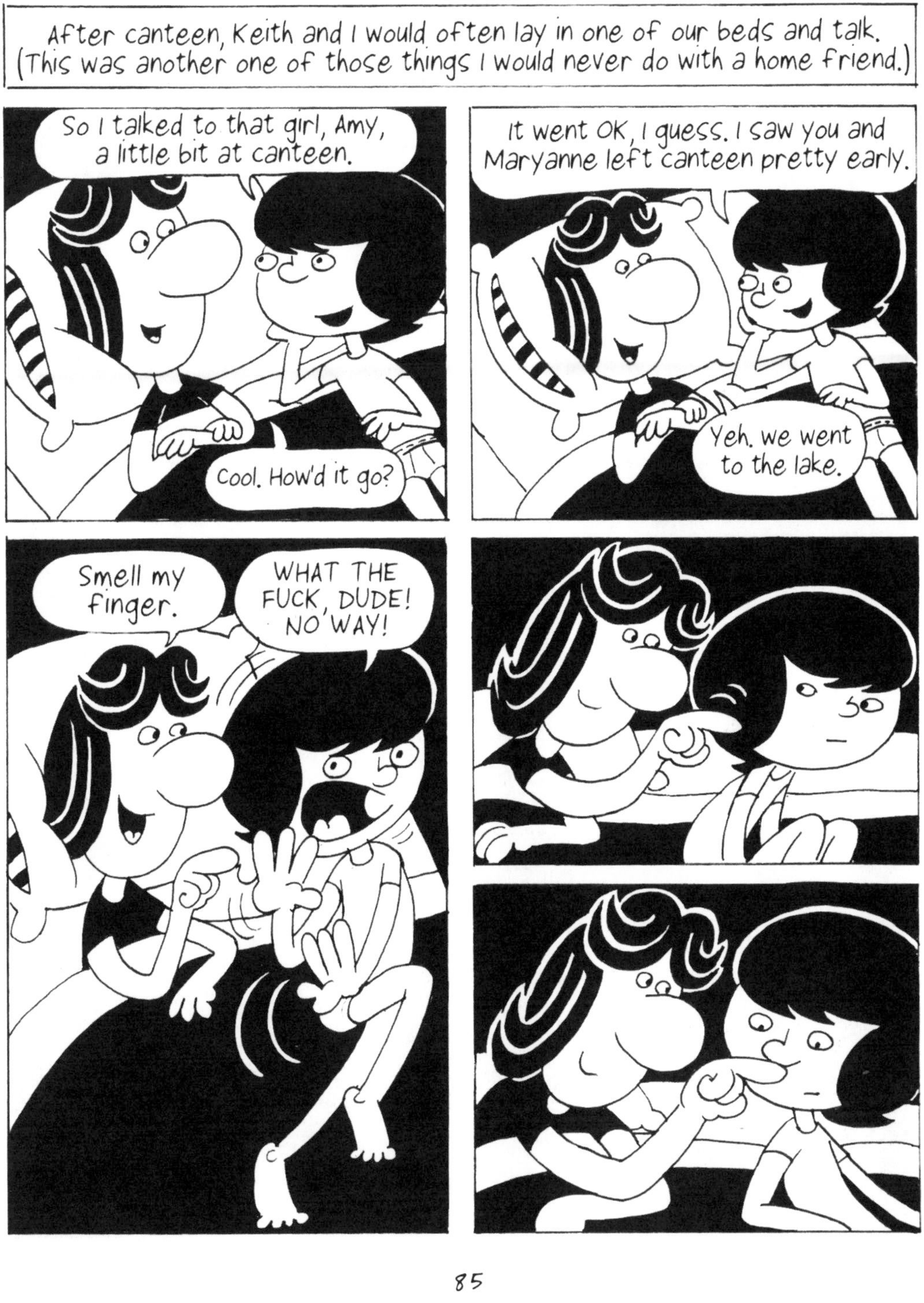
After canteen, Keith and I would often lay in one of our beds and talk. (This was another one of those things I would never do with a home friend.)
So I talked to that girl, Amy, a little bit at canteen.
Cool. How'd it go?
It went OK, I guess. I saw you and Maryanne left canteen pretty early.
Yeh. we went to the lake.
Smell my finger.
WHAT THE FUCK, DUDE! NO WAY!

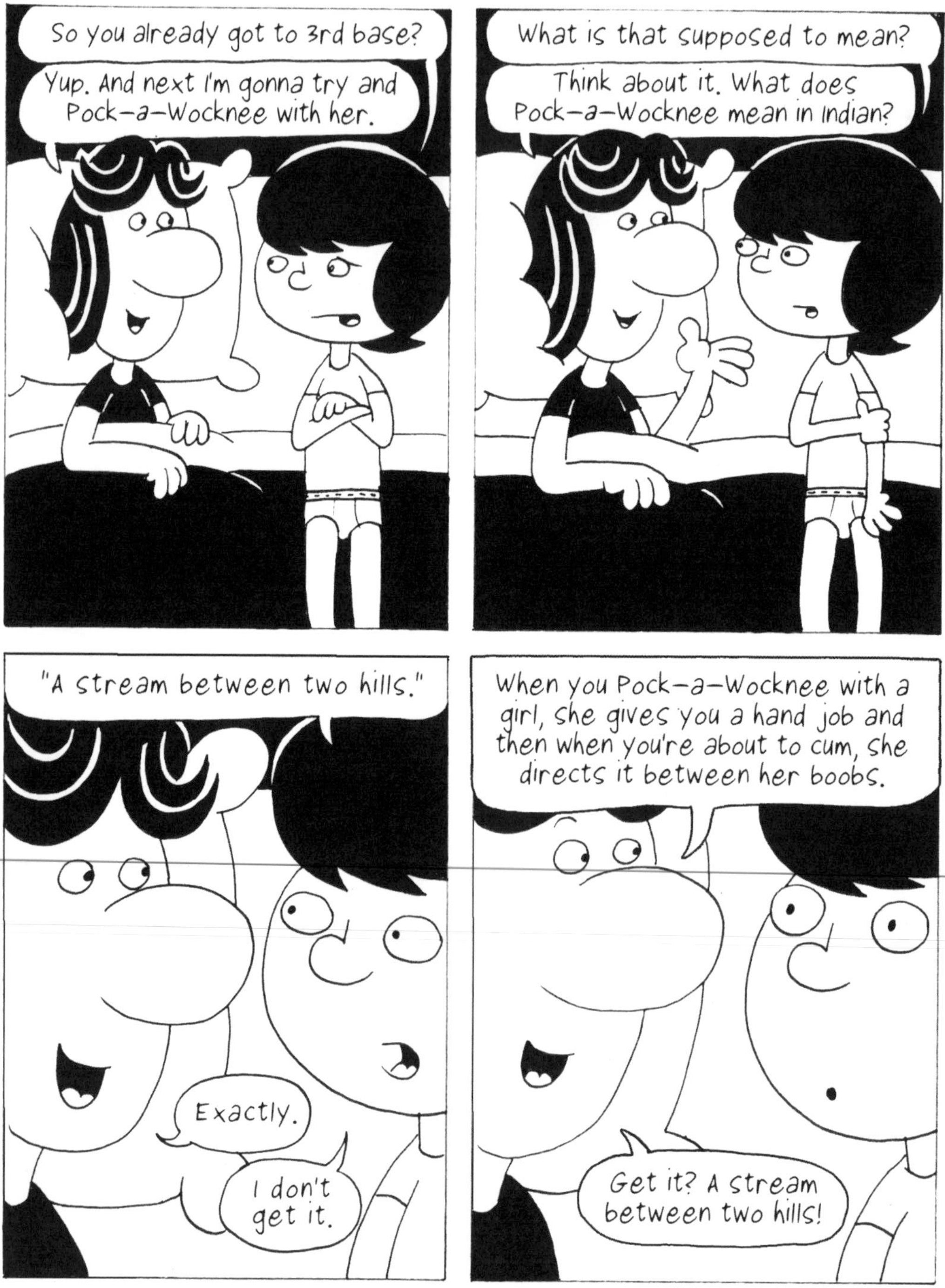

So you already got to 3rd base?
Yup. And next I'm gonna try and Pock-a-Wocknee with her.
What is that supposed to mean?
Think about it. What does Pock-a-Wocknee mean in Indian?
"A stream between two hills."
Exactly.
I don't get it.
When you Pock-a-Wocknee with a girl, she gives you a hand job and then when you're about to cum, she directs it between her boobs.
Get it? A stream between two hills!

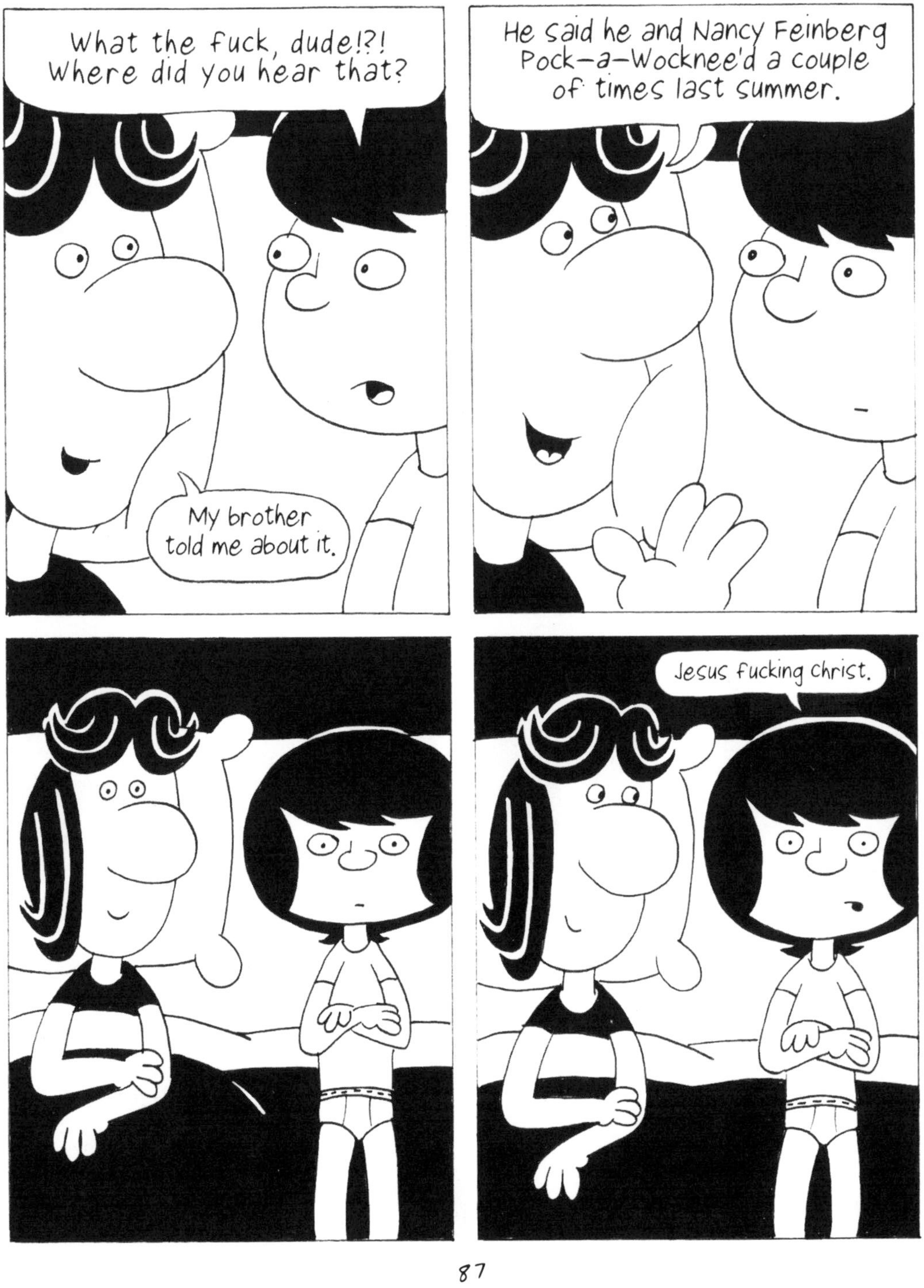
What the fuck, dude!?! Where did you hear that?
My brother told me about it.
He said he and Nancy Feinberg Pock-a-Wocknee'd a couple of times last summer.
Jesus fucking christ.

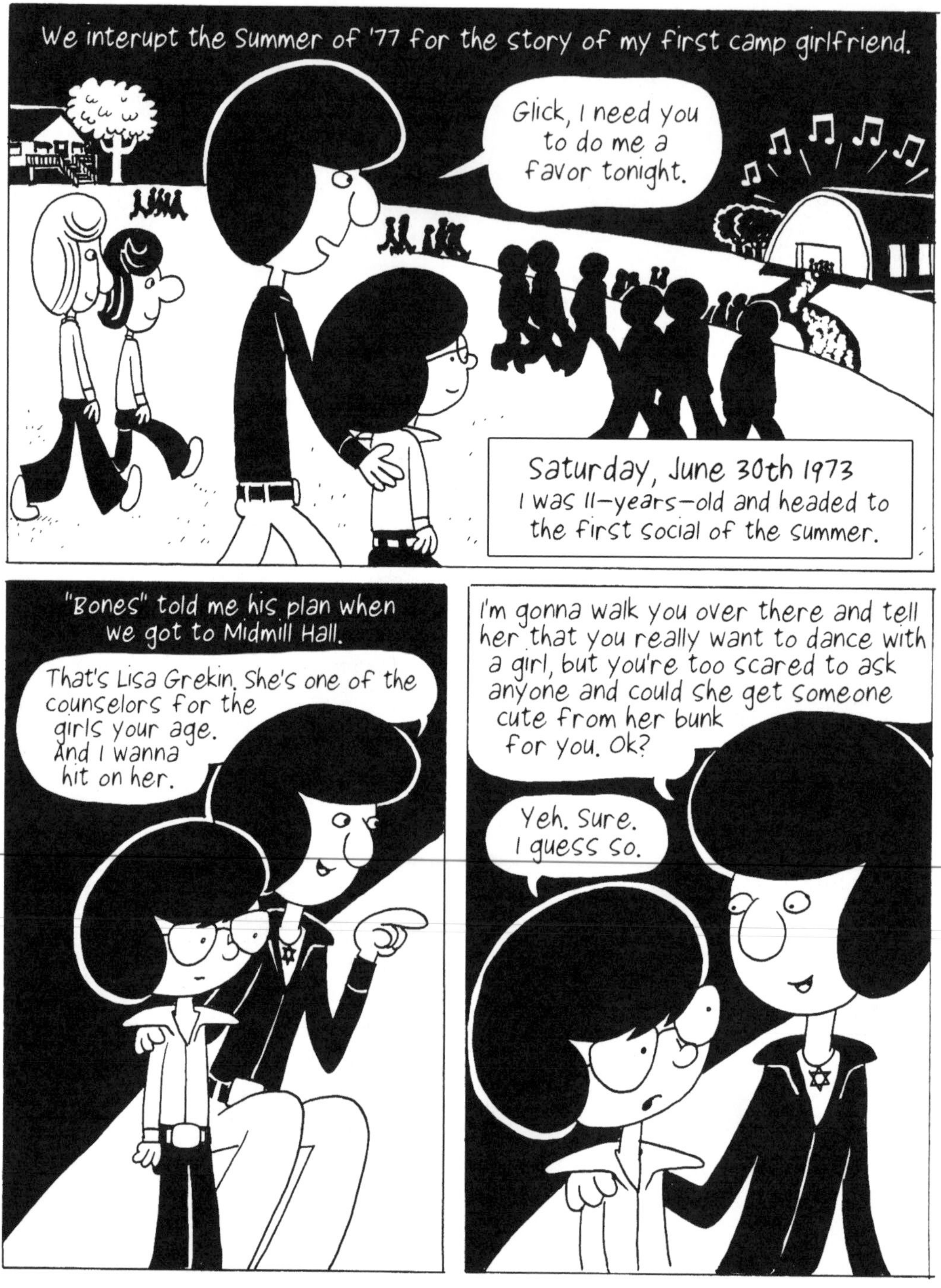
We interupt the Summer of '77 for the story of my first camp girlfriend.
Glick, I need you to do me a favor tonight.
Saturday, June 30th 1973
I was 11-years-old and headed to the first social of the summer.
"Bones" told me his plan when we got to Midmill Hall.
That's Lisa Grekin. She's one of the counselors for the girls your age. And I wanna hit on her.
I'm gonna walk you over there and tell her that you really want to dance with a girl, but you're too scared to ask anyone and could she get someone cute from her bunk for you. Ok?
Yeh. Sure. I guess so.

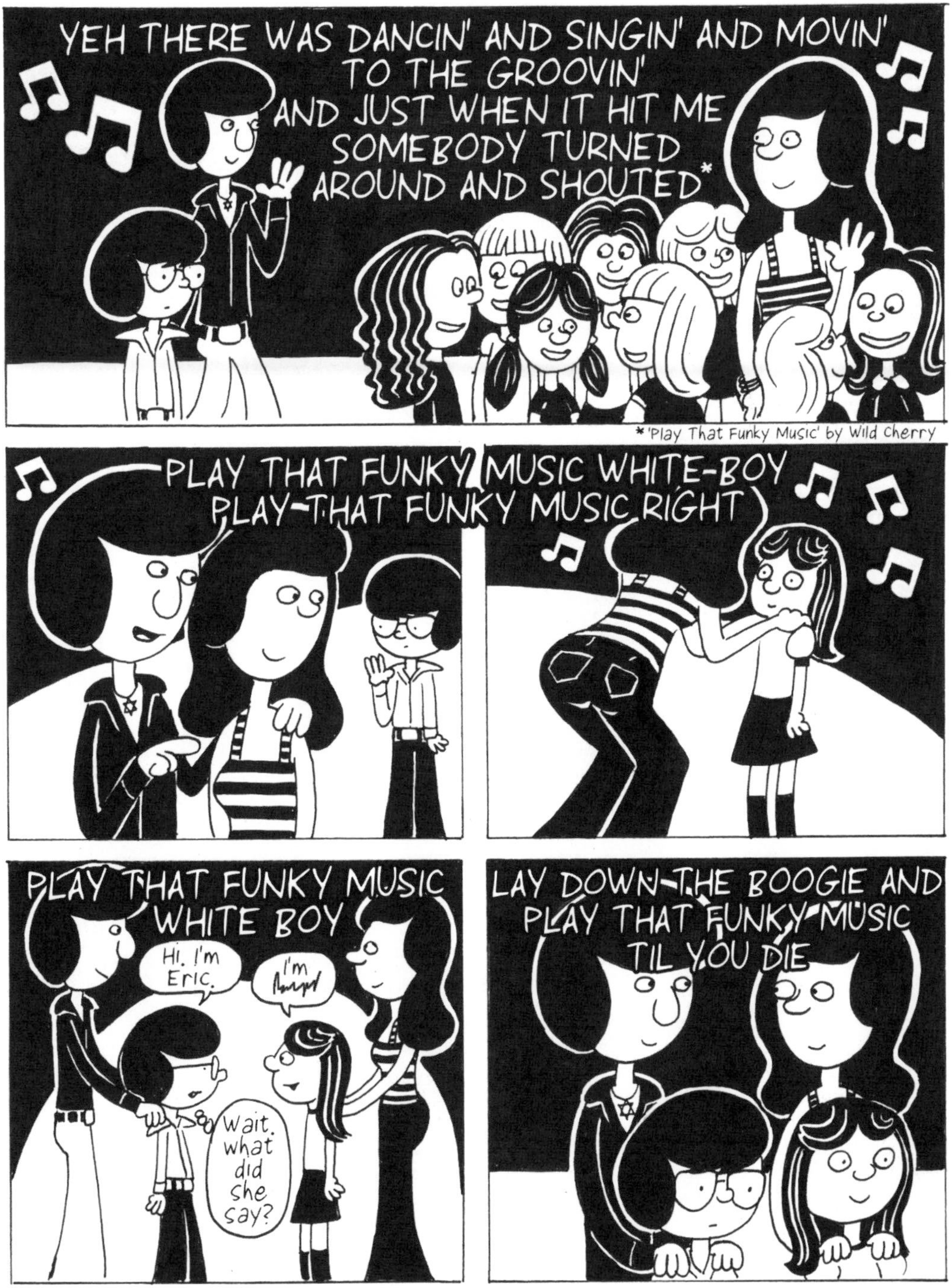
YEH THERE WAS DANCIN' AND SINGIN' AND MOVIN' TO THE GROOVIN' AND JUST WHEN IT HIT ME SOMEBODY TURNED AROUND AND SHOUTED*
* 'Play That Funky Music' by Wild Cherry
PLAY THAT FUNKY MUSIC WHITE-BOY PLAY THAT FUNKY MUSIC RIGHT
PLAY THAT FUNKY MUSIC WHITE BOY
Hi. I'm Eric.
I'm
Wait. what did she say?
LAY DOWN THE BOOGIE AND PLAY THAT FUNKY MUSIC TIL YOU DIE

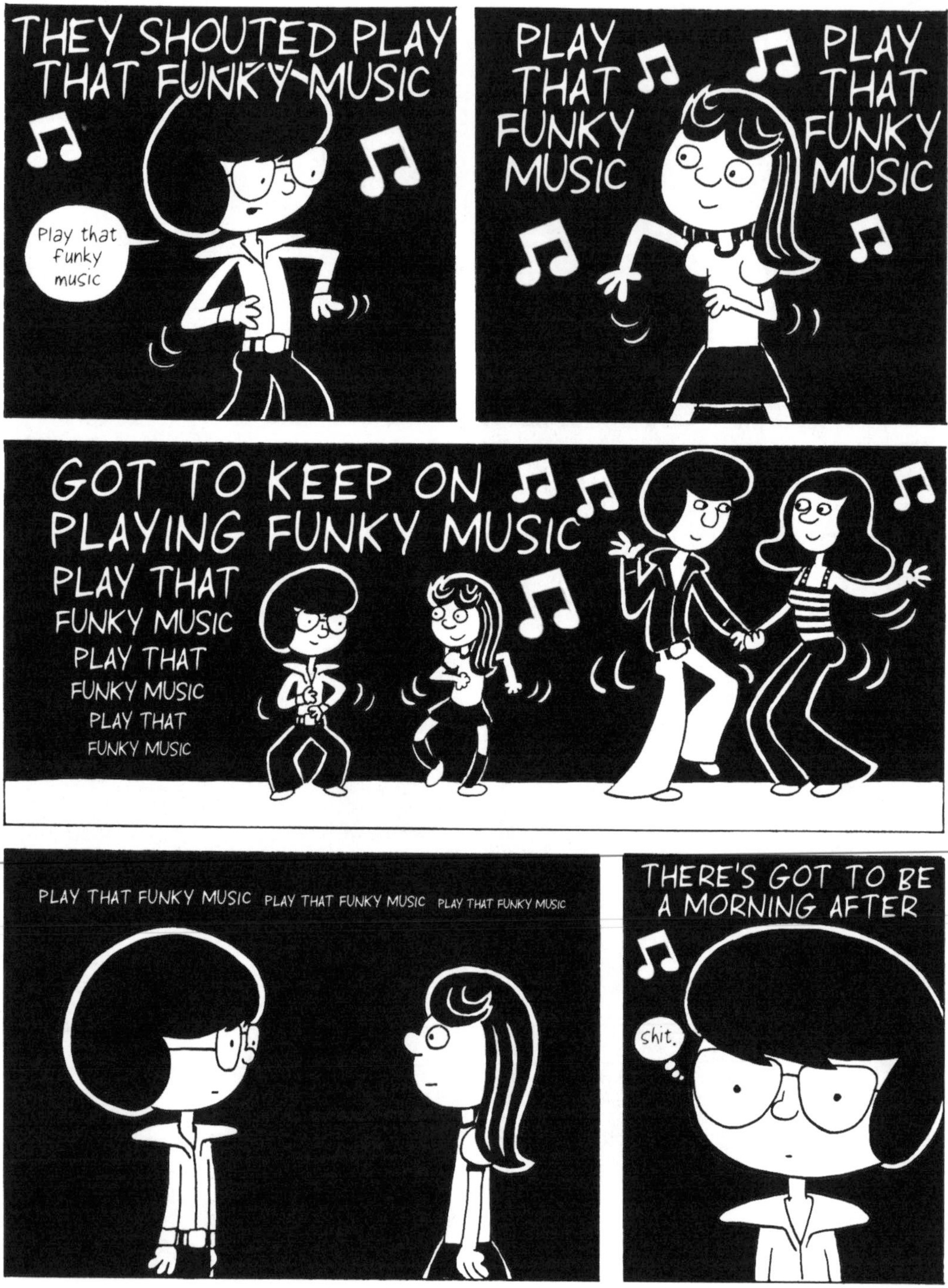
THEY SHOUTED PLAY THAT FUNKY MUSIC
Play that funky music
PLAY THAT FUNKY MUSIC
PLAY THAT FUNKY MUSIC
GOT TO KEEP ON PLAYING FUNKY MUSIC
PLAY THAT FUNKY MUSIC
PLAY THAT FUNKY MUSIC
PLAY THAT FUNKY MUSIC
PLAY THAT FUNKY MUSIC PLAY THAT FUNKY MUSIC PLAY THAT FUNKY MUSIC
THERE'S GOT TO BE A MORNING AFTER
shit.

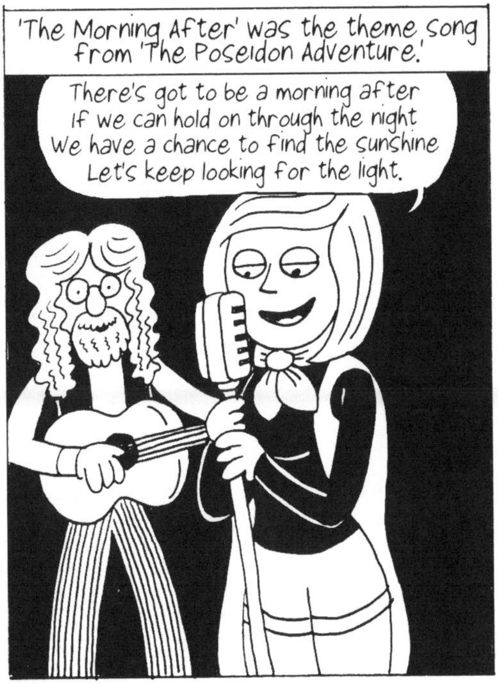
'The Morning After' was the theme song from 'The Poseidon Adventure.'
There's got to be a morning after
If we can hold on through the night
We have a chance to find the sunshine
Let's keep looking for the light.

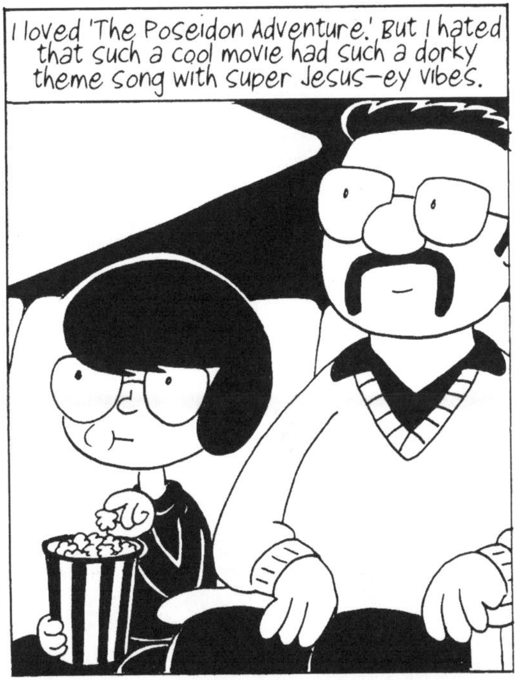
I loved 'The Poseidon Adventure.' But I hated that such a cool movie had such a dorky theme song with super Jesus-ey vibes.

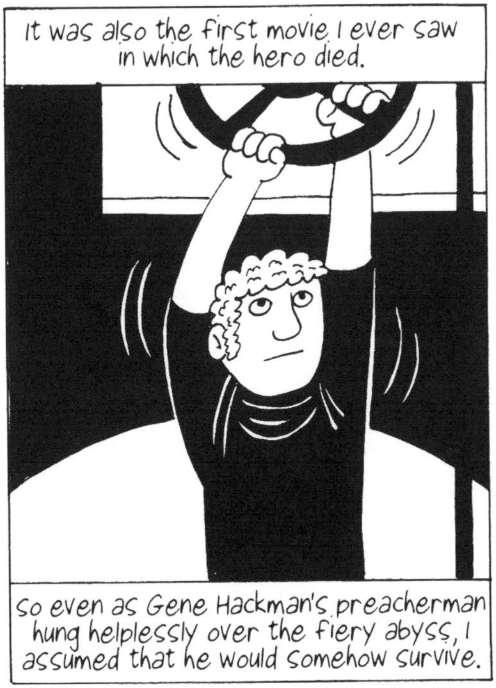
It was also the first movie I ever saw in which the hero died.
So even as Gene Hackman's preacherman hung helplessly over the fiery abyss, I assumed that he would somehow survive.

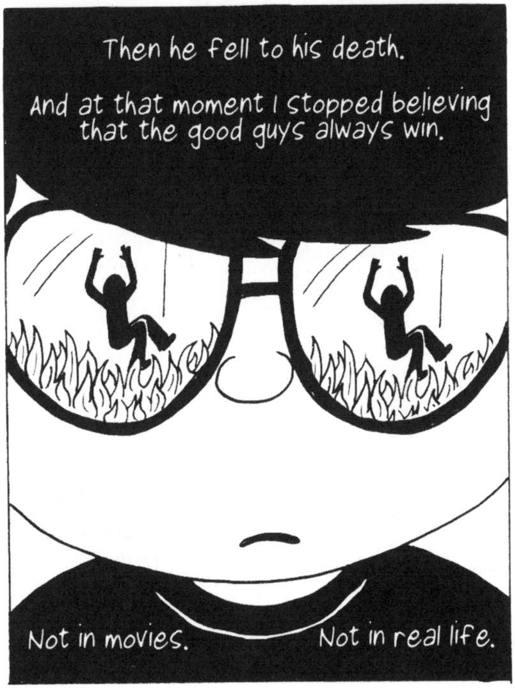
Then he fell to his death.
And at that moment I stopped believing that the good guys always win.
Not in movies.
Not in real life.

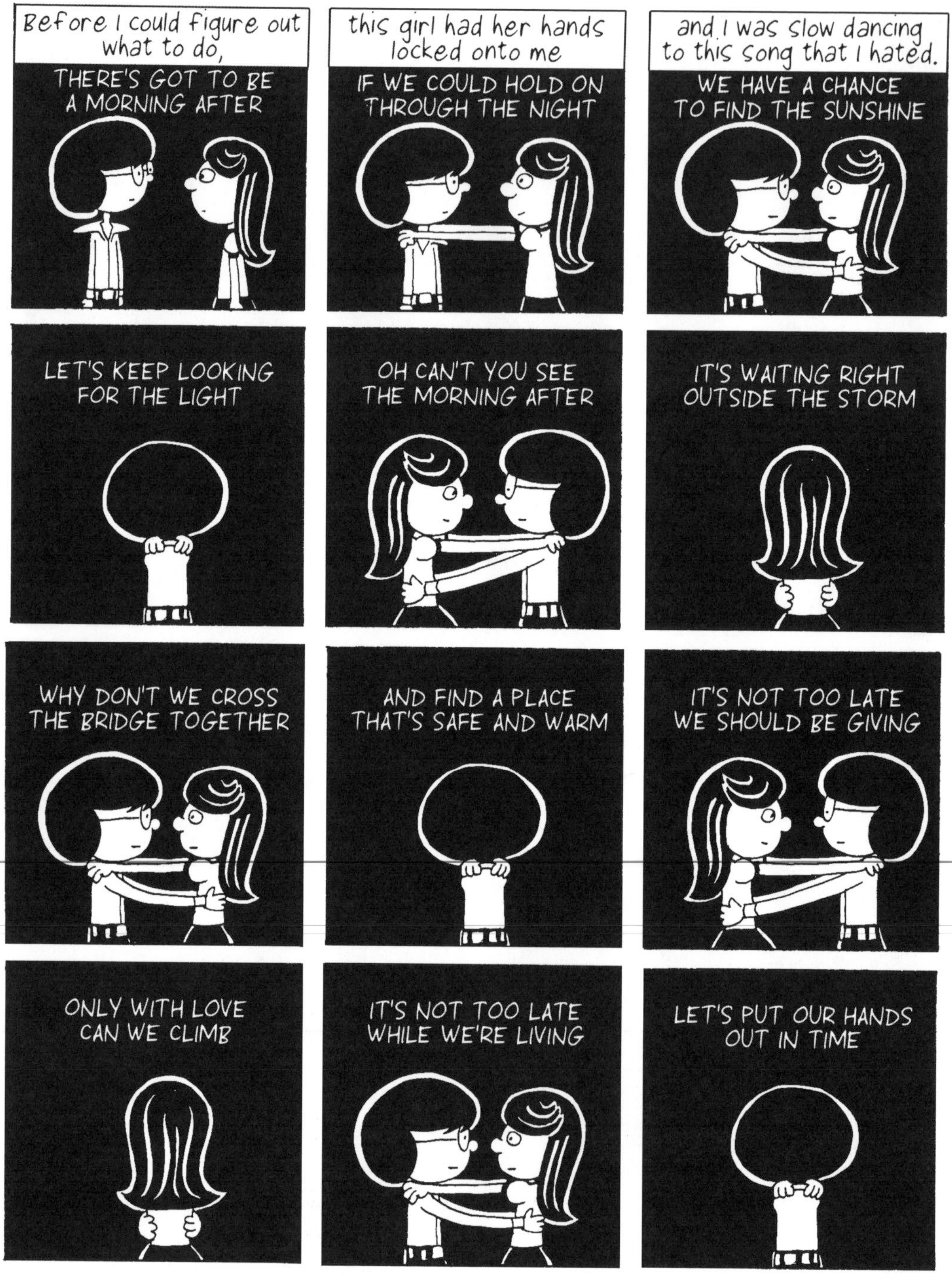
Before I could figure out what to do,
THERE'S GOT TO BE A MORNING AFTER
this girl had her hands locked onto me
IF WE COULD HOLD ON THROUGH THE NIGHT
and I was slow dancing to this song that I hated.
WE HAVE A CHANCE TO FIND THE SUNSHINE
LET'S KEEP LOOKING FOR THE LIGHT
OH CAN'T YOU SEE THE MORNING AFTER
IT'S WAITING RIGHT OUTSIDE THE STORM
WHY DON'T WE CROSS THE BRIDGE TOGETHER
AND FIND A PLACE THAT'S SAFE AND WARM
IT'S NOT TOO LATE WE SHOULD BE GIVING
ONLY WITH LOVE CAN WE CLIMB
IT'S NOT TOO LATE WHILE WE'RE LIVING
LET'S PUT OUR HANDS OUT IN TIME

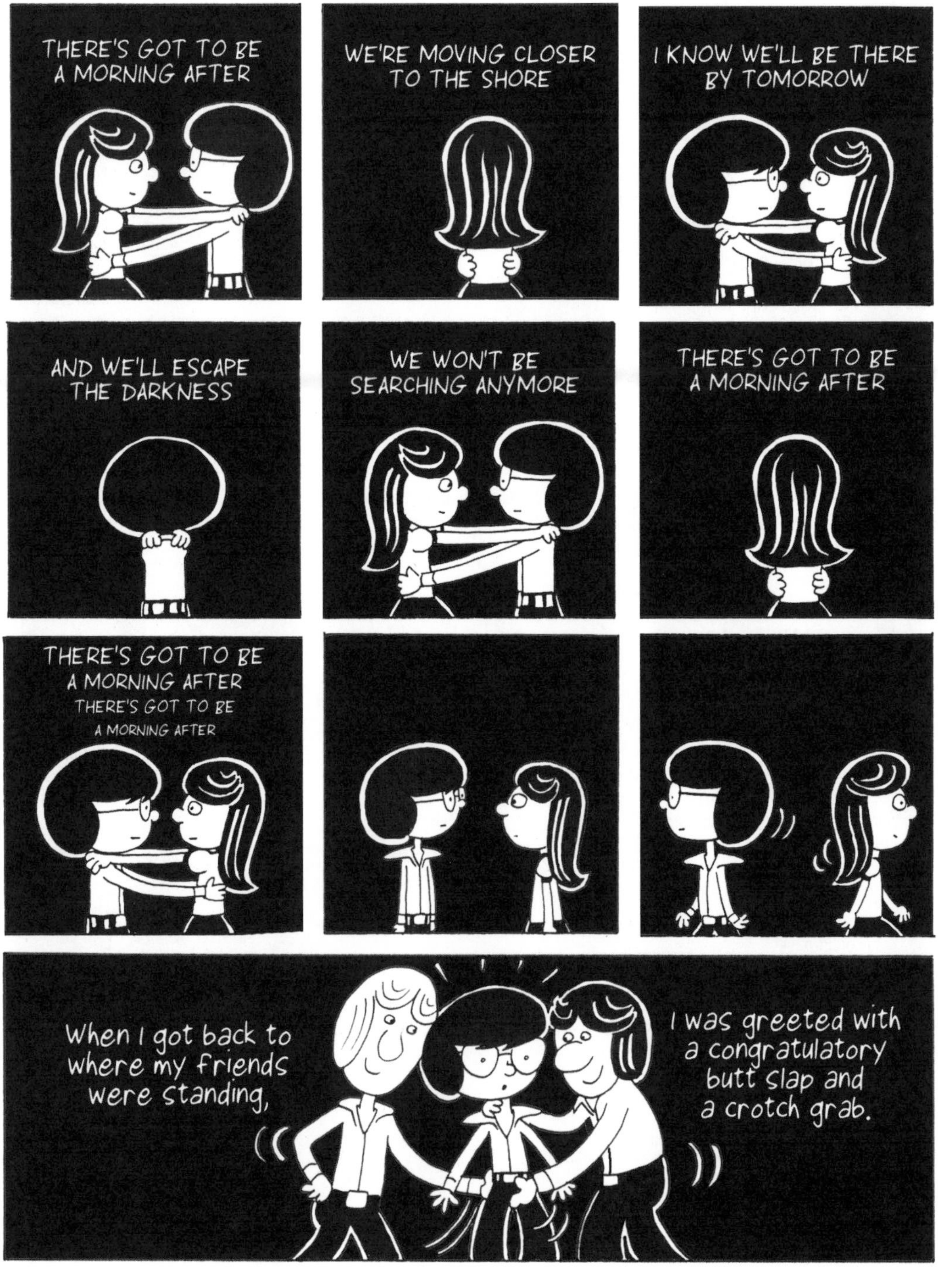
THERE'S GOT TO BE A MORNING AFTER
WE'RE MOVING CLOSER TO THE SHORE
I KNOW WE'LL BE THERE BY TOMORROW
AND WE'LL ESCAPE THE DARKNESS
WE WON'T BE SEARCHING ANYMORE
THERE'S GOT TO BE A MORNING AFTER
THERE'S GOT TO BE A MORNING AFTER
THERE'S GOT TO BE A MORNING AFTER
When I got back to where my friends were standing,
I was greeted with a congratulatory butt slap and a crotch grab.

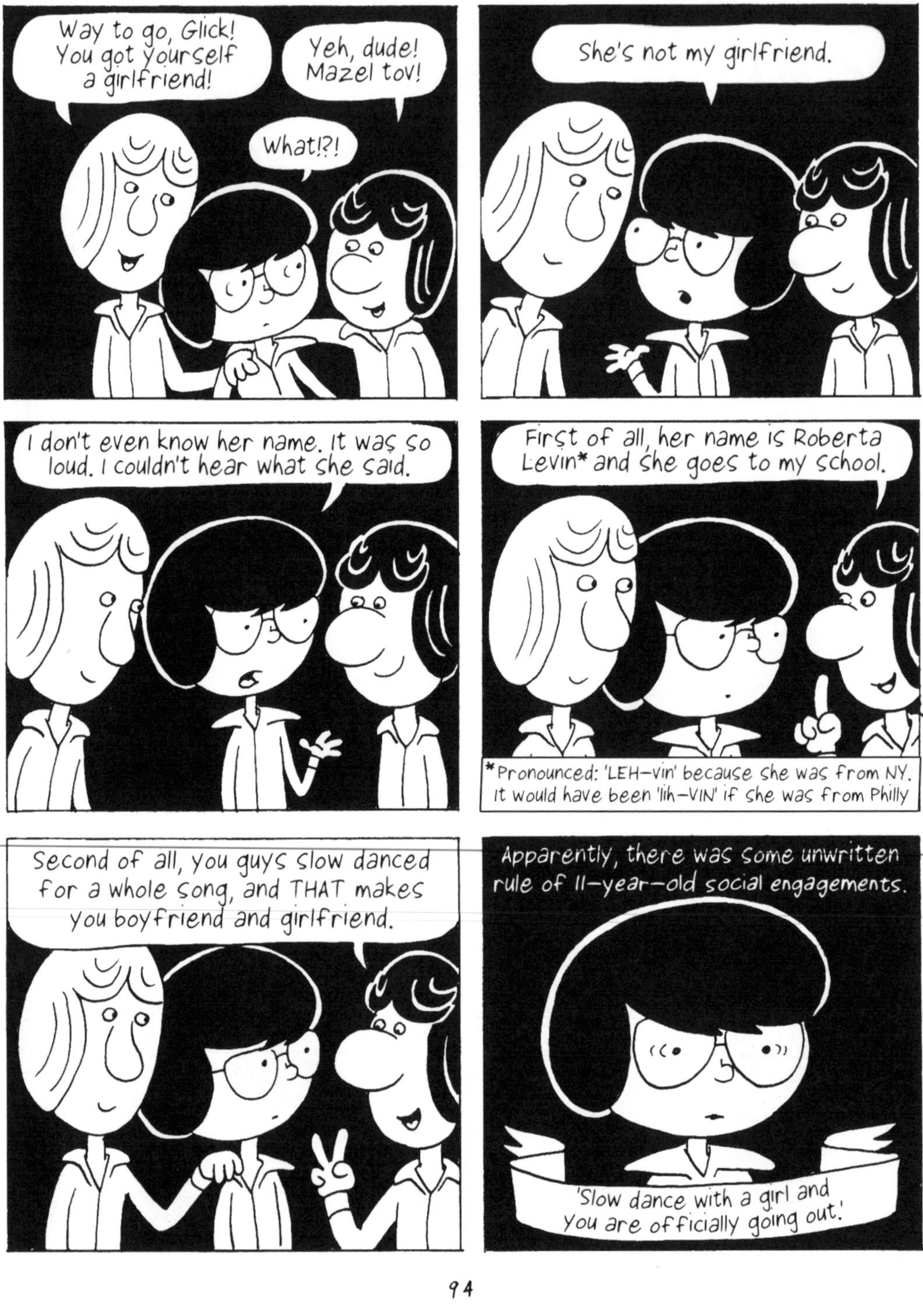
Way to go, Glick! You got yourself a girlfriend!
Yeh, dude! Mazel tov!
What!?!
She's not my girlfriend.
I don't even know her name. It was so loud. I couldn't hear what she said.
First of all, her name is Roberta Levin* and she goes to my school.
*Pronounced: 'LEH—vin' because she was from NY. It would have been 'lih—VIN' if she was from Philly
Second of all, you guys slow danced for a whole song, and THAT makes you boyfriend and girlfriend.
Apparently, there was some unwritten rule of 11—year—old social engagements.
'Slow dance with a girl and you are officially going out.'

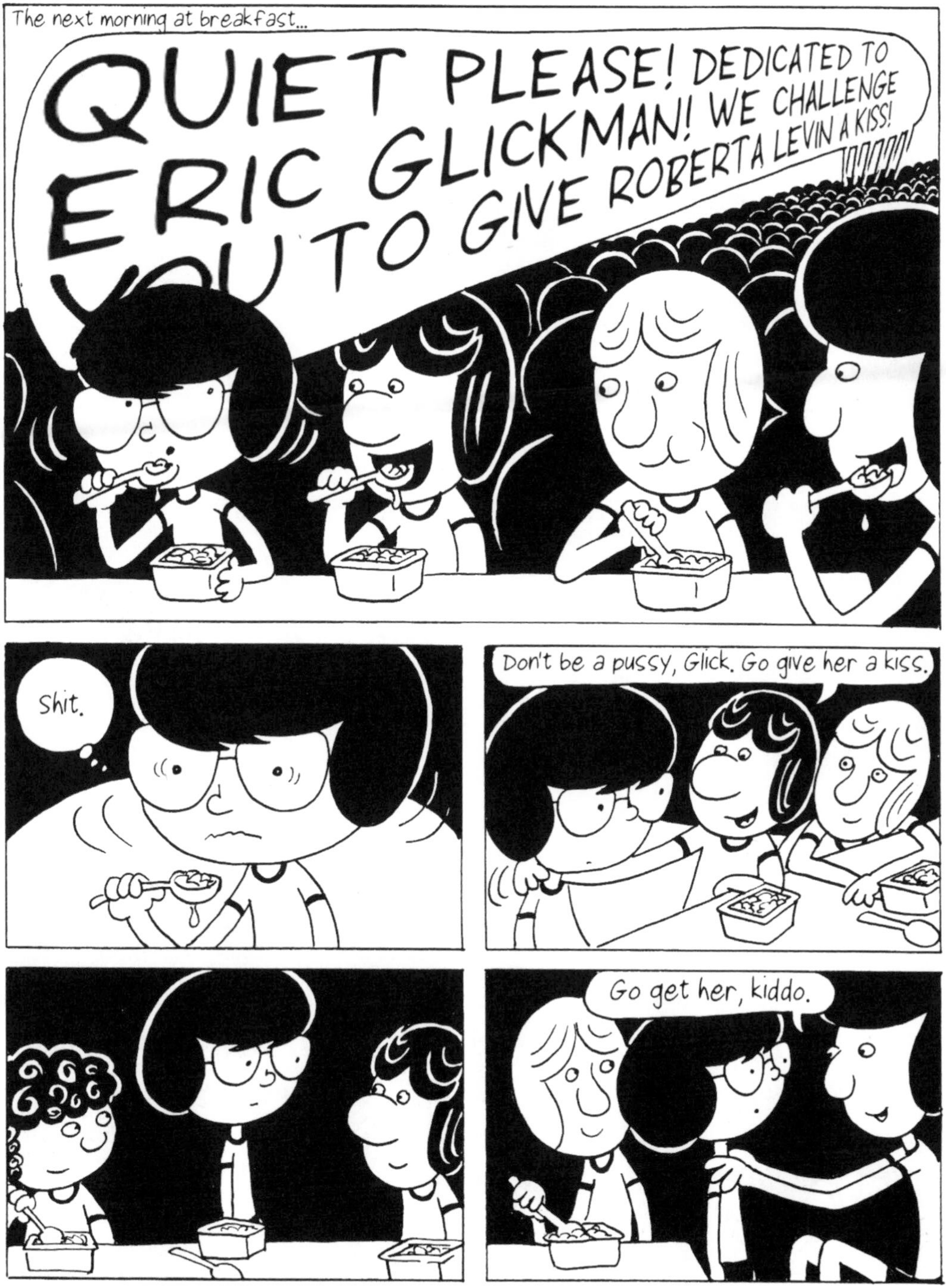
The next morning at breakfast...
QUIET PLEASE! DEDICATED TO ERIC GLICKMAN! WE CHALLENGE YOU TO GIVE ROBERTA LEVIN A KISS!
Shit.
Don't be a pussy, Glick. Go give her a kiss.
Go get her, kiddo.

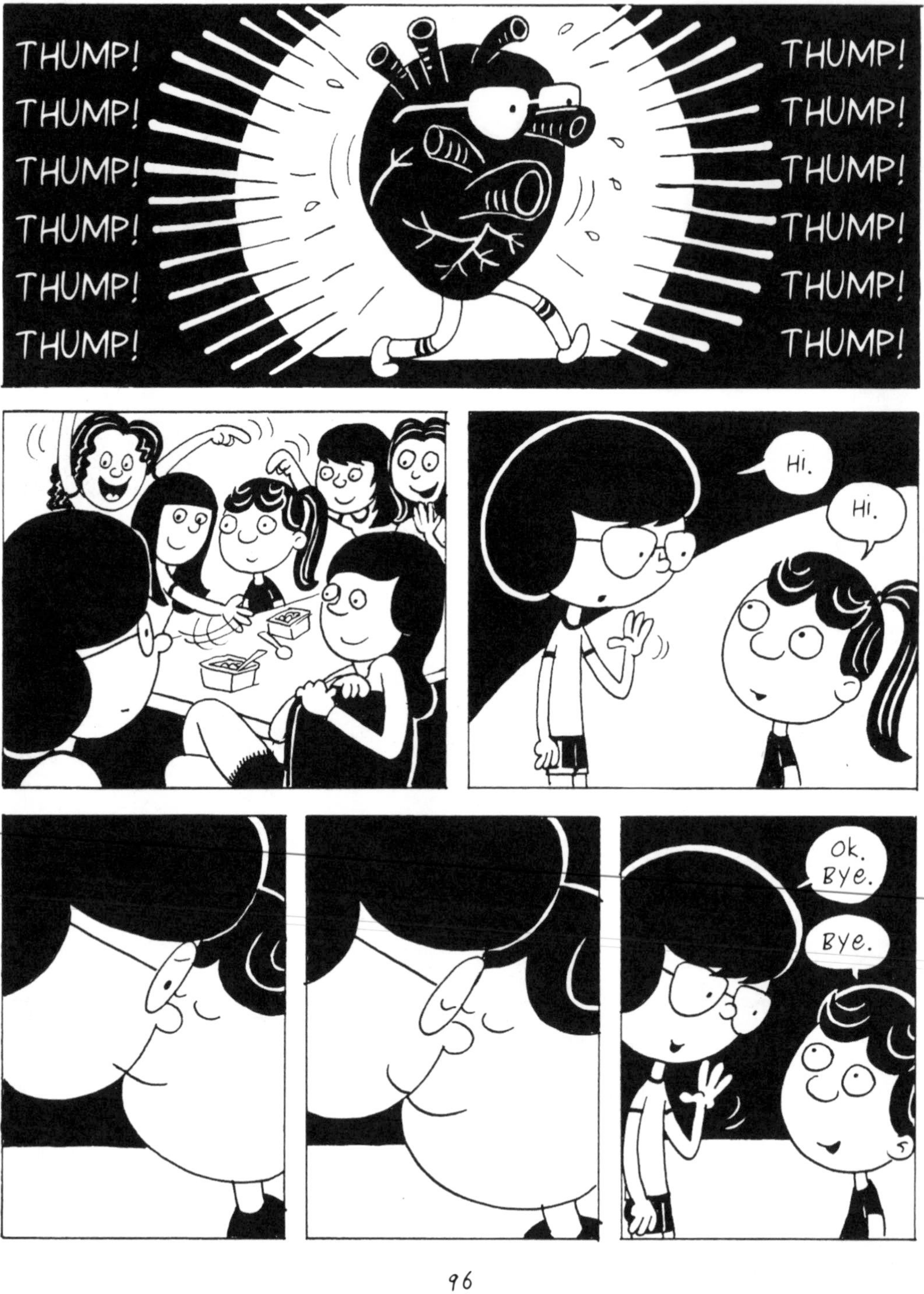
THUMP!
THUMP!
THUMP!
THUMP!
THUMP!
THUMP!
THUMP!
THUMP!
THUMP!
THUMP!
THUMP!
THUMP!
Hi.
Hi.
Ok. Bye.
Bye.

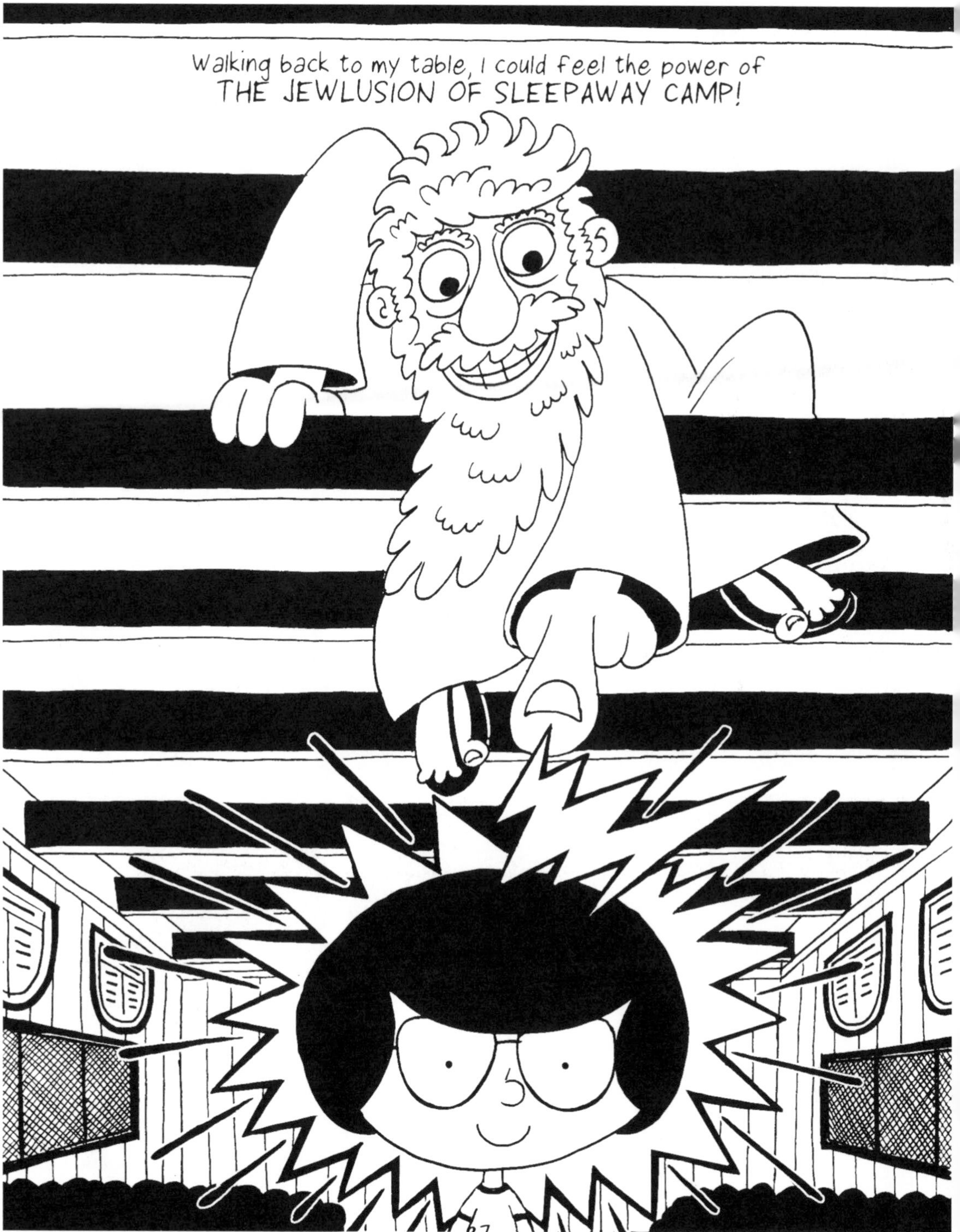
Walking back to my table, I could feel the power of
THE JEWLUSION OF SLEEPAWAY CAMP!

From that point on, we did what 11-year-old couples did.

We sat together on movie nights.

We shared our canteen candy.

We danced with each other at socials.

♪ Little Willy, Willy won't go home!* ♪

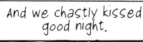

*"Little Willy" by The Sweet

We held hands and roller skated on the tennis courts behind Midmill Hall after Friday night services.

And we chastly kissed good night.

On the last day of camp she gave me a bus note covered in perfume.

Over the next 10 months, there wasn't any communication between us except for a brief moment at reunion at camp in October.

Hi.

Hi.

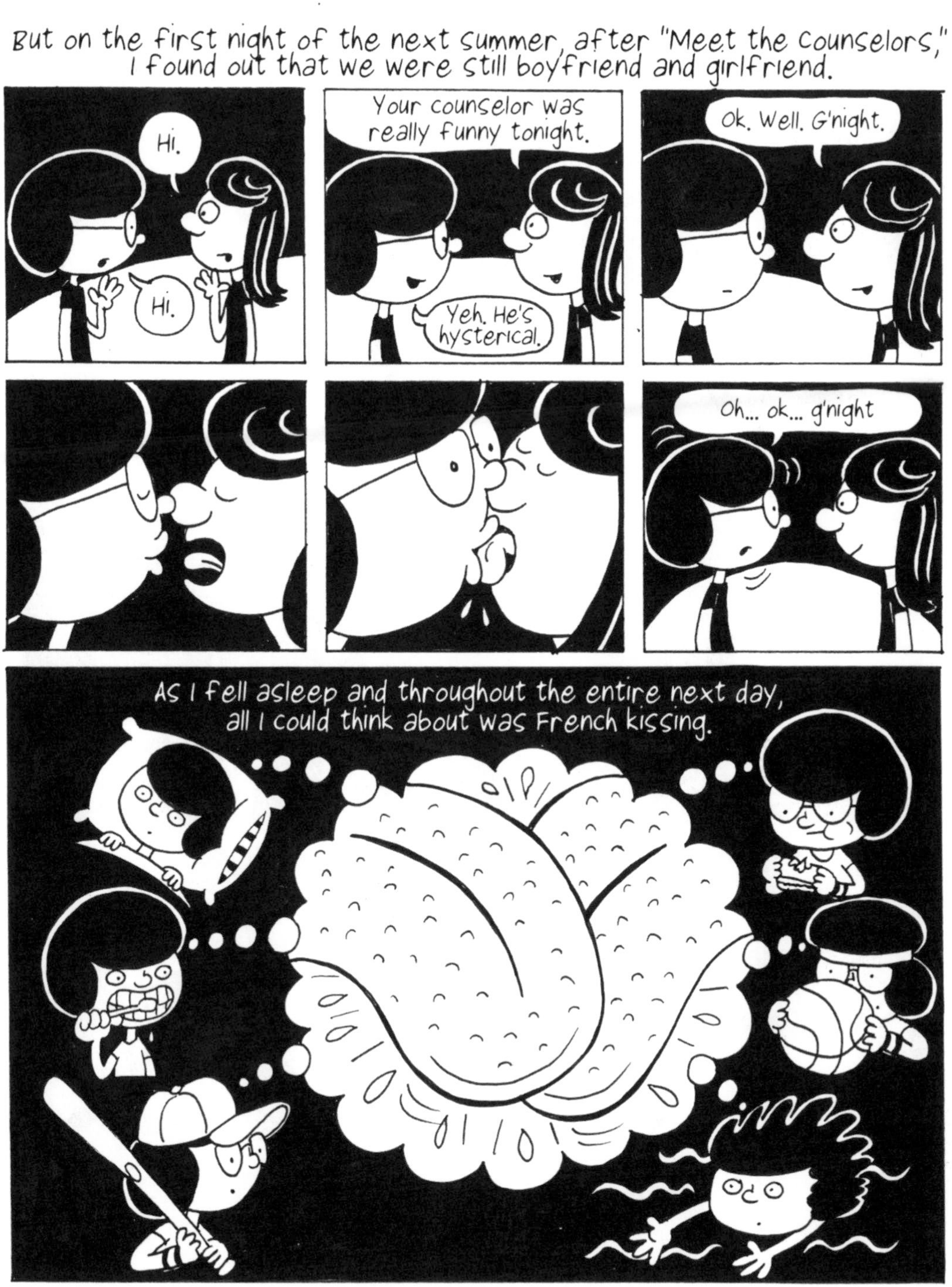
But on the first night of the next summer, after "Meet the Counselors," I found out that we were still boyfriend and girlfriend.
Hi.
Hi.
Your counselor was really funny tonight.
Yeh. He's hysterical.
Ok. Well. G'night.
Oh... ok... g'night
As I fell asleep and throughout the entire next day, all I could think about was French kissing.

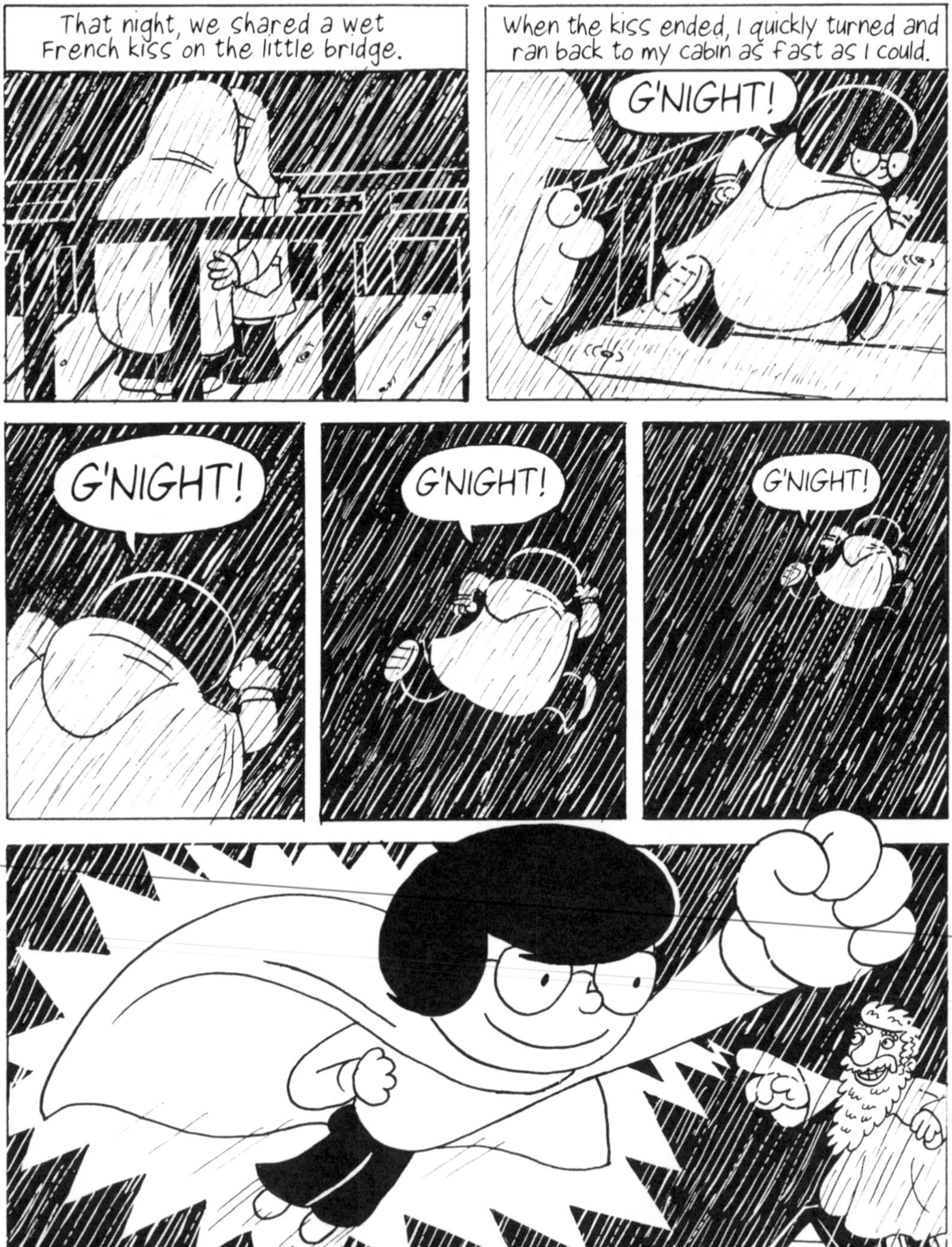
That night, we shared a wet French kiss on the little bridge.
When the kiss ended, I quickly turned and ran back to my cabin as fast as I could.
G'NIGHT!
G'NIGHT!
G'NIGHT!
G'NIGHT!

My second summer with a girlfriend was just like my first . . . only more.

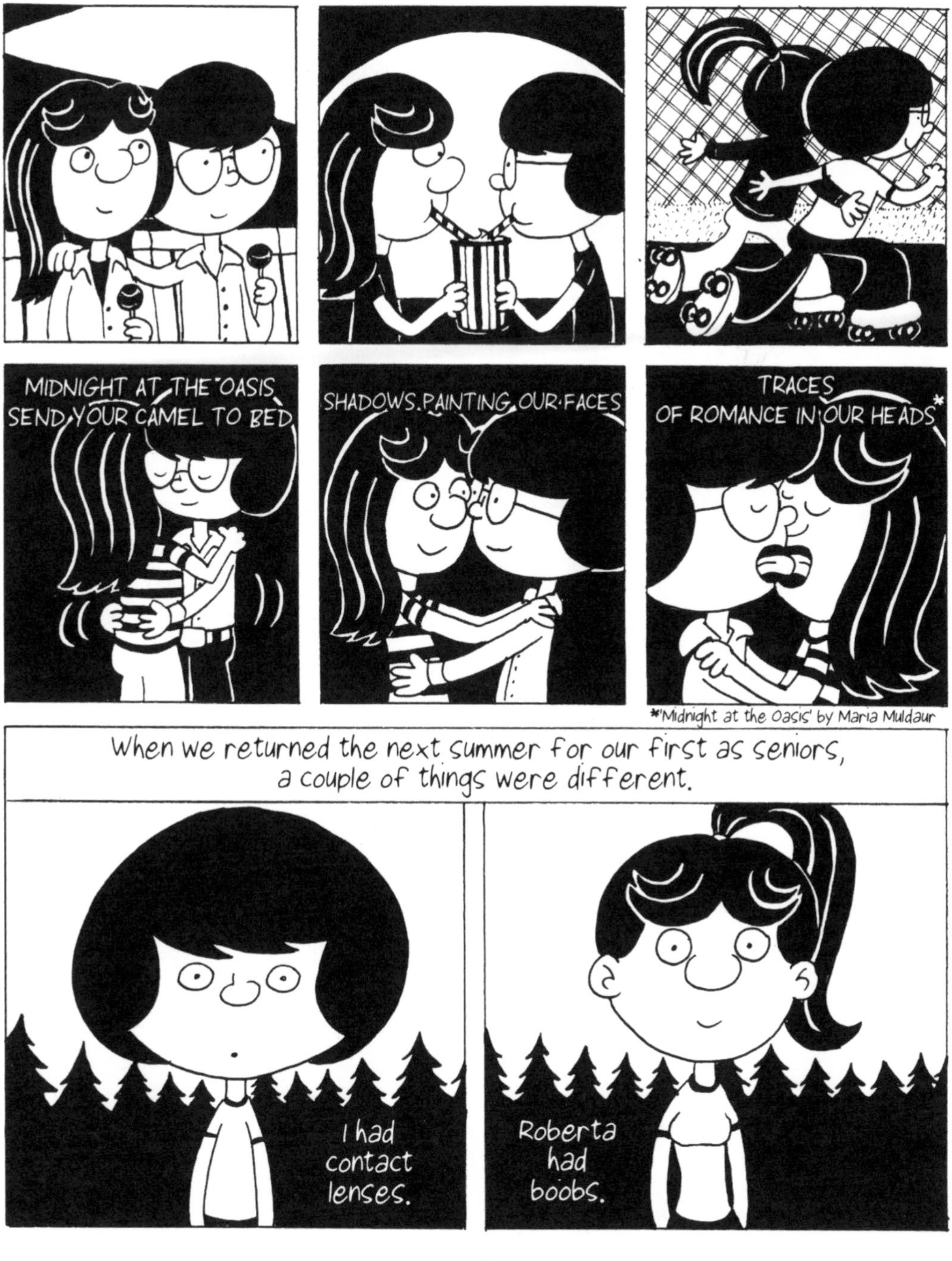
MIDNIGHT AT THE OASIS
SEND YOUR CAMEL TO BED
SHADOWS PAINTING OUR FACES
TRACES
OF ROMANCE IN OUR HEADS*
*'Midnight at the Oasis' by Maria Muldaur
When we returned the next summer for our first as seniors, a couple of things were different.
I had contact lenses.
Roberta had boobs.

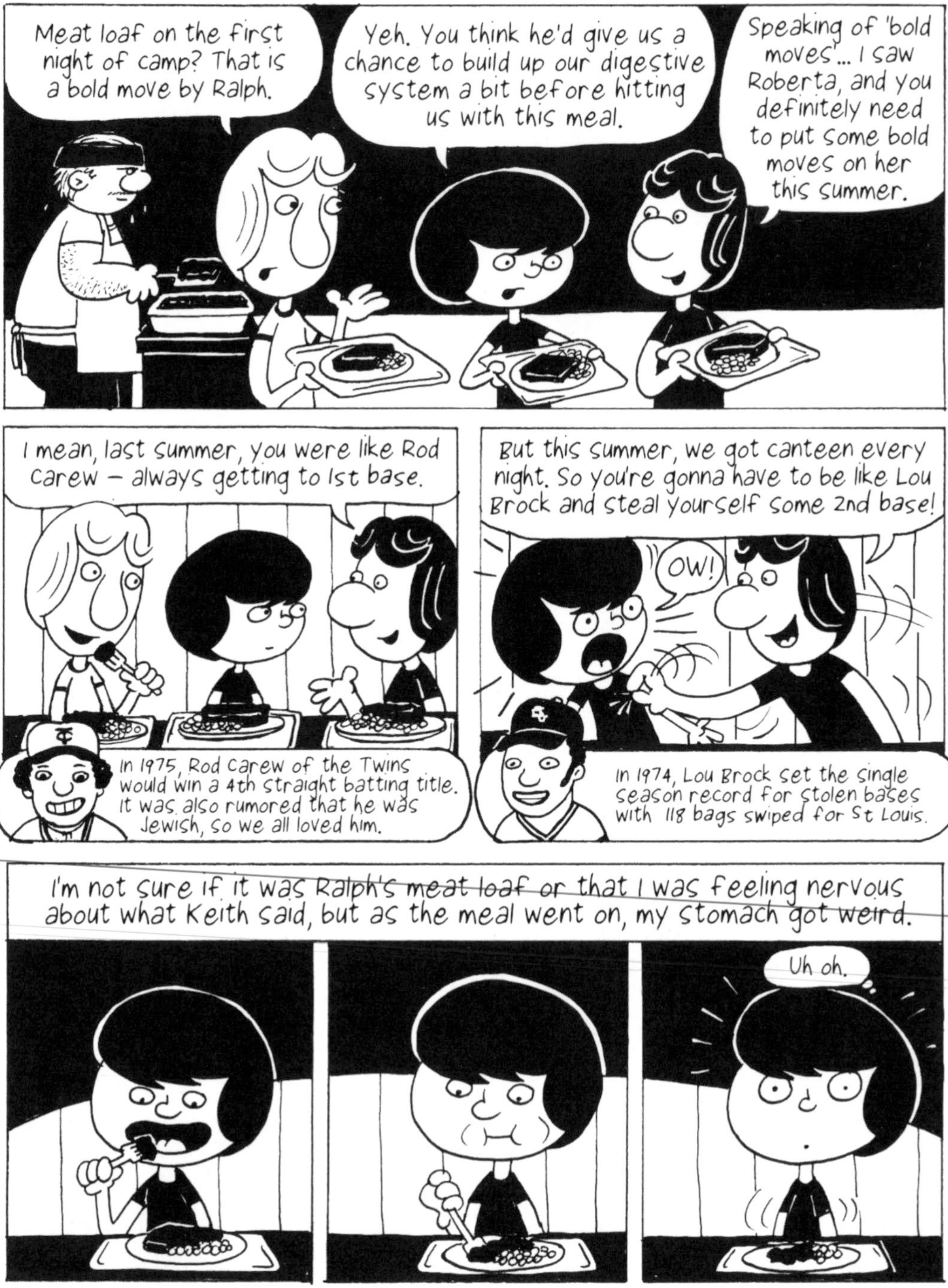
Meat loaf on the first night of camp? That is a bold move by Ralph.
Yeh. You think he'd give us a chance to build up our digestive system a bit before hitting us with this meal.
Speaking of 'bold moves'... I saw Roberta, and you definitely need to put some bold moves on her this summer.
I mean, last summer, you were like Rod Carew – always getting to 1st base.
In 1975, Rod Carew of the Twins would win a 4th straight batting title. It was also rumored that he was Jewish, so we all loved him.
But this summer, we got canteen every night. So you're gonna have to be like Lou Brock and steal yourself some 2nd base!
OW!
In 1974, Lou Brock set the single season record for stolen bases with 118 bags swiped for St Louis.
I'm not sure if it was Ralph's meat loaf or that I was feeling nervous about what Keith said, but as the meal went on, my stomach got weird.
Uh oh.

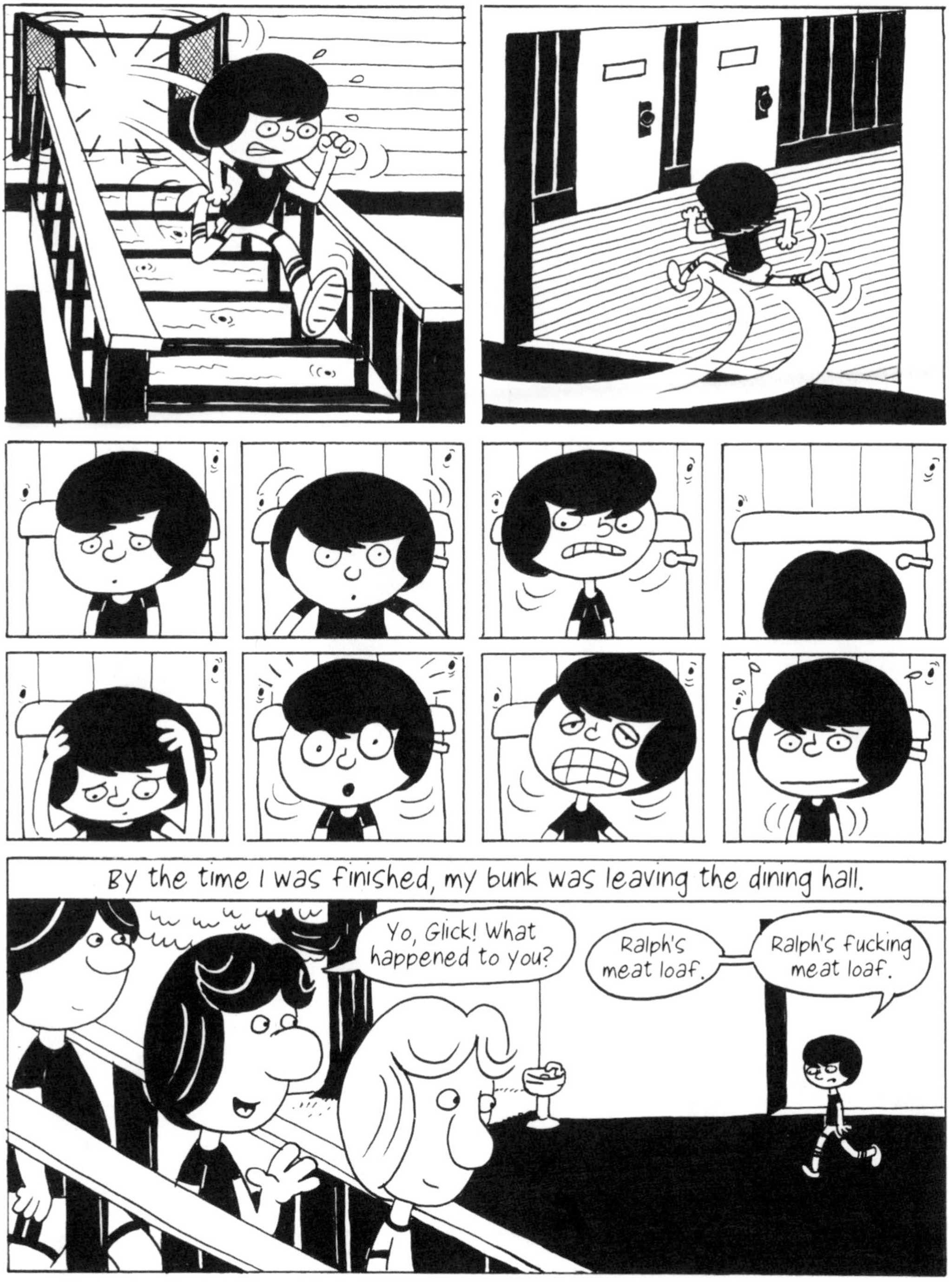

By the time I was finished, my bunk was leaving the dining hall.
Yo, Glick! What happened to you?
Ralph's meat loaf.
Ralph's fucking meat loaf.

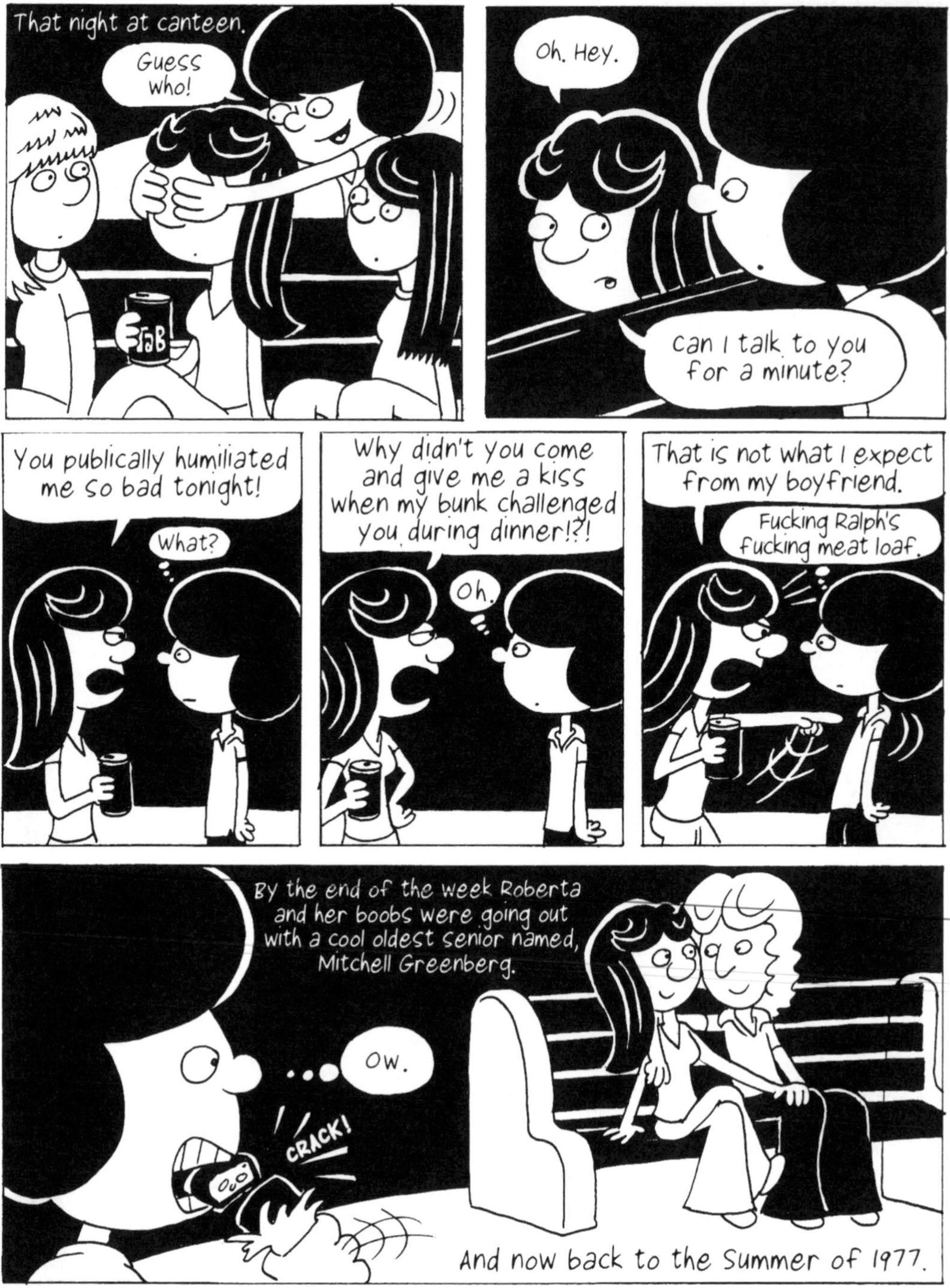
That night at canteen.
Guess who!
Oh. Hey.
Can I talk to you for a minute?
You publically humiliated me so bad tonight!
What?
Why didn't you come and give me a kiss when my bunk challenged you during dinner!?!
Oh.
That is not what I expect from my boyfriend.
Fucking Ralph's fucking meat loaf.
By the end of the week Roberta and her boobs were going out with a cool oldest senior named, Mitchell Greenberg.
Ow.
CRACK!
And now back to the Summer of 1977.

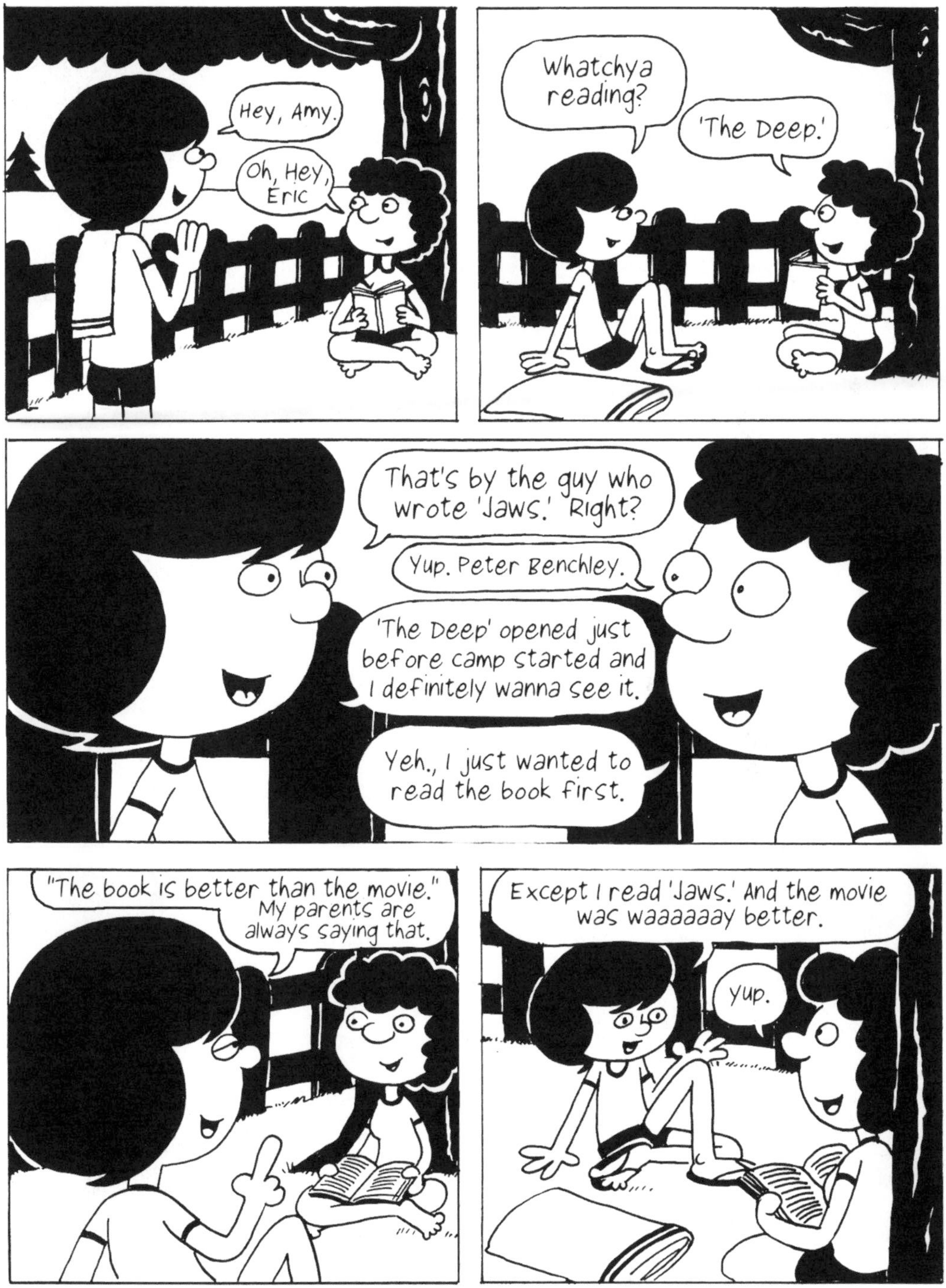
Hey, Amy.
Oh, Hey, Eric
Whatchya reading?
'The Deep.'
That's by the guy who wrote 'Jaws.' Right?
Yup. Peter Benchley.
'The Deep' opened just before camp started and I definitely wanna see it.
Yeh., I just wanted to read the book first.
"The book is better than the movie." My parents are always saying that.
Except I read 'Jaws.' And the movie was waaaaaay better.
Yup.

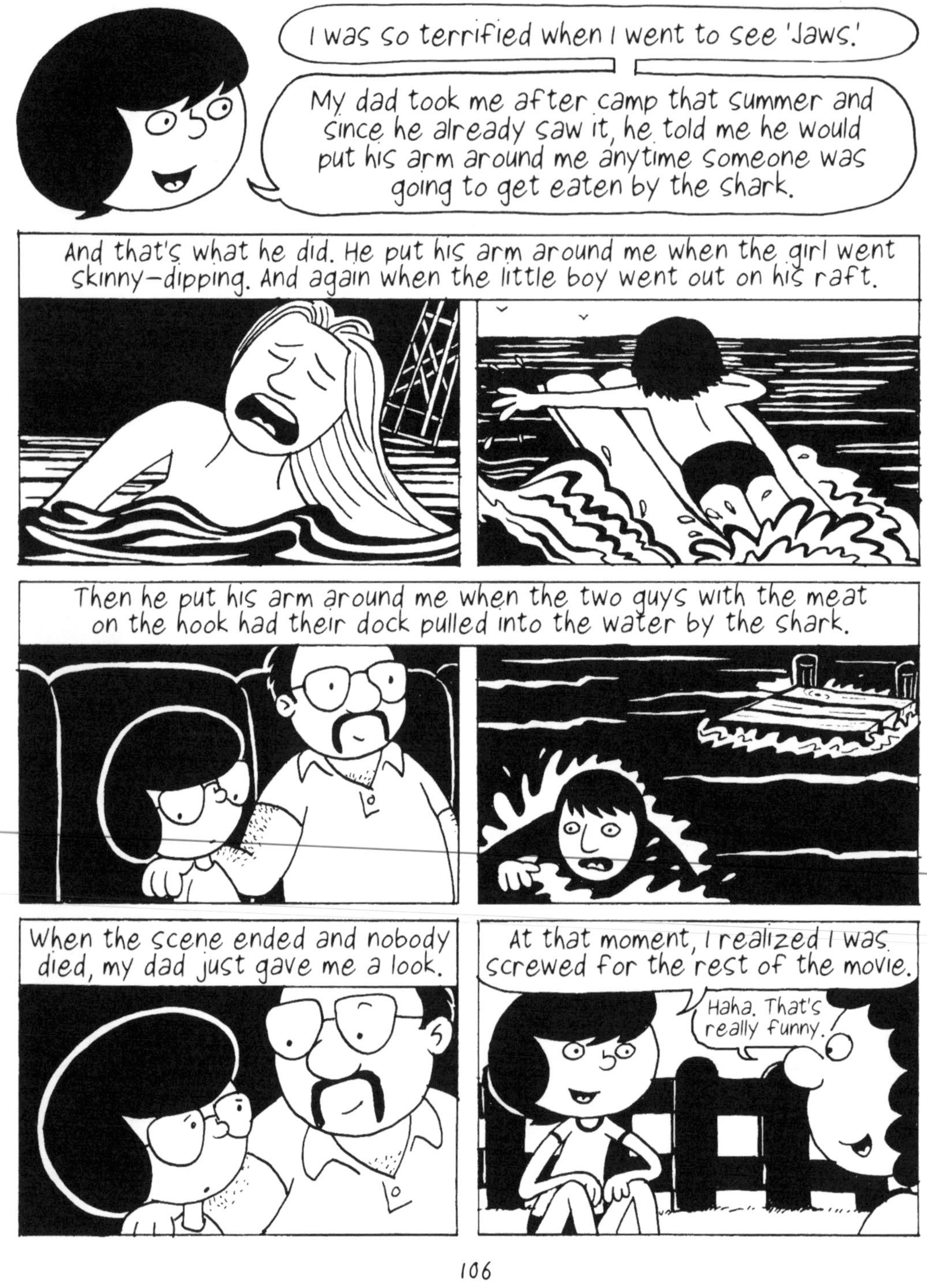

I was so terrified when I went to see 'Jaws.'
My dad took me after camp that summer and since he already saw it, he told me he would put his arm around me anytime someone was going to get eaten by the shark.
And that's what he did. He put his arm around me when the girl went skinny-dipping. And again when the little boy went out on his raft.
Then he put his arm around me when the two guys with the meat on the hook had their dock pulled into the water by the shark.
When the scene ended and nobody died, my dad just gave me a look.
At that moment, I realized I was screwed for the rest of the movie.
Haha. That's really funny.

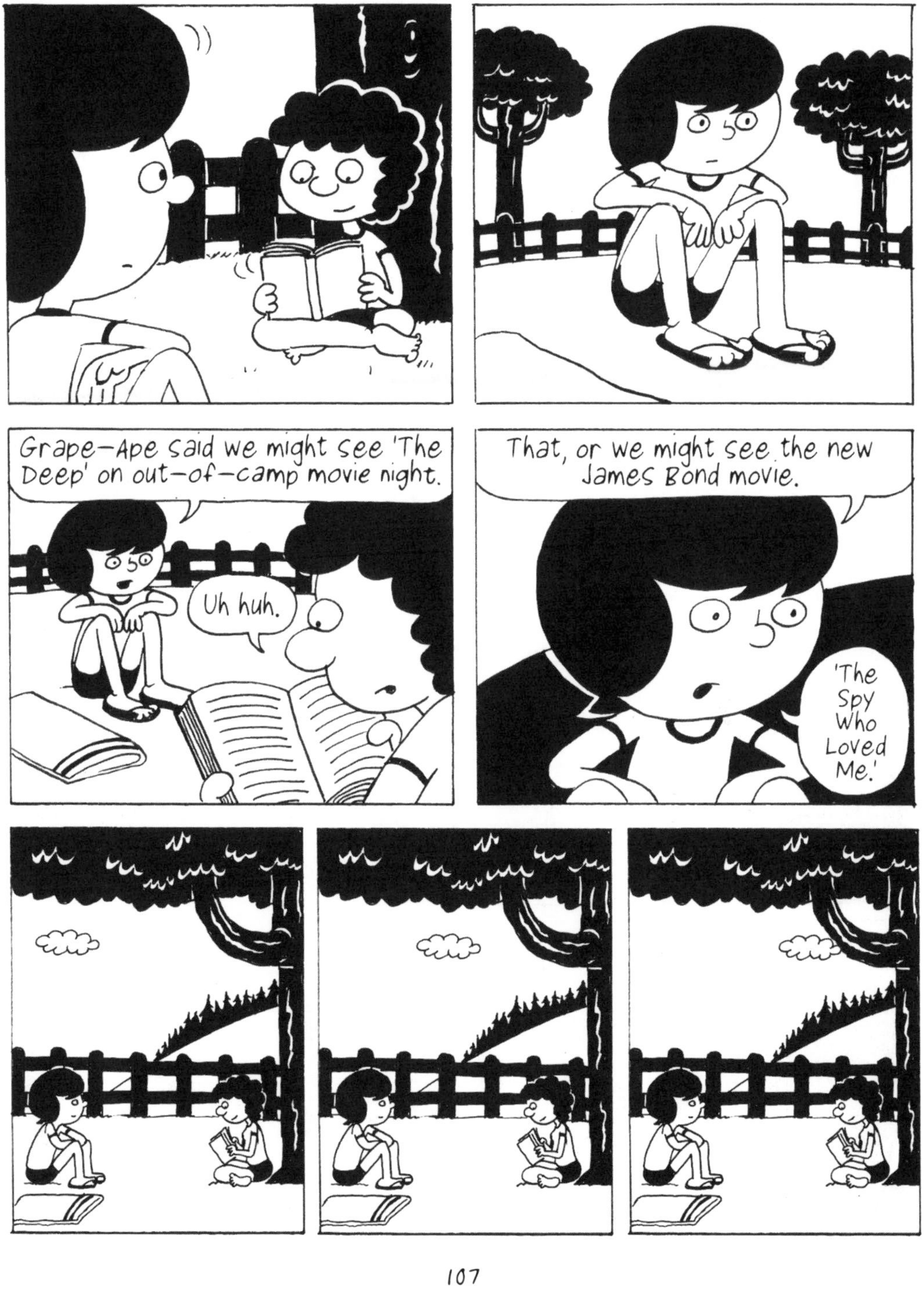
Grape-Ape said we might see 'The Deep' on out-of-camp movie night.
Uh huh.
That, or we might see the new James Bond movie.
'The Spy Who Loved Me.'

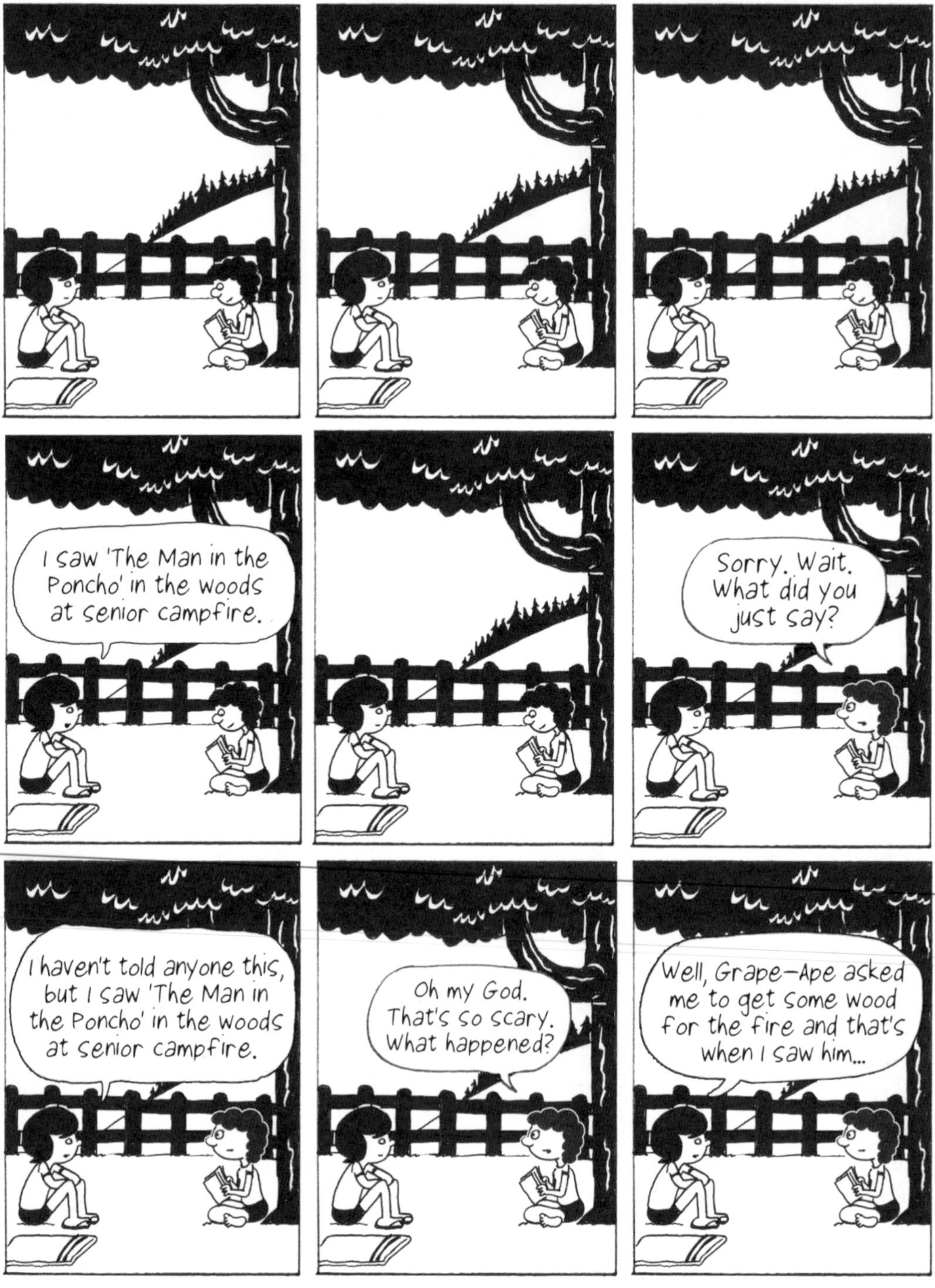
I saw 'The Man in the Poncho' in the woods at senior campfire.
Sorry. Wait. What did you just say?
I haven't told anyone this, but I saw 'The Man in the Poncho' in the woods at senior campfire.
Oh my God. That's so scary. What happened?
Well, Grape-Ape asked me to get some wood for the fire and that's when I saw him...

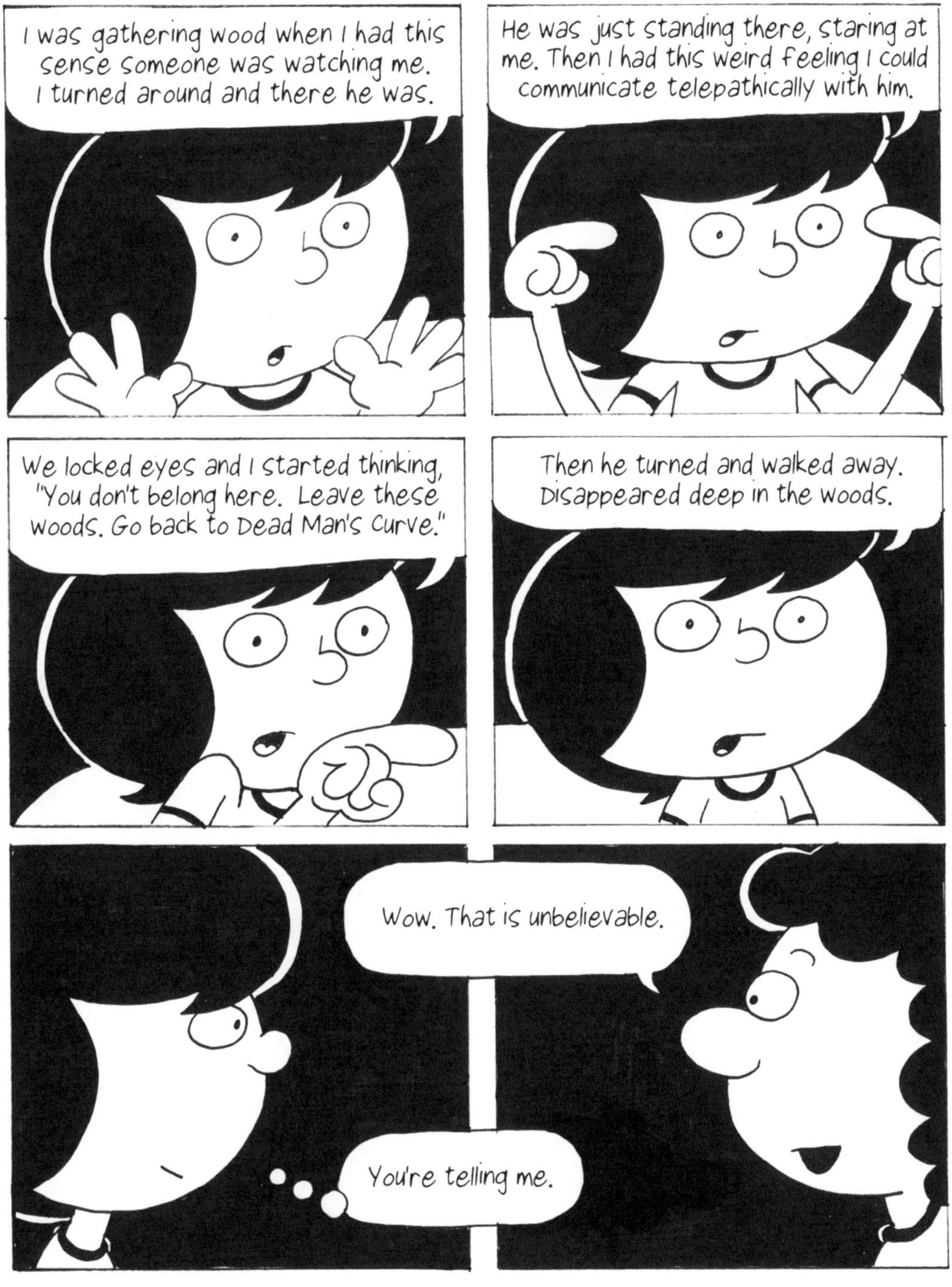
I was gathering wood when I had this sense someone was watching me. I turned around and there he was.
He was just standing there, staring at me. Then I had this weird feeling I could communicate telepathically with him.
We locked eyes and I started thinking, "You don't belong here. Leave these woods. Go back to Dead Man's Curve."
Then he turned and walked away. Disappeared deep in the woods.
Wow. That is unbelievable.
You're telling me.

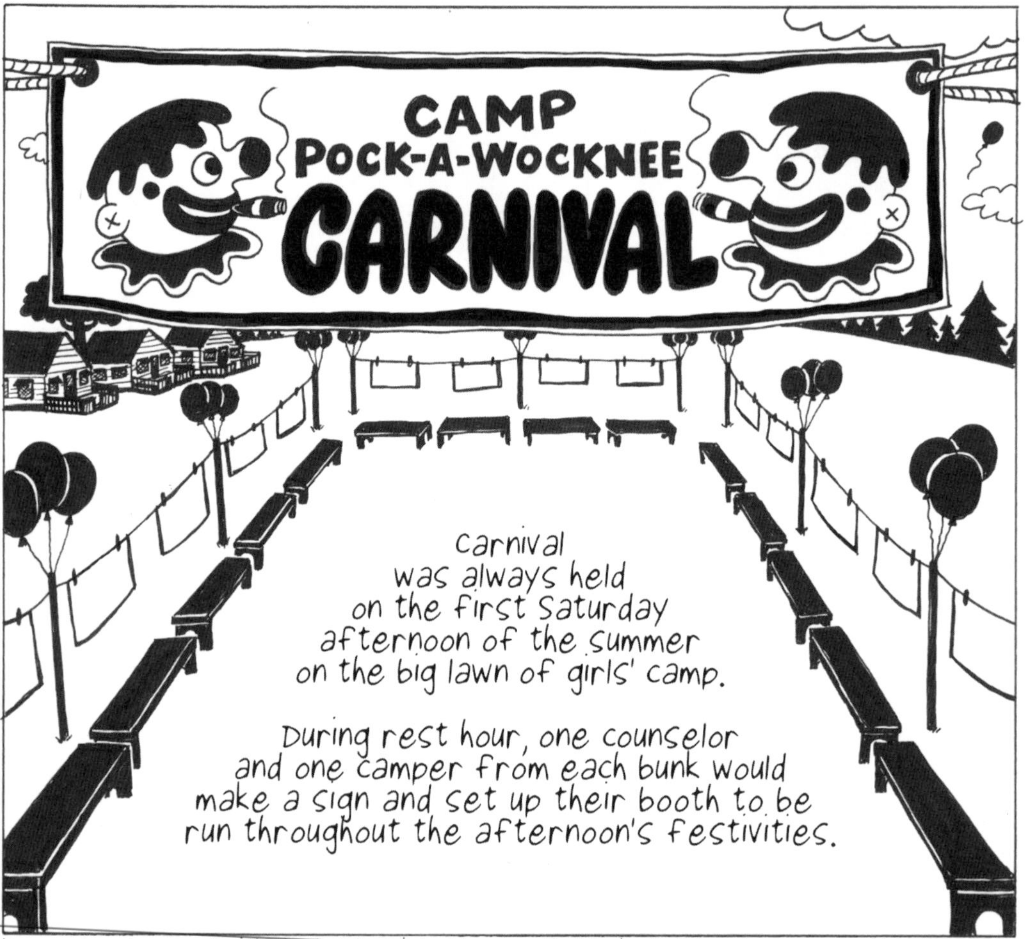
CAMP
POCK-A-WOCKNEE
CARNIVAL
Carnival
was always held
on the first Saturday
afternoon of the summer
on the big lawn of girls' camp.
During rest hour, one counselor
and one camper from each bunk would
make a sign and set up their booth to be
run throughout the afternoon's festivities.

(I was also obsessed with the hand-painted banner that looked at least 20 years old and always hung over carnival. I always wondered: who painted those two cigar-smoking clowns? And why?)

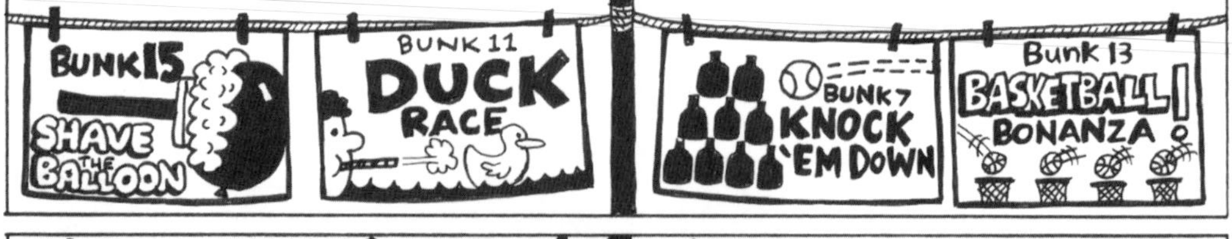
BUNK 15
SHAVE THE BALLOON
BUNK 11
DUCK RACE
BUNK 7
KNOCK 'EM DOWN
Bunk 13
BASKETBALL BONANZA!

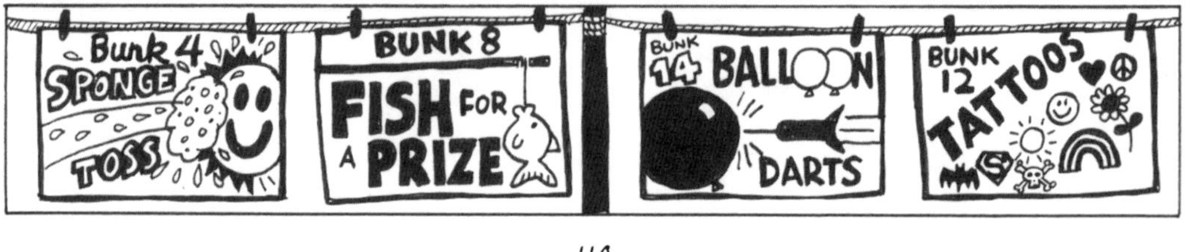
Bunk 4
SPONGE
TOSS
BUNK 8
FISH FOR A PRIZE
BUNK 14
BALLOON
DARTS
BUNK 12
TATTOOS

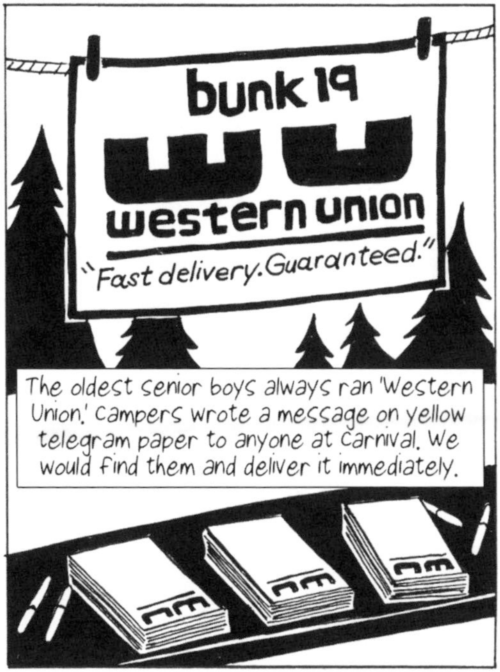
bunk 19
western union
"Fast delivery. Guaranteed."
The oldest senior boys always ran 'Western Union.' Campers wrote a message on yellow telegram paper to anyone at Carnival. We would find them and deliver it immediately.

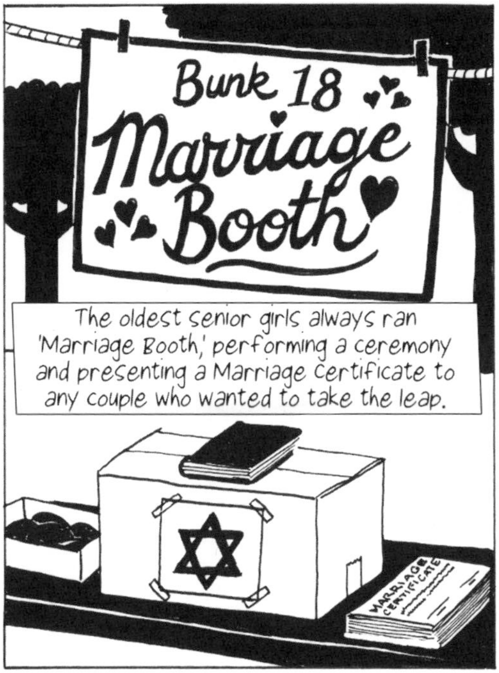
Bunk 18
Marriage Booth
The oldest senior girls always ran 'Marriage Booth,' performing a ceremony and presenting a Marriage Certificate to any couple who wanted to take the leap.
MARRIAGE CERTIFICATE

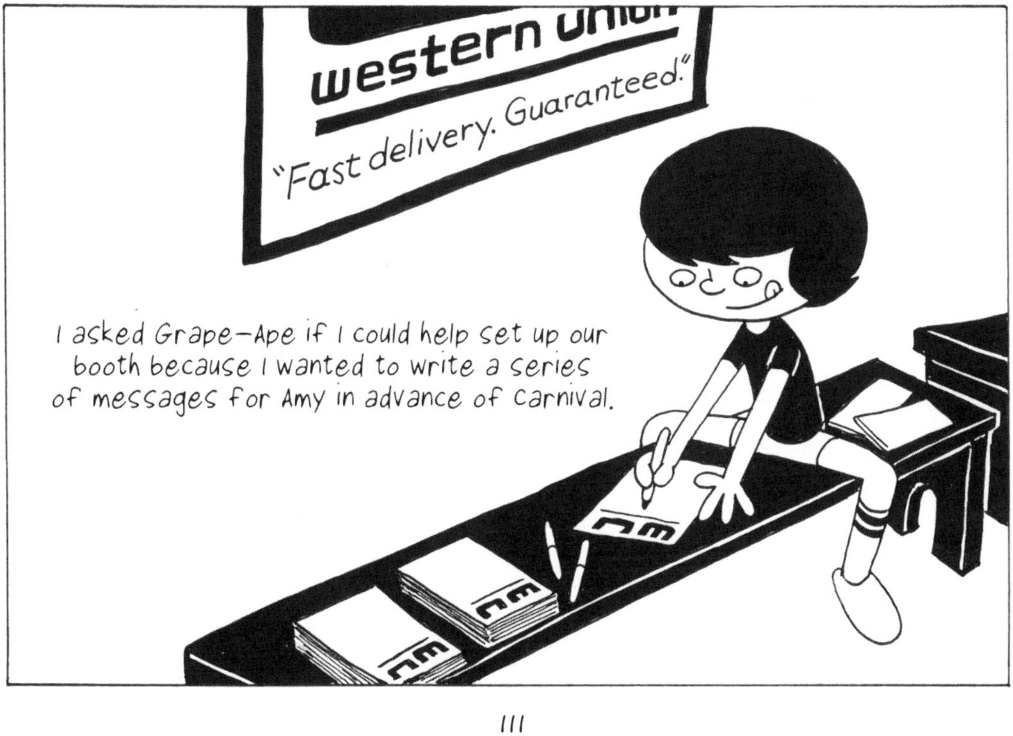
western union
"Fast delivery. Guaranteed."
I asked Grape-Ape if I could help set up our booth because I wanted to write a series of messages for Amy in advance of Carnival.

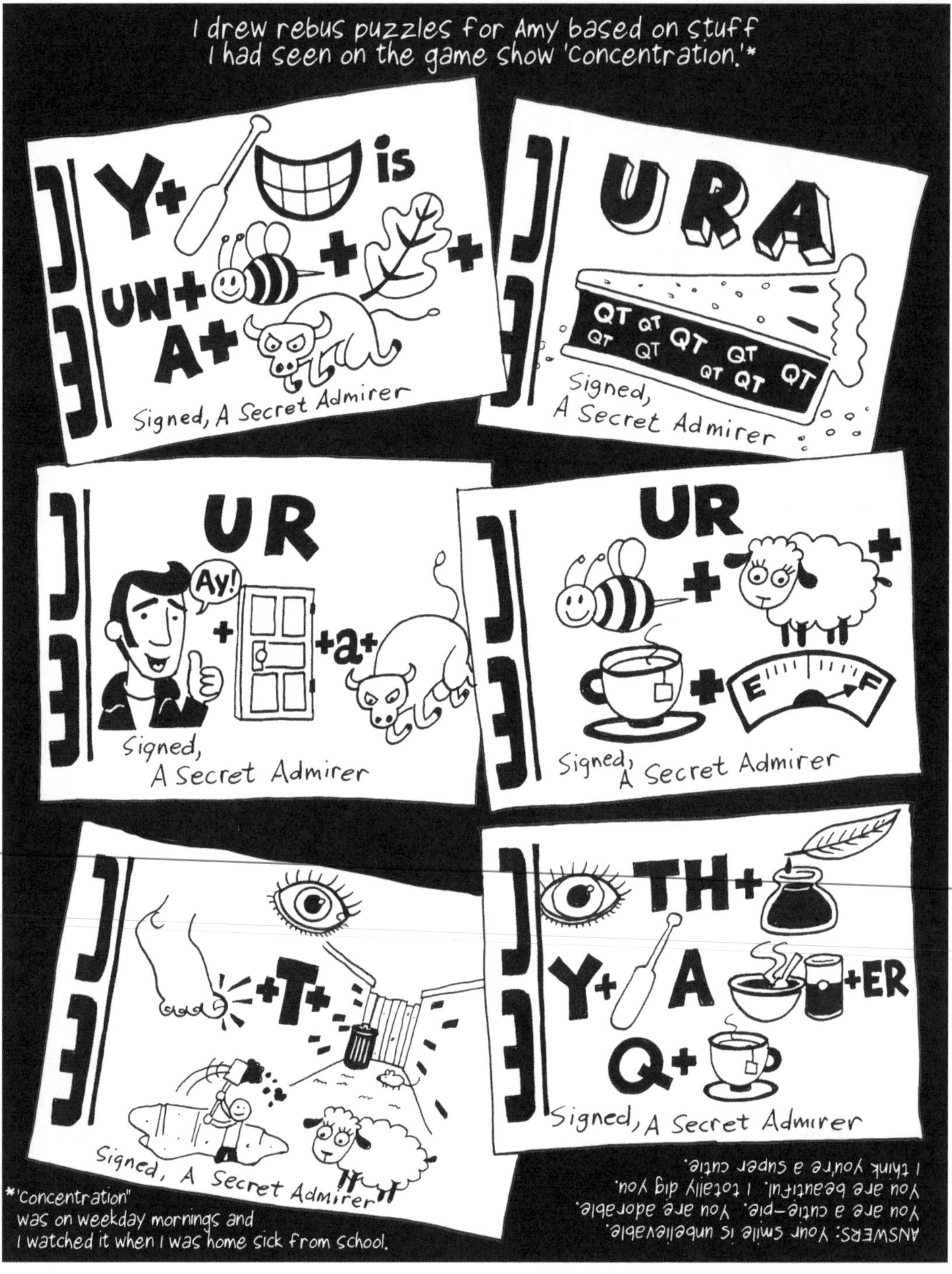
I drew rebus puzzles for Amy based on stuff I had seen on the game show 'Concentration.'*
Y+ is
UN+ + +
A+
Signed, A Secret Admirer
URA
QT QT QT QT QT QT QT QT QT
Signed, A Secret Admirer
UR
Ay!
+ +a+
Signed, A Secret Admirer
UR
+ +
+
E F
Signed, A Secret Admirer
+T+
Signed, A Secret Admirer
TH+
Y+ A +ER
Q+
Signed, A Secret Admirer
*"Concentration" was on weekday mornings and I watched it when I was home sick from school.
ANSWERS: Your smile is unbelievable. You are a cutie-pie. You are adorable. You are beautiful. I totally dig you. I think you're a super cutie.

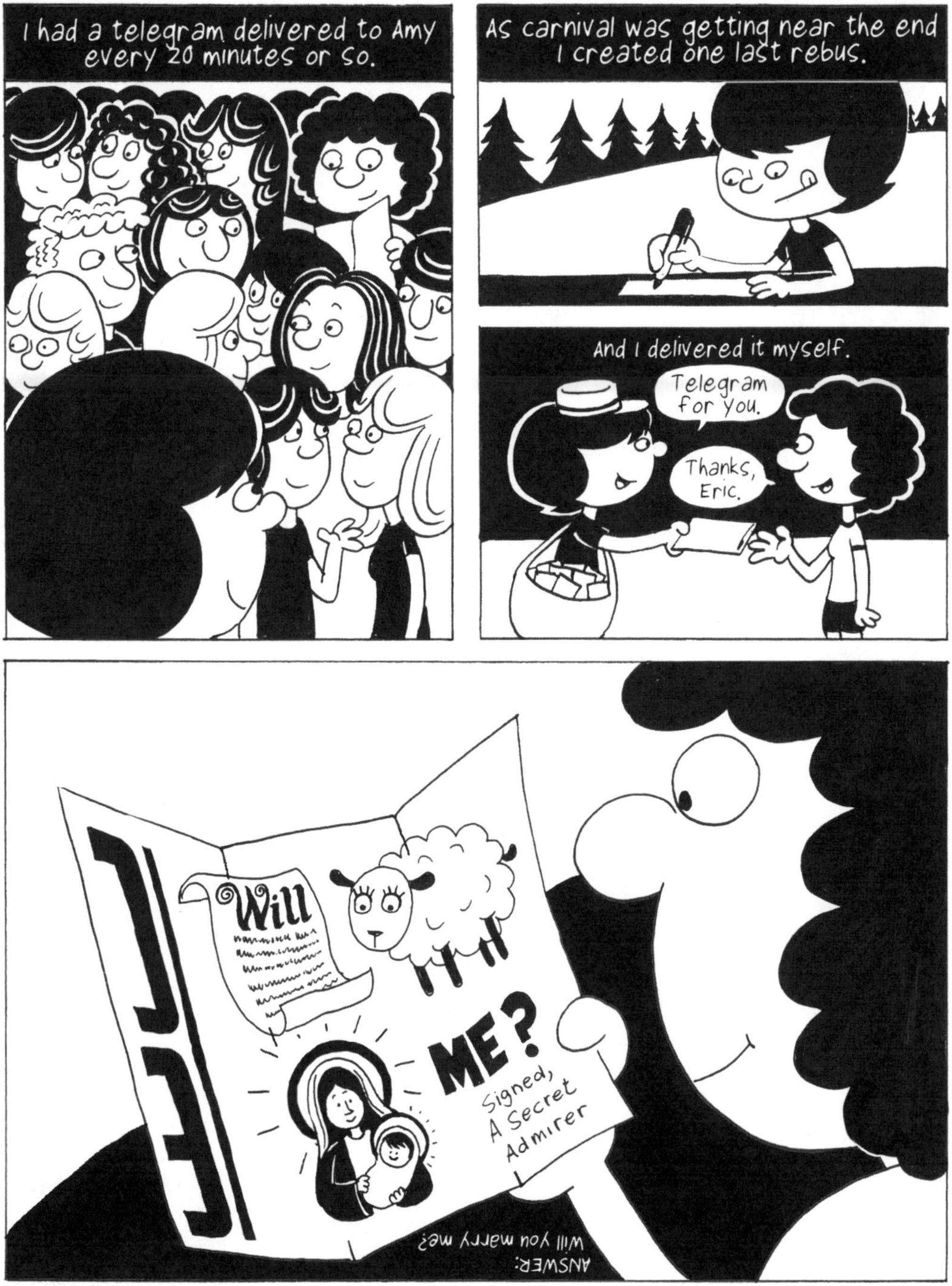
I had a telegram delivered to Amy every 20 minutes or so.
As carnival was getting near the end I created one last rebus.
And I delivered it myself.
Telegram for you.
Thanks, Eric.
Will
ME?
Signed, A Secret Admirer
ANSWER: Will you marry me?

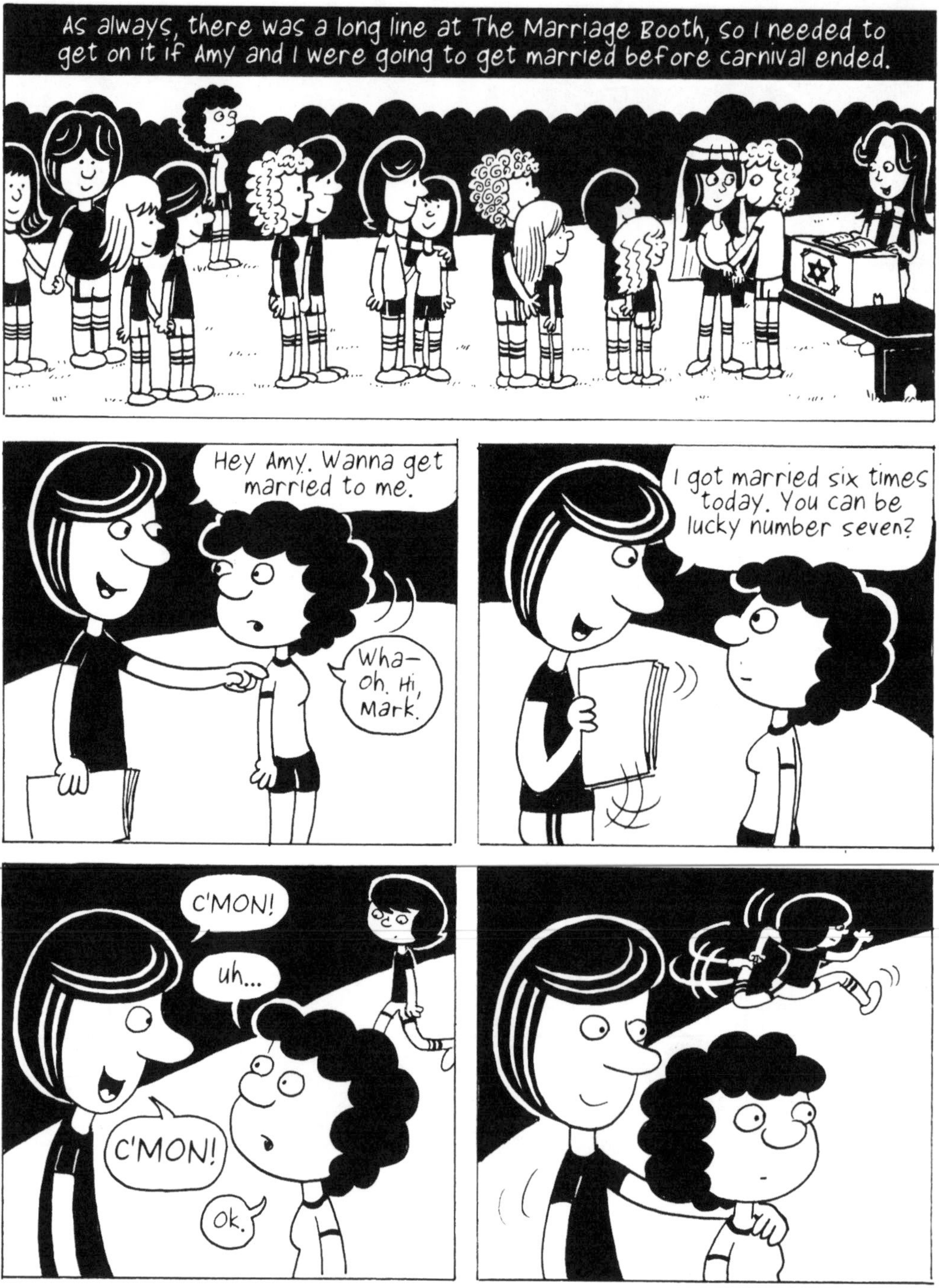
As always, there was a long line at The Marriage Booth, so I needed to get on it if Amy and I were going to get married before carnival ended.
Hey Amy. Wanna get married to me.
Wha- Oh. Hi, Mark.
I got married six times today. You can be lucky number seven?
C'MON!
uh...
C'MON!
Ok.

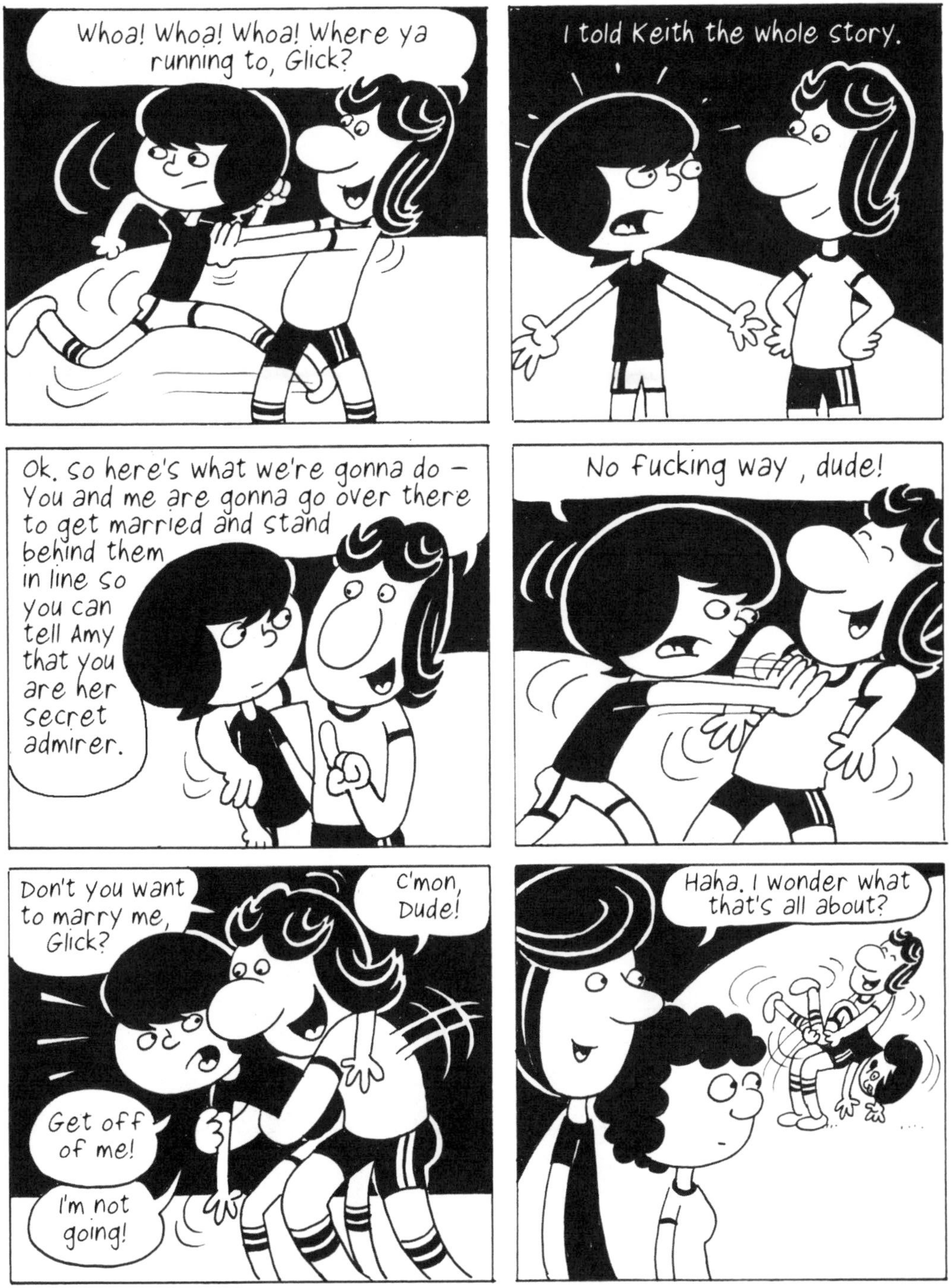
Whoa! Whoa! Whoa! Where ya running to, Glick?
I told Keith the whole story.
Ok. So here's what we're gonna do – You and me are gonna go over there to get married and stand behind them in line so you can tell Amy that you are her secret admirer.
No fucking way , dude!
Don't you want to marry me, Glick?
C'mon, Dude!
Get off of me!
I'm not going!
Haha. I wonder what that's all about?

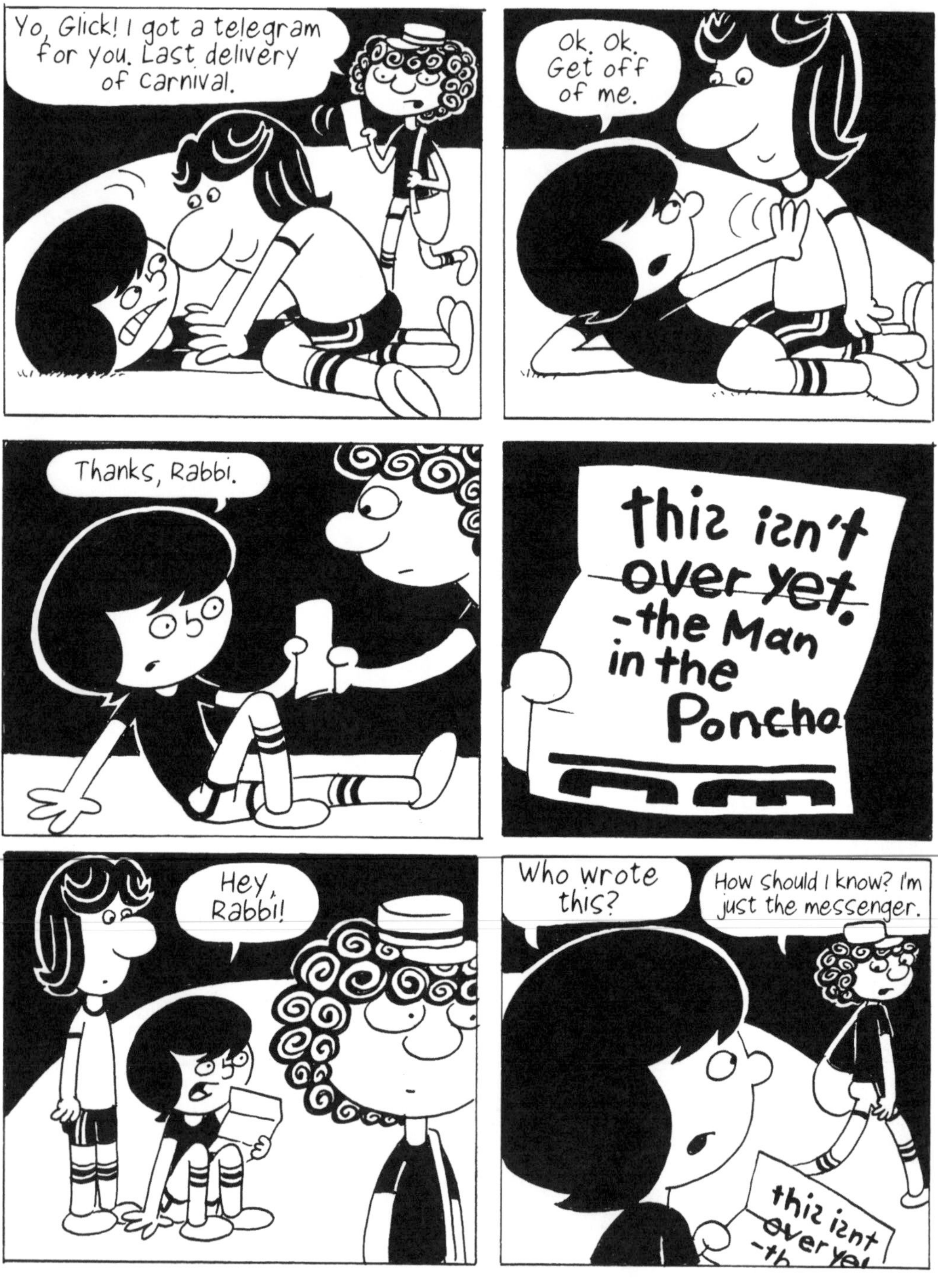
Yo, Glick! I got a telegram for you. Last delivery of carnival.
Ok. Ok. Get off of me.
Thanks, Rabbi.
this isn't over yet. -the Man in the Poncho
Hey, Rabbi!
Who wrote this?
How should I know? I'm just the messenger.

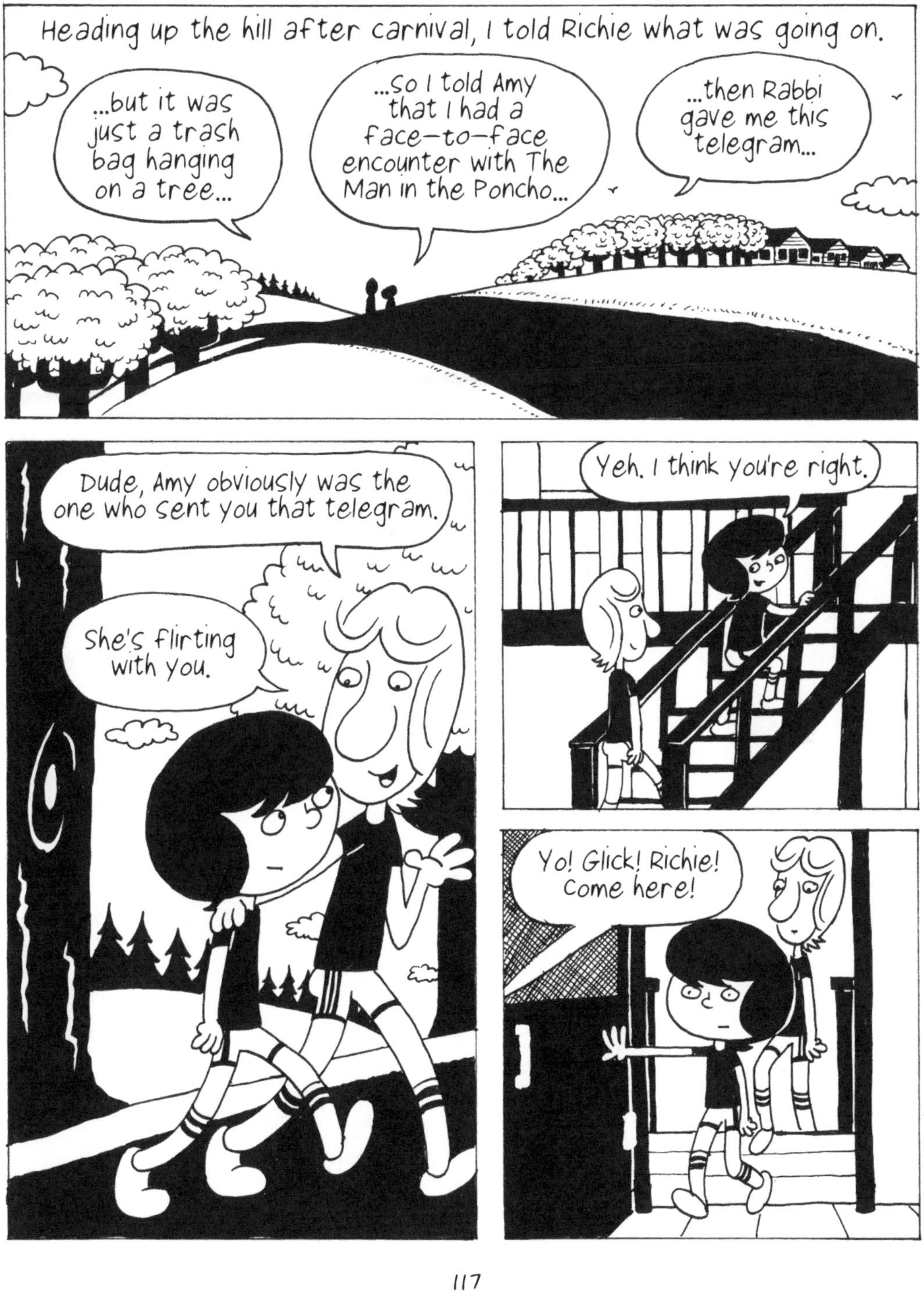
Heading up the hill after carnival, I told Richie what was going on.
...but it was just a trash bag hanging on a tree...
...so I told Amy that I had a face-to-face encounter with The Man in the Poncho...
...then Rabbi gave me this telegram...
Dude, Amy obviously was the one who sent you that telegram.
She's flirting with you.
Yeh. I think you're right.
Yo! Glick! Richie! Come here!

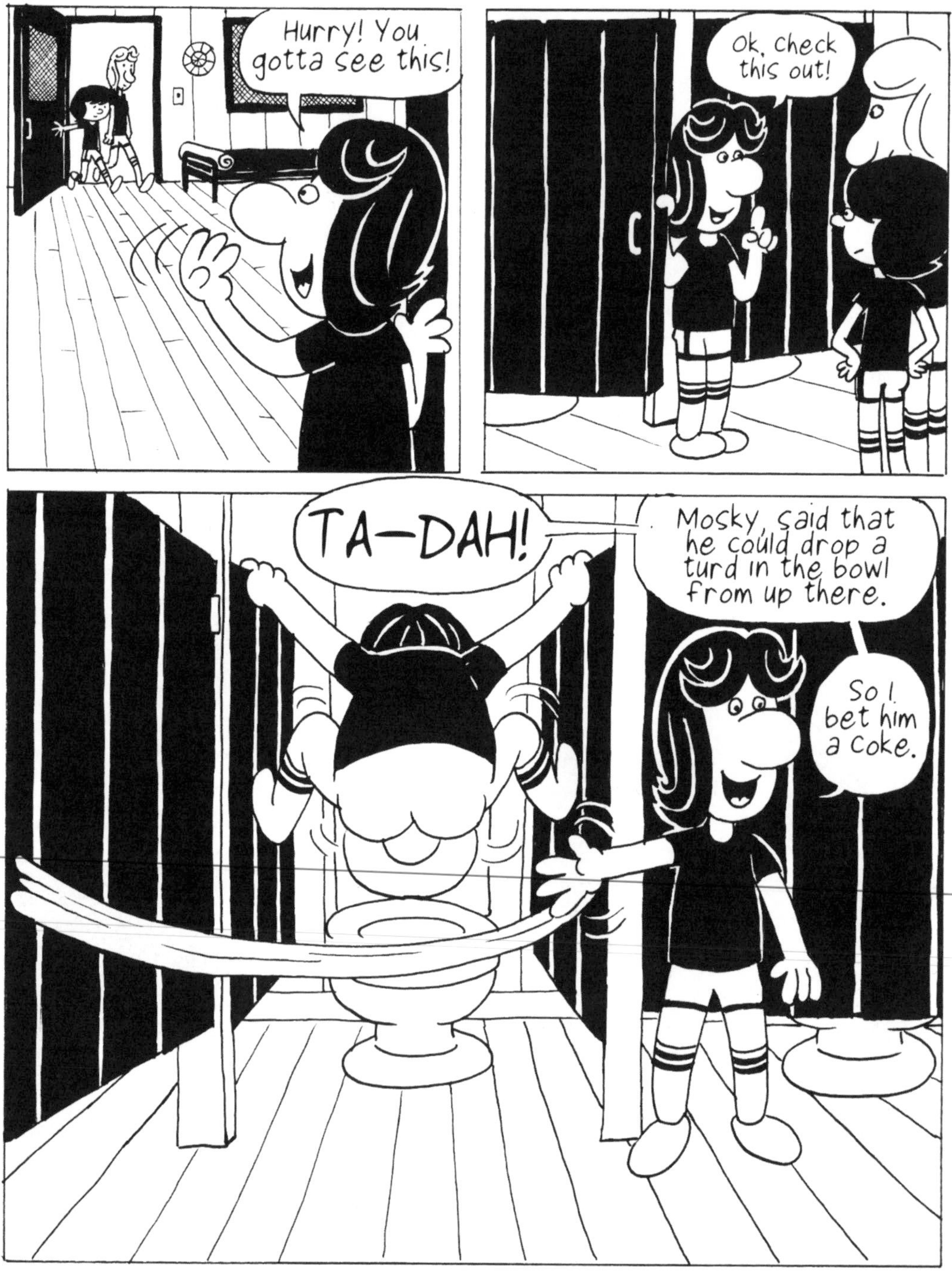
Hurry! You gotta see this!
Ok, check this out!
TA—DAH!
Mosky, said that he could drop a turd in the bowl from up there.
So I bet him a coke.

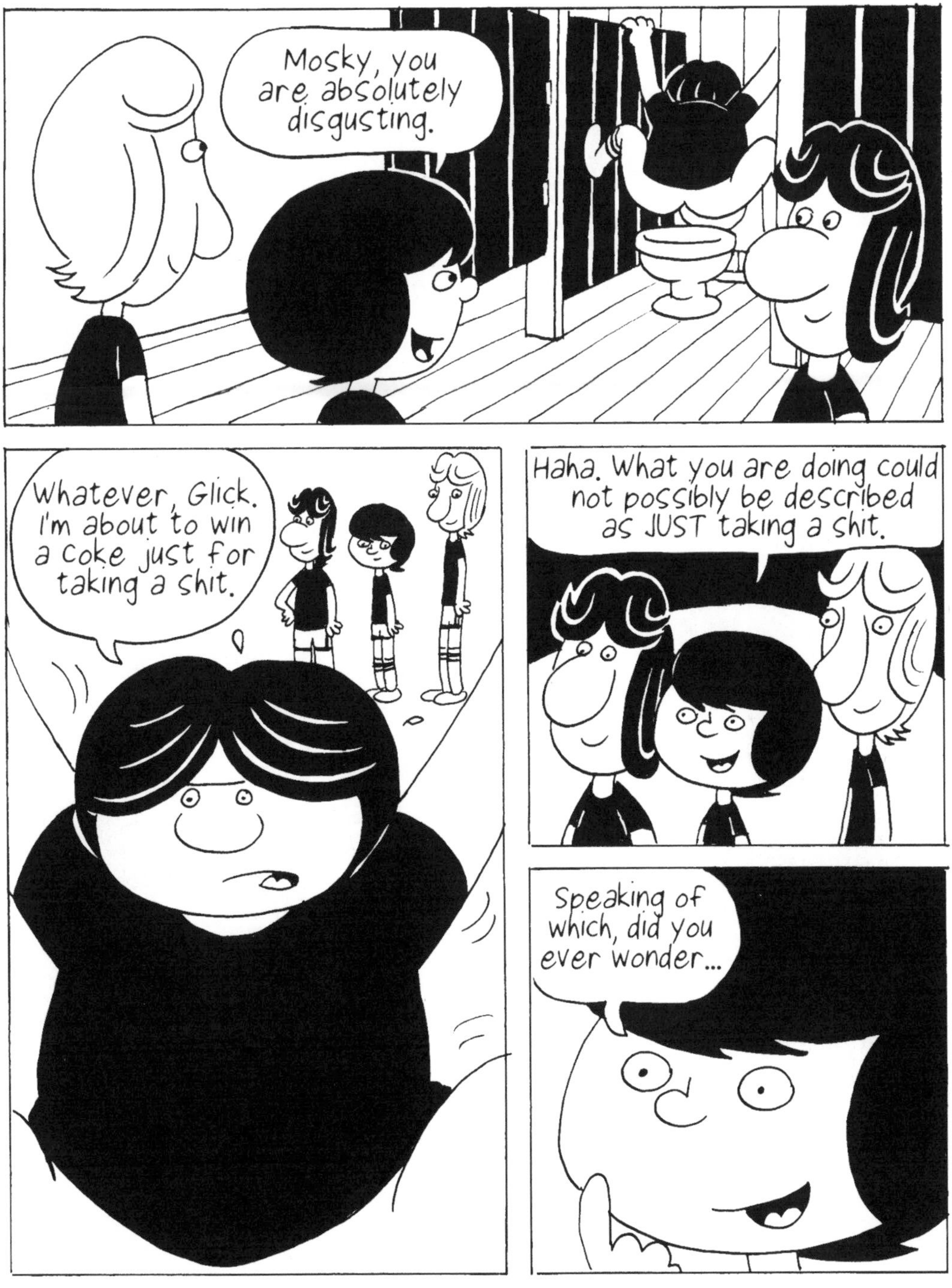
Mosky, you are absolutely disgusting.
Whatever, Glick. I'm about to win a coke just for taking a shit.
Haha. What you are doing could not possibly be described as JUST taking a shit.
Speaking of which, did you ever wonder...

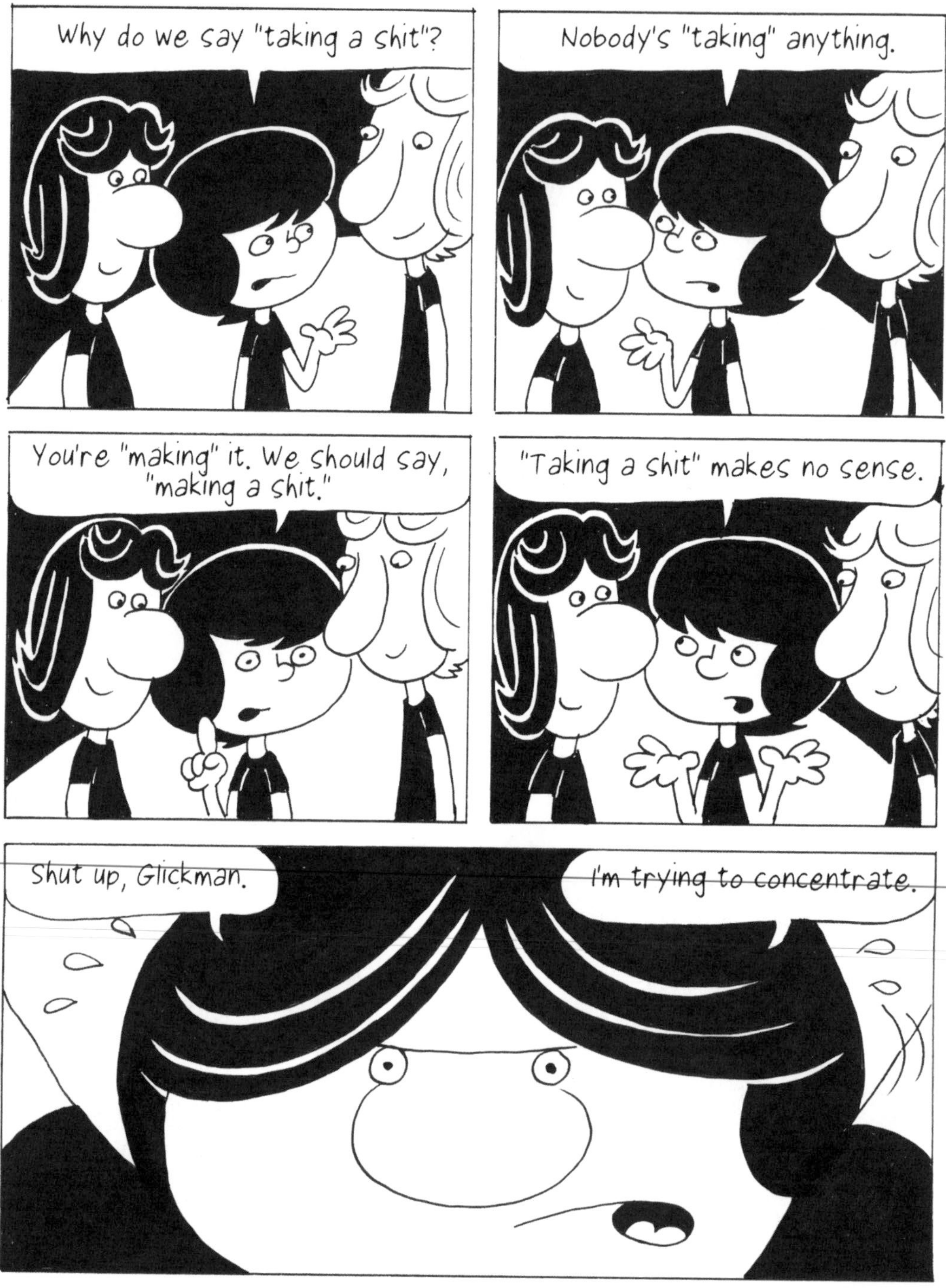
Why do we say "taking a shit"?
Nobody's "taking" anything.
You're "making" it. We should say, "making a shit."
"Taking a shit" makes no sense.
Shut up, Glickman.
I'm trying to concentrate.

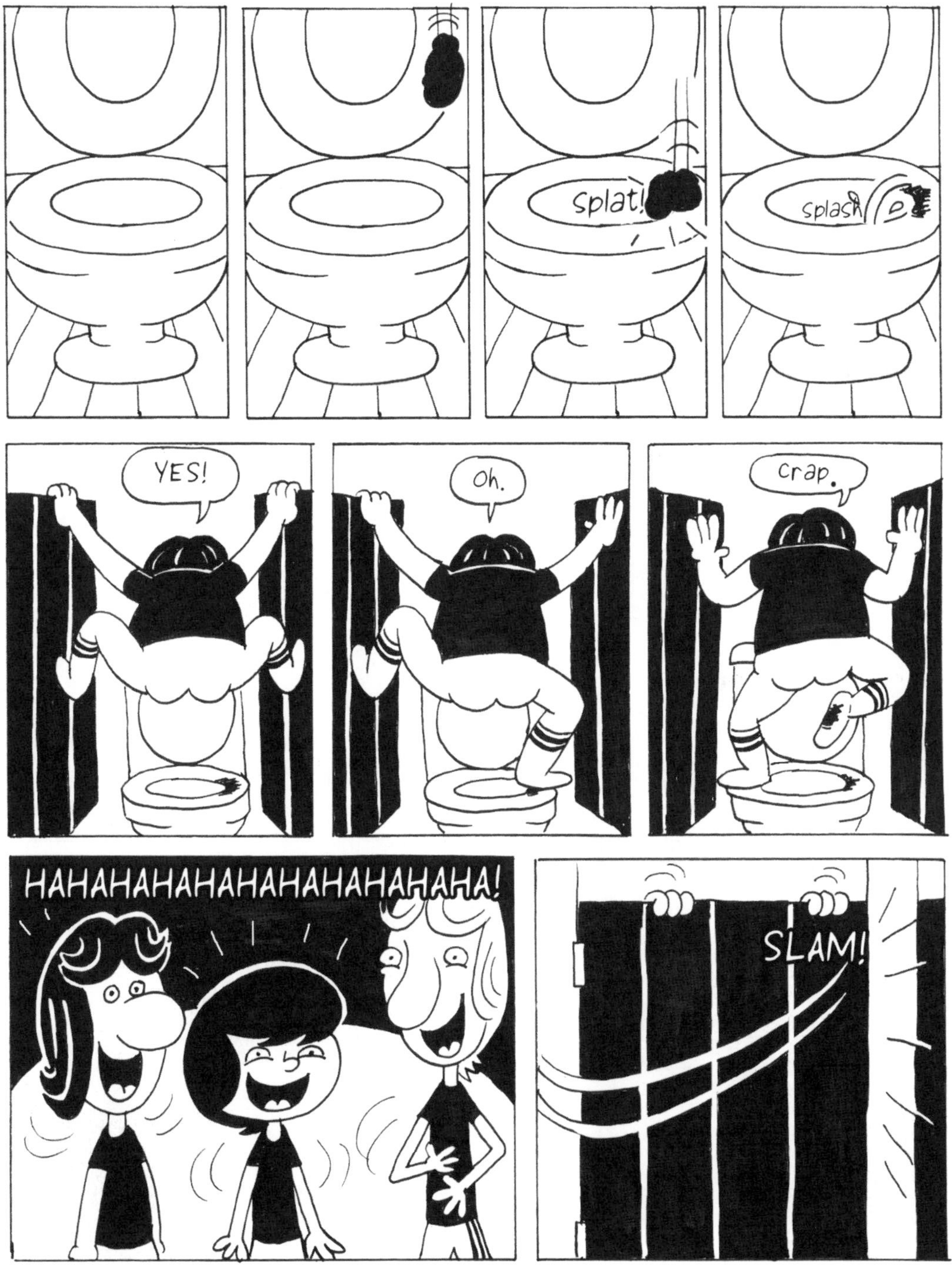
splat!
splash
YES!
Oh.
crap.
HAHAHAHAHAHAHAHAHAHAHA!
SLAM!

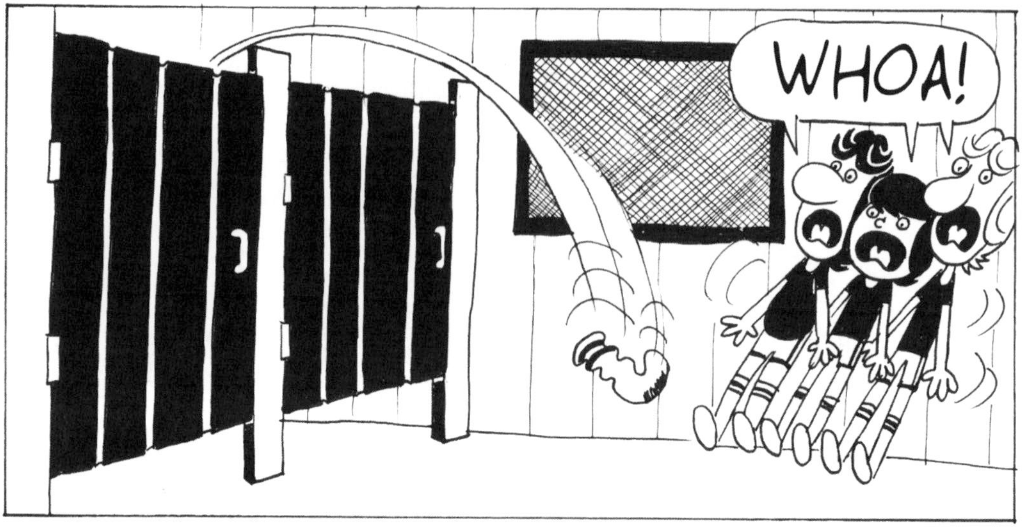
WHOA!

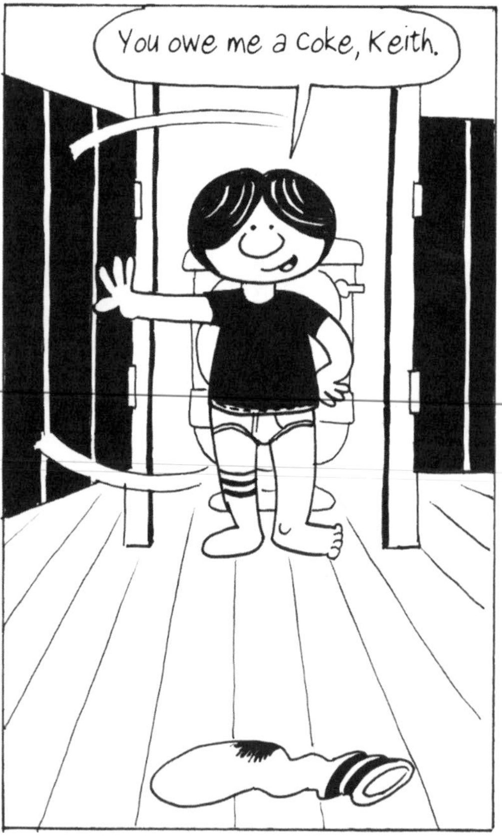
You owe me a coke, Keith.

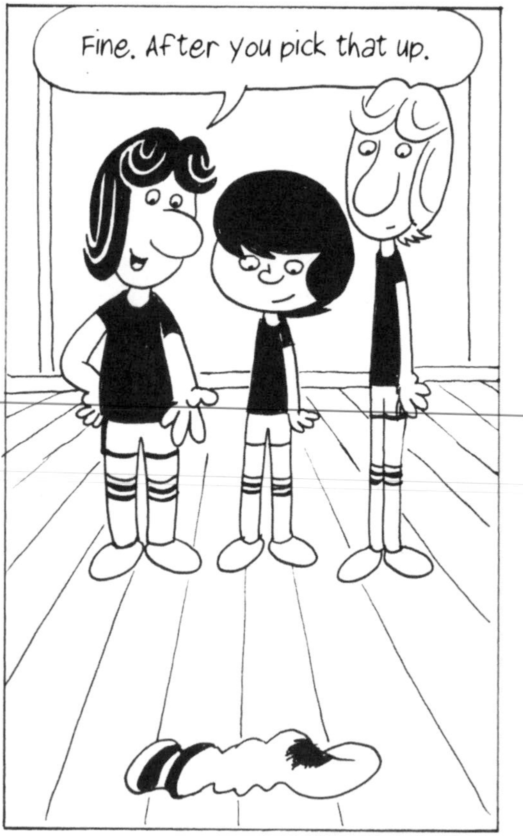
Fine. After you pick that up.

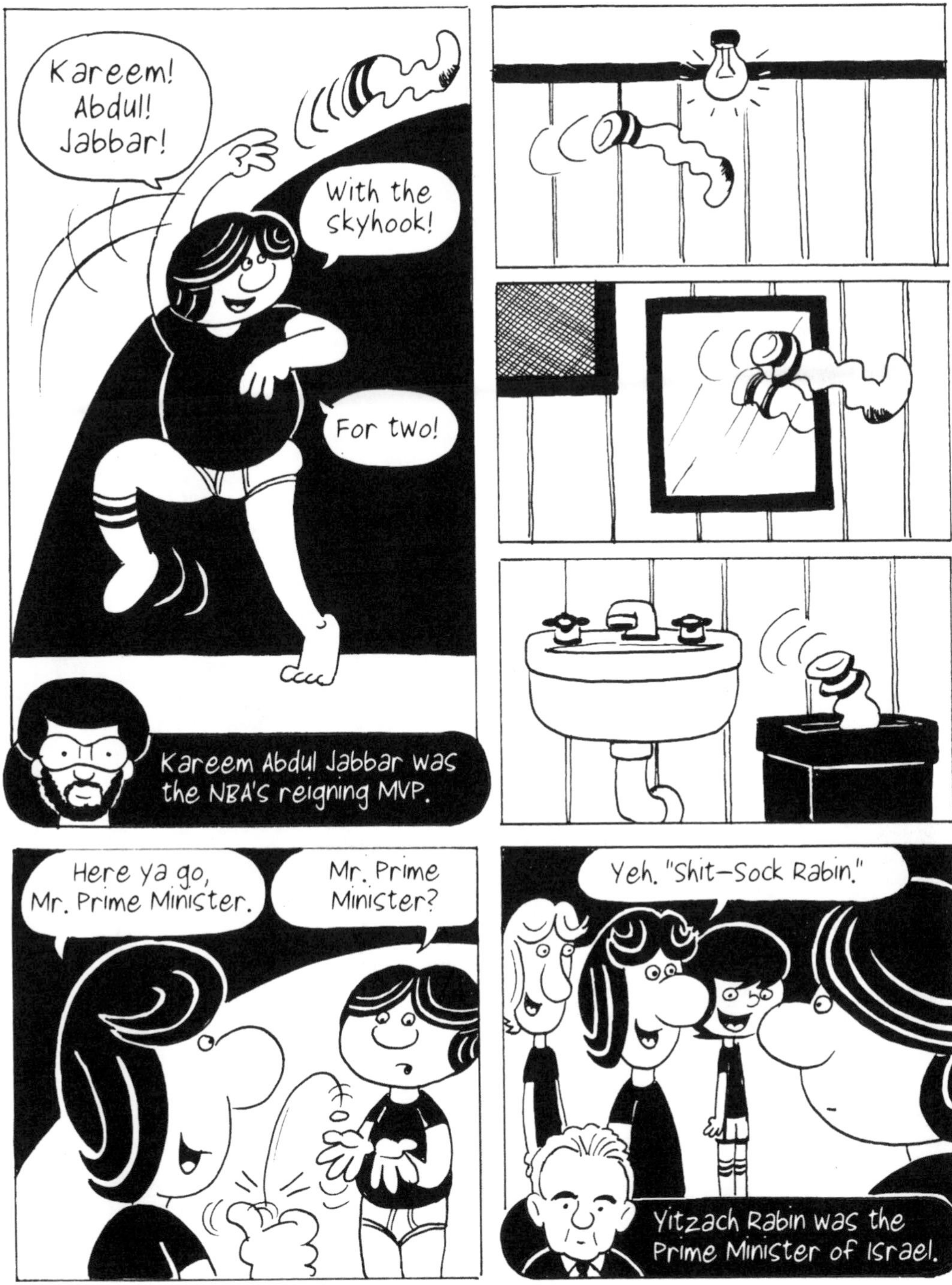
Kareem! Abdul! Jabbar!
With the skyhook!
For two!
Kareem Abdul Jabbar was the NBA's reigning MVP.
Here ya go, Mr. Prime Minister.
Mr. Prime Minister?
Yeh. "Shit-Sock Rabin."
Yitzach Rabin was the Prime Minister of Israel.

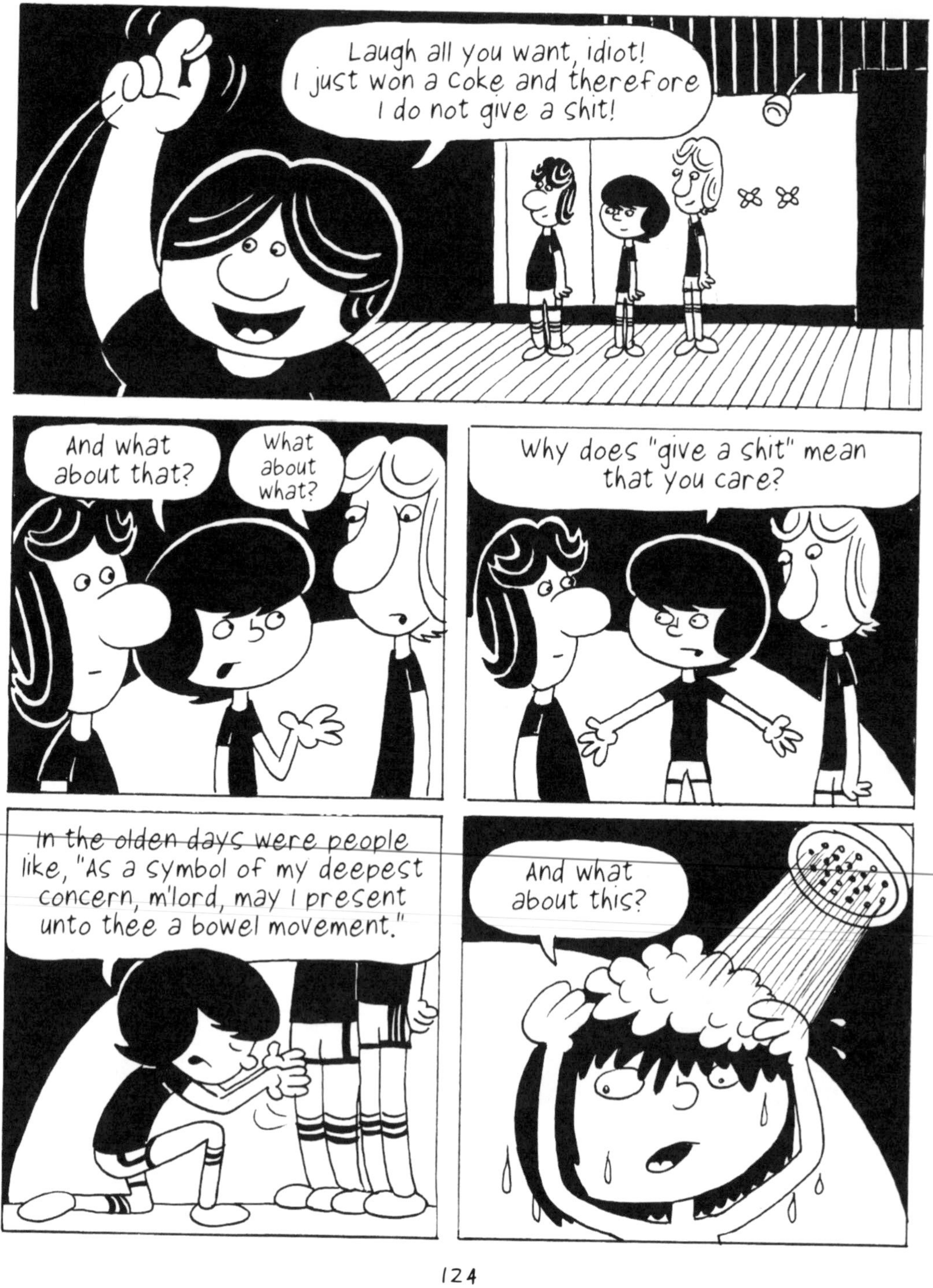
Laugh all you want, idiot! I just won a Coke and therefore I do not give a shit!
And what about that?
What about what?
Why does "give a shit" mean that you care?
In the olden days were people like, "As a symbol of my deepest concern, m'lord, may I present unto thee a bowel movement."
And what about this?

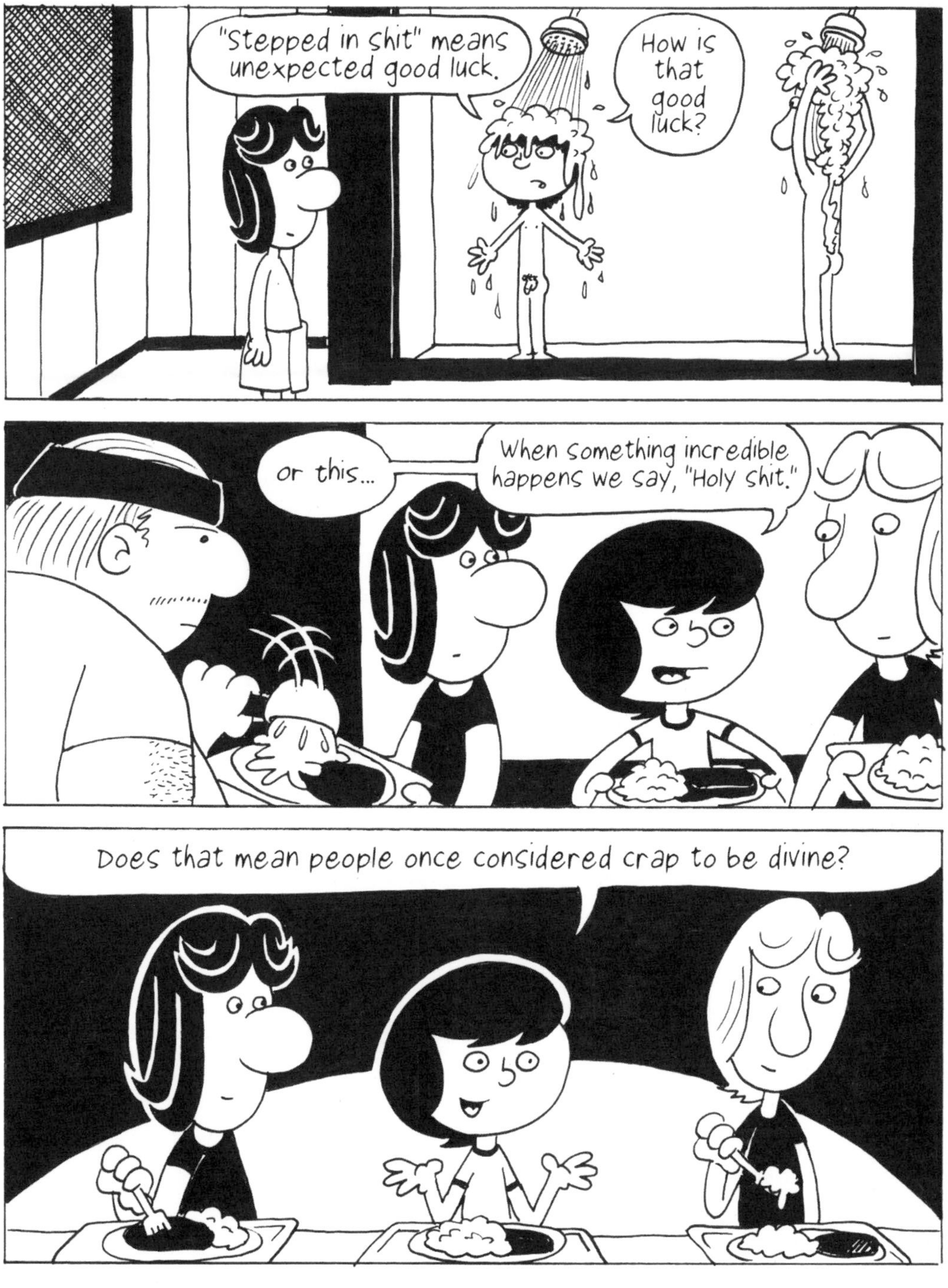
"Stepped in shit" means unexpected good luck.
How is that good luck?
or this...
When something incredible happens we say, "Holy shit."
Does that mean people once considered crap to be divine?

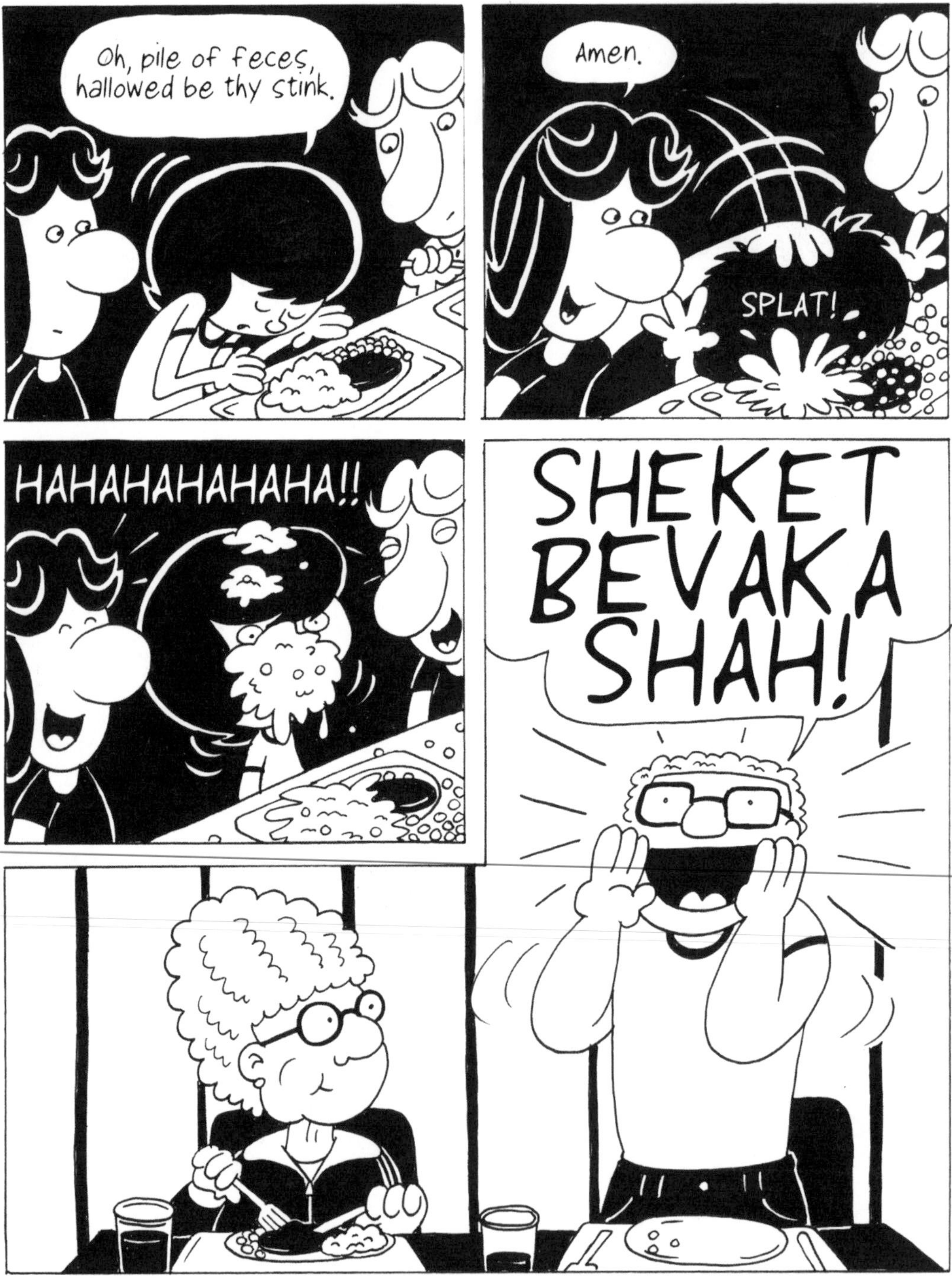
Oh, pile of feces, hallowed be thy stink.
Amen.
SPLAT!
HAHAHAHAHAHA!!
SHEKET BEVAKA SHAH!

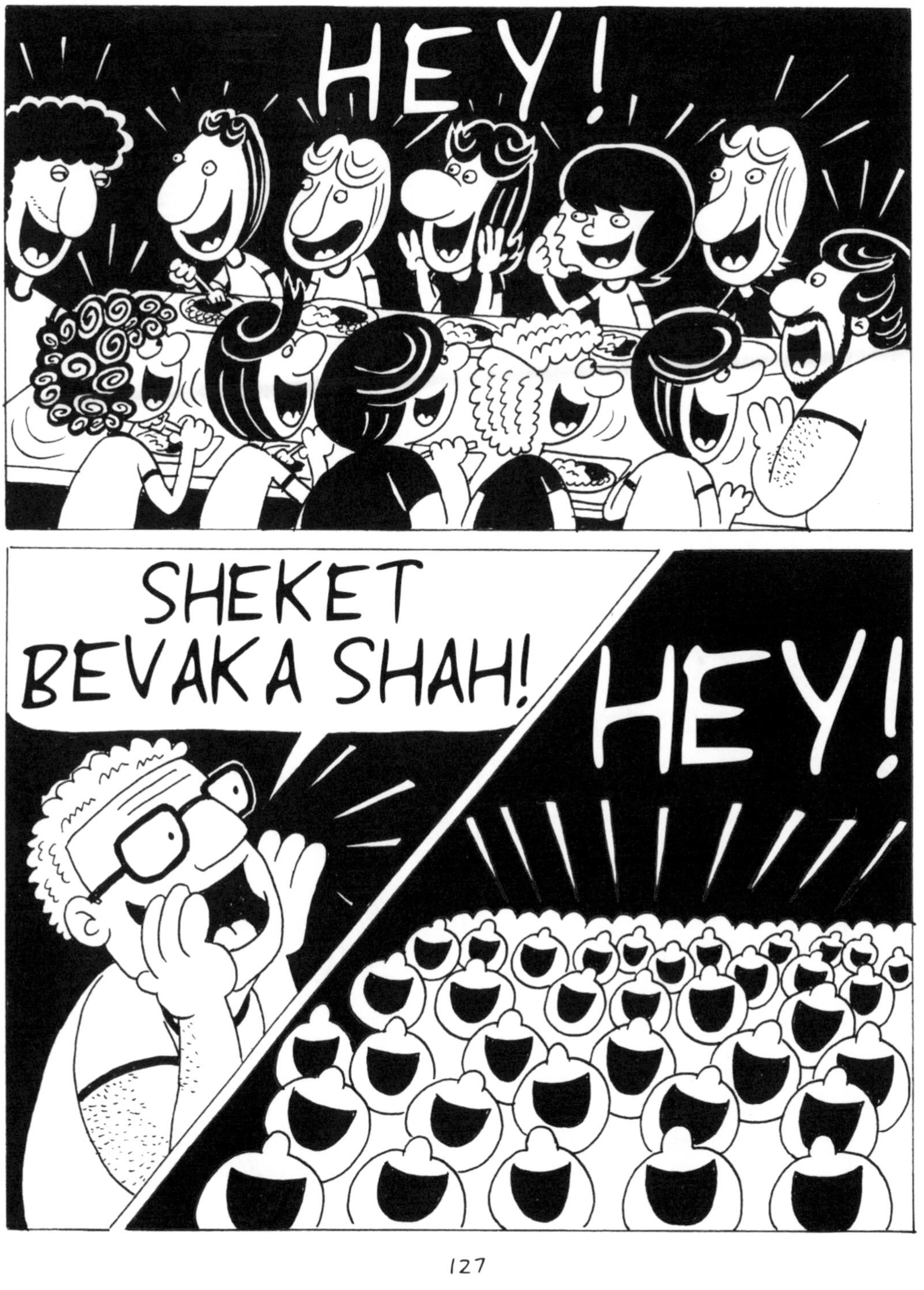
HEY!
SHEKET BEVAKA SHAH!
HEY!

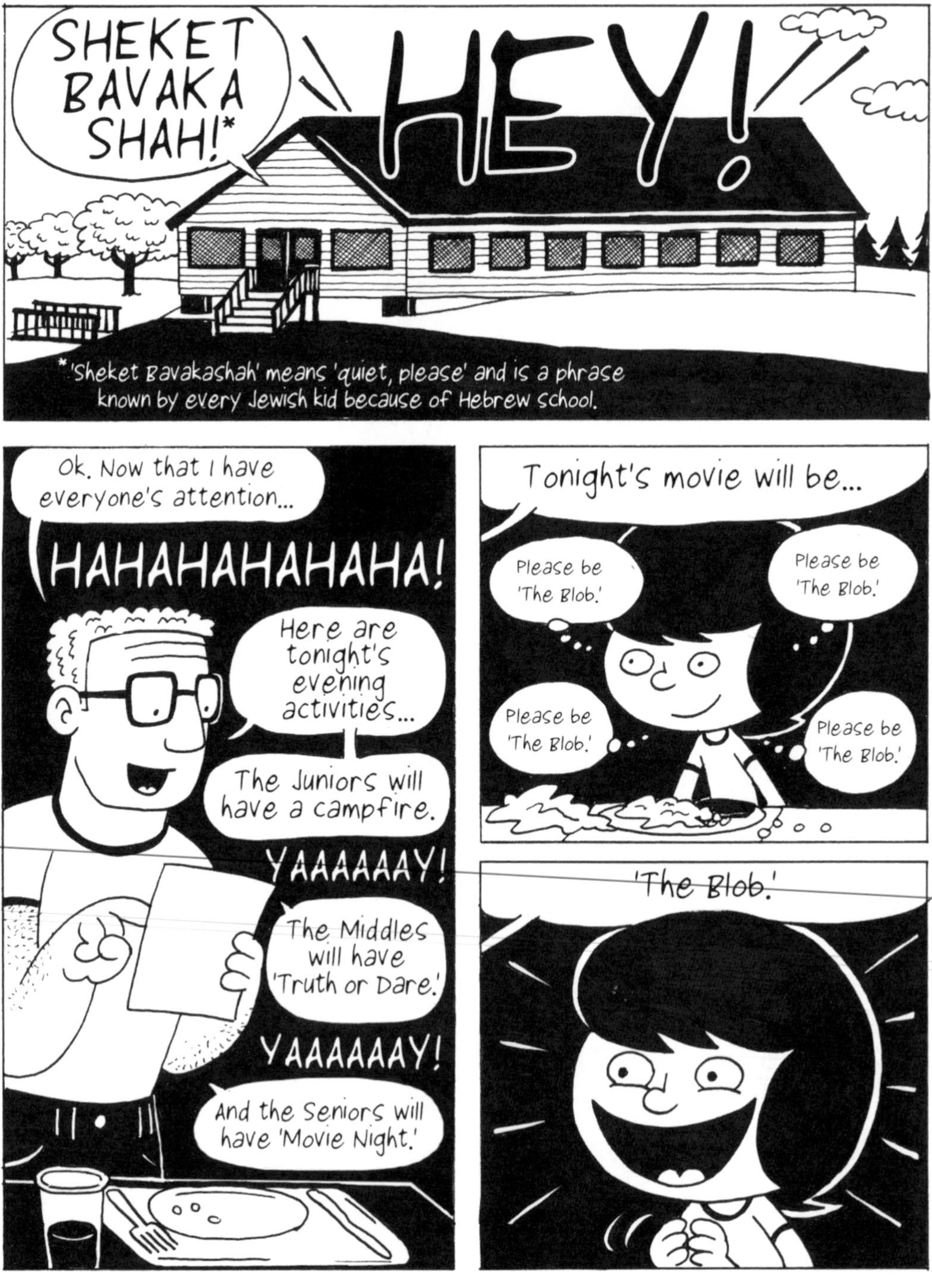
SHEKET BAVAKA SHAH!*
HEY!
*'Sheket Bavakashah' means 'quiet, please' and is a phrase known by every Jewish kid because of Hebrew school.
Ok. Now that I have everyone's attention...
HAHAHAHAHAHA!
Here are tonight's evening activities...
The Juniors will have a campfire.
YAAAAAAY!
The Middles will have 'Truth or Dare.'
YAAAAAAY!
And the Seniors will have 'Movie Night.'
Tonight's movie will be...
Please be 'The Blob.'
Please be 'The Blob.'
Please be 'The Blob.'
Please be 'The Blob.'
'The Blob.'

Camp Pock-a-Wocknee owned 35mm prints of four films and showed those same four films to the seniors every summer. In my mind, 'The Blob' was the perfect movie to ask Amy to watch with me as our 'first date.'

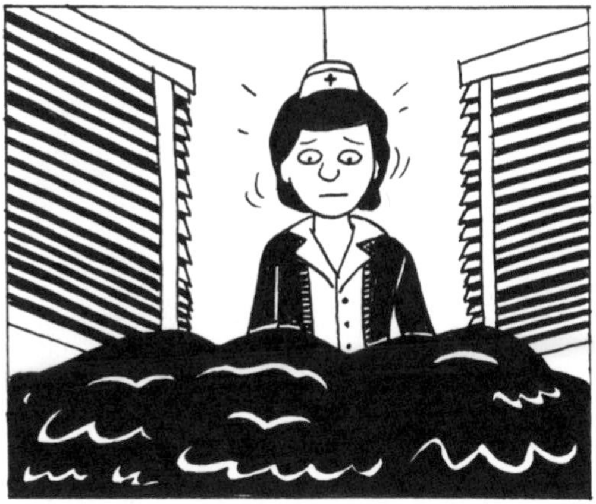

'THE BLOB' 1958
A highly enjoyable, sci-fi, B movie about an alien organism that arrives in a small town on a meteor, then goes on a rampage, growing bigger and bigger as it absorbs town folks along the way.

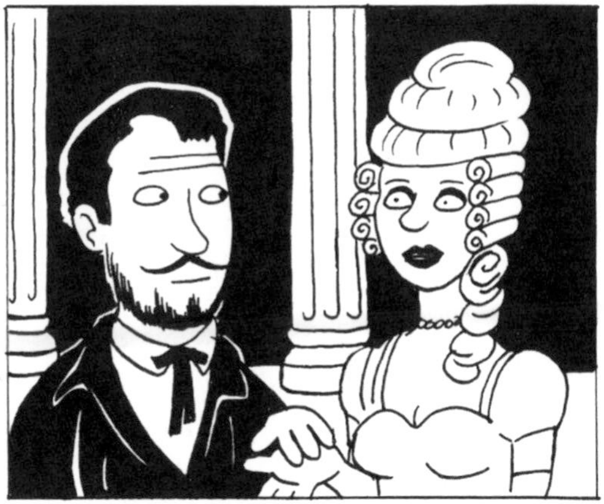

'THE HOUSE OF WAX' 1953
A surprisingly scary horror movie starring the legendary Vincent Price as an insane sculptor who murders people, dips them in wax, and puts them on display in his museum.

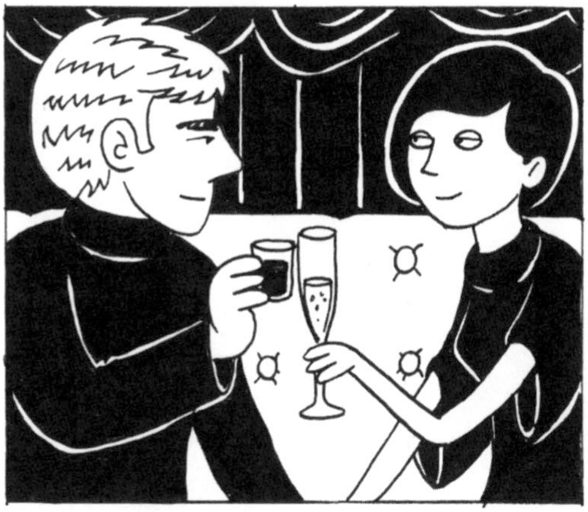

'IN LIKE FLINT' 1967
An American, James Bond rip-off starring James Coburn as Derek Flint who must save the U.S. from an international feminist organization's attempt to overthrow the patriarchy.

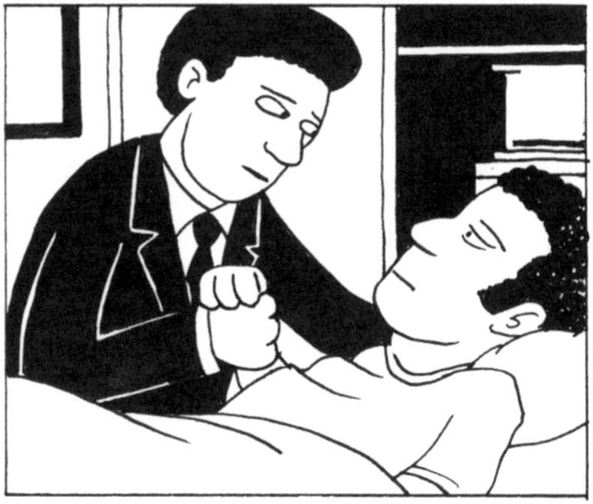

'BRIAN'S SONG' 1971
A true story and incredible tear-jerker starring Billy Dee Williams and James Caan as Chicago Bears teammates and best friends: Hall of Fame running back, Gale Sayers and Brian Piccolo, who is dying of cancer.

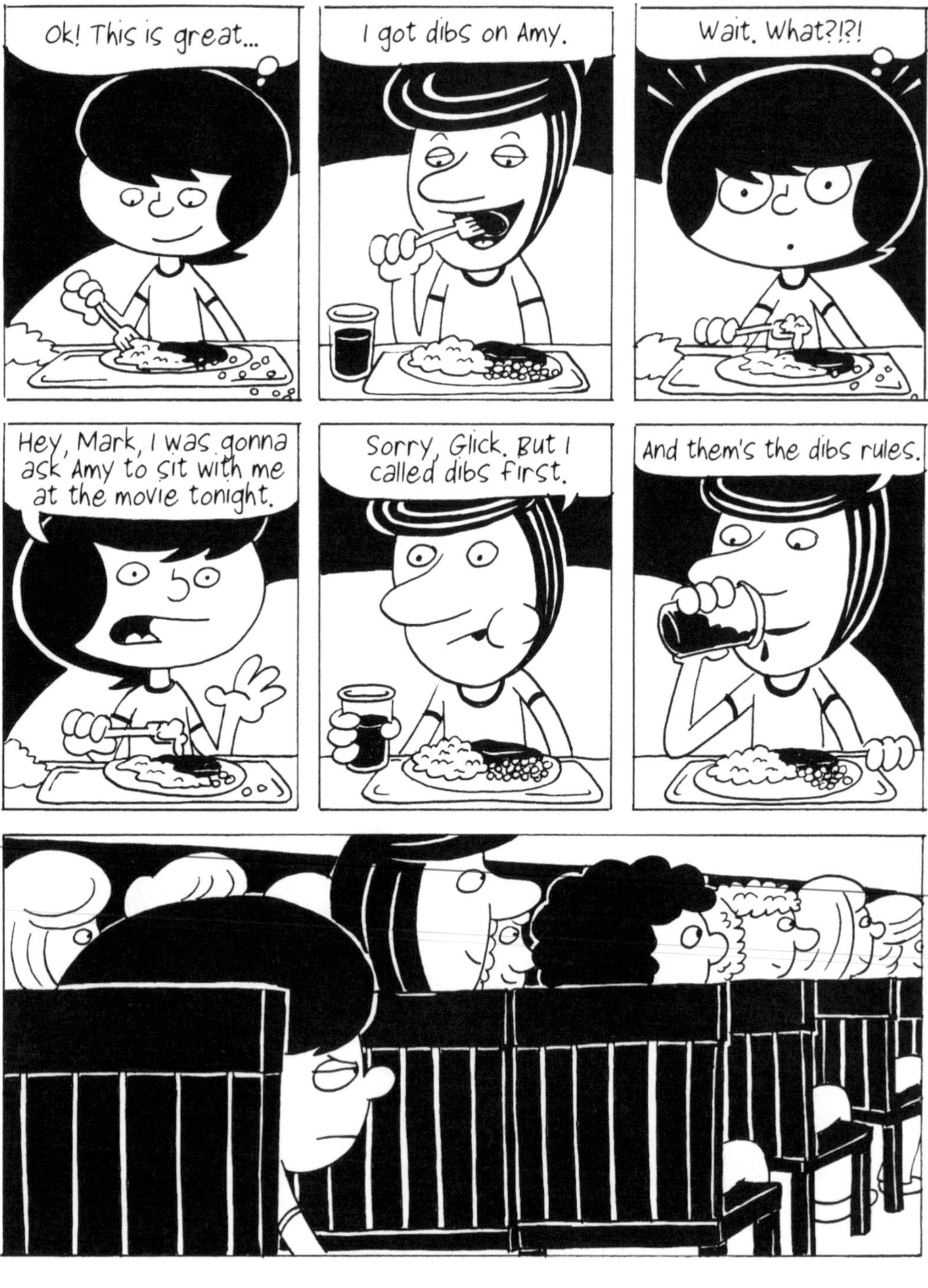
Ok! This is great...
I got dibs on Amy.
Wait. What?!?!
Hey, Mark, I was gonna ask Amy to sit with me at the movie tonight.
Sorry, Glick. But I called dibs first.
And them's the dibs rules.

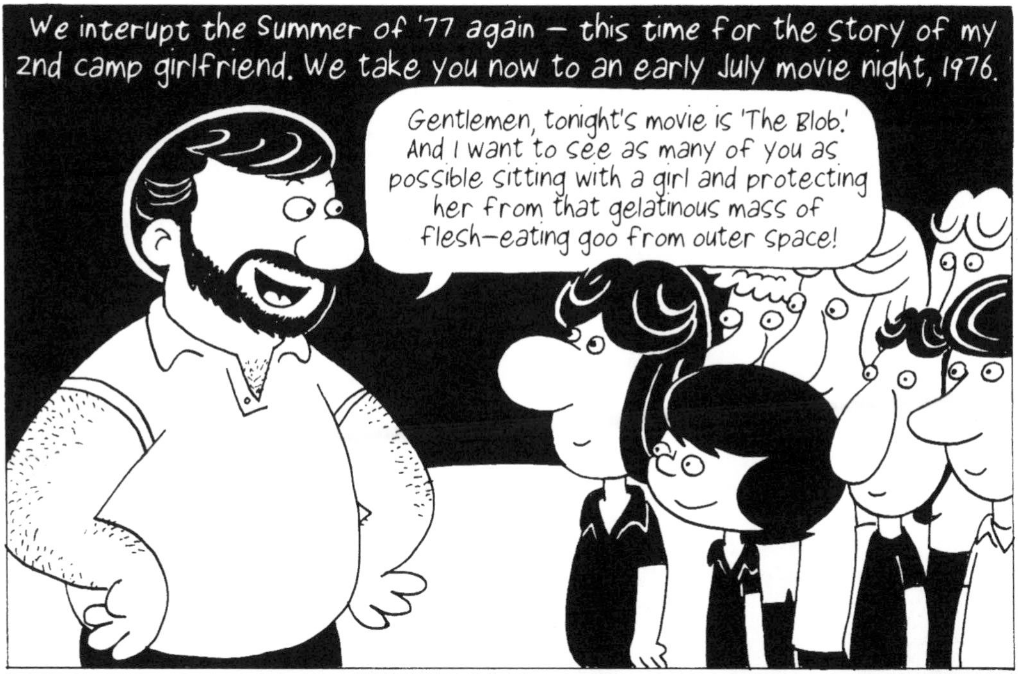
We interupt the Summer of '77 again – this time for the story of my 2nd camp girlfriend. We take you now to an early July movie night, 1976.
Gentlemen, tonight's movie is 'The Blob.' And I want to see as many of you as possible sitting with a girl and protecting her from that gelatinous mass of flesh-eating goo from outer space!

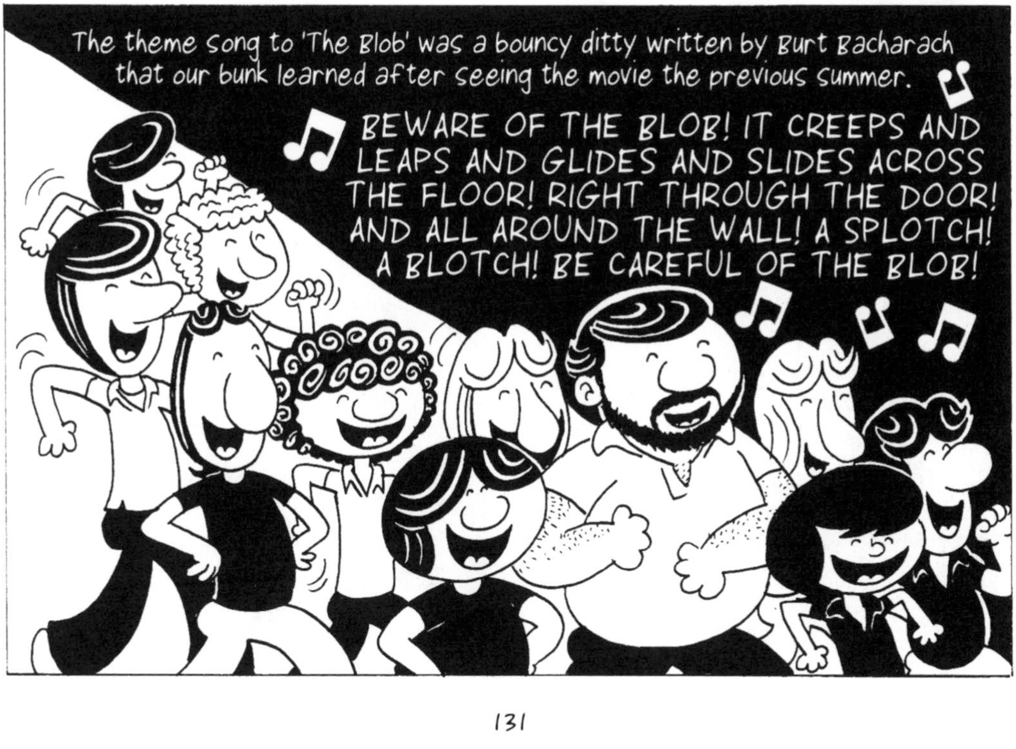
The theme song to 'The Blob' was a bouncy ditty written by Burt Bacharach that our bunk learned after seeing the movie the previous summer.
BEWARE OF THE BLOB! IT CREEPS AND LEAPS AND GLIDES AND SLIDES ACROSS THE FLOOR! RIGHT THROUGH THE DOOR! AND ALL AROUND THE WALL! A SPLOTCH! A BLOTCH! BE CAREFUL OF THE BLOB!

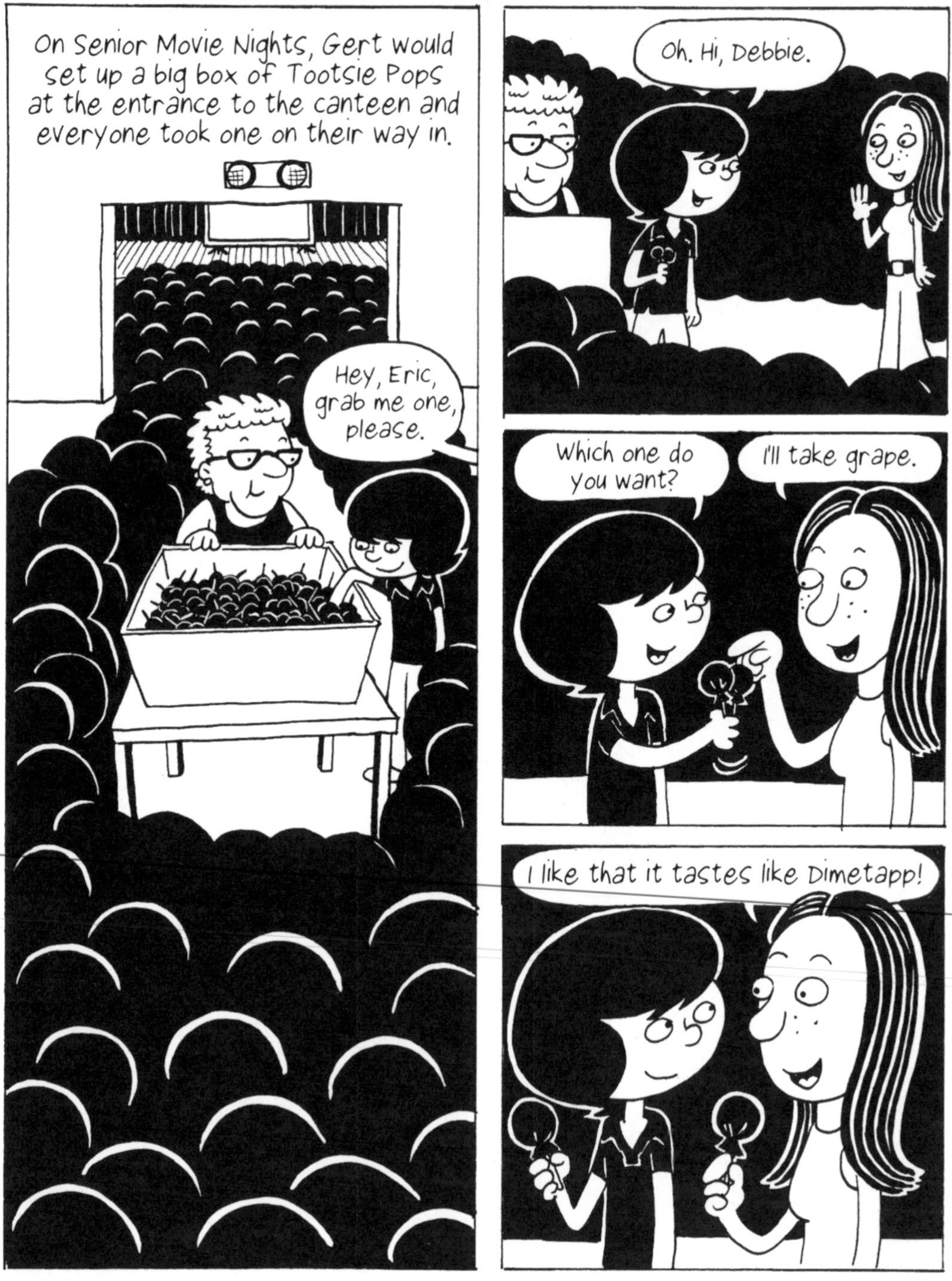
On Senior Movie Nights, Gert would set up a big box of Tootsie Pops at the entrance to the canteen and everyone took one on their way in.
Hey, Eric, grab me one, please.
Oh. Hi, Debbie.
Which one do you want?
I'll take grape.
I like that it tastes like Dimetapp!

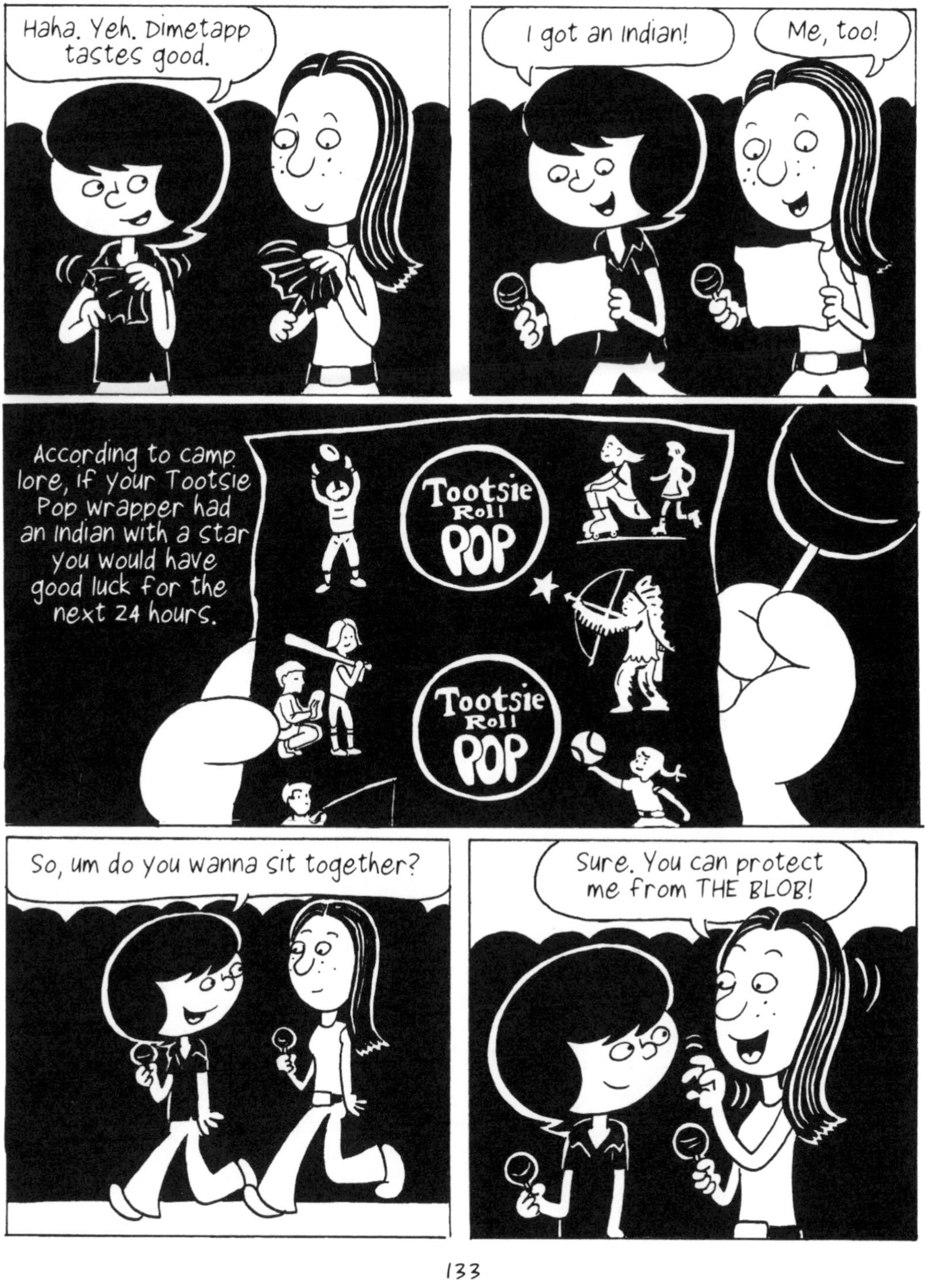
Haha. Yeh. Dimetapp tastes good.
I got an Indian!
Me, too!
According to camp lore, if your Tootsie Pop wrapper had an Indian with a star you would have good luck for the next 24 hours.
Tootsie Roll POP
Tootsie Roll POP
So, um do you wanna sit together?
Sure. You can protect me from THE BLOB!

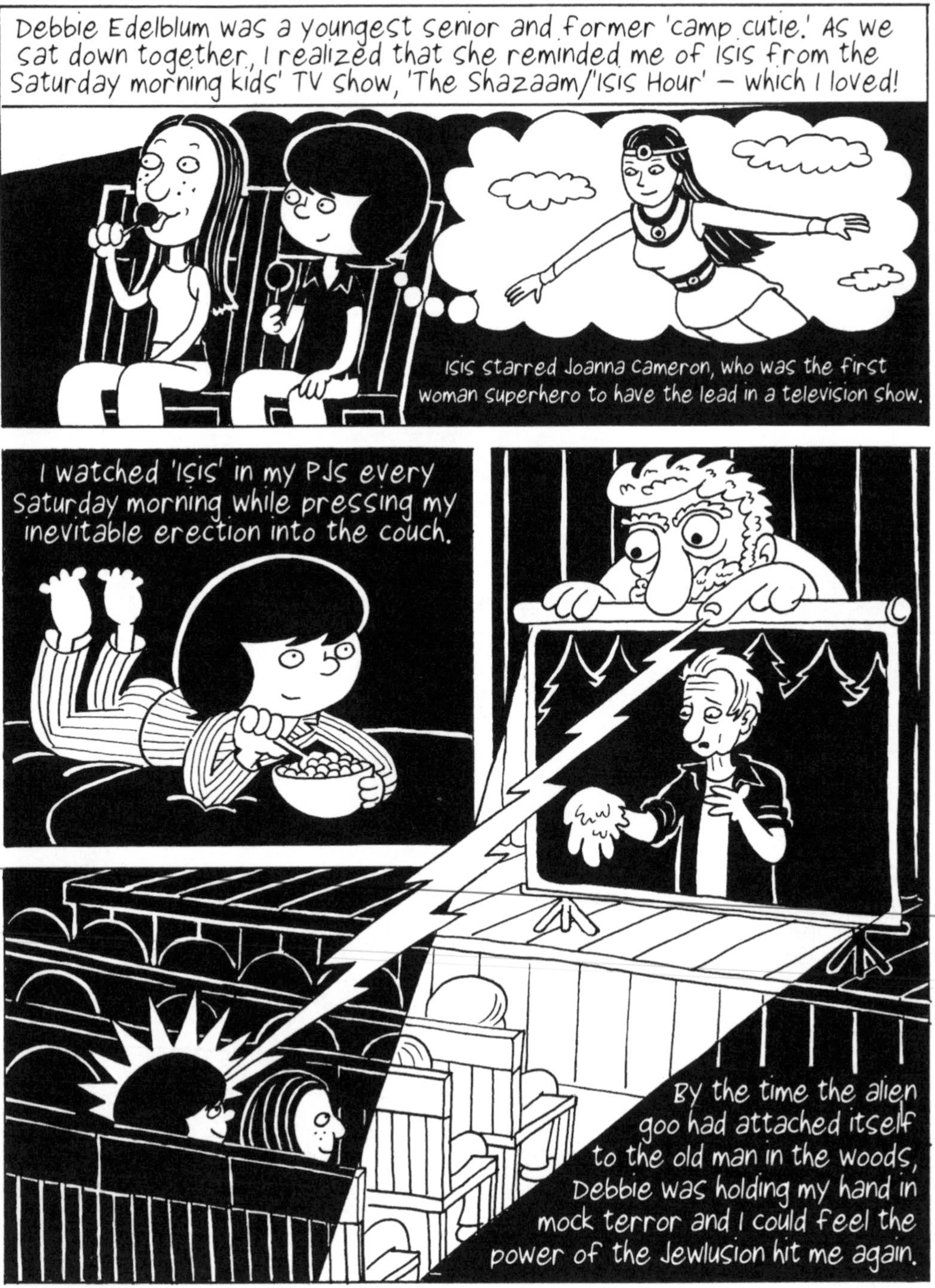

Debbie Edelblum was a youngest senior and former 'camp cutie.' As we sat down together, I realized that she reminded me of Isis from the Saturday morning kids' TV show, 'The Shazaam/'Isis Hour' – which I loved!
Isis starred Joanna Cameron, who was the first woman superhero to have the lead in a television show.
I watched 'Isis' in my PJs every Saturday morning while pressing my inevitable erection into the couch.
By the time the alien goo had attached itself to the old man in the woods, Debbie was holding my hand in mock terror and I could feel the power of the Jewlusion hit me again.

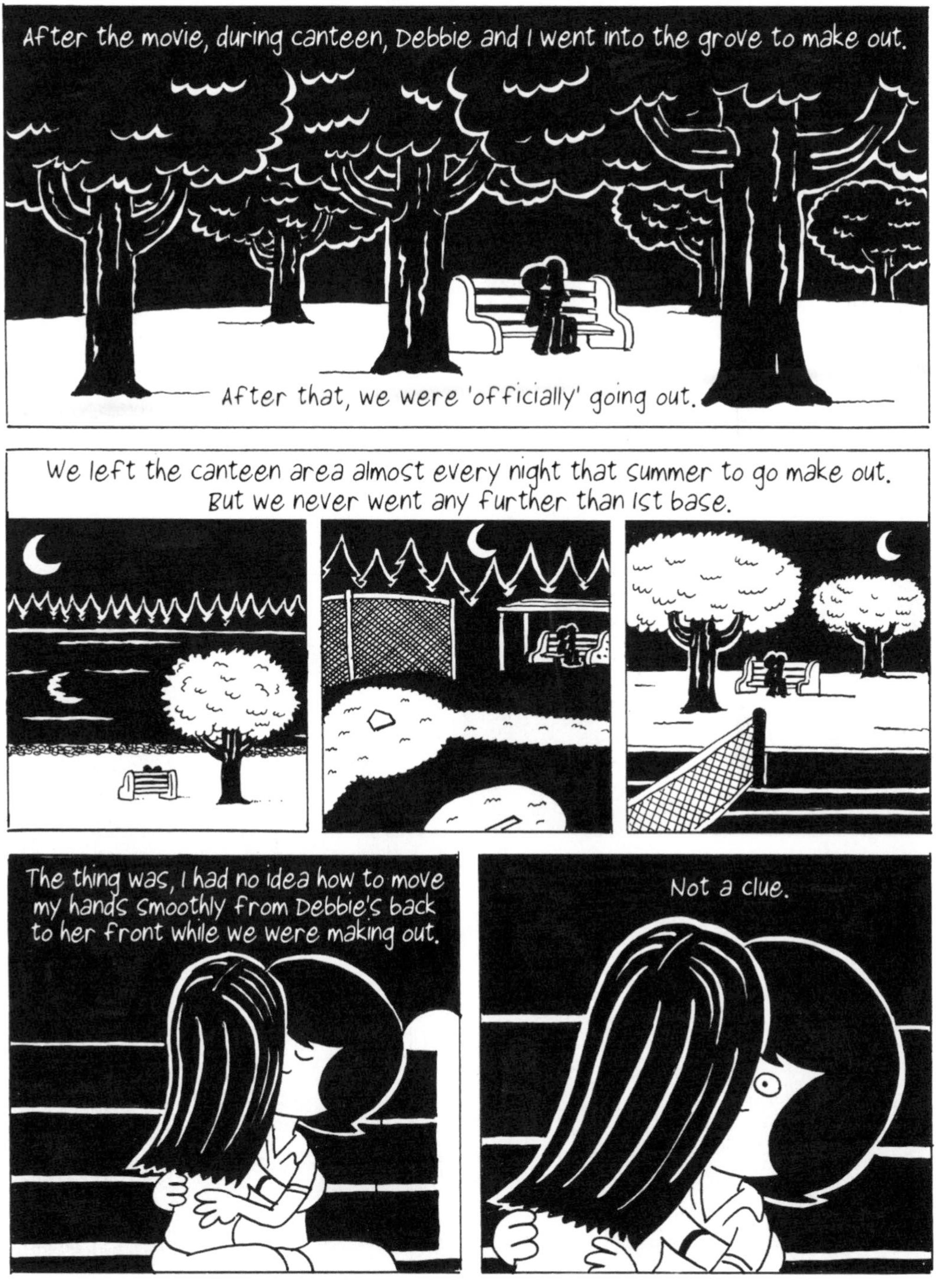
After the movie, during canteen, Debbie and I went into the grove to make out.
After that, we were 'officially' going out.
We left the canteen area almost every night that summer to go make out.
But we never went any further than 1st base.
The thing was, I had no idea how to move my hands smoothly from Debbie's back to her front while we were making out.
Not a clue.

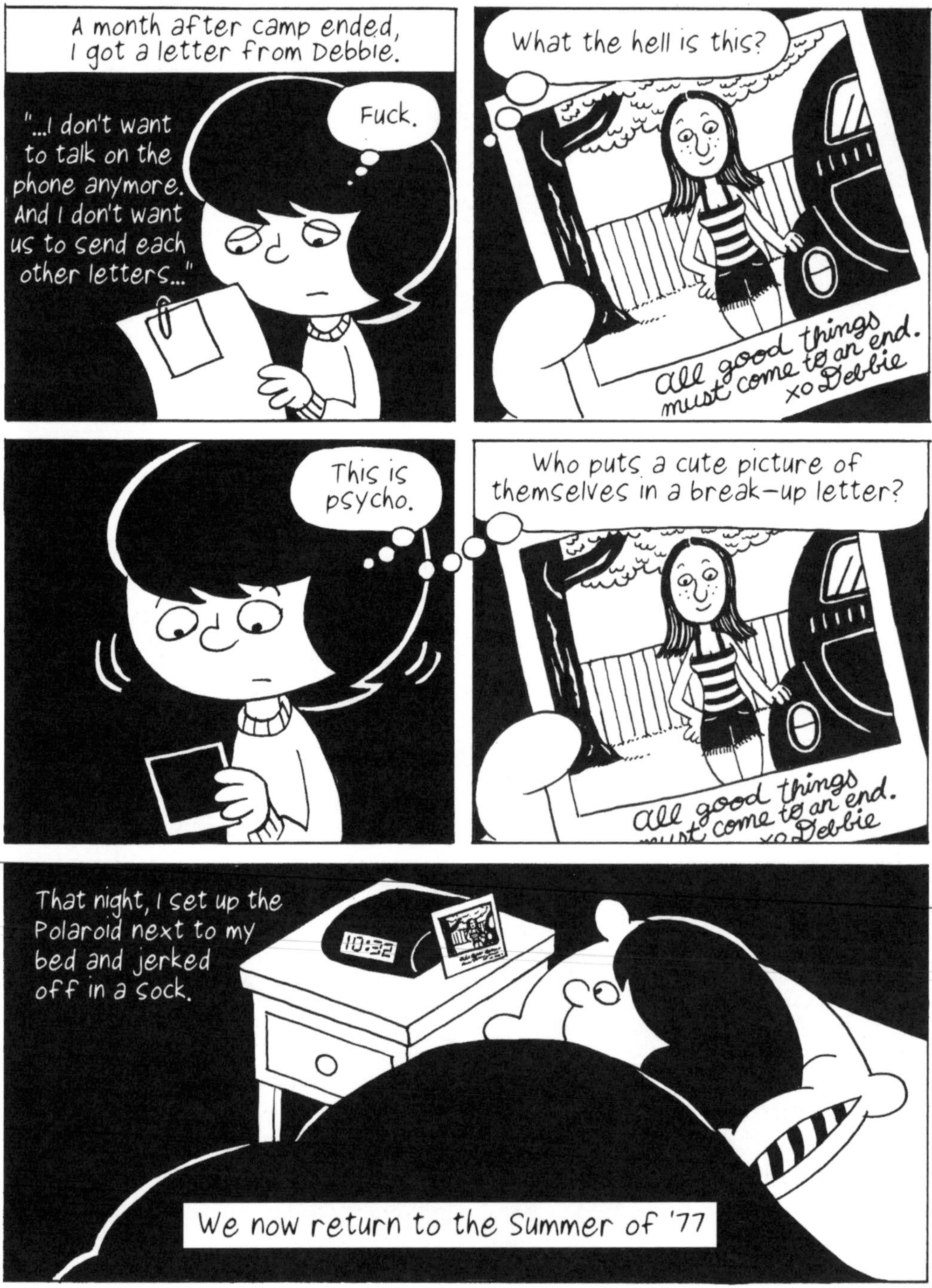
A month after camp ended, I got a letter from Debbie.
"...I don't want to talk on the phone anymore. And I don't want us to send each other letters..."
Fuck.
What the hell is this?
All good things must come to an end. xo Debbie
This is psycho.
Who puts a cute picture of themselves in a break-up letter?
All good things must come to an end. xo Debbie
That night, I set up the Polaroid next to my bed and jerked off in a sock.
10:32
We now return to the Summer of '77

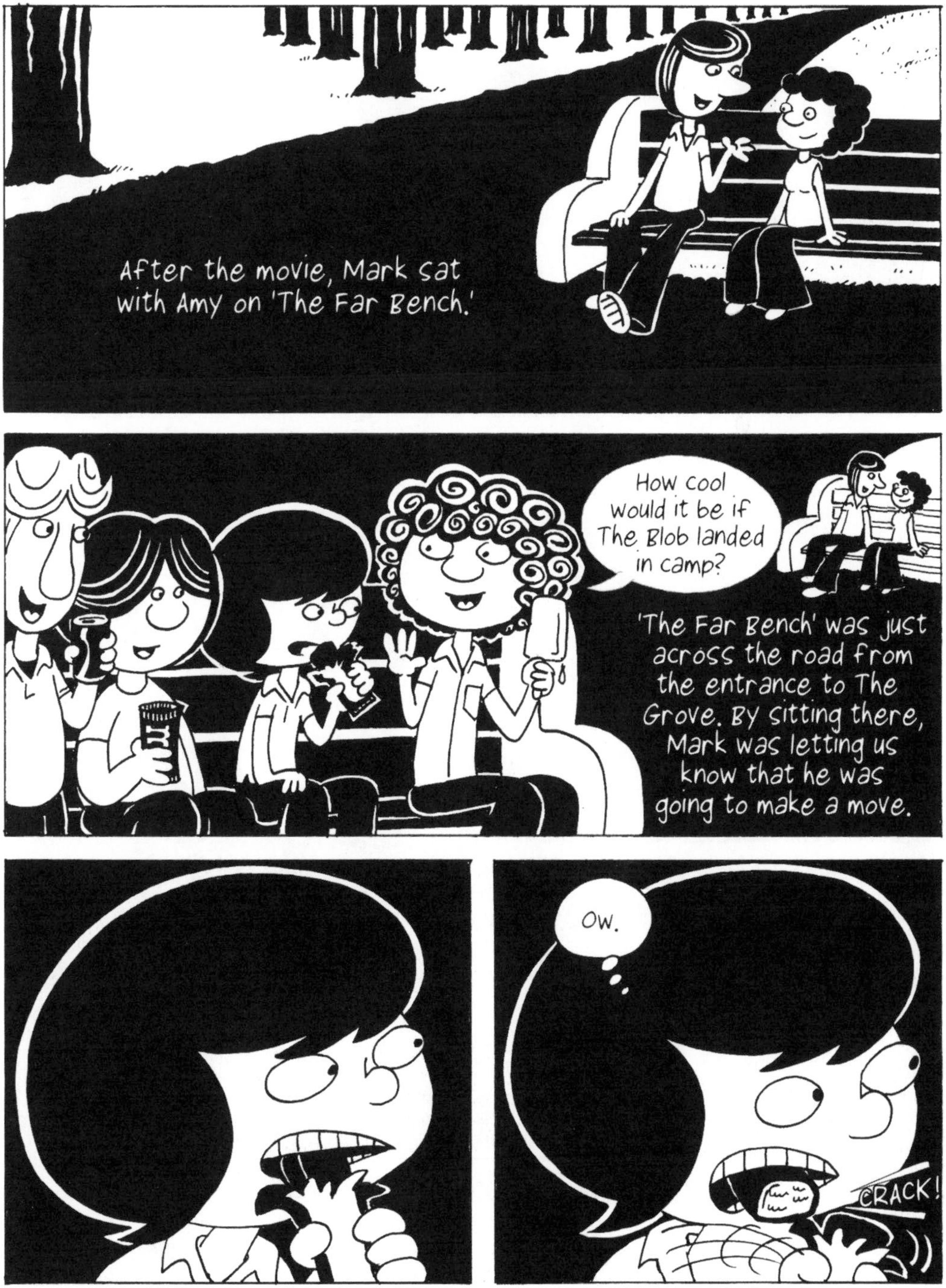
After the movie, Mark sat with Amy on 'The Far Bench.'
How cool would it be if The Blob landed in camp?
'The Far Bench' was just across the road from the entrance to The Grove. By sitting there, Mark was letting us know that he was going to make a move.
OW.
CRACK!

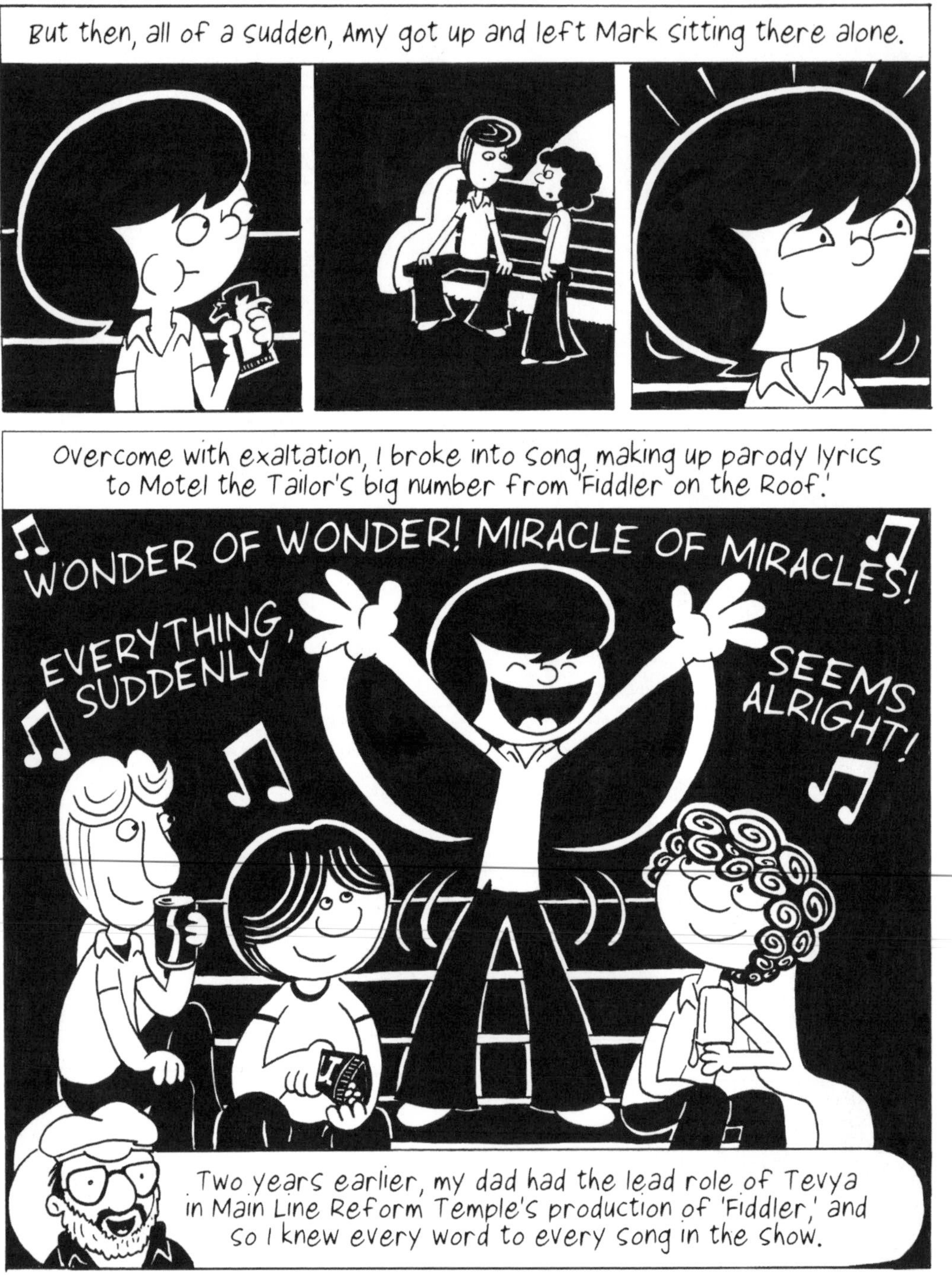
But then, all of a sudden, Amy got up and left Mark sitting there alone.
Overcome with exaltation, I broke into song, making up parody lyrics to Motel the Tailor's big number from 'Fiddler on the Roof.'
WONDER OF WONDER! MIRACLE OF MIRACLES!
EVERYTHING, SUDDENLY
SEEMS ALRIGHT!
Two years earlier, my dad had the lead role of Tevya in Main Line Reform Temple's production of 'Fiddler,' and so I knew every word to every song in the show.

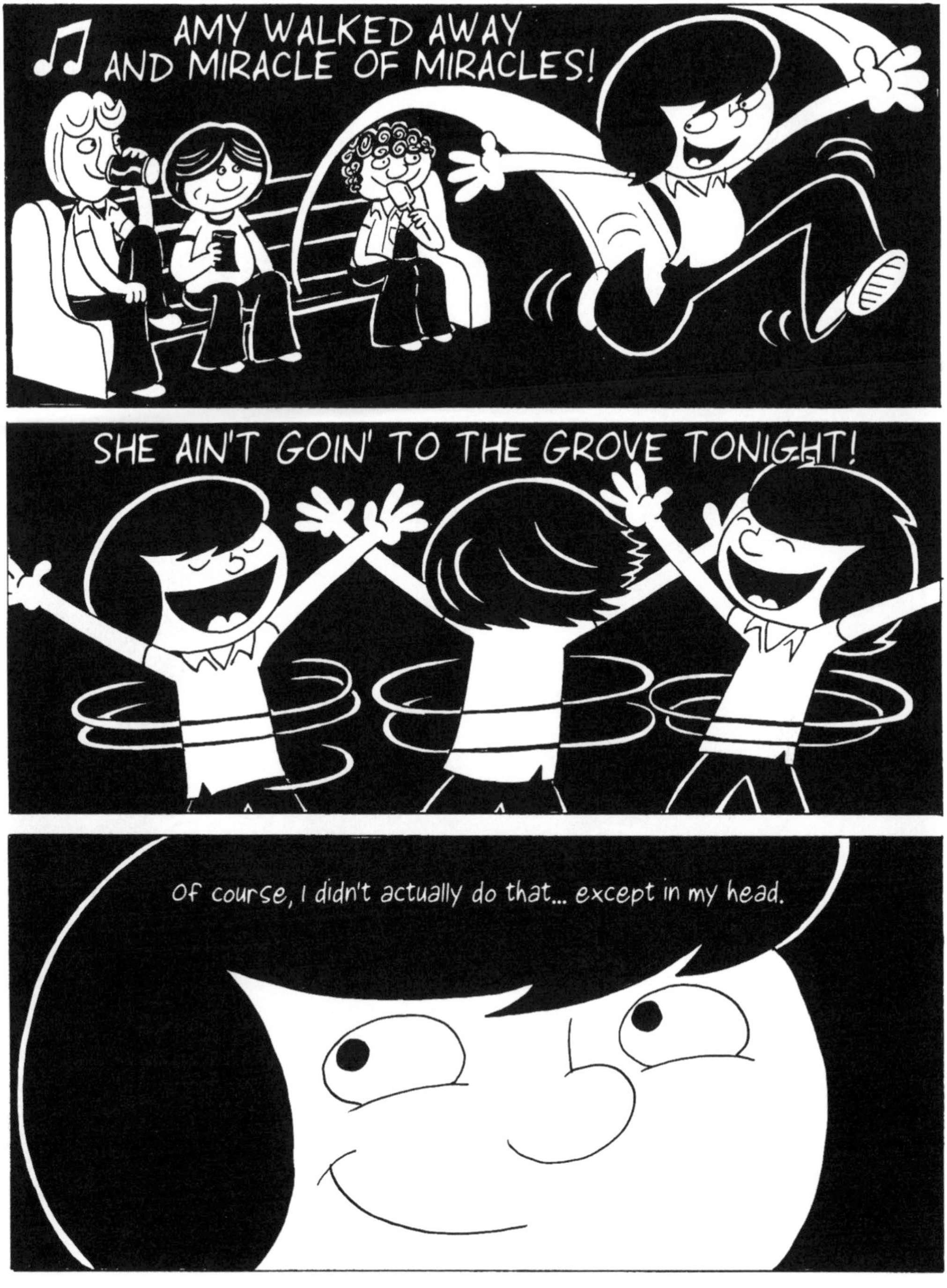
♫ AMY WALKED AWAY
AND MIRACLE OF MIRACLES!
SHE AIN'T GOIN' TO THE GROVE TONIGHT!
Of course, I didn't actually do that... except in my head.

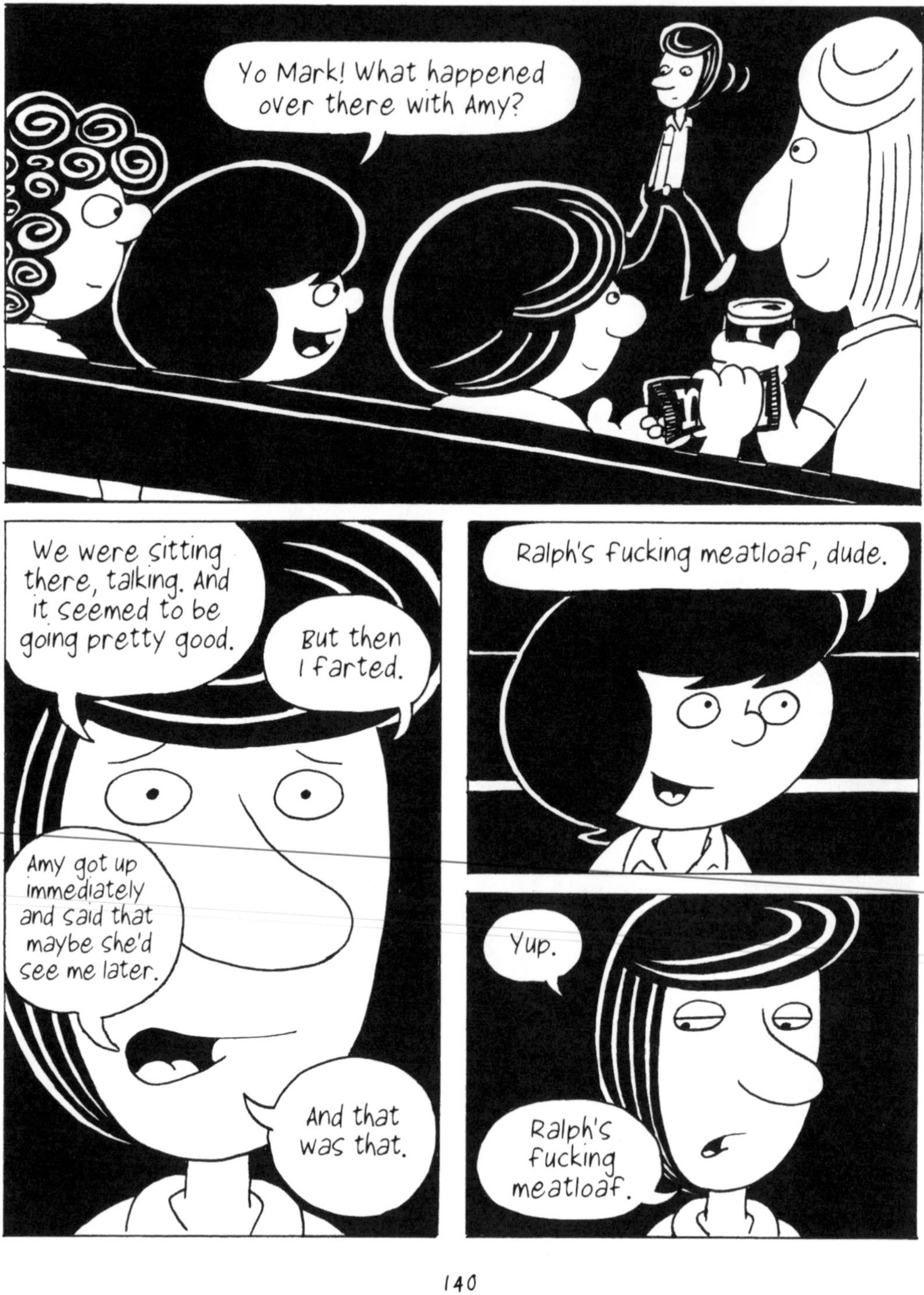
Yo Mark! What happened over there with Amy?
We were sitting there, talking. And it seemed to be going pretty good.
But then I farted.
Amy got up immediately and said that maybe she'd see me later.
And that was that.
Ralph's fucking meatloaf, dude.
Yup.
Ralph's fucking meatloaf.

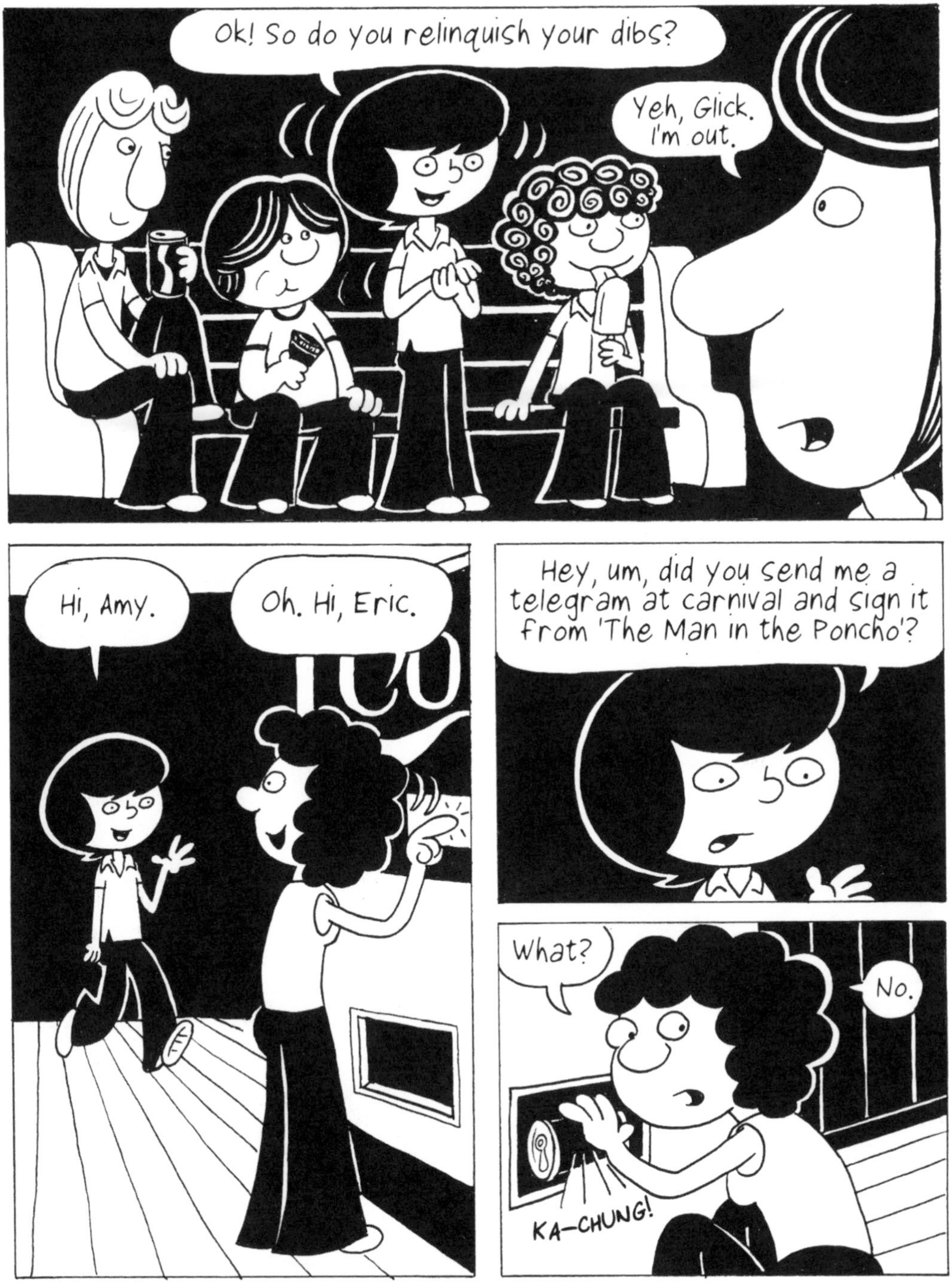
Ok! So do you relinquish your dibs?
Yeh, Glick. I'm out.
Hi, Amy.
Oh. Hi, Eric.
Hey, um, did you send me a telegram at carnival and sign it from 'The Man in the Poncho'?
What?
No.
KA-CHUNG!

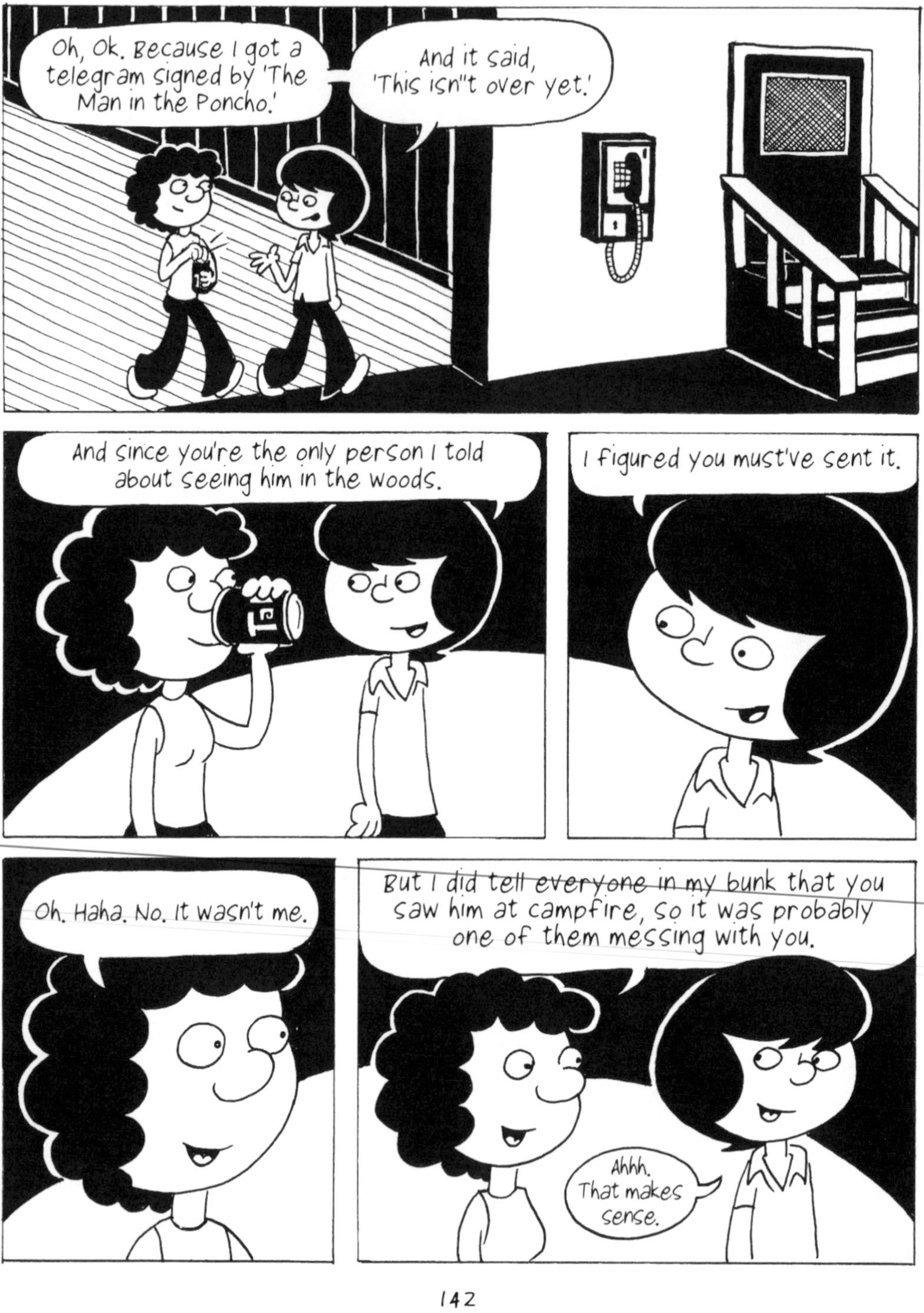
Oh, Ok. Because I got a telegram signed by 'The Man in the Poncho.'
And it said, 'This isn"t over yet.'
And since you're the only person I told about seeing him in the woods.
I figured you must've sent it.
Oh. Haha. No. It wasn't me.
But I did tell everyone in my bunk that you saw him at campfire, so it was probably one of them messing with you.
Ahhh. That makes sense.

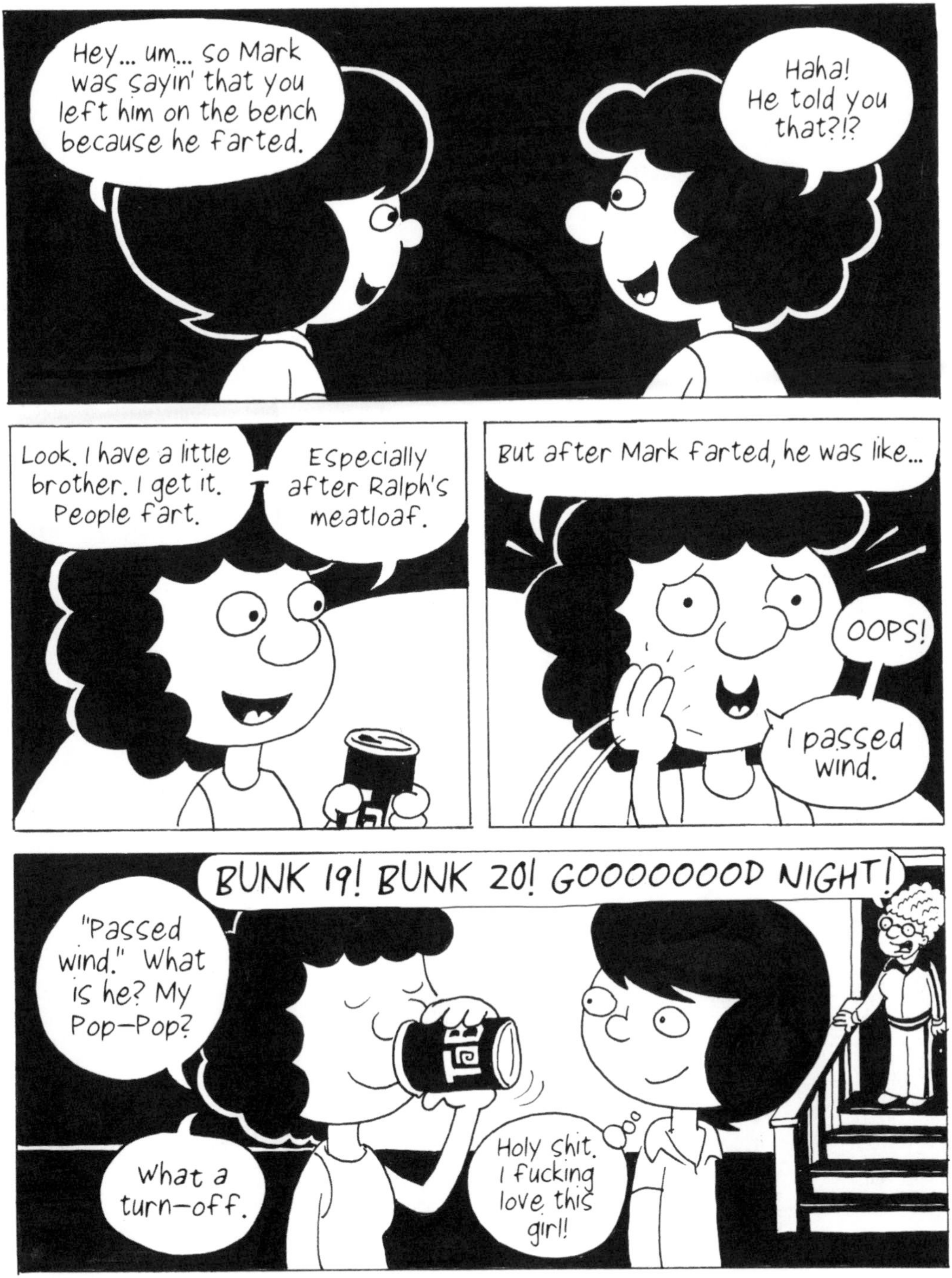
Hey... um... So Mark was sayin' that you left him on the bench because he farted.
Haha! He told you that?!?
Look. I have a little brother. I get it. People fart.
Especially after Ralph's meatloaf.
But after Mark farted, he was like...
OOPS!
I passed wind.
BUNK 19! BUNK 20! GOOOOOOOD NIGHT!
"Passed wind." What is he? My Pop-Pop?
What a turn-off.
Holy shit. I fucking love this girl!

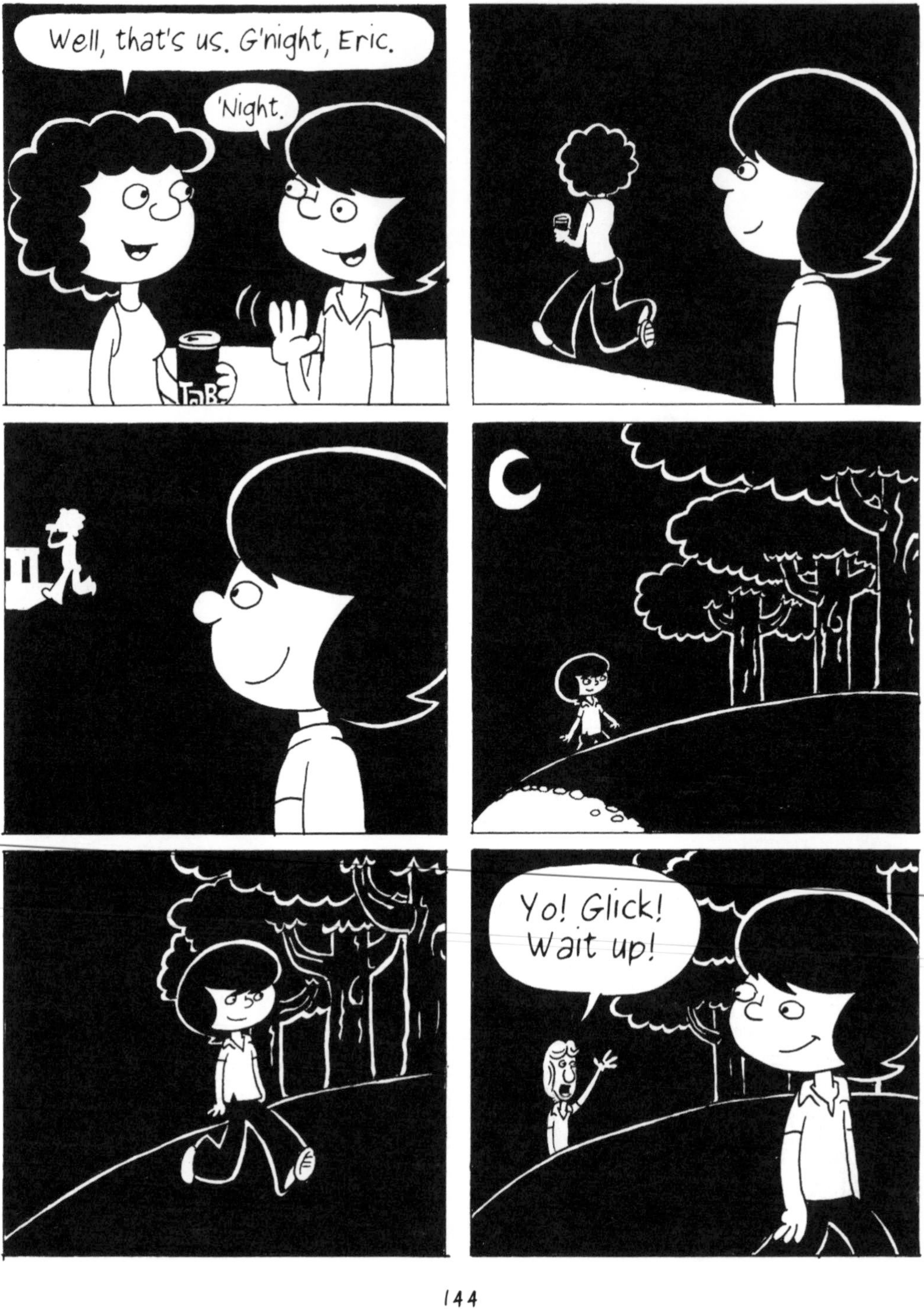
Well, that's us. G'night, Eric.
'Night.
TaB
Yo! Glick! Wait up!

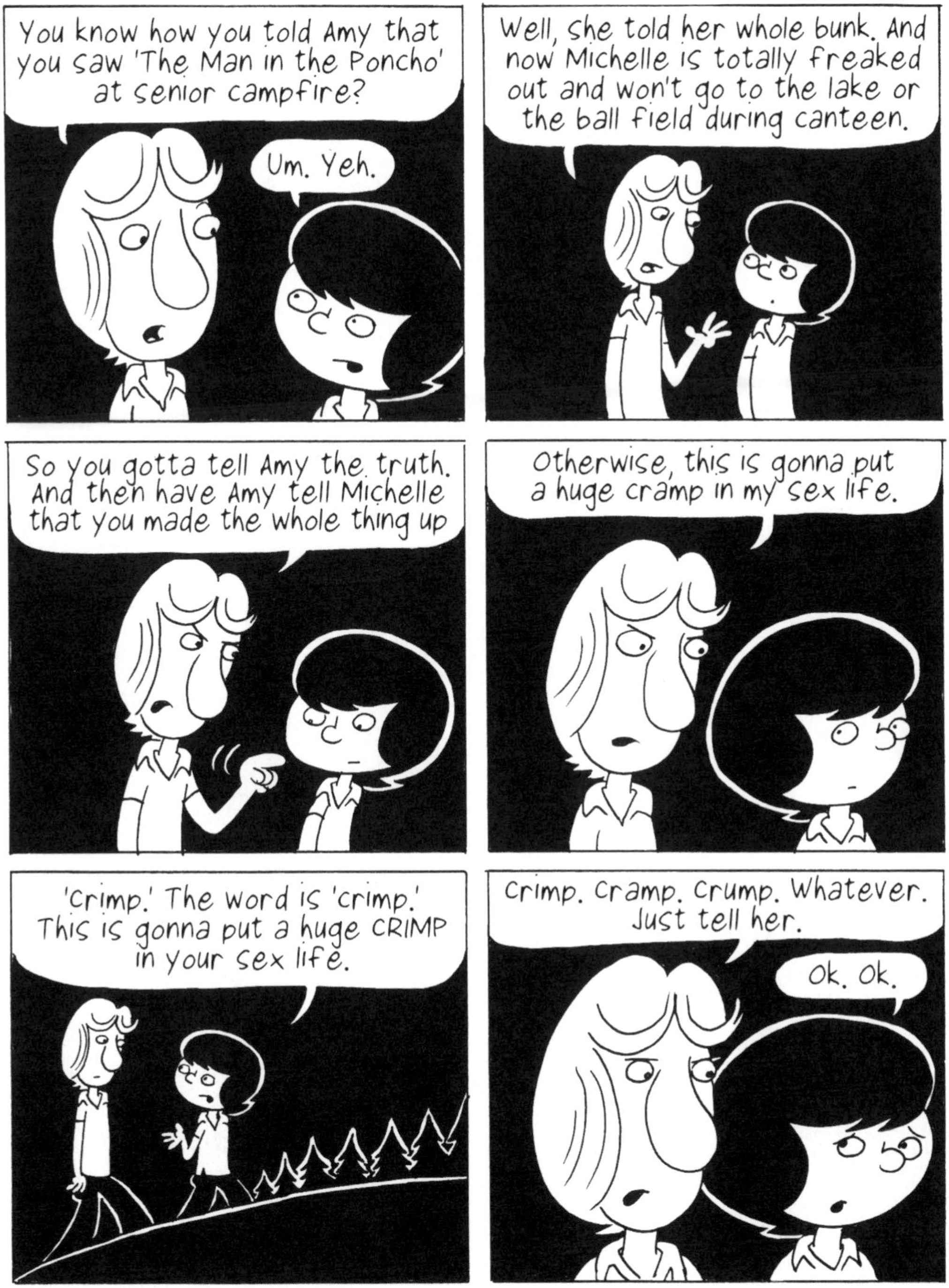
You know how you told Amy that you saw 'The Man in the Poncho' at senior campfire?
Um. Yeh.
Well, she told her whole bunk. And now Michelle is totally freaked out and won't go to the lake or the ball field during canteen.
So you gotta tell Amy the truth. And then have Amy tell Michelle that you made the whole thing up
Otherwise, this is gonna put a huge cramp in my sex life.
'Crimp.' The word is 'crimp.' This is gonna put a huge CRIMP in your sex life.
Crimp. Cramp. Crump. Whatever. Just tell her.
Ok. Ok.

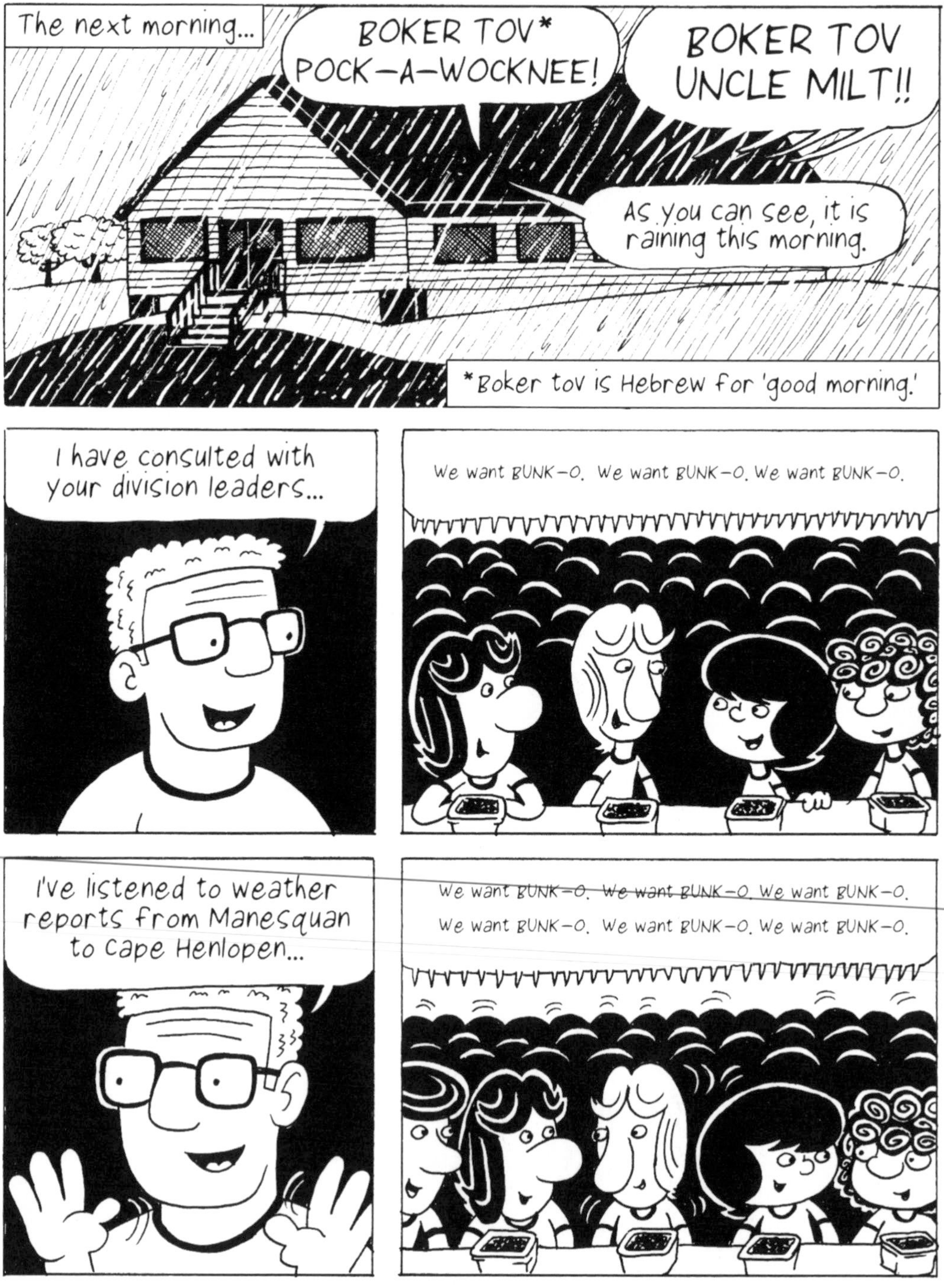
The next morning...
BOKER TOV* POCK-A-WOCKNEE!
BOKER TOV UNCLE MILT!!
As you can see, it is raining this morning.
*Boker tov is Hebrew for 'good morning.'
I have consulted with your division leaders...
We want BUNK-O. We want BUNK-O. We want BUNK-O.
I've listened to weather reports from Manesquan to Cape Henlopen...
We want BUNK-O. We want BUNK-O. We want BUNK-O.
We want BUNK-O. We want BUNK-O. We want BUNK-O.

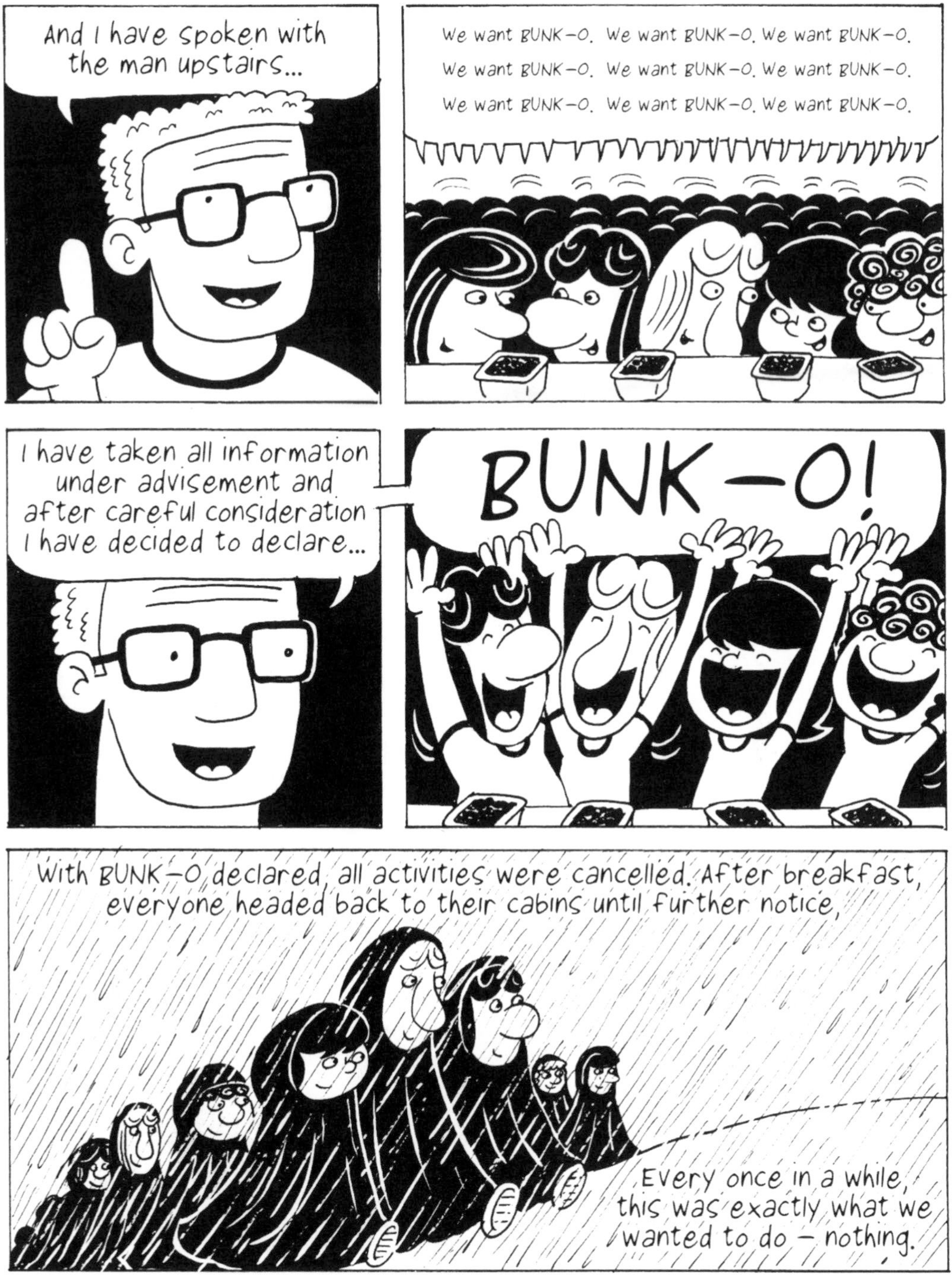

And I have spoken with the man upstairs...
We want BUNK-O. We want BUNK-O. We want BUNK-O.
We want BUNK-O. We want BUNK-O. We want BUNK-O.
We want BUNK-O. We want BUNK-O. We want BUNK-O.
I have taken all information under advisement and after careful consideration I have decided to declare...
BUNK-O!
With BUNK-O declared, all activities were cancelled. After breakfast, everyone headed back to their cabins until further notice,
Every once in a while, this was exactly what we wanted to do - nothing.

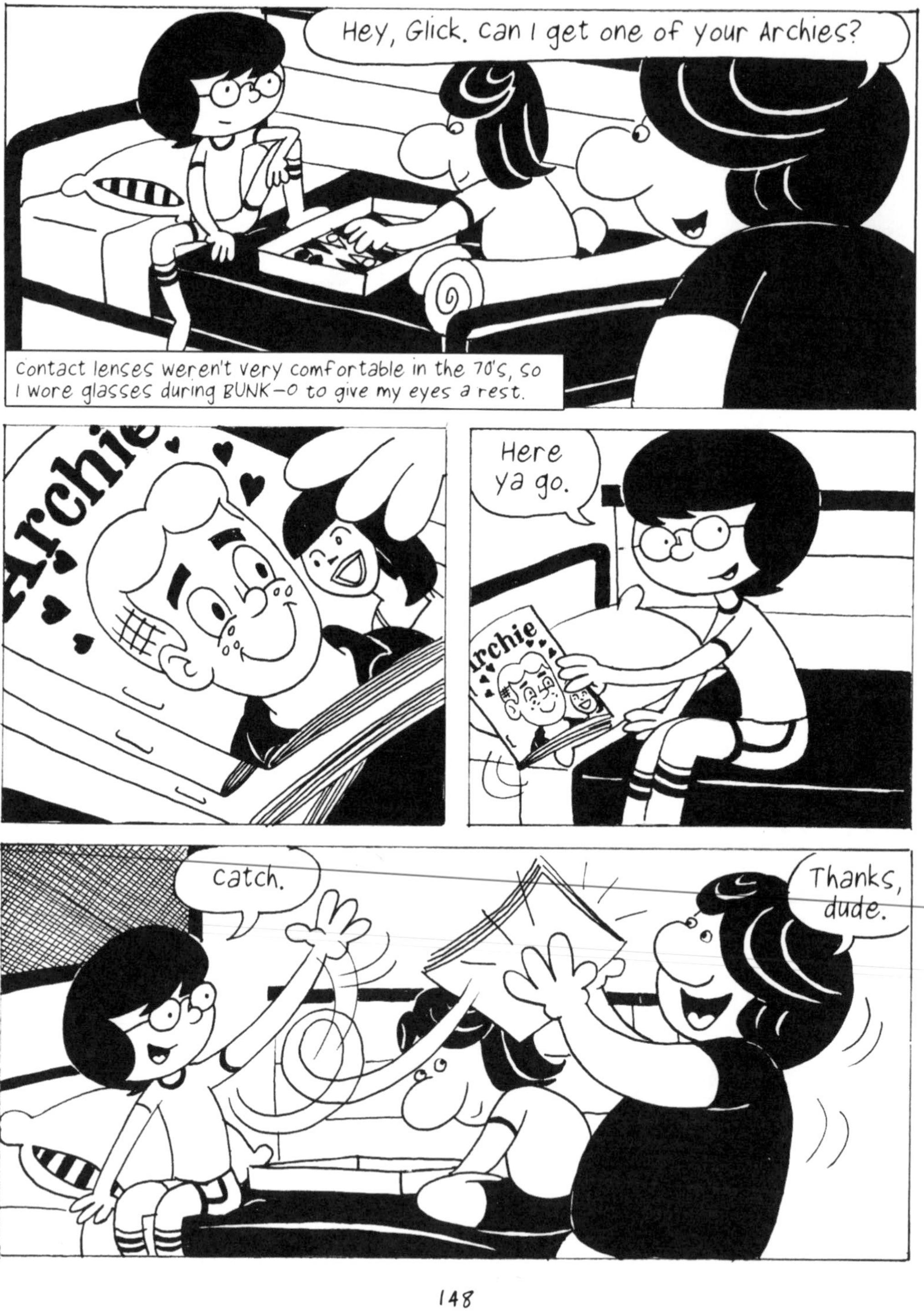
Hey, Glick. Can I get one of your Archies?
Contact lenses weren't very comfortable in the 70's, so I wore glasses during BUNK-O to give my eyes a rest.
Archie
Here ya go.
Archie
Catch.
Thanks, dude.

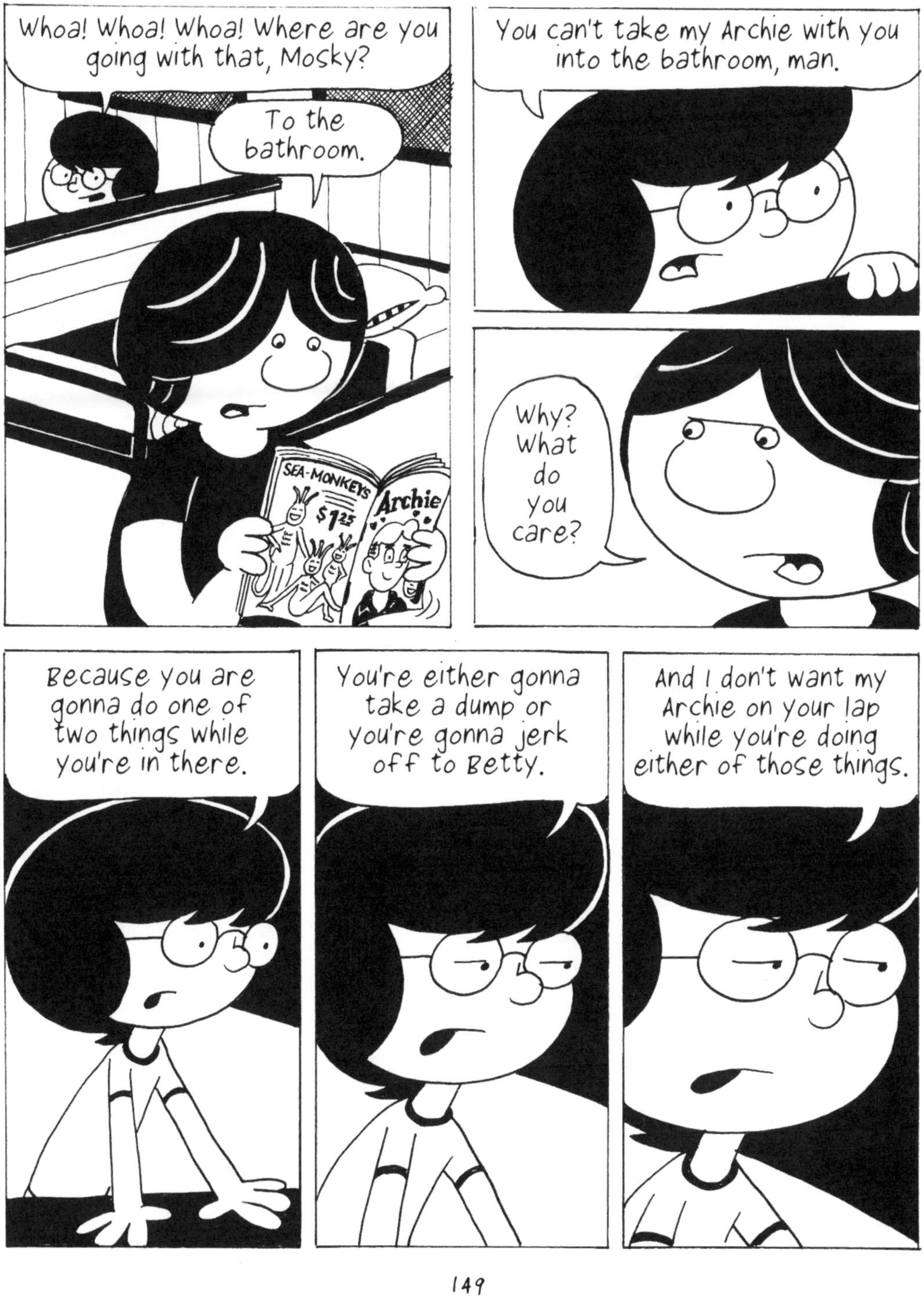
Whoa! Whoa! Whoa! Where are you going with that, Mosky?
To the bathroom.
SEA-MONKEYS
$1.25
Archie
You can't take my Archie with you into the bathroom, man.
Why? What do you care?
Because you are gonna do one of two things while you're in there.
You're either gonna take a dump or you're gonna jerk off to Betty.
And I don't want my Archie on your lap while you're doing either of those things.

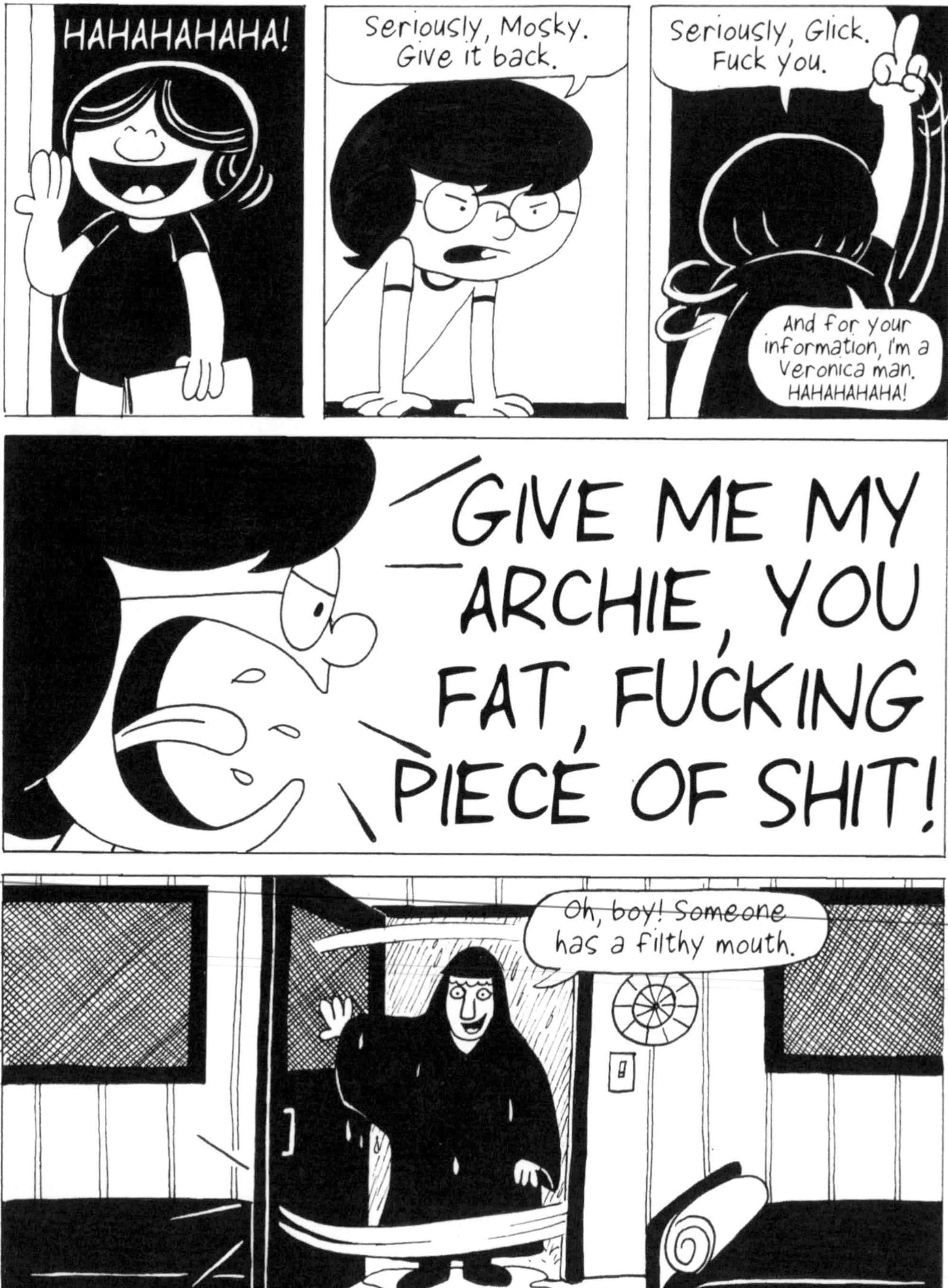
HAHAHAHAHA!
Seriously, Mosky. Give it back.
Seriously, Glick. Fuck you.
And for your information, I'm a Veronica man. HAHAHAHAHA!
GIVE ME MY ARCHIE, YOU FAT, FUCKING PIECE OF SHIT!
Oh, boy! Someone has a filthy mouth.

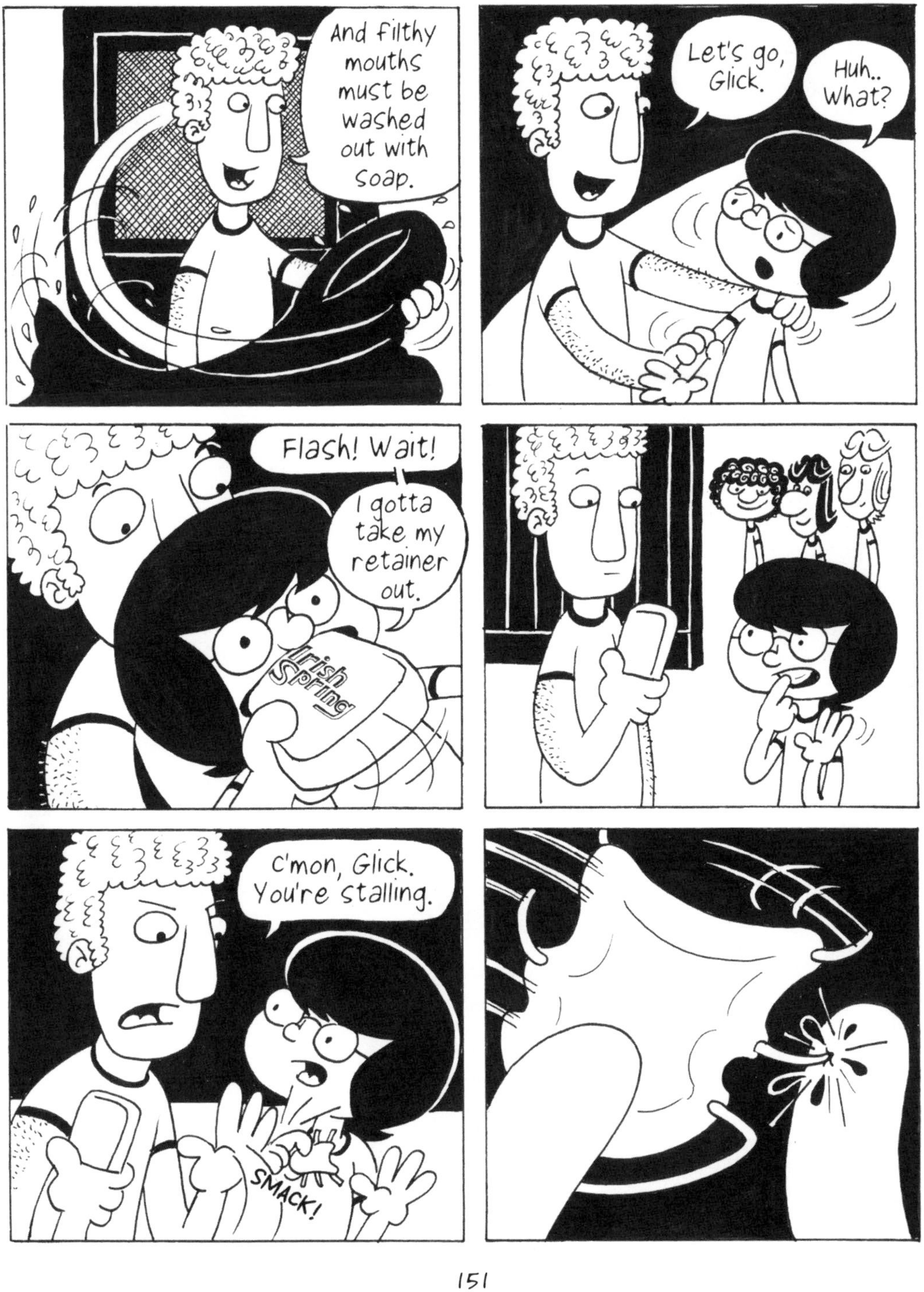
And filthy mouths must be washed out with soap.
Let's go, Glick.
Huh.. What?
Flash! Wait!
I gotta take my retainer out.
Irish Spring
C'mon, Glick. You're stalling.
SMACK!

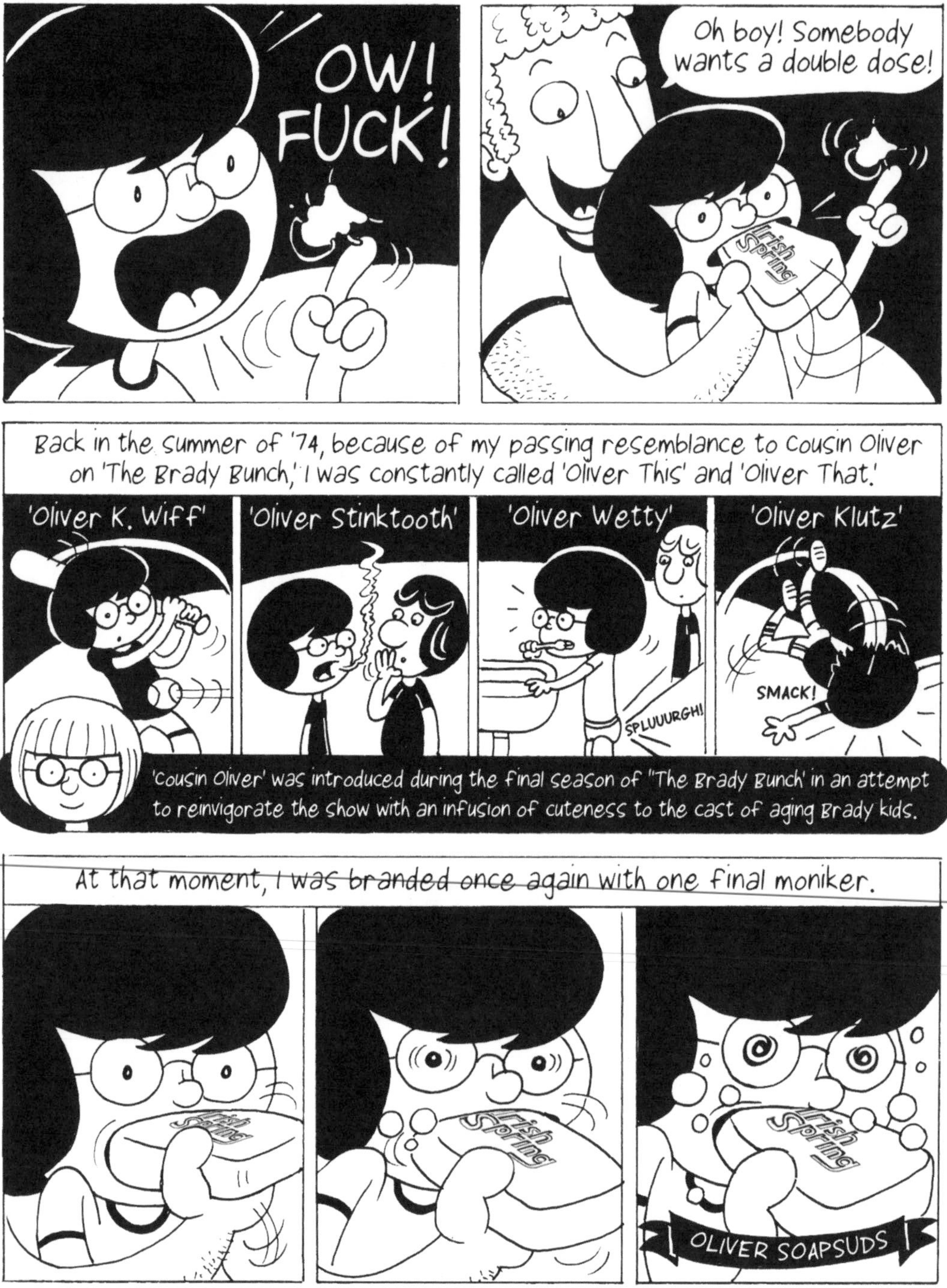
OW! FUCK!
Oh boy! Somebody wants a double dose!
Irish Spring
Back in the summer of '74, because of my passing resemblance to Cousin Oliver on 'The Brady Bunch,' I was constantly called 'Oliver This' and 'Oliver That.'
'Oliver K. Wiff'
'Oliver Stinktooth'
'Oliver Wetty'
SPLUUURGH!
'Oliver Klutz'
SMACK!
'Cousin Oliver' was introduced during the final season of "The Brady Bunch' in an attempt to reinvigorate the show with an infusion of cuteness to the cast of aging Brady kids.
At that moment, I was branded once again with one final moniker.
Irish Spring
Irish Spring
Irish Spring
OLIVER SOAPSUDS

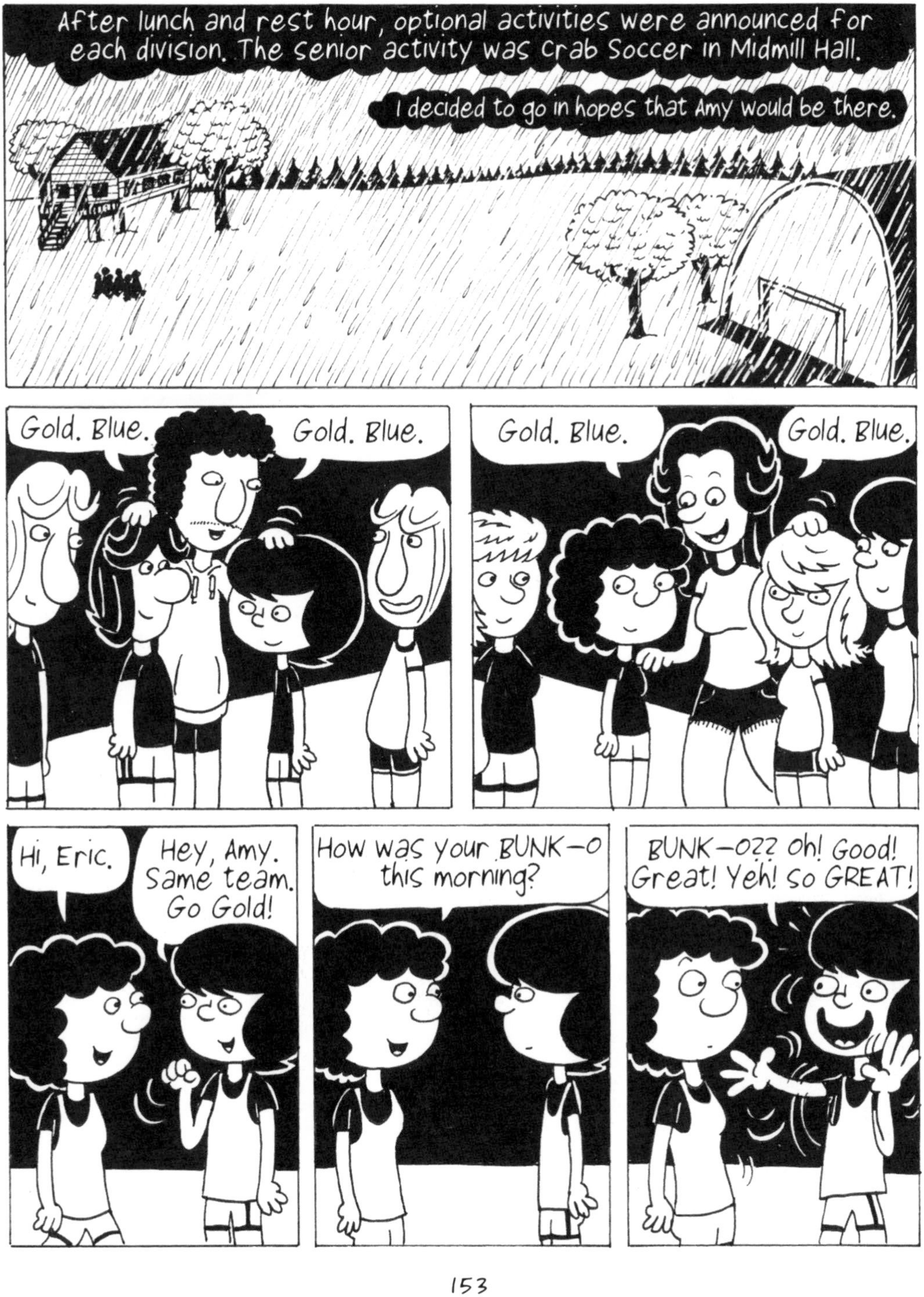
After lunch and rest hour, optional activities were announced for each division. The senior activity was Crab Soccer in Midmill Hall.
I decided to go in hopes that Amy would be there.
Gold. Blue.
Gold. Blue.
Gold. Blue.
Gold. Blue.
Hi, Eric.
Hey, Amy. Same team. Go Gold!
How was your BUNK-O this morning?
BUNK-O?? Oh! Good! Great! Yeh! So GREAT!

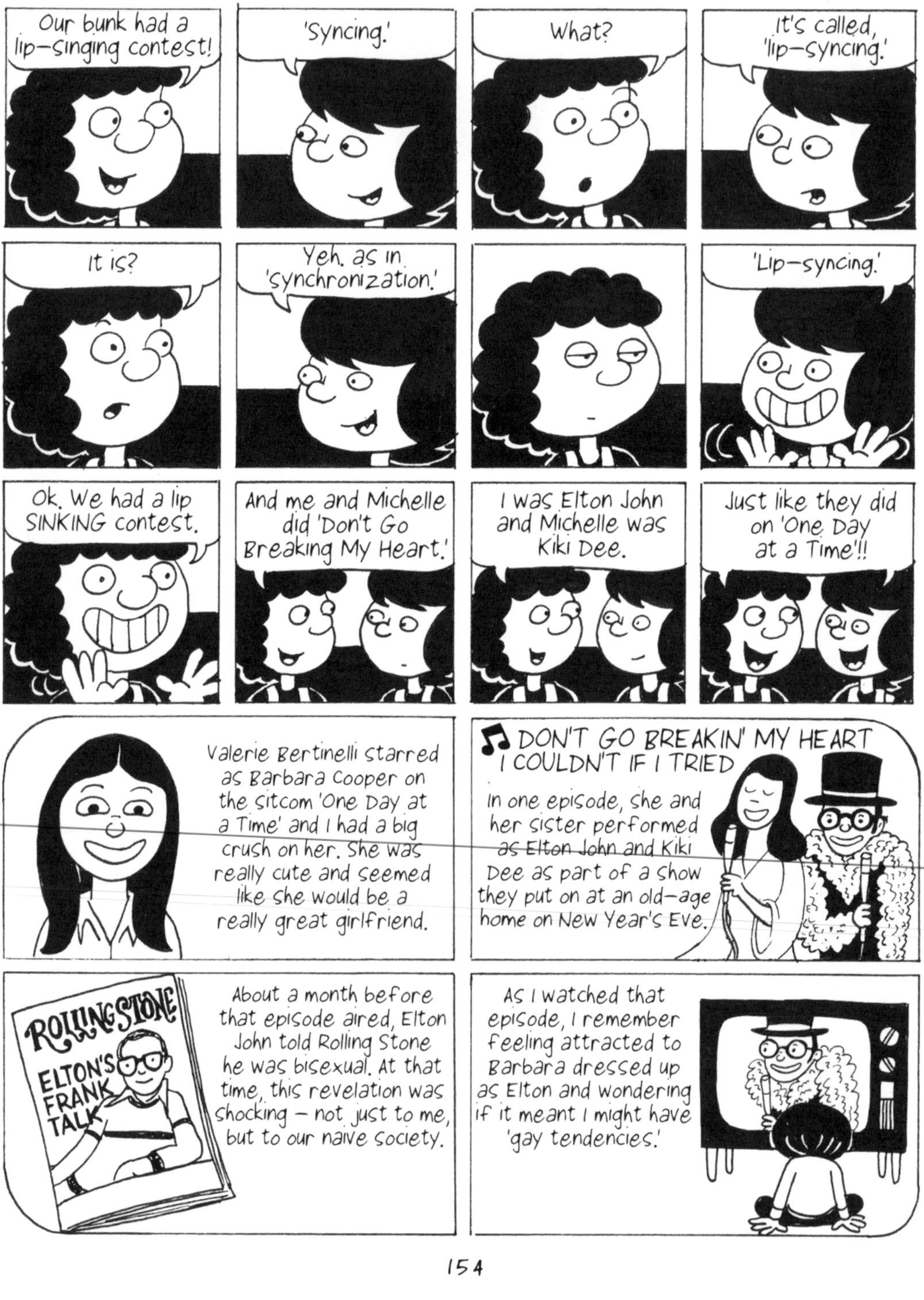
Our bunk had a lip-singing contest!
'Syncing.'
What?
It's called, 'lip-syncing.'
It is?
Yeh. as in 'synchronization.'
'Lip-syncing.'
Ok. We had a lip SINKING contest.
And me and Michelle did 'Don't Go Breaking My Heart.'
I was Elton John and Michelle was Kiki Dee.
Just like they did on 'One Day at a Time'!!
Valerie Bertinelli starred as Barbara Cooper on the sitcom 'One Day at a Time' and I had a big crush on her. She was really cute and seemed like she would be a really great girlfriend.
DON'T GO BREAKIN' MY HEART I COULDN'T IF I TRIED
In one episode, she and her sister performed as Elton John and Kiki Dee as part of a show they put on at an old-age home on New Year's Eve.
ROLLING STONE
ELTON'S FRANK TALK
About a month before that episode aired, Elton John told Rolling Stone he was bisexual. At that time, this revelation was shocking – not just to me, but to our naive society.
As I watched that episode, I remember feeling attracted to Barbara dressed up as Elton and wondering if it meant I might have 'gay tendencies.'

Everyone thought we were really good, so I think we're gonna do it for Talent Show.

TWEET!

Ok, people! Let's go! Line it up! Blue on this side! Gold over there!

ugh.

LET'S GET CRABBY!

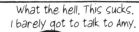

What the hell. This sucks. I barely got to talk to Amy.

And there's no way to look cool playing crab soccer.

BONK!

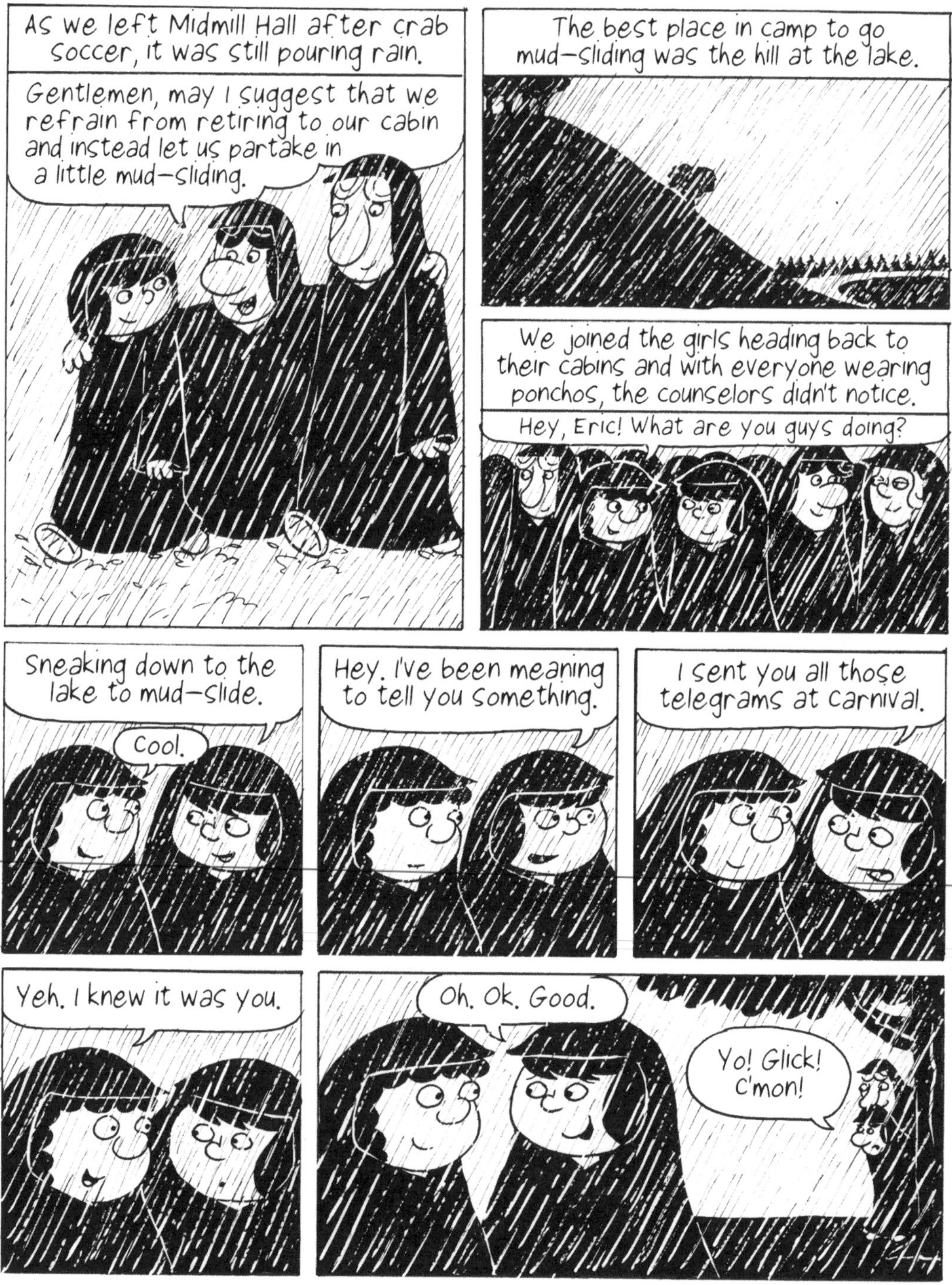
As we left Midmill Hall after crab soccer, it was still pouring rain.
Gentlemen, may I suggest that we refrain from retiring to our cabin and instead let us partake in a little mud-sliding.
The best place in camp to go mud-sliding was the hill at the lake.
We joined the girls heading back to their cabins and with everyone wearing ponchos, the counselors didn't notice.
Hey, Eric! What are you guys doing?
Sneaking down to the lake to mud-slide.
Cool.
Hey. I've been meaning to tell you something.
I sent you all those telegrams at carnival.
Yeh. I knew it was you.
Oh. Ok. Good.
Yo! Glick! C'mon!

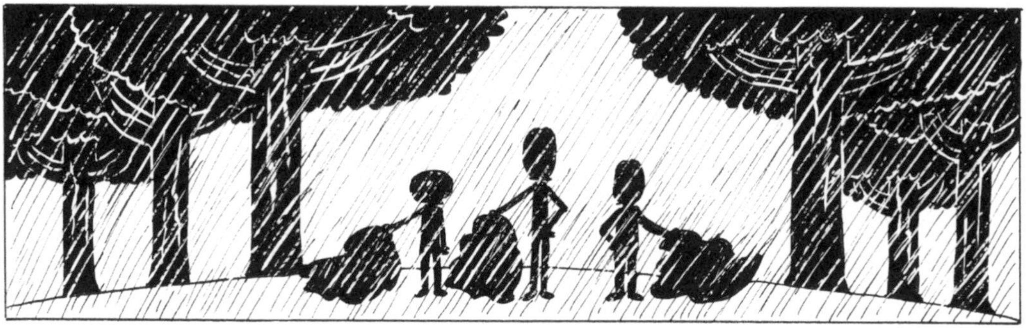

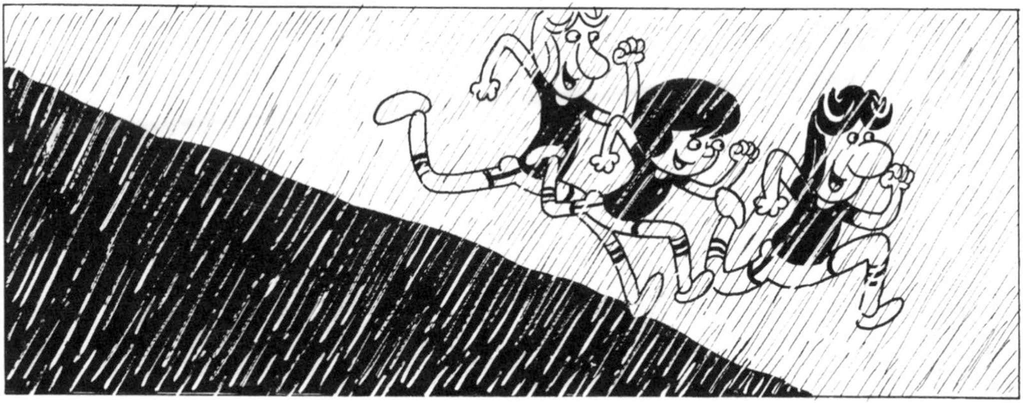

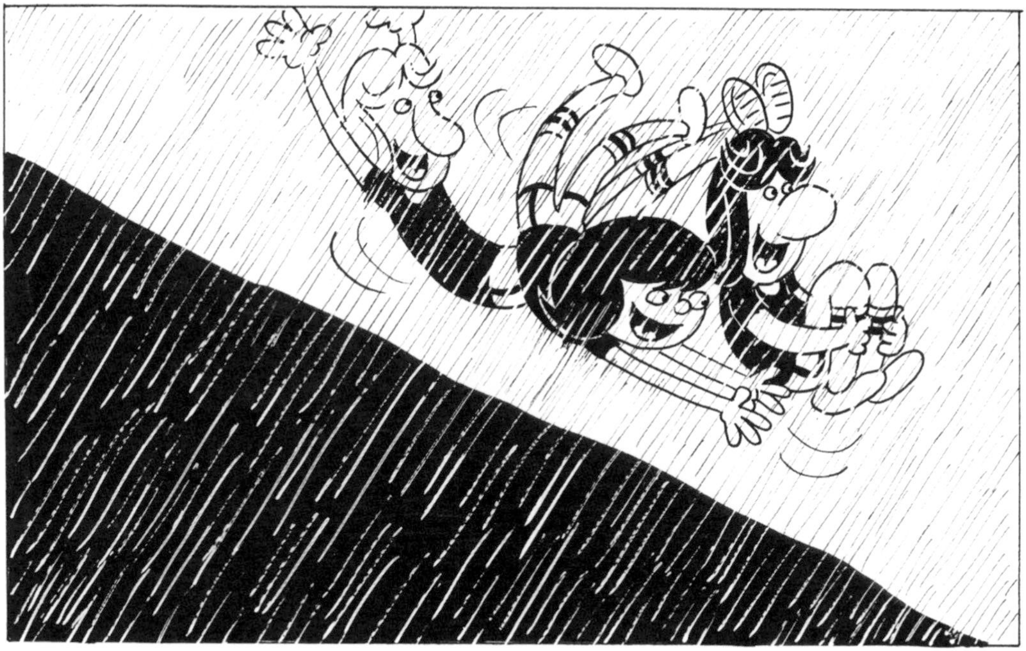

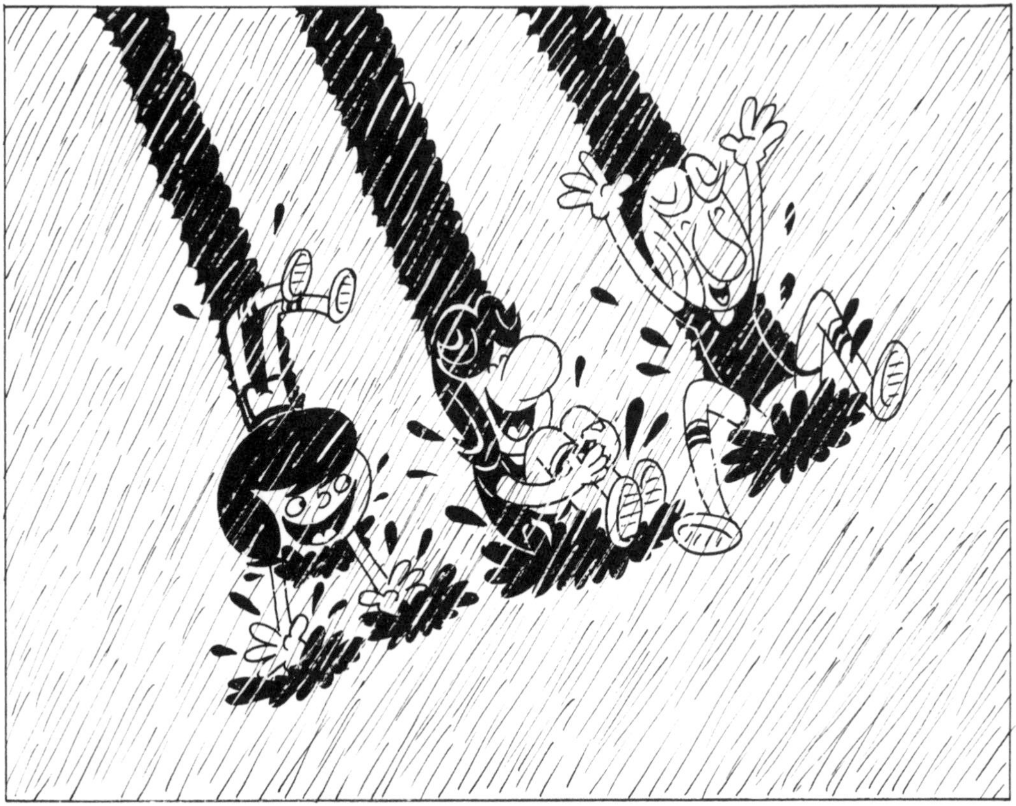

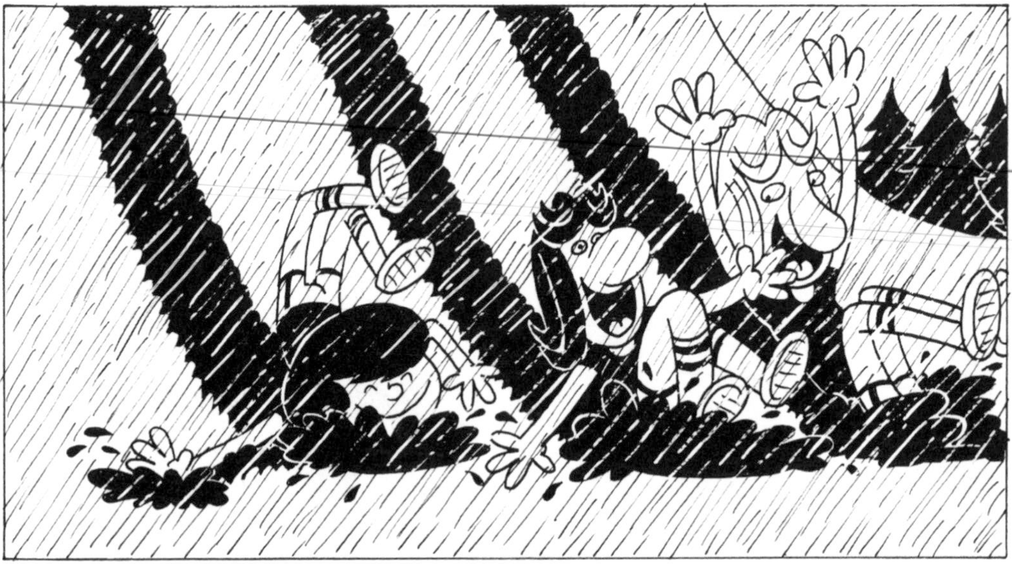

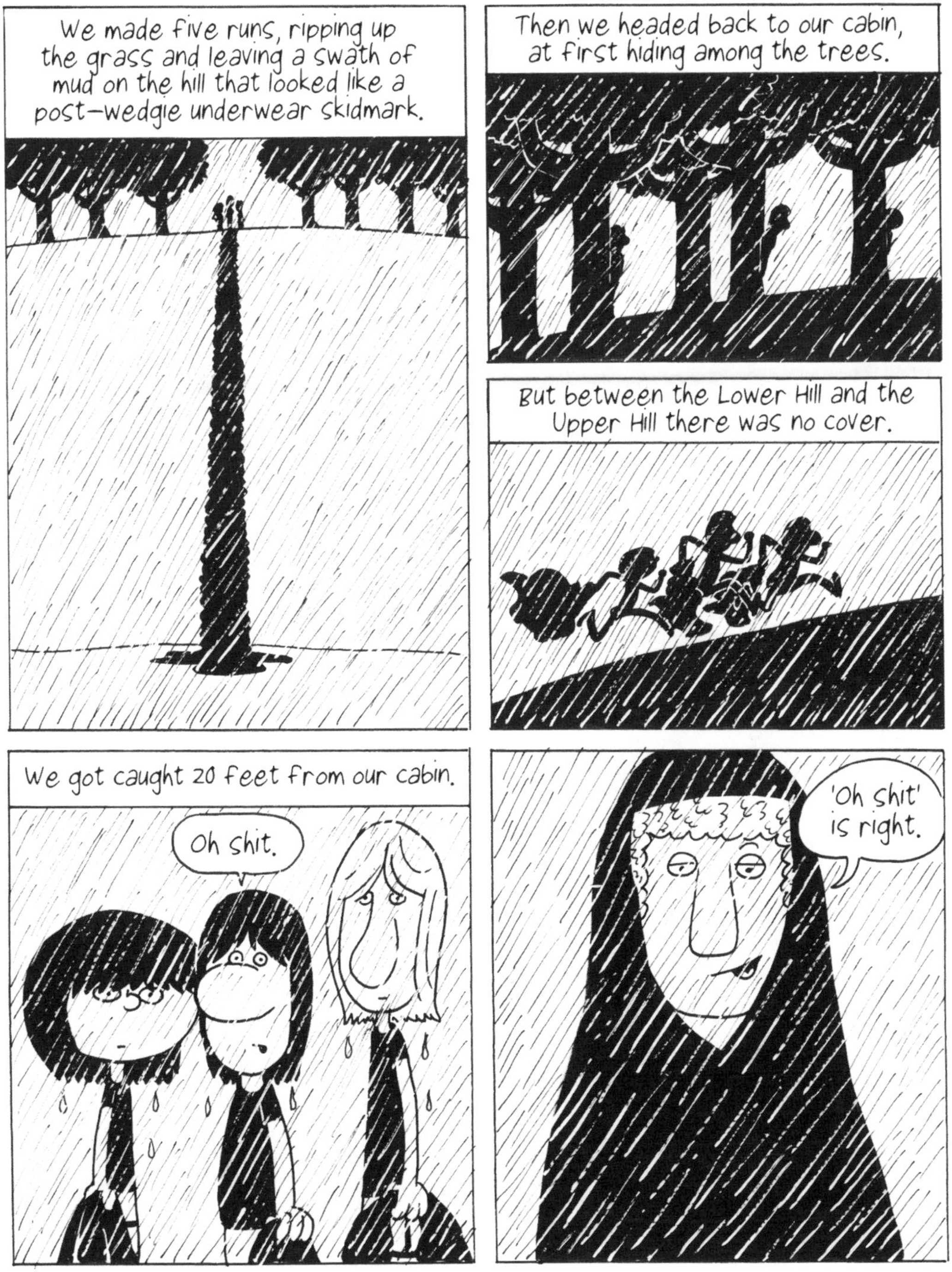
We made five runs, ripping up the grass and leaving a swath of mud on the hill that looked like a post—wedgie underwear skidmark.
Then we headed back to our cabin, at first hiding among the trees.
But between the Lower Hill and the Upper Hill there was no cover.
We got caught 20 feet from our cabin.
Oh shit.
'Oh shit' is right.

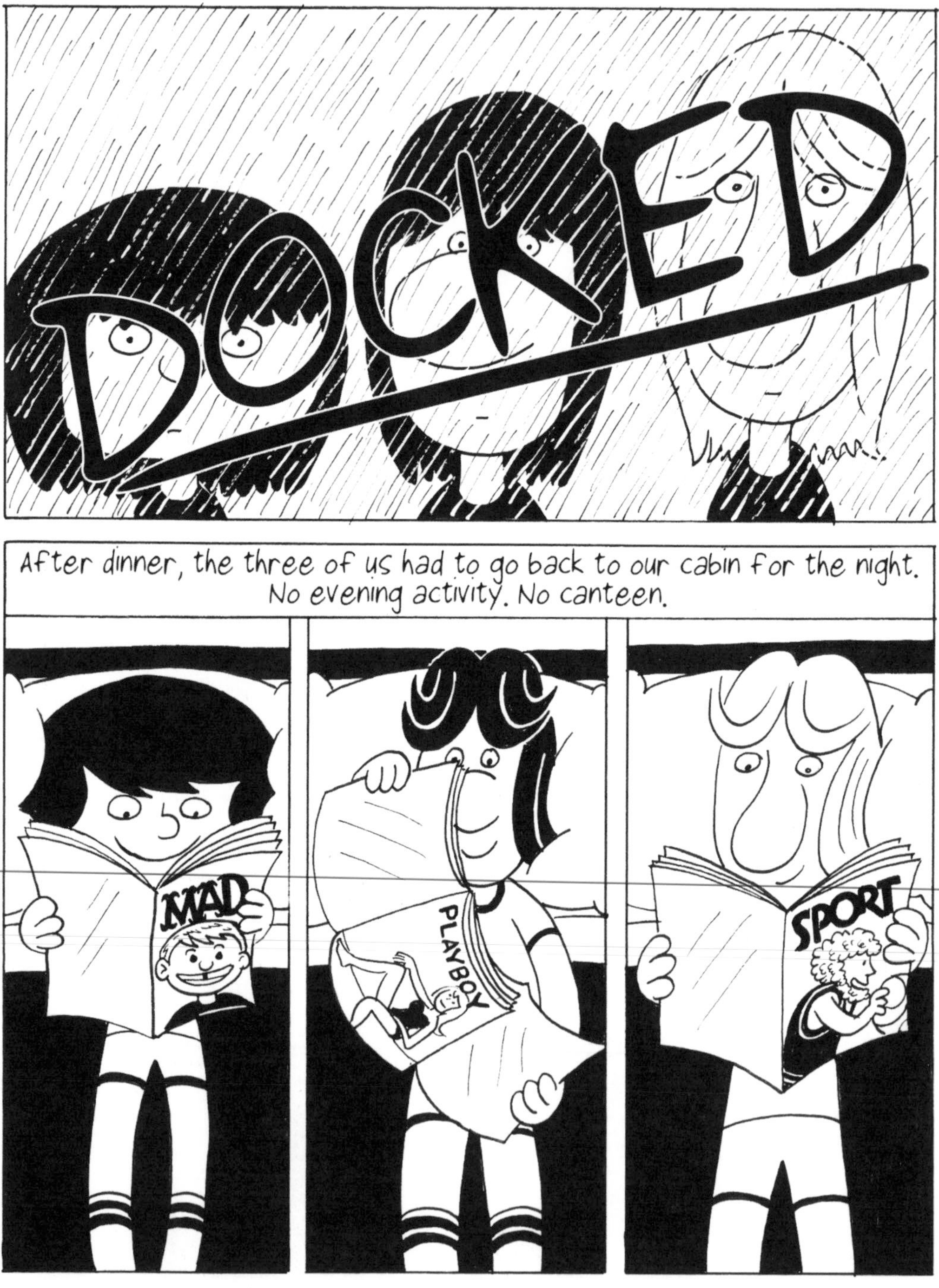
DOCKED
After dinner, the three of us had to go back to our cabin for the night. No evening activity. No canteen.
MAD
PLAYBOY
SPORT

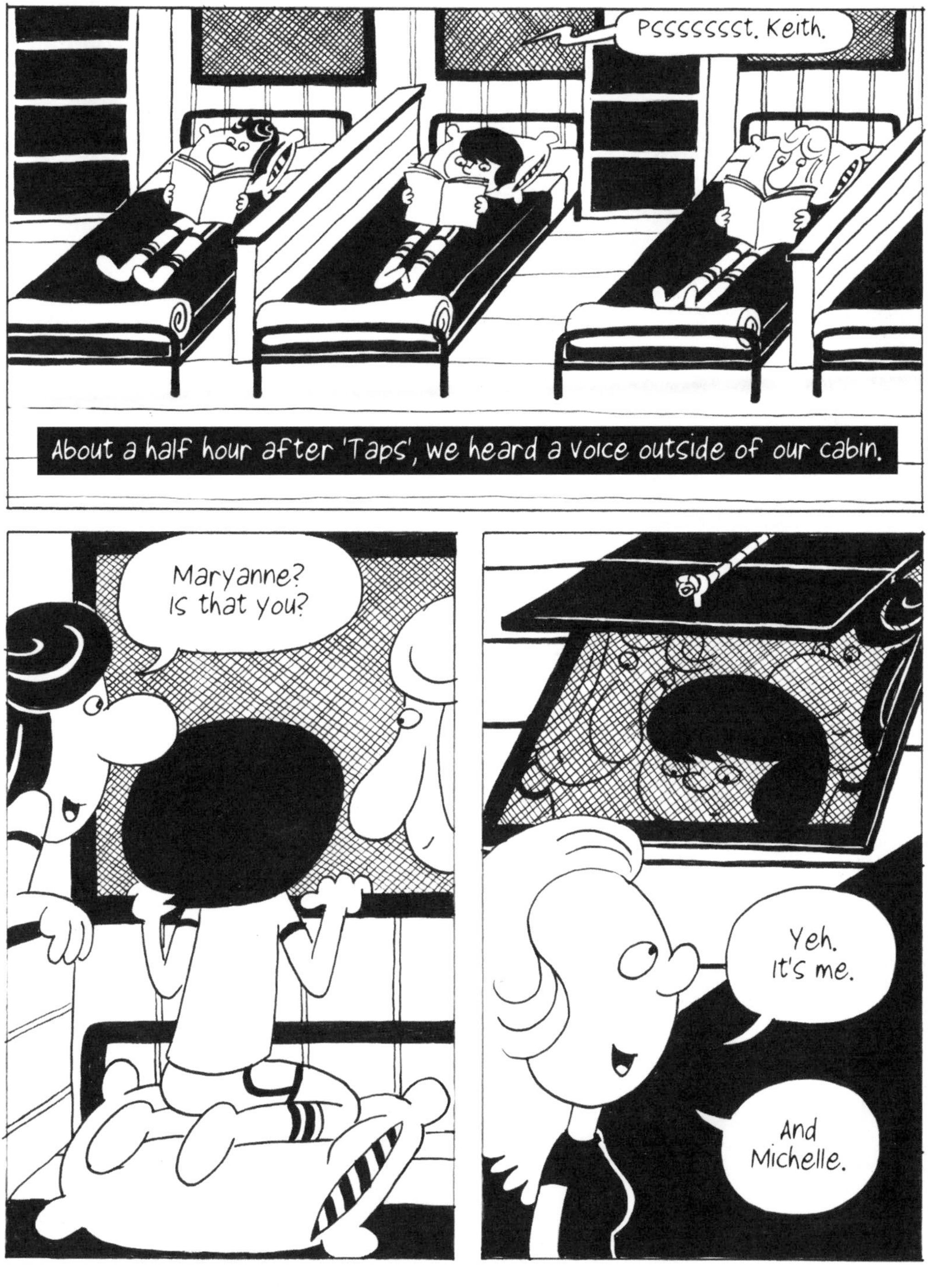
Psssssst. Keith.
About a half hour after 'Taps', we heard a voice outside of our cabin.
Maryanne? Is that you?
Yeh. It's me.
And Michelle.

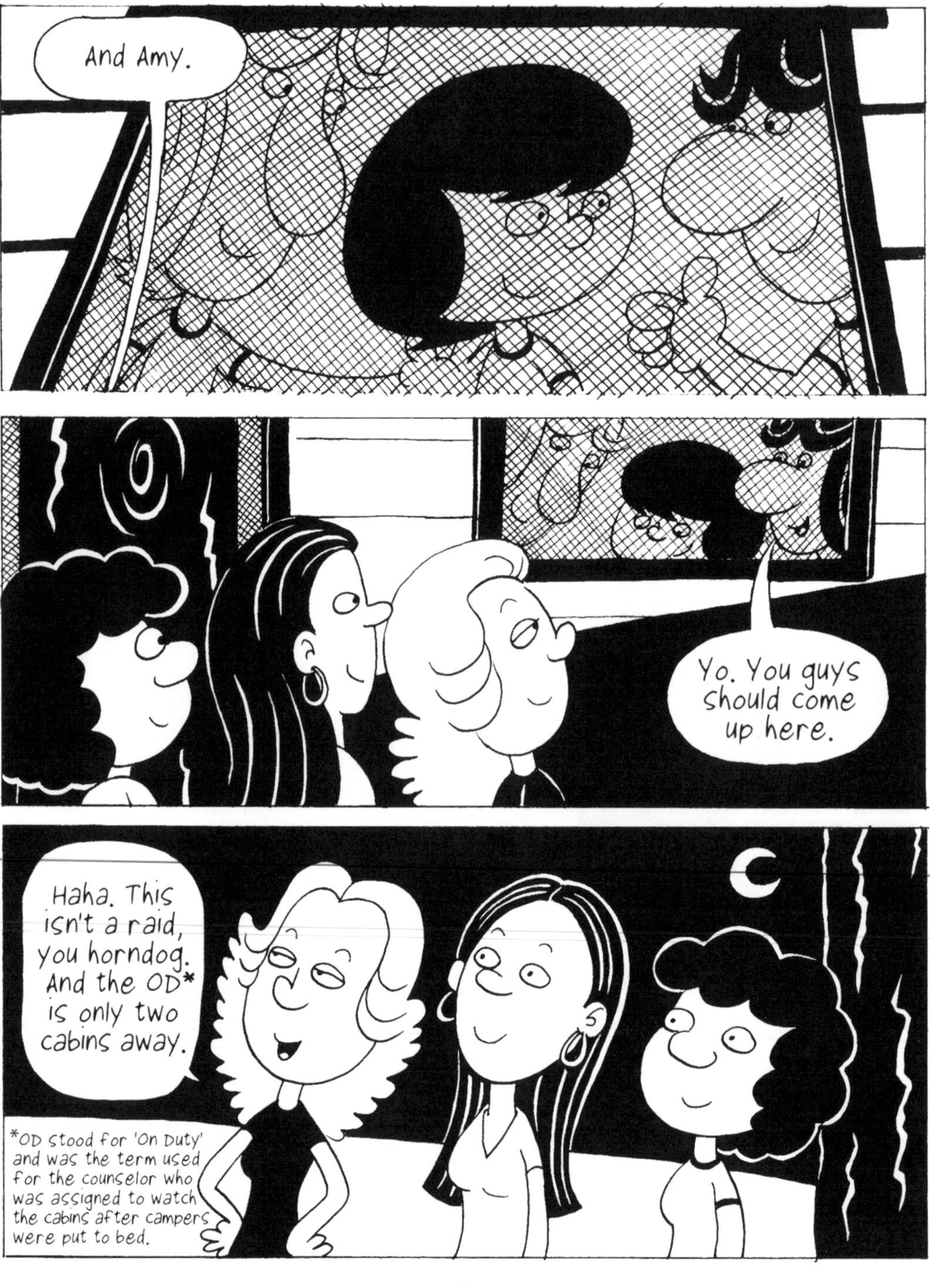
And Amy.
Yo. You guys should come up here.
Haha. This isn't a raid, you horndog. And the OD* is only two cabins away.
*OD stood for 'On Duty' and was the term used for the counselor who was assigned to watch the cabins after campers were put to bed.

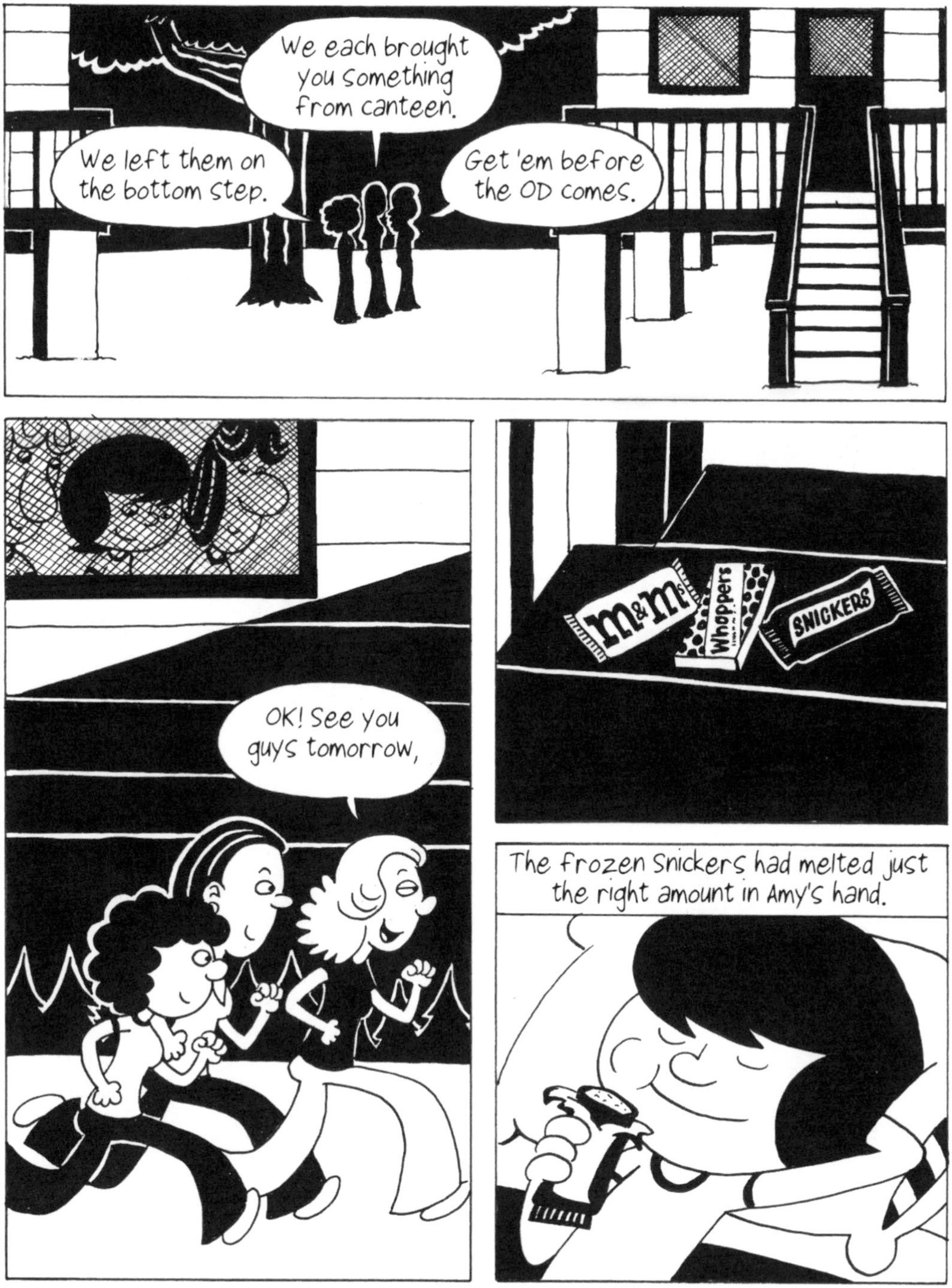
We each brought you something from canteen.
We left them on the bottom step.
Get 'em before the OD comes.
OK! See you guys tomorrow,
m&m's
Whoppers
SNICKERS
The frozen Snickers had melted just the right amount in Amy's hand.

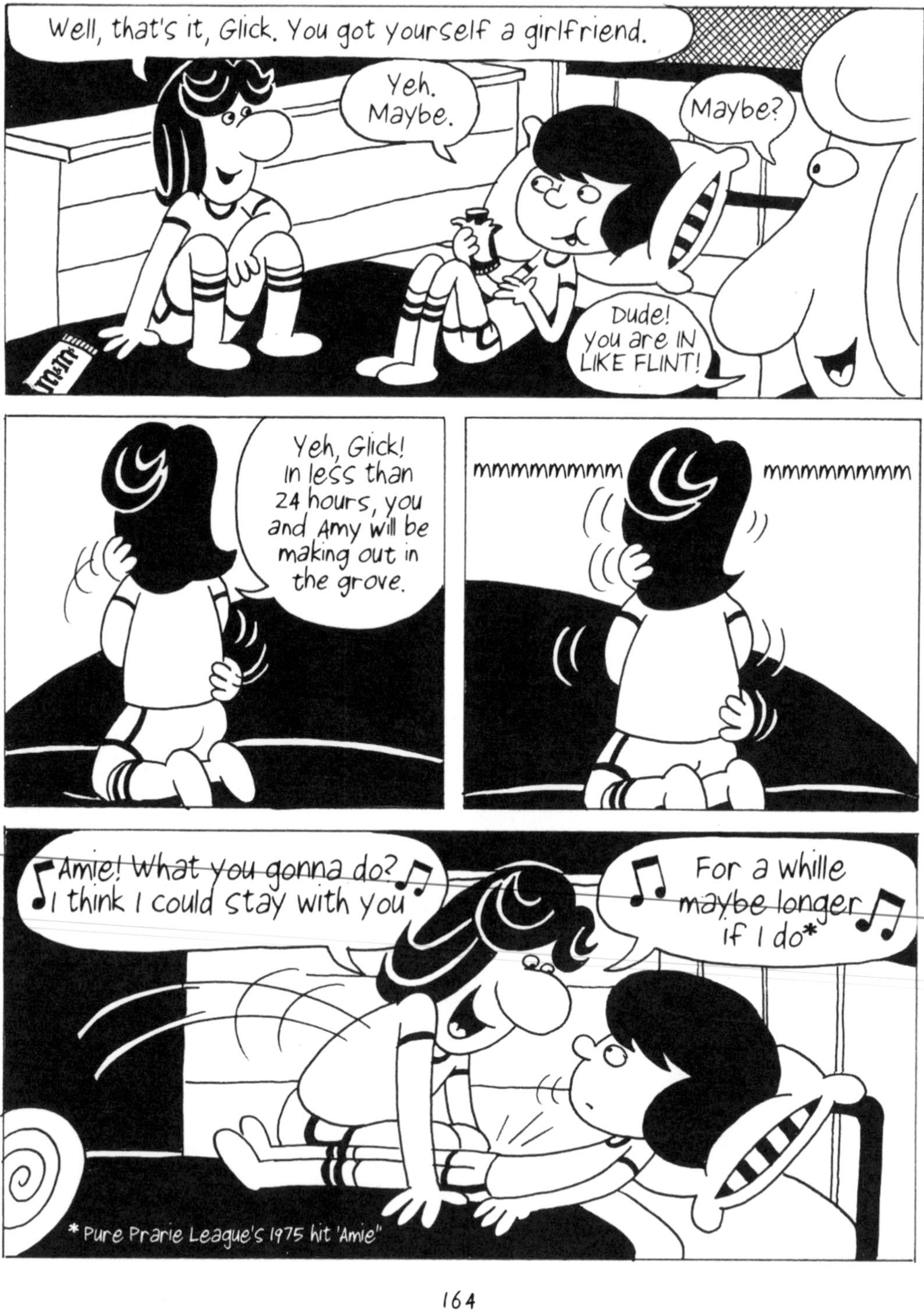
Well, that's it, Glick. You got yourself a girlfriend.
Yeh. Maybe.
Maybe?
Dude! You are IN LIKE FLINT!
M&M's
Yeh, Glick! In less than 24 hours, you and Amy will be making out in the grove.
mmmmmmmm
mmmmmmmm
♫Amie! What you gonna do? ♫ I think I could stay with you
♫ For a while maybe longer ♫ if I do*
* Pure Prarie League's 1975 hit 'Amie"

And then in another night or so, you'll be getting a handful of—

OH MY GOD!! Get the fuck off of me!

I desperately wanted to change the subject...

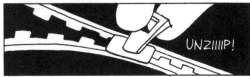

UNZIIIIP!

Yo! check this out!

What the hell, Glick?

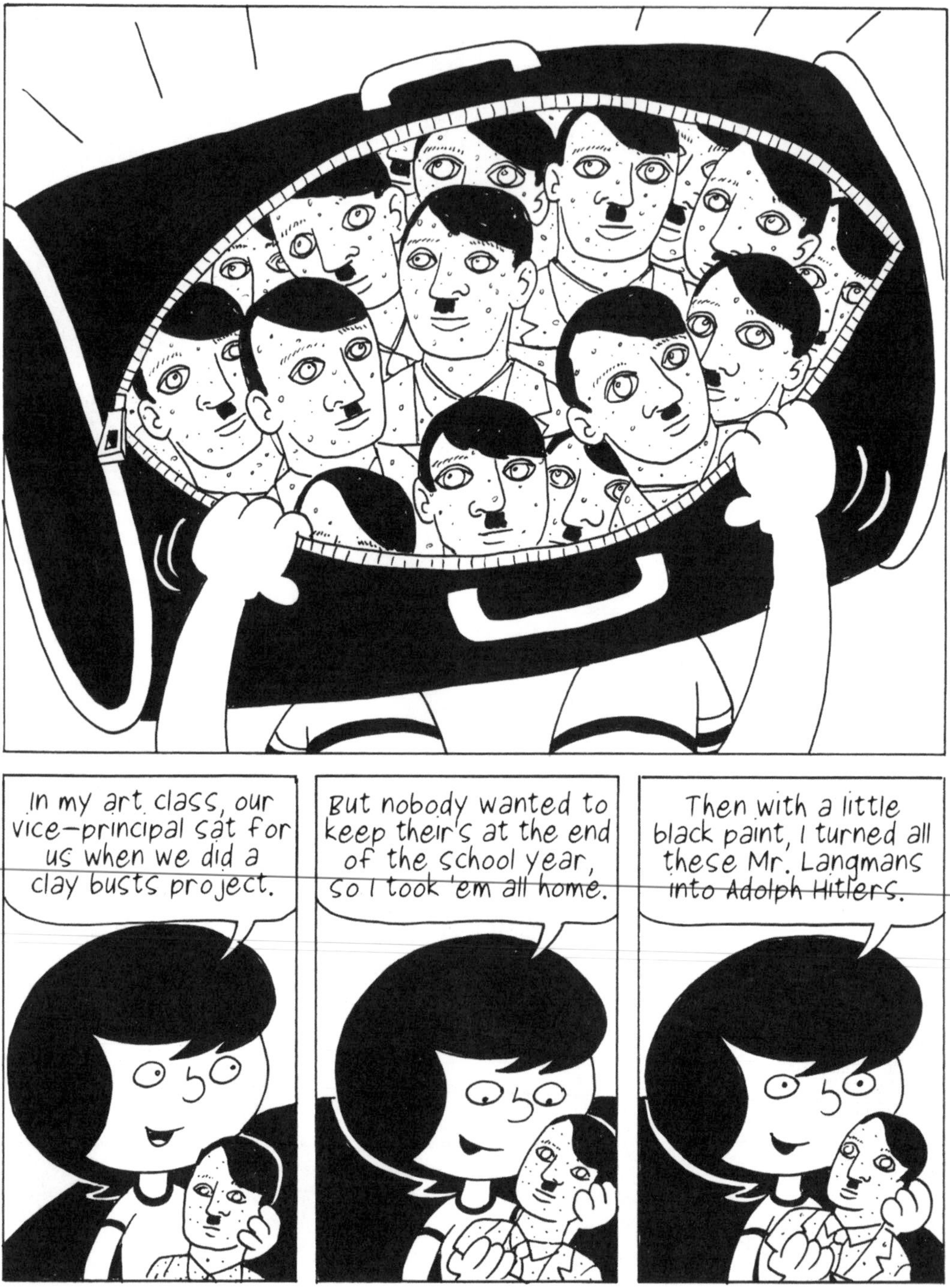
In my art class, our vice-principal sat for us when we did a clay busts project.
But nobody wanted to keep their's at the end of the school year, so I took 'em all home.
Then with a little black paint, I turned all these Mr. Langmans into Adolph Hitlers.

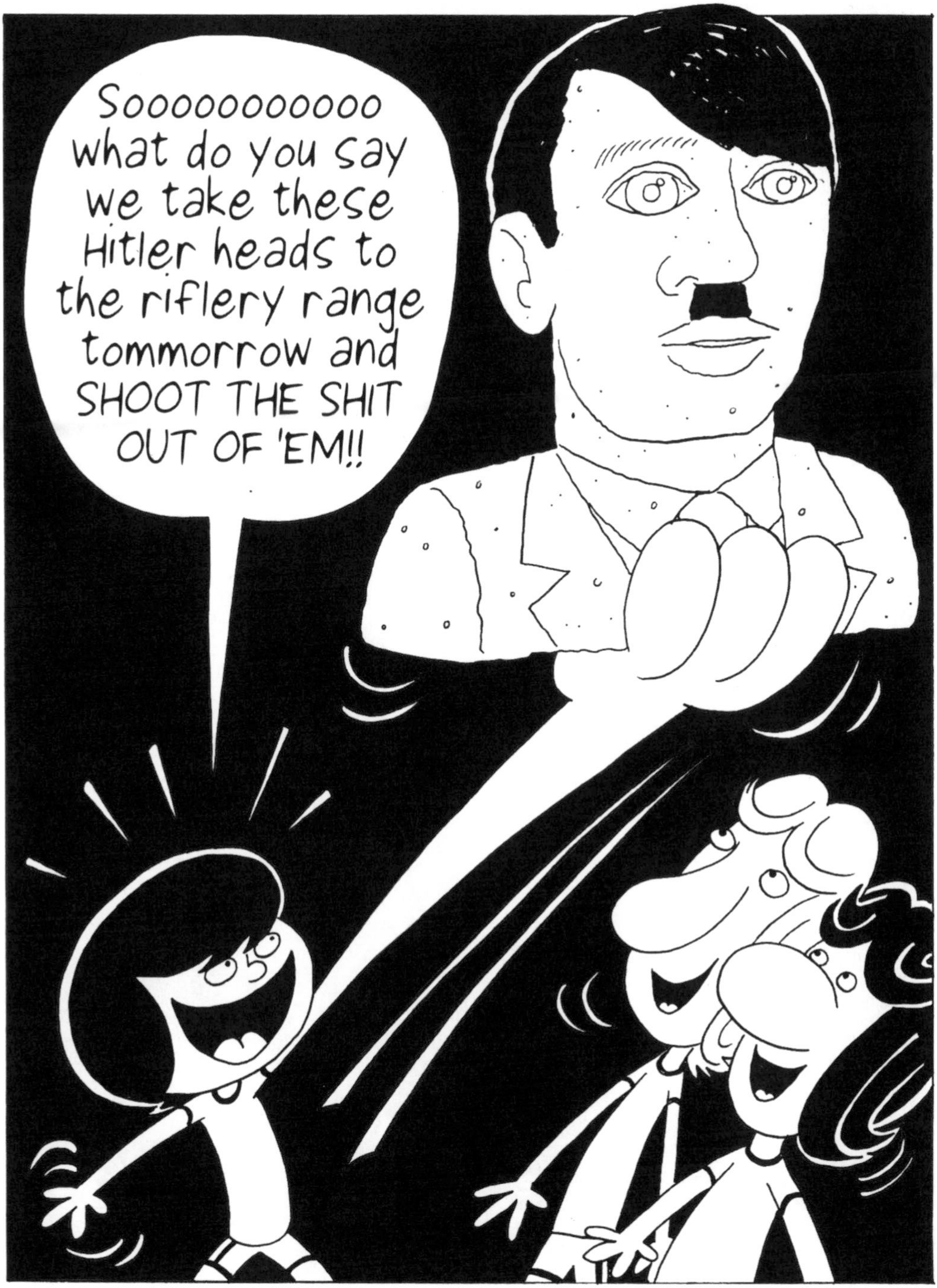
Sooooooooooo what do you say we take these Hitler heads to the riflery range tommorrow and SHOOT THE SHIT OUT OF 'EM!!

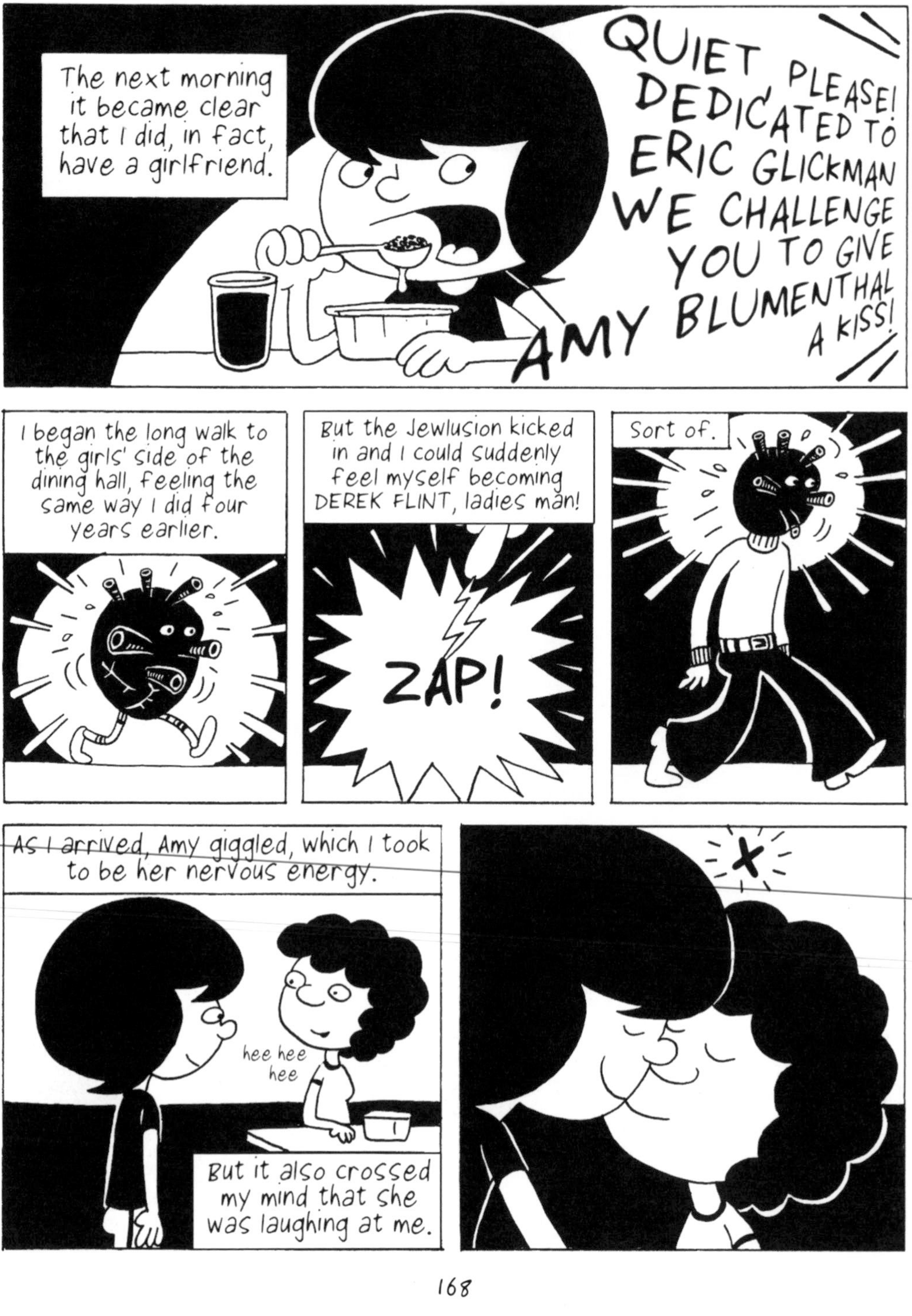

The next morning it became clear that I did, in fact, have a girlfriend.
QUIET PLEASE! DEDICATED TO ERIC GLICKMAN WE CHALLENGE YOU TO GIVE AMY BLUMENTHAL A KISS!
I began the long walk to the girls' side of the dining hall, feeling the same way I did four years earlier.
But the Jewlusion kicked in and I could suddenly feel myself becoming DEREK FLINT, ladies man!
ZAP!
Sort of.
As I arrived, Amy giggled, which I took to be her nervous energy.
hee hee hee
But it also crossed my mind that she was laughing at me.

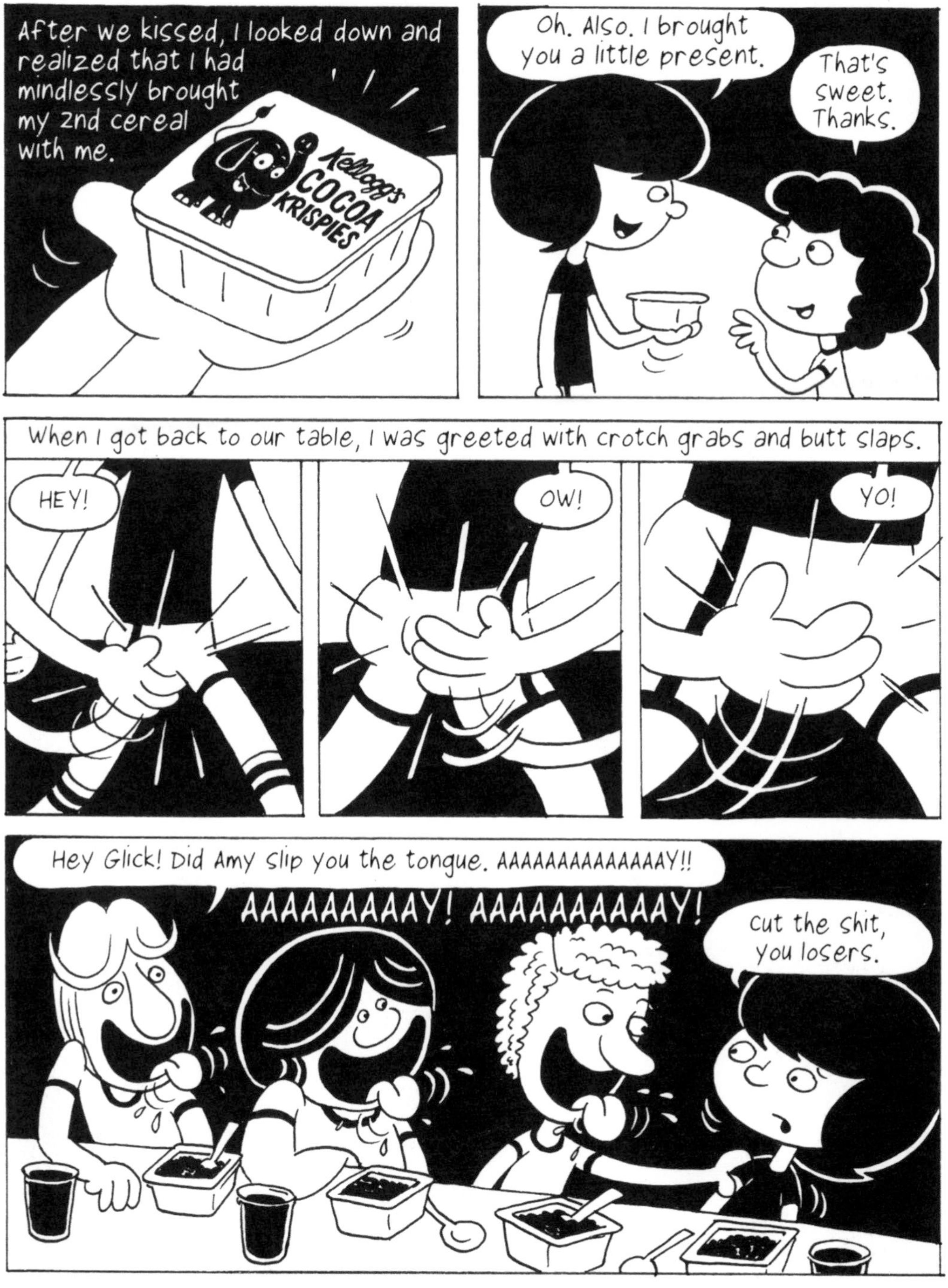
After we kissed, I looked down and realized that I had mindlessly brought my 2nd cereal with me.
Kellogg's COCOA KRISPIES
Oh. Also. I brought you a little present.
That's sweet. Thanks.
When I got back to our table, I was greeted with crotch grabs and butt slaps.
HEY!
OW!
YO!
Hey Glick! Did Amy slip you the tongue. AAAAAAAAAAAAAY!!
AAAAAAAAAY! AAAAAAAAAAY!
Cut the shit, you losers.

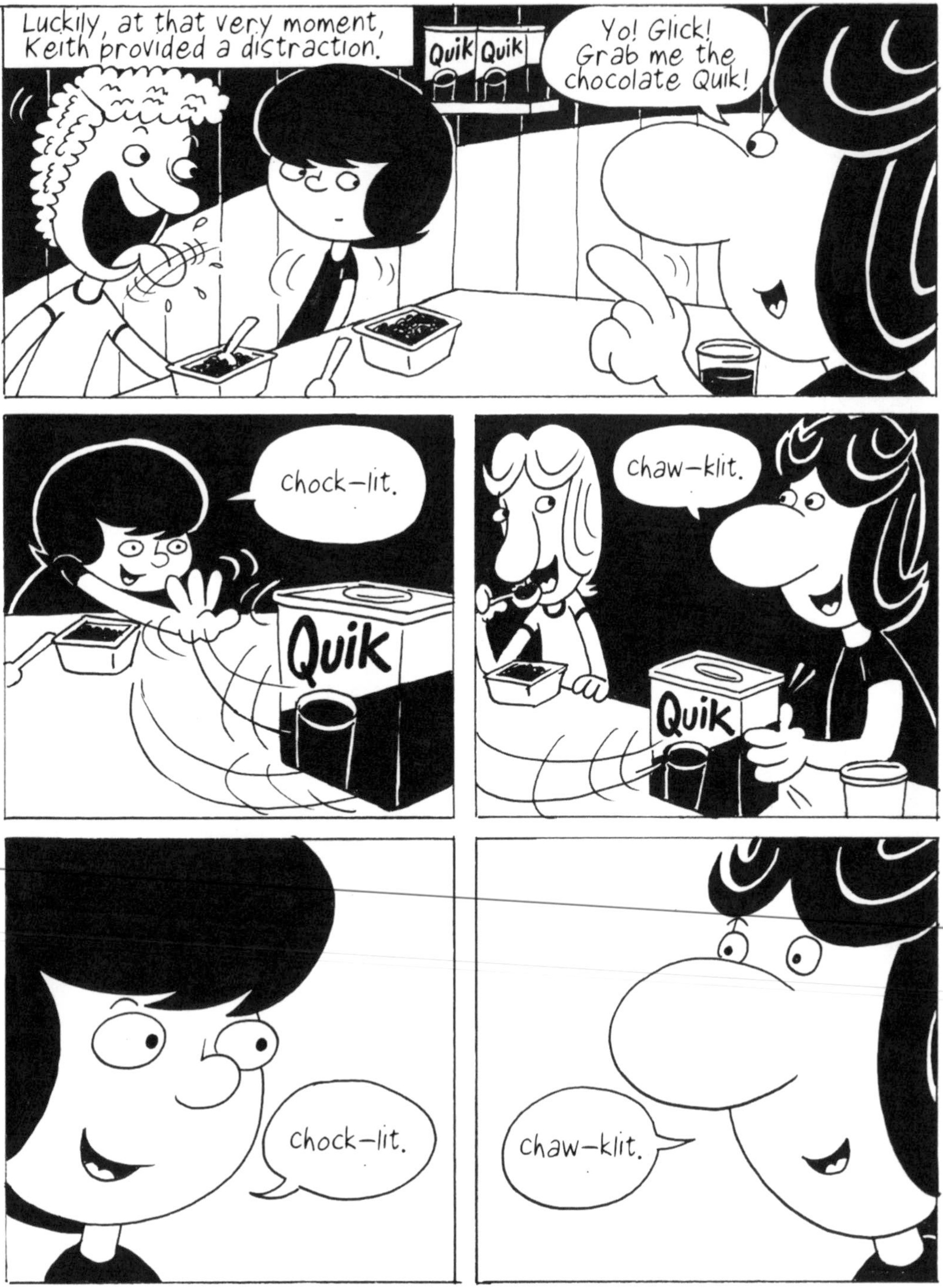
Luckily, at that very moment, Keith provided a distraction.
Quik
Quik
Yo! Glick! Grab me the chocolate Quik!
chock-lit.
Quik
chaw-klit.
Quik
chock-lit.
chaw-klit.

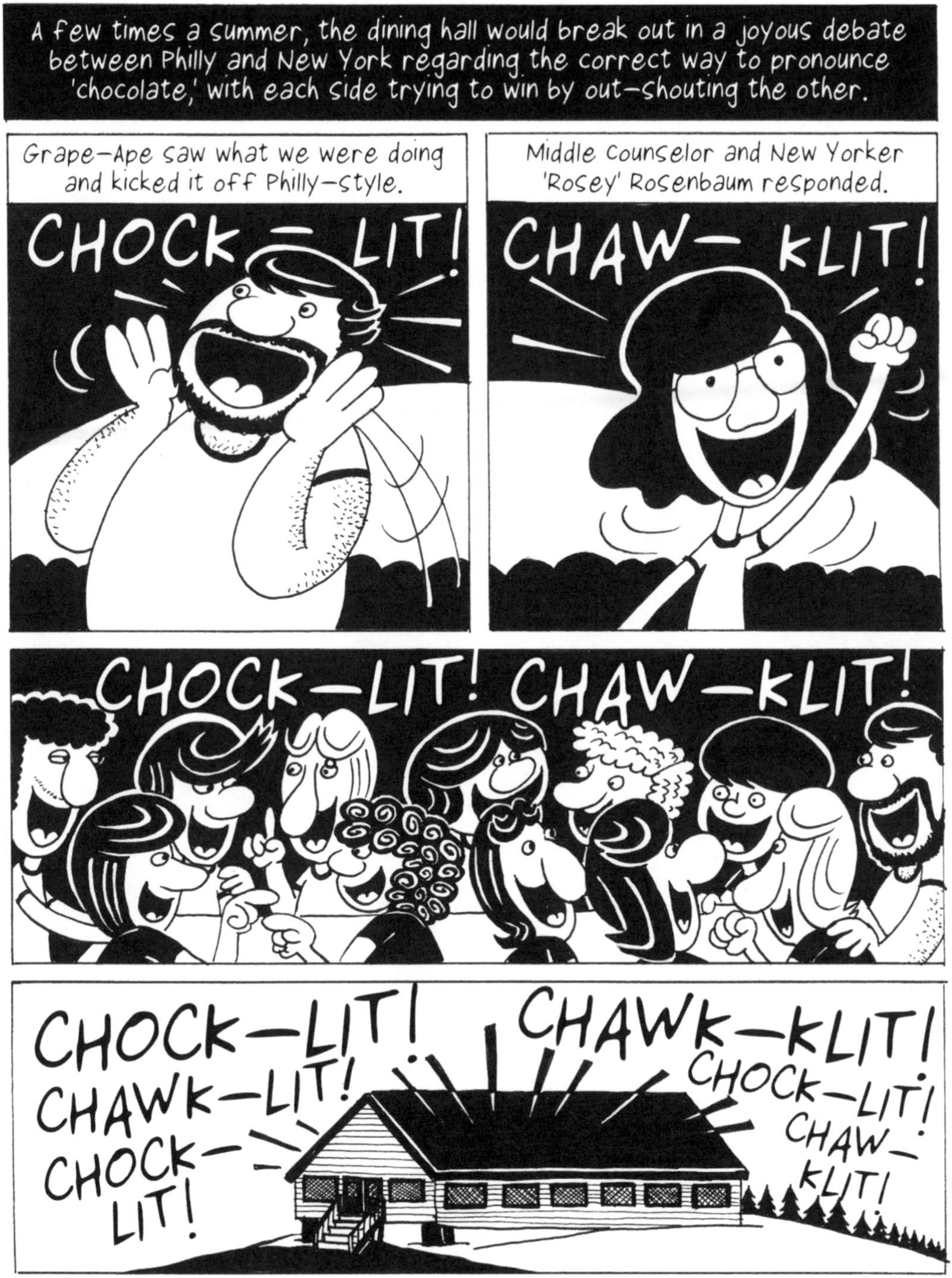
A few times a summer, the dining hall would break out in a joyous debate between Philly and New York regarding the correct way to pronounce 'chocolate,' with each side trying to win by out-shouting the other.
Grape-Ape saw what we were doing and kicked it off Philly-style.
CHOCK — LIT!
Middle Counselor and New Yorker 'Rosey' Rosenbaum responded.
CHAW— KLIT!
CHOCK—LIT! CHAW—KLIT!
CHOCK—LIT!
CHAWK—LIT!
CHOCK— LIT!
CHAWK—KLIT!
CHOCK—LIT!
CHAW— KLIT!

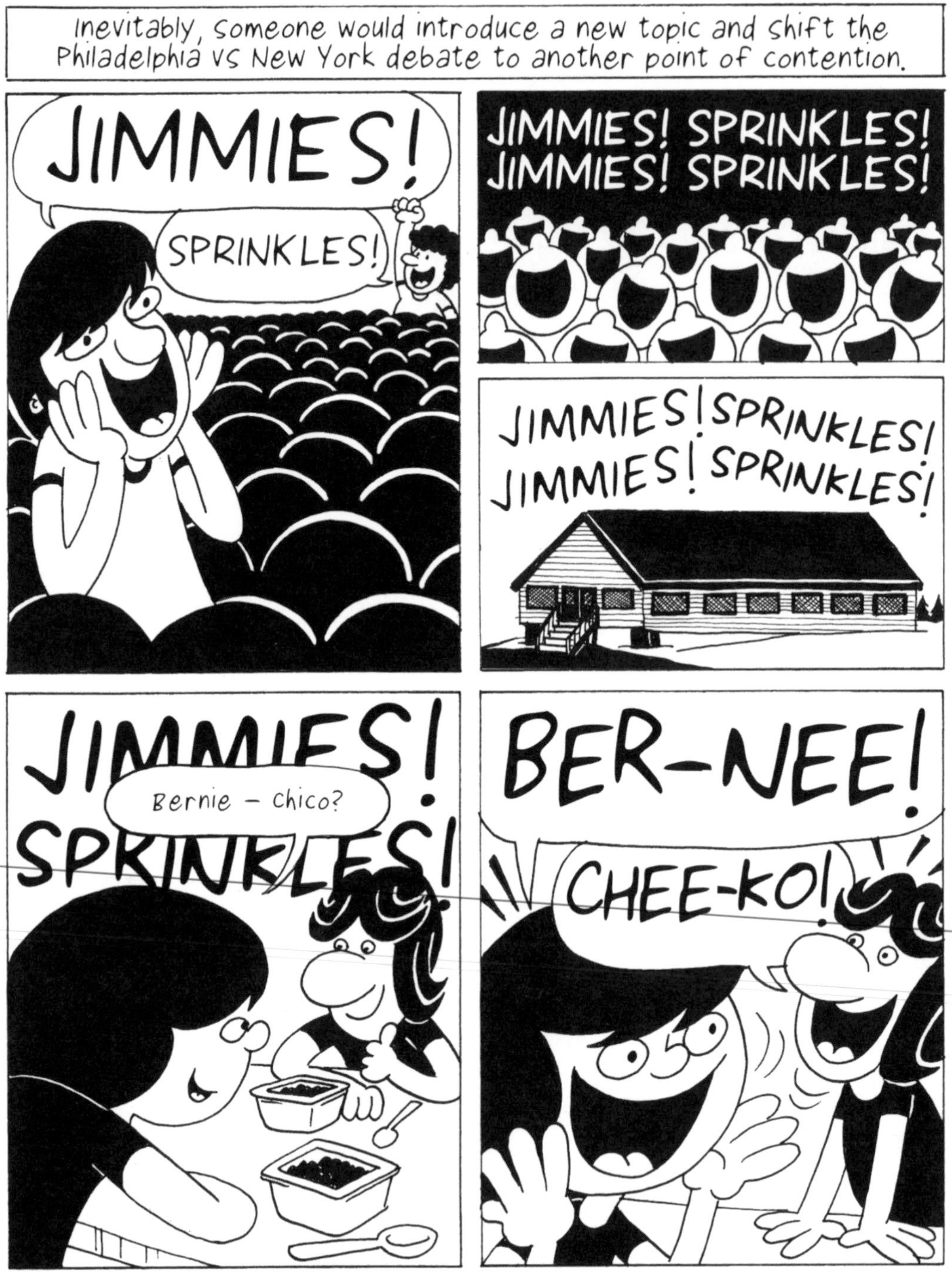
Inevitably, someone would introduce a new topic and shift the Philadelphia vs New York debate to another point of contention.
JIMMIES!
SPRINKLES!
JIMMIES! SPRINKLES! JIMMIES! SPRINKLES!
JIMMIES! SPRINKLES! JIMMIES! SPRINKLES!
JIMMIES! SPRINKLES!
Bernie – Chico?
BER-NEE!
CHEE-KO!

In the summer of 1977, kids from Philly and New York loved their hockey teams and their goalies more than just about anything.

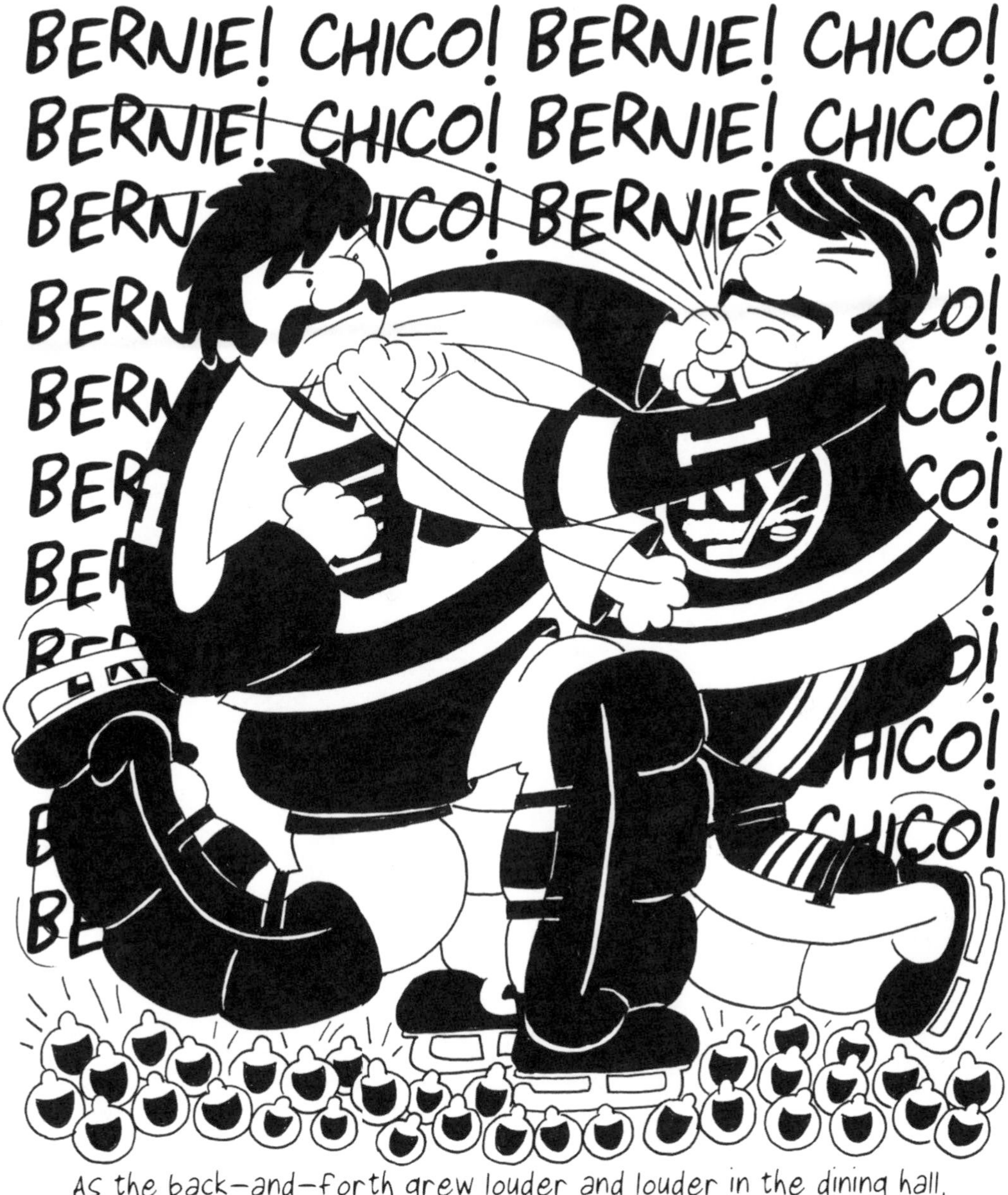
BERNIE! CHICO! BERNIE! CHICO!
BERNIE! CHICO! BERNIE! CHICO!

As the back-and-forth grew louder and louder in the dining hall, it felt as if we were conjuring apparitions of Bernie Parent and 'Chico' Resch to pummel each other with every shout of their name.

Fink was in charge of the riflery range and was totally cool with us shooting the Hitler heads, so we brought all 13 of them to hobbies.
Campers, when you are ready, you may commence shooting.

Die, you fucking Nazi. Die.

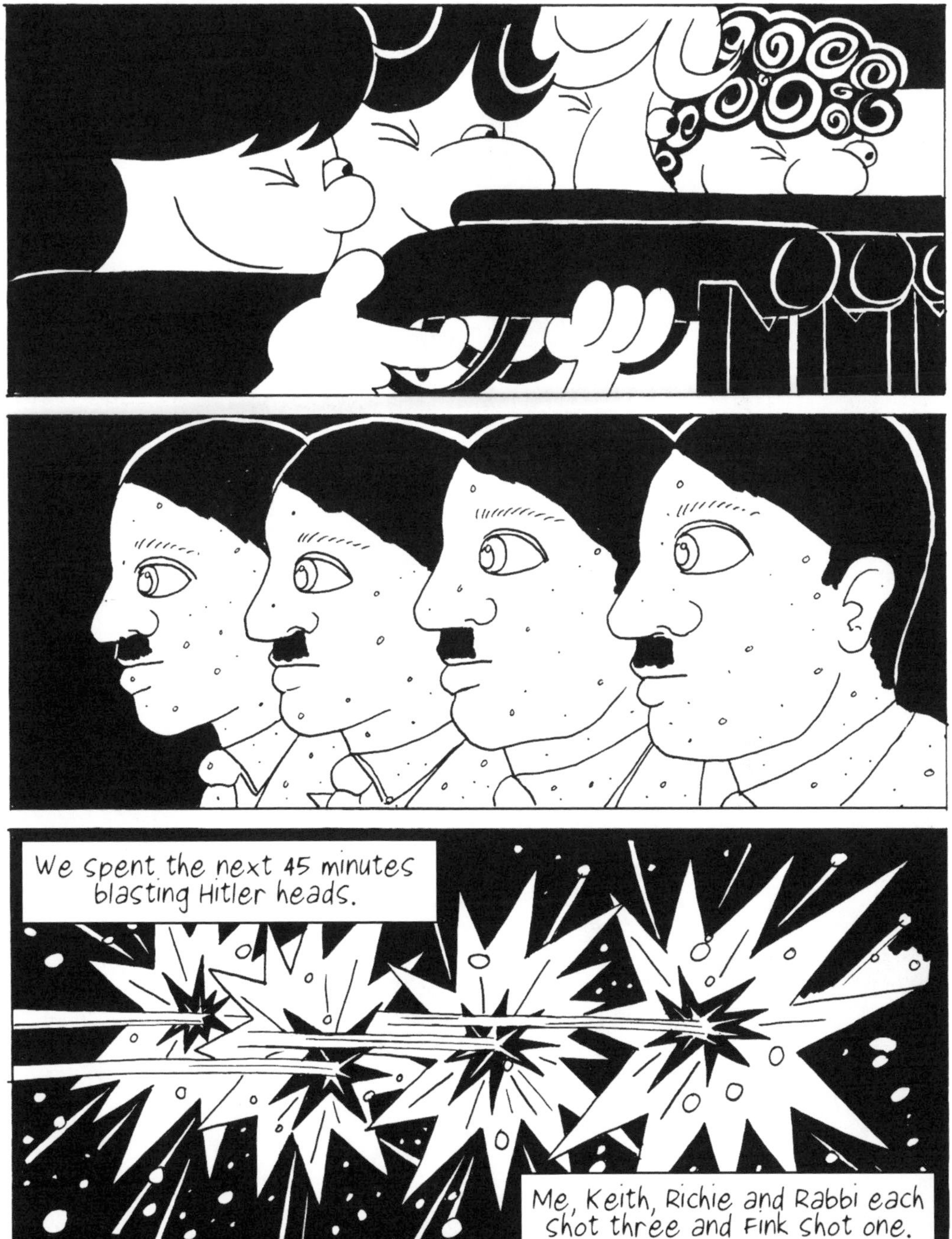
We spent the next 45 minutes blasting Hitler heads.
Me, Keith, Richie and Rabbi each shot three and Fink shot one.

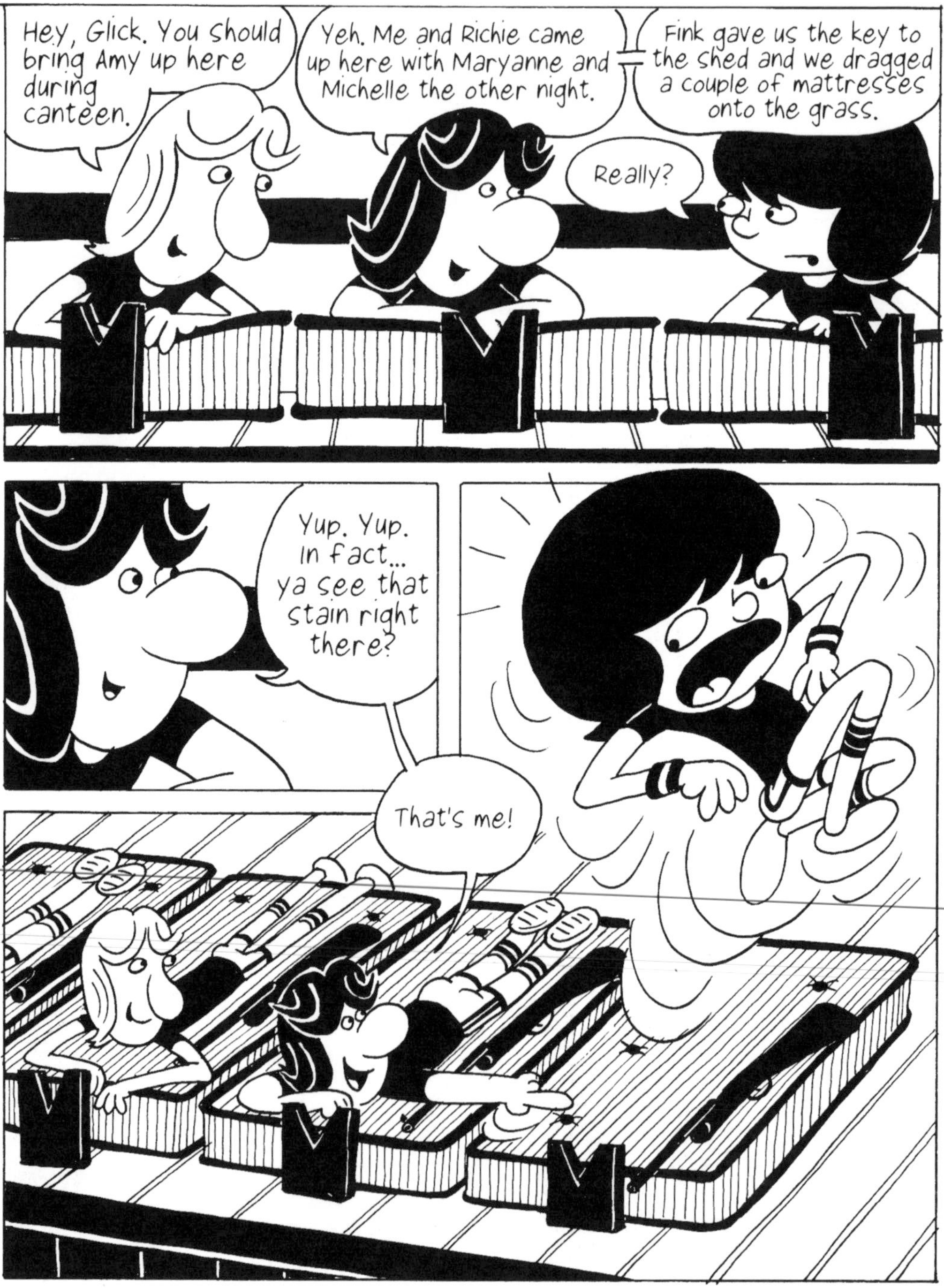
Hey, Glick. You should bring Amy up here during canteen.
Yeh. Me and Richie came up here with Maryanne and Michelle the other night.
Fink gave us the key to the shed and we dragged a couple of mattresses onto the grass.
Really?
Yup. Yup. In fact... ya see that stain right there?
That's me!

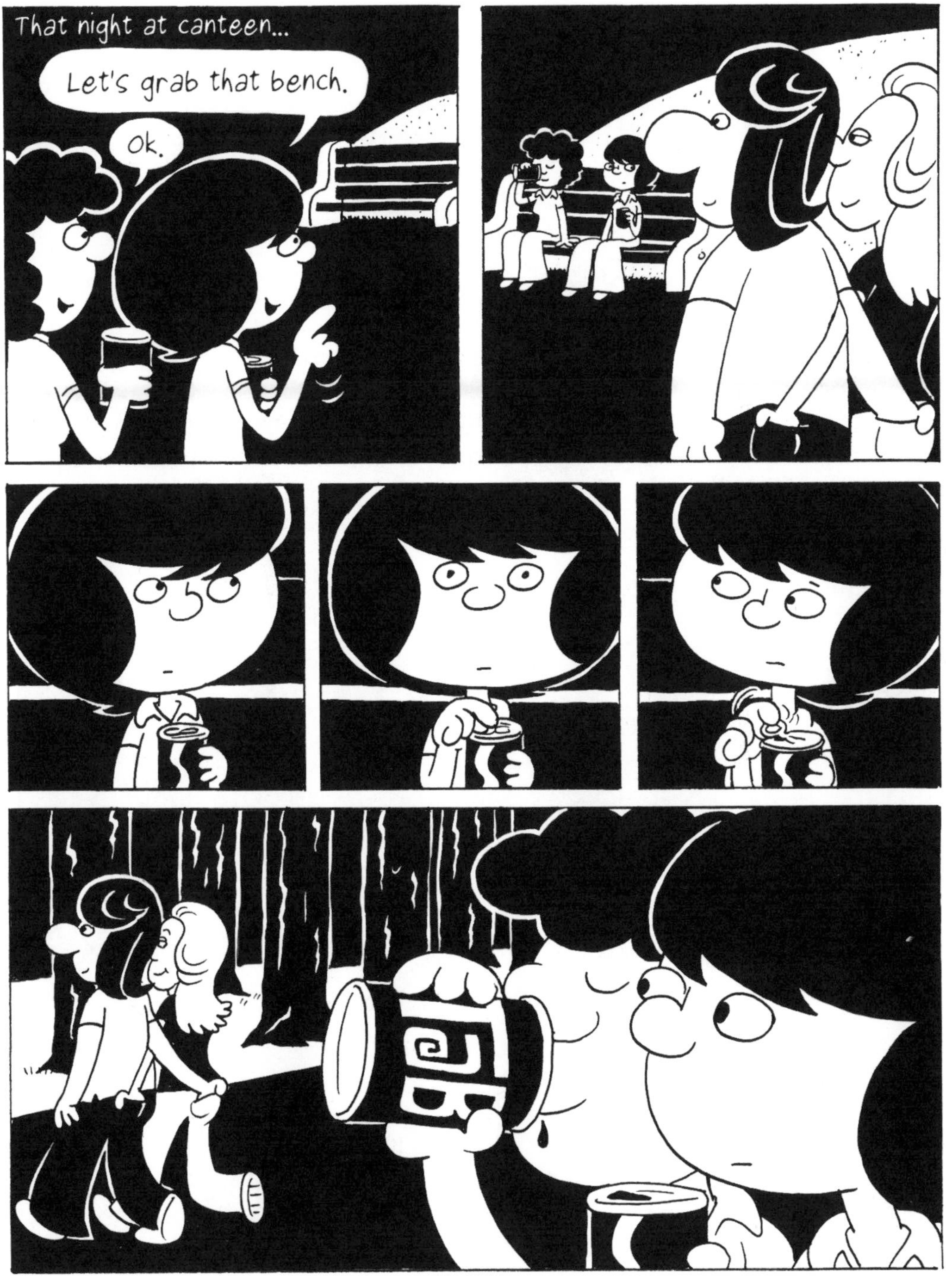
That night at canteen...
Let's grab that bench.
Ok.

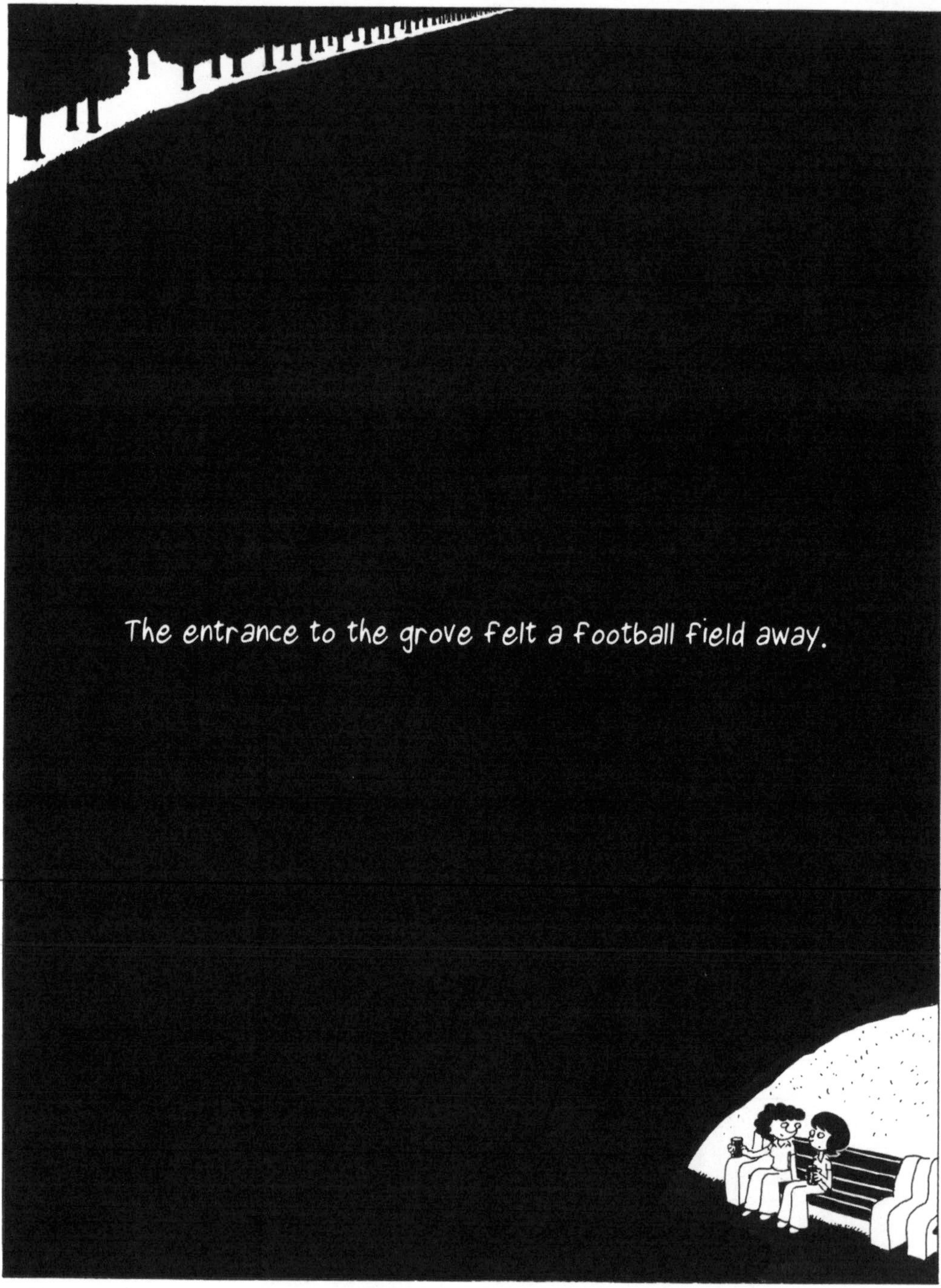
The entrance to the grove felt a football field away.

Earth to Eric.
Huh. Sorry. What?
I said, "can I have your ring tab?"
Oh. Yeh. Here.
Back in the 70s, soda cans opened with a ring tab that needed to be completely pulled off the can.
FANTA ORANGE SODA
FANTA ORANGE SODA
FANTA ORANGE SODA
To keep camp clean, all the girls' bunks collected soda can tabs and made chains out of them that hung across the rafters of their cabins
During the last week of camp, they would lay their chains out on the grass and the bunk with the longest chain got a pizza party.

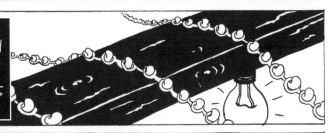

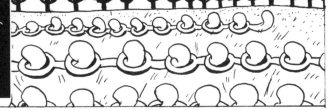

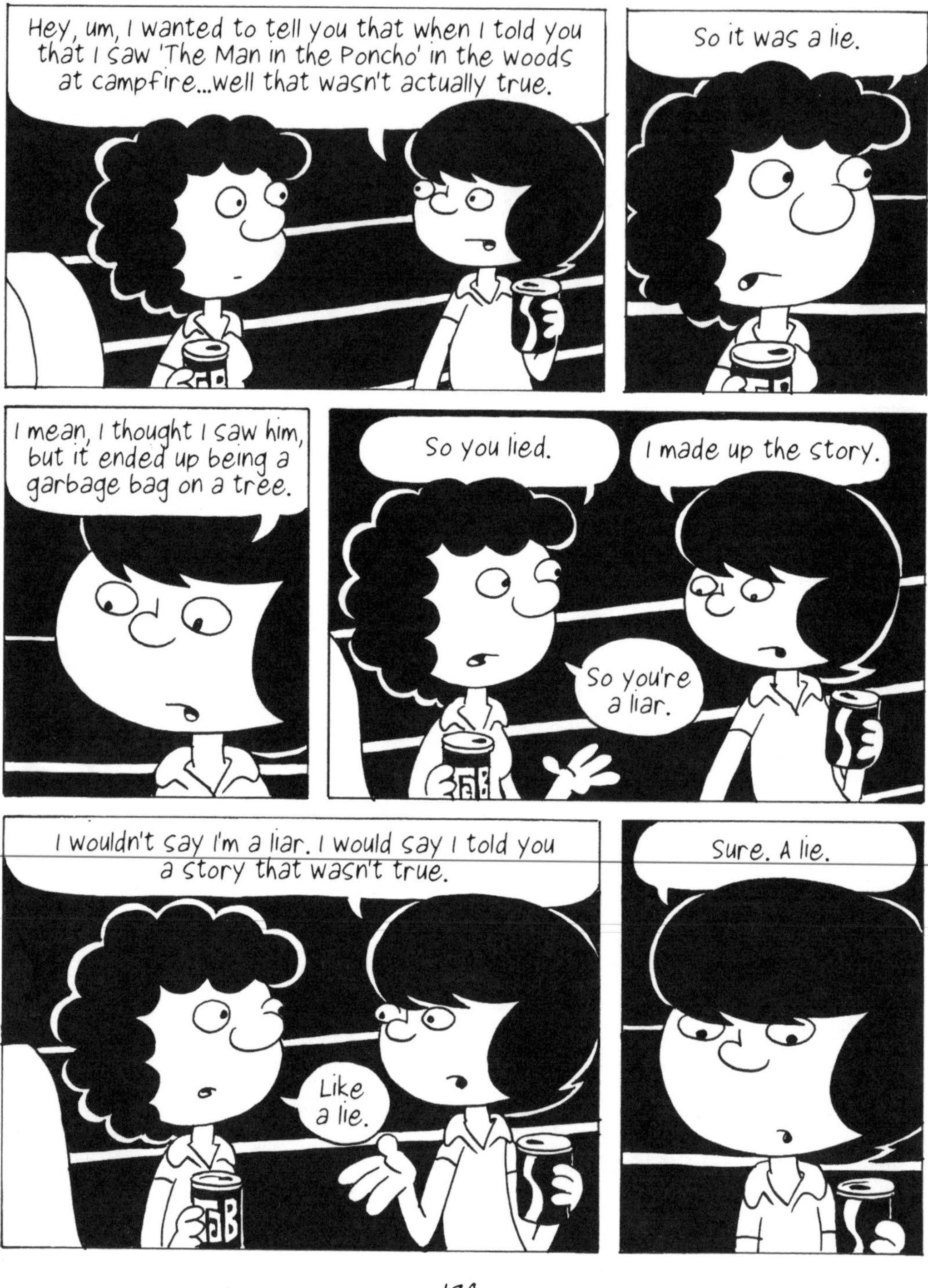
Hey, um, I wanted to tell you that when I told you that I saw 'The Man in the Poncho' in the woods at campfire...well that wasn't actually true.
So it was a lie.
I mean, I thought I saw him, but it ended up being a garbage bag on a tree.
So you lied.
I made up the story.
So you're a liar.
I wouldn't say I'm a liar. I would say I told you a story that wasn't true.
Like a lie.
Sure. A lie.

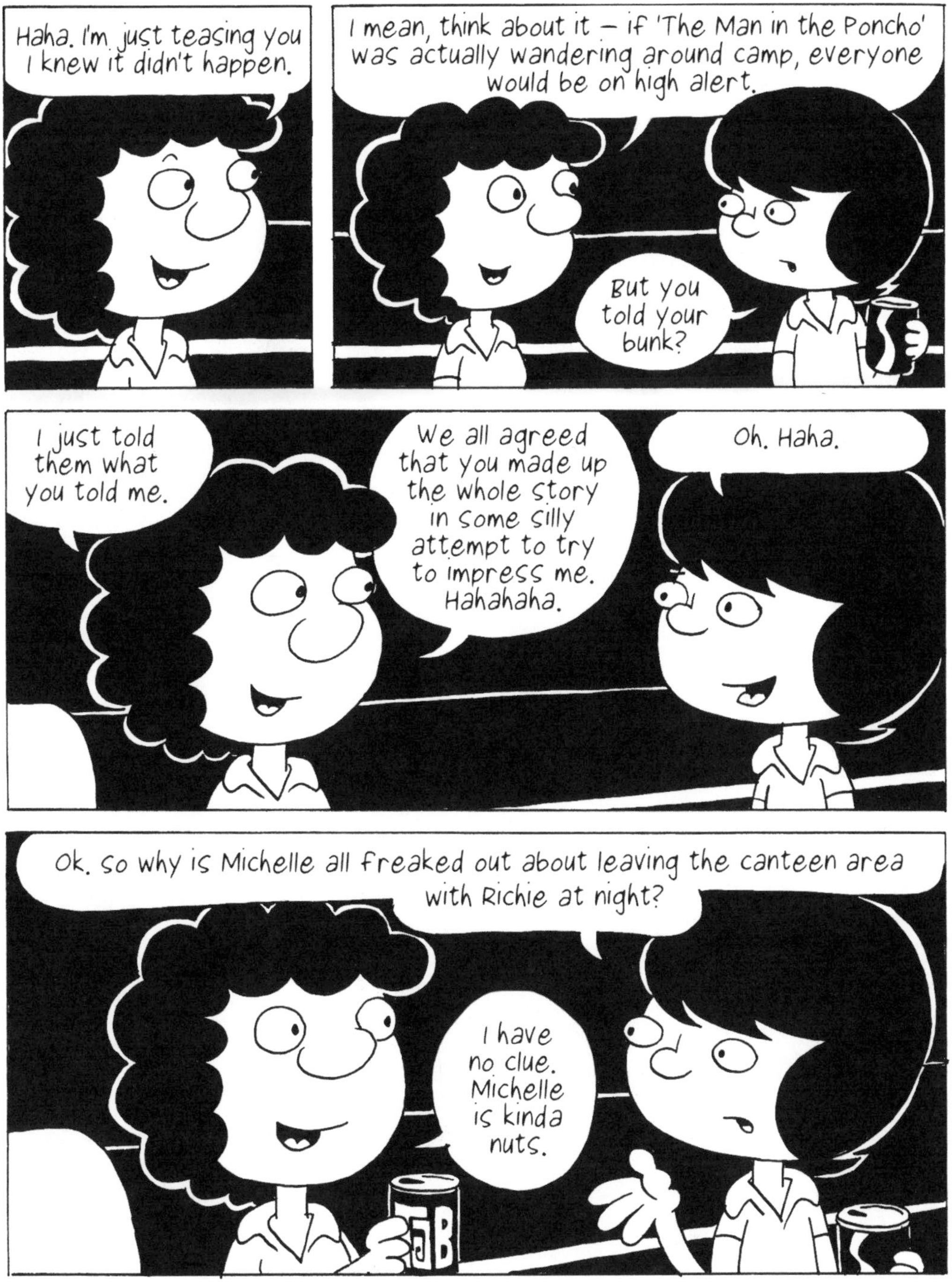
Haha. I'm just teasing you I knew it didn't happen.
I mean, think about it – if 'The Man in the Poncho' was actually wandering around camp, everyone would be on high alert.
But you told your bunk?
I just told them what you told me.
We all agreed that you made up the whole story in some silly attempt to try to impress me. Hahahaha.
Oh. Haha.
Ok. So why is Michelle all freaked out about leaving the canteen area with Richie at night?
I have no clue. Michelle is kinda nuts.
TaB

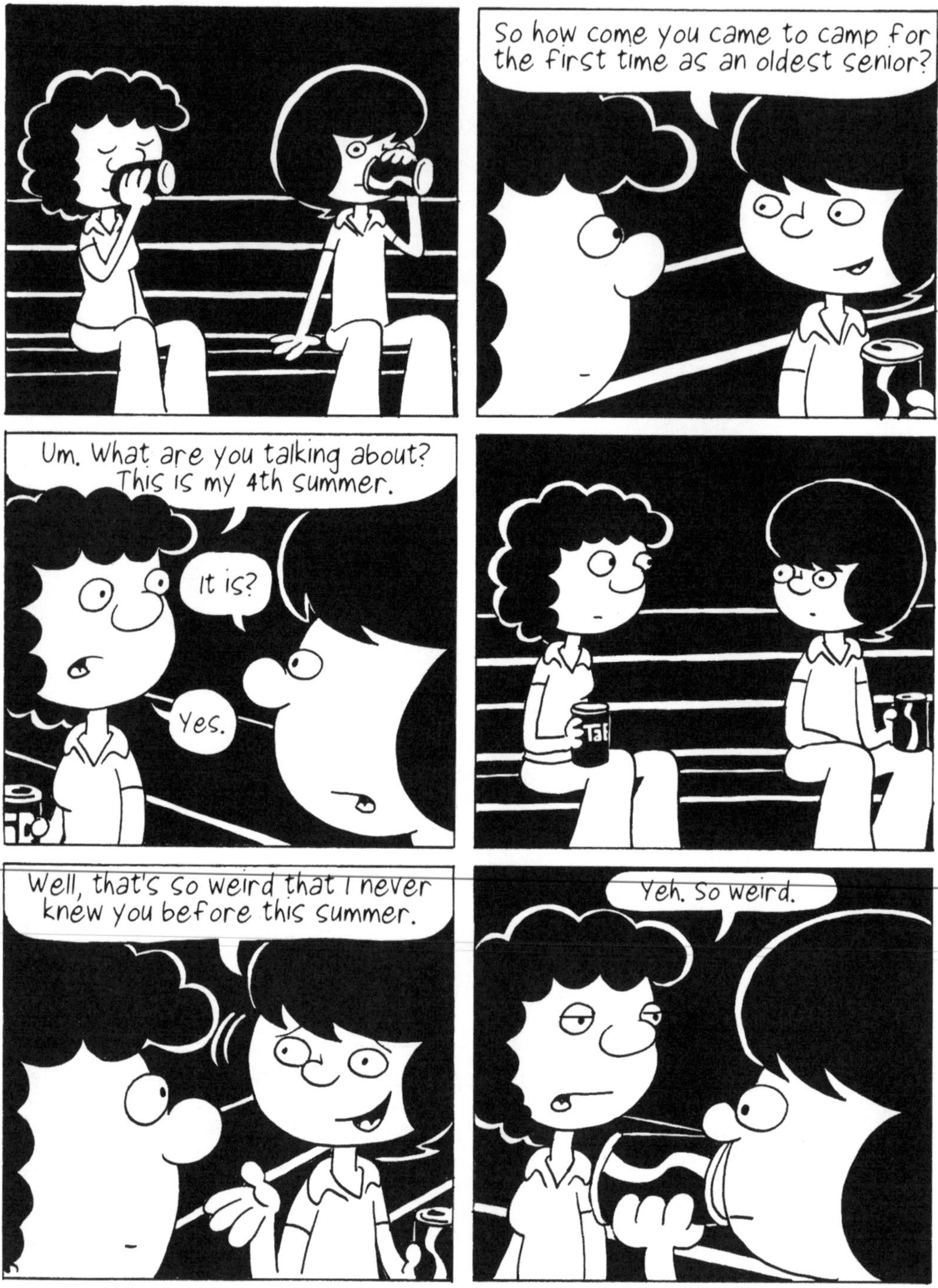
So how come you came to camp for the first time as an oldest senior?
Um. What are you talking about? This is my 4th summer.
It is?
Yes.
Well, that's so weird that I never knew you before this summer.
Yeh. So weird.

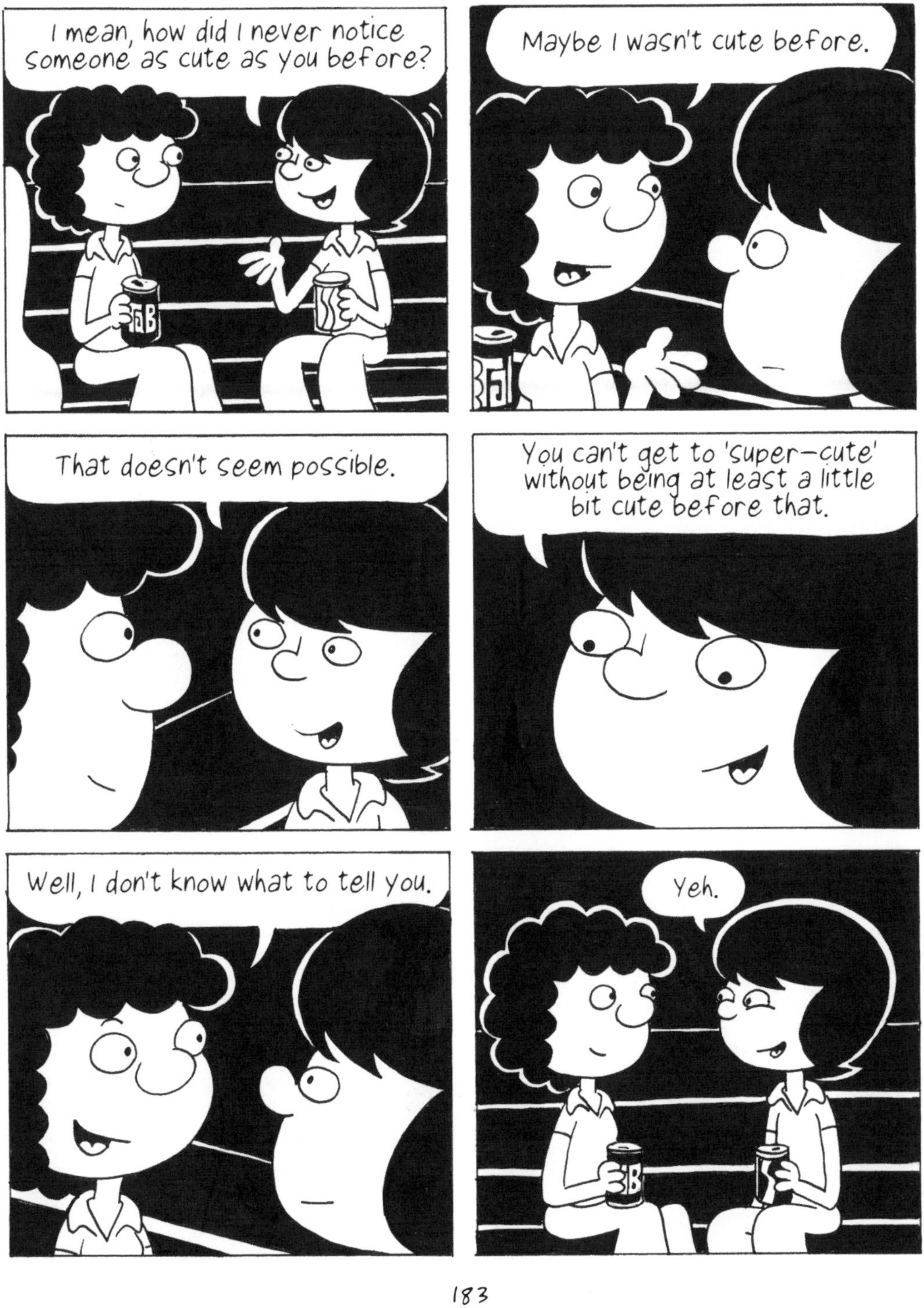
I mean, how did I never notice someone as cute as you before?
Maybe I wasn't cute before.
That doesn't seem possible.
You can't get to 'super-cute' without being at least a little bit cute before that.
Well, I don't know what to tell you.
Yeh.

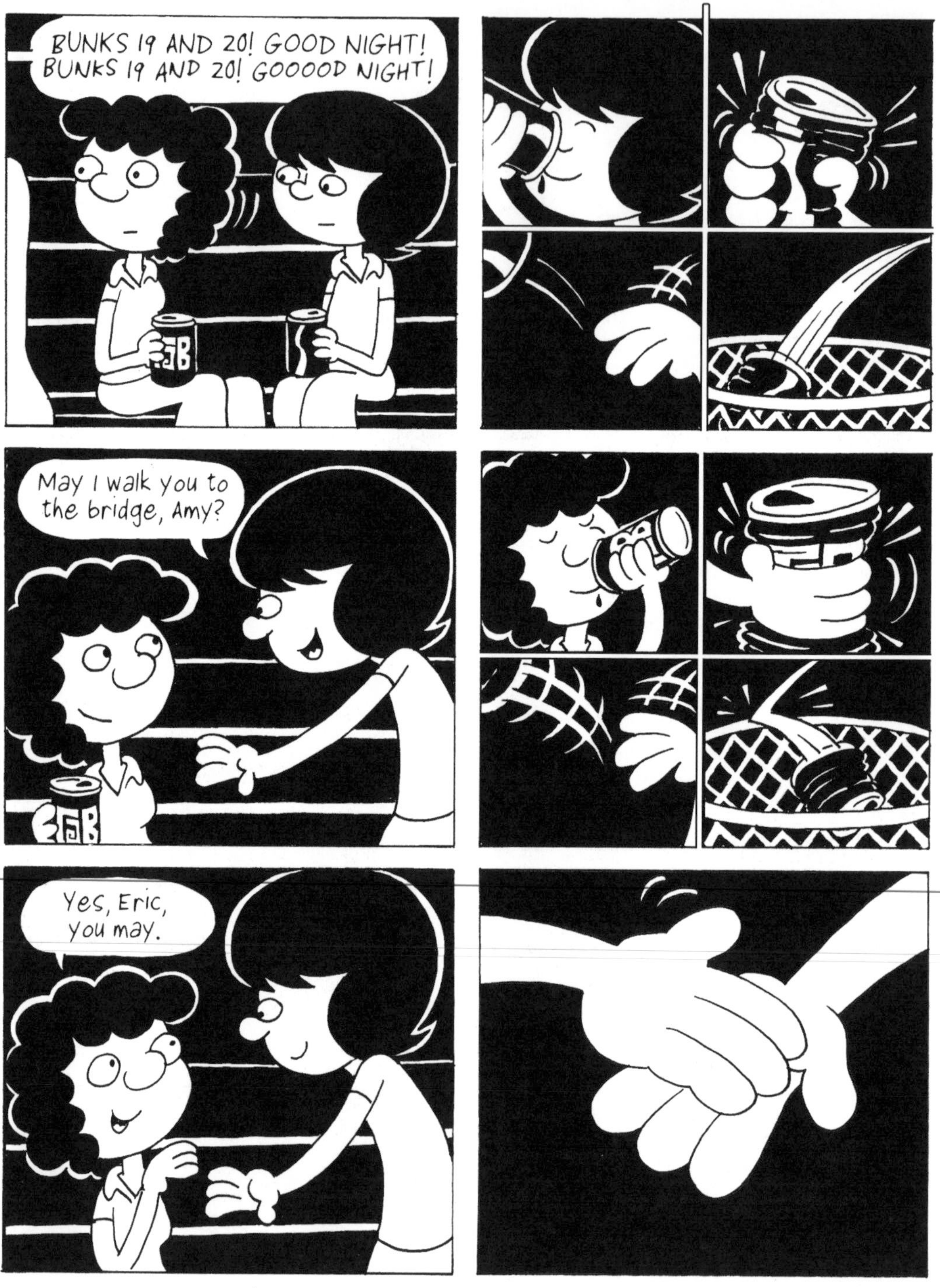
BUNKS 19 AND 20! GOOD NIGHT! BUNKS 19 AND 20! GOOOOD NIGHT!
May I walk you to the bridge, Amy?
Yes, Eric, you may.

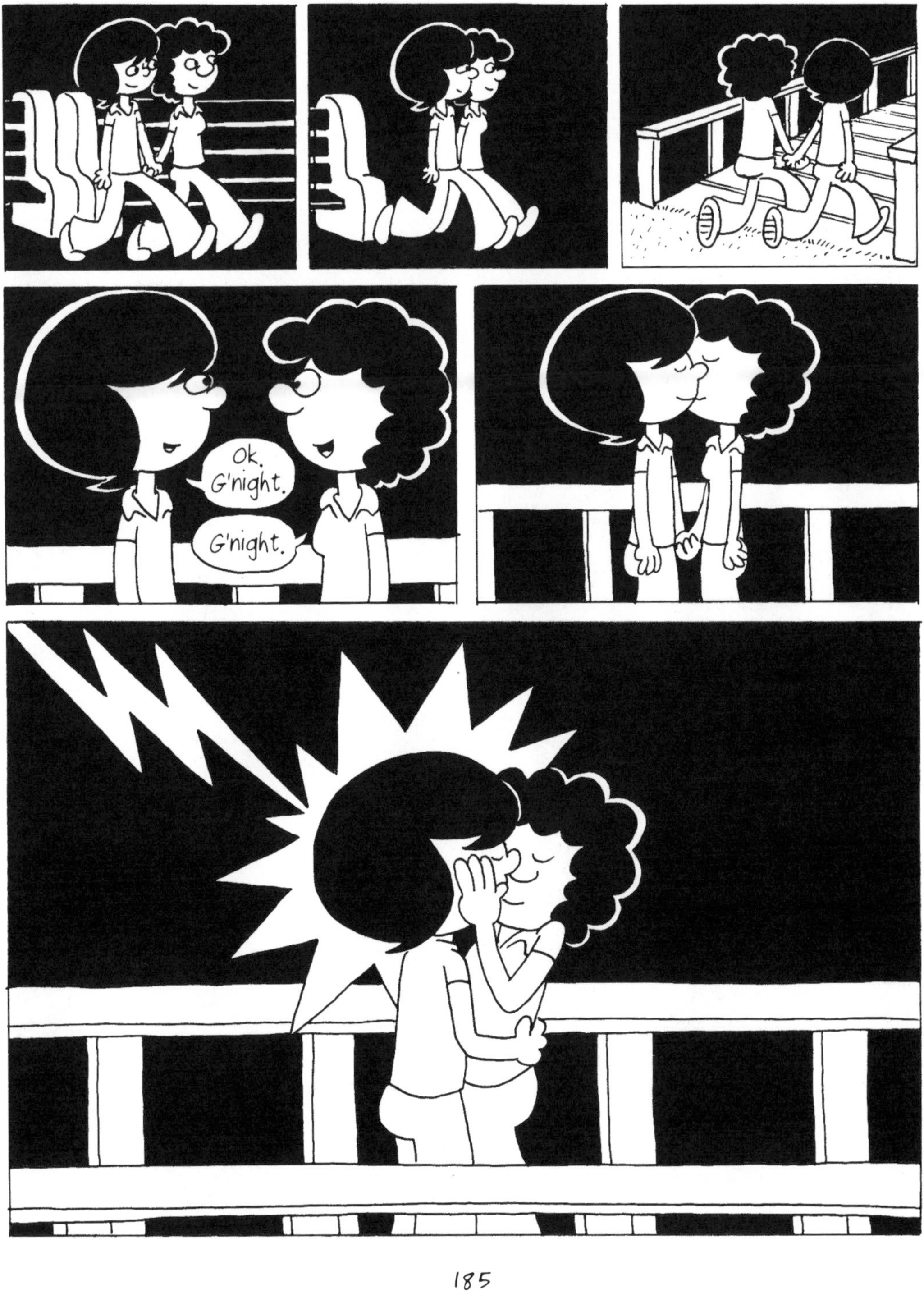
Ok. G'night.
G'night.

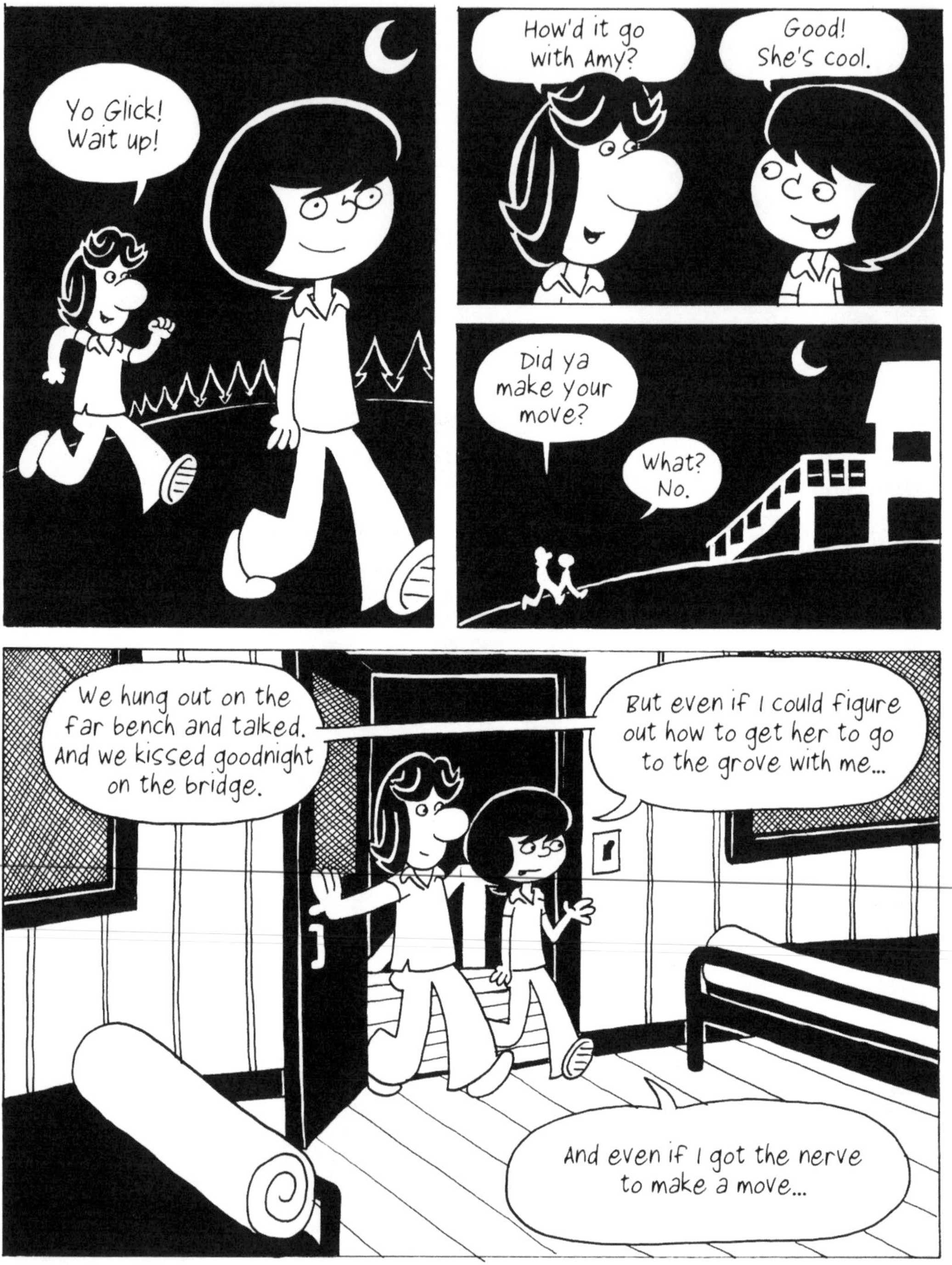
Yo Glick! Wait up!
How'd it go with Amy?
Good! She's cool.
Did ya make your move?
What? No.
We hung out on the far bench and talked. And we kissed goodnight on the bridge.
But even if I could figure out how to get her to go to the grove with me...
And even if I got the nerve to make a move...

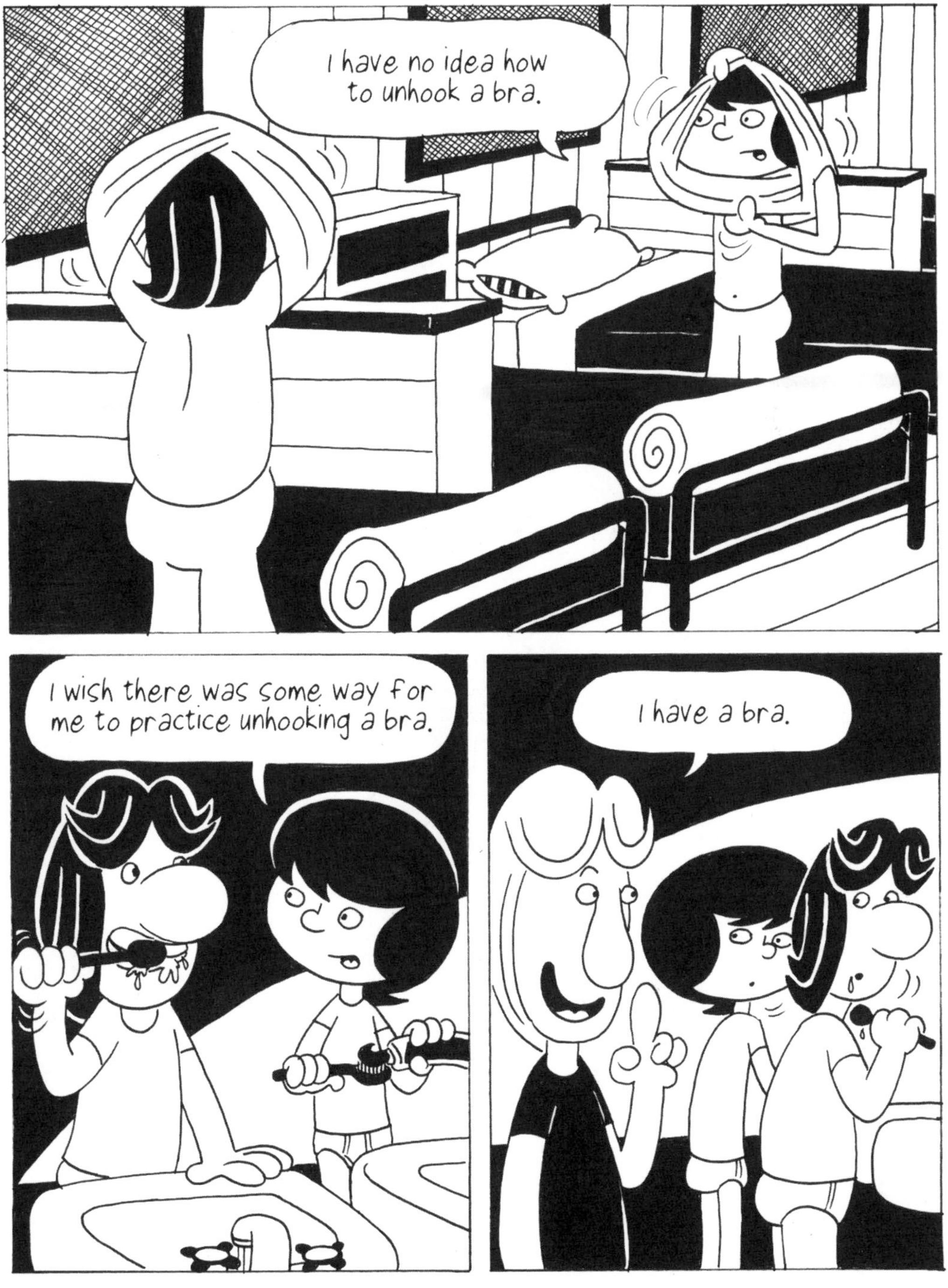
I have no idea how to unhook a bra.
I wish there was some way for me to practice unhooking a bra.
I have a bra.

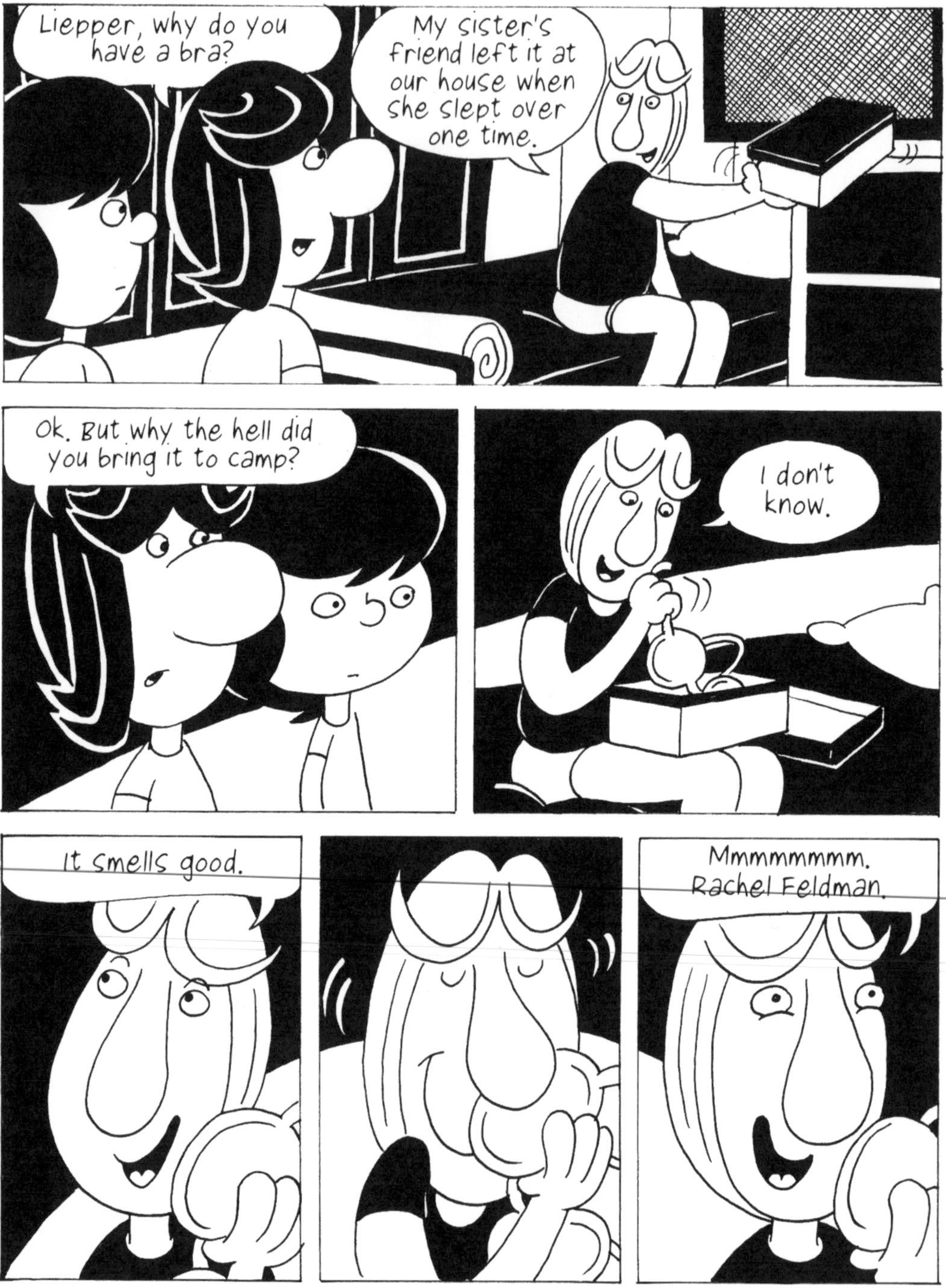
Liepper, why do you have a bra?
My sister's friend left it at our house when she slept over one time.
Ok. But why the hell did you bring it to camp?
I don't know.
It smells good.
Mmmmmmmm. Rachel Feldman.

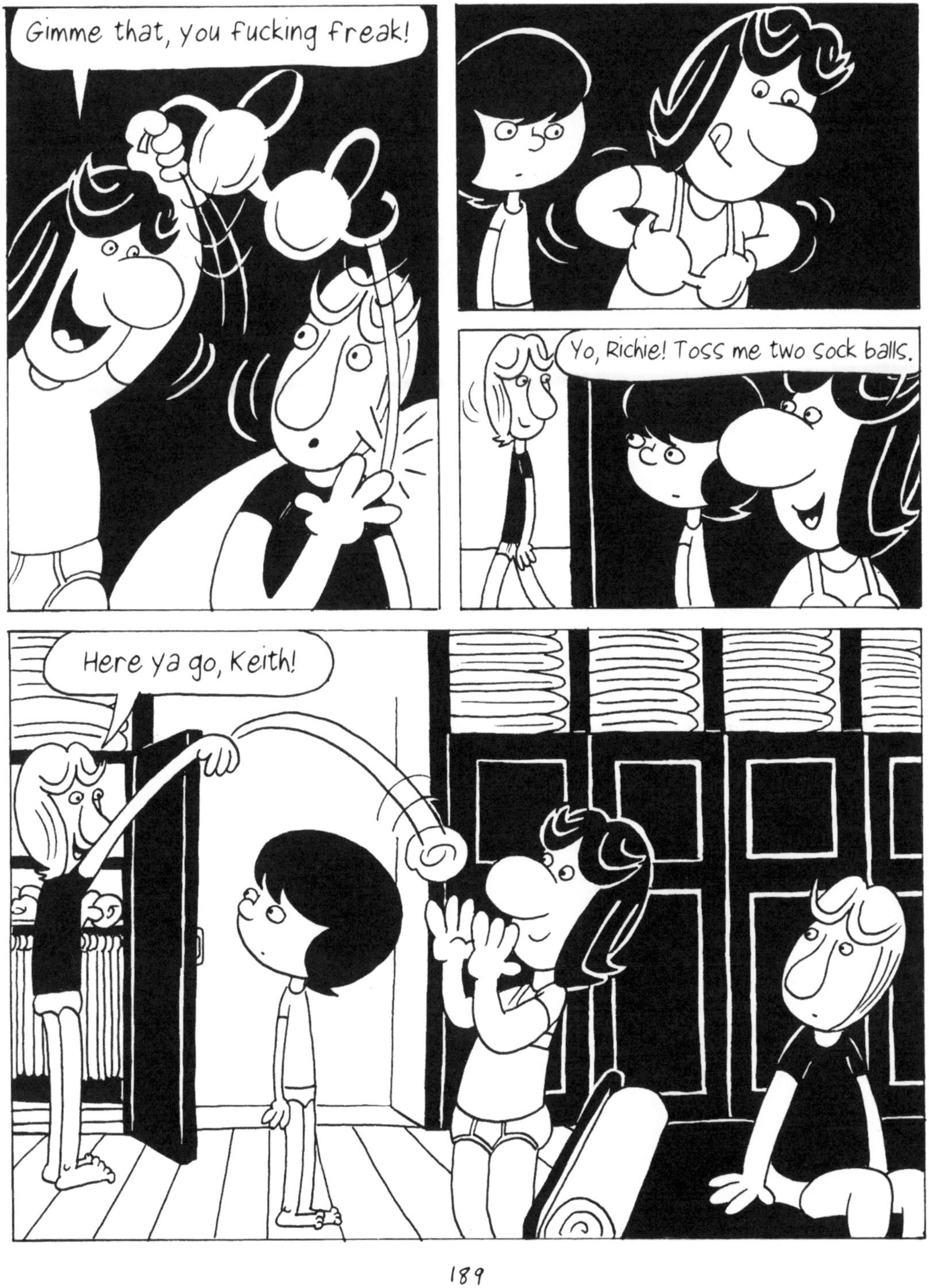
Gimme that, you fucking freak!
Yo, Richie! Toss me two sock balls.
Here ya go, Keith!

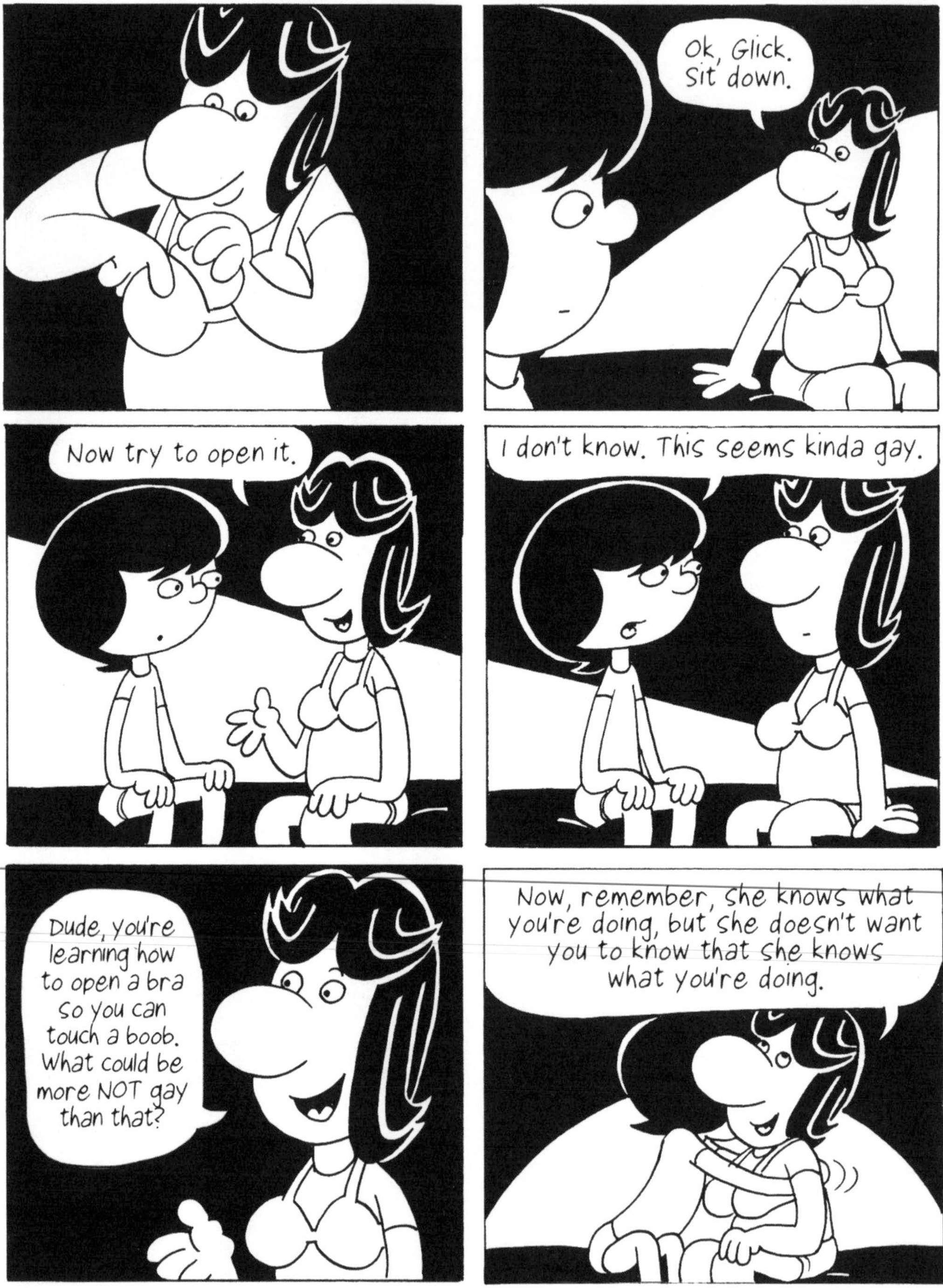
Ok, Glick. Sit down.
Now try to open it.
I don't know. This seems kinda gay.
Dude, you're learning how to open a bra so you can touch a boob. What could be more NOT gay than that?
Now, remember, she knows what you're doing, but she doesn't want you to know that she knows what you're doing.

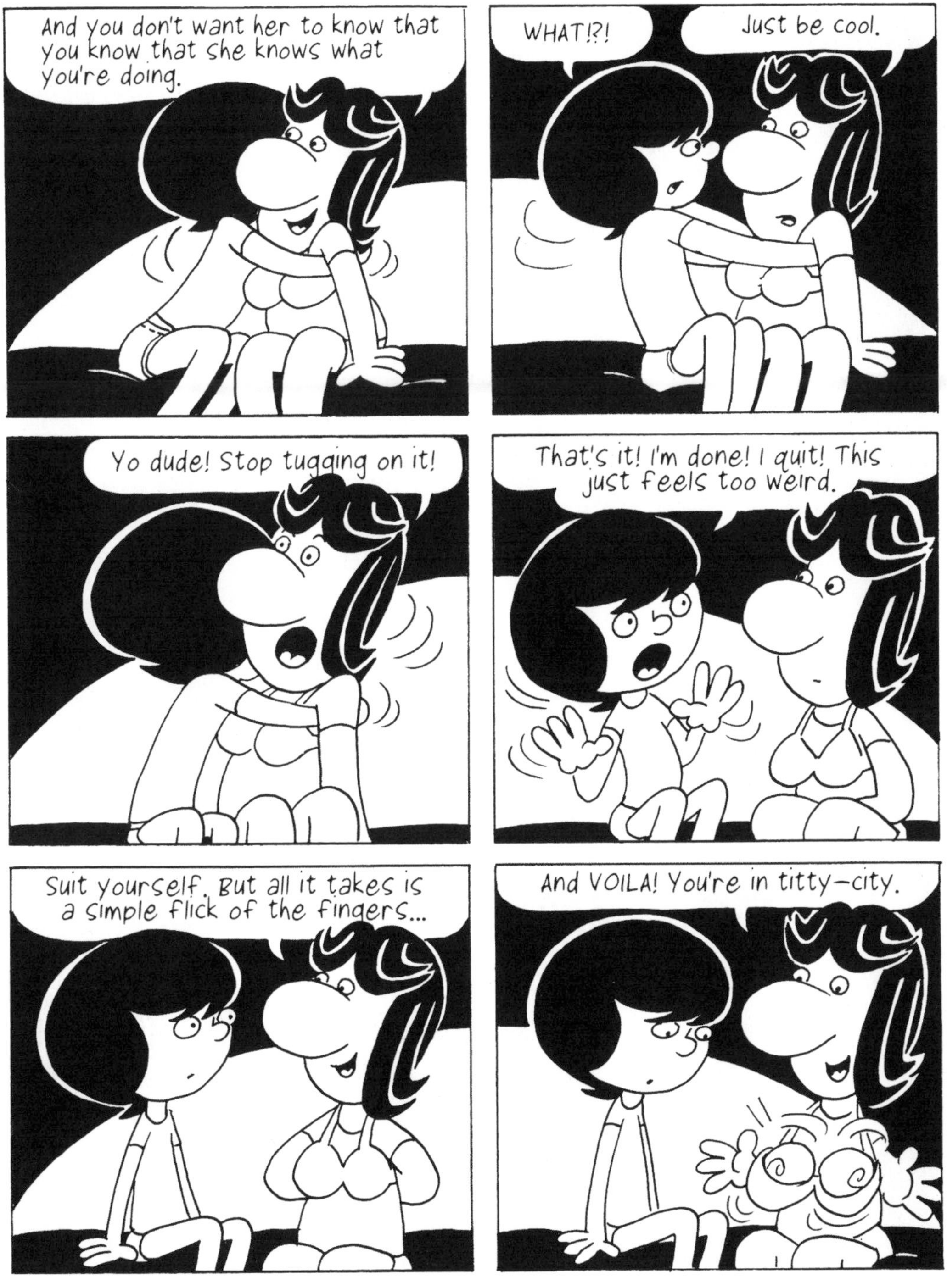
And you don't want her to know that you know that she knows what you're doing.
WHAT!?!
Just be cool.
Yo dude! Stop tugging on it!
That's it! I'm done! I quit! This just feels too weird.
Suit yourself. But all it takes is a simple flick of the fingers...
And VOILA! You're in titty-city.

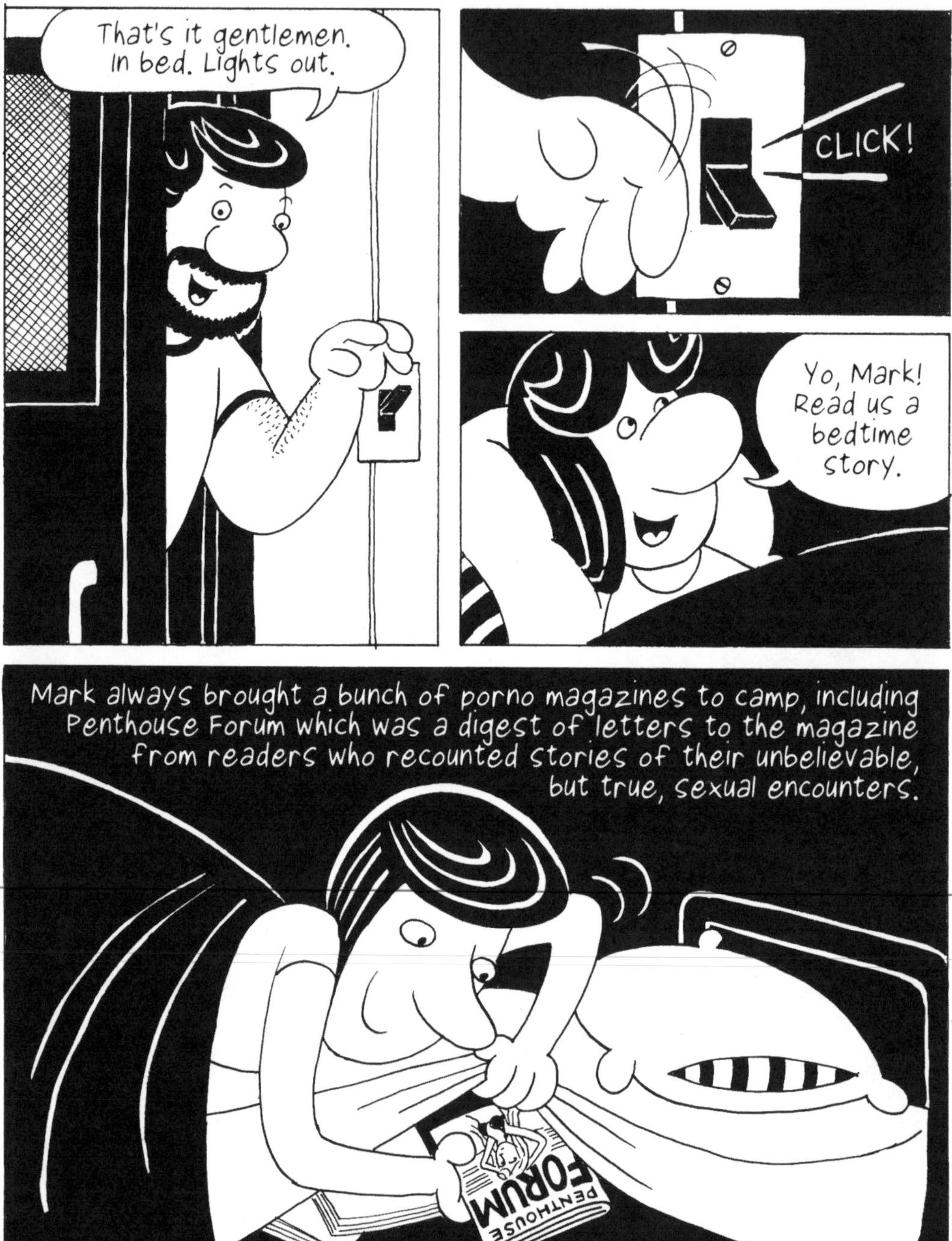
That's it gentlemen. In bed. Lights out.
CLICK!
Yo, Mark! Read us a bedtime story.
Mark always brought a bunch of porno magazines to camp, including Penthouse Forum which was a digest of letters to the magazine from readers who recounted stories of their unbelievable, but true, sexual encounters.
PENTHOUSE FORUM

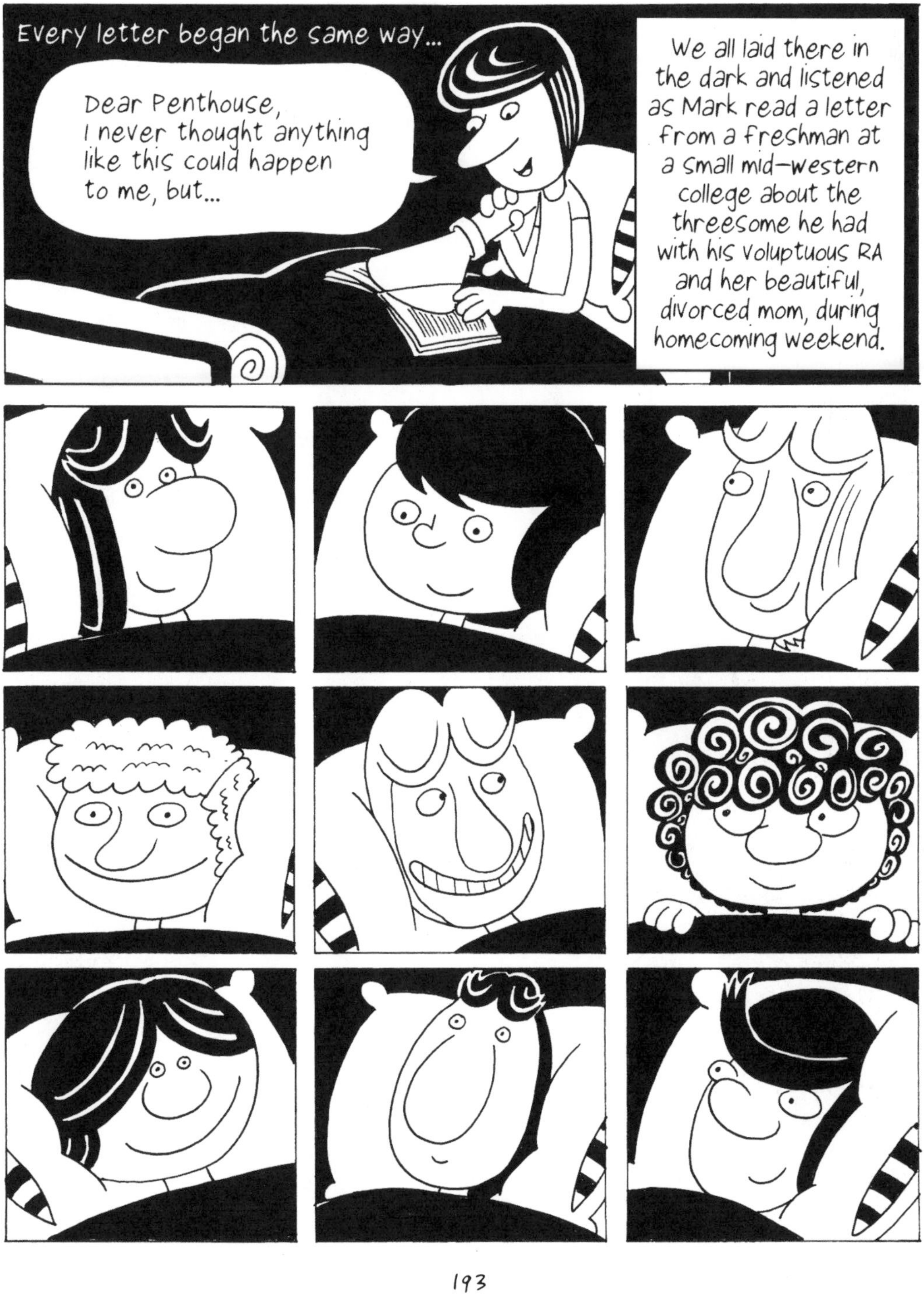

Every letter began the same way...
Dear Penthouse, I never thought anything like this could happen to me, but...
We all laid there in the dark and listened as Mark read a letter from a freshman at a small mid-western college about the threesome he had with his voluptuous RA and her beautiful, divorced mom, during homecoming weekend.

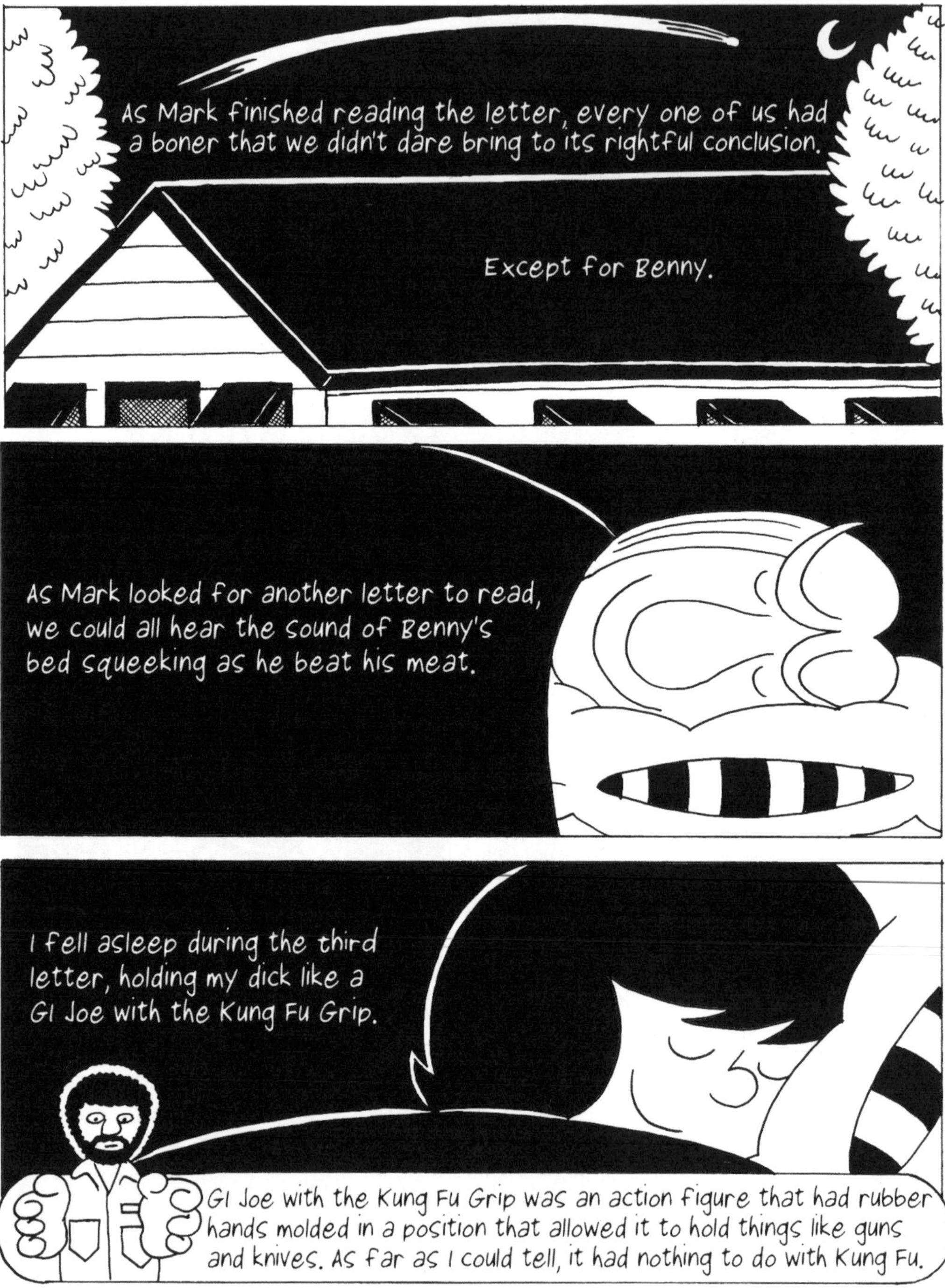

As Mark finished reading the letter, every one of us had a boner that we didn't dare bring to its rightful conclusion.
Except for Benny.
As Mark looked for another letter to read, we could all hear the sound of Benny's bed squeeking as he beat his meat.
I fell asleep during the third letter, holding my dick like a GI Joe with the Kung Fu Grip.
GI Joe with the Kung Fu Grip was an action figure that had rubber hands molded in a position that allowed it to hold things like guns and knives. As far as I could tell, it had nothing to do with Kung Fu.

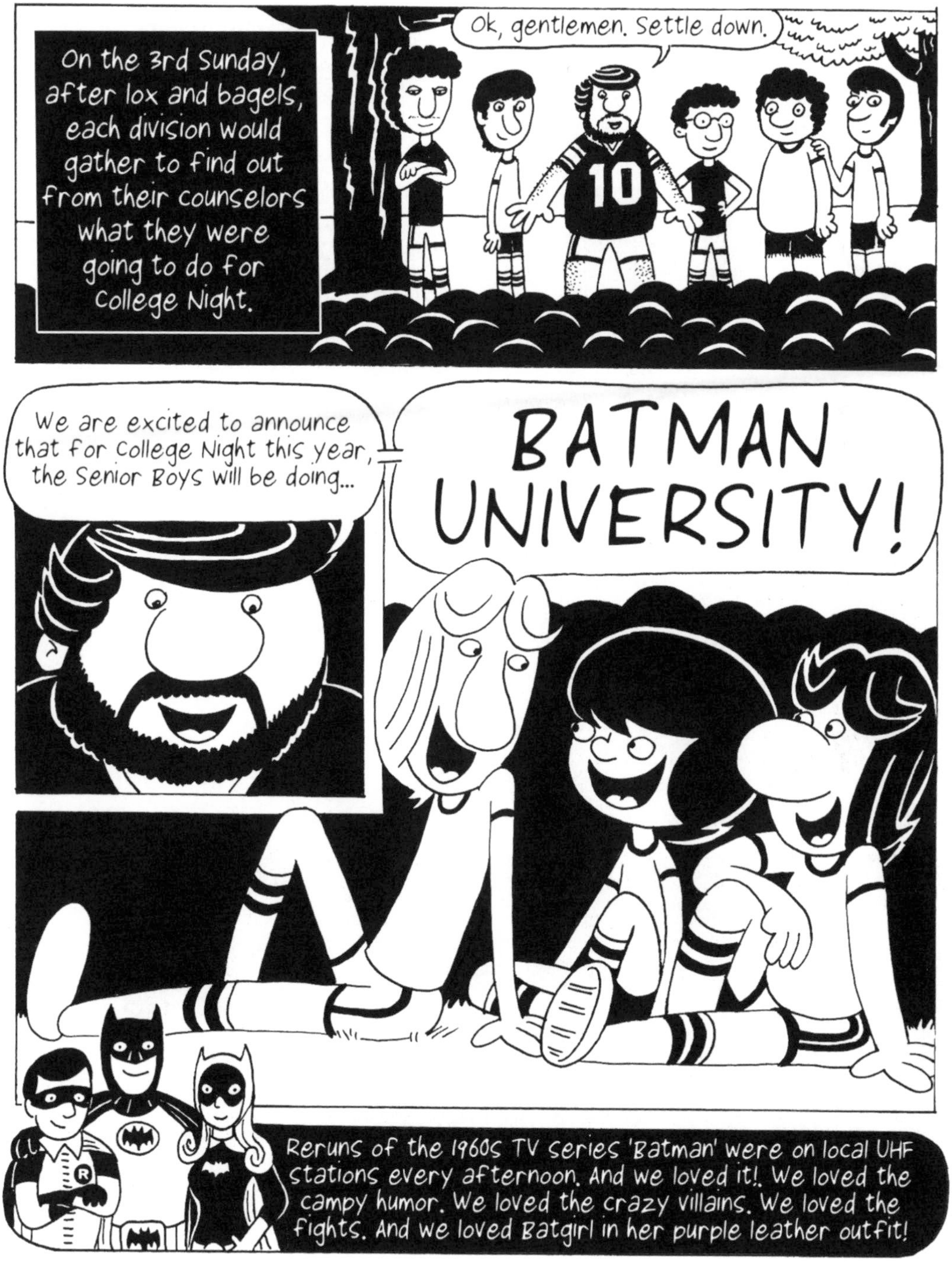
On the 3rd Sunday, after lox and bagels, each division would gather to find out from their counselors what they were going to do for College Night.
Ok, gentlemen. Settle down.
10
We are excited to announce that for College Night this year, the Senior Boys will be doing...
BATMAN UNIVERSITY!
R
Reruns of the 1960s TV series 'Batman' were on local UHF stations every afternoon. And we loved it!. We loved the campy humor. We loved the crazy villains. We loved the fights. And we loved Batgirl in her purple leather outfit!

Over the next week, we prepared for College Night.

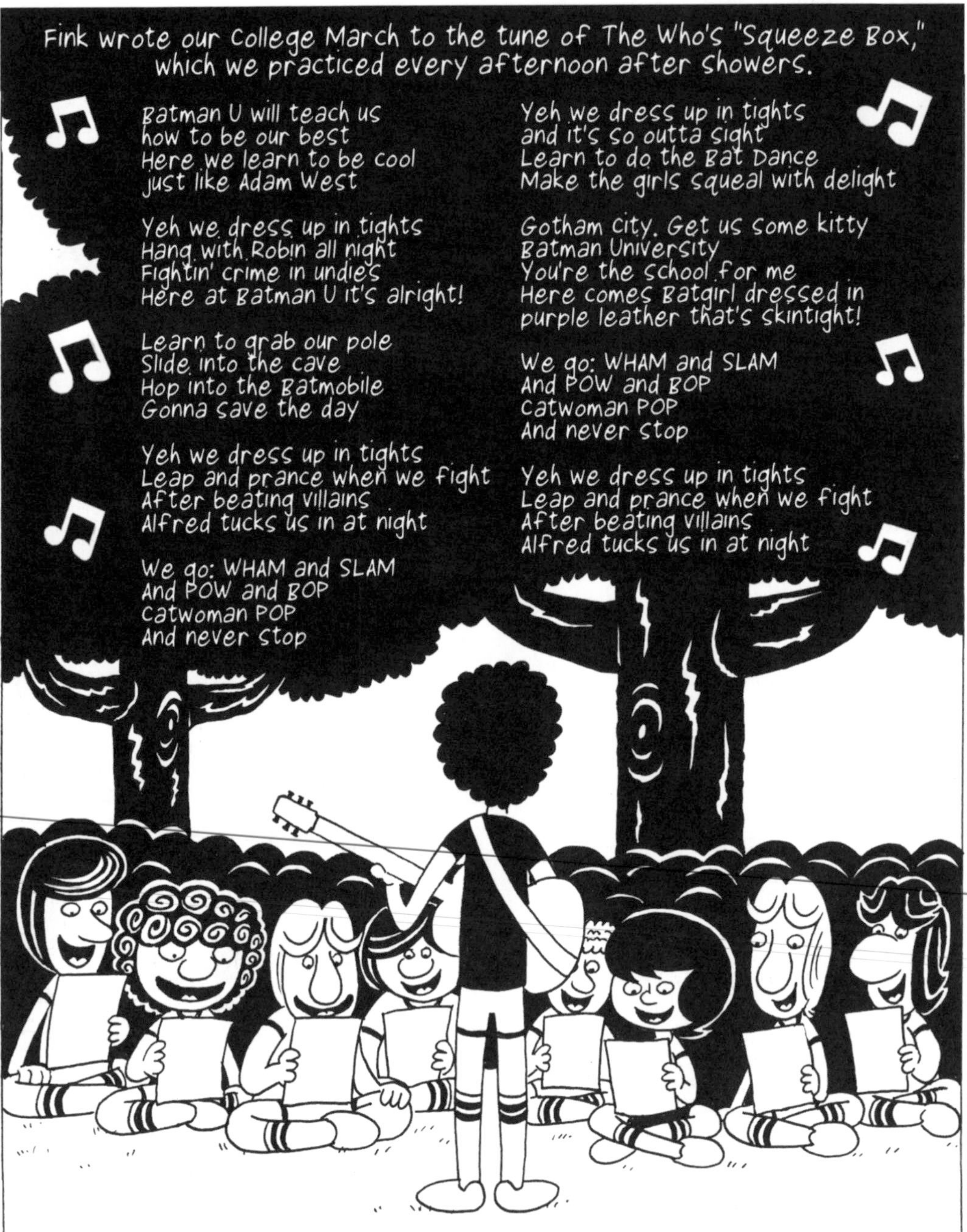
Fink wrote our College March to the tune of The Who's "Squeeze Box," which we practiced every afternoon after showers.
Batman U will teach us
how to be our best
Here we learn to be cool
just like Adam West
Yeh we dress up in tights
Hang with Robin all night
Fightin' crime in undies
Here at Batman U it's alright!
Learn to grab our pole
Slide into the cave
Hop into the Batmobile
Gonna save the day
Yeh we dress up in tights
Leap and prance when we fight
After beating villains
Alfred tucks us in at night
We go: WHAM and SLAM
And POW and BOP
Catwoman POP
And never stop
Yeh we dress up in tights
and it's so outta sight
Learn to do the Bat Dance
Make the girls squeal with delight
Gotham City. Get us some kitty
Batman University
You're the school for me
Here comes Batgirl dressed in
purple leather that's skintight!
We go: WHAM and SLAM
And POW and BOP
Catwoman POP
And never stop
Yeh we dress up in tights
Leap and prance when we fight
After beating villains
Alfred tucks us in at night

We rehearsed choreography that Grape-Ape created to go with the March.

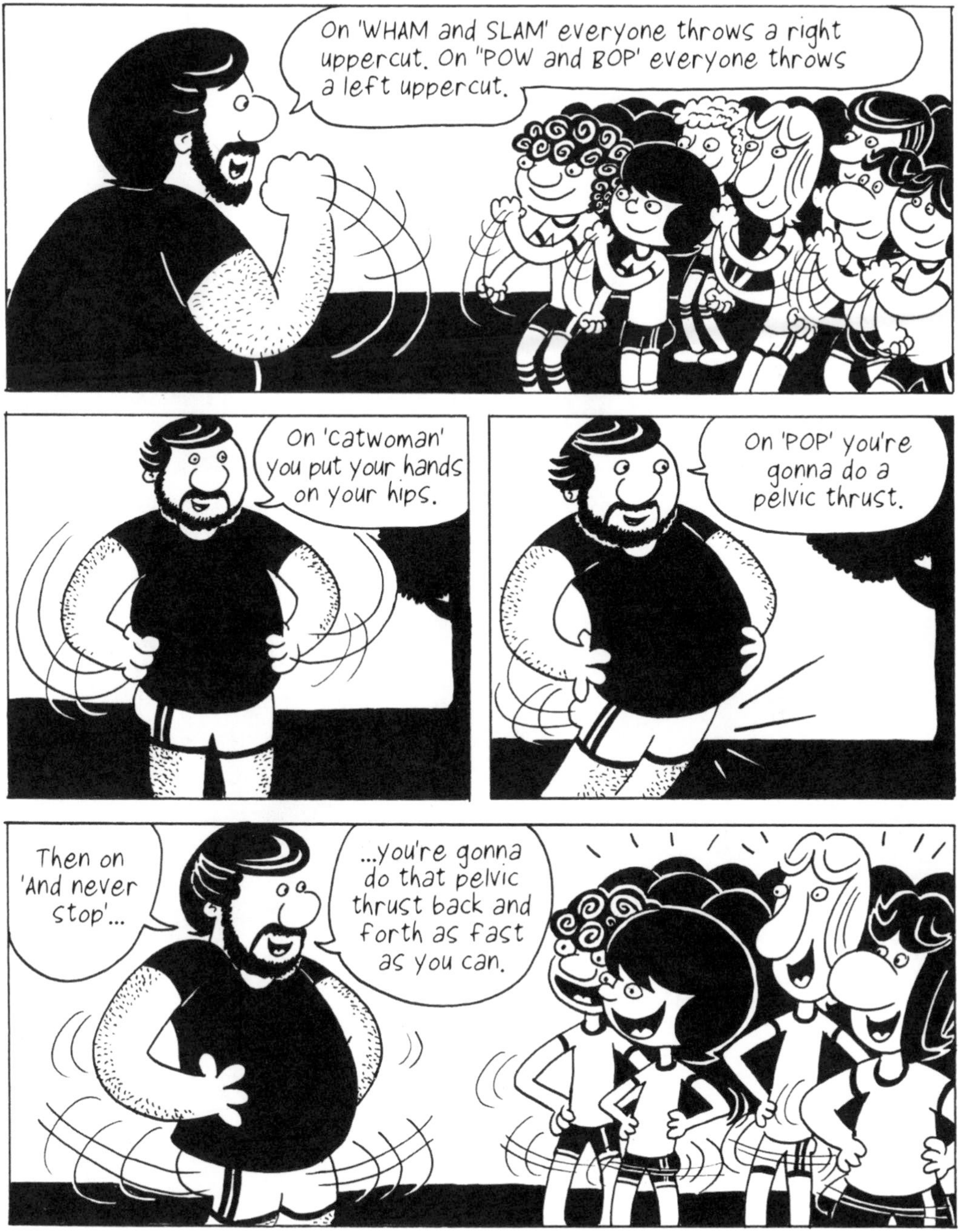
On 'WHAM and SLAM' everyone throws a right uppercut. On "POW and BOP' everyone throws a left uppercut.
On 'Catwoman' you put your hands on your hips.
On 'POP' you're gonna do a pelvic thrust.
Then on 'And never stop'...
...you're gonna do that pelvic thrust back and forth as fast as you can.

We put together costumes for every senior camper and counselor.

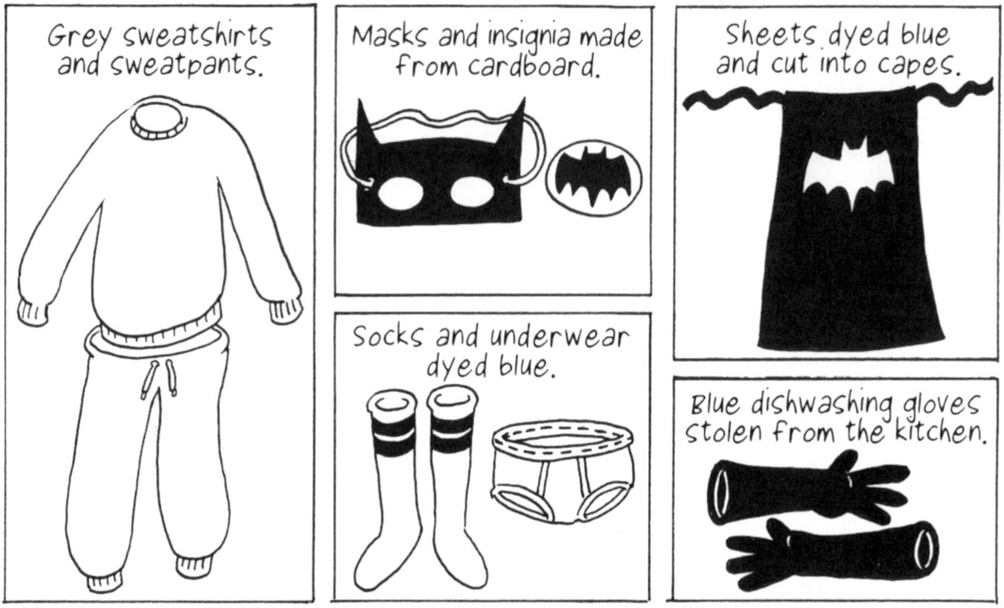
Grey sweatshirts and sweatpants.
Masks and insignia made from cardboard.
Sheets dyed blue and cut into capes.
Socks and underwear dyed blue.
Blue dishwashing gloves stolen from the kitchen.

I designed our banner and painted it on a large sheet.

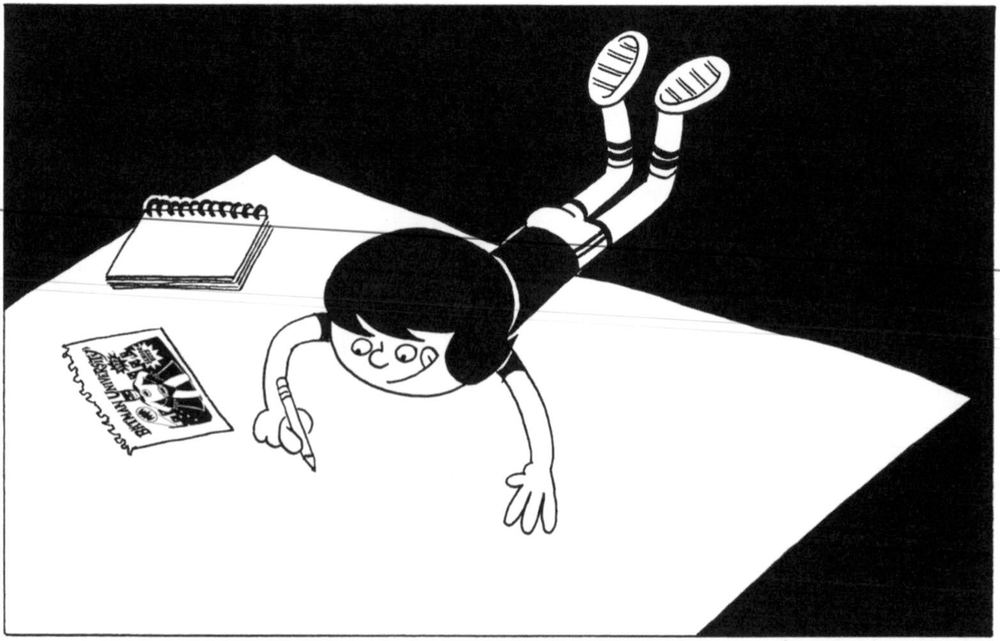

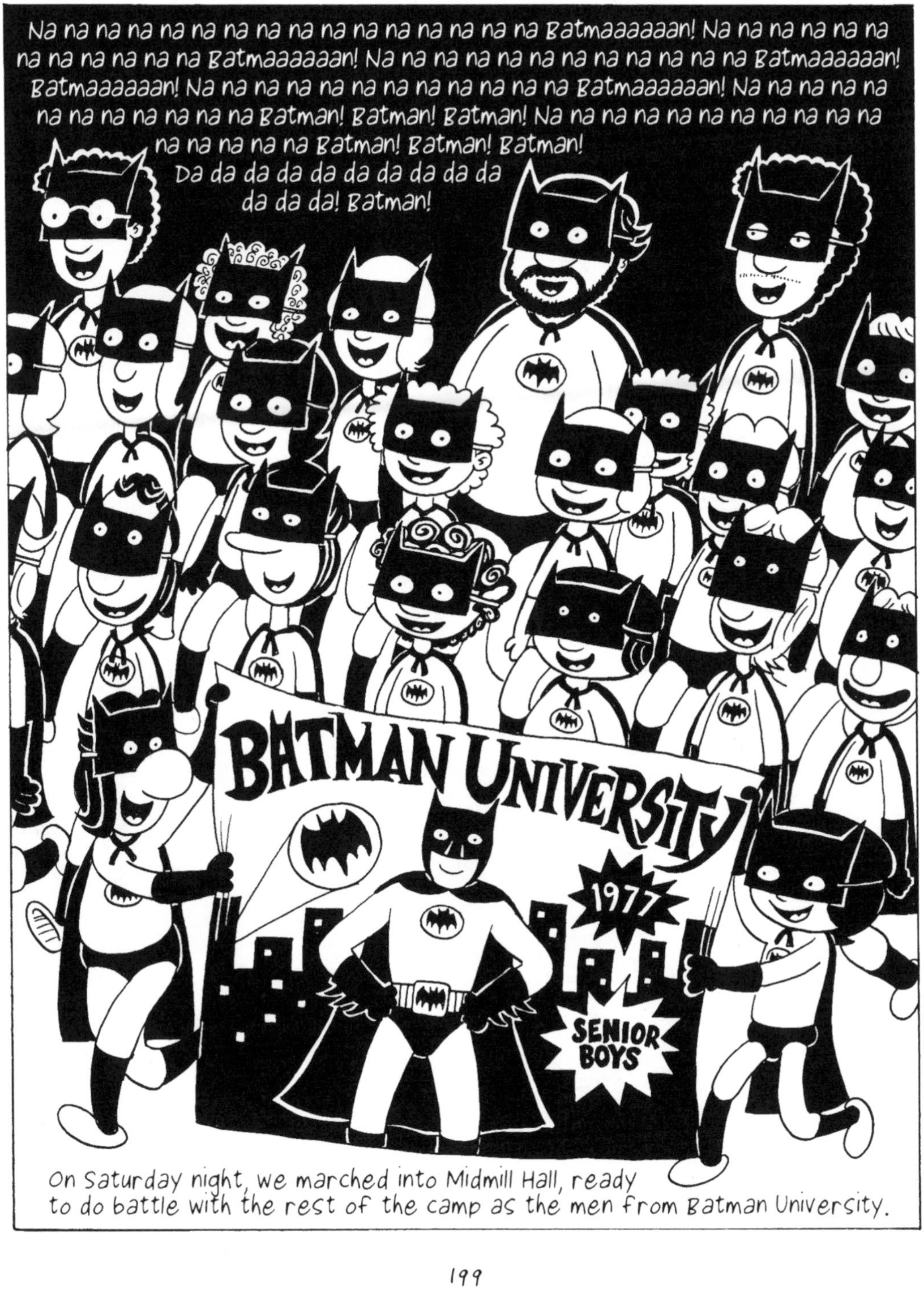
Na na na na na na na na na na na na na na na na Batmaaaaaaan! Na na na na na na na na na na na na Batmaaaaaaan! Na na na na na na na na na na na na Batmaaaaaaan! Batmaaaaaaan! Na na na na na na na na na na na na Batmaaaaaaan! Na na na na na na na na na na na na Batman! Batman! Batman! Na na na na na na na na na na na na na na na na Batman! Batman! Batman!
Da da da da da da da da da da da da da! Batman!
BATMAN UNIVERSITY
1977
SENIOR BOYS
On Saturday night, we marched into Midmill Hall, ready to do battle with the rest of the camp as the men from Batman University.

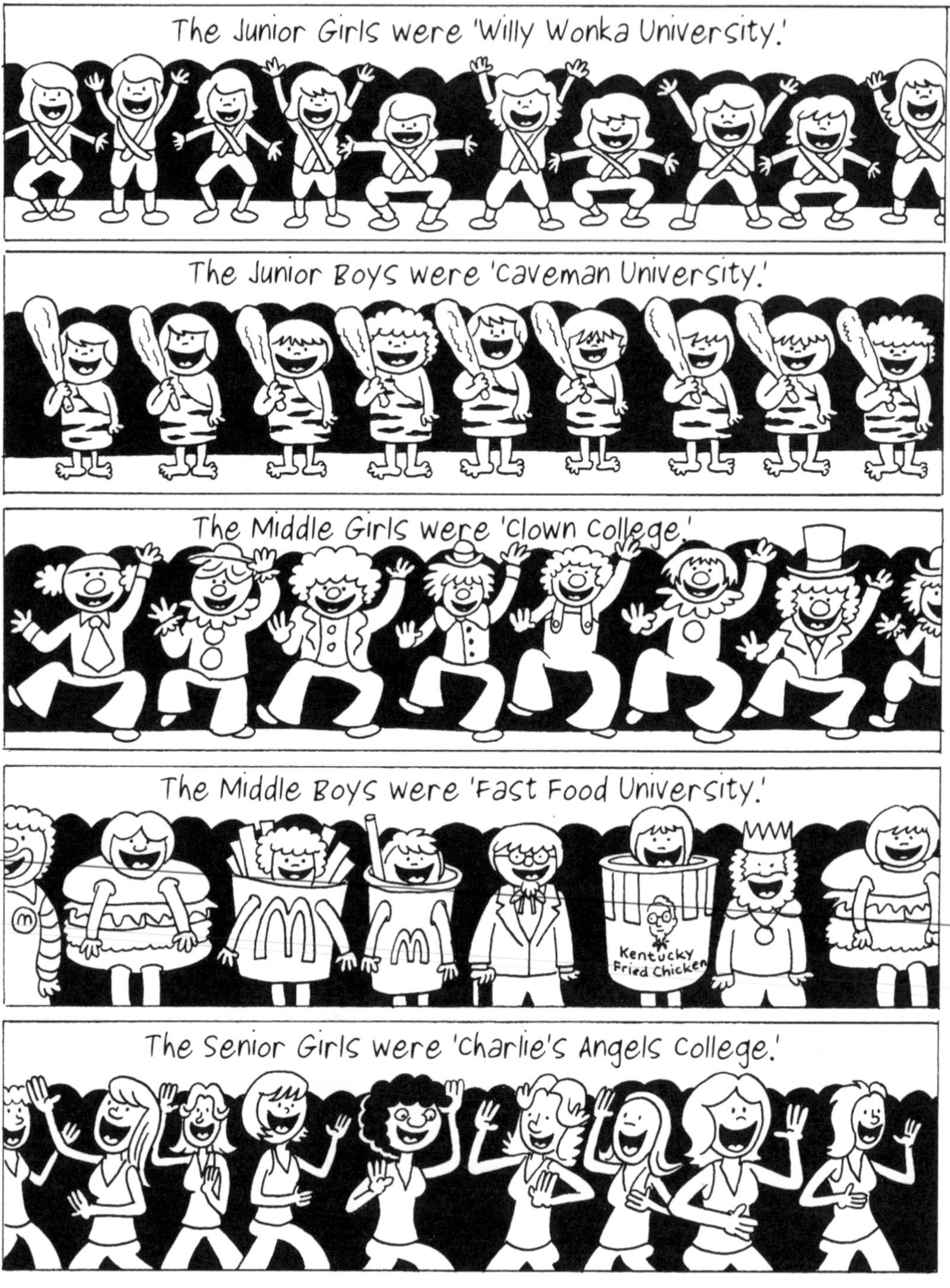
The Junior Girls were 'Willy Wonka University.'
The Junior Boys were 'Caveman University.'
The Middle Girls were 'Clown College.'
The Middle Boys were 'Fast Food University.'
Kentucky Fried Chicken
The Senior Girls were 'Charlie's Angels College.'

The Junior Girls march was sung to 'The Oompa Loompa Song' from the movie "Willy Wonka and the Chocolate Factory."

Willy Wonka! Doopity Doo!
If you love candy, this school's for you
Willy Wonka! Doopity Dee!
CHOCK—LIT or CHAWK—LIT
we'll never agree

The Junior Boys march was sung to 'Hooked on a Feeling' by Blue Swede.

OOGA CHAHKA! OOGA OOGA! OOGA CHAHKA! OOGA OOGA!

We discovered fire   Dino—burgers   Ah—ah—ahhhhhhhh!
that was a big deal   fill our bellies   that cro—magnum feeling
Then we took a big rock   Wooly mammoth   is oh so appealing
and we made a wheel   Keep us warm at night   Right here at caveman U

The Middle Girls march was sung to 'Get Down Tonight' by KC and the Sunshine Band.

Do a goofy dance! Sing a silly song!   Let's clown, let's clown,
Let's clown tonight! Let's clown tonight!   let's clown, let's clown,
Do a goofy dance! Sing a silly song!   let's clown tonight, Bozo!
Let's clown tonight! Let's clown tonight!

The Middle Boys march was sung to 'Saturday Night' by The Bay City Rollers.

F—A—S—T—F—O—O—D—U!
F—A—S—T—F—O—O—D—U!

The Senior Girls march was sung to 'Rhinestone Cowboy' by Glenn Campbell

Charlie's Angels College
Learn to fight in gowns and 6—inch high stillettos
At Charlie's Angels College
Never wear a bra, so we jiggle like a bowl of Jell—O
And our hair's always perfectly blown

Each division also did a skit. Our skit was a peek inside classes at Batman U. Fink was the professor for 'Batpole 101.'

Ok class. First, you want to grab your pole and get a real good grip on it.

Next, you'll want to get your pole between your legs.

Then you're gonna want to start sliding on your pole real slow.

Ok. Good. Now slide on your pole a little faster. Good! Now faster. Faster. Faster.

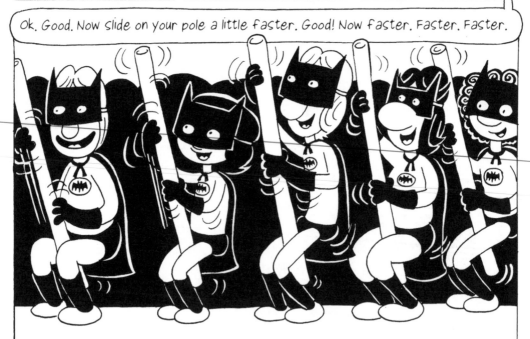

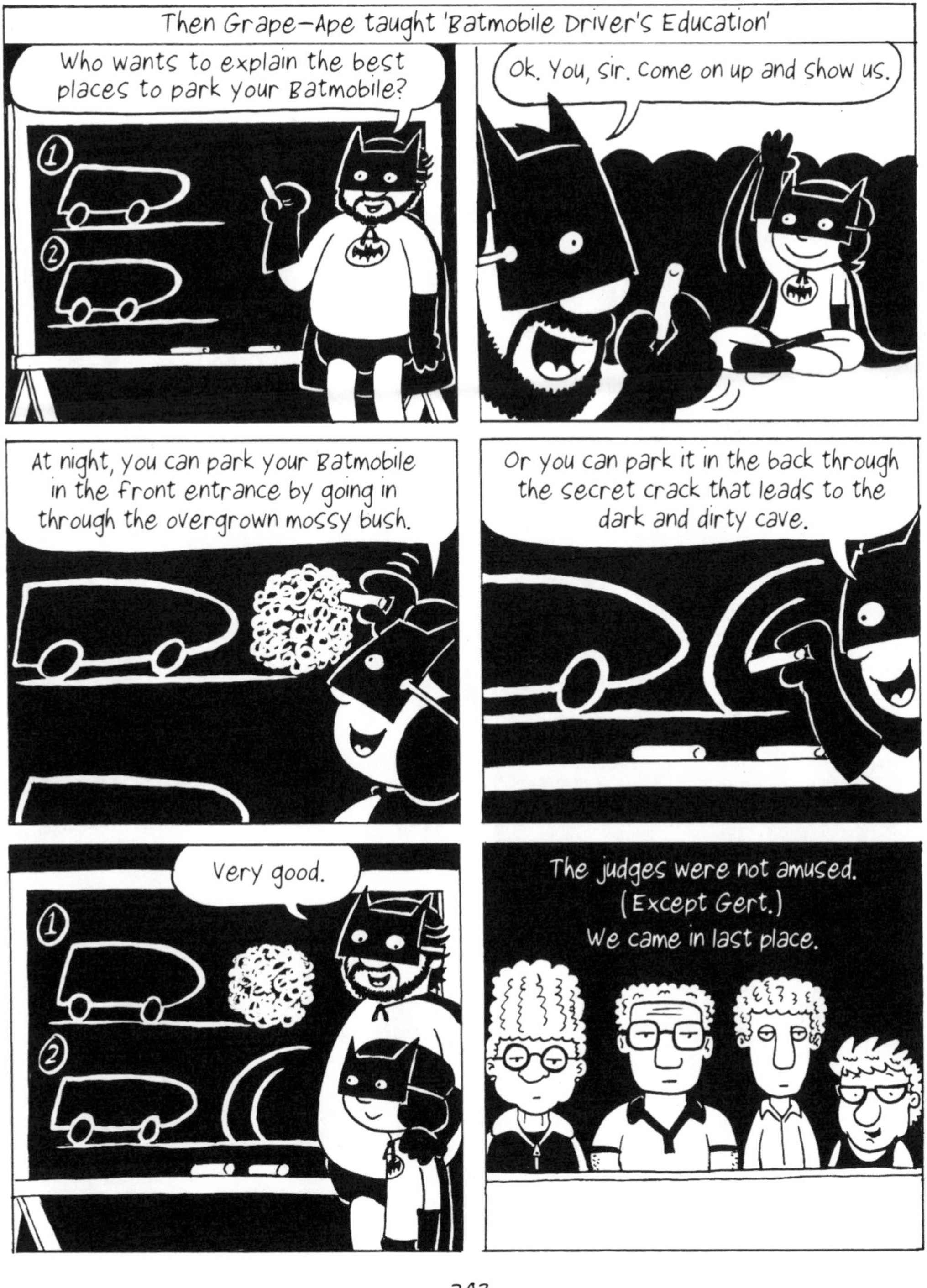
Then Grape-Ape taught 'Batmobile Driver's Education'
Who wants to explain the best places to park your Batmobile?
Ok. You, sir. Come on up and show us.
At night, you can park your Batmobile in the front entrance by going in through the overgrown mossy bush.
Or you can park it in the back through the secret crack that leads to the dark and dirty cave.
Very good.
The judges were not amused. (Except Gert.) We came in last place.

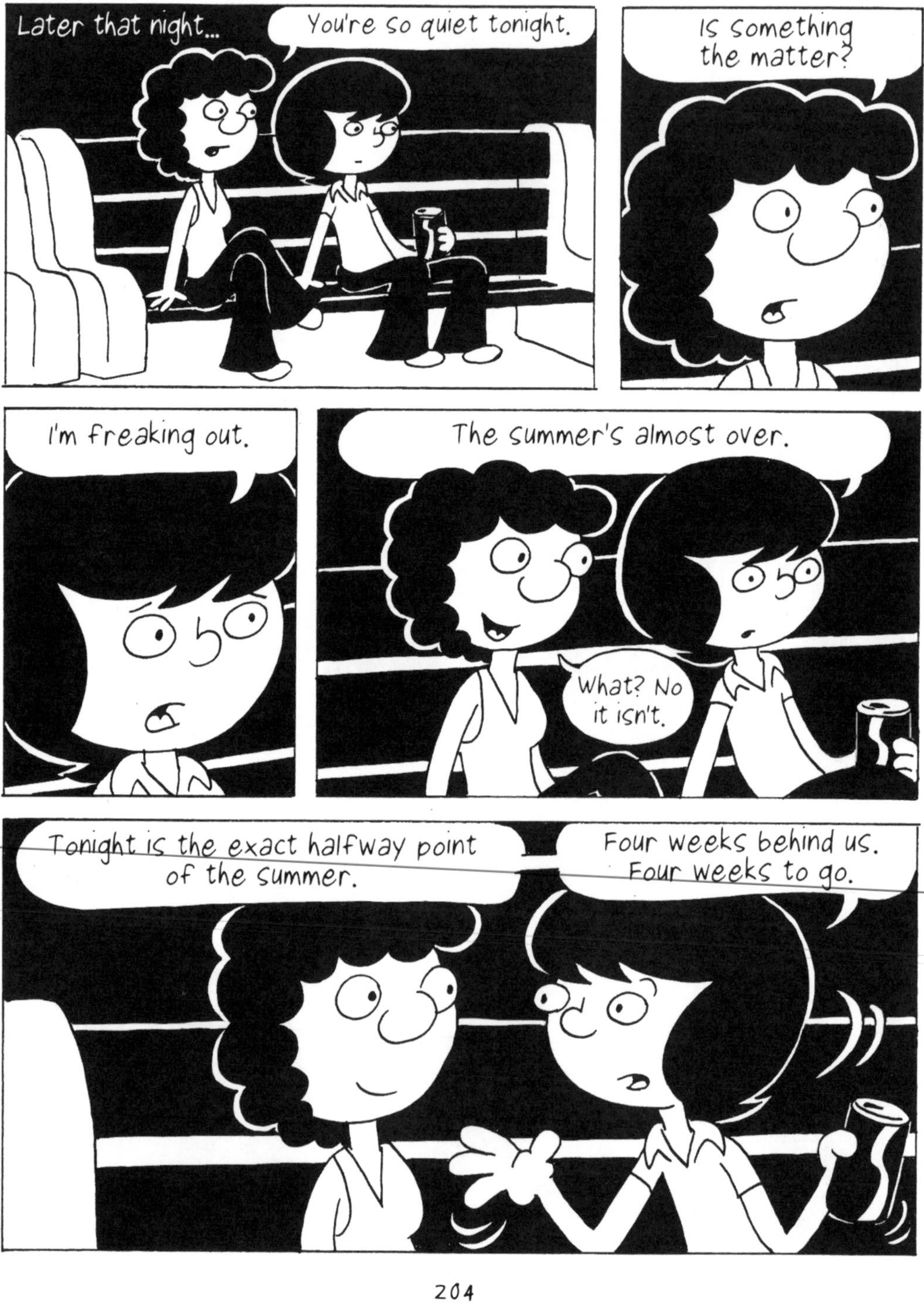
Later that night...
You're so quiet tonight.
Is something the matter?
I'm freaking out.
The summer's almost over.
What? No it isn't.
Tonight is the exact halfway point of the summer.
Four weeks behind us. Four weeks to go.

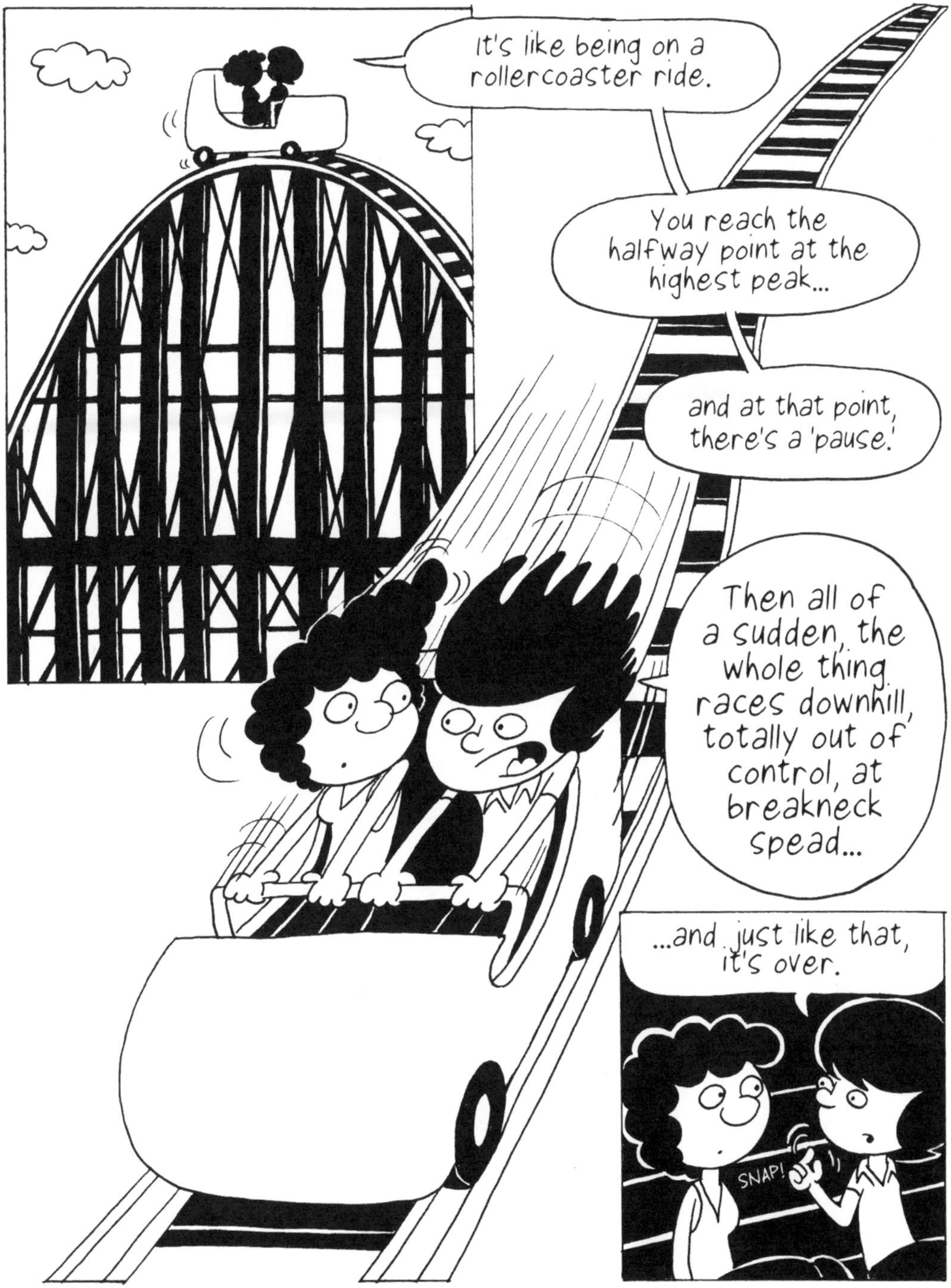
It's like being on a rollercoaster ride.
You reach the halfway point at the highest peak...
and at that point, there's a 'pause.'
Then all of a sudden, the whole thing races downhill, totally out of control, at breakneck spead...
...and just like that, it's over.
SNAP!

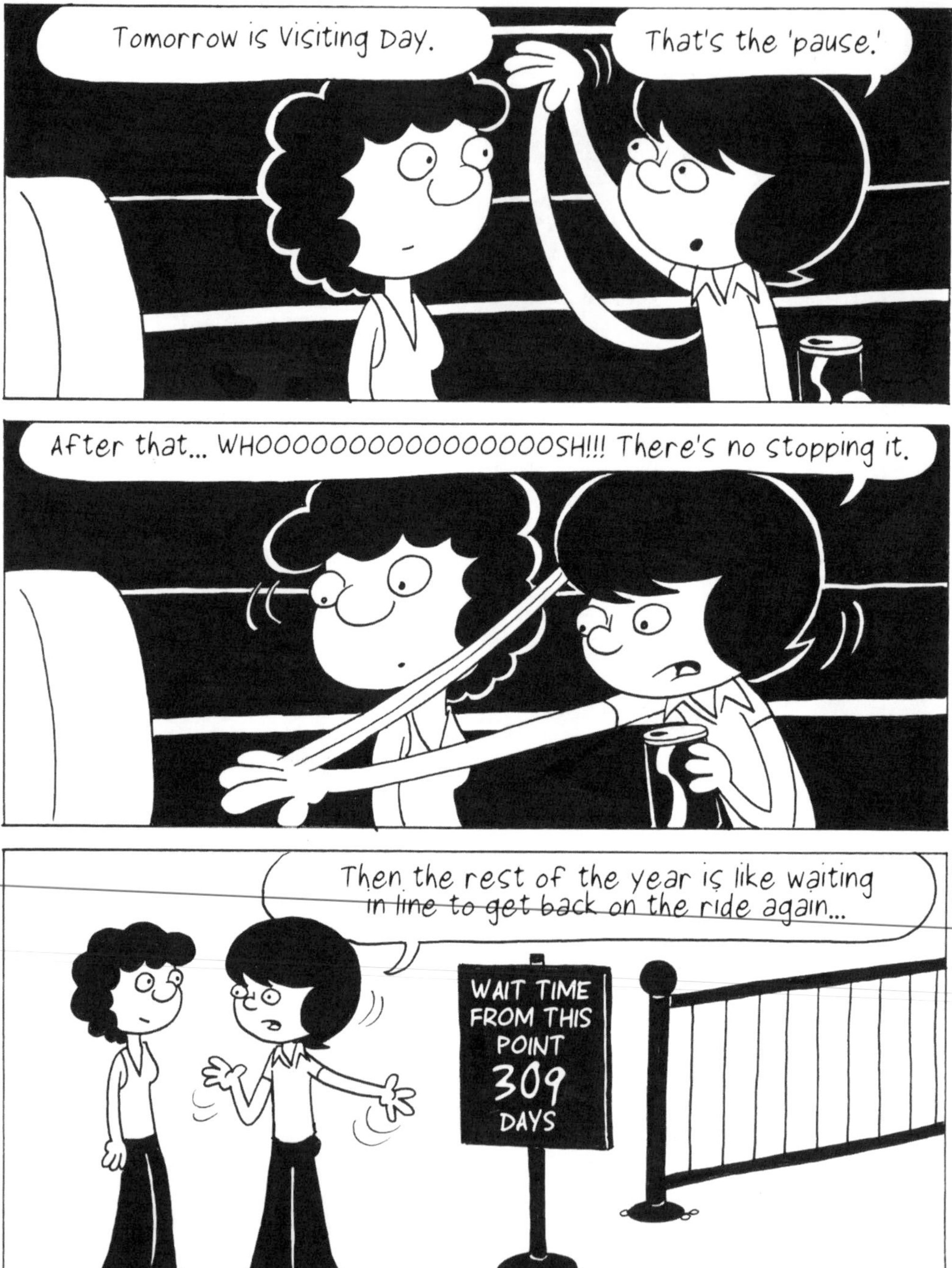
Tomorrow is Visiting Day.
That's the 'pause.'
After that... WHOOOOOOOOOOOOOOOOOSH!!! There's no stopping it.
Then the rest of the year is like waiting in line to get back on the ride again...
WAIT TIME FROM THIS POINT 309 DAYS

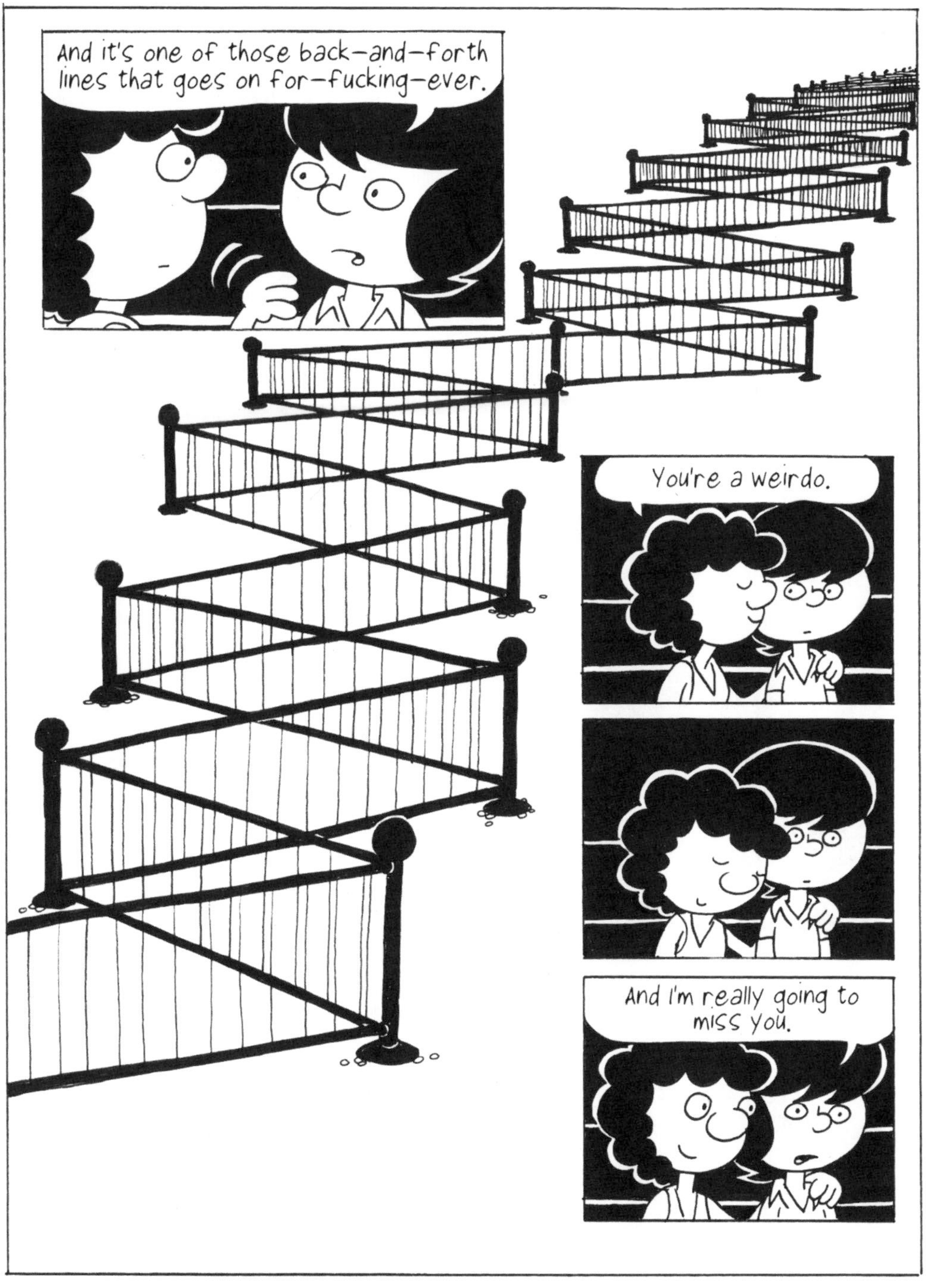
And it's one of those back-and-forth lines that goes on for-fucking-ever.
You're a weirdo.
And I'm really going to miss you.

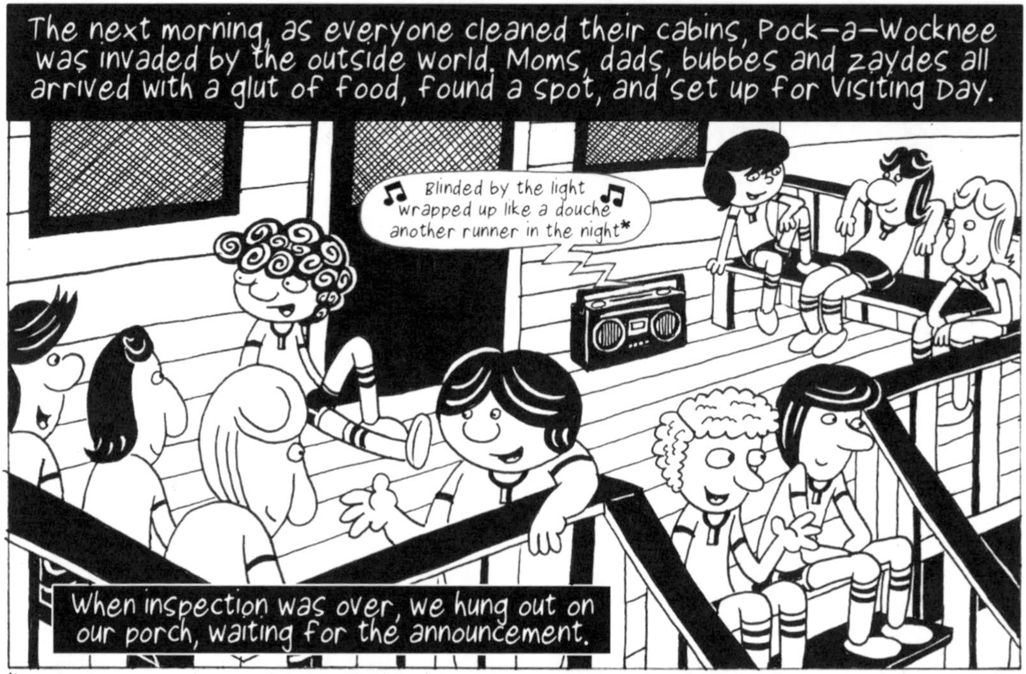
The next morning, as everyone cleaned their cabins, Pock-a-Wocknee was invaded by the outside world. Moms, dads, bubbes and zaydes all arrived with a glut of food, found a spot, and set up for Visiting Day.
♫ Blinded by the light wrapped up like a douche another runner in the night* ♫
When inspection was over, we hung out on our porch, waiting for the announcement.

*Manfred Mann's version of 'Blinded by the Light.' (I know those aren't the lyrics, but that's what we thought he was singing.)

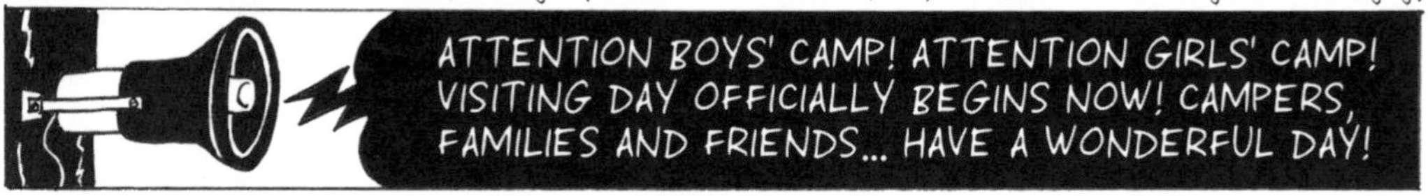
ATTENTION BOYS' CAMP! ATTENTION GIRLS' CAMP! VISITING DAY OFFICIALLY BEGINS NOW! CAMPERS, FAMILIES AND FRIENDS... HAVE A WONDERFUL DAY!

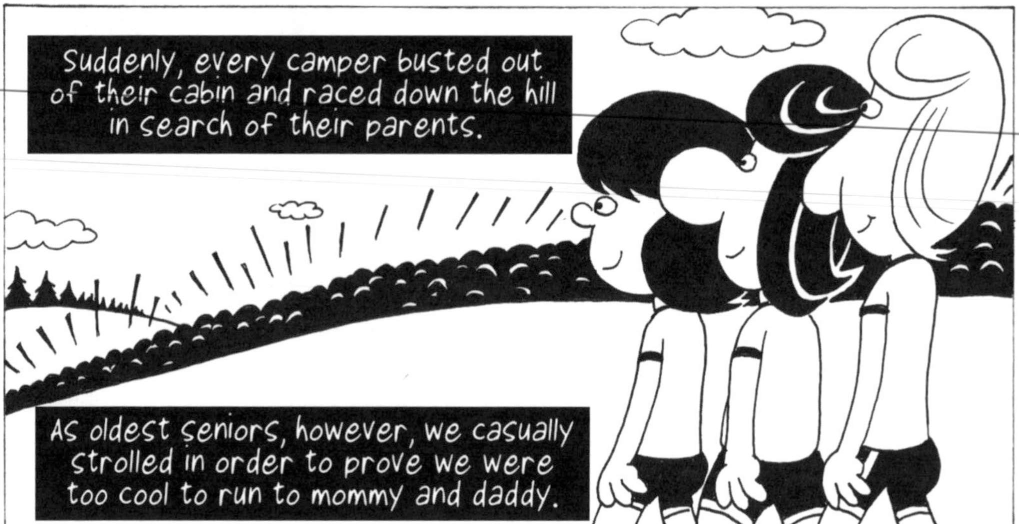
Suddenly, every camper busted out of their cabin and raced down the hill in search of their parents.
As oldest seniors, however, we casually strolled in order to prove we were too cool to run to mommy and daddy.

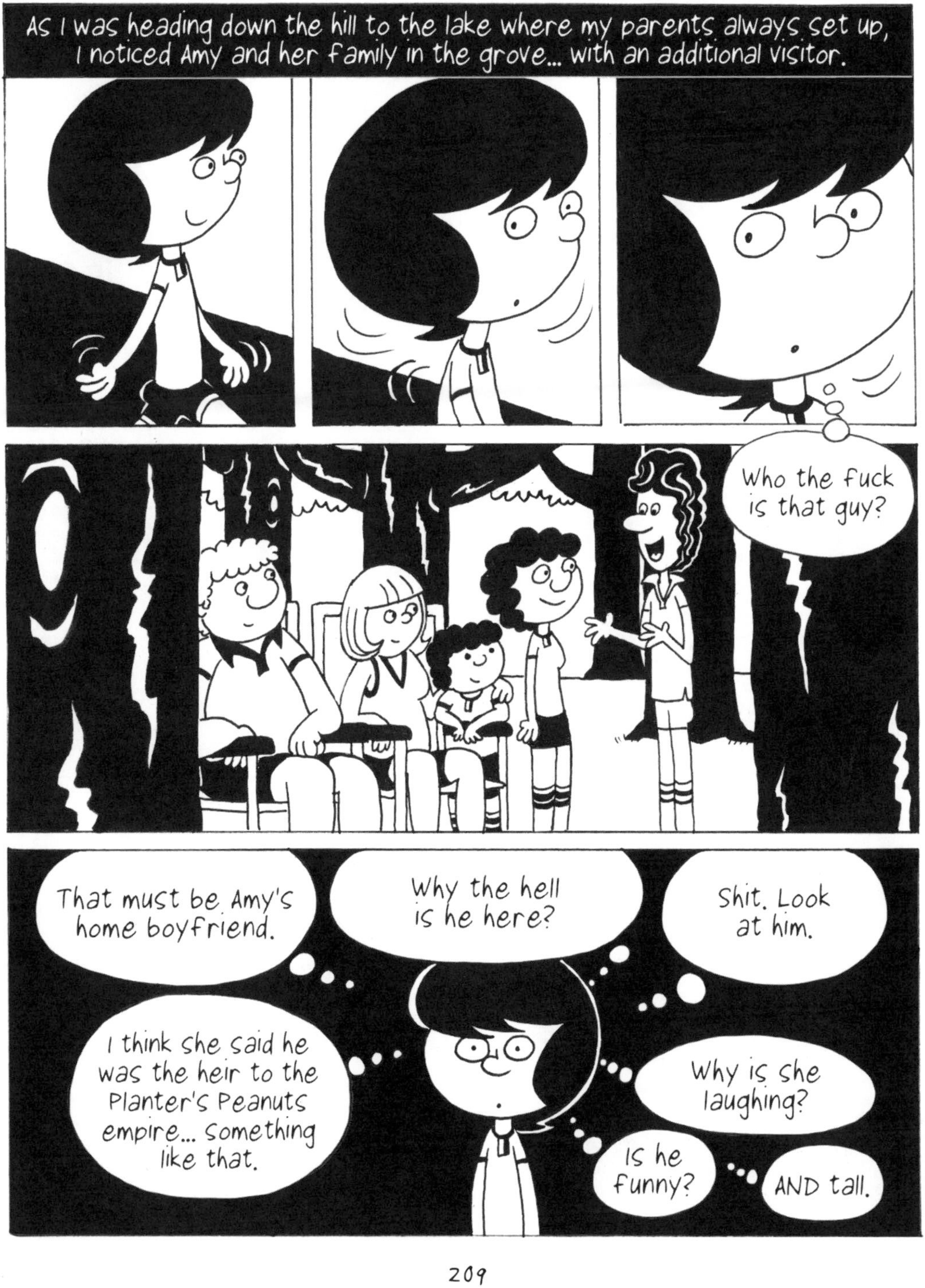
As I was heading down the hill to the lake where my parents always set up, I noticed Amy and her family in the grove... with an additional visitor.
Who the fuck is that guy?
That must be Amy's home boyfriend.
Why the hell is he here?
Shit. Look at him.
I think she said he was the heir to the Planter's Peanuts empire... something like that.
Why is she laughing?
Is he funny?
AND tall.

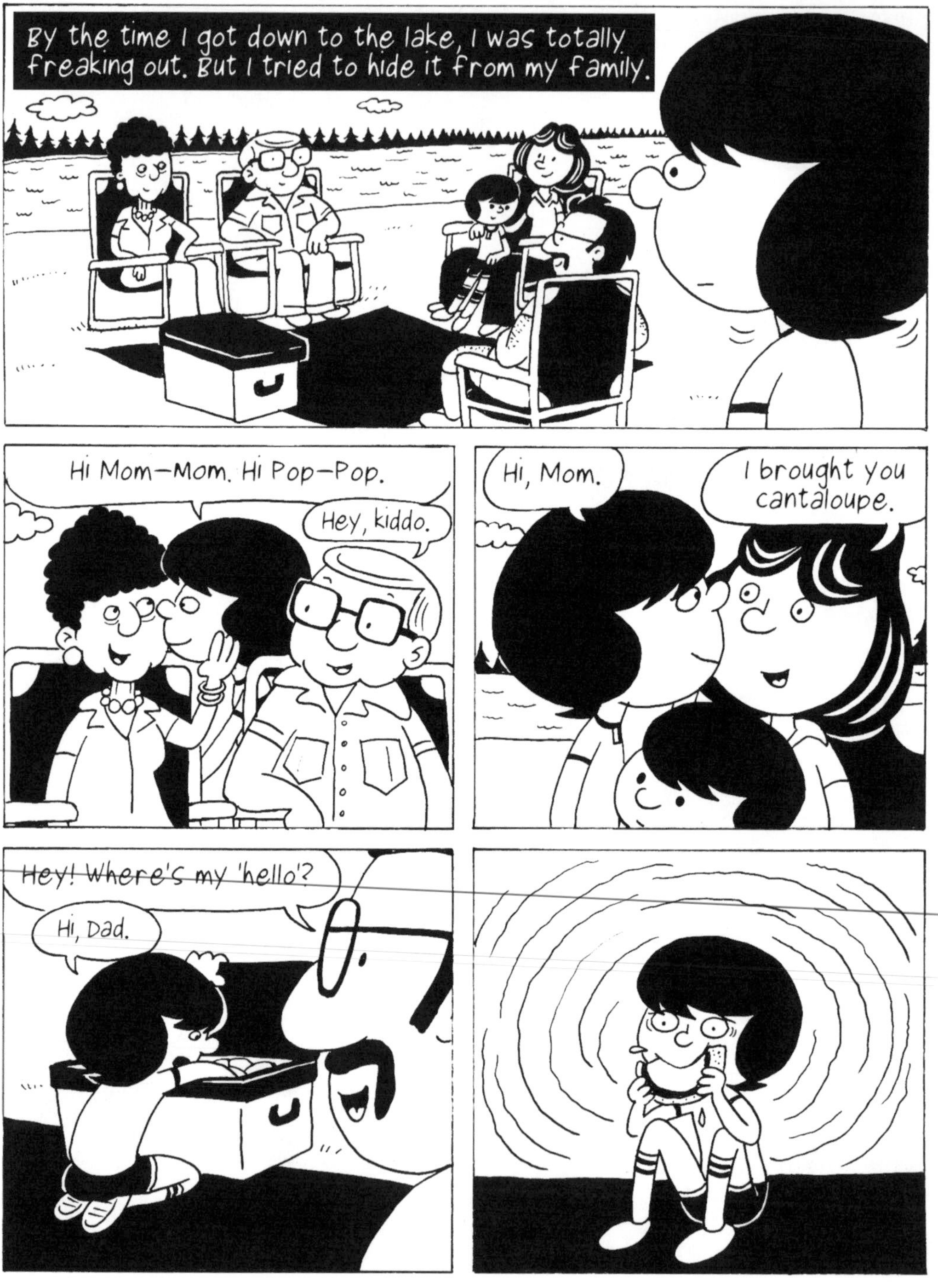
By the time I got down to the lake, I was totally freaking out. But I tried to hide it from my family.
Hi Mom—Mom. Hi Pop—Pop.
Hey, kiddo.
Hi, Mom.
I brought you cantaloupe.
Hey! Where's my 'hello'?
Hi, Dad.

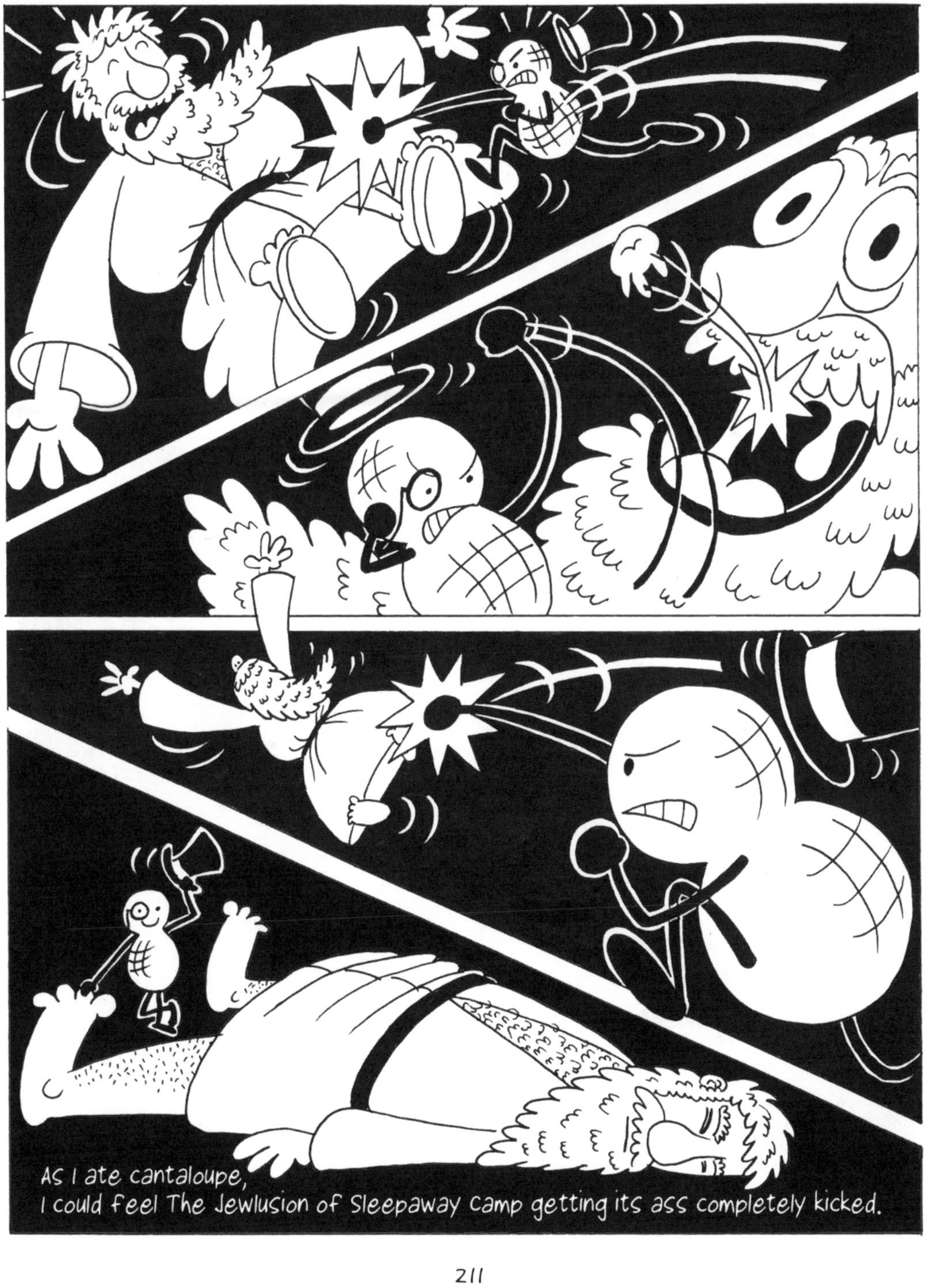
As I ate cantaloupe,
I could feel The Jewlusion of Sleepaway Camp getting its ass completely kicked.

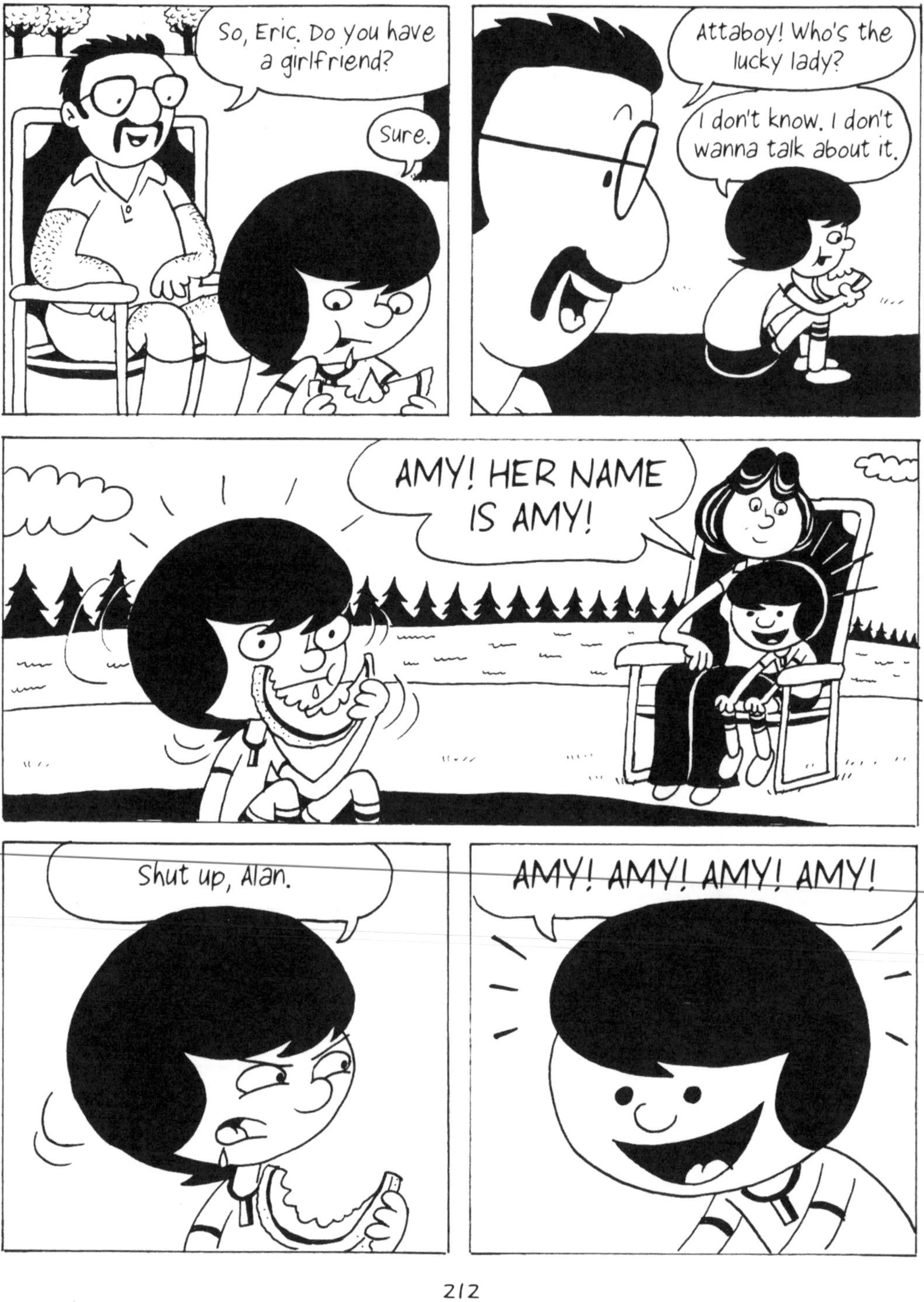
So, Eric. Do you have a girlfriend?
Sure.
Attaboy! Who's the lucky lady?
I don't know. I don't wanna talk about it.
AMY! HER NAME IS AMY!
Shut up, Alan.
AMY! AMY! AMY! AMY!

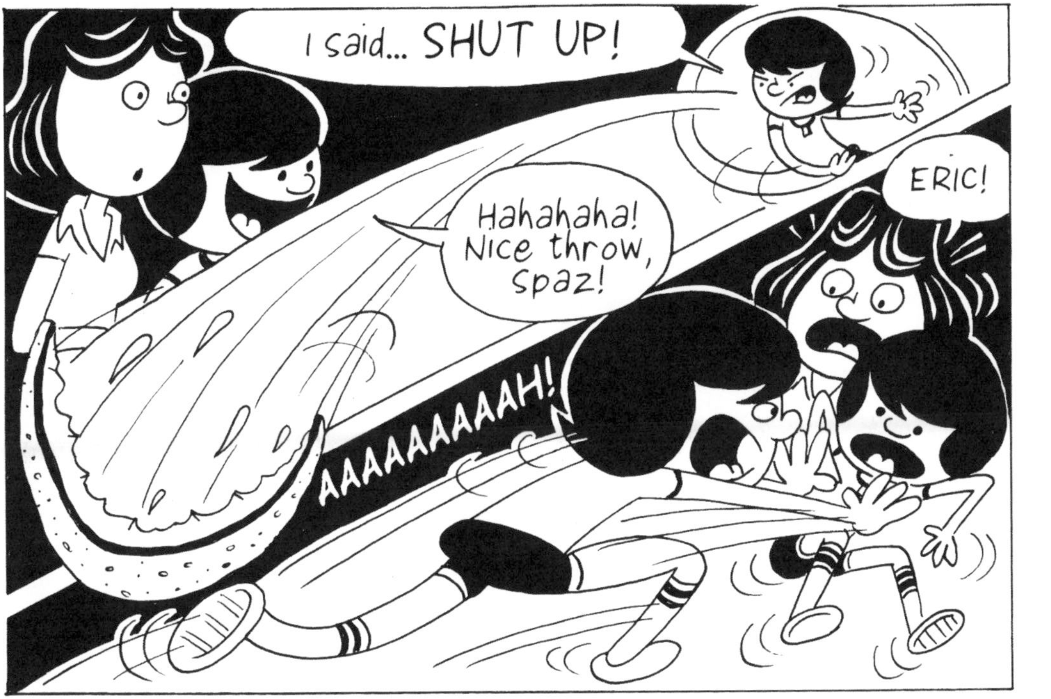
I said... SHUT UP!
Hahahaha! Nice throw, spaz!
ERIC!
AAAAAAAAAH!

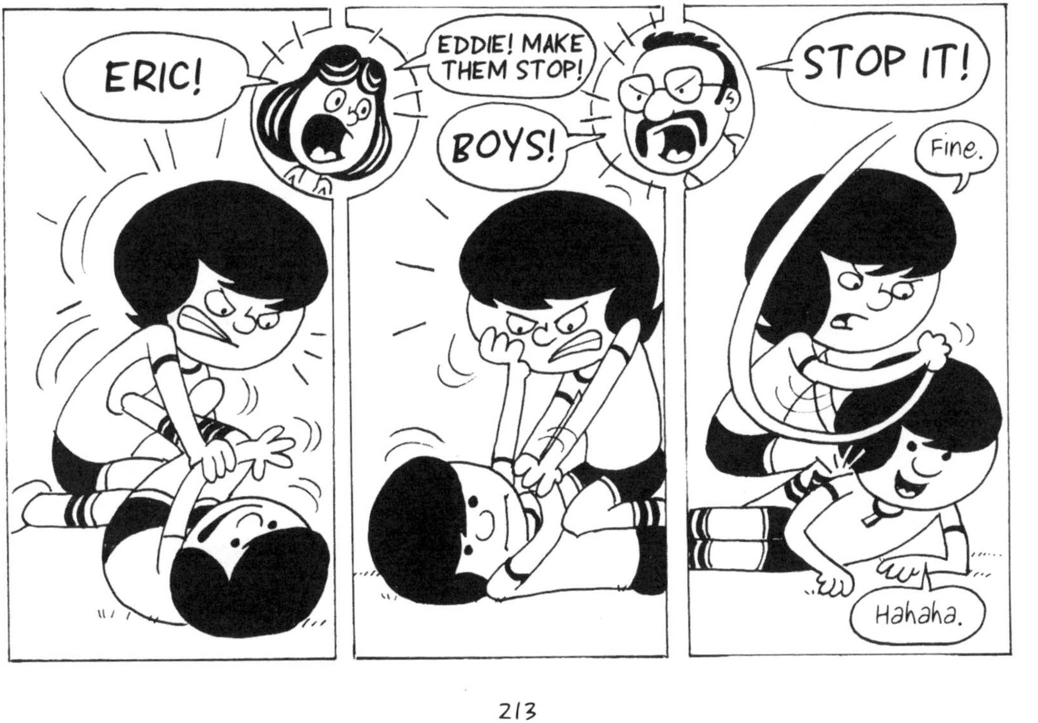
ERIC!
EDDIE! MAKE THEM STOP!
BOYS!
STOP IT!
Fine.
Hahaha.

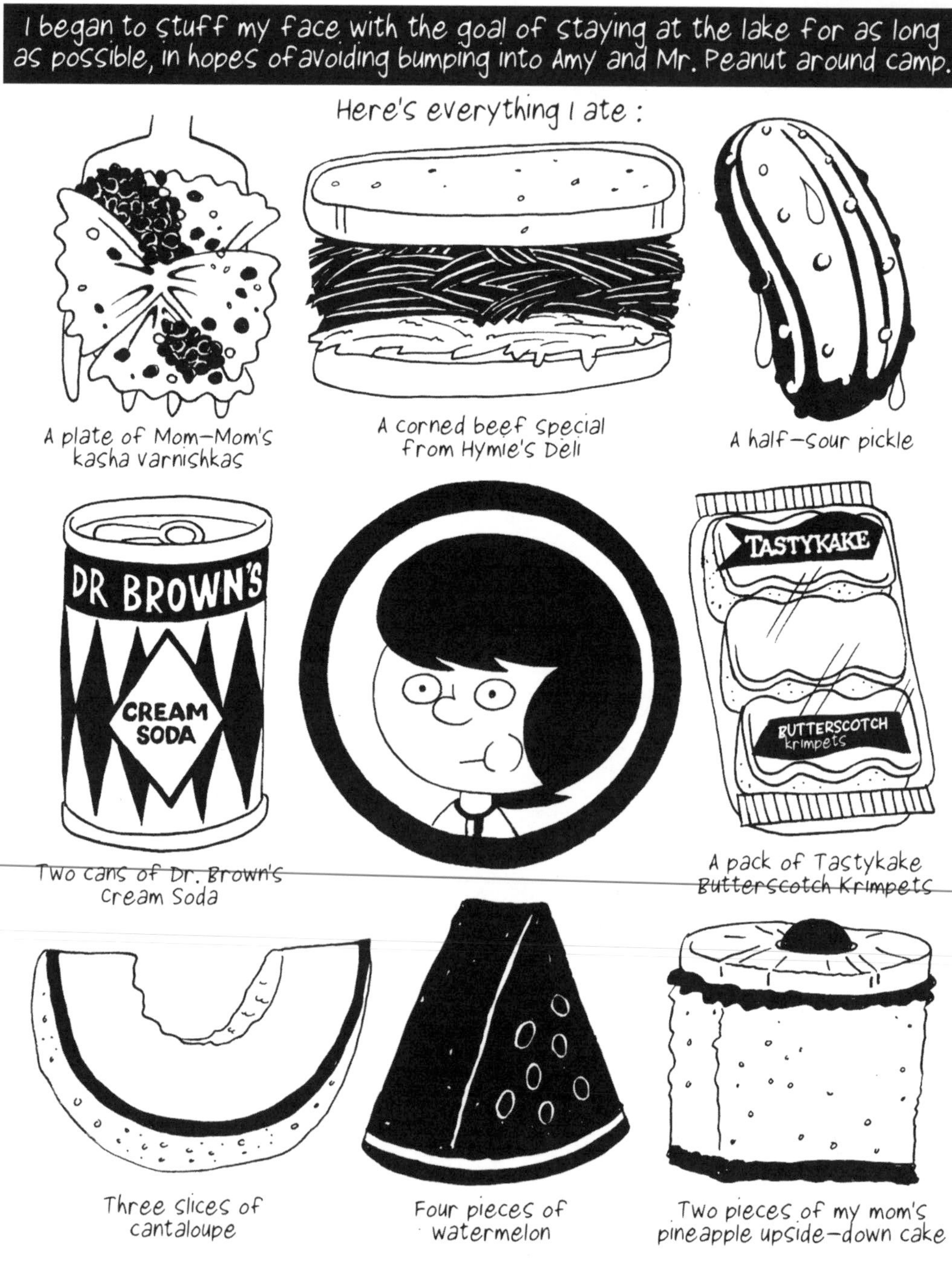
I began to stuff my face with the goal of staying at the lake for as long as possible, in hopes of avoiding bumping into Amy and Mr. Peanut around camp.
Here's everything I ate:
A plate of Mom-Mom's kasha varnishkas
A corned beef special from Hymie's Deli
A half-sour pickle
DR BROWN'S
CREAM SODA
TASTYKAKE
BUTTERSCOTCH krimpets
Two cans of Dr. Brown's Cream Soda
A pack of Tastykake Butterscotch Krimpets
Three slices of cantaloupe
Four pieces of watermelon
Two pieces of my mom's pineapple upside-down cake

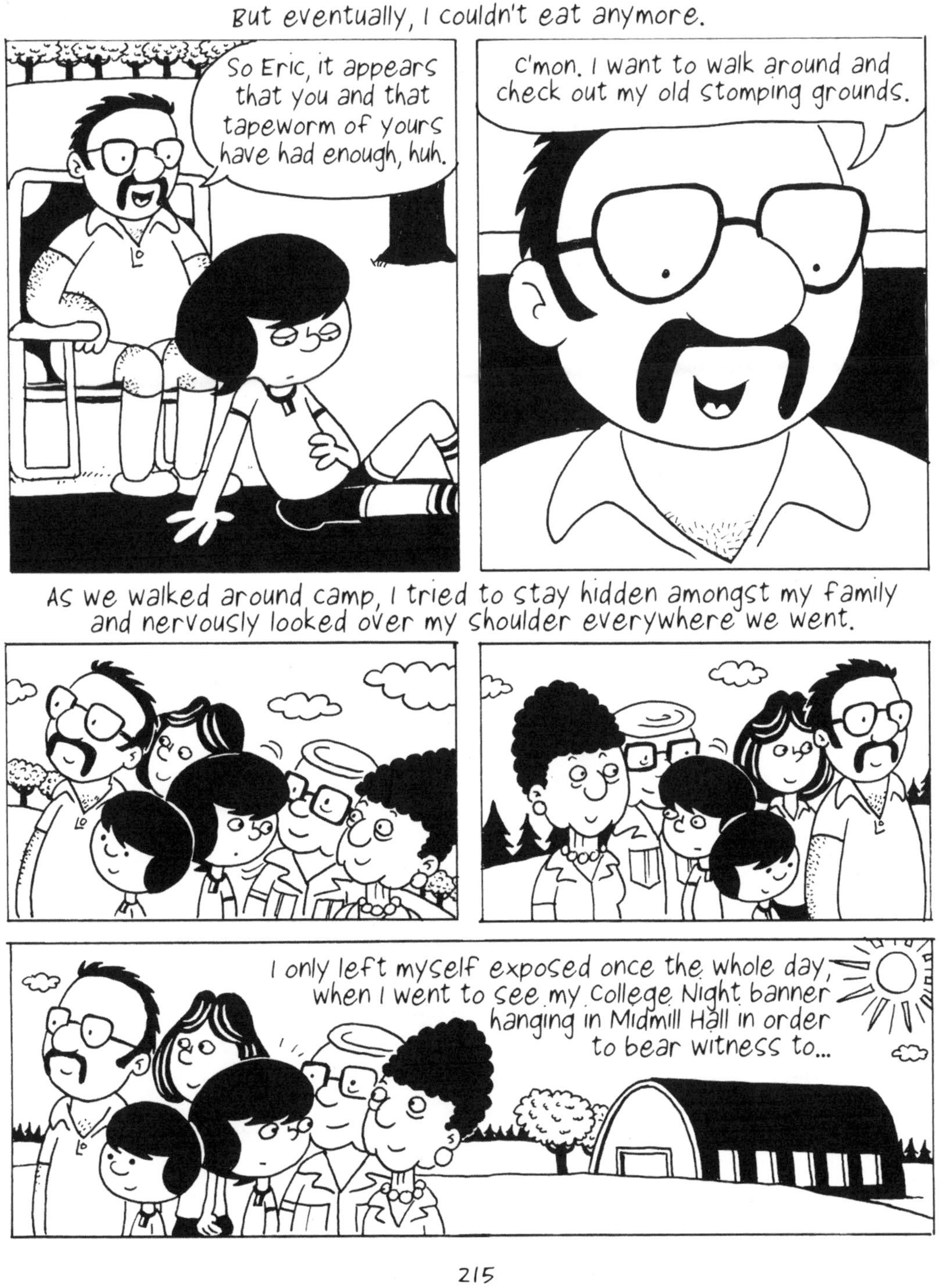
But eventually, I couldn't eat anymore.
So Eric, it appears that you and that tapeworm of yours have had enough, huh.
C'mon. I want to walk around and check out my old stomping grounds.
As we walked around camp, I tried to stay hidden amongst my family and nervously looked over my shoulder everywhere we went.
I only left myself exposed once the whole day, when I went to see my College Night banner hanging in Midmill Hall in order to bear witness to...

The Revenge of BATMANU.

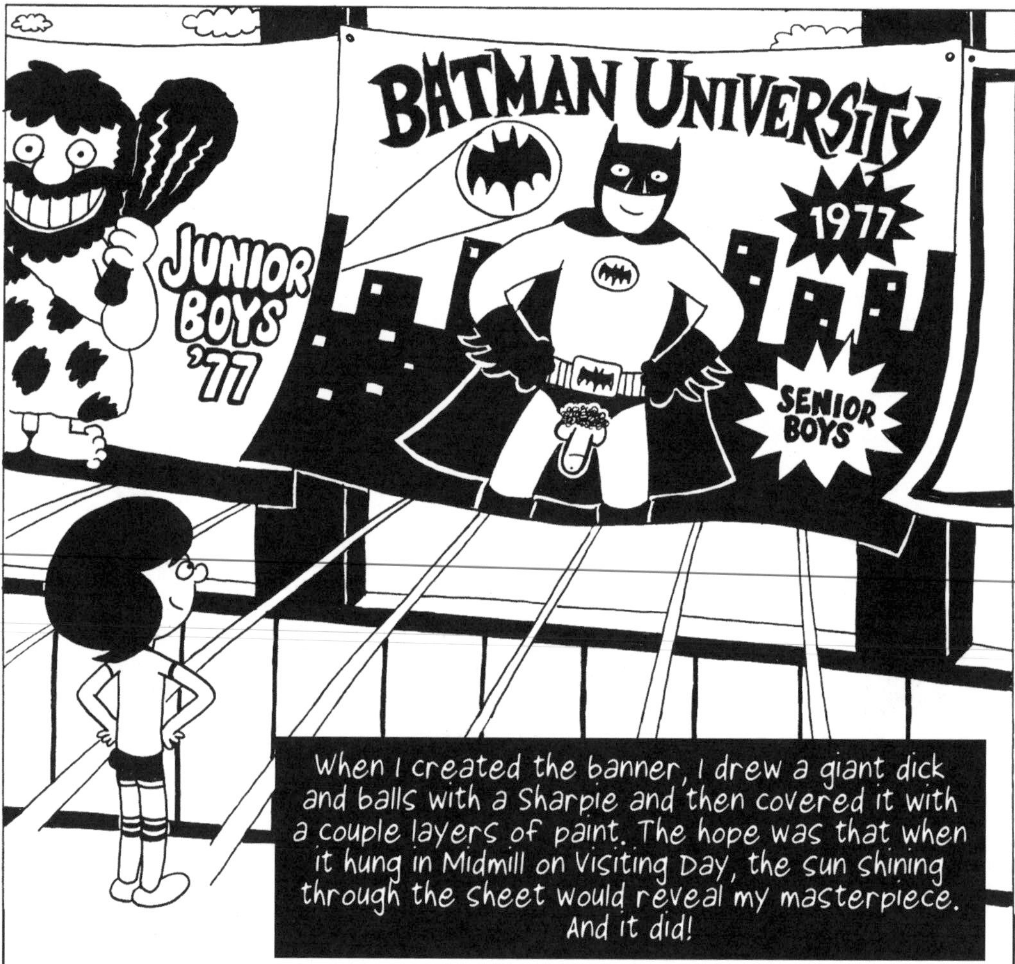
BATMAN UNIVERSITY
1977
SENIOR BOYS
JUNIOR BOYS '77
When I created the banner, I drew a giant dick and balls with a Sharpie and then covered it with a couple layers of paint. The hope was that when it hung in Midmill on Visiting Day, the sun shining through the sheet would reveal my masterpiece. And it did!

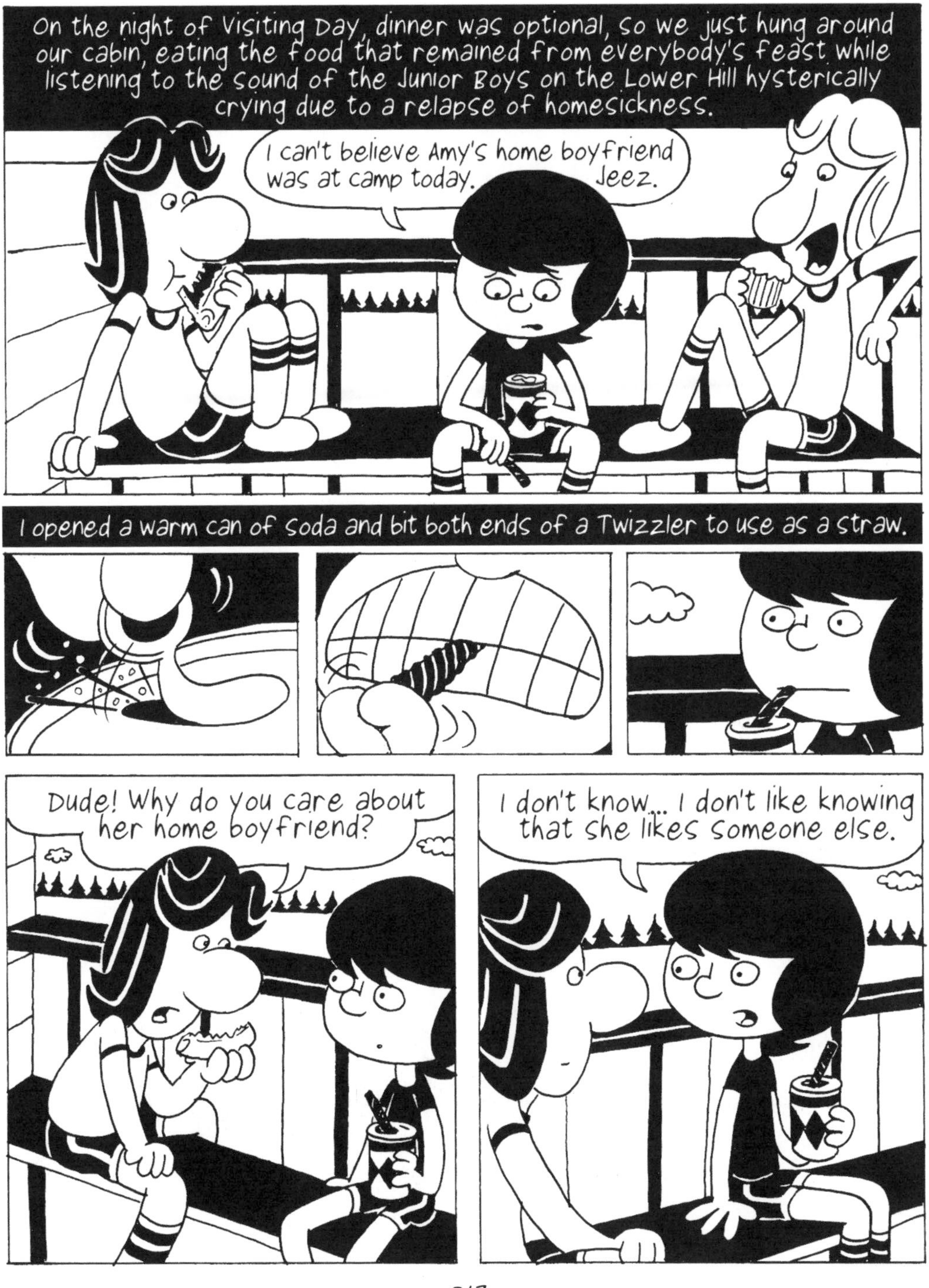
On the night of Visiting Day, dinner was optional, so we just hung around our cabin, eating the food that remained from everybody's feast while listening to the sound of the Junior Boys on the Lower Hill hysterically crying due to a relapse of homesickness.
I can't believe Amy's home boyfriend was at camp today. Jeez.
I opened a warm can of soda and bit both ends of a Twizzler to use as a straw.
Dude! Why do you care about her home boyfriend?
I don't know... I don't like knowing that she likes someone else.

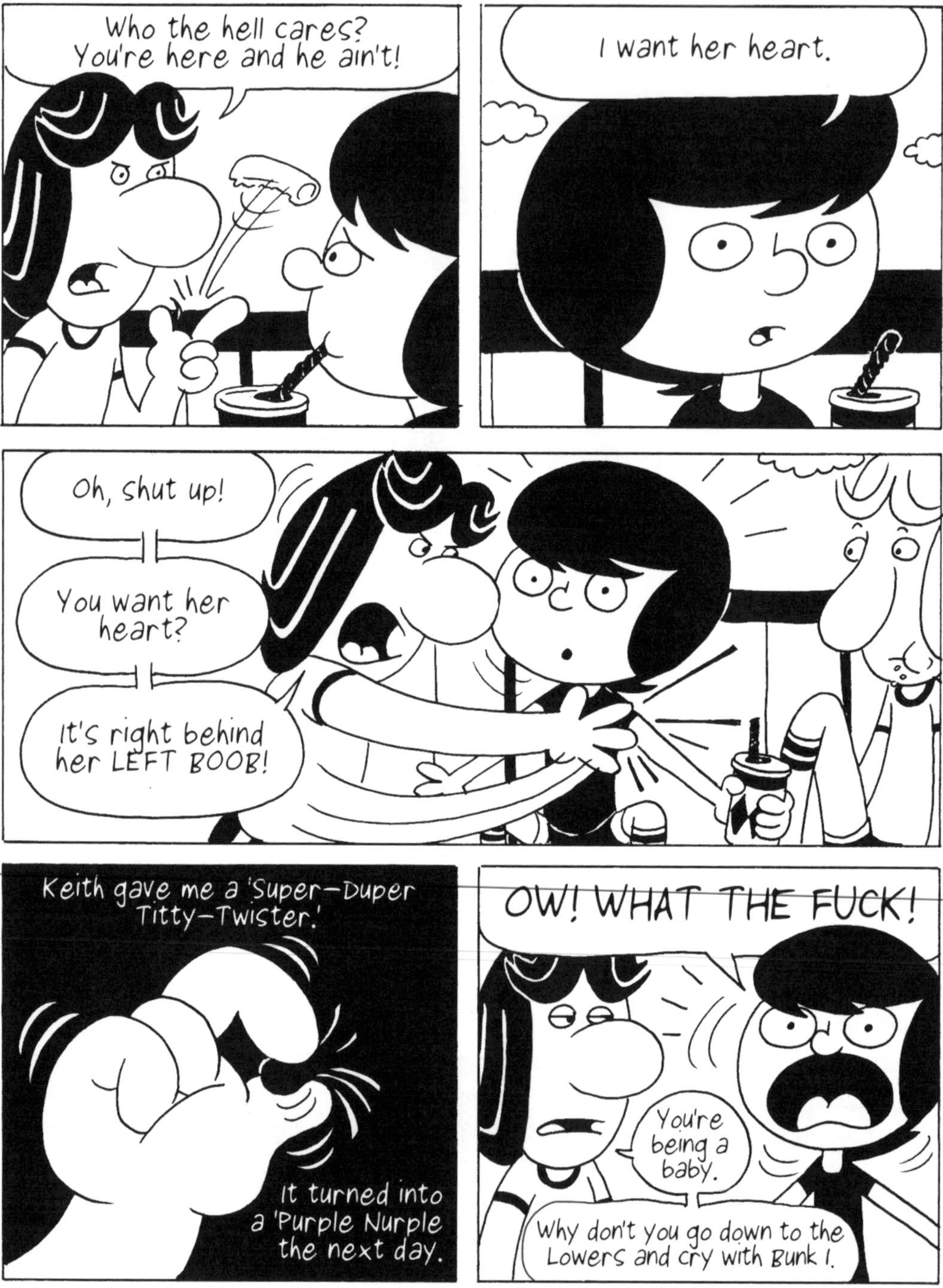
Who the hell cares? You're here and he ain't!
I want her heart.
Oh, shut up!
You want her heart?
It's right behind her LEFT BOOB!
Keith gave me a 'Super-Duper Titty-Twister.'
It turned into a 'Purple Nurple the next day.
OW! WHAT THE FUCK!
You're being a baby.
Why don't you go down to the Lowers and cry with Bunk 1.

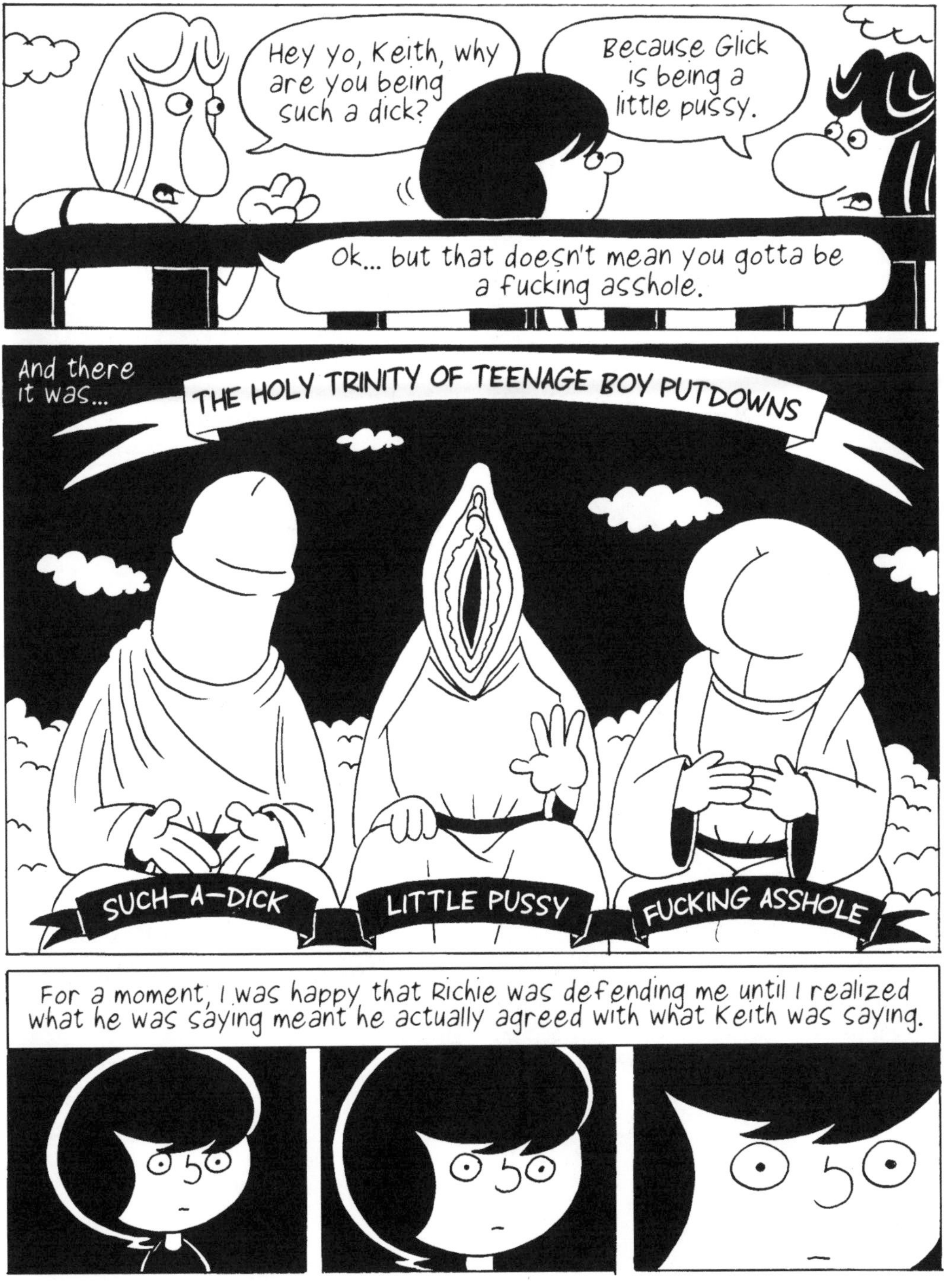
Hey yo, Keith, why are you being such a dick?
Because Glick is being a little pussy.
Ok... but that doesn't mean you gotta be a fucking asshole.
And there it was...
THE HOLY TRINITY OF TEENAGE BOY PUTDOWNS
SUCH-A-DICK
LITTLE PUSSY
FUCKING ASSHOLE
For a moment, I was happy that Richie was defending me until I realized what he was saying meant he actually agreed with what Keith was saying.

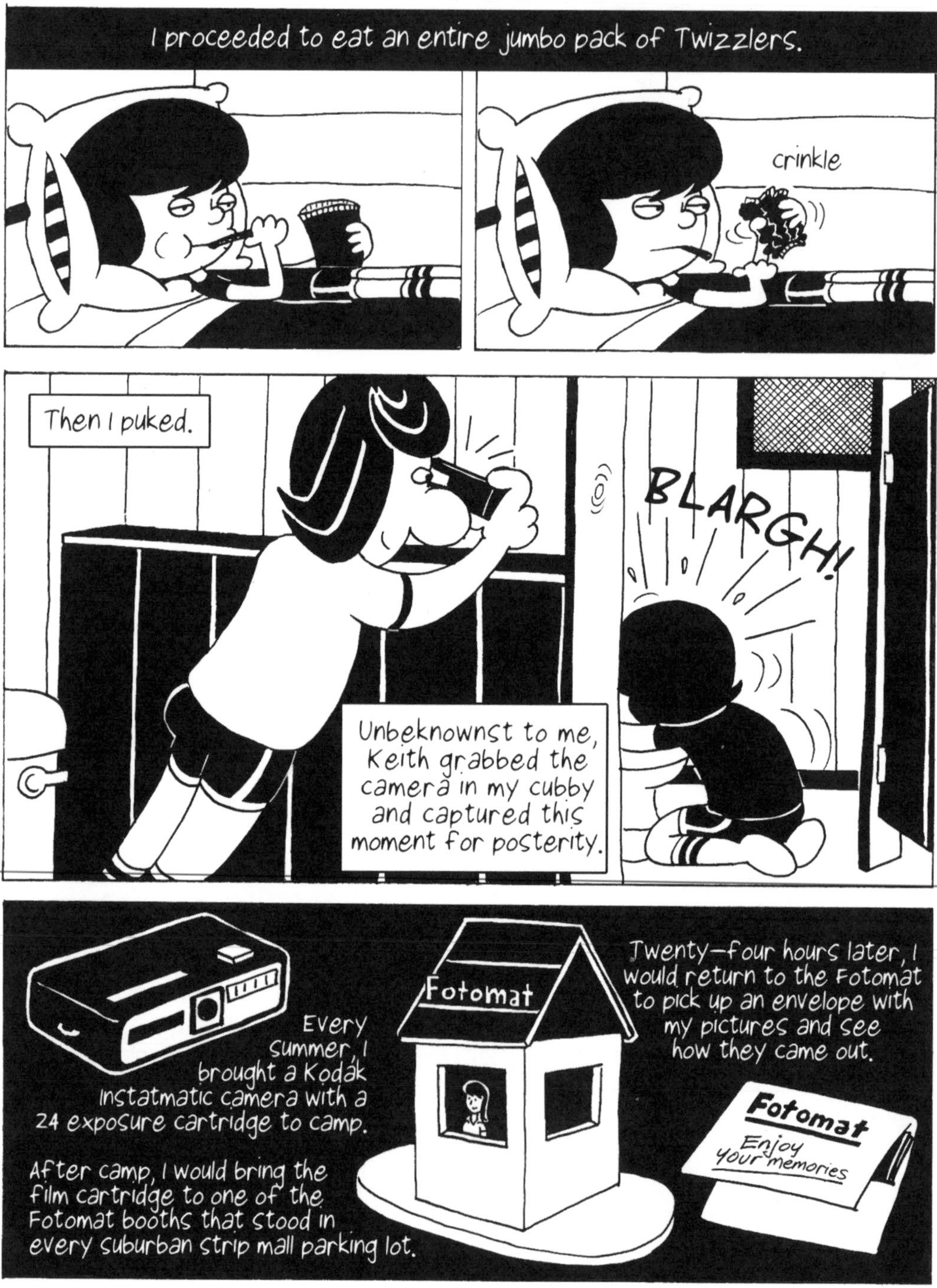
I proceeded to eat an entire jumbo pack of Twizzlers.
crinkle
Then I puked.
BLARGH!
Unbeknownst to me, Keith grabbed the camera in my cubby and captured this moment for posterity.
Every summer, I brought a Kodák Instatmatic camera with a 24 exposure cartridge to camp.
After camp, I would bring the film cartridge to one of the Fotomat booths that stood in every suburban strip mall parking lot.
Fotomat
Twenty-four hours later, I would return to the Fotomat to pick up an envelope with my pictures and see how they came out.
Fotomat
Enjoy your memories

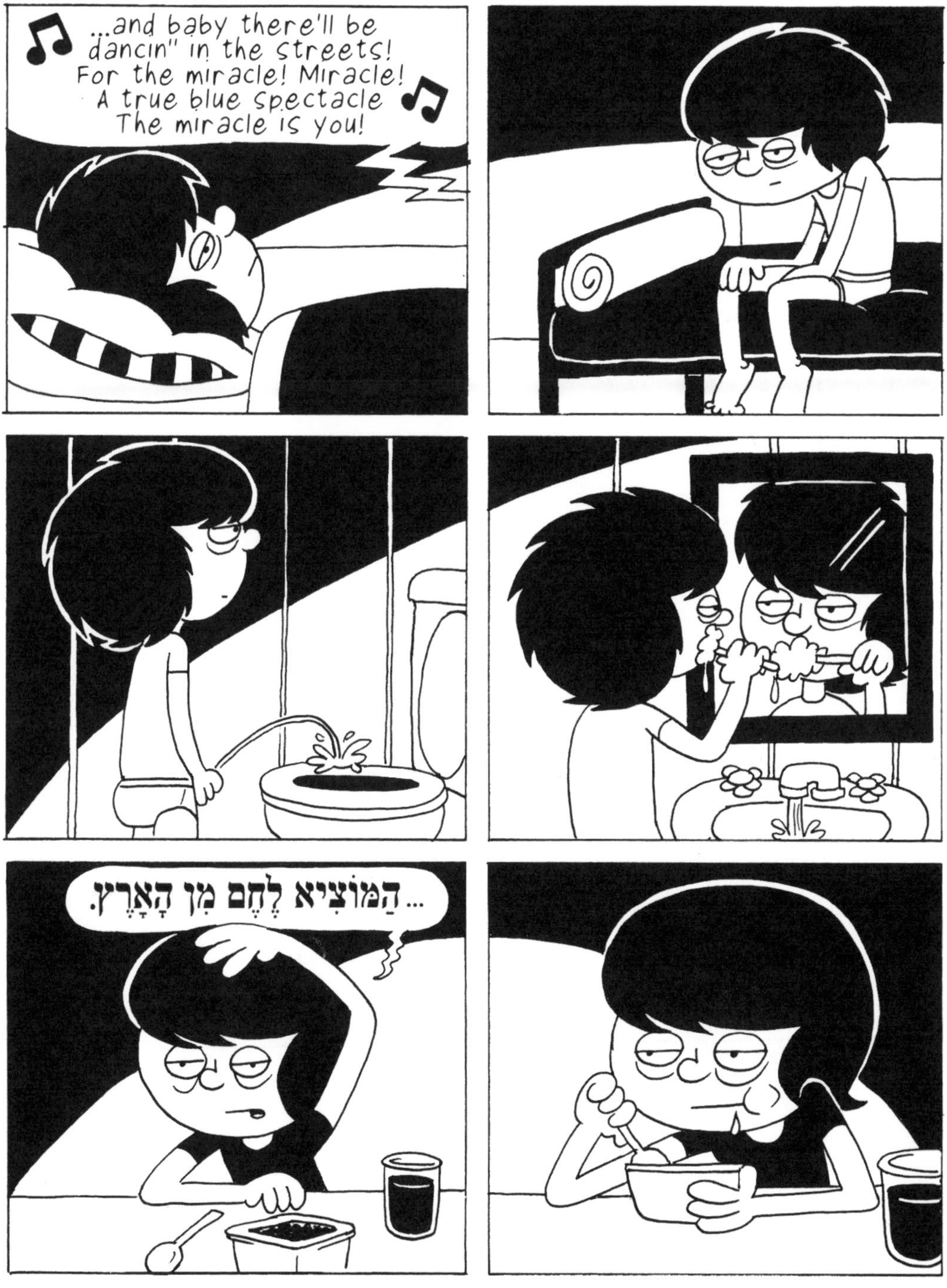
...and baby there'll be dancin'' in the streets! For the miracle! Miracle! A true blue spectacle The miracle is you!
הַמּוֹצִיא לֶחֶם מִן הָאָרֶץ...

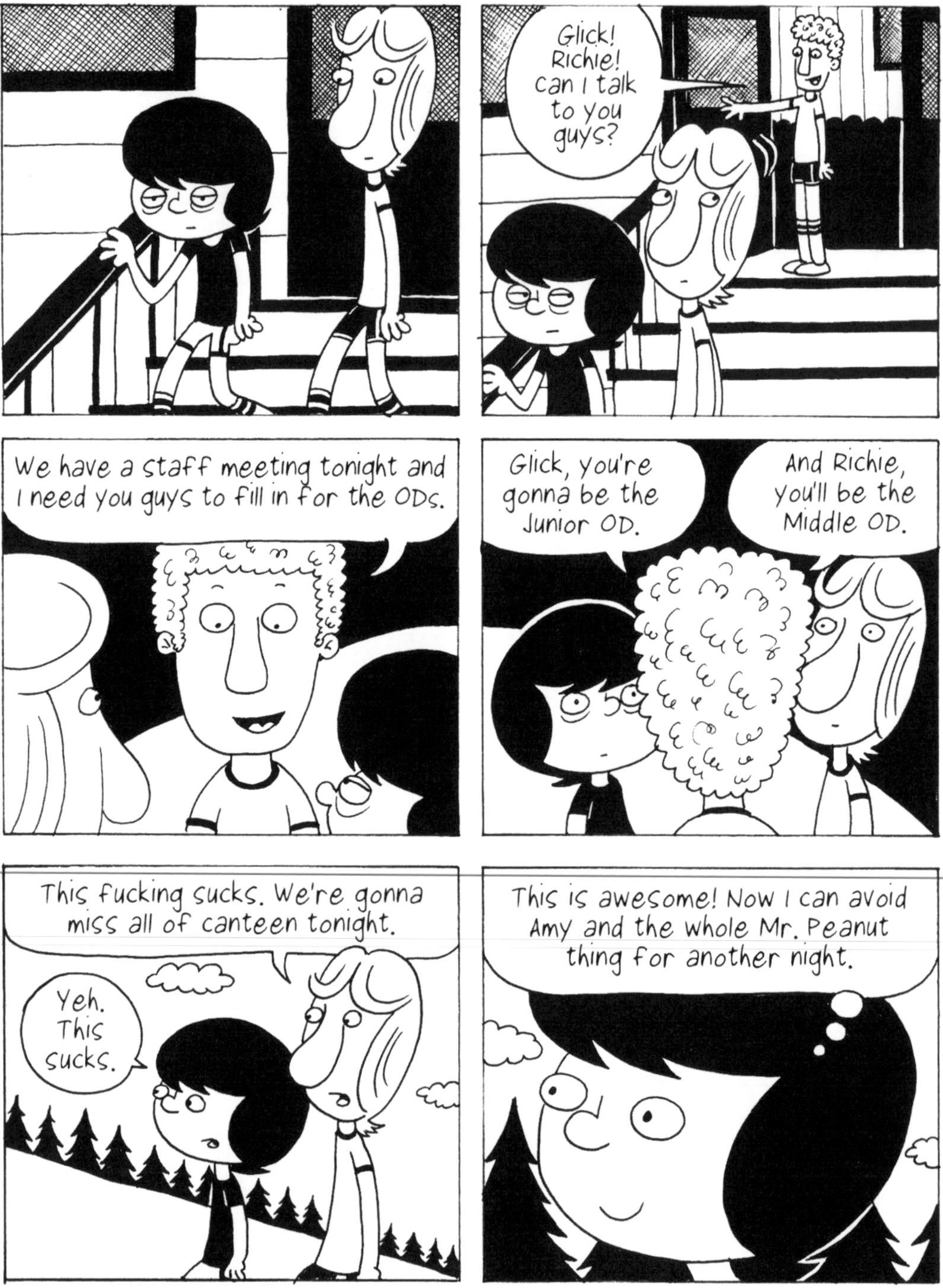
Glick! Richie! can I talk to you guys?
We have a staff meeting tonight and I need you guys to fill in for the ODs.
Glick, you're gonna be the Junior OD.
And Richie, you'll be the Middle OD.
This fucking sucks. We're gonna miss all of canteen tonight.
Yeh. This sucks.
This is awesome! Now I can avoid Amy and the whole Mr. Peanut thing for another night.

I decided to tell the 10-year-olds of Bunk 5 my favorite scary camp tale: The Story of the Green Man.

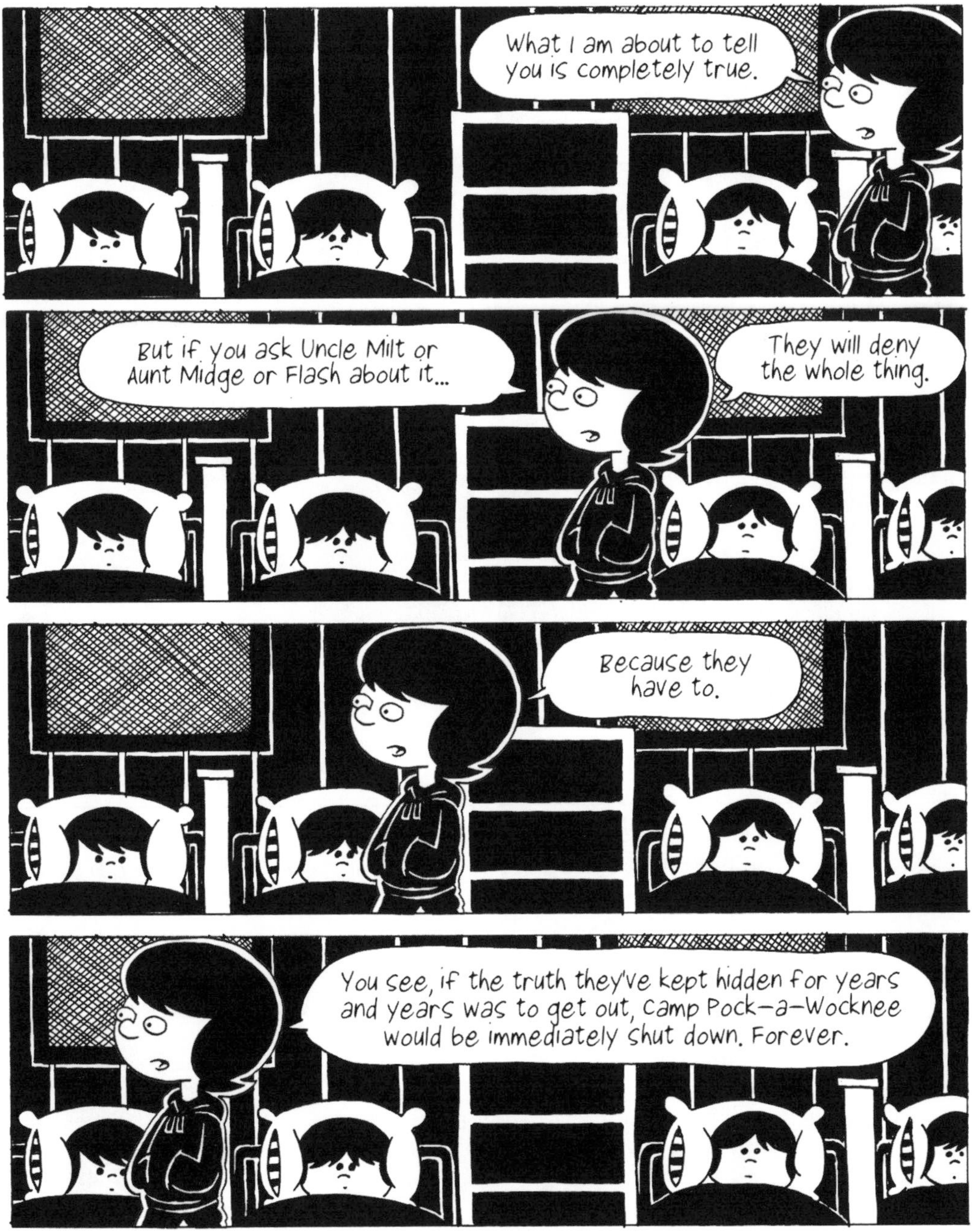
What I am about to tell you is completely true.
But if you ask Uncle Milt or Aunt Midge or Flash about it...
They will deny the whole thing.
Because they have to.
You see, if the truth they've kept hidden for years and years was to get out, Camp Pock-a-Wocknee would be immediately shut down. Forever.

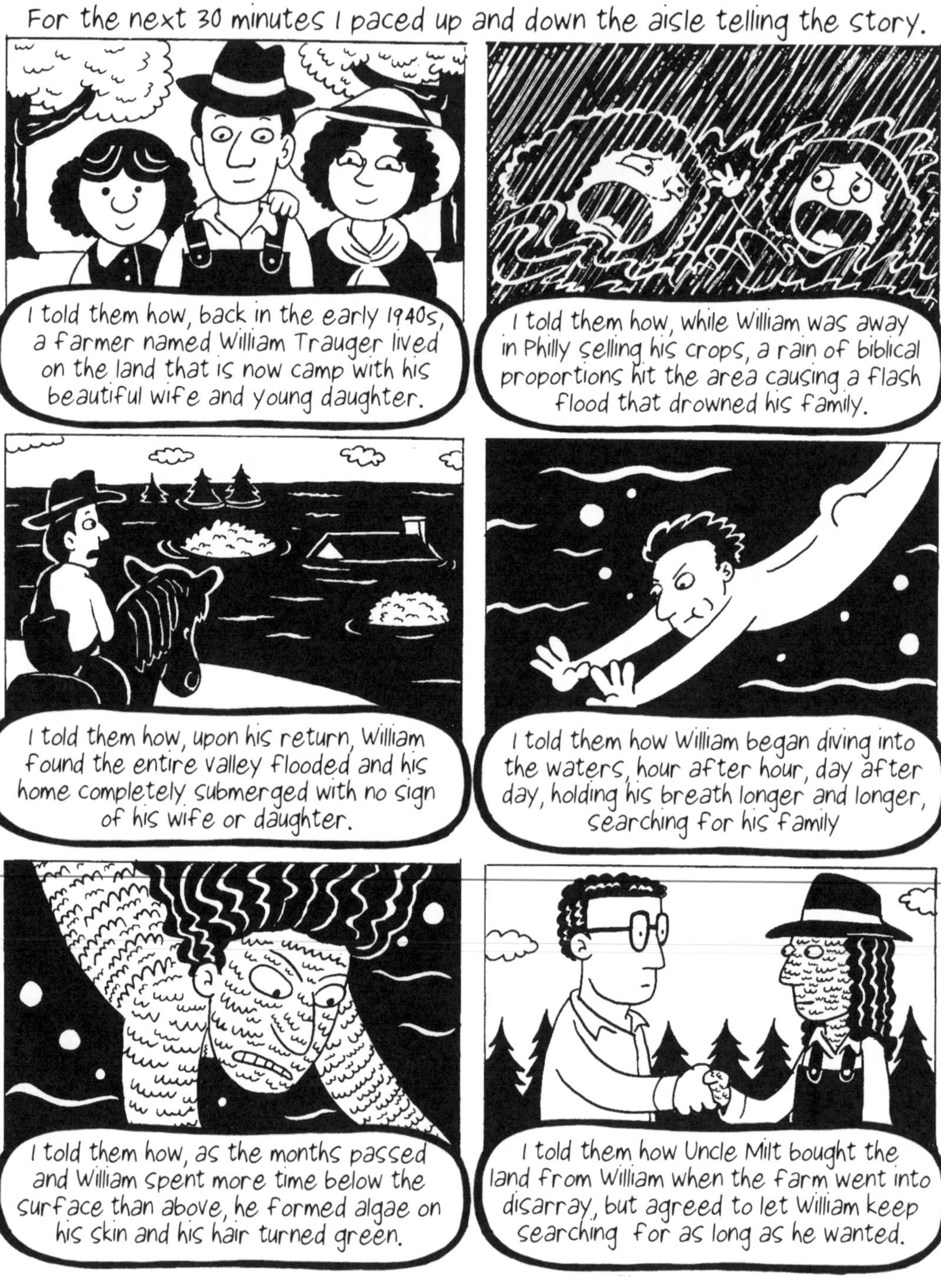
For the next 30 minutes I paced up and down the aisle telling the story.
I told them how, back in the early 1940s, a farmer named William Trauger lived on the land that is now camp with his beautiful wife and young daughter.
I told them how, while William was away in Philly selling his crops, a rain of biblical proportions hit the area causing a flash flood that drowned his family.
I told them how, upon his return, William found the entire valley flooded and his home completely submerged with no sign of his wife or daughter.
I told them how William began diving into the waters, hour after hour, day after day, holding his breath longer and longer, searching for his family
I told them how, as the months passed and William spent more time below the surface than above, he formed algae on his skin and his hair turned green.
I told them how Uncle Milt bought the land from William when the farm went into disarray, but agreed to let William keep searching for as long as he wanted.

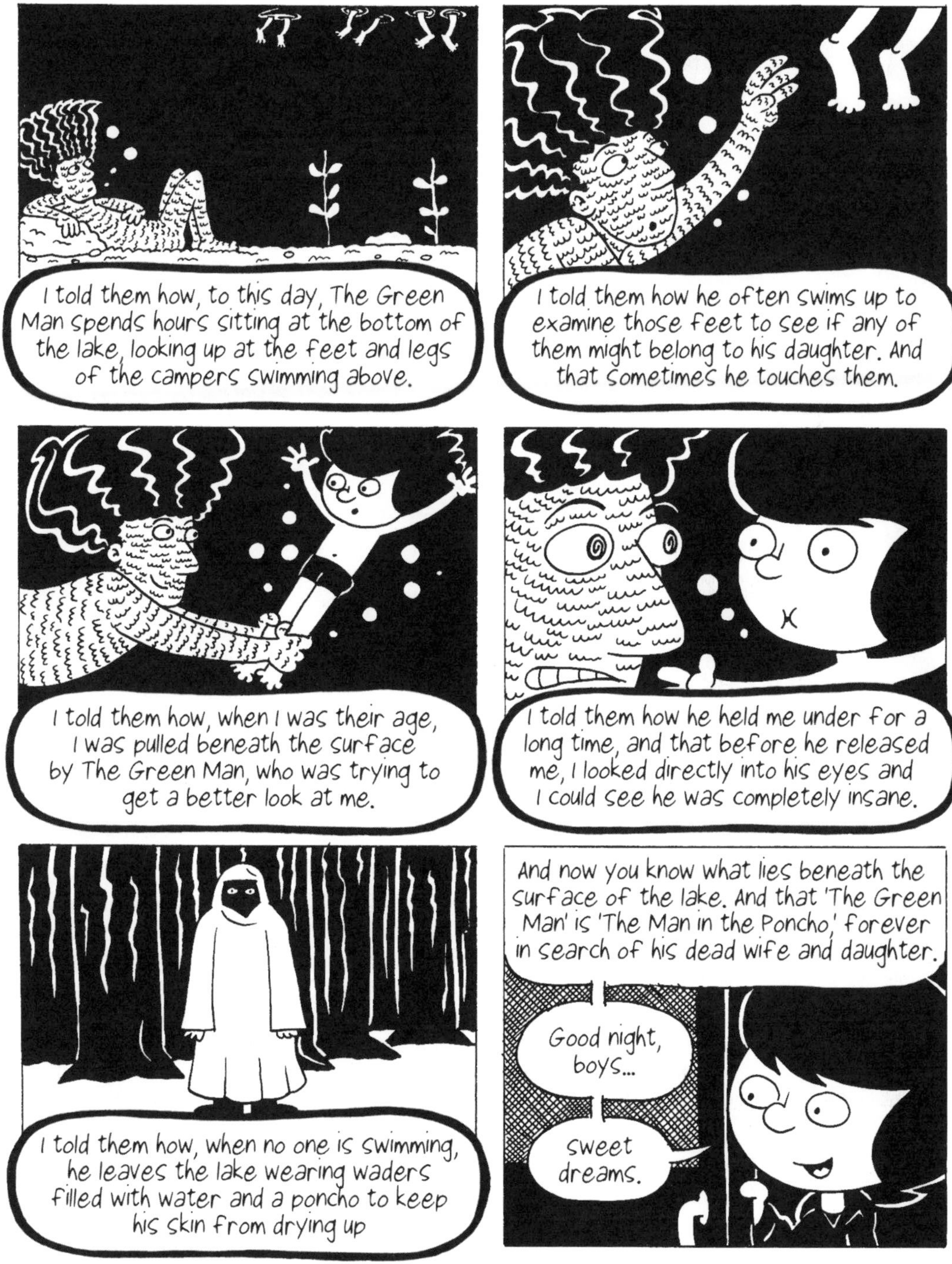
I told them how, to this day, The Green Man spends hours sitting at the bottom of the lake, looking up at the feet and legs of the campers swimming above.
I told them how he often swims up to examine those feet to see if any of them might belong to his daughter. And that sometimes he touches them.
I told them how, when I was their age, I was pulled beneath the surface by The Green Man, who was trying to get a better look at me.
I told them how he held me under for a long time, and that before he released me, I looked directly into his eyes and I could see he was completely insane.
I told them how, when no one is swimming, he leaves the lake wearing waders filled with water and a poncho to keep his skin from drying up
And now you know what lies beneath the surface of the lake. And that 'The Green Man' is 'The Man in the Poncho,' forever in search of his dead wife and daughter.
Good night, boys...
Sweet dreams.

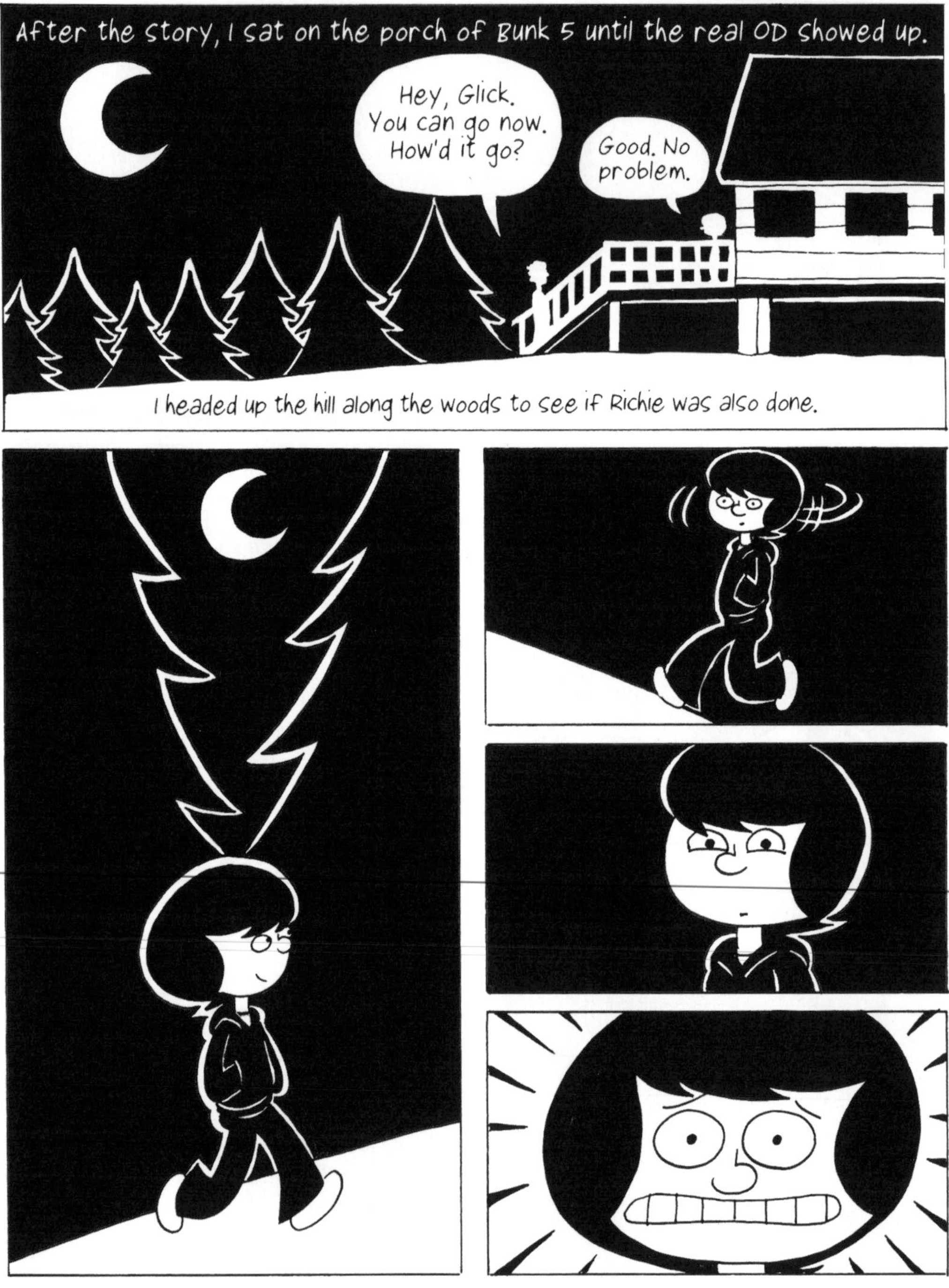
After the story, I sat on the porch of Bunk 5 until the real OD showed up.
Hey, Glick. You can go now. How'd it go?
Good. No problem.
I headed up the hill along the woods to see if Richie was also done.

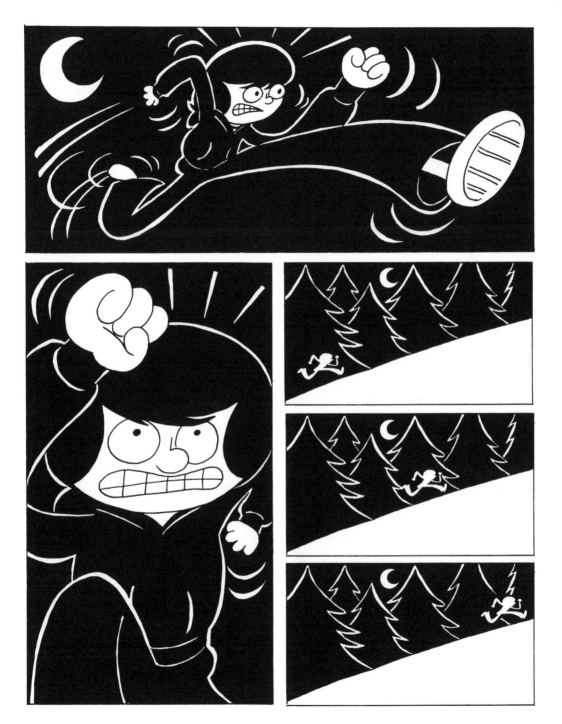

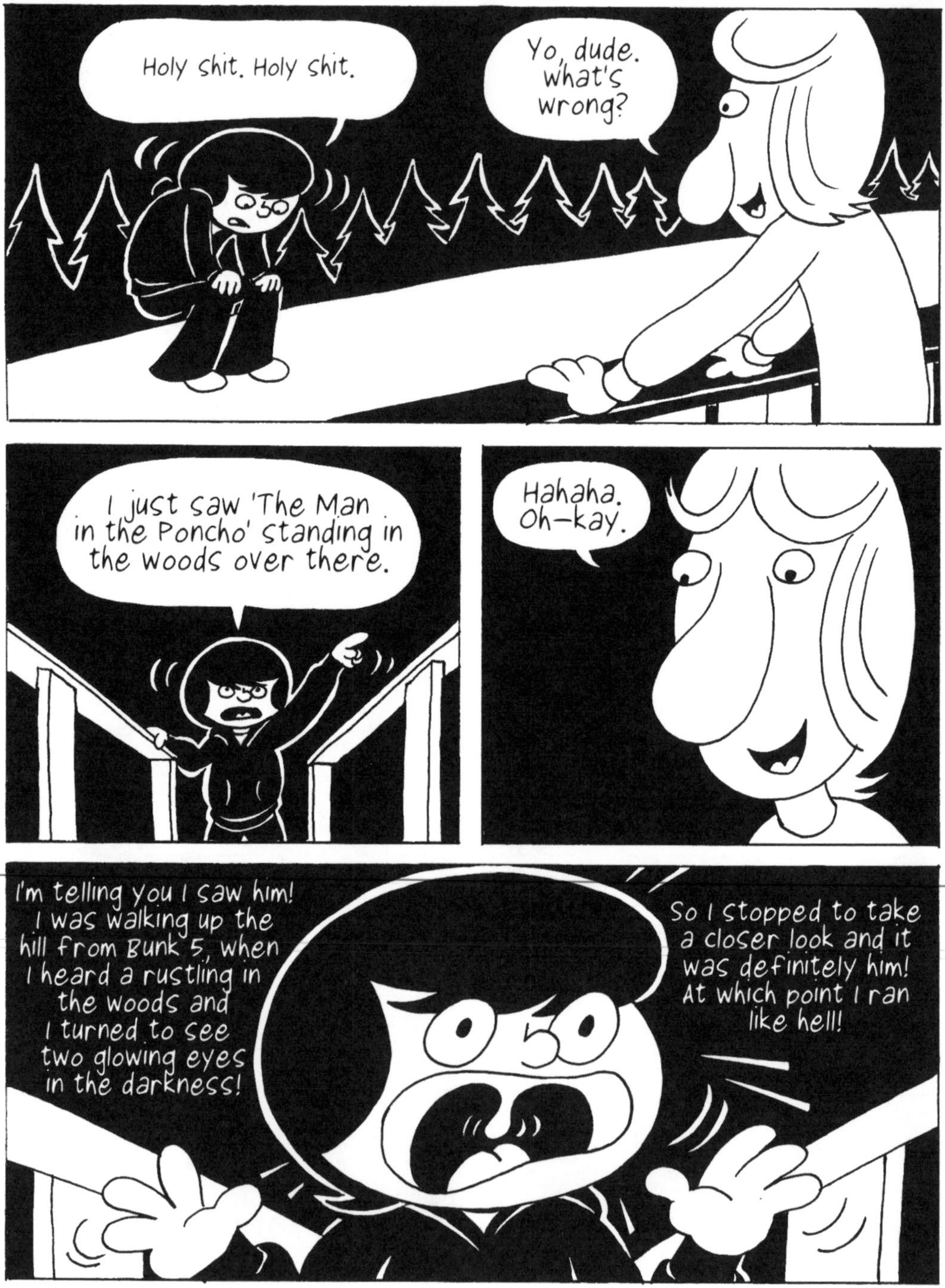
Holy shit. Holy shit.
Yo, dude. What's wrong?
I just saw 'The Man in the Poncho' standing in the woods over there.
Hahaha. Oh-kay.
I'm telling you I saw him! I was walking up the hill from Bunk 5, when I heard a rustling in the woods and I turned to see two glowing eyes in the darkness!
So I stopped to take a closer look and it was definitely him! At which point I ran like hell!

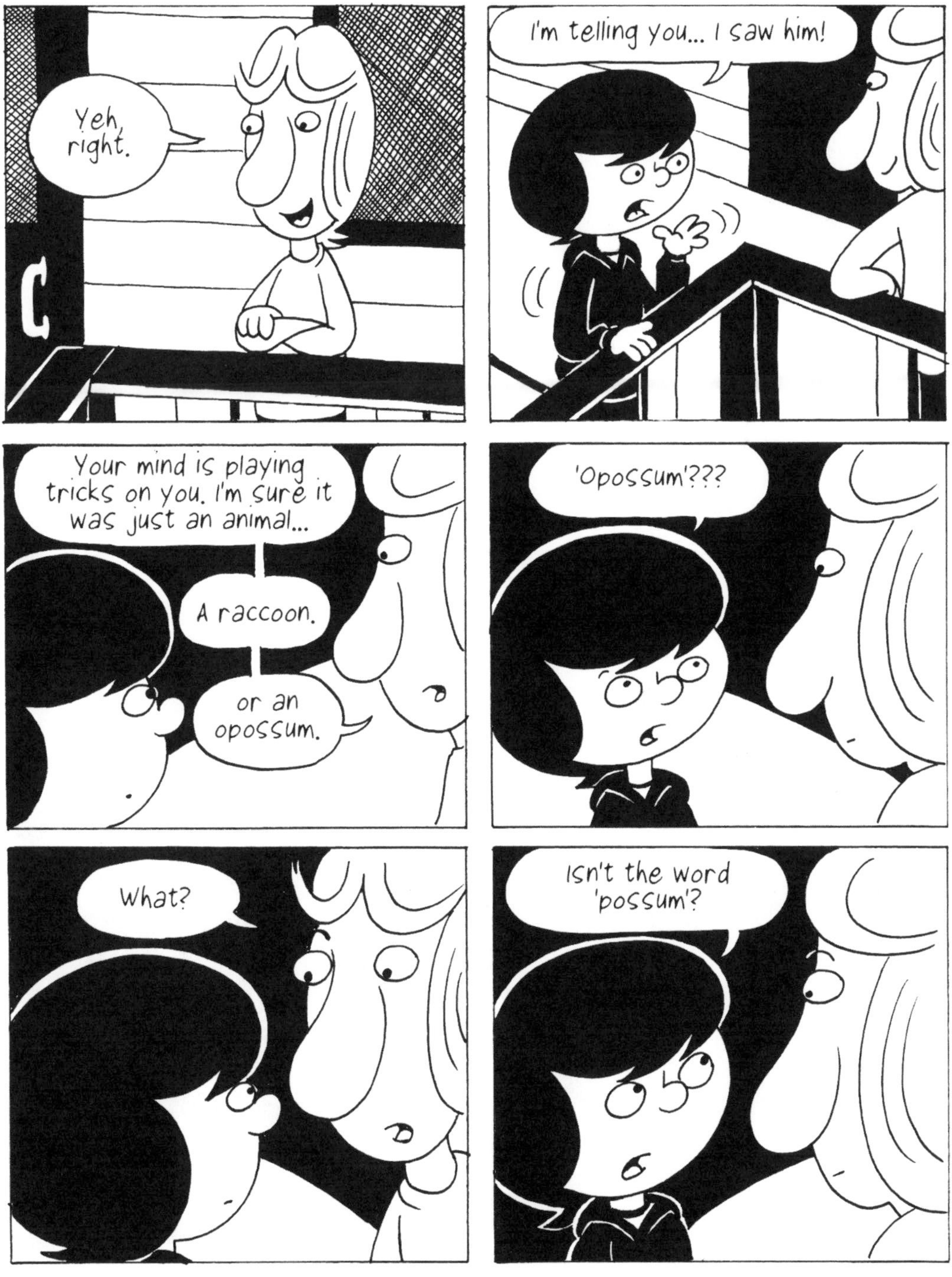
Yeh, right.
I'm telling you... I saw him!
Your mind is playing tricks on you. I'm sure it was just an animal...
A raccoon.
or an opossum.
'Opossum'???
What?
Isn't the word 'possum'?

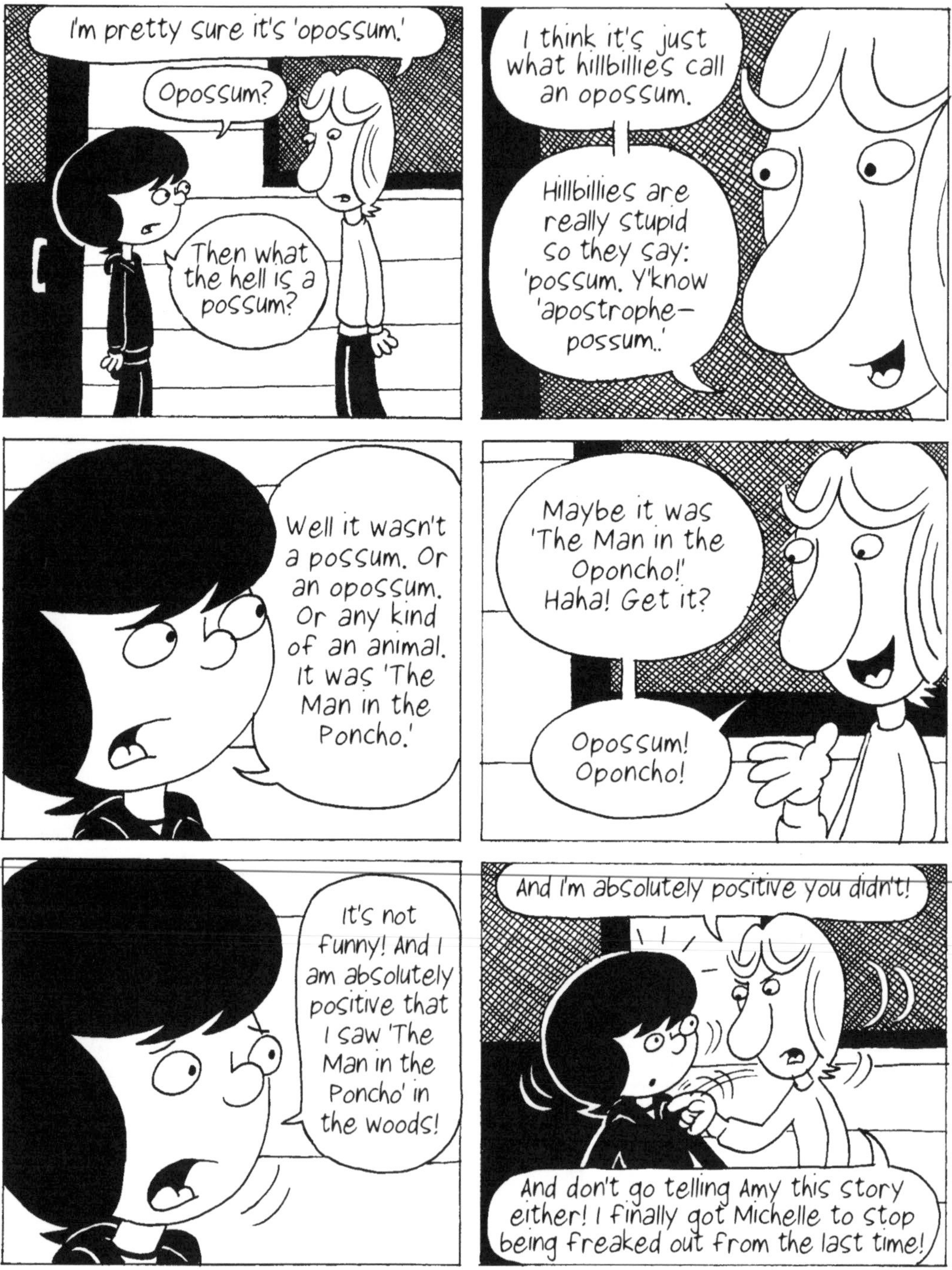
I'm pretty sure it's 'opossum.'
Opossum?
Then what the hell is a possum?
I think it's just what hillbillies call an opossum.
Hillbillies are really stupid so they say: 'possum. Y'know 'apostrophe-possum..'
Well it wasn't a possum. Or an opossum. Or any kind of an animal. It was 'The Man in the Poncho.'
Maybe it was 'The Man in the Oponcho!' Haha! Get it?
Opossum! Oponcho!
It's not funny! And I am absolutely positive that I saw 'The Man in the Poncho' in the woods!
And I'm absolutely positive you didn't!
And don't go telling Amy this story either! I finally got Michelle to stop being freaked out from the last time!

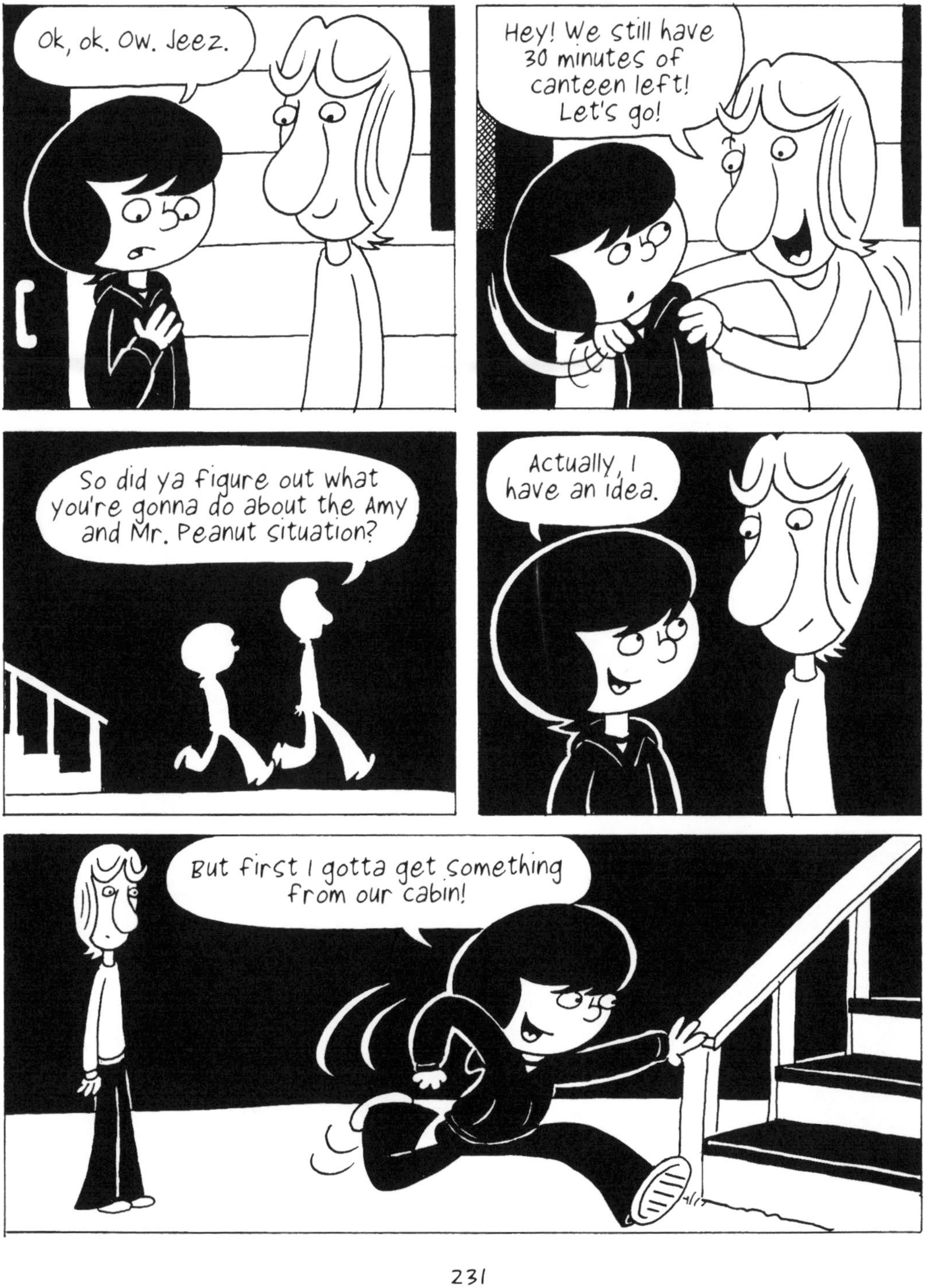
Ok, ok. Ow. Jeez.
Hey! We still have 30 minutes of canteen left! Let's go!
So did ya figure out what you're gonna do about the Amy and Mr. Peanut situation?
Actually, I have an idea.
But first I gotta get something from our cabin!

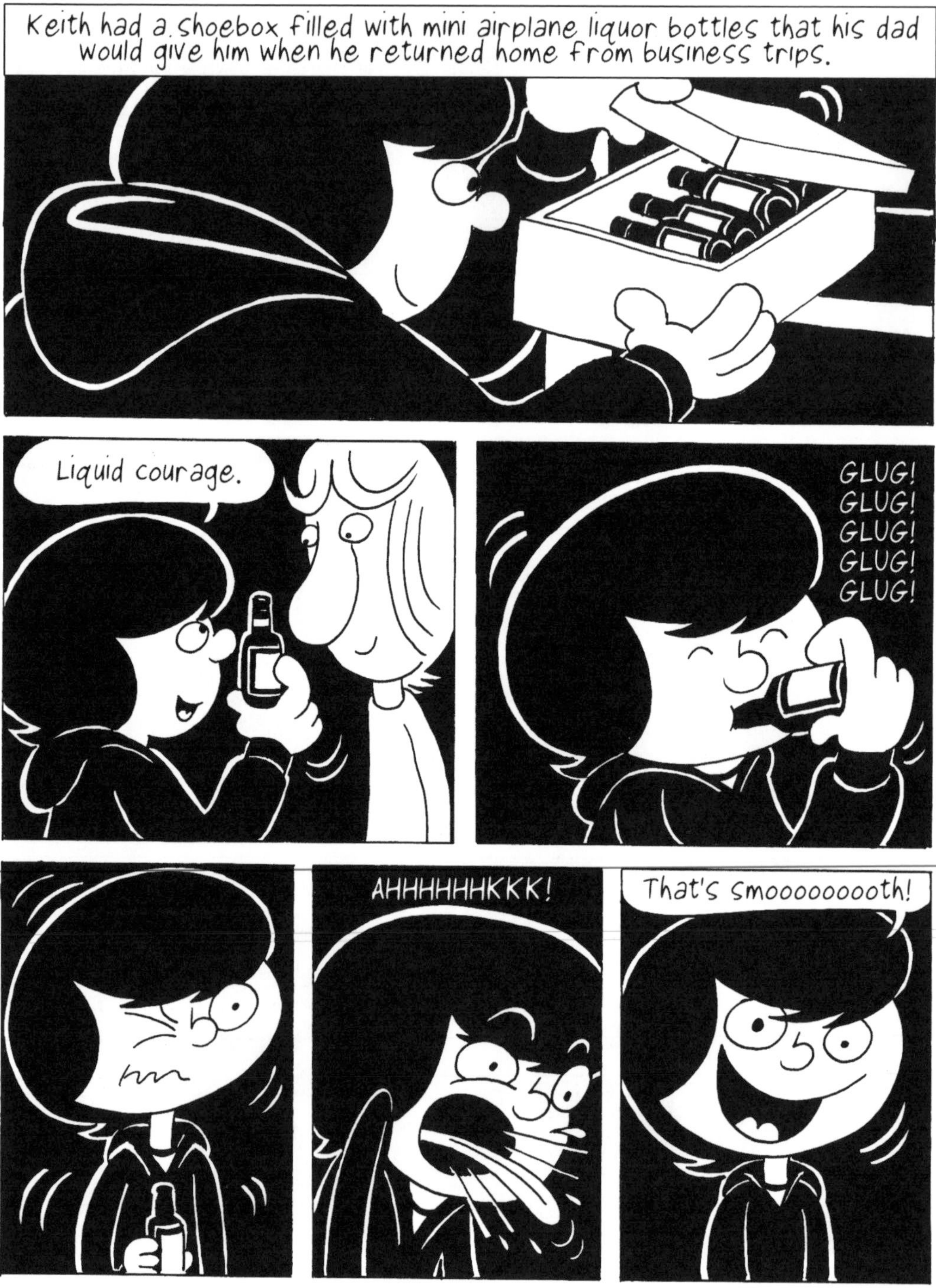
Keith had a shoebox filled with mini airplane liquor bottles that his dad would give him when he returned home from business trips.
Liquid courage.
GLUG! GLUG! GLUG! GLUG! GLUG!
AHHHHHHKKK!
That's smoooooooooth!

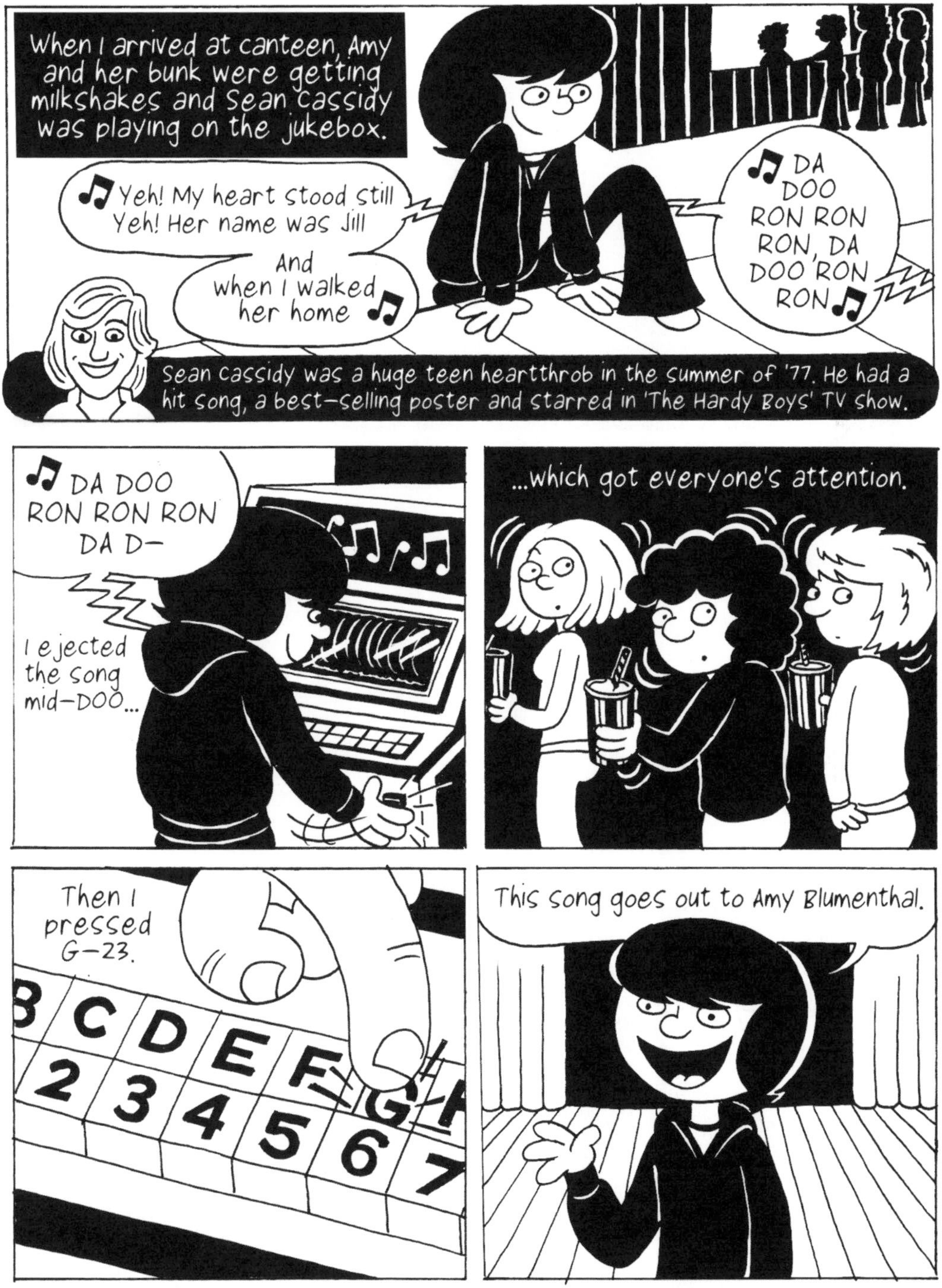

When I arrived at canteen, Amy and her bunk were getting milkshakes and Sean Cassidy was playing on the jukebox.
♫ Yeh! My heart stood still Yeh! Her name was Jill
And when I walked her home ♫
♫ DA DOO RON RON RON, DA DOO RON RON ♫
Sean Cassidy was a huge teen heartthrob in the summer of '77. He had a hit song, a best-selling poster and starred in 'The Hardy Boys' TV show.
♫ DA DOO RON RON RON DA D–
I ejected the song mid–DOO...
...which got everyone's attention.
Then I pressed G–23.
B C D E F G H
2 3 4 5 6 7
This song goes out to Amy Blumenthal.

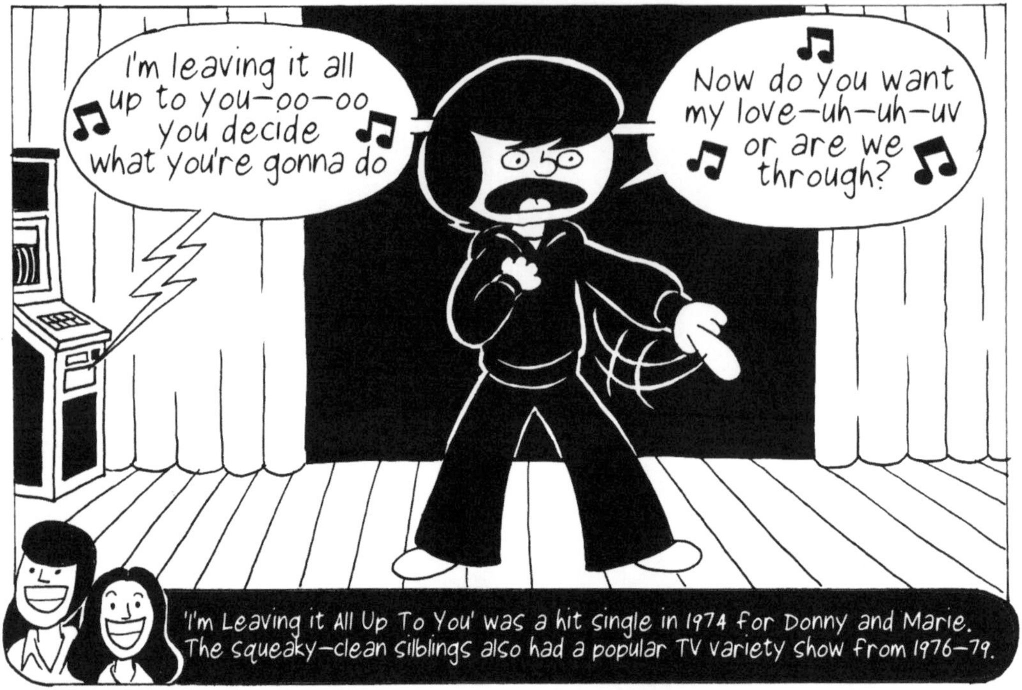
I'm leaving it all up to you-oo-oo you decide what you're gonna do
Now do you want my love-uh-uh-uv or are we through?
'I'm Leaving it All Up To You' was a hit single in 1974 for Donny and Marie. The squeaky-clean siblings also had a popular TV variety show from 1976-79.

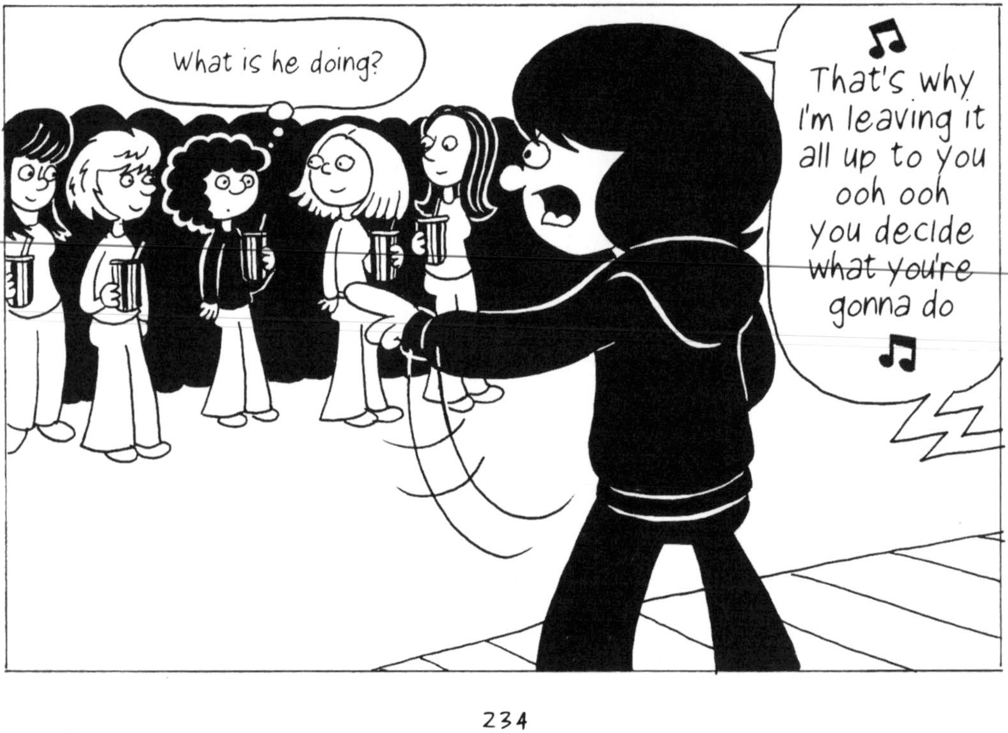
That's why I'm leaving it all up to you ooh ooh you decide what you're gonna do
What is he doing?

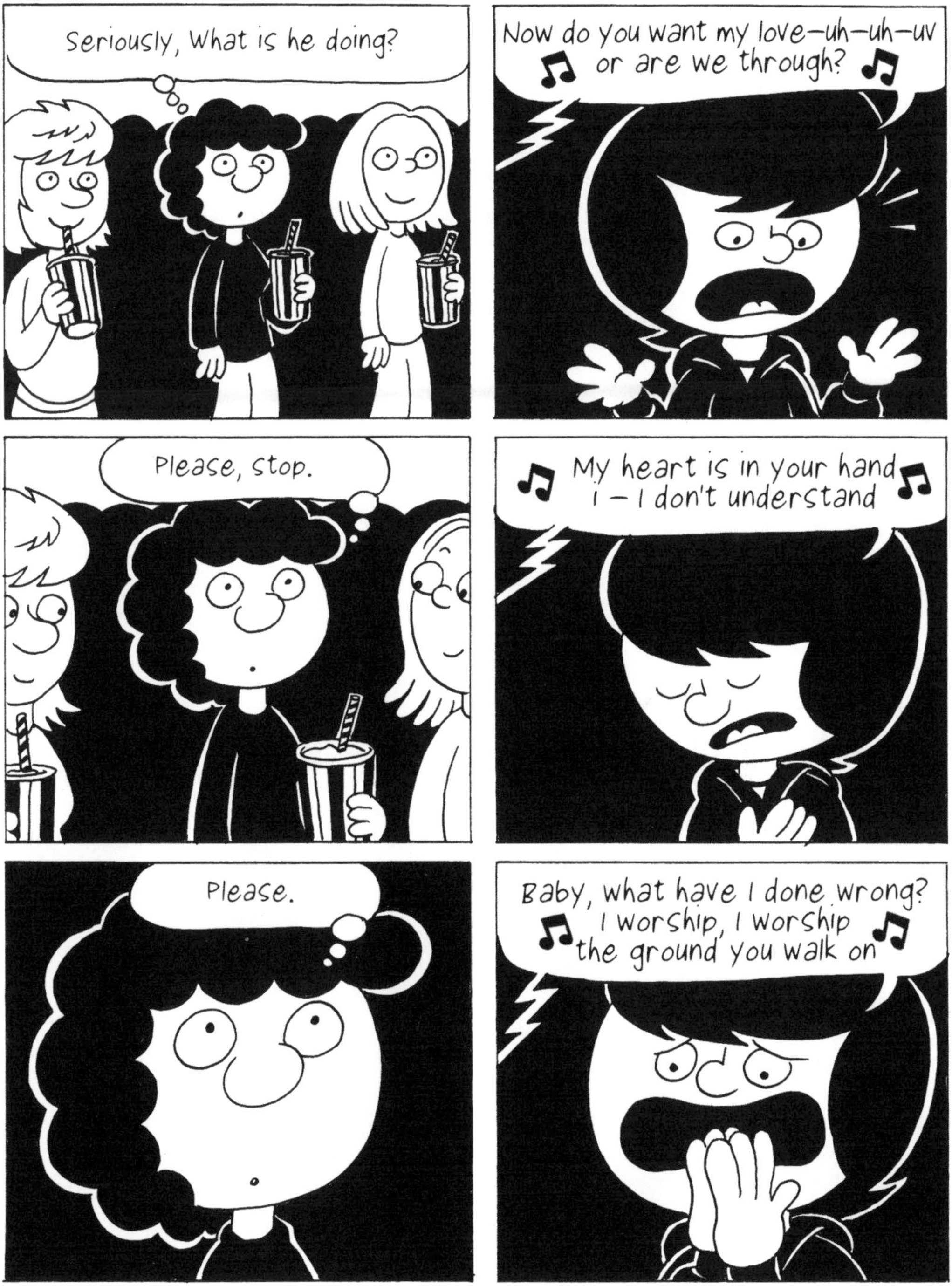
Seriously, What is he doing?
Now do you want my love-uh-uh-uv or are we through?
Please, stop.
My heart is in your hand i - I don't understand
Please.
Baby, what have I done wrong? I worship, I worship the ground you walk on

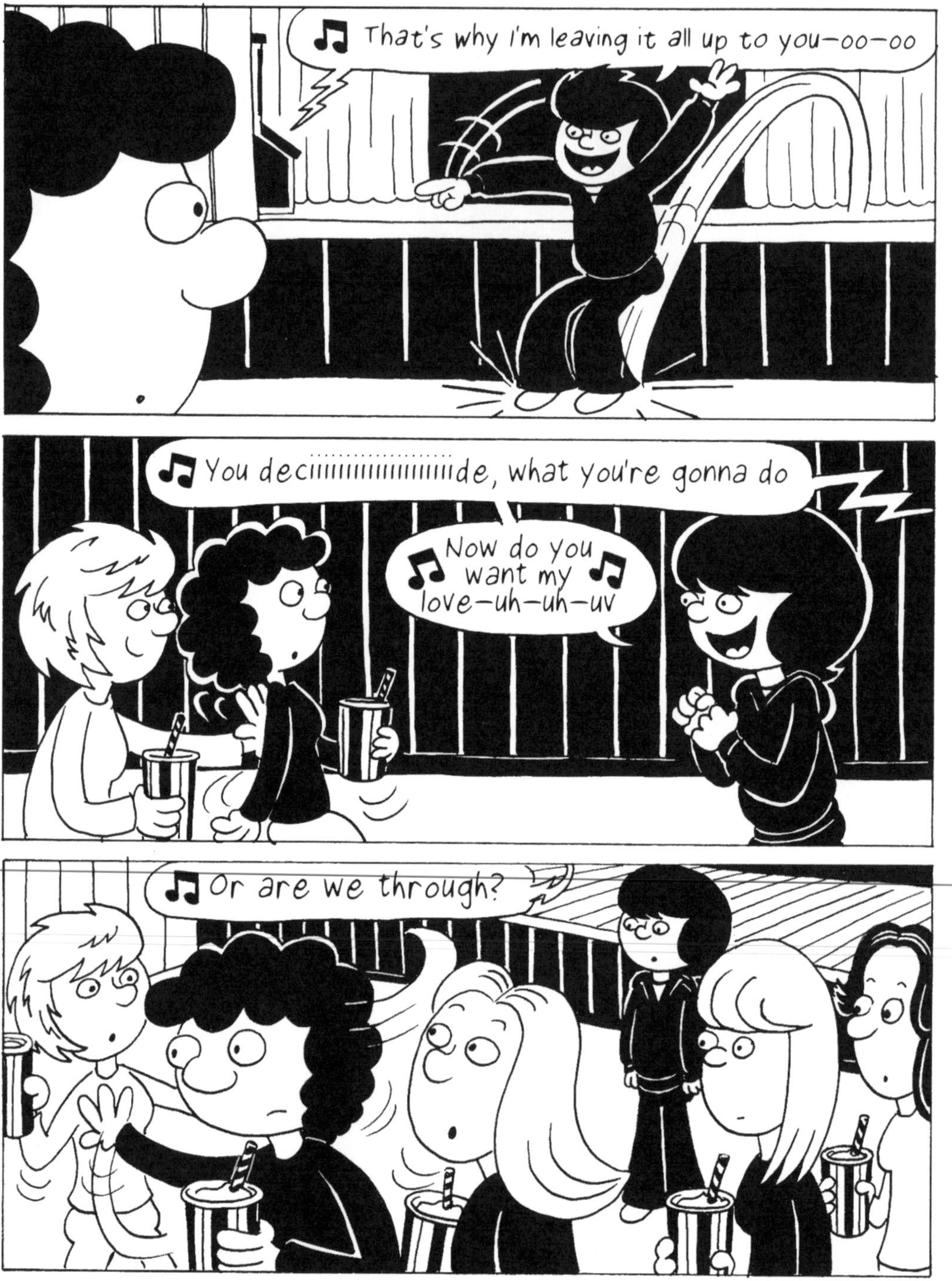
That's why I'm leaving it all up to you—oo—oo
You deciiiiiiiiiiiiiiiiiiiiide, what you're gonna do
Now do you want my love—uh—uh—uv
Or are we through?

What is wrong with you!?! What was that all about!?!

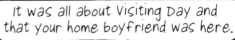

It was all about Visiting Day and that your home boyfriend was here.

Oh my God!

First of all, I didn't invite him. My parents did it to surprise me.

Second of all, I told my parents that was really uncool and that they need to stay out of my relationships.

And third of all, I told David that I was breaking up with him because I had met someone at camp.

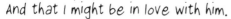

And that I might be in love with him.

Well, I might be in love with you, too.

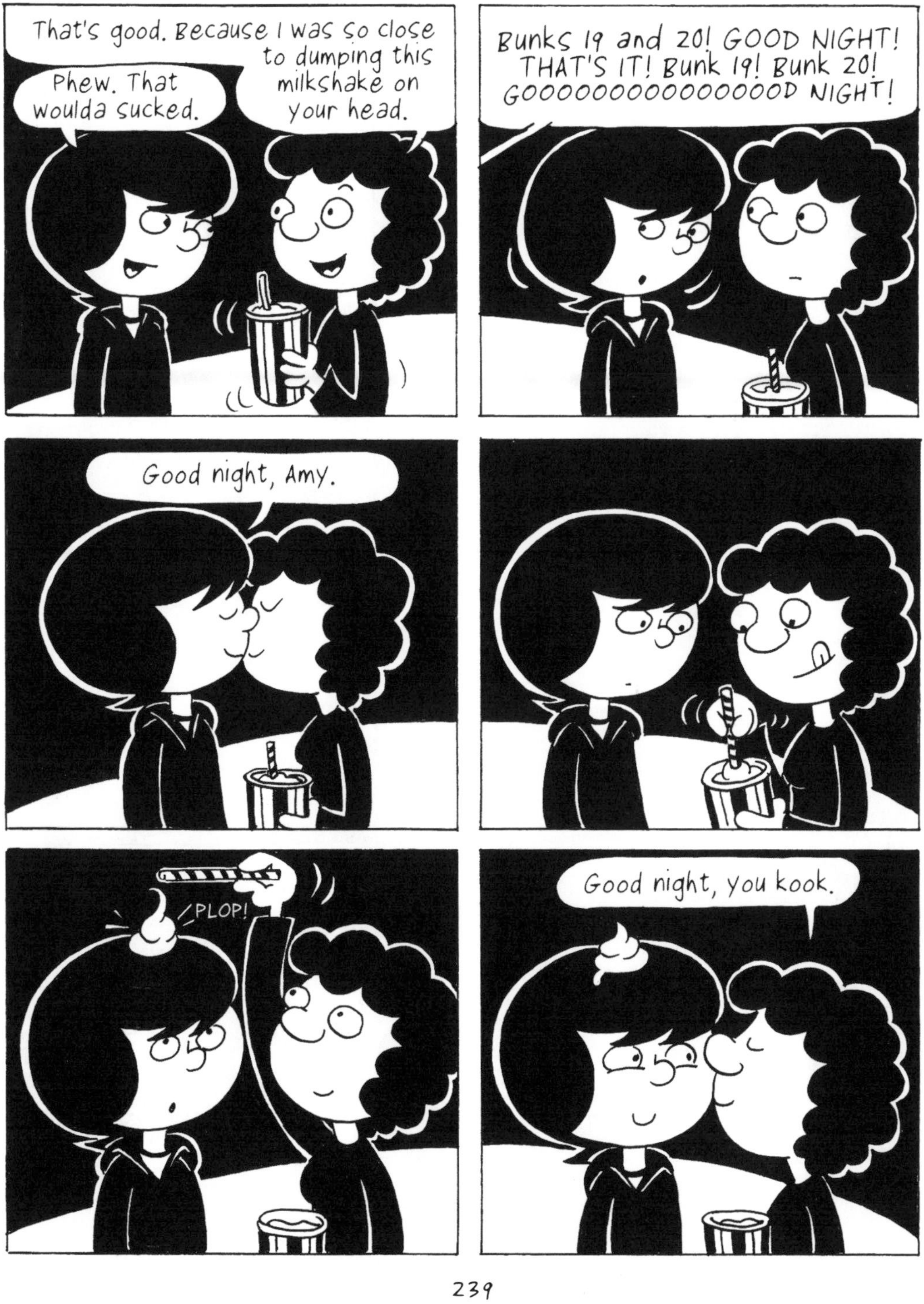
Phew. That woulda sucked.
That's good. Because I was so close to dumping this milkshake on your head.
Bunks 19 and 20! GOOD NIGHT! THAT'S IT! Bunk 19! Bunk 20! GOOOOOOOOOOOOOOOD NIGHT!
Good night, Amy.
PLOP!
Good night, you kook.

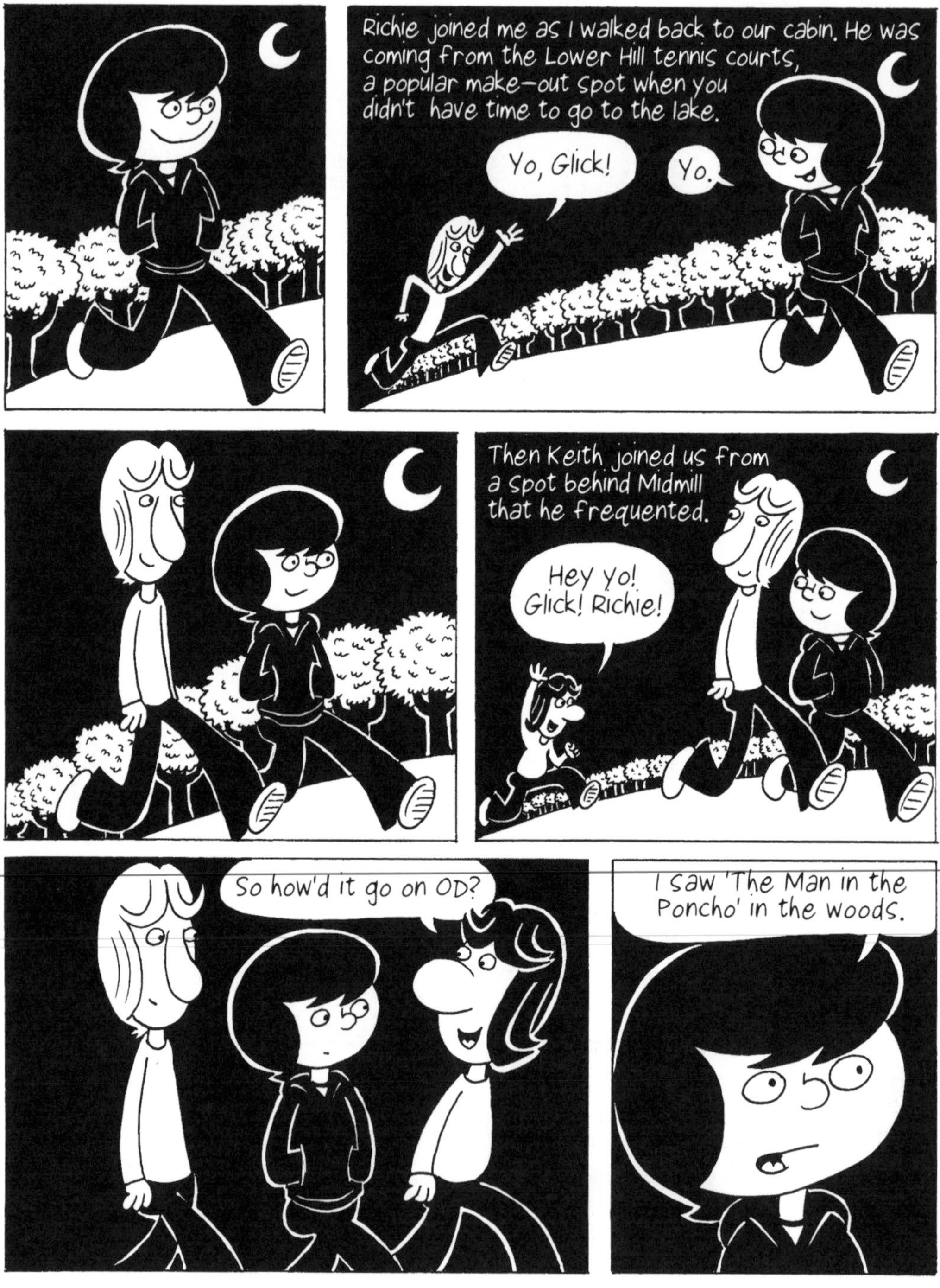
Richie joined me as I walked back to our cabin. He was coming from the Lower Hill tennis courts, a popular make-out spot when you didn't have time to go to the lake.
Yo, Glick!
Yo.
Then Keith joined us from a spot behind Midmill that he frequented.
Hey yo! Glick! Richie!
So how'd it go on OD?
I saw 'The Man in the Poncho' in the woods.

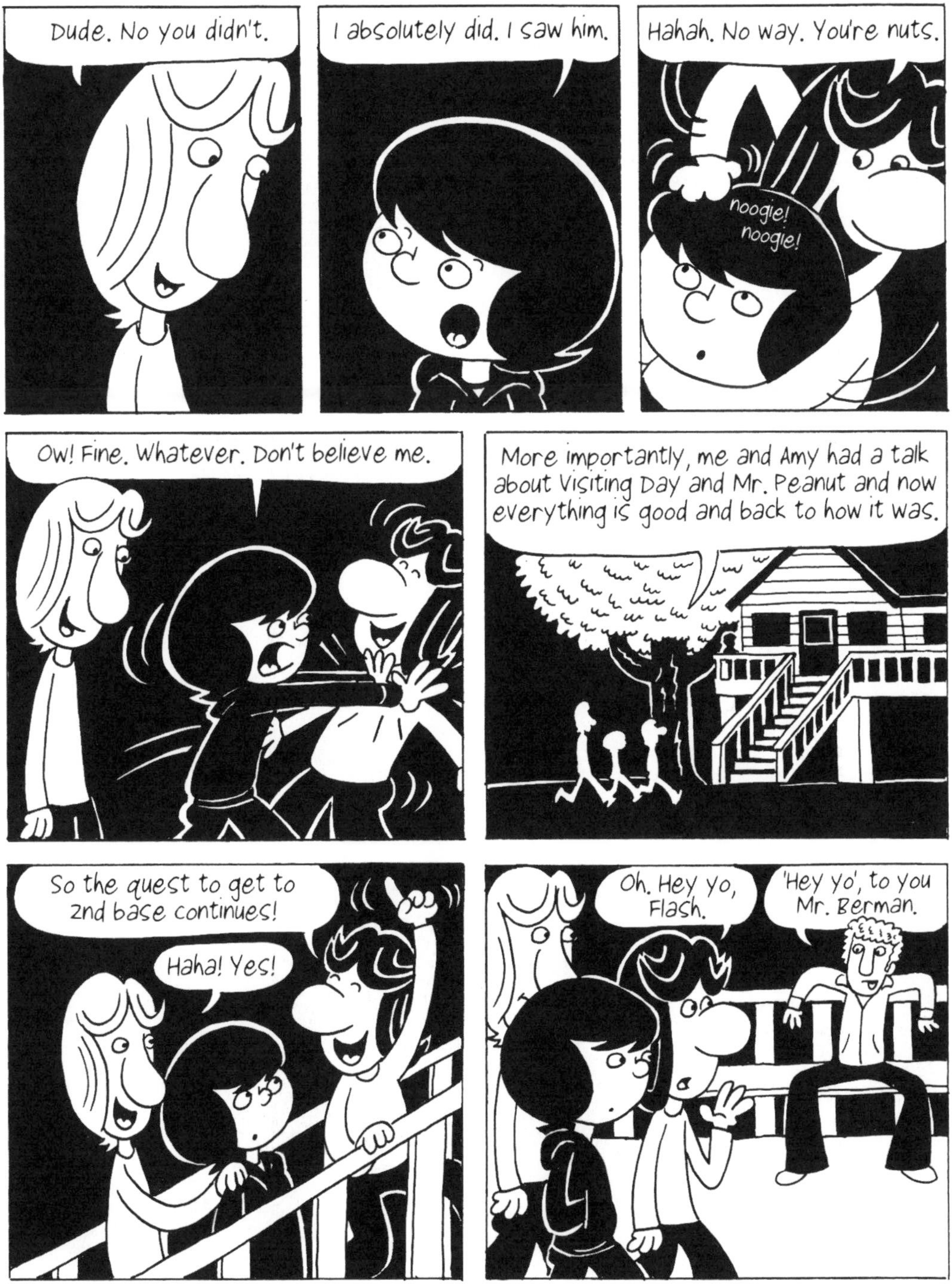
Dude. No you didn't.
I absolutely did. I saw him.
Hahah. No way. You're nuts.
noogie! noogie!
Ow! Fine. Whatever. Don't believe me.
More importantly, me and Amy had a talk about Visiting Day and Mr. Peanut and now everything is good and back to how it was.
So the quest to get to 2nd base continues!
Haha! Yes!
Oh. Hey yo, Flash.
'Hey yo', to you Mr. Berman.

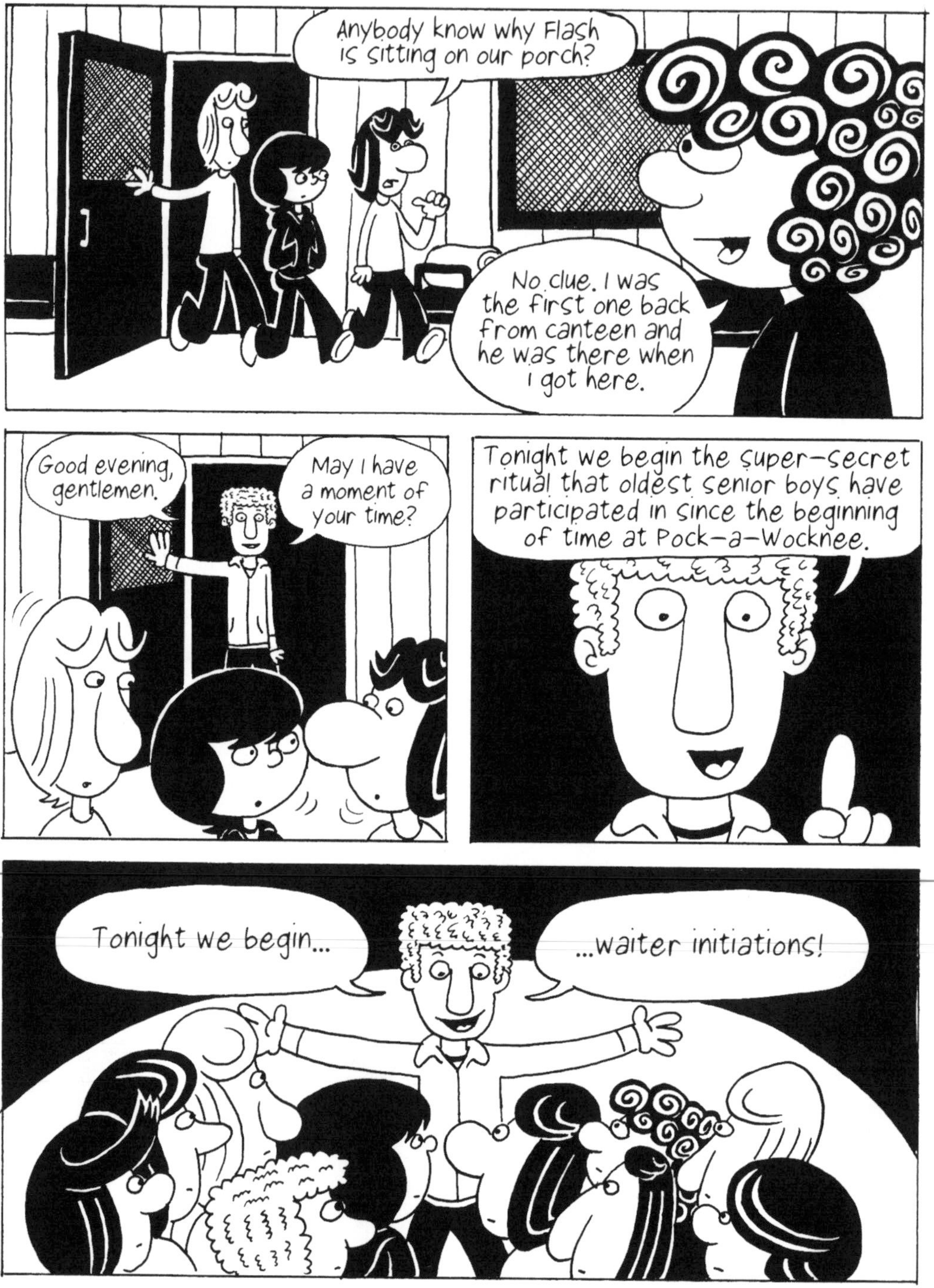

Anybody know why Flash is sitting on our porch?
No clue. I was the first one back from canteen and he was there when I got here.
Good evening, gentlemen.
May I have a moment of your time?
Tonight we begin the super-secret ritual that oldest senior boys have participated in since the beginning of time at Pock-a-Wocknee.
Tonight we begin...
...waiter initiations!

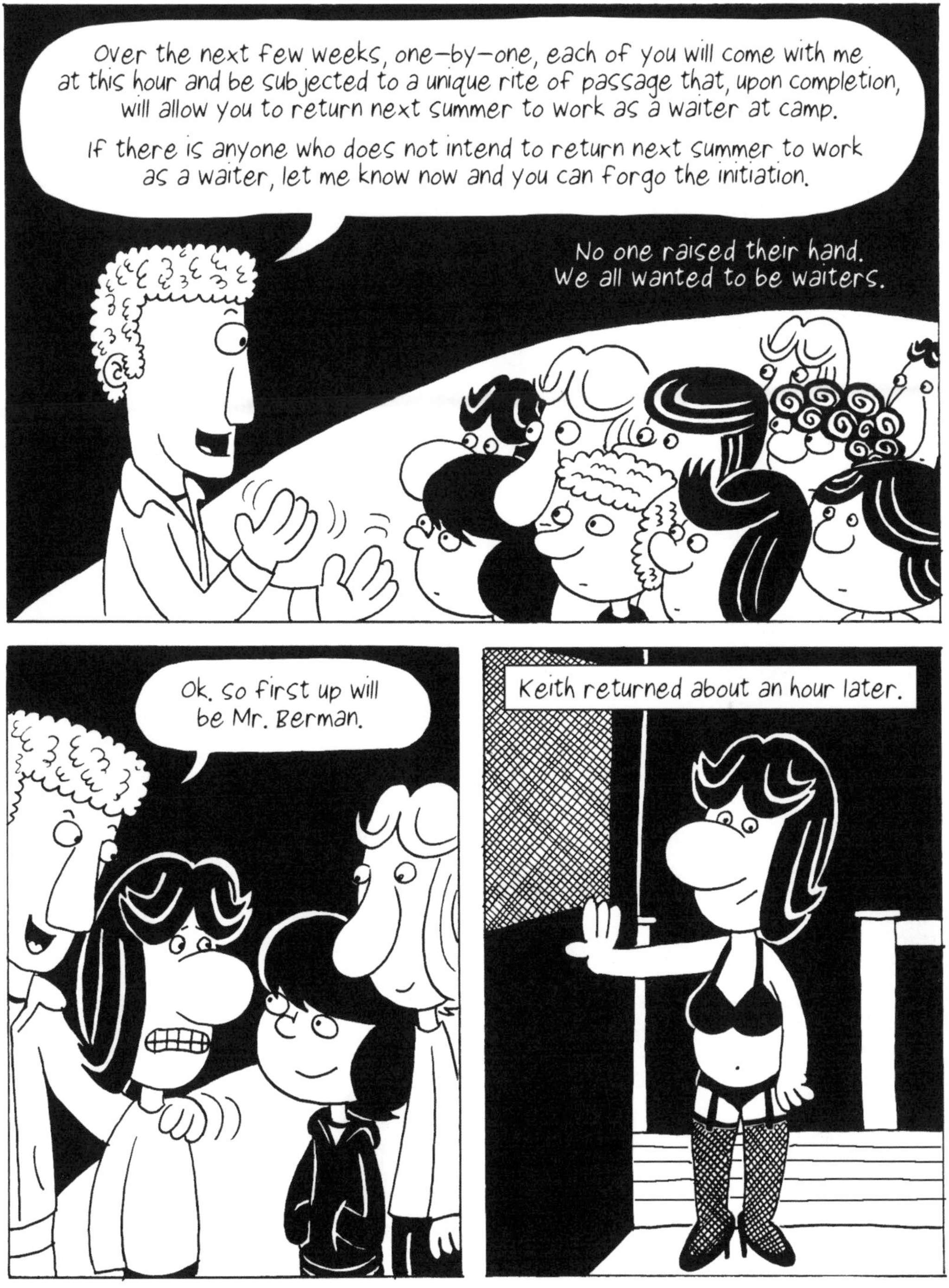
Over the next few weeks, one-by-one, each of you will come with me at this hour and be subjected to a unique rite of passage that, upon completion, will allow you to return next summer to work as a waiter at camp.
If there is anyone who does not intend to return next summer to work as a waiter, let me know now and you can forgo the initiation.
No one raised their hand. We all wanted to be waiters.
Ok. So first up will be Mr. Berman.
Keith returned about an hour later.

Every few nights, Flash showed up after canteen and took someone for initiation.

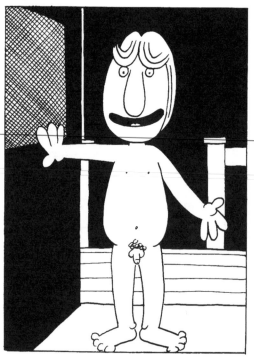

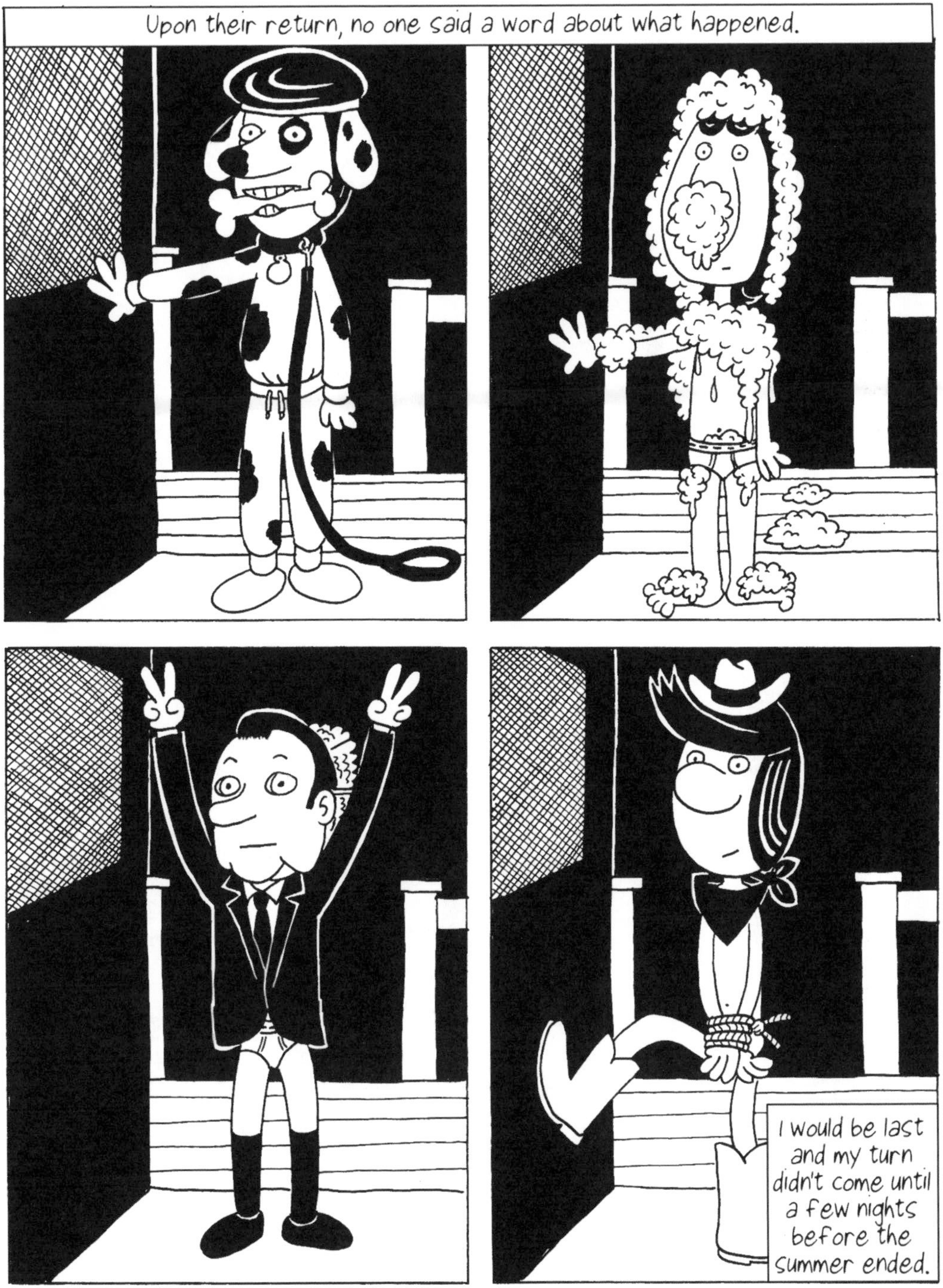
Upon their return, no one said a word about what happened.
I would be last and my turn didn't come until a few nights before the summer ended.

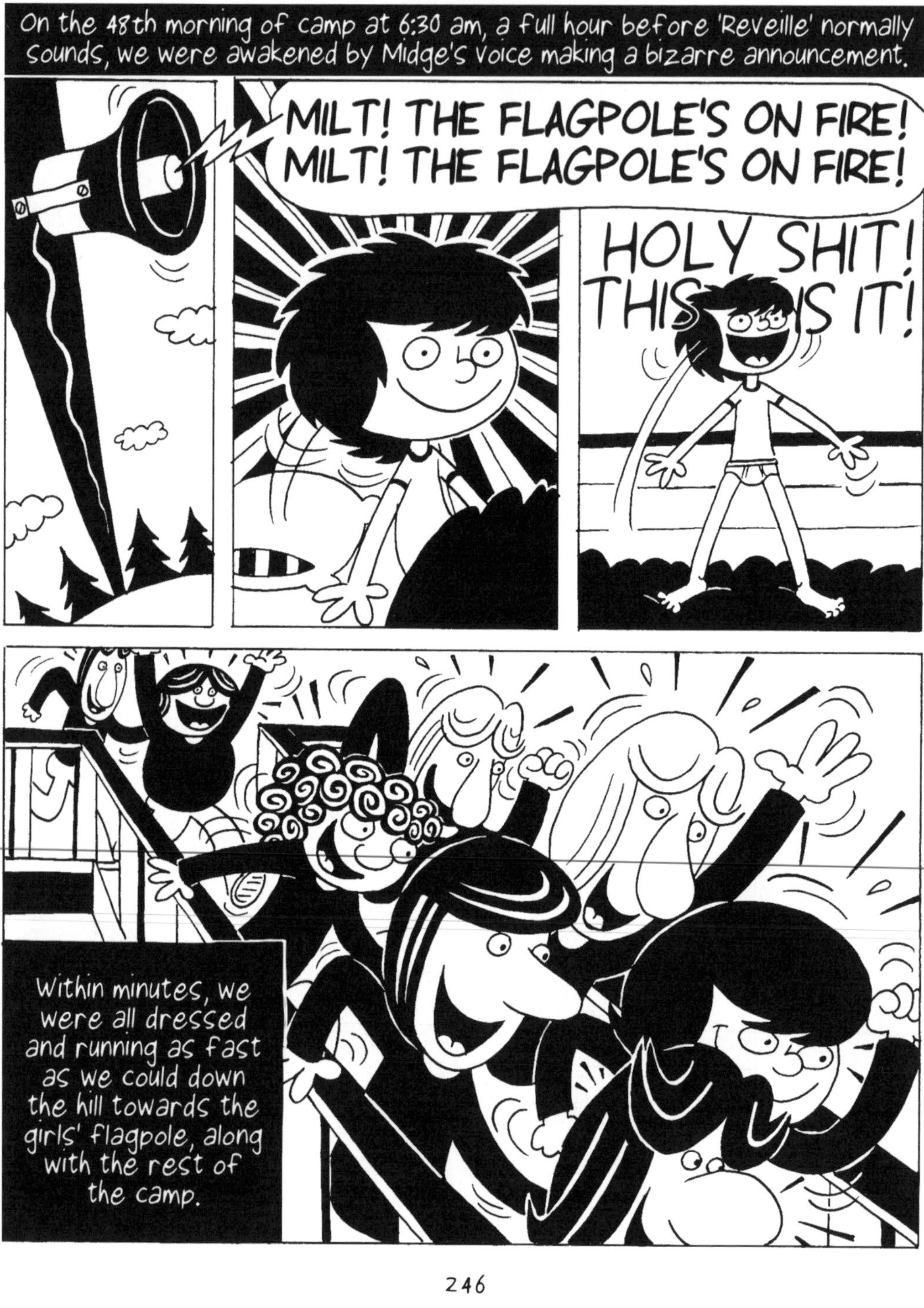
On the 48th morning of camp at 6:30 am, a full hour before 'Reveille' normally sounds, we were awakened by Midge's voice making a bizarre announcement.
MILT! THE FLAGPOLE'S ON FIRE! MILT! THE FLAGPOLE'S ON FIRE!
HOLY SHIT! THIS IS IT!
Within minutes, we were all dressed and running as fast as we could down the hill towards the girls' flagpole, along with the rest of the camp.

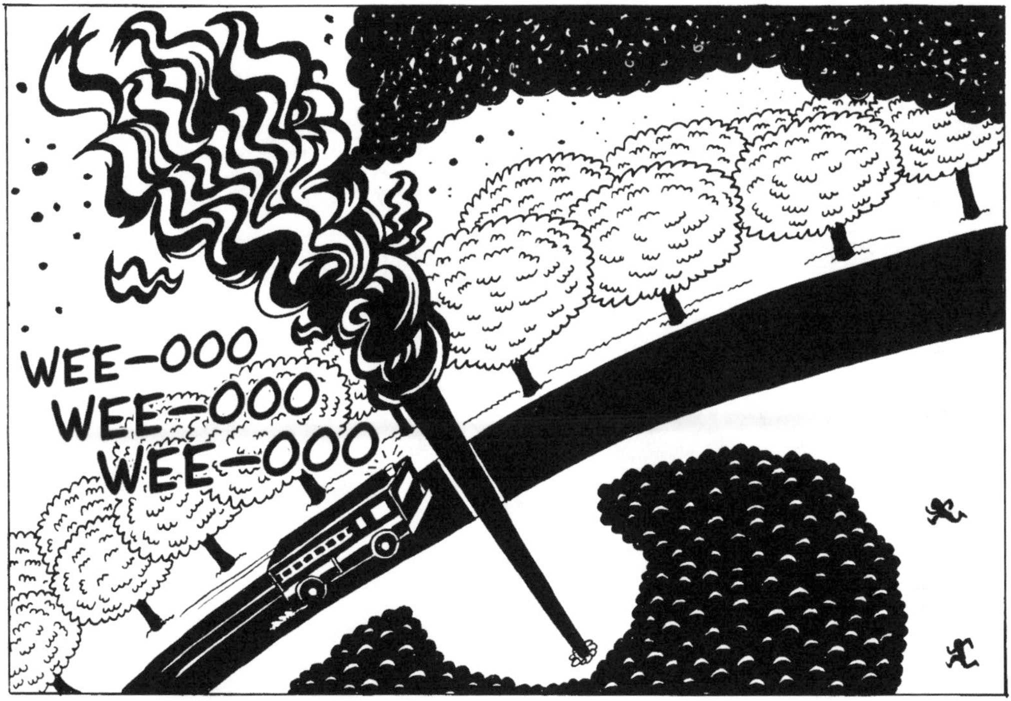
WEE-OOO
WEE-OOO
WEE-OOO

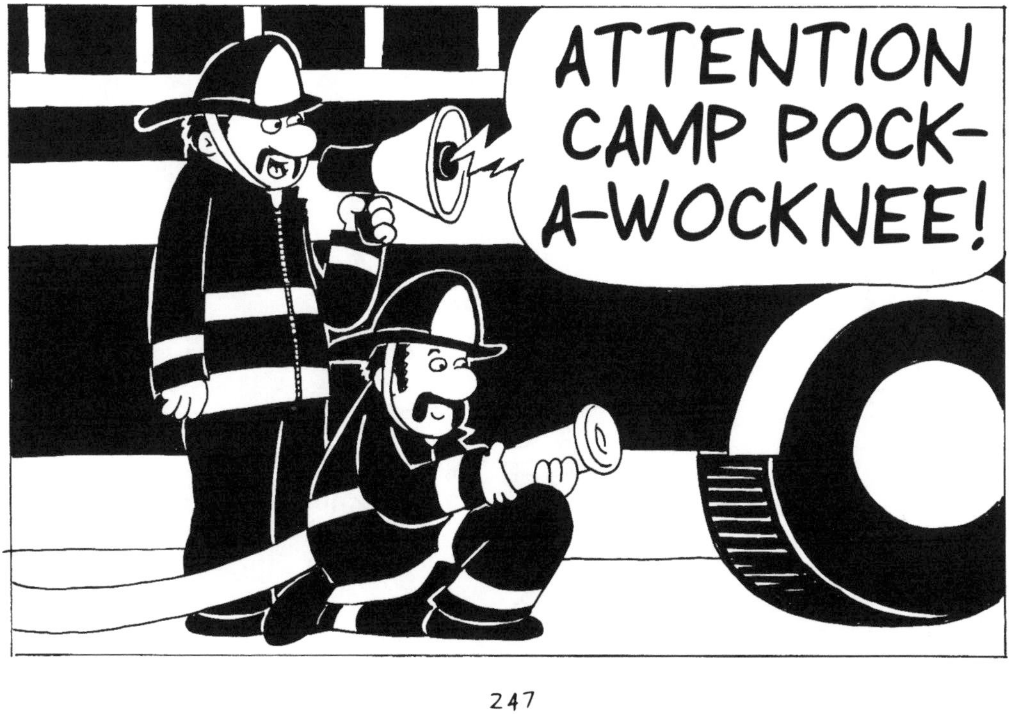
ATTENTION CAMP POCK-A-WOCKNEE!

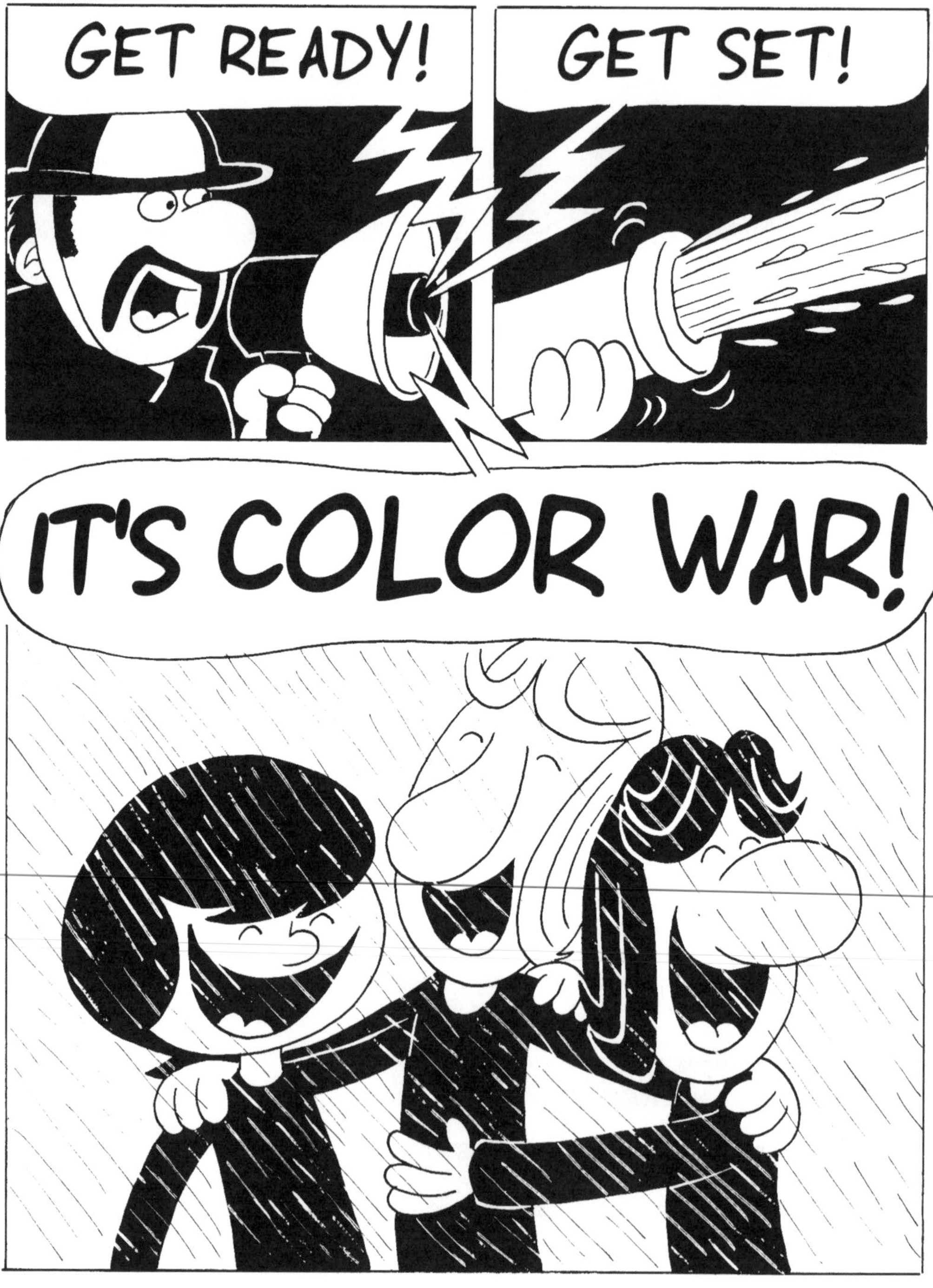
GET READY!
GET SET!
IT'S COLOR WAR!

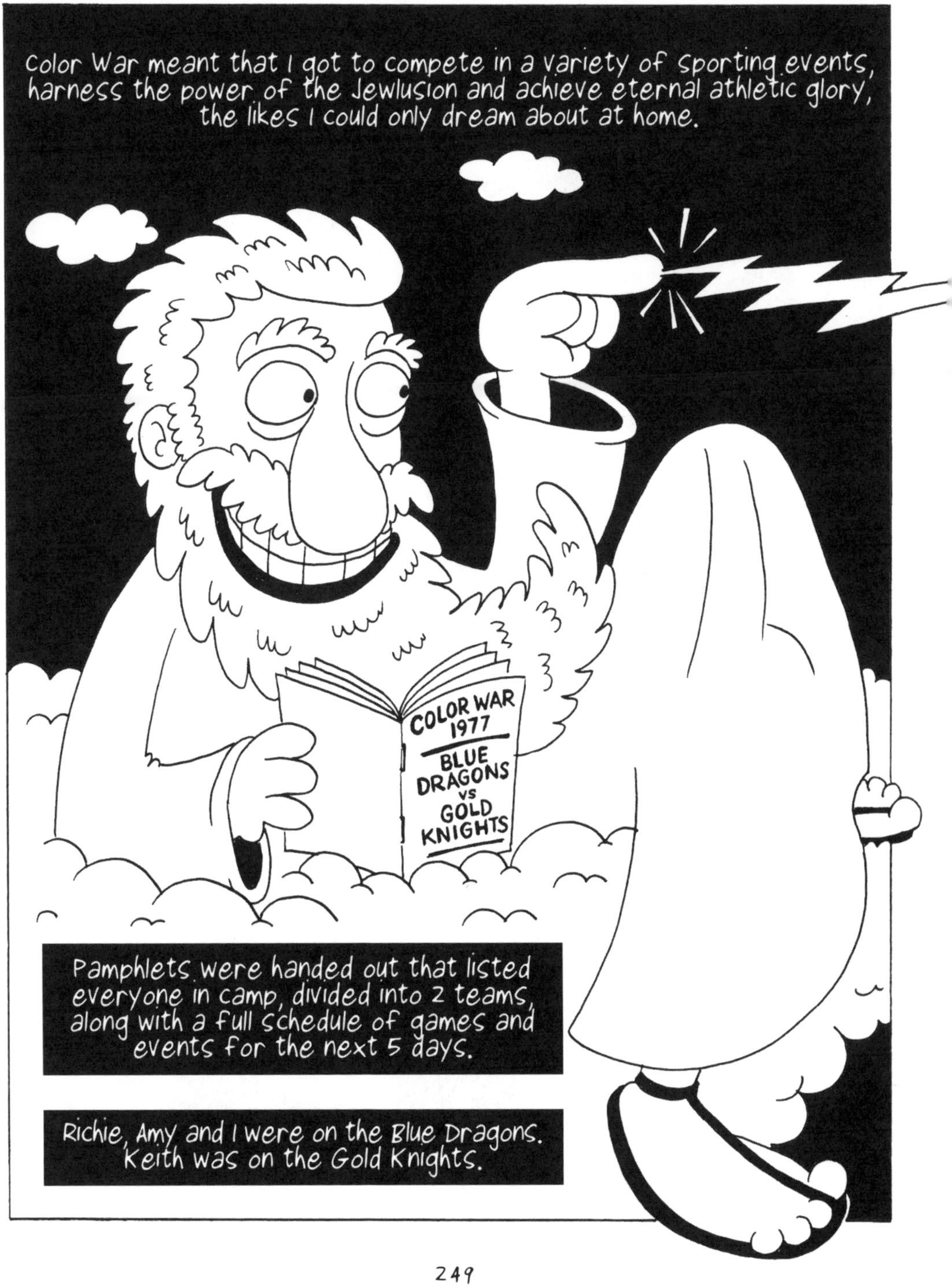
Color War meant that I got to compete in a variety of sporting events, harness the power of the Jewlusion and achieve eternal athletic glory, the likes I could only dream about at home.
COLOR WAR 1977
BLUE DRAGONS VS GOLD KNIGHTS
Pamphlets were handed out that listed everyone in camp, divided into 2 teams, along with a full schedule of games and events for the next 5 days.
Richie, Amy and I were on the Blue Dragons. Keith was on the Gold Knights.

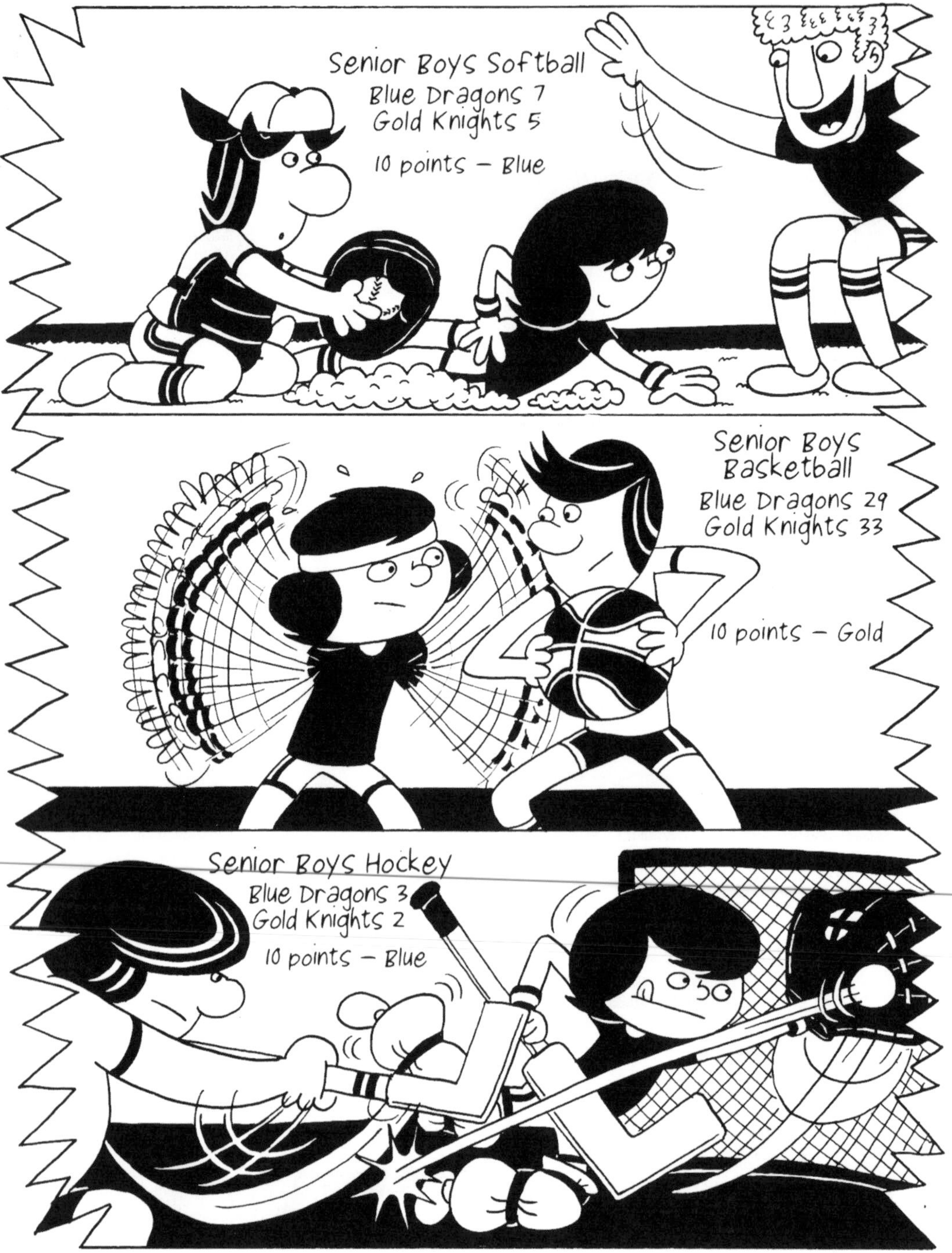
Senior Boys Softball
Blue Dragons 7
Gold Knights 5
10 points – Blue
Senior Boys Basketball
Blue Dragons 29
Gold Knights 33
10 points – Gold
Senior Boys Hockey
Blue Dragons 3
Gold Knights 2
10 points – Blue

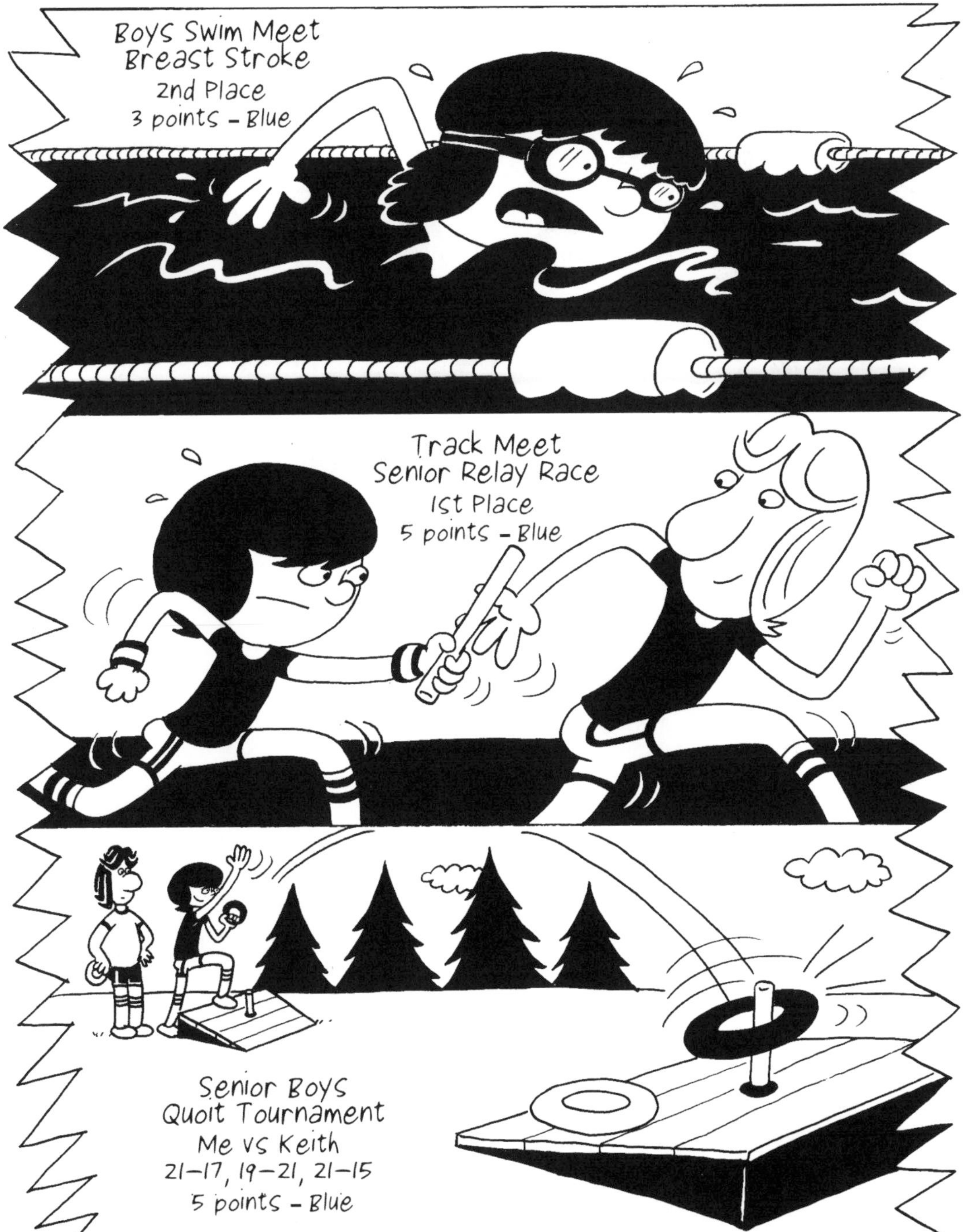
Boys Swim Meet
Breast Stroke
2nd Place
3 points - Blue
Track Meet
Senior Relay Race
1st Place
5 points - Blue
Senior Boys
Quoit Tournament
Me vs Keith
21-17, 19-21, 21-15
5 points - Blue

The first event of Color War was always an all-camp competition called "ALL GOD'S CHILDREN GOT SHOES."

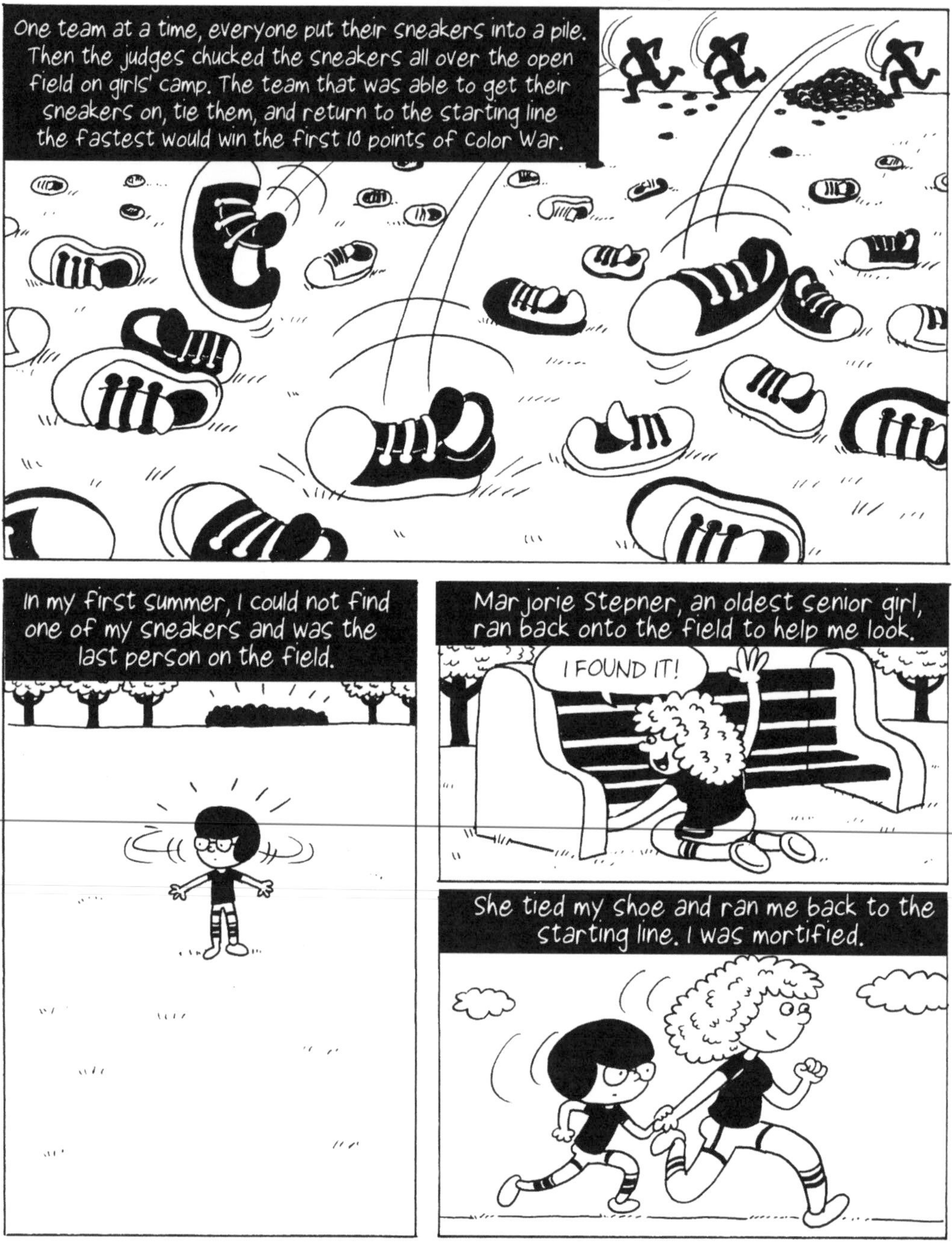

One team at a time, everyone put their sneakers into a pile. Then the judges chucked the sneakers all over the open field on girls' camp. The team that was able to get their sneakers on, tie them, and return to the starting line the fastest would win the first 10 points of Color War.
In my first summer, I could not find one of my sneakers and was the last person on the field.
Marjorie Stepner, an oldest senior girl, ran back onto the field to help me look.
I FOUND IT!
She tied my shoe and ran me back to the starting line. I was mortified.

Because of that incident, I was determined to help every little kid on the Blue Dragons find their sneakers and get off the field as quickly as possible.

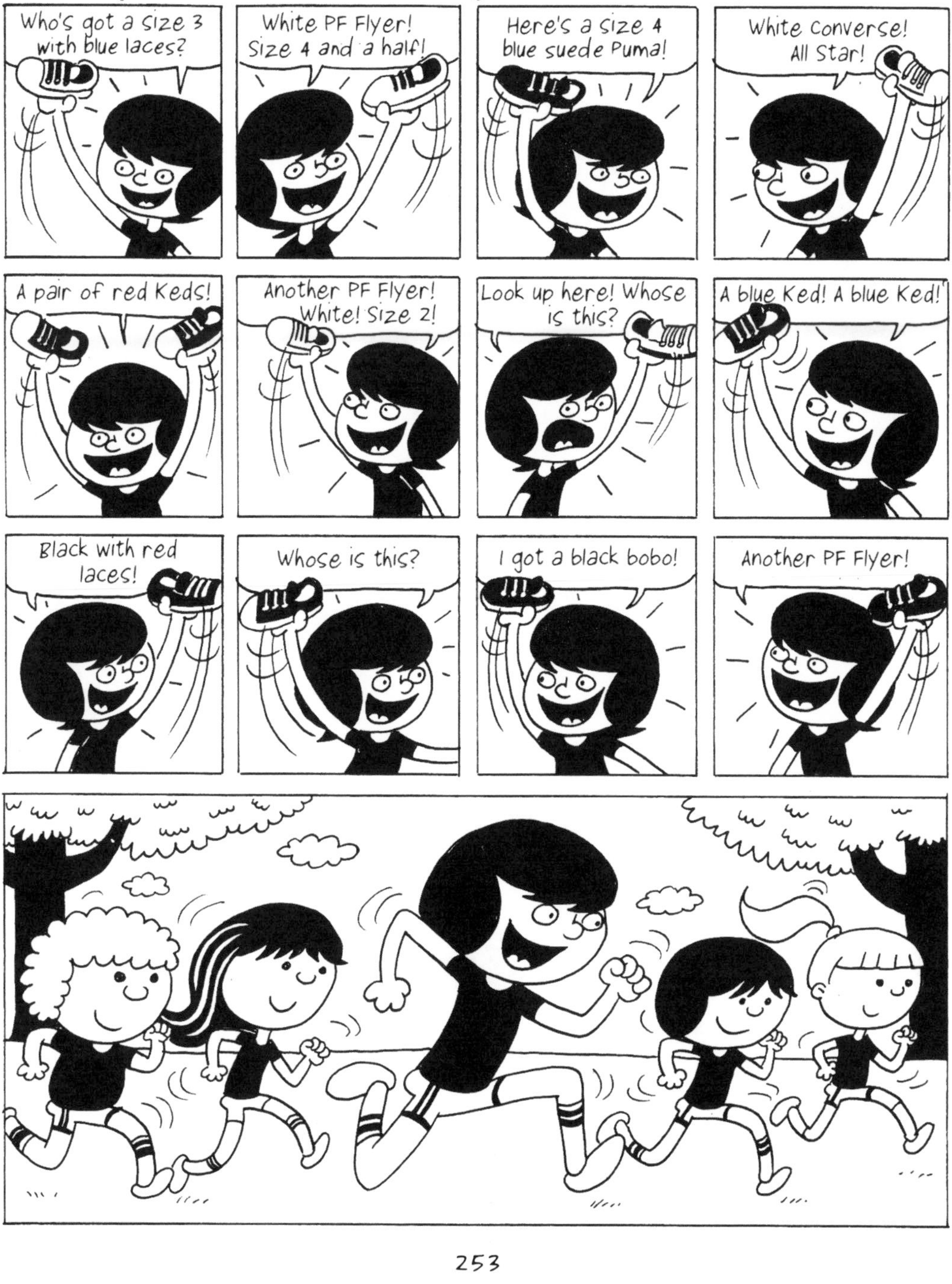
Who's got a size 3 with blue laces?
White PF Flyer! Size 4 and a half!
Here's a size 4 blue suede Puma!
White Converse! All Star!
A pair of red Keds!
Another PF Flyer! White! Size 2!
Look up here! Whose is this?
A blue Ked! A blue Ked!
Black with red laces!
Whose is this?
I got a black bobo!
Another PF Flyer!

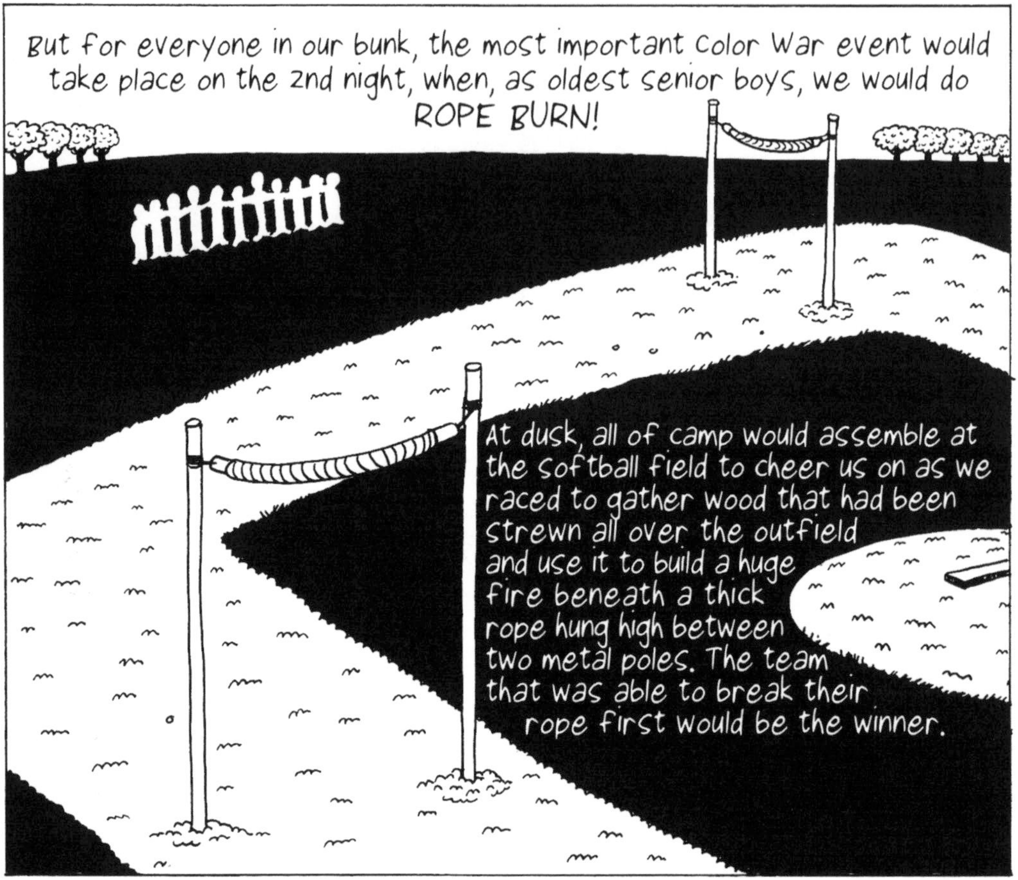
But for everyone in our bunk, the most important Color War event would take place on the 2nd night, when, as oldest senior boys, we would do
ROPE BURN!
At dusk, all of camp would assemble at the softball field to cheer us on as we raced to gather wood that had been strewn all over the outfield and use it to build a huge fire beneath a thick rope hung high between two metal poles. The team that was able to break their rope first would be the winner.

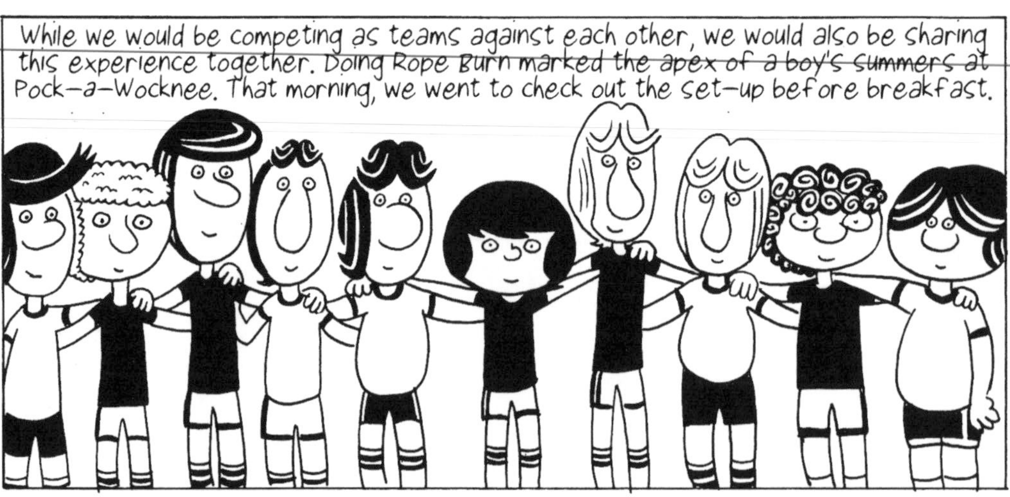
While we would be competing as teams against each other, we would also be sharing this experience together. Doing Rope Burn marked the apex of a boy's summers at Pock-a-Wocknee. That morning, we went to check out the set-up before breakfast.

Then we marched into the dining hall, alternating members of Blue and Gold, as our names were chanted by our respective teams.

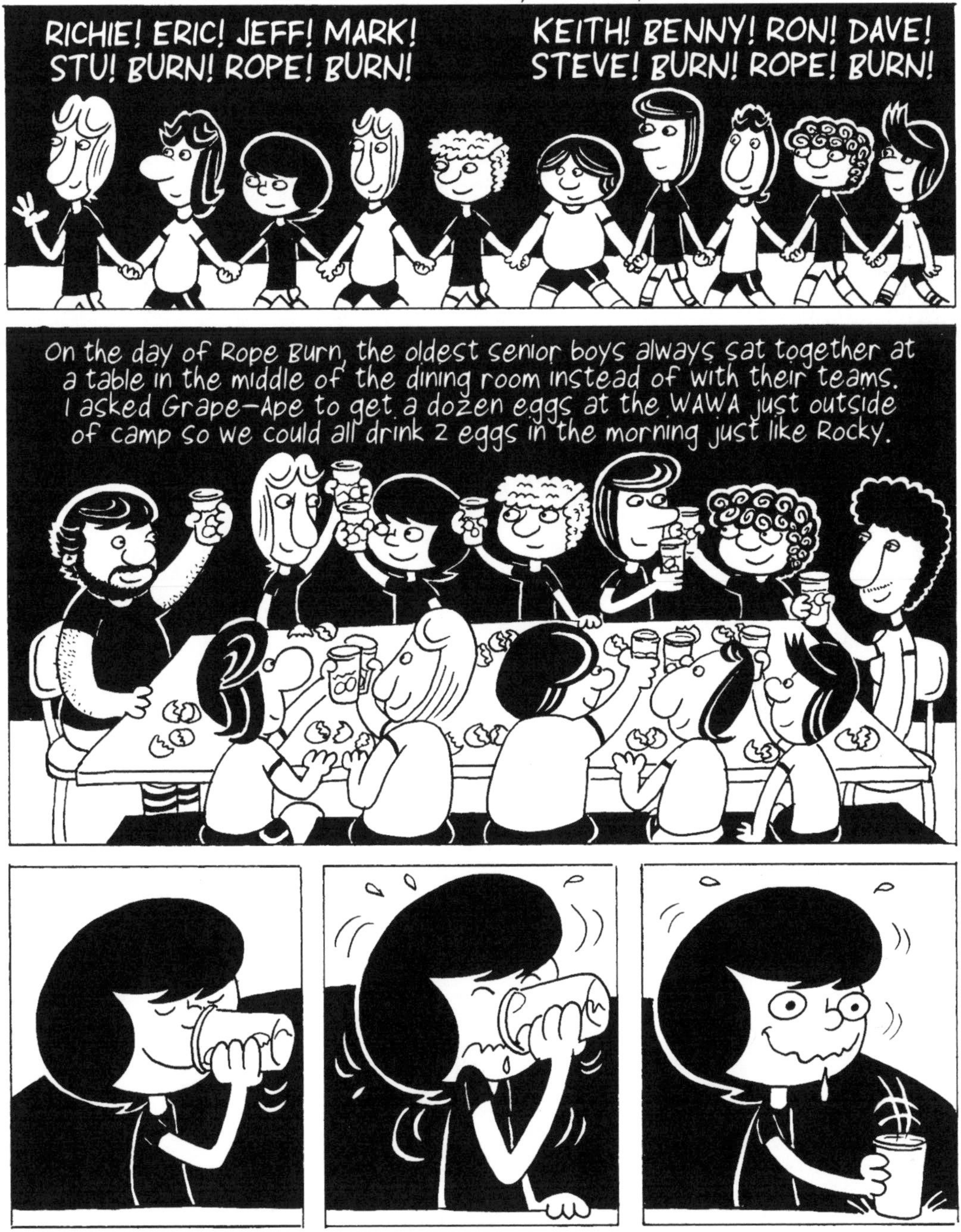
RICHIE! ERIC! JEFF! MARK! STU! BURN! ROPE! BURN!
KEITH! BENNY! RON! DAVE! STEVE! BURN! ROPE! BURN!
On the day of Rope Burn, the oldest senior boys always sat together at a table in the middle of the dining room instead of with their teams. I asked Grape-Ape to get a dozen eggs at the WAWA just outside of camp so we could all drink 2 eggs in the morning just like Rocky.

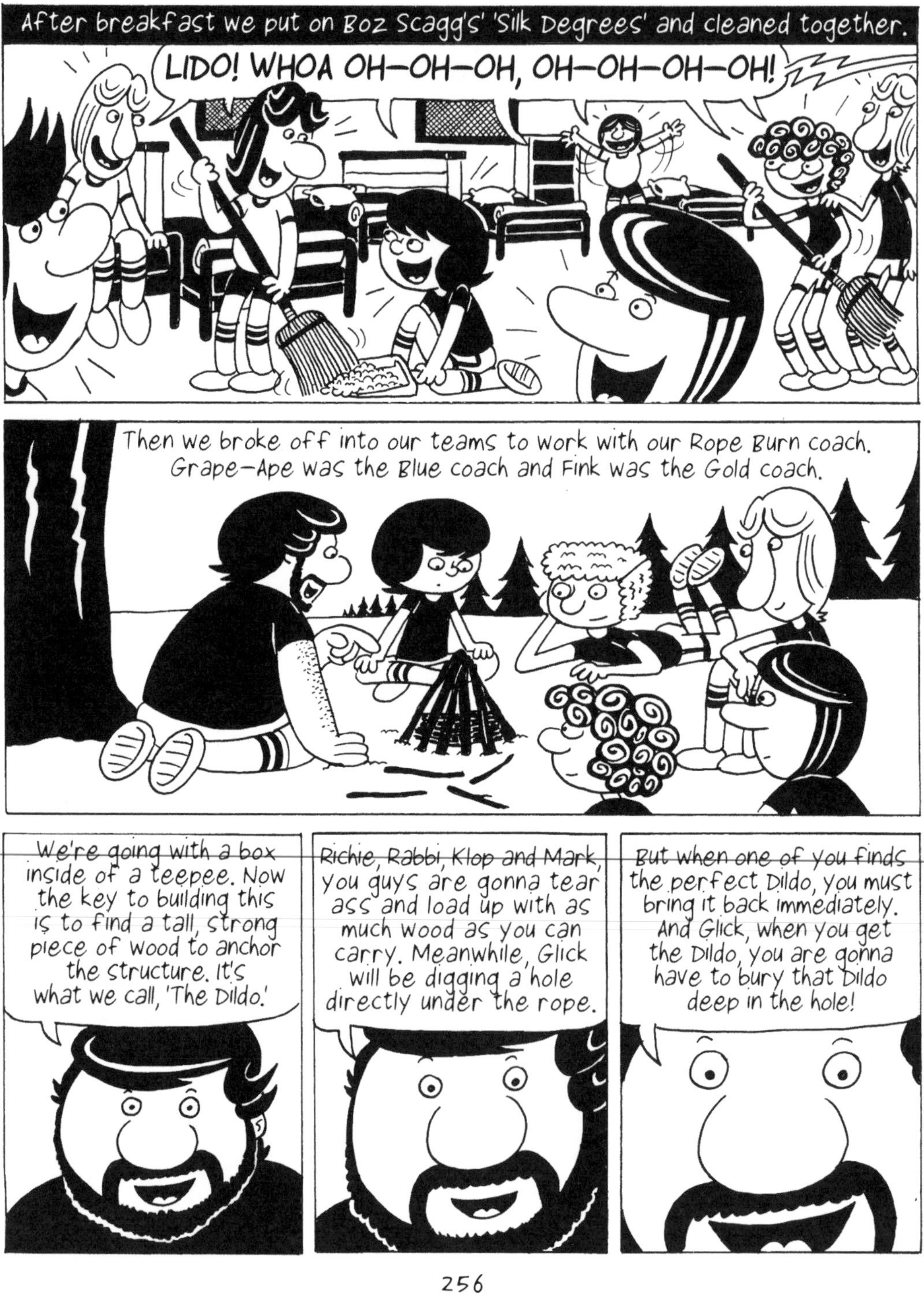
After breakfast we put on Boz Scagg's' 'Silk Degrees' and cleaned together.
LIDO! WHOA OH-OH-OH, OH-OH-OH-OH!
Then we broke off into our teams to work with our Rope Burn coach. Grape-Ape was the Blue coach and Fink was the Gold coach.
We're going with a box inside of a teepee. Now the key to building this is to find a tall, strong piece of wood to anchor the structure. It's what we call, 'The Dildo.'
Richie, Rabbi, Klop and Mark, you guys are gonna tear ass and load up with as much wood as you can carry. Meanwhile, Glick will be digging a hole directly under the rope.
But when one of you finds the perfect Dildo, you must bring it back immediately. And Glick, when you get the Dildo, you are gonna have to bury that Dildo deep in the hole!

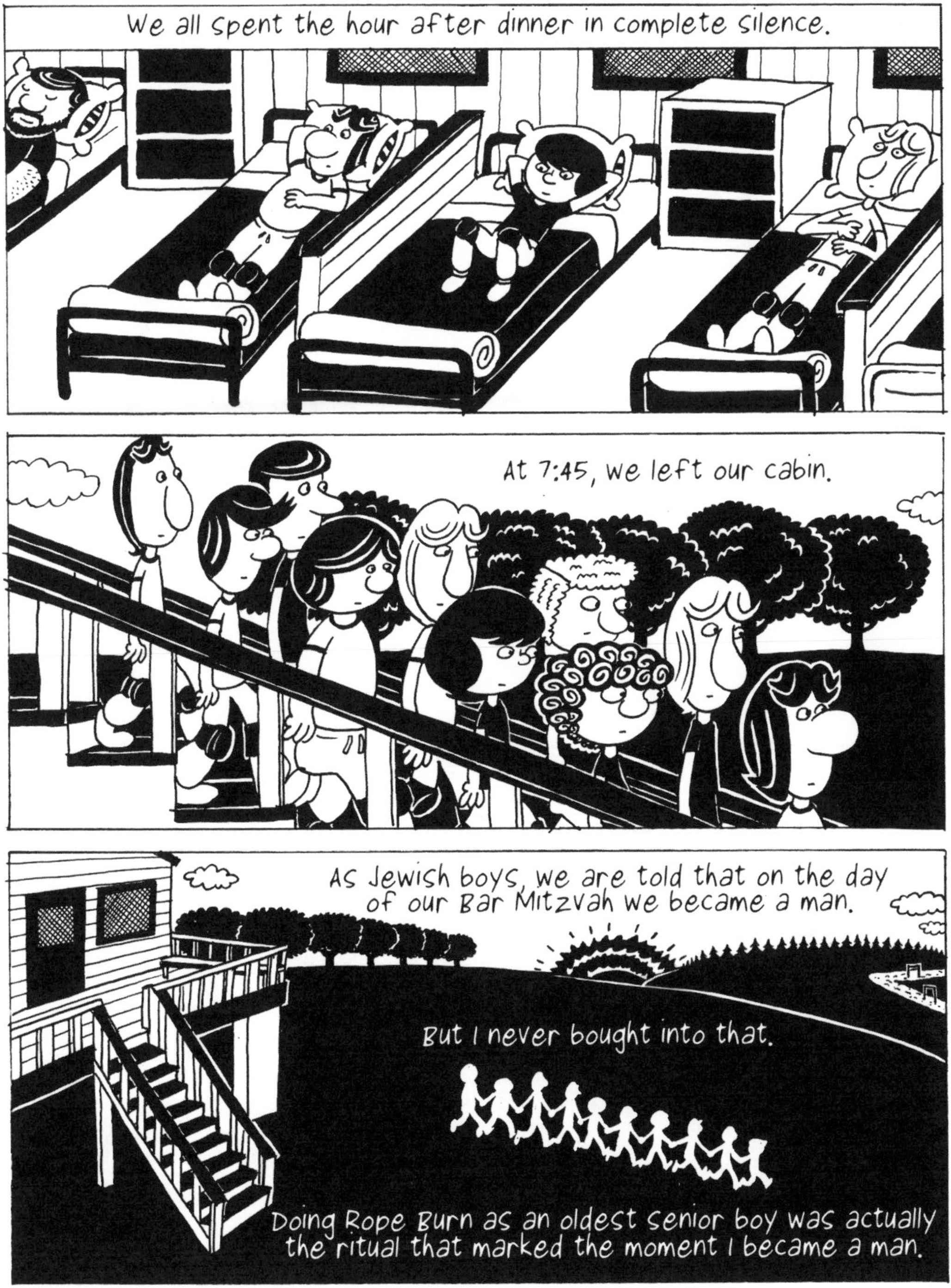
We all spent the hour after dinner in complete silence.
At 7:45, we left our cabin.
As Jewish boys, we are told that on the day of our Bar Mitzvah we became a man.
But I never bought into that.
Doing Rope Burn as an oldest senior boy was actually the ritual that marked the moment I became a man.

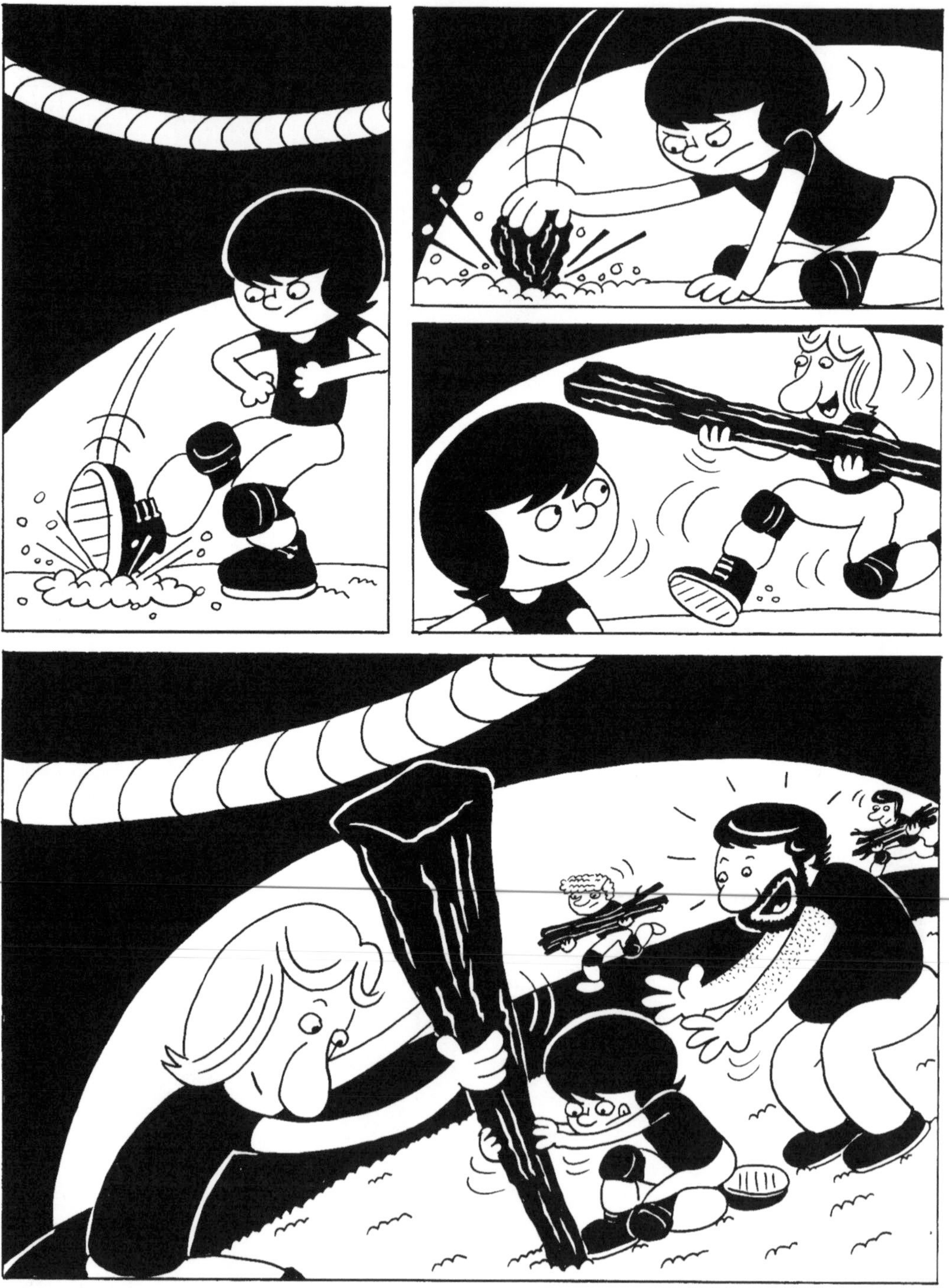

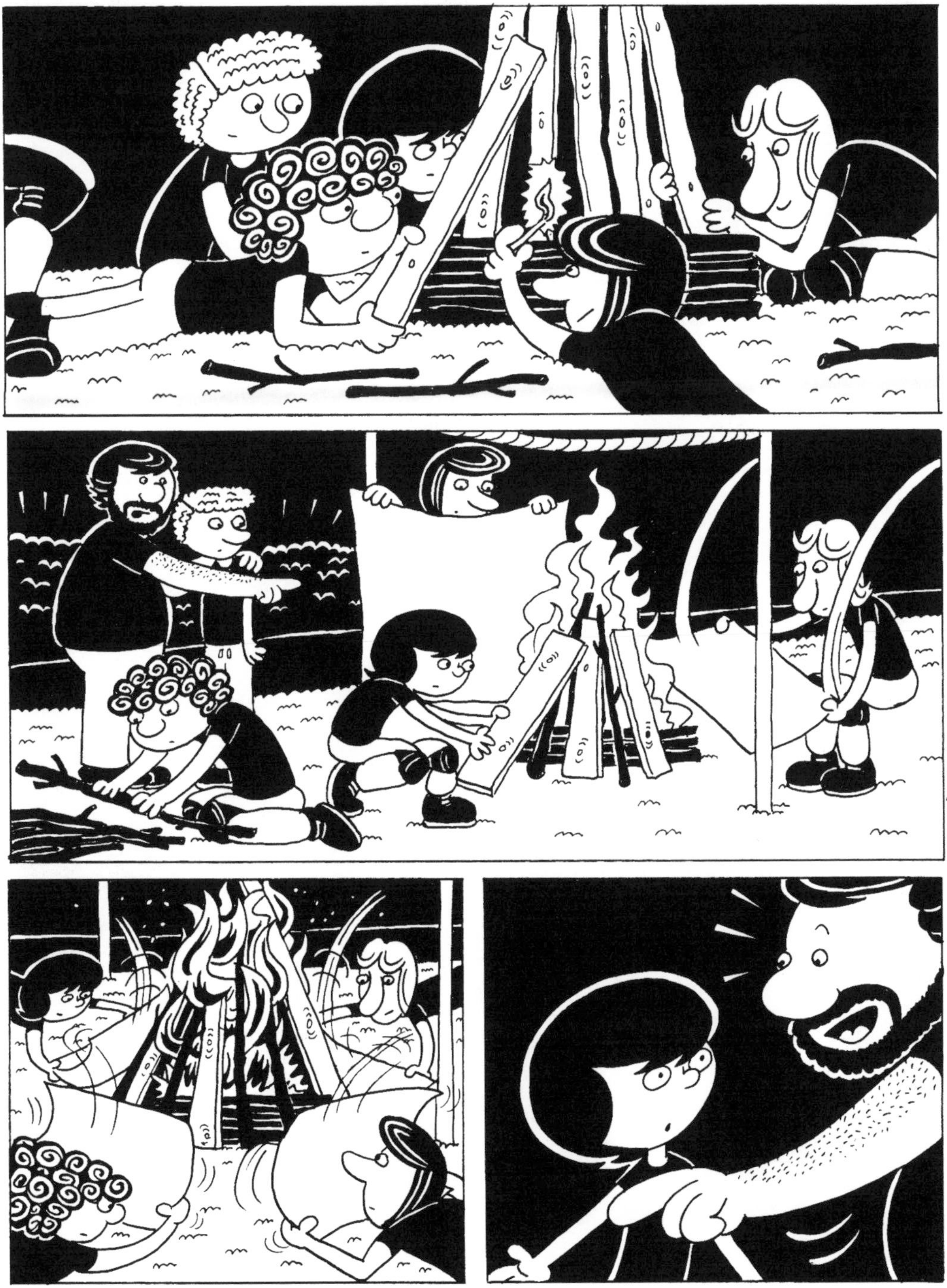

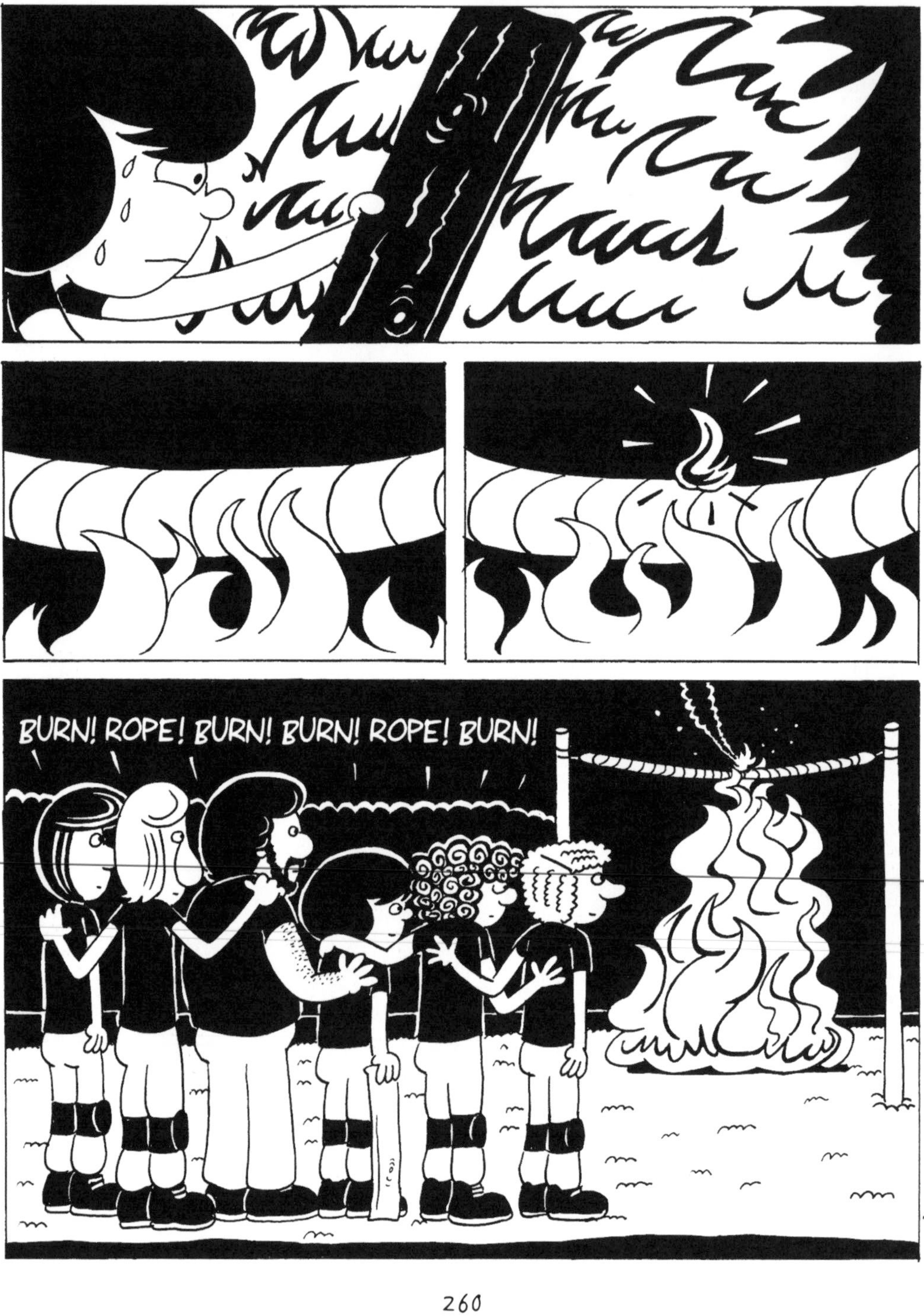
BURN! ROPE! BURN! BURN! ROPE! BURN!

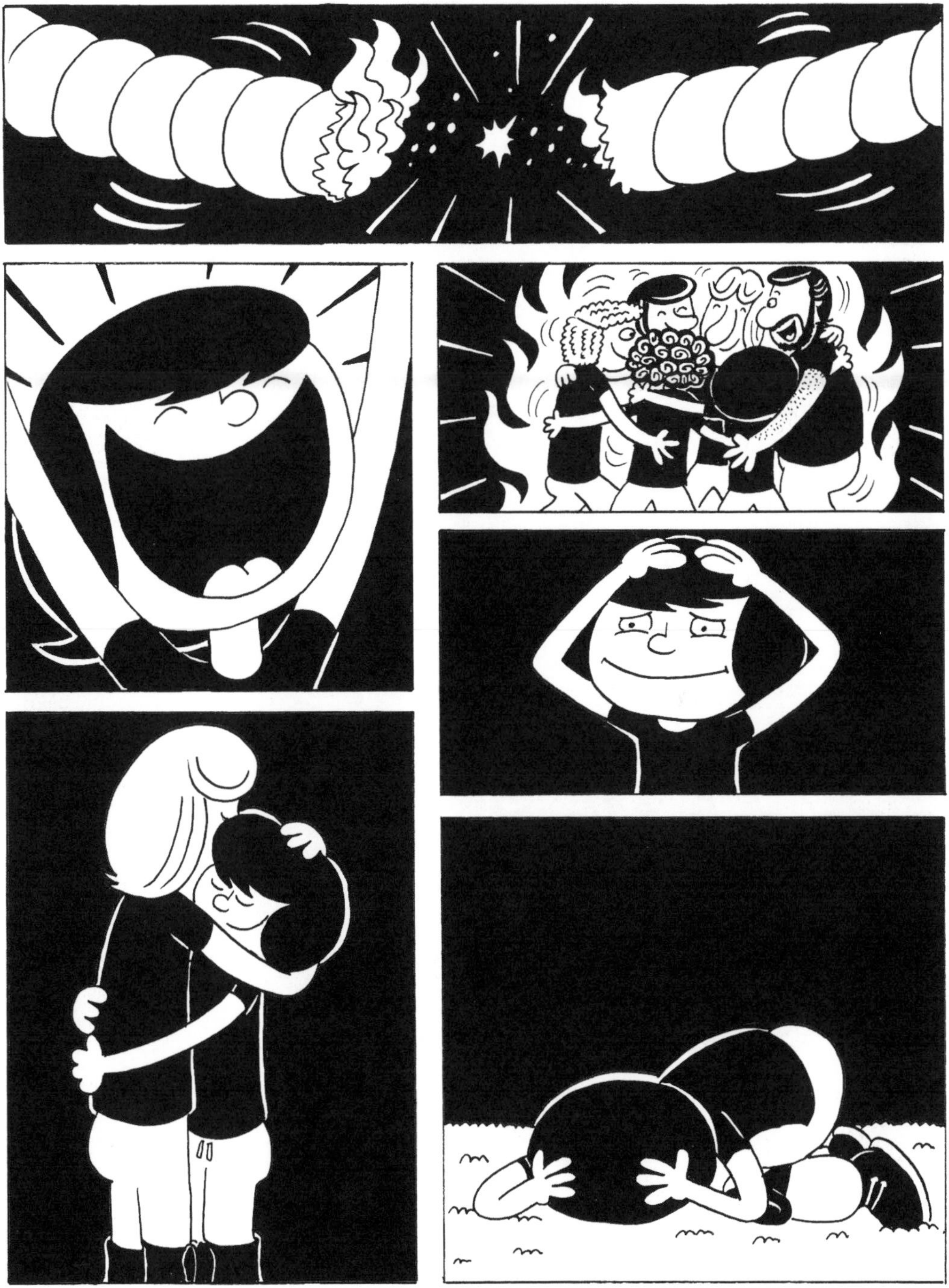

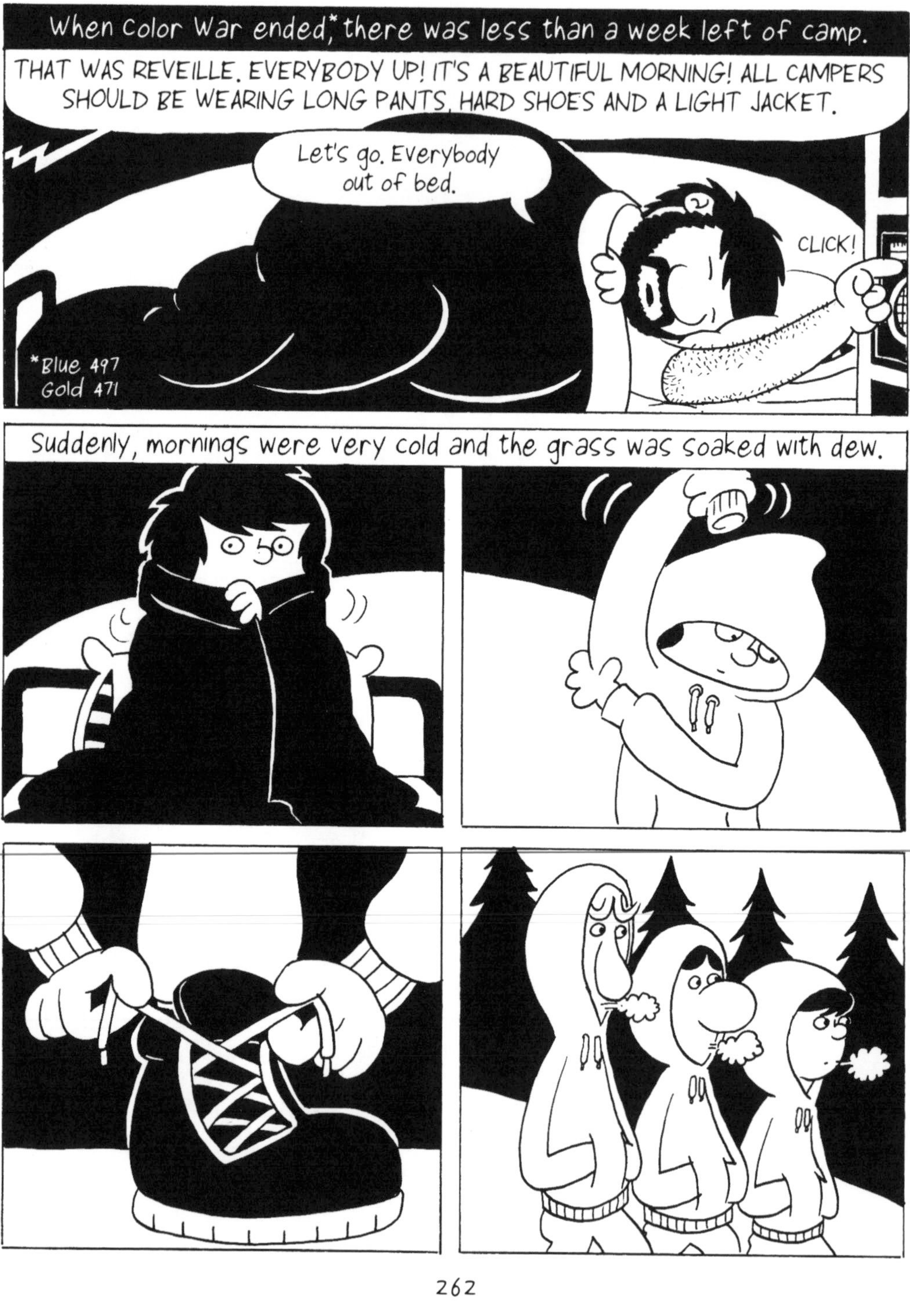
When Color War ended,* there was less than a week left of camp.
THAT WAS REVEILLE. EVERYBODY UP! IT'S A BEAUTIFUL MORNING! ALL CAMPERS SHOULD BE WEARING LONG PANTS, HARD SHOES AND A LIGHT JACKET.
Let's go. Everybody out of bed.
CLICK!
*Blue 497 Gold 471
Suddenly, mornings were very cold and the grass was soaked with dew.

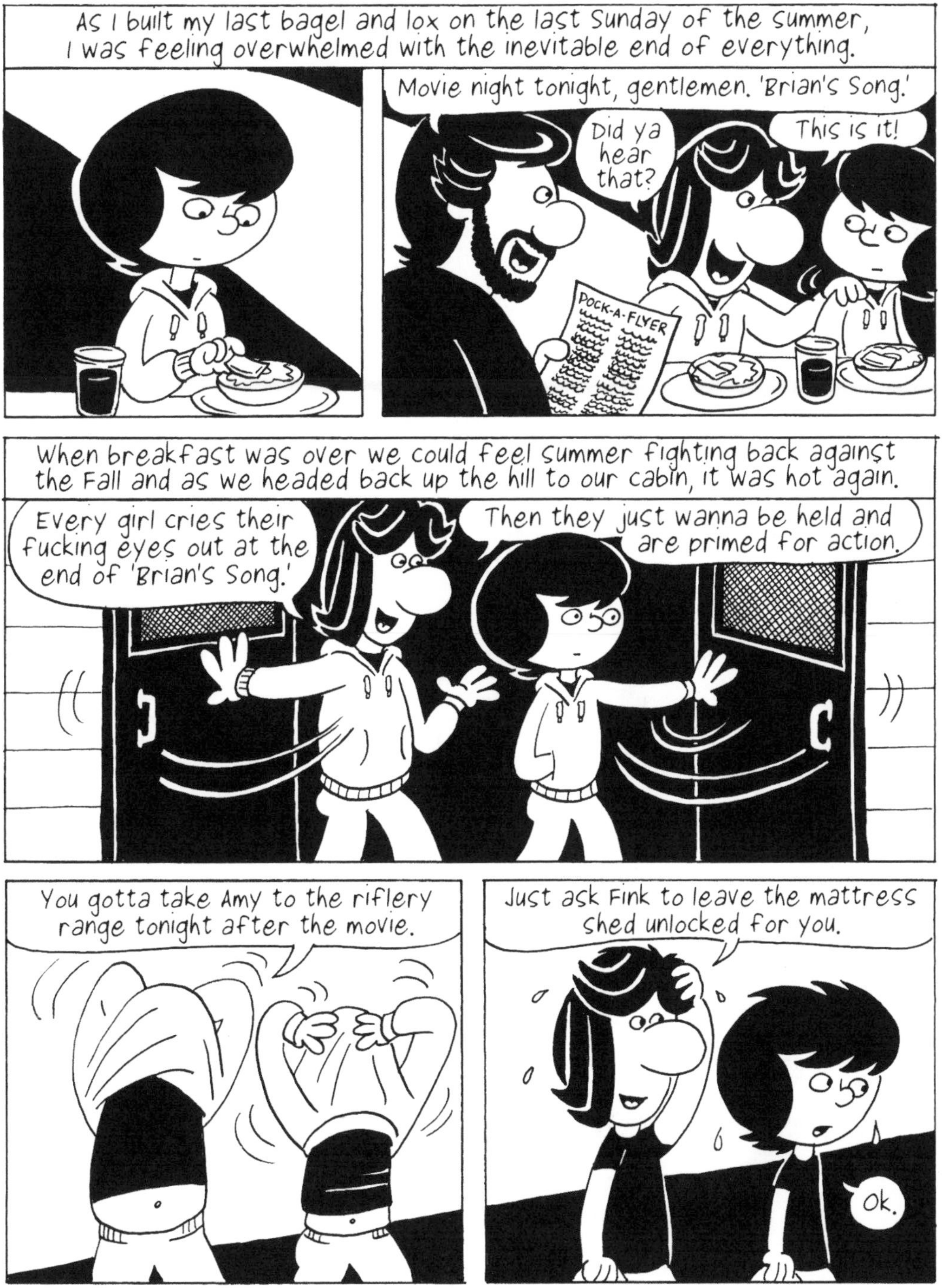
As I built my last bagel and lox on the last Sunday of the summer, I was feeling overwhelmed with the inevitable end of everything.
Movie night tonight, gentlemen. 'Brian's Song.'
Did ya hear that?
This is it!
POCK-A-FLYER
When breakfast was over we could feel summer fighting back against the Fall and as we headed back up the hill to our cabin, it was hot again.
Every girl cries their fucking eyes out at the end of 'Brian's Song.'
Then they just wanna be held and are primed for action.
You gotta take Amy to the riflery range tonight after the movie.
Just ask Fink to leave the mattress shed unlocked for you.
Ok.

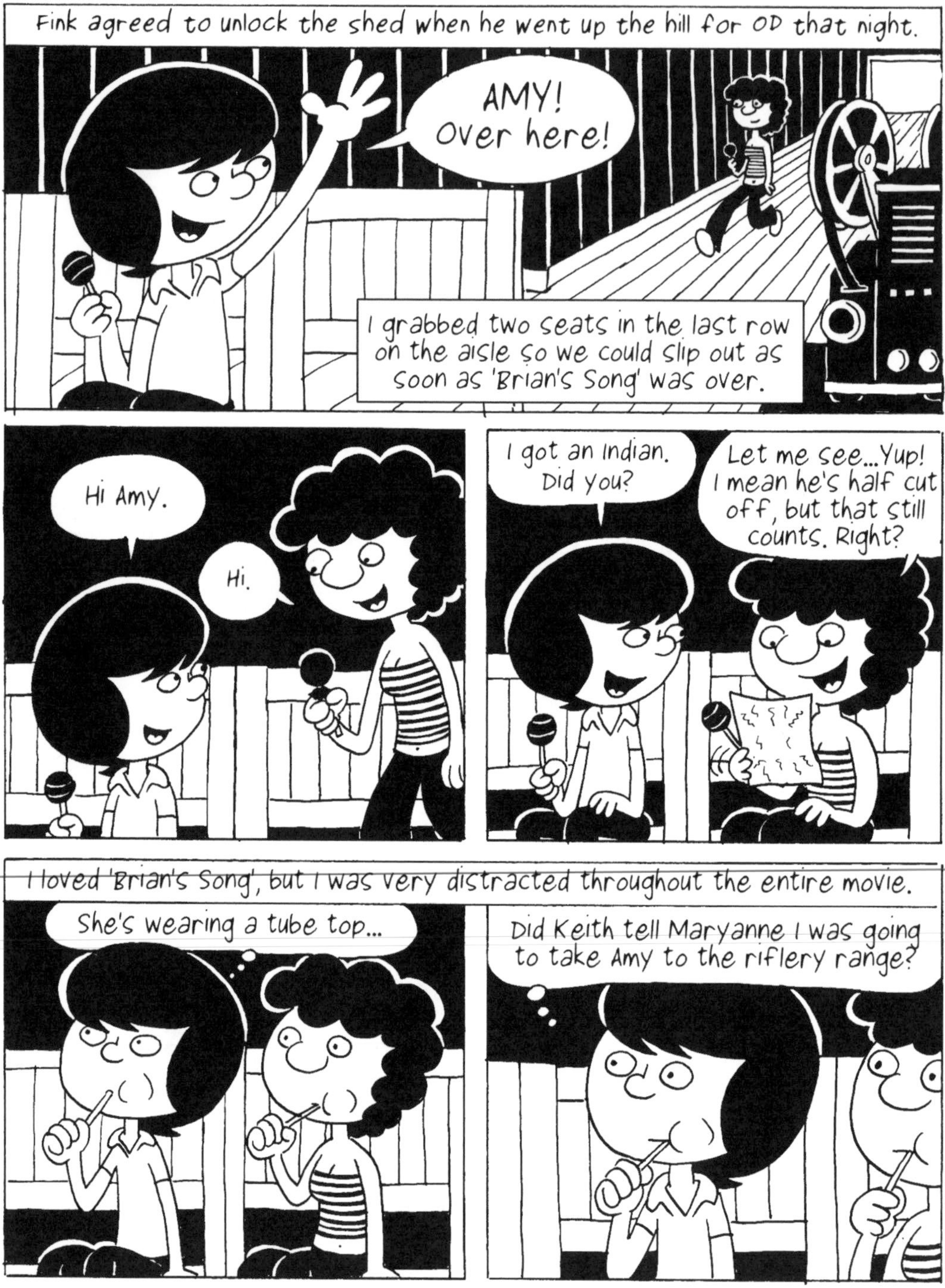

Fink agreed to unlock the shed when he went up the hill for OD that night.
AMY! Over here!
I grabbed two seats in the last row on the aisle so we could slip out as soon as 'Brian's Song' was over.
Hi Amy.
Hi.
I got an Indian. Did you?
Let me see...Yup! I mean he's half cut off, but that still counts. Right?
I loved 'Brian's Song', but I was very distracted throughout the entire movie.
She's wearing a tube top...
Did Keith tell Maryanne I was going to take Amy to the riflery range?

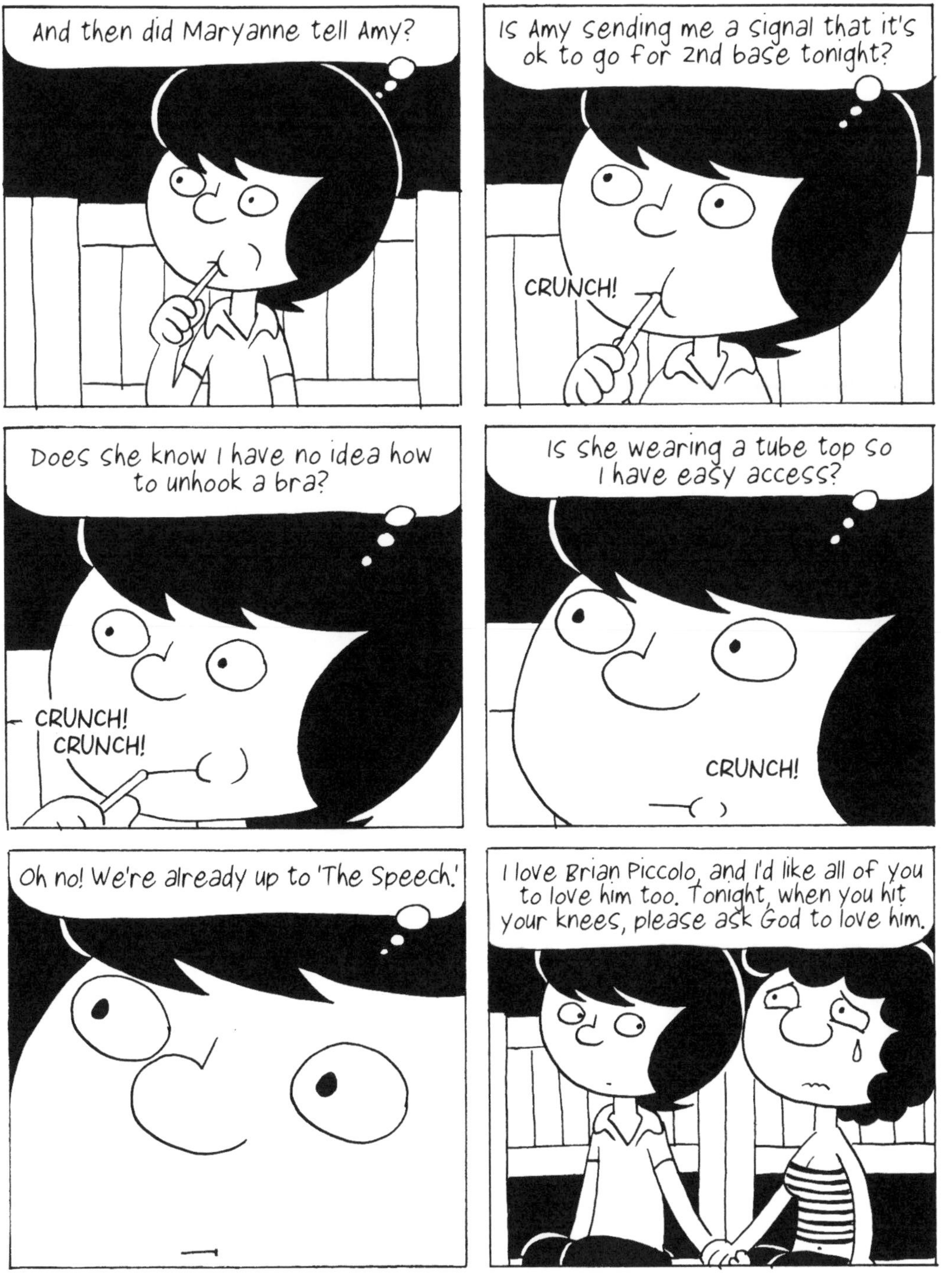
And then did Maryanne tell Amy?
Is Amy sending me a signal that it's ok to go for 2nd base tonight?
CRUNCH!
Does she know I have no idea how to unhook a bra?
CRUNCH!
CRUNCH!
Is she wearing a tube top so I have easy access?
CRUNCH!
Oh no! We're already up to 'The Speech.'
I love Brian Piccolo, and I'd like all of you to love him too. Tonight, when you hit your knees, please ask God to love him.

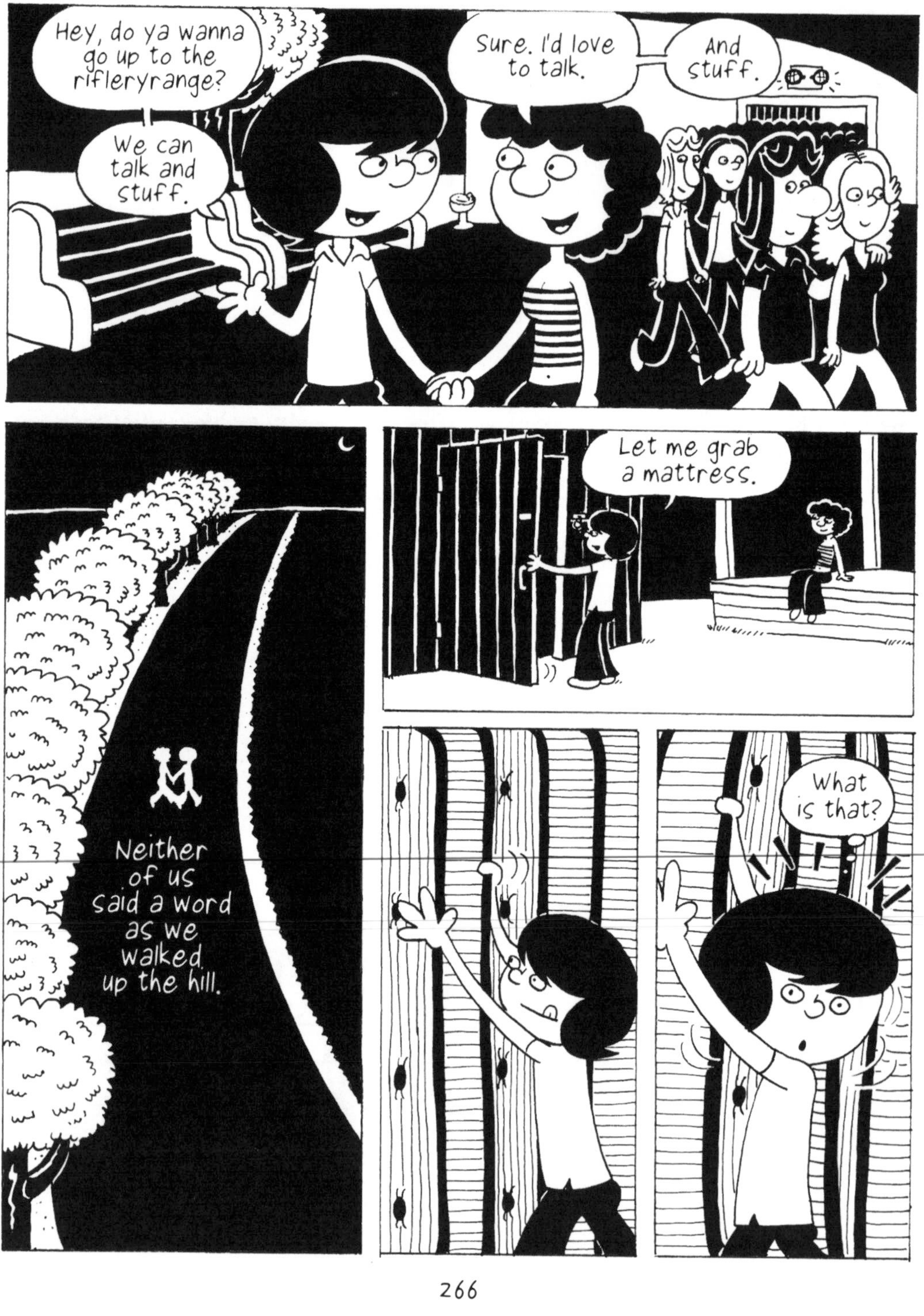
Hey, do ya wanna go up to the rifleryrange?
We can talk and stuff.
Sure. I'd love to talk.
And stuff.
Neither of us said a word as we walked up the hill.
Let me grab a mattress.
What is that?

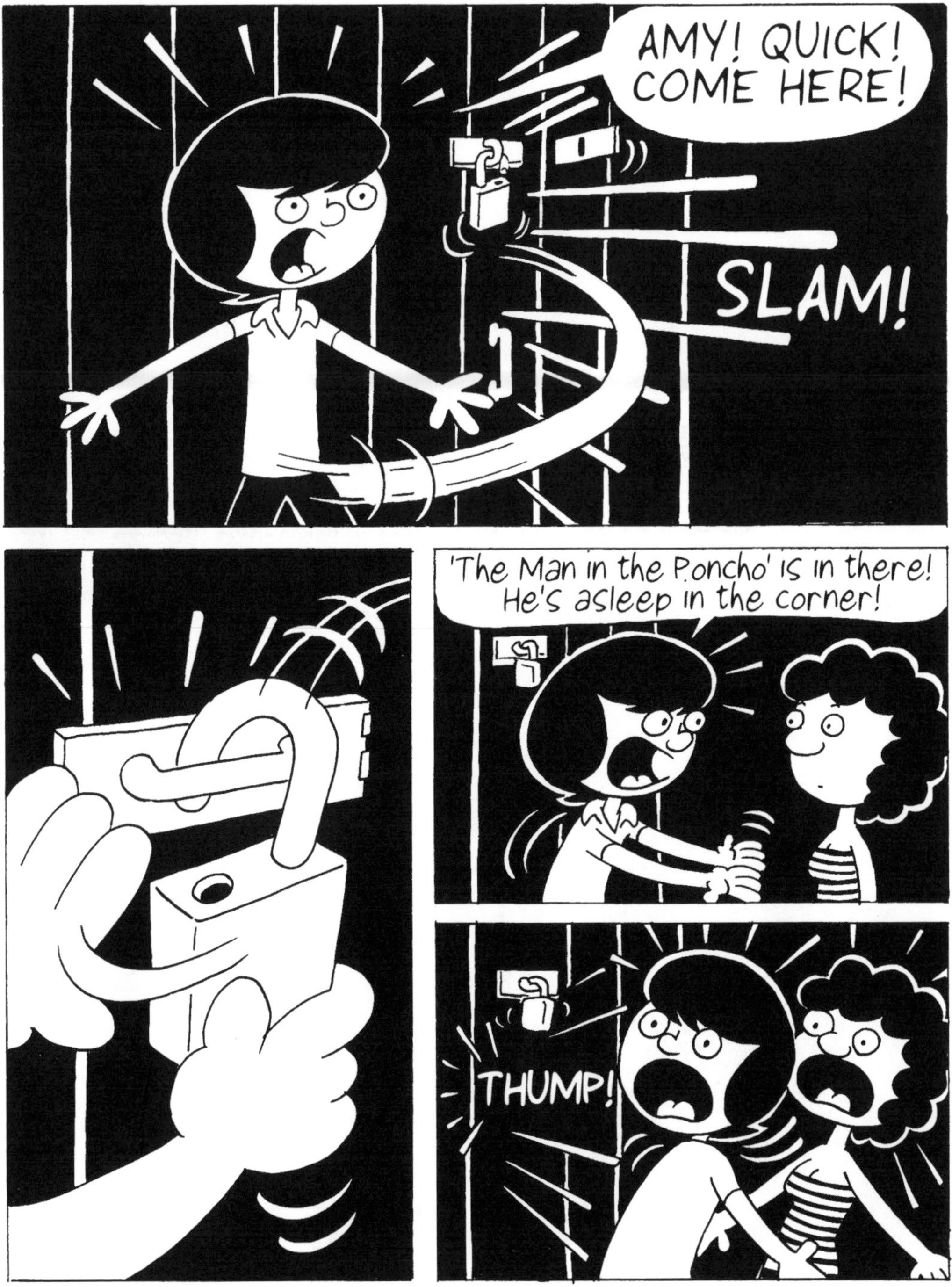
AMY! QUICK! COME HERE!
SLAM!
'The Man in the Poncho' is in there! He's asleep in the corner!
THUMP!

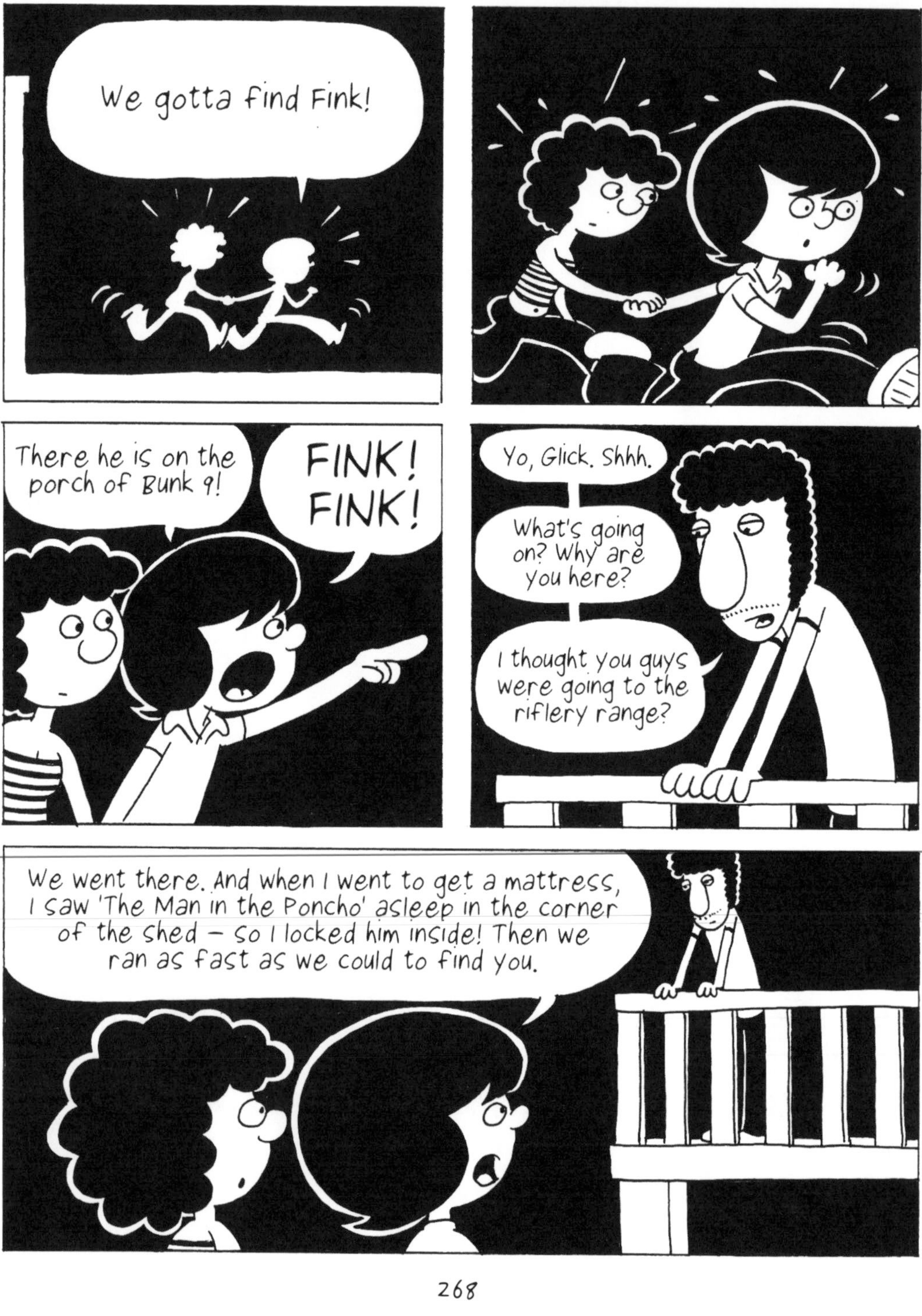
We gotta find Fink!
There he is on the porch of Bunk 9!
FINK! FINK!
Yo, Glick. Shhh.
What's going on? Why are you here?
I thought you guys were going to the riflery range?
We went there. And when I went to get a mattress, I saw 'The Man in the Poncho' asleep in the corner of the shed – so I locked him inside! Then we ran as fast as we could to find you.

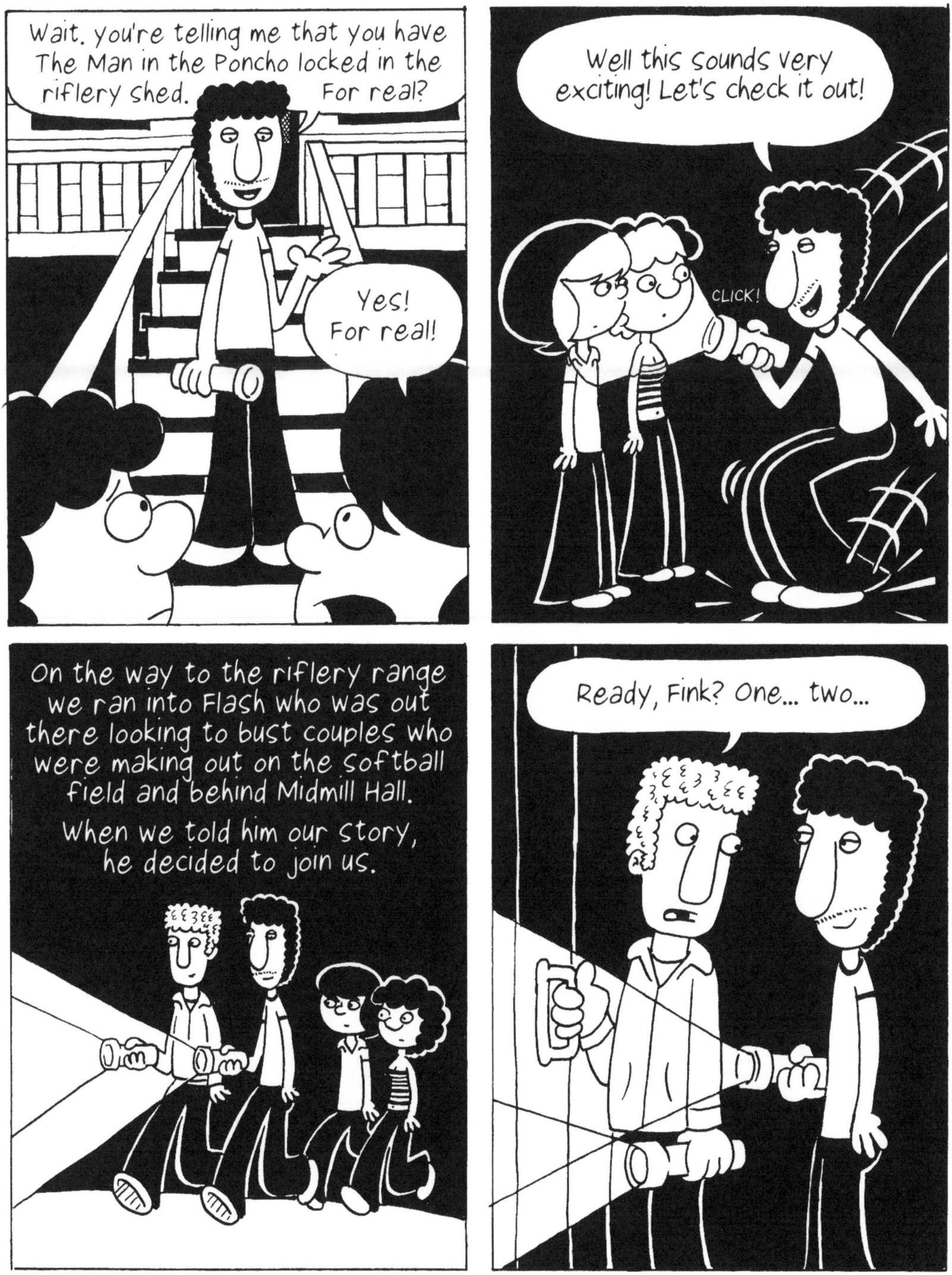
Wait. you're telling me that you have The Man in the Poncho locked in the riflery shed.
For real?
Yes! For real!
Well this sounds very exciting! Let's check it out!
CLICK!
On the way to the riflery range we ran into Flash who was out there looking to bust couples who were making out on the softball field and behind Midmill Hall.
When we told him our story, he decided to join us.
Ready, Fink? One... two...

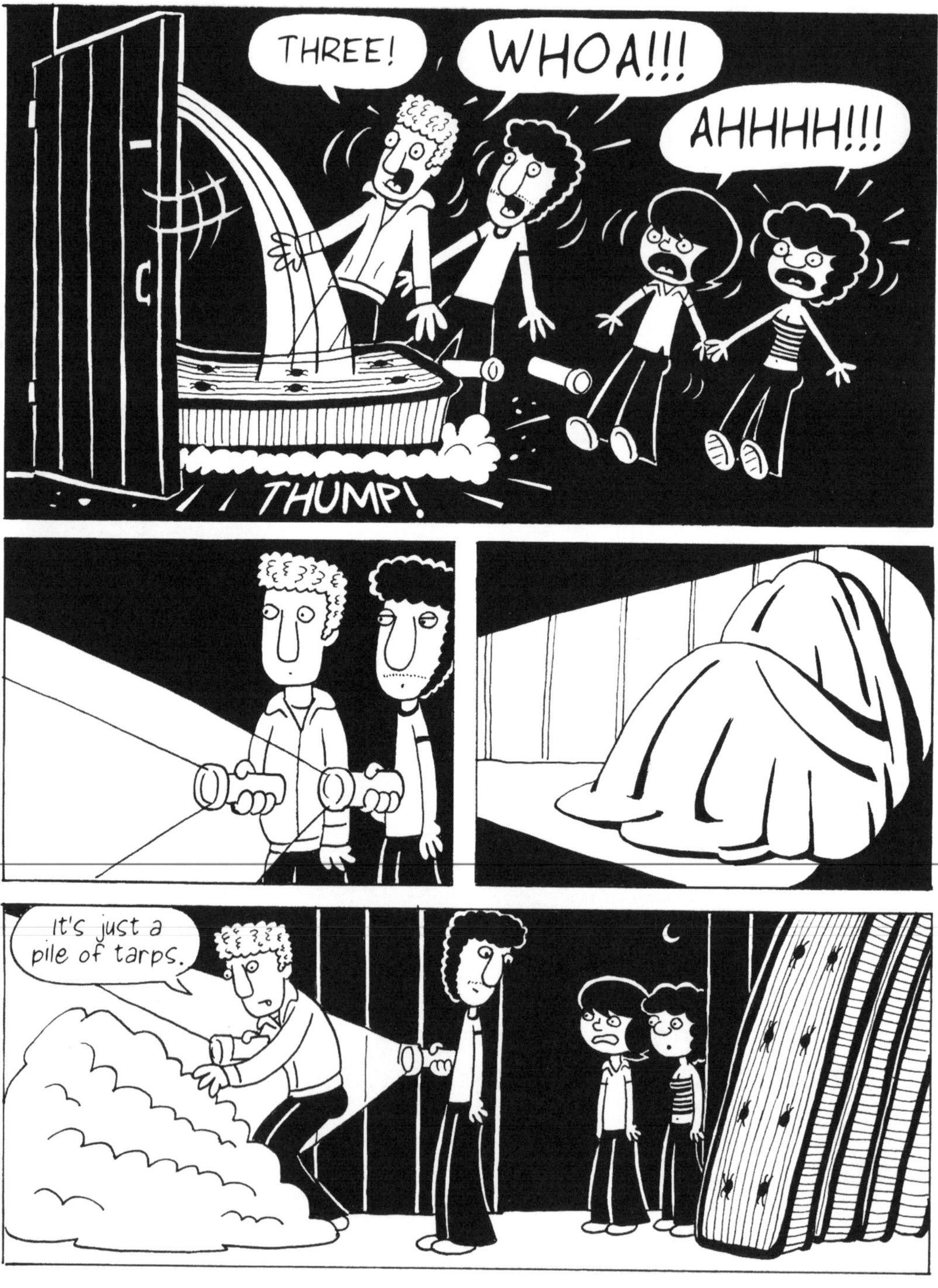
THREE!
WHOA!!!
AHHHH!!!
THUMP!
It's just a pile of tarps.

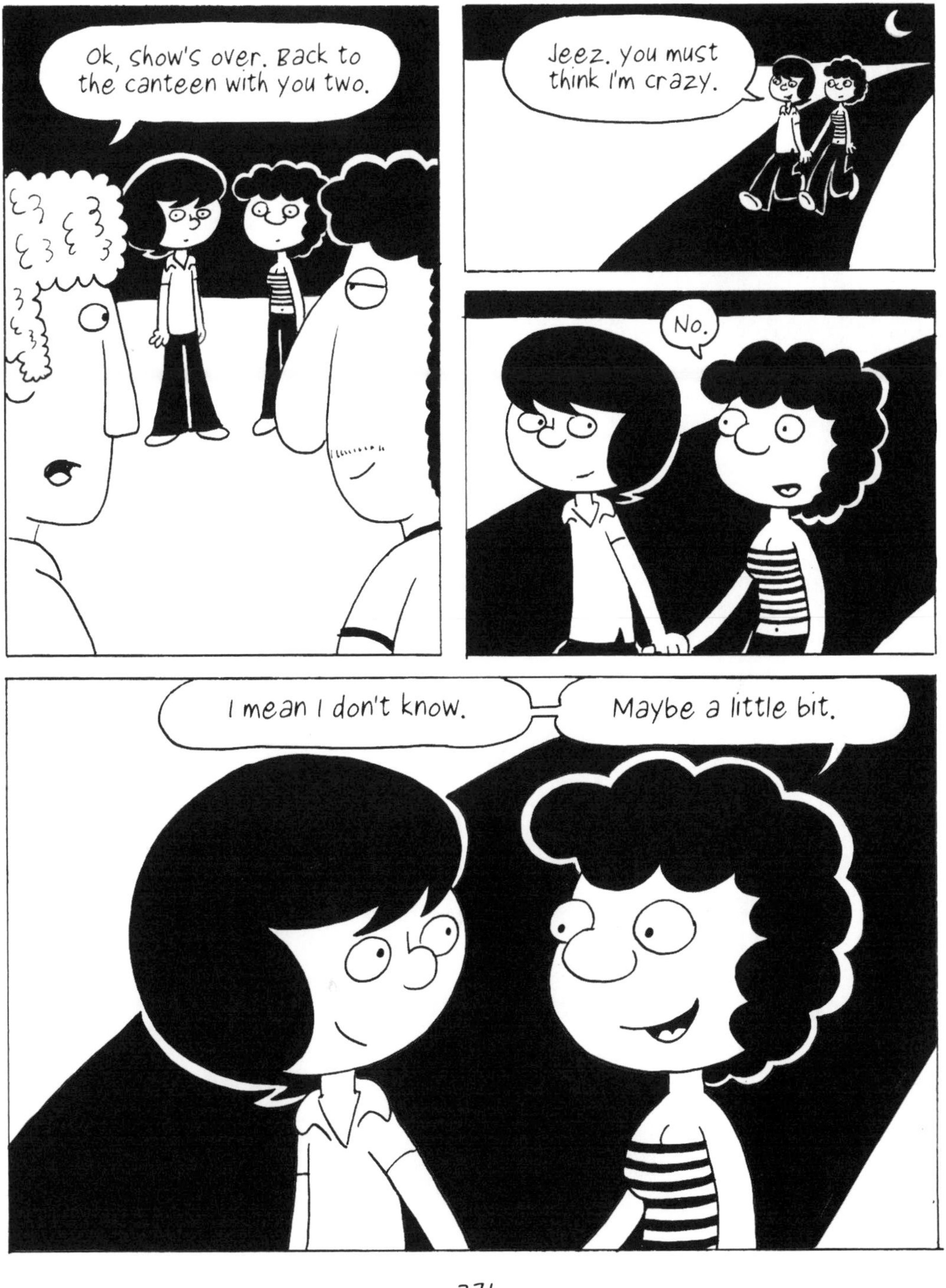
Ok, show's over. Back to the canteen with you two.
Jeez. you must think I'm crazy.
No.
I mean I don't know.
Maybe a little bit.

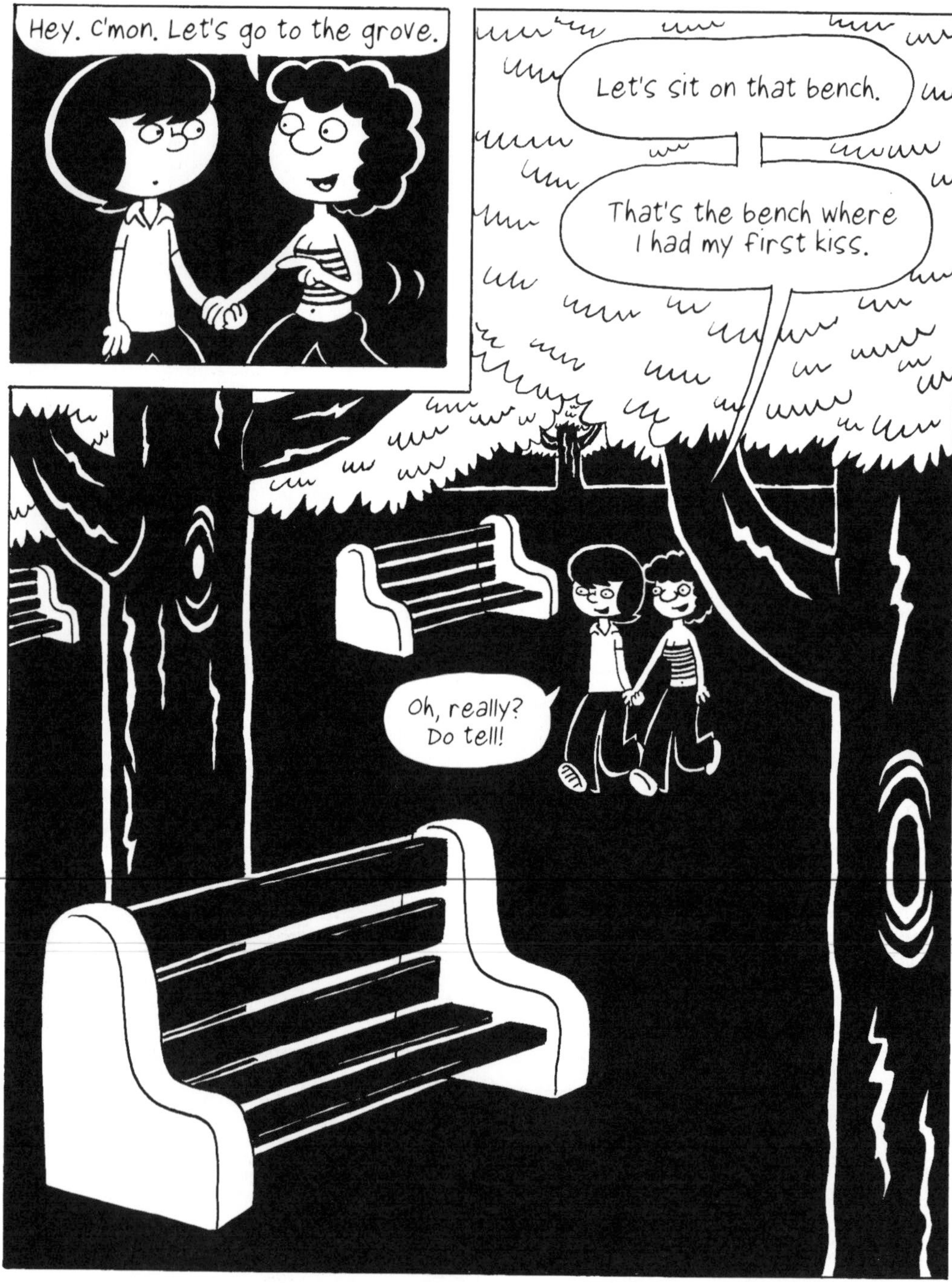
Hey. C'mon. Let's go to the grove.
Let's sit on that bench.
That's the bench where I had my first kiss.
Oh, really? Do tell!

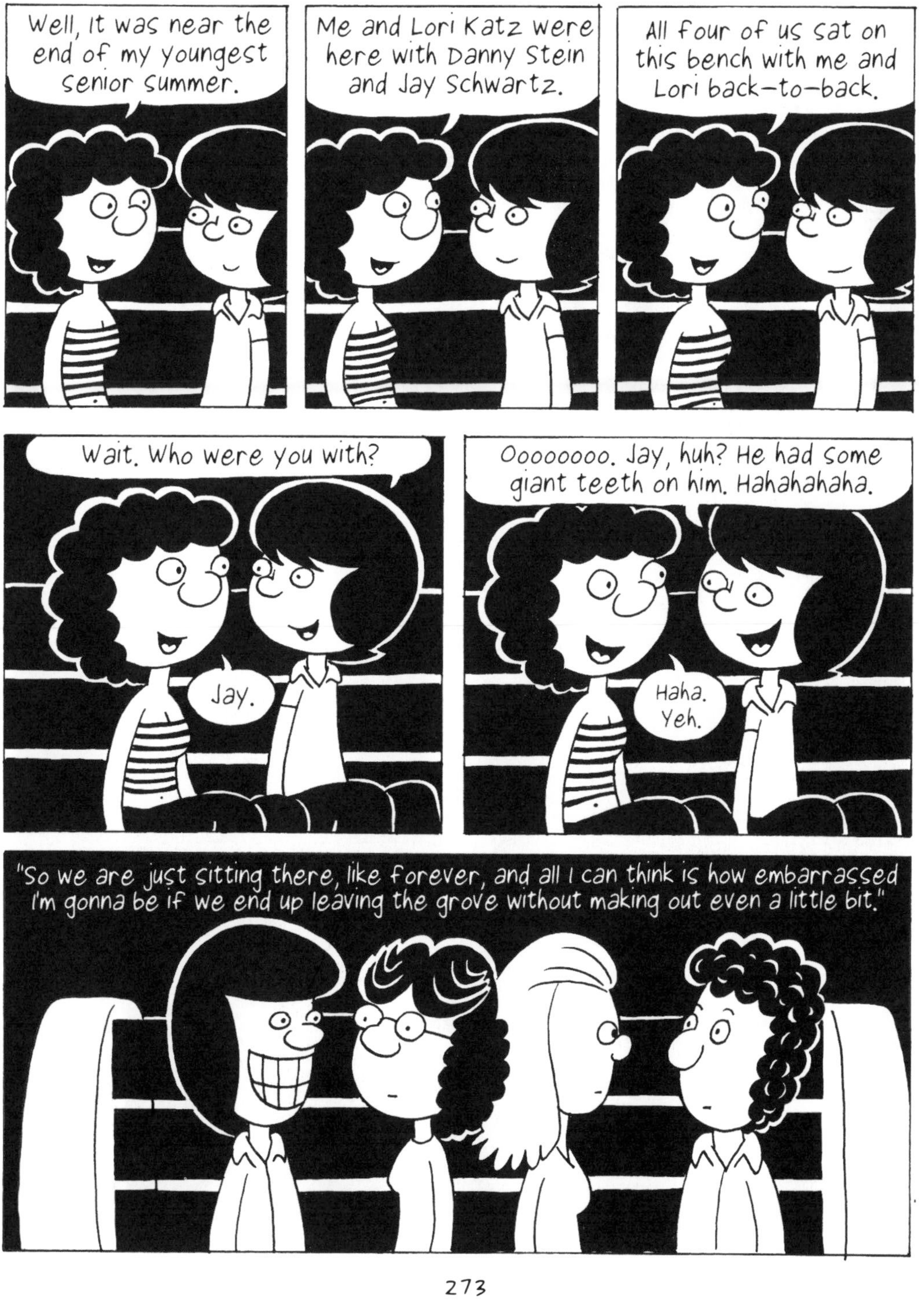
Well, it was near the end of my youngest senior summer.
Me and Lori Katz were here with Danny Stein and Jay Schwartz.
All four of us sat on this bench with me and Lori back-to-back.
Wait. Who were you with?
Jay.
Ooooooo. Jay, huh? He had some giant teeth on him. Hahahahaha.
Haha. Yeh.
"So we are just sitting there, like forever, and all I can think is how embarrassed I'm gonna be if we end up leaving the grove without making out even a little bit."

"All of a sudden, we heard a voice come out from the darkness...."

You guys are taking waaaaay too long.

I'm gonna count you in. OK?

READY. 1... 2... 3...

GO!

"I closed my eyes and Jay came in pretty hard with his mouth open."

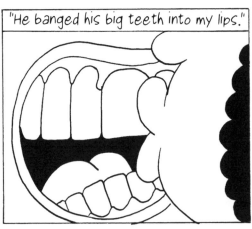

"He banged his big teeth into my lips."

"Then we kissed for about 10 seconds."

"When we were done, we heard applause coming from the darkness."

CLAP!
CLAP!
CLAP!
CLAP!
CLAP!
CLAP!
CLAP!
CLAP!
CLAP!

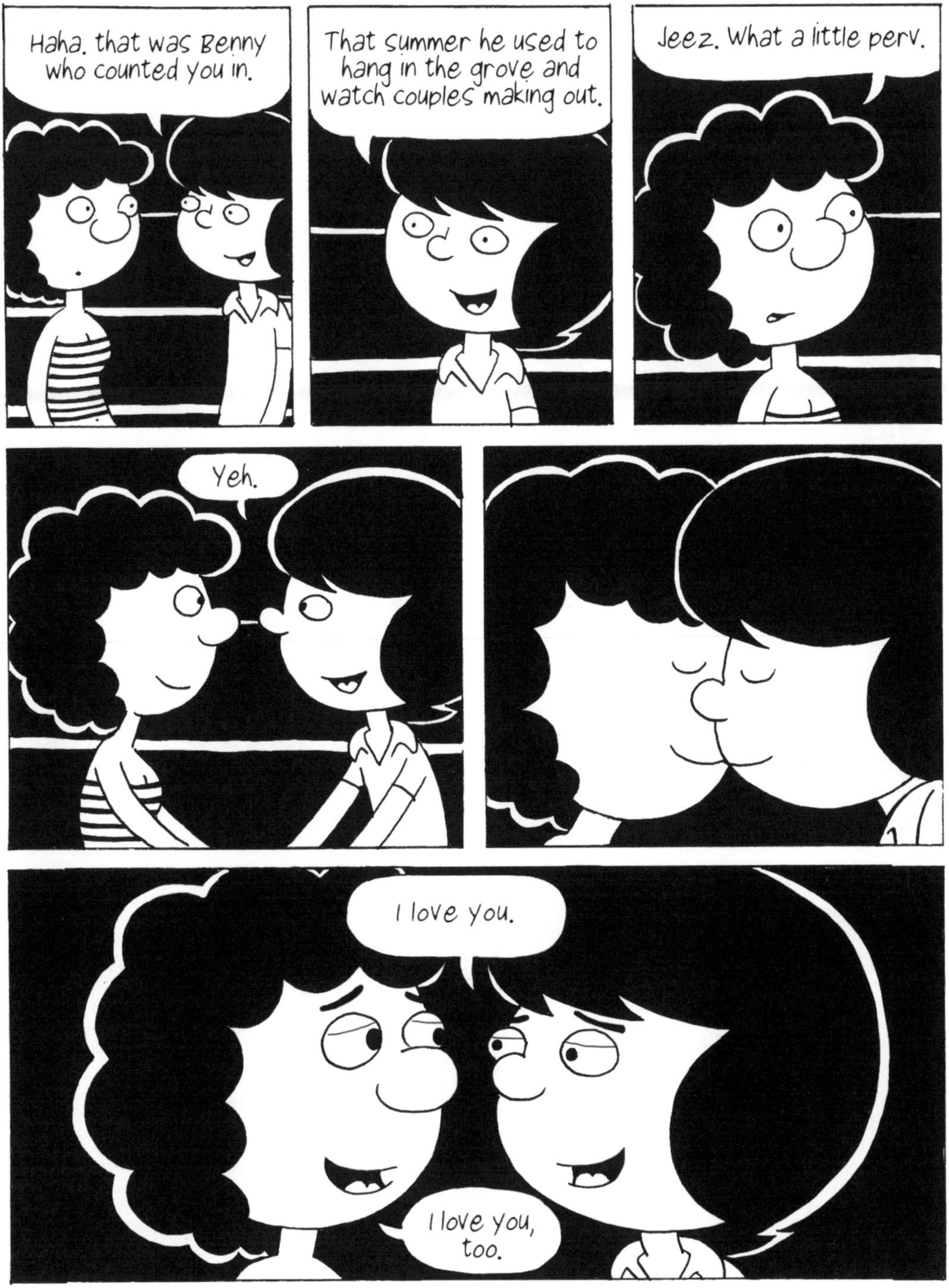
Haha. that was Benny who counted you in.
That summer he used to hang in the grove and watch couples making out.
Jeez. What a little perv.
Yeh.
I love you.
I love you, too.

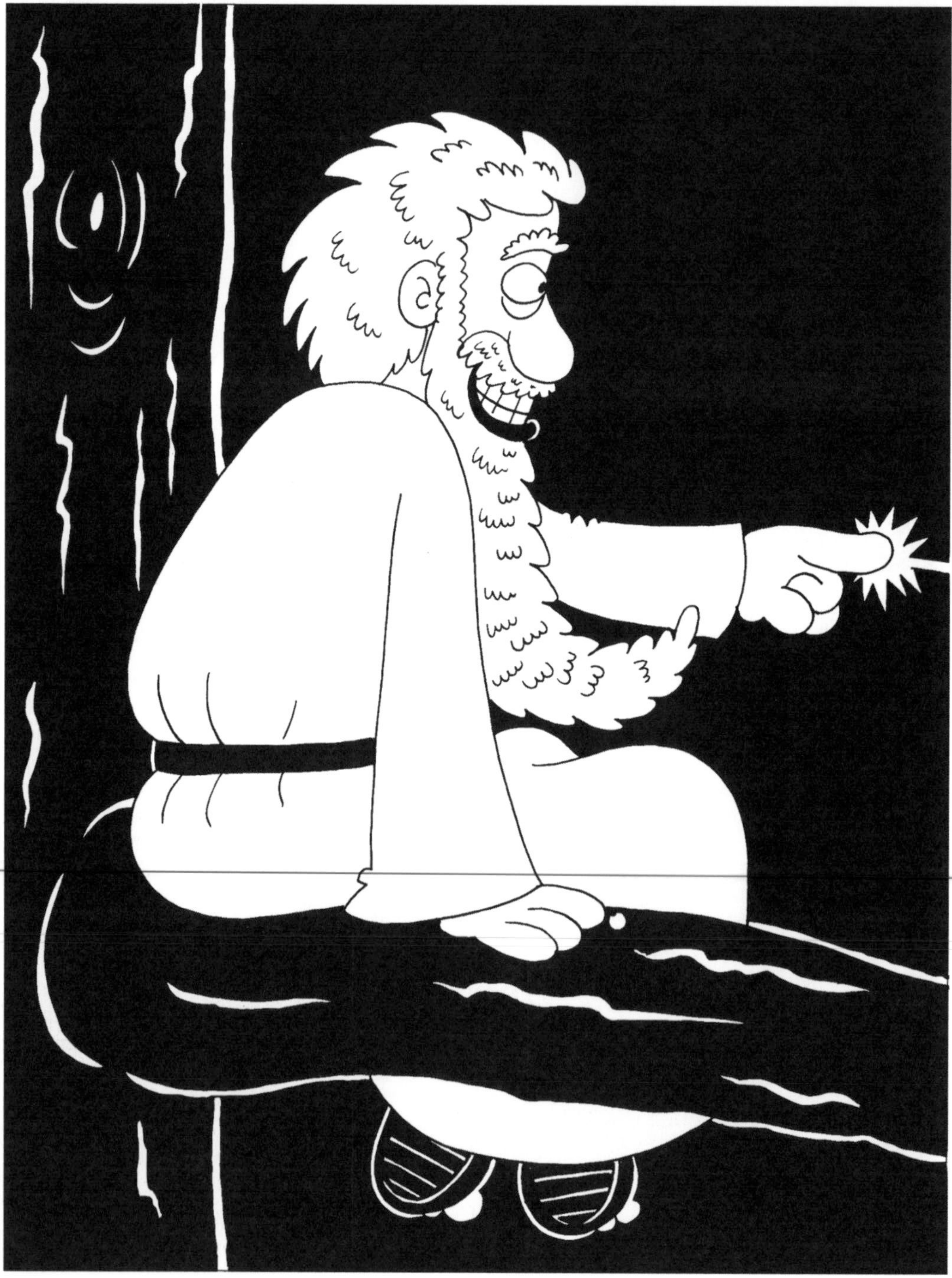

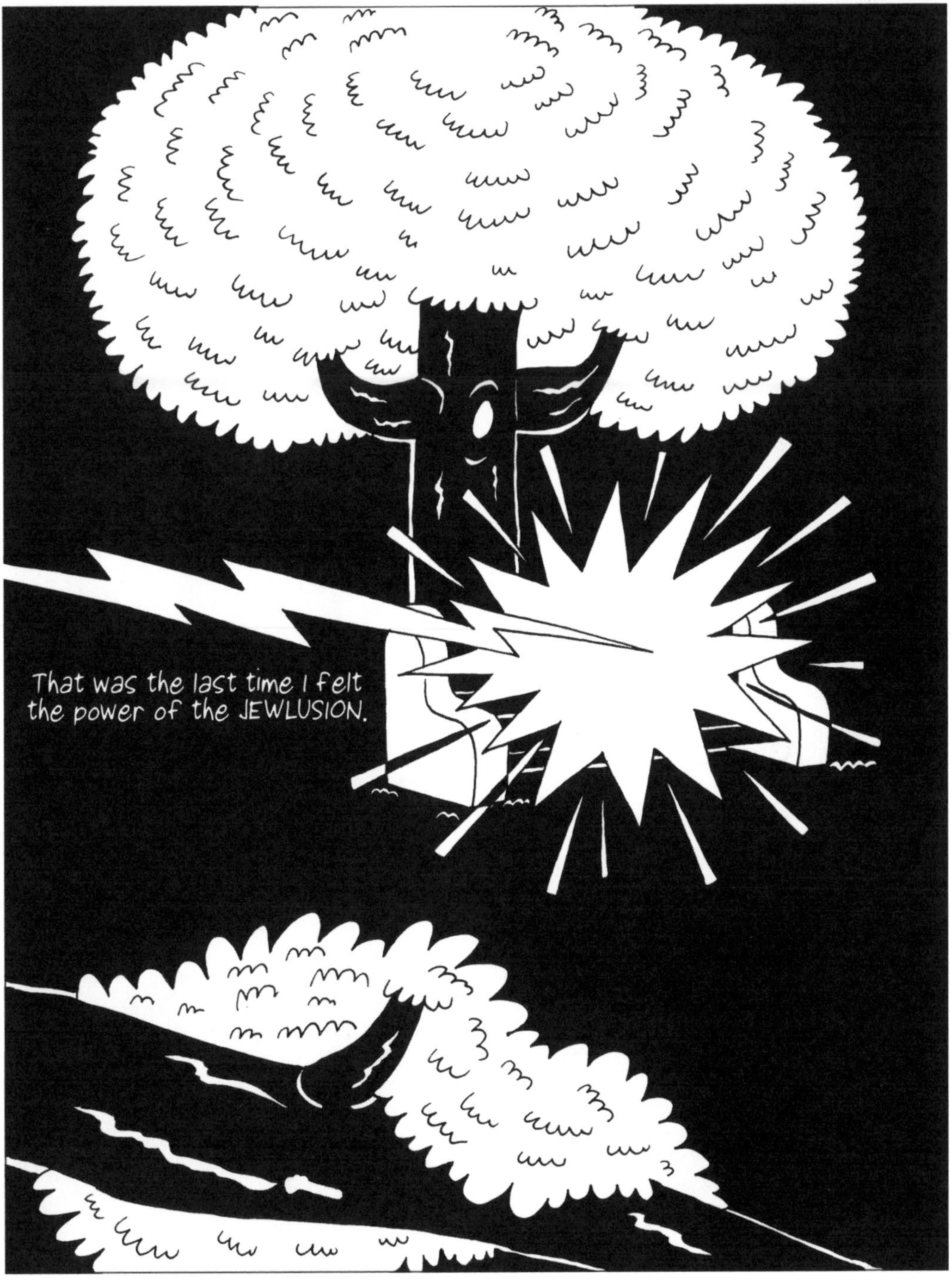
That was the last time I felt the power of the JEWLUSION.

There he is.

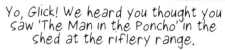

Yo, Glick! We heard you thought you saw 'The Man in the Poncho' in the shed at the riflery range.

And that you totally freaked out.

Haha. Yeh.

So I have a theory.

You had the perfect opportunity and it was all gonna happen with Amy.

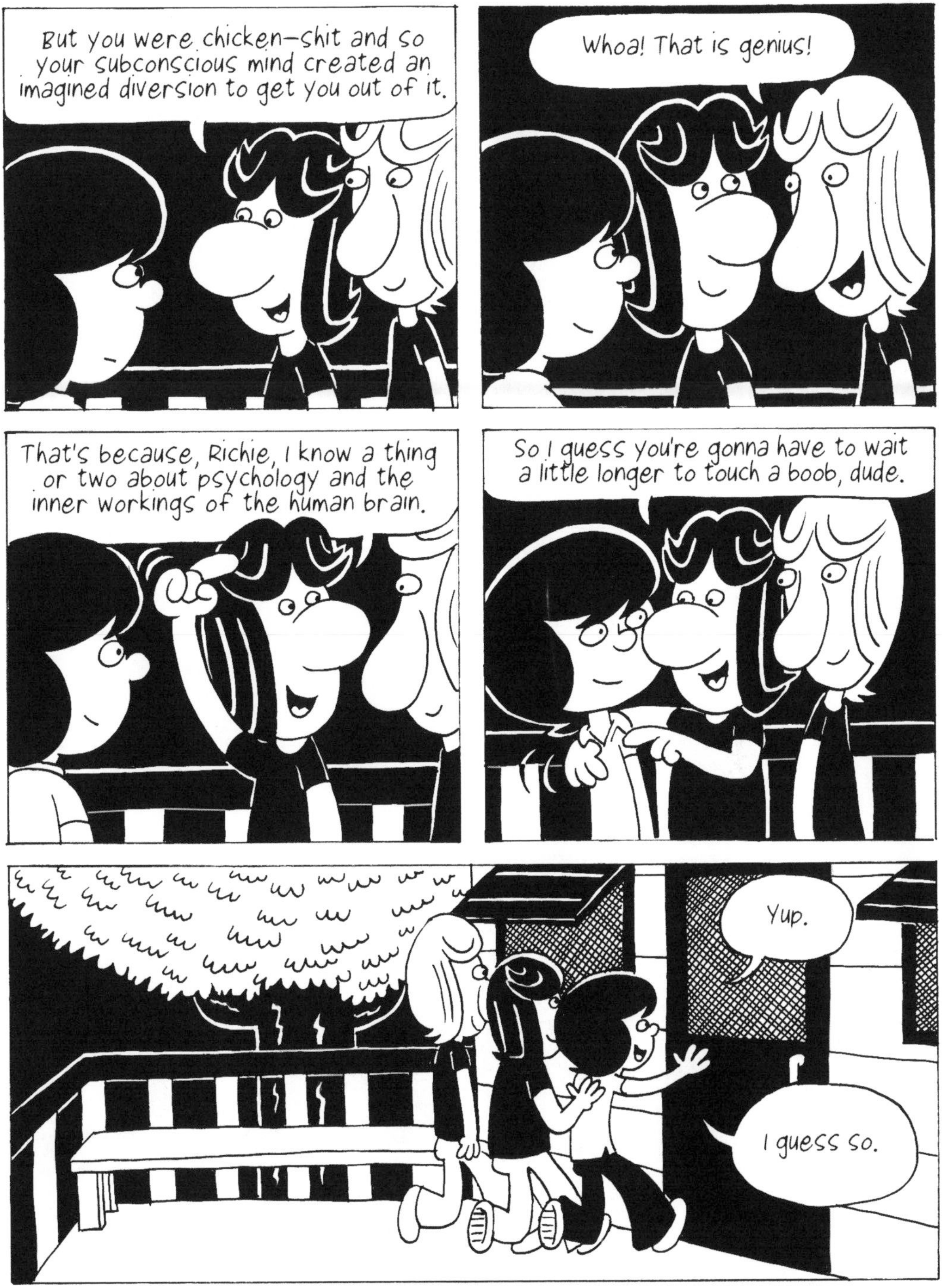
But you were chicken–shit and so your subconscious mind created an imagined diversion to get you out of it.
Whoa! That is genius!
That's because, Richie, I know a thing or two about psychology and the inner workings of the human brain.
So I guess you're gonna have to wait a little longer to touch a boob, dude.
Yup.
I guess so.

As I took my contacts out, I sang the theme to 'The Spy Who Loved Me' in my head.

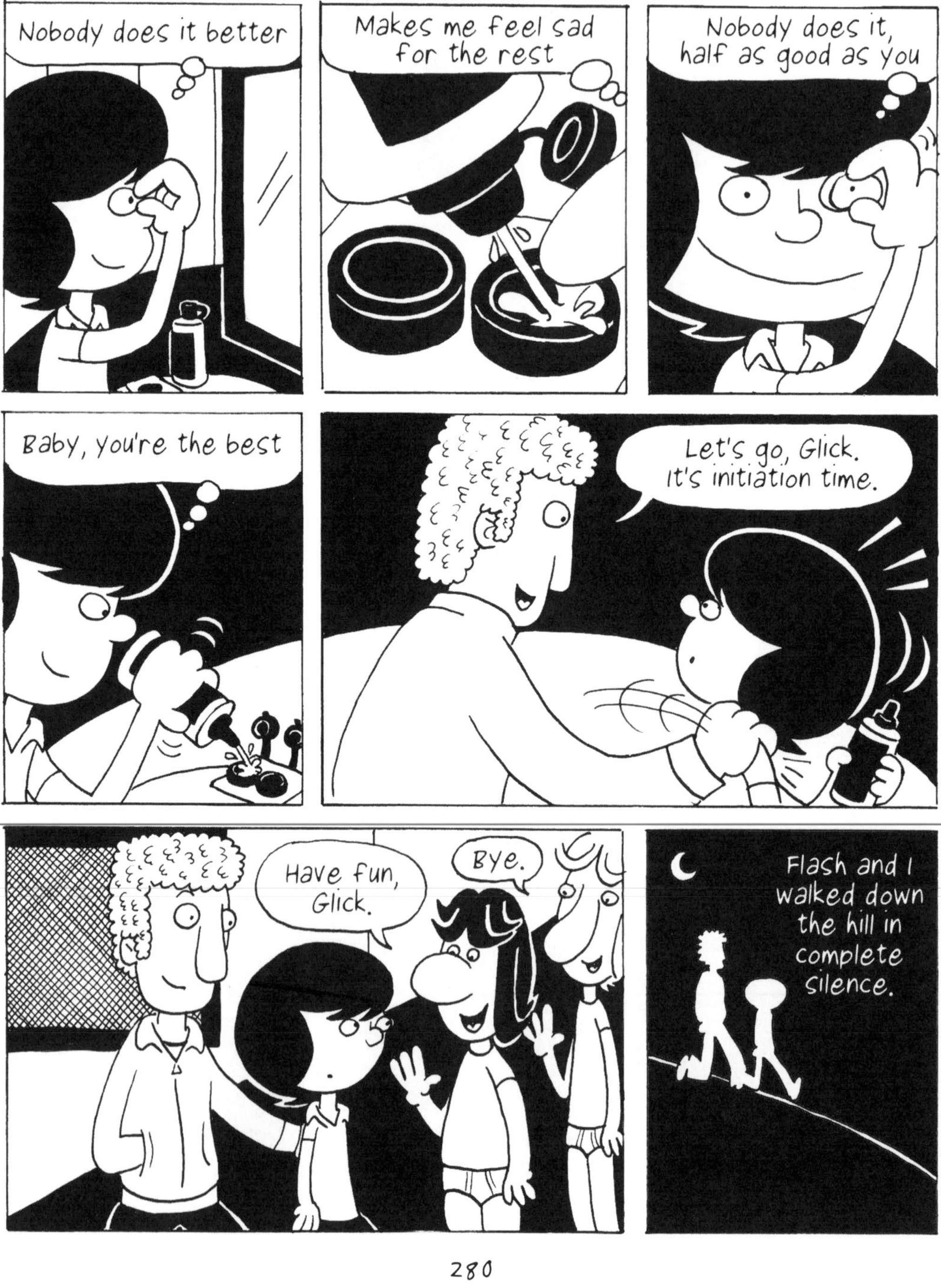
Nobody does it better
Makes me feel sad for the rest
Nobody does it, half as good as you
Baby, you're the best
Let's go, Glick. It's initiation time.
Have fun, Glick.
Bye.
Flash and I walked down the hill in complete silence.

When we reached the canteen, I saw Midge's Cadillac Eldorado parked there.

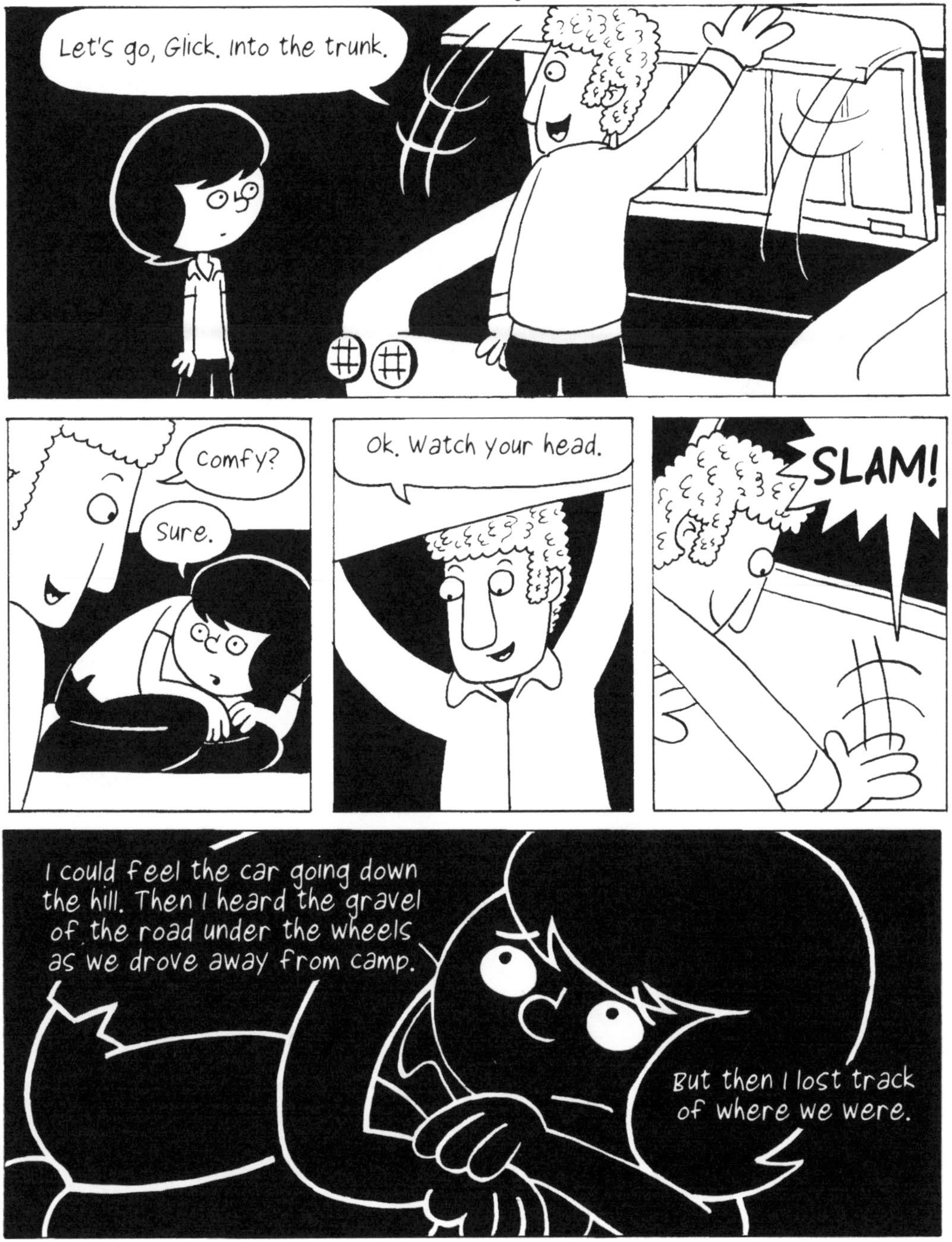

Let's go, Glick. Into the trunk.
Comfy?
Sure.
Ok. Watch your head.
SLAM!
I could feel the car going down the hill. Then I heard the gravel of the road under the wheels as we drove away from camp.
But then I lost track of where we were.

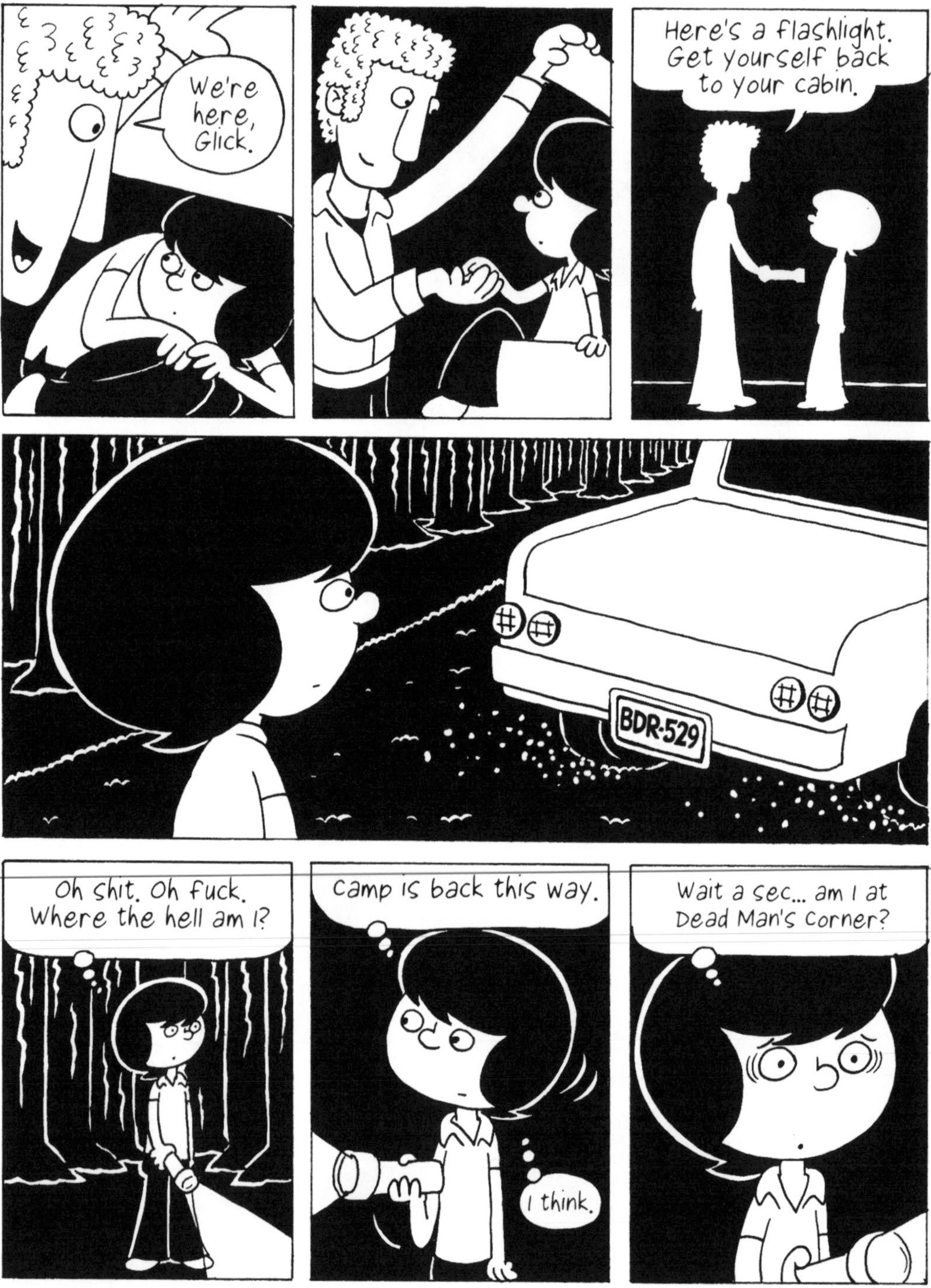

We're here, Glick.
Here's a flashlight. Get yourself back to your cabin.
BDR-529
Oh shit. Oh fuck. Where the hell am I?
Camp is back this way.
I think.
Wait a sec... am I at Dead Man's Corner?

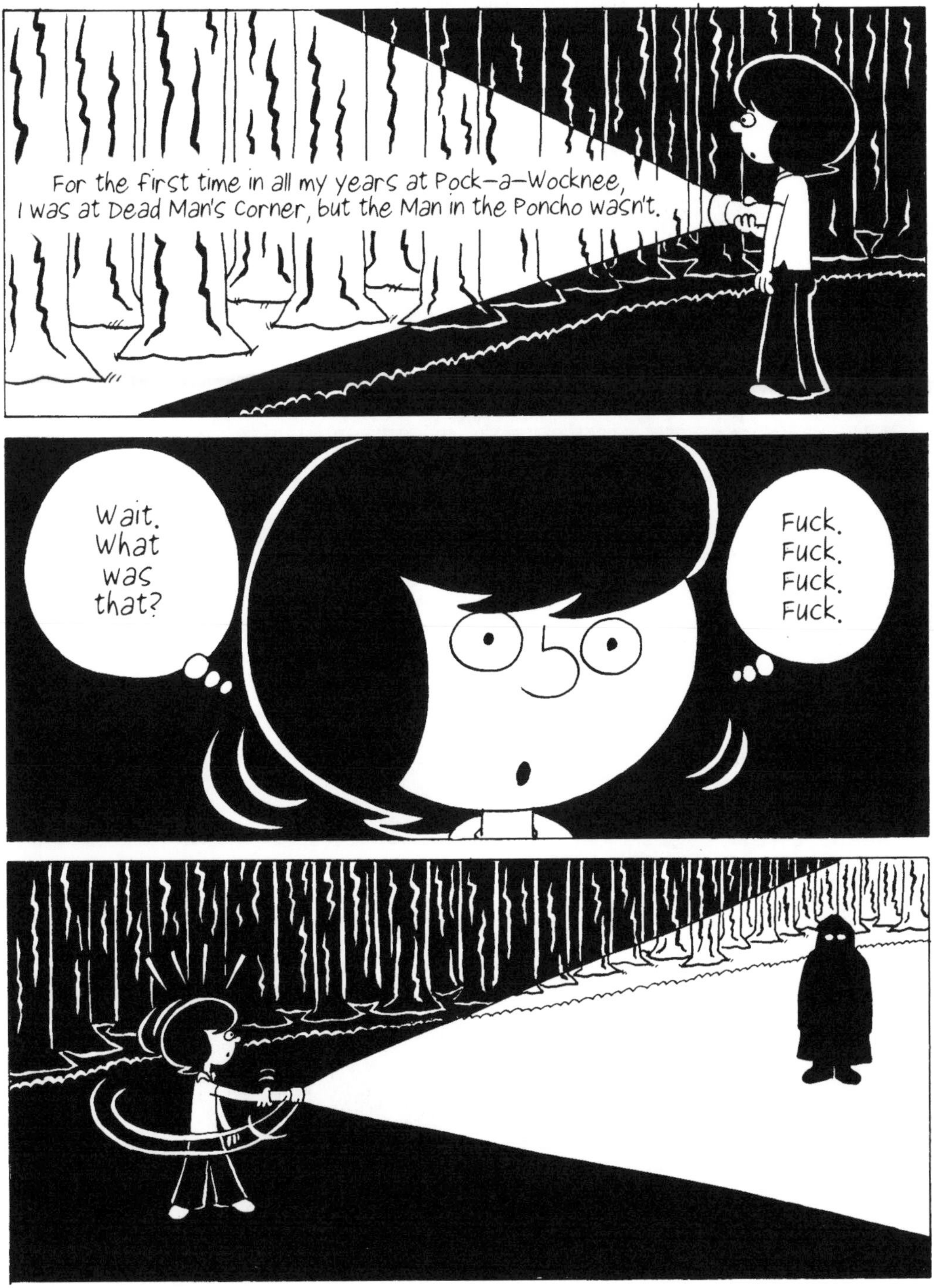

For the first time in all my years at Pock-a-Wocknee, I was at Dead Man's Corner, but the Man in the Poncho wasn't.
Wait. What was that?
Fuck. Fuck. Fuck. Fuck.

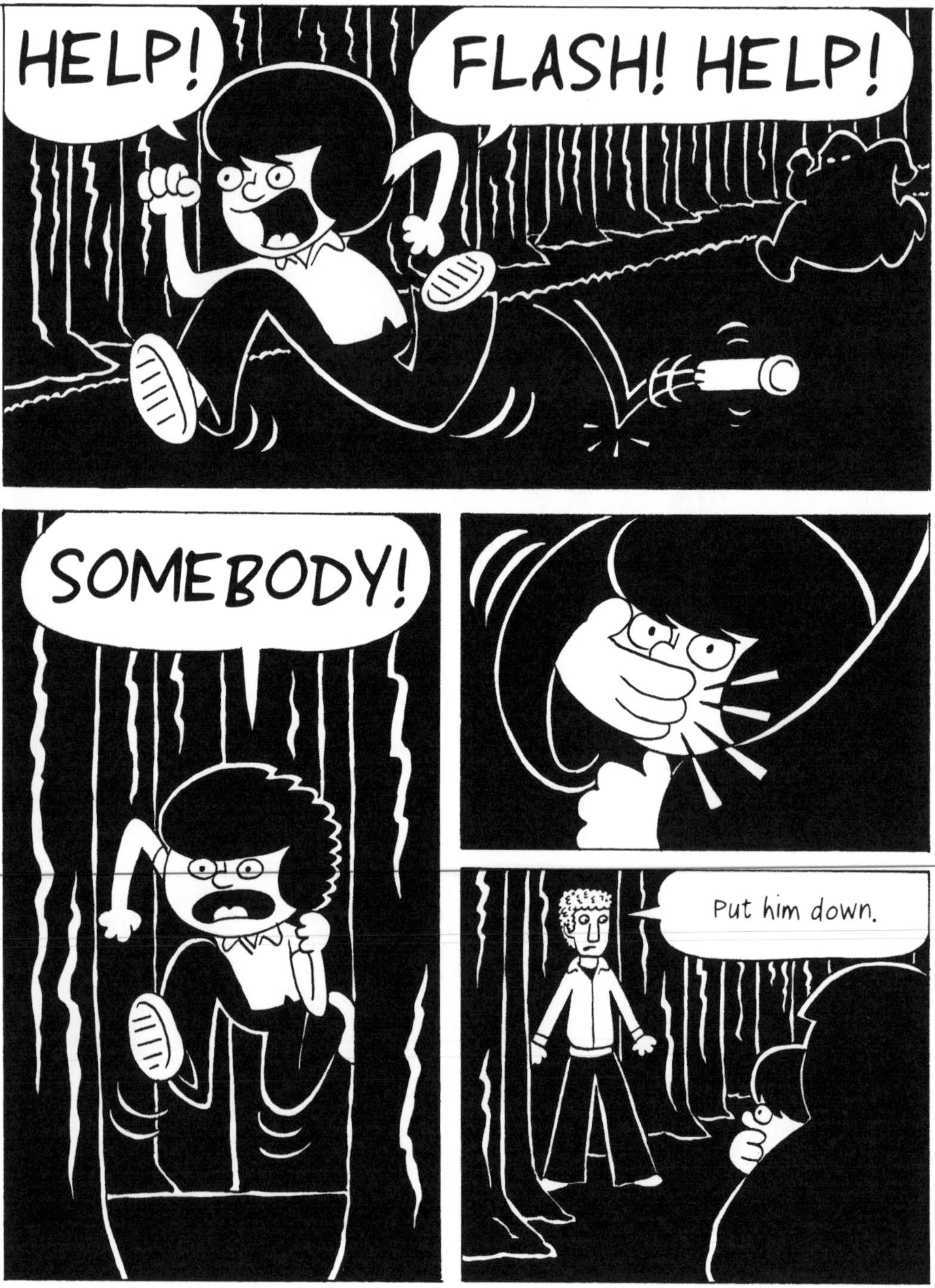
HELP!
FLASH! HELP!
SOMEBODY!
Put him down.

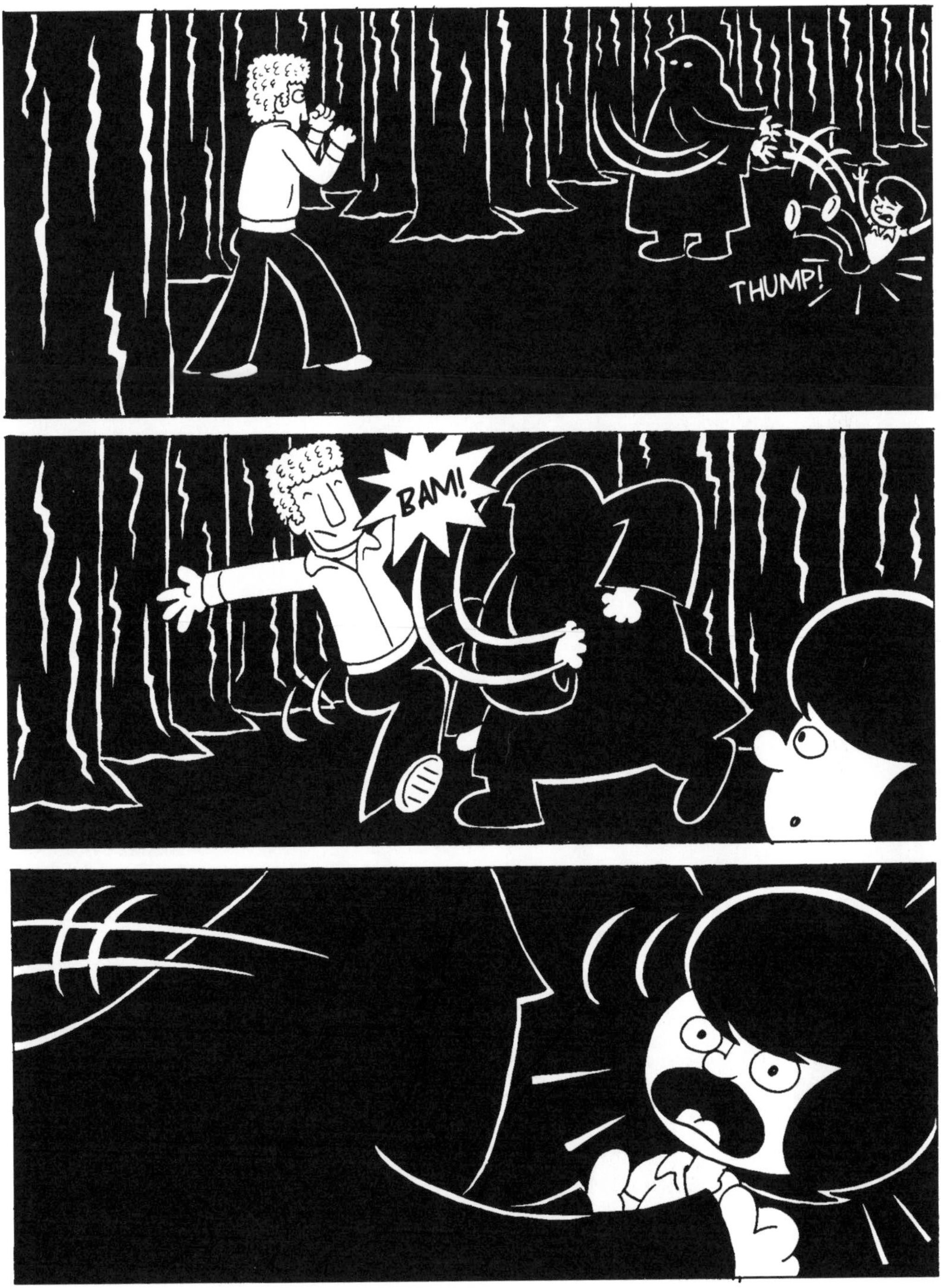
THUMP!
BAM!

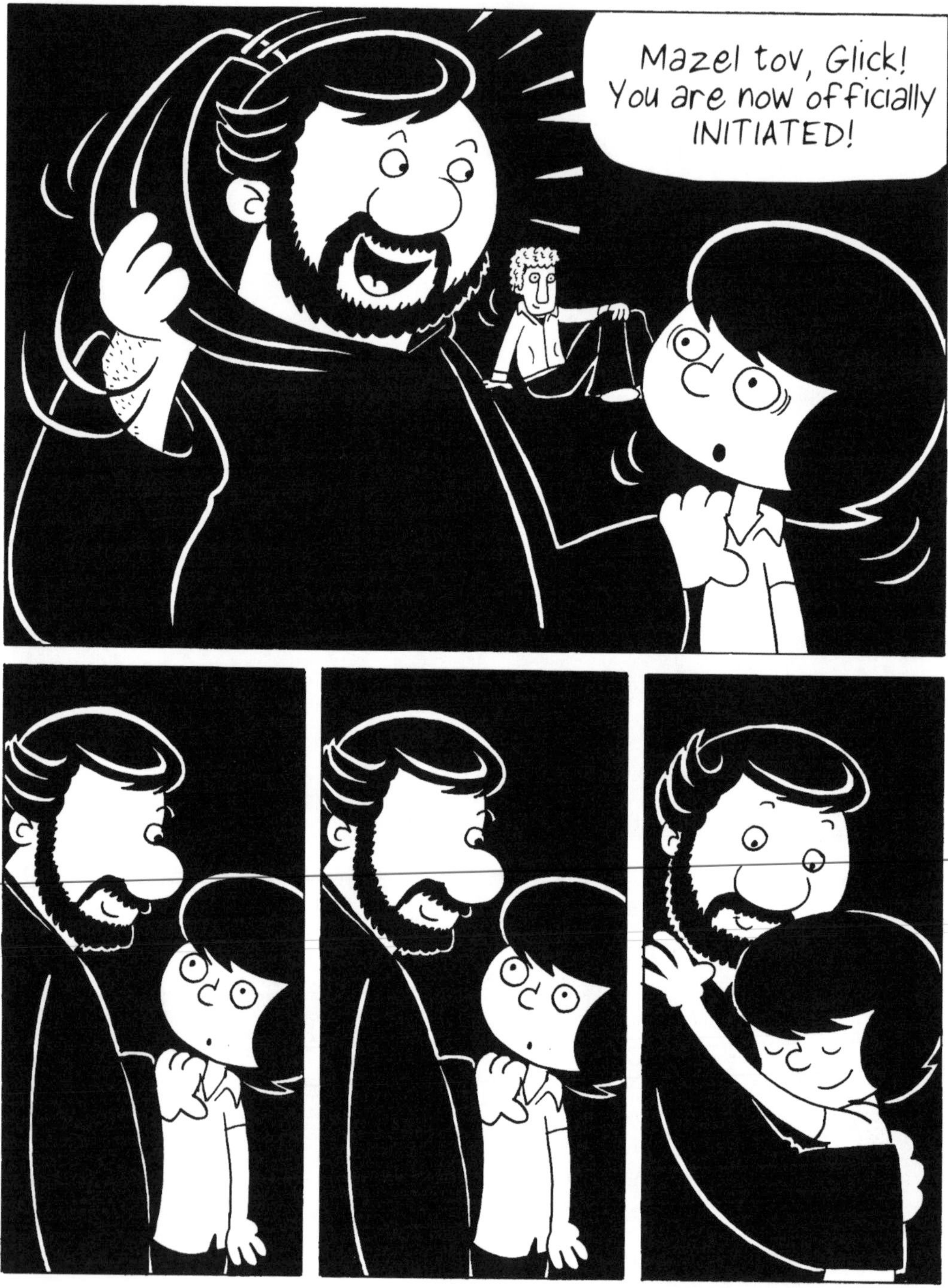
Mazel tov, Glick! You are now officially INITIATED!

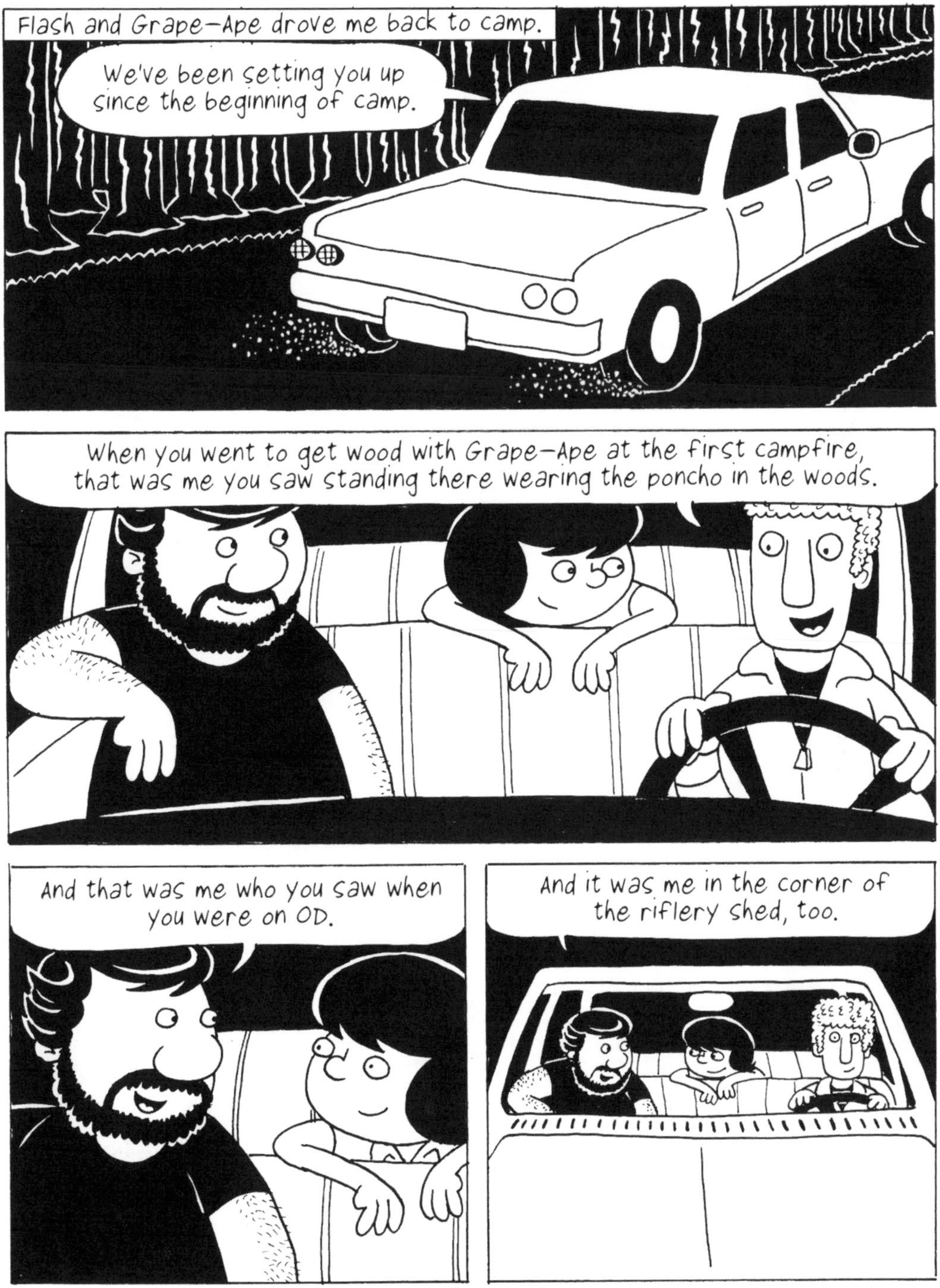
Flash and Grape-Ape drove me back to camp.
We've been setting you up since the beginning of camp.
When you went to get wood with Grape-Ape at the first campfire, that was me you saw standing there wearing the poncho in the woods.
And that was me who you saw when you were on OD.
And it was me in the corner of the riflery shed, too.

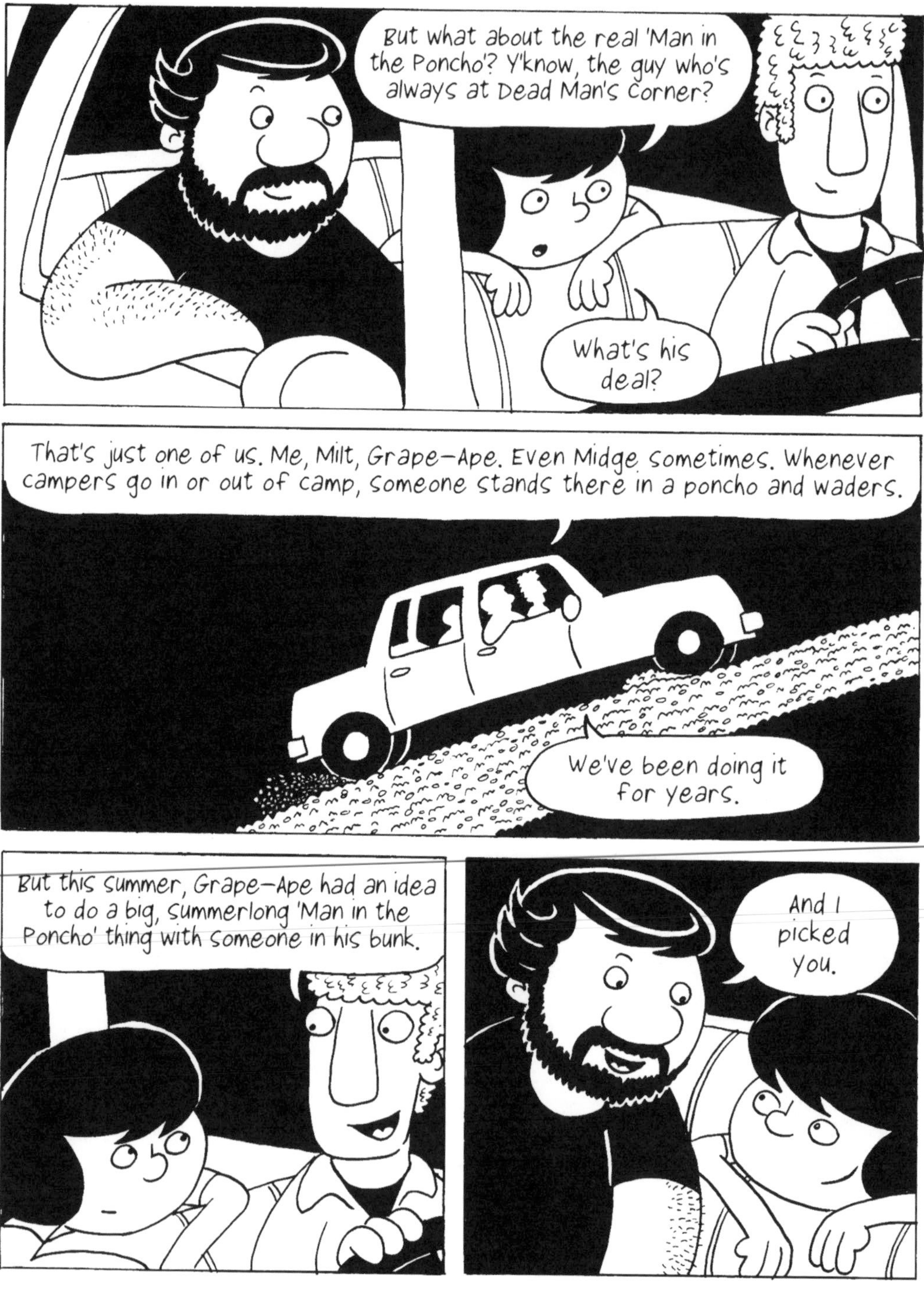
But what about the real 'Man in the Poncho'? Y'know, the guy who's always at Dead Man's Corner?
What's his deal?
That's just one of us. Me, Milt, Grape—Ape. Even Midge sometimes. Whenever campers go in or out of camp, someone stands there in a poncho and waders.
We've been doing it for years.
But this summer, Grape—Ape had an idea to do a big, summerlong 'Man in the Poncho' thing with someone in his bunk.
And I picked you.

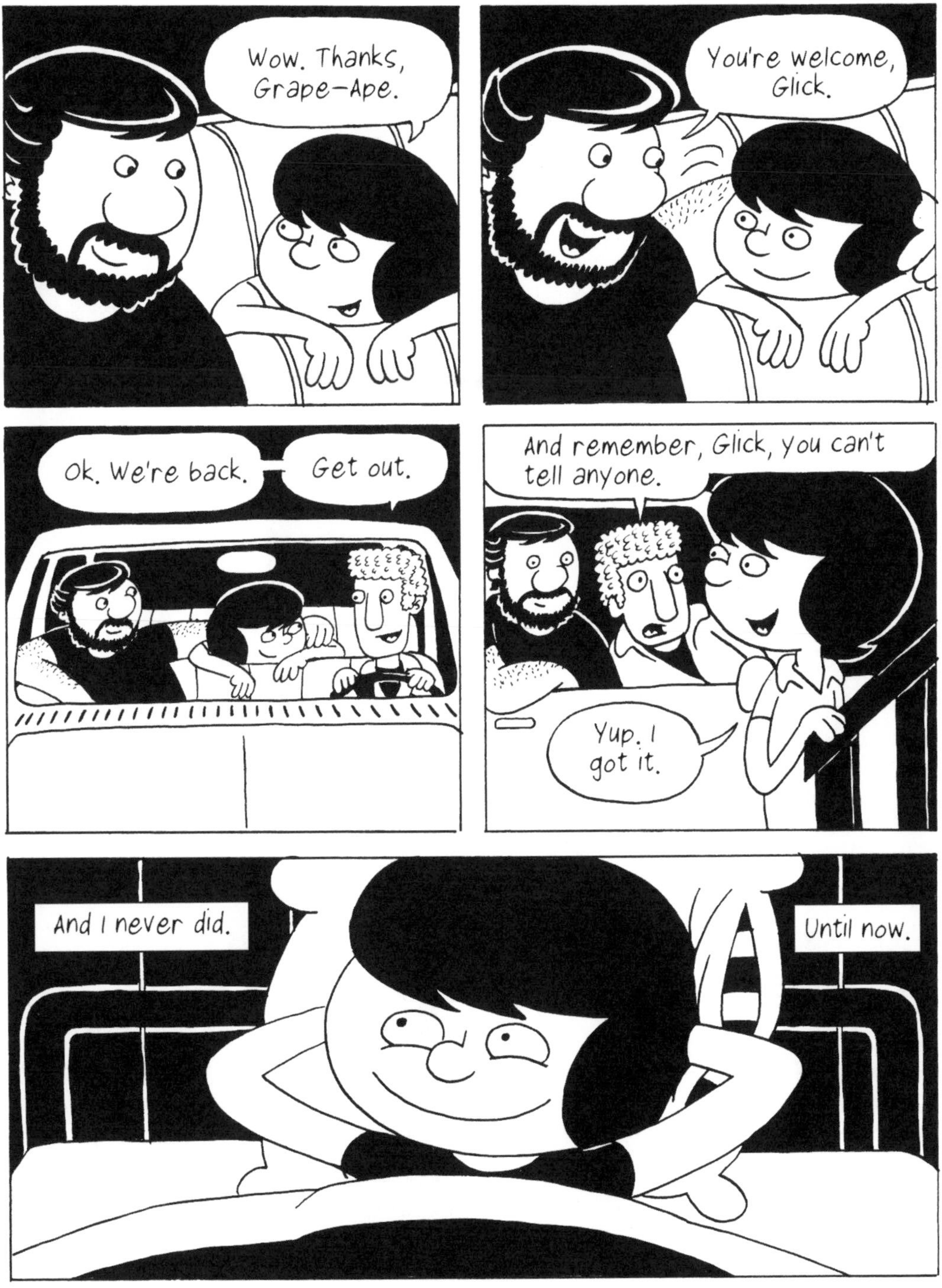
Wow. Thanks, Grape-Ape.
You're welcome, Glick.
Ok. We're back.
Get out.
And remember, Glick, you can't tell anyone.
Yup. I got it.
And I never did.
Until now.

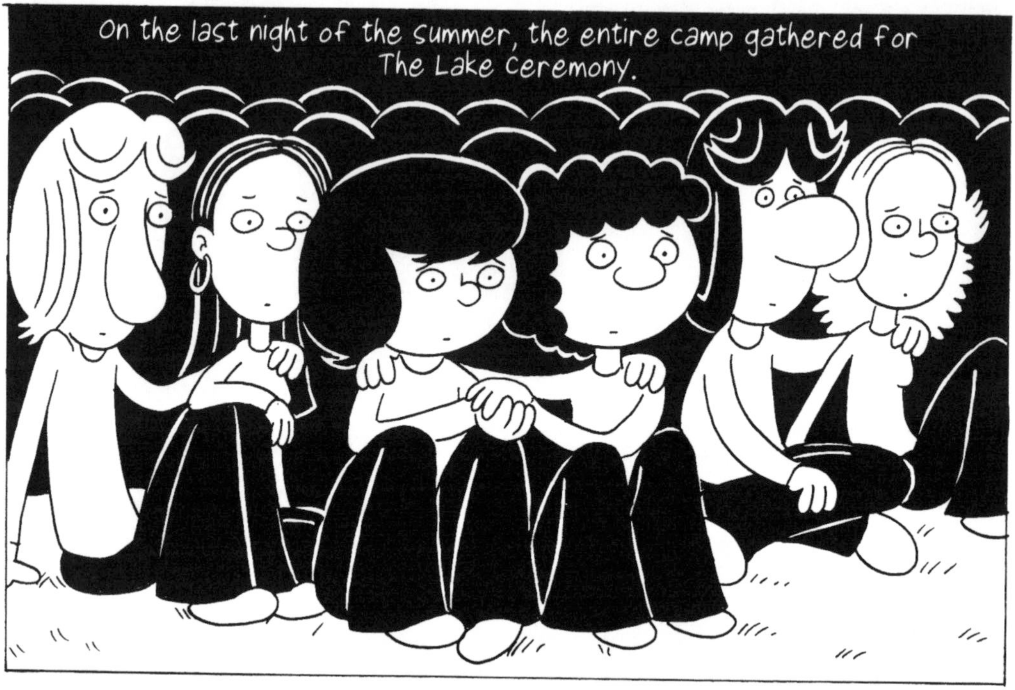
On the last night of the summer, the entire camp gathered for The Lake ceremony.

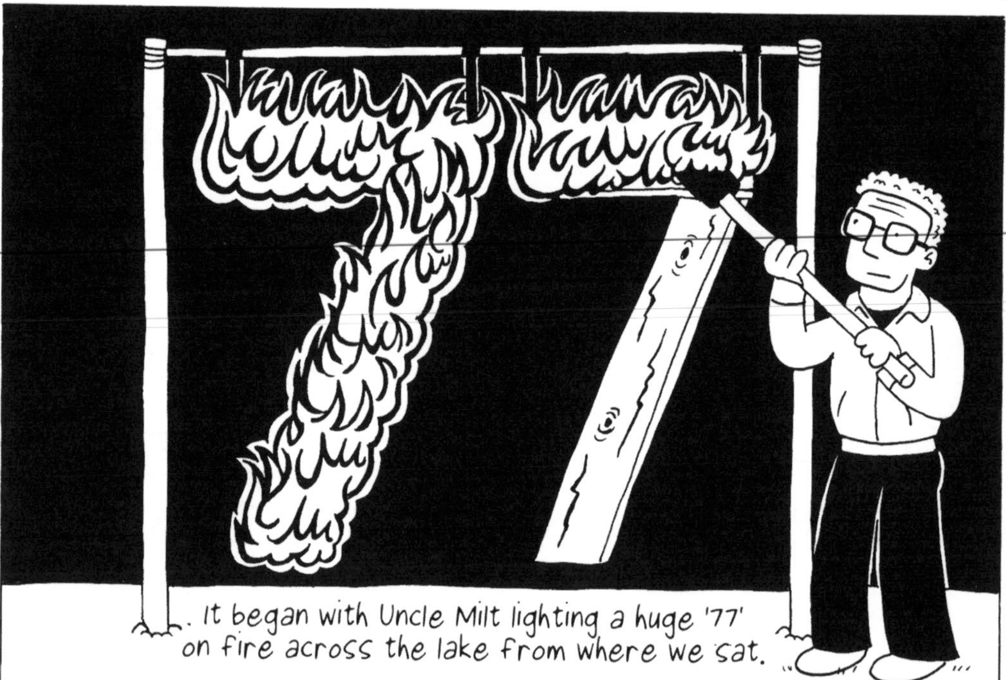
It began with Uncle Milt lighting a huge '77' on fire across the lake from where we sat.

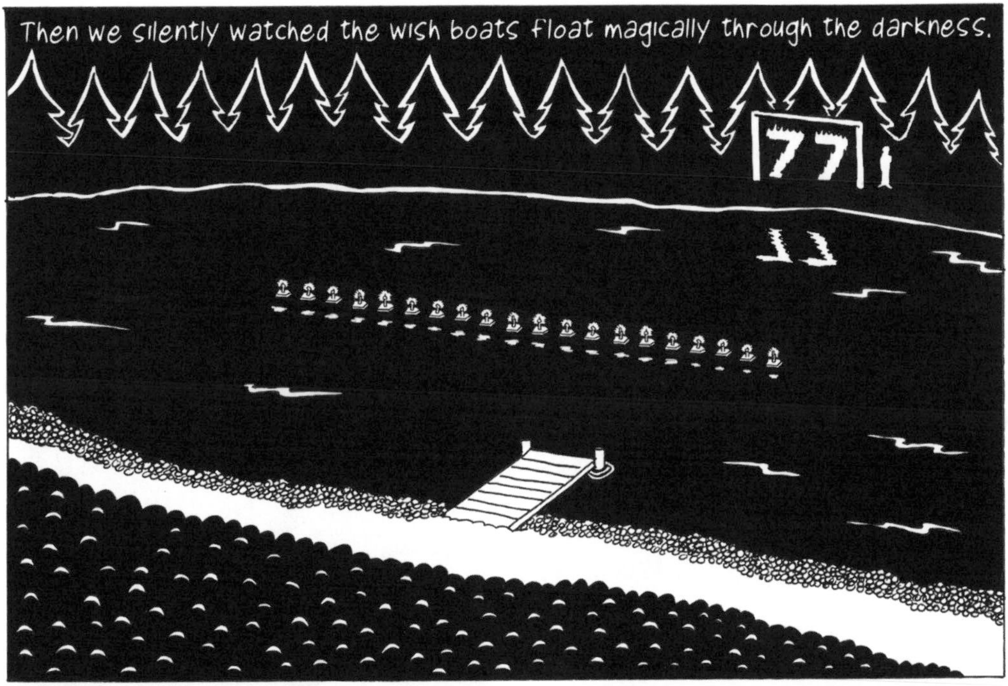
Then we silently watched the wish boats float magically through the darkness.
77

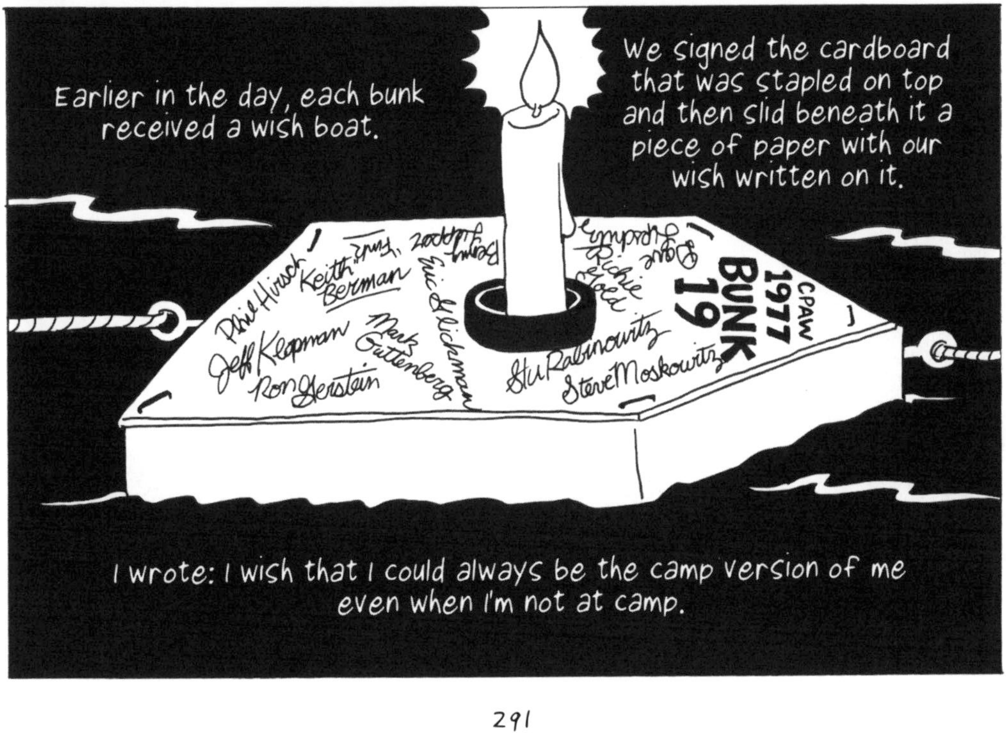
Earlier in the day, each bunk received a wish boat.
We signed the cardboard that was stapled on top and then slid beneath it a piece of paper with our wish written on it.
CPAW 1977 BUNK 19
Phil Hirsch
Keith Berman
Jeff Klapman
Mark Guttenberg
Ron Gerstein
Eric Glickman
Richie Gold
Stu Rabinowitz
Steve Moskowitz
I wrote: I wish that I could always be the camp version of me even when I'm not at camp.

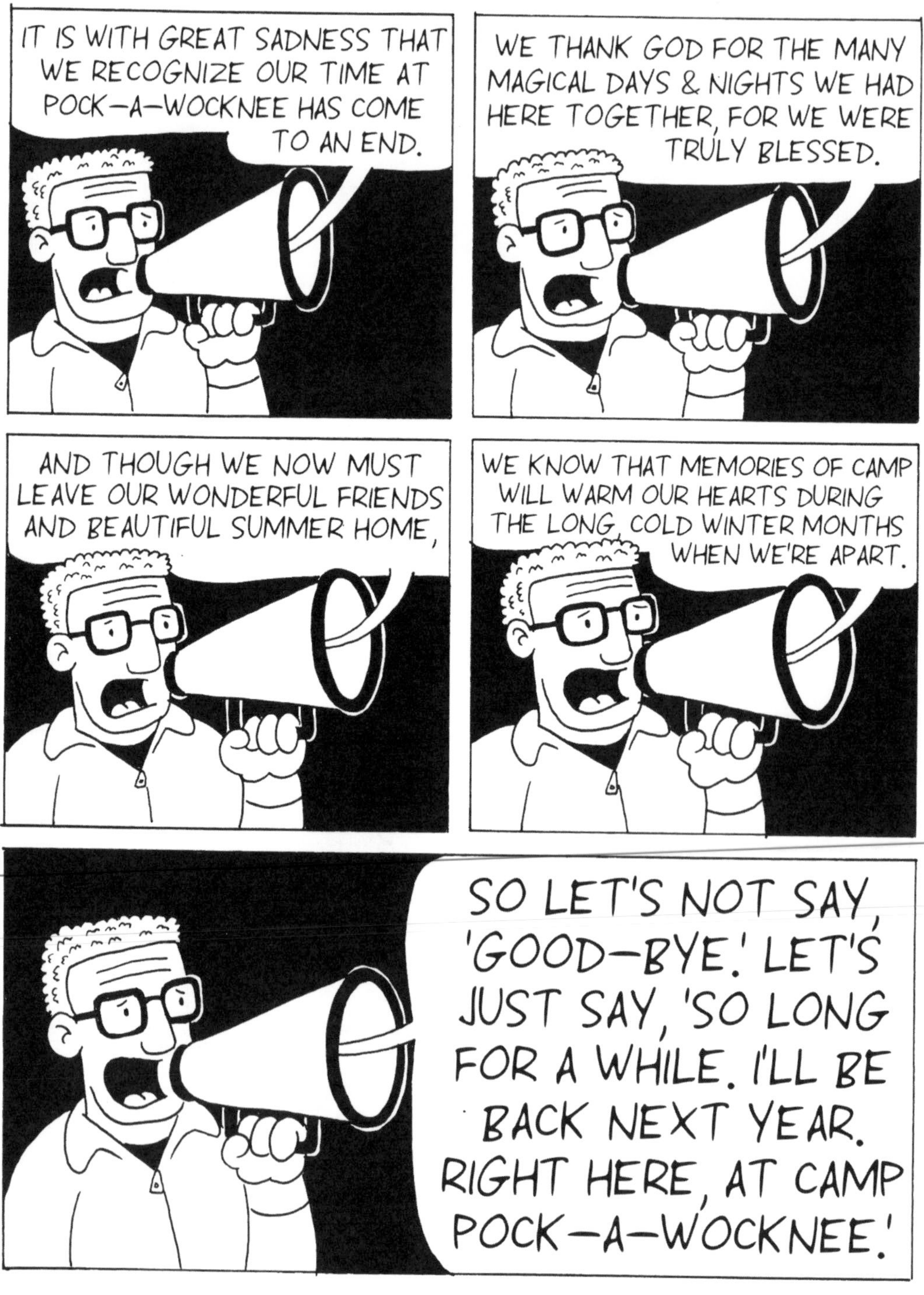
IT IS WITH GREAT SADNESS THAT WE RECOGNIZE OUR TIME AT POCK-A-WOCKNEE HAS COME TO AN END.
WE THANK GOD FOR THE MANY MAGICAL DAYS & NIGHTS WE HAD HERE TOGETHER, FOR WE WERE TRULY BLESSED.
AND THOUGH WE NOW MUST LEAVE OUR WONDERFUL FRIENDS AND BEAUTIFUL SUMMER HOME,
WE KNOW THAT MEMORIES OF CAMP WILL WARM OUR HEARTS DURING THE LONG, COLD WINTER MONTHS WHEN WE'RE APART.
SO LET'S NOT SAY, 'GOOD-BYE.' LET'S JUST SAY, 'SO LONG FOR A WHILE. I'LL BE BACK NEXT YEAR. RIGHT HERE, AT CAMP POCK-A-WOCKNEE.'

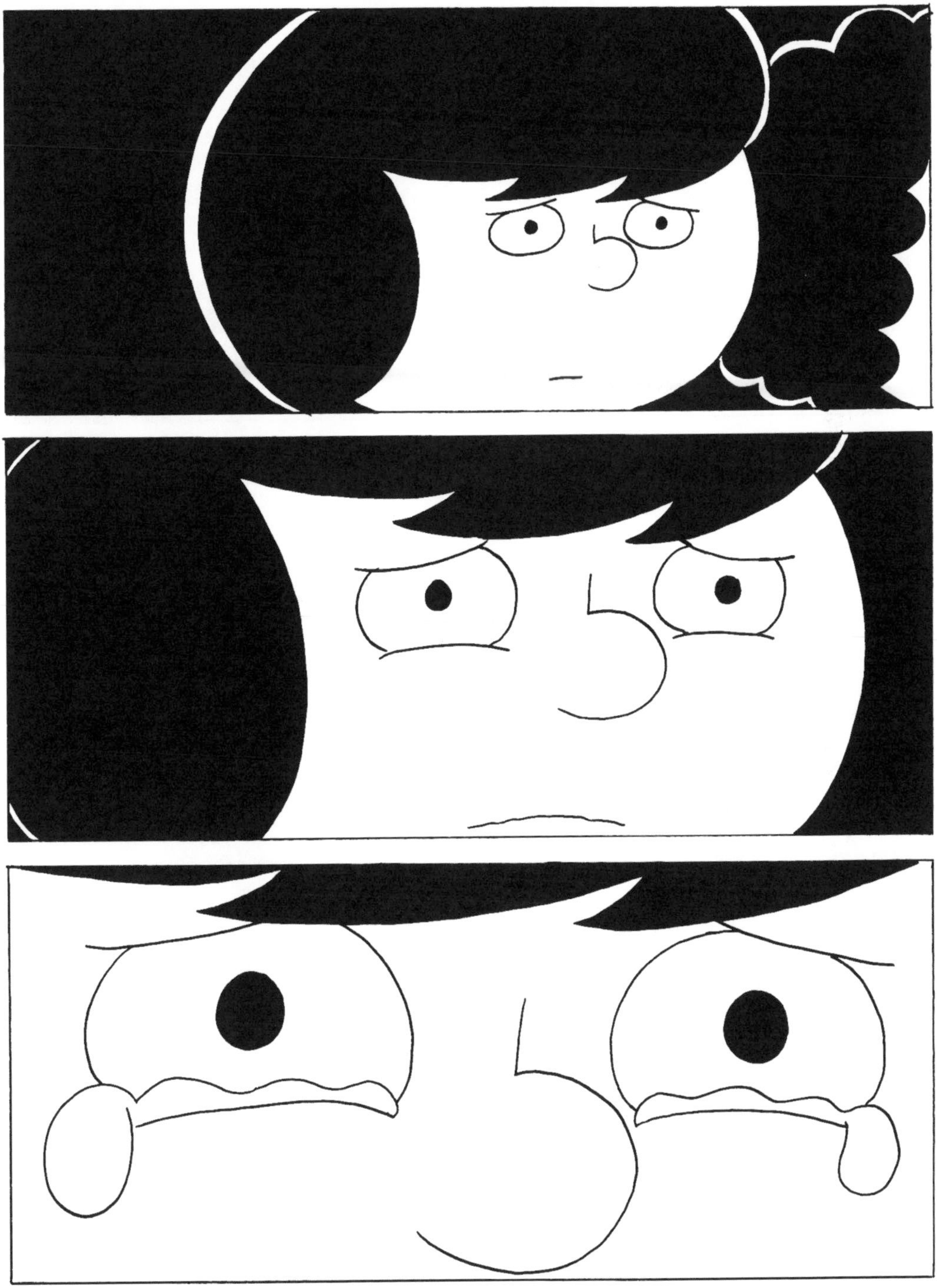

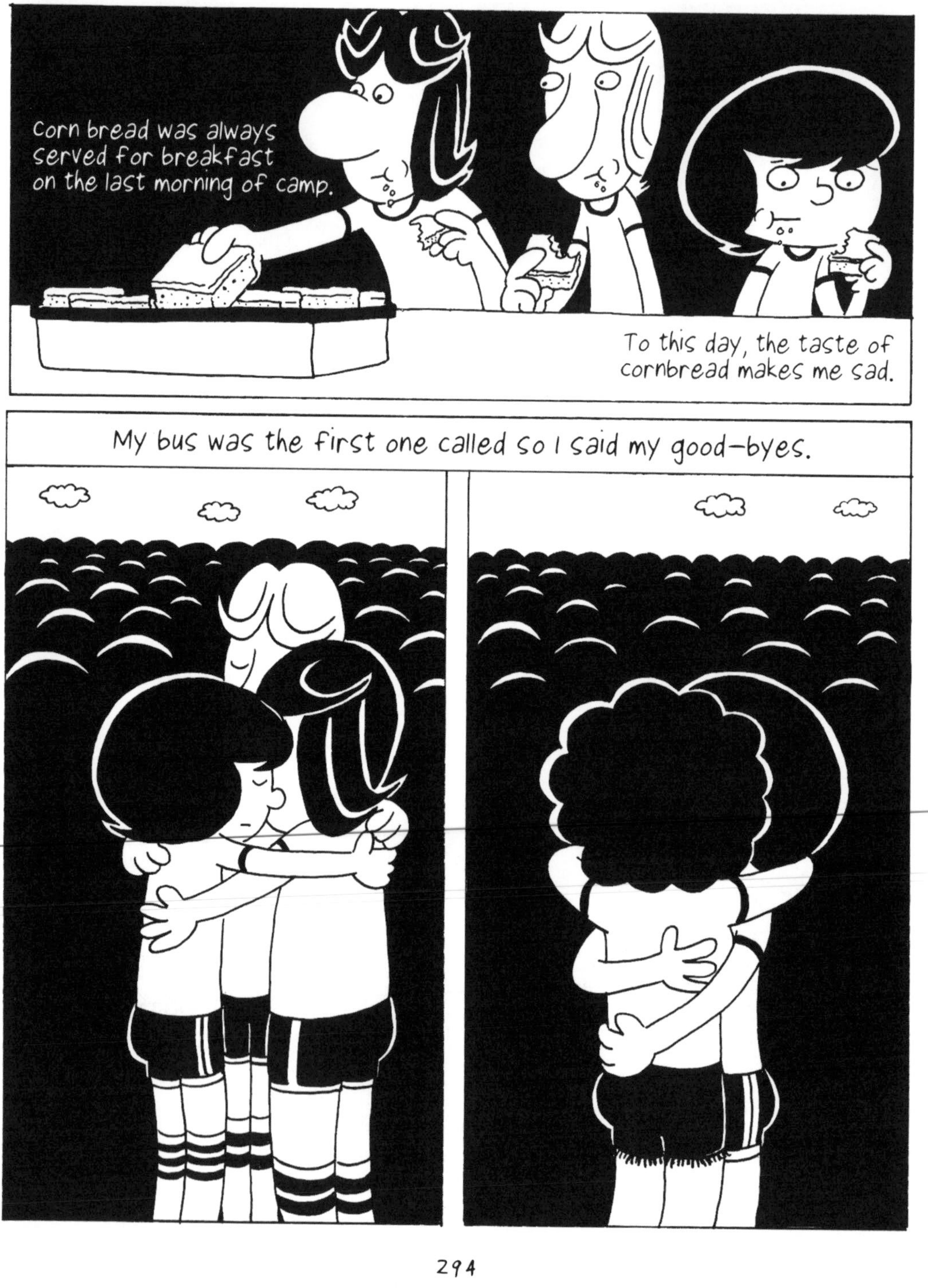
Corn bread was always served for breakfast on the last morning of camp.
To this day, the taste of cornbread makes me sad.
My bus was the first one called so I said my good-byes.

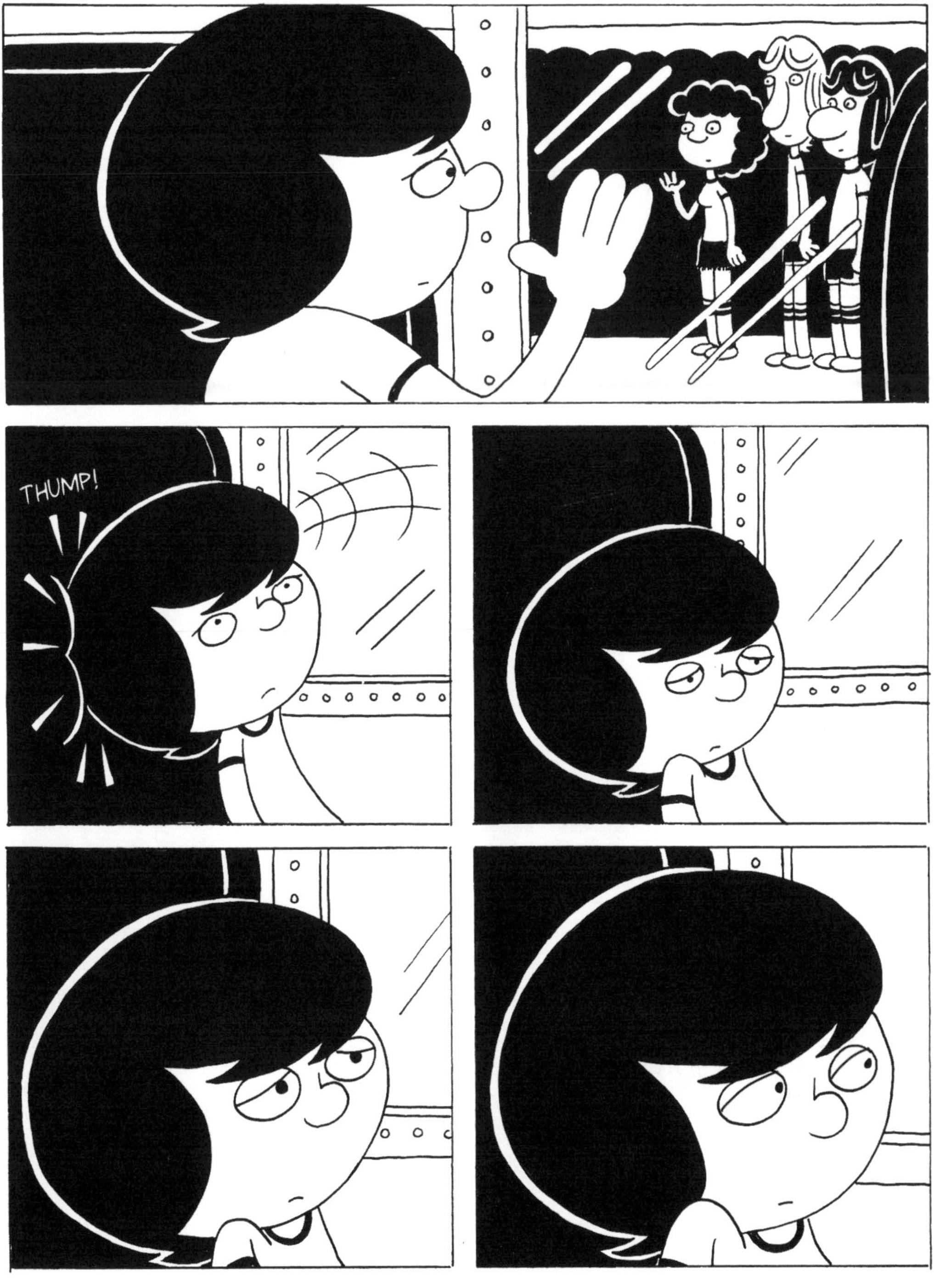
THUMP!

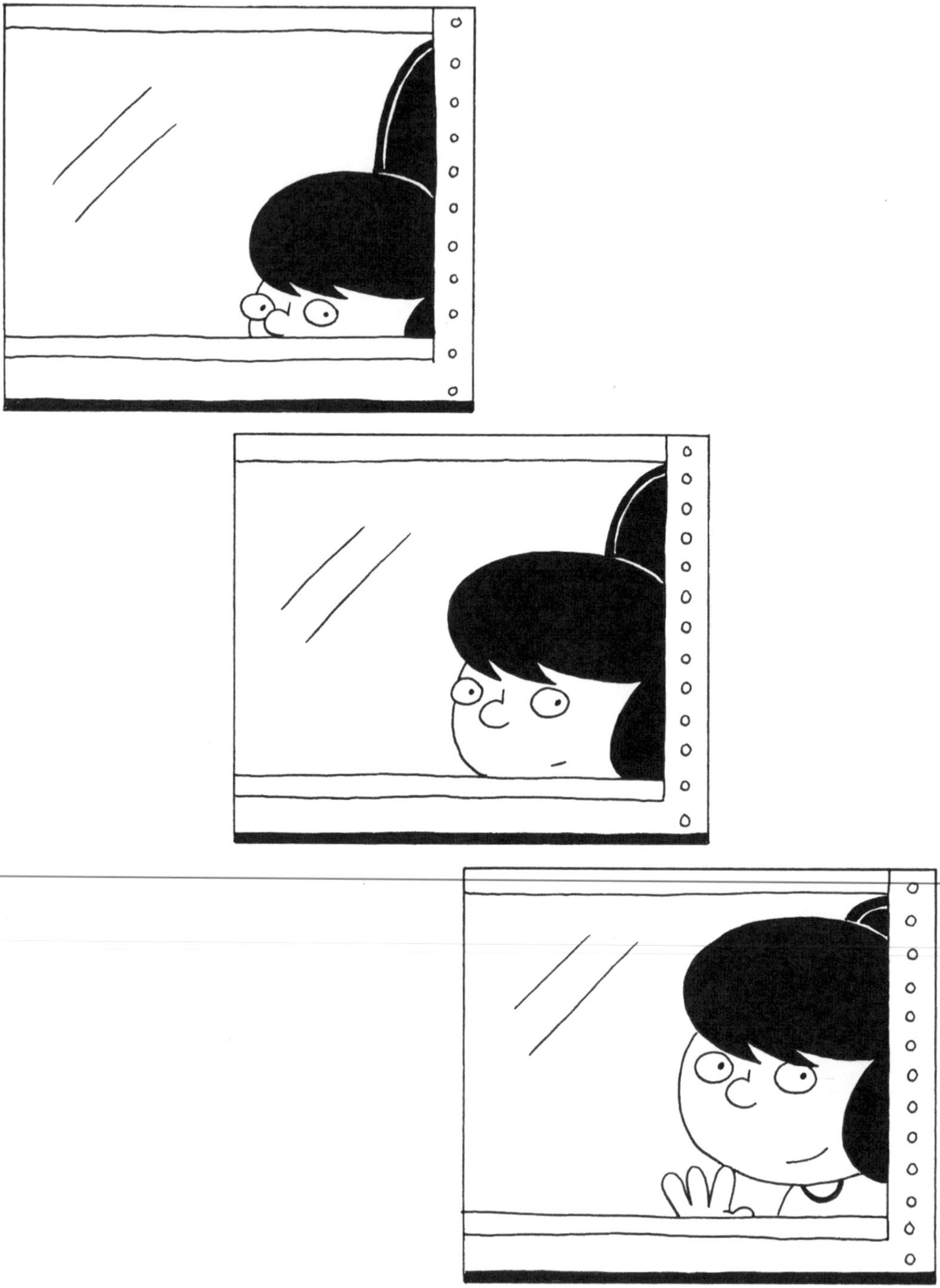

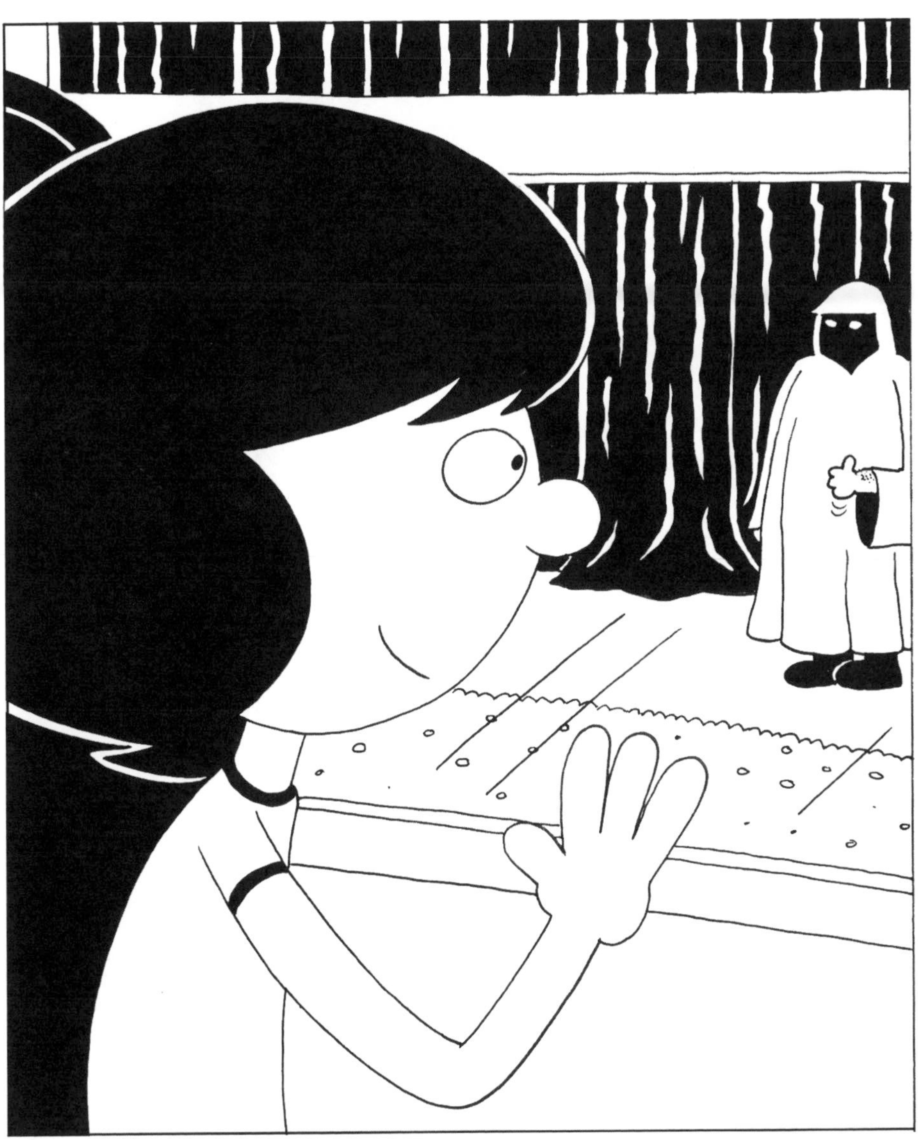

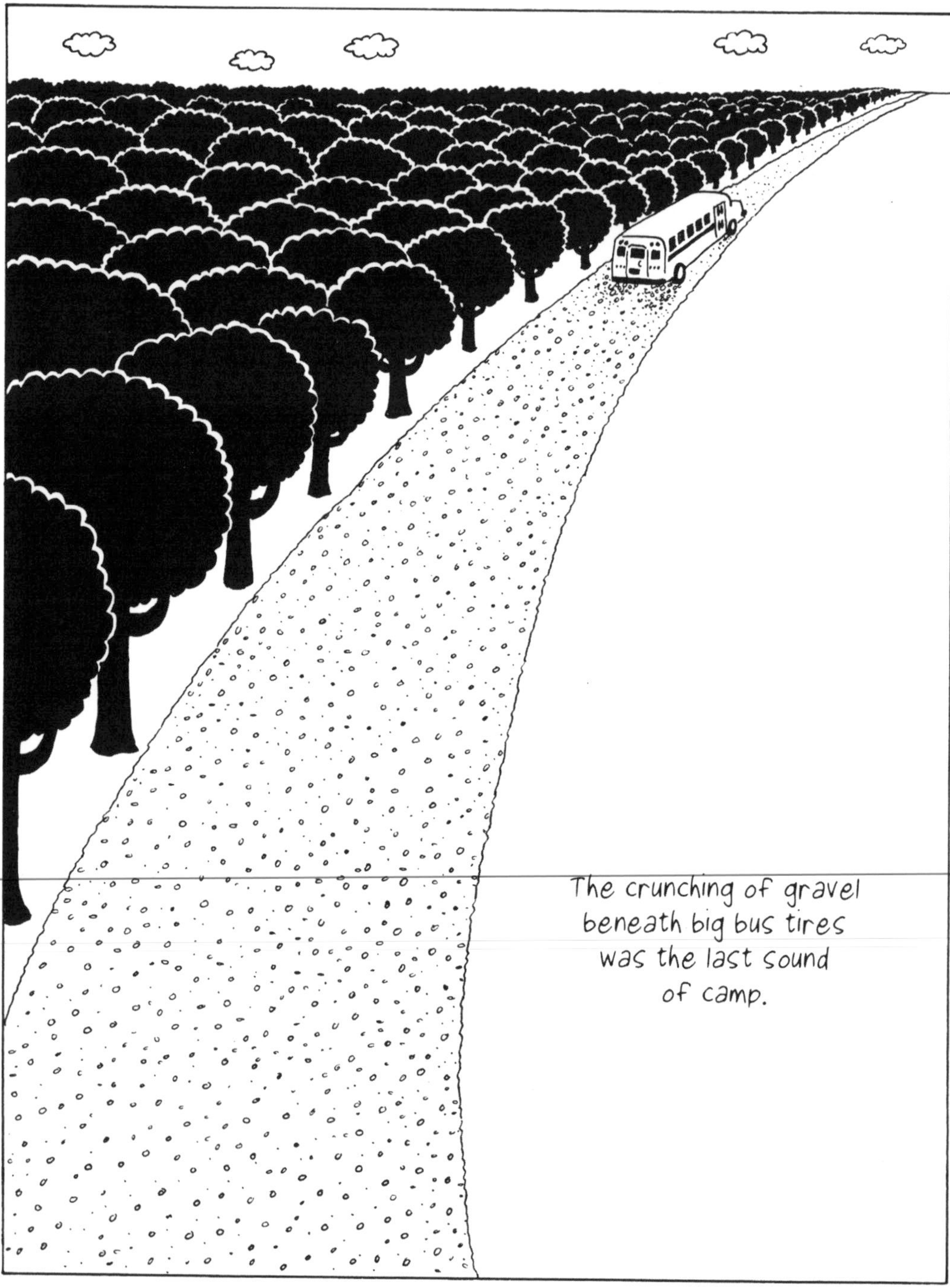
The crunching of gravel beneath big bus tires was the last sound of camp.

Back at home, I would often wake up in the middle of the night
and think I was still at camp.

Incredibly, more than 40 years later,
it still happens every now and then.

And in that hazy moment between sleep and consciousness,
it feels as if my days at camp were all a dream...

which they were.

The author (center) as a counselor at camp with the real Keith and Amy, 1981